Gaea

Gaea

This is a work of fiction. As such, any persons, places, things or ideas appearing in this book that resemble those of the real world, living or dead, ugly or beautiful, are either coincidental or used fictitiously.

GAEA
Book Two of the Mother Trilogy

First Edition

Cover art and design by Ferdinand Ladera
Maps by Jacob Gamber

Font: 11 pt Sylfaen
209,600 words
Printed in the USA

Idea Engine Press LLC
850 Euclid Ave Ste 819 #4020,
Cleveland OH 44114, US

The Mother Trilogy: Book Two

- GAEA -

Jacob Gamber

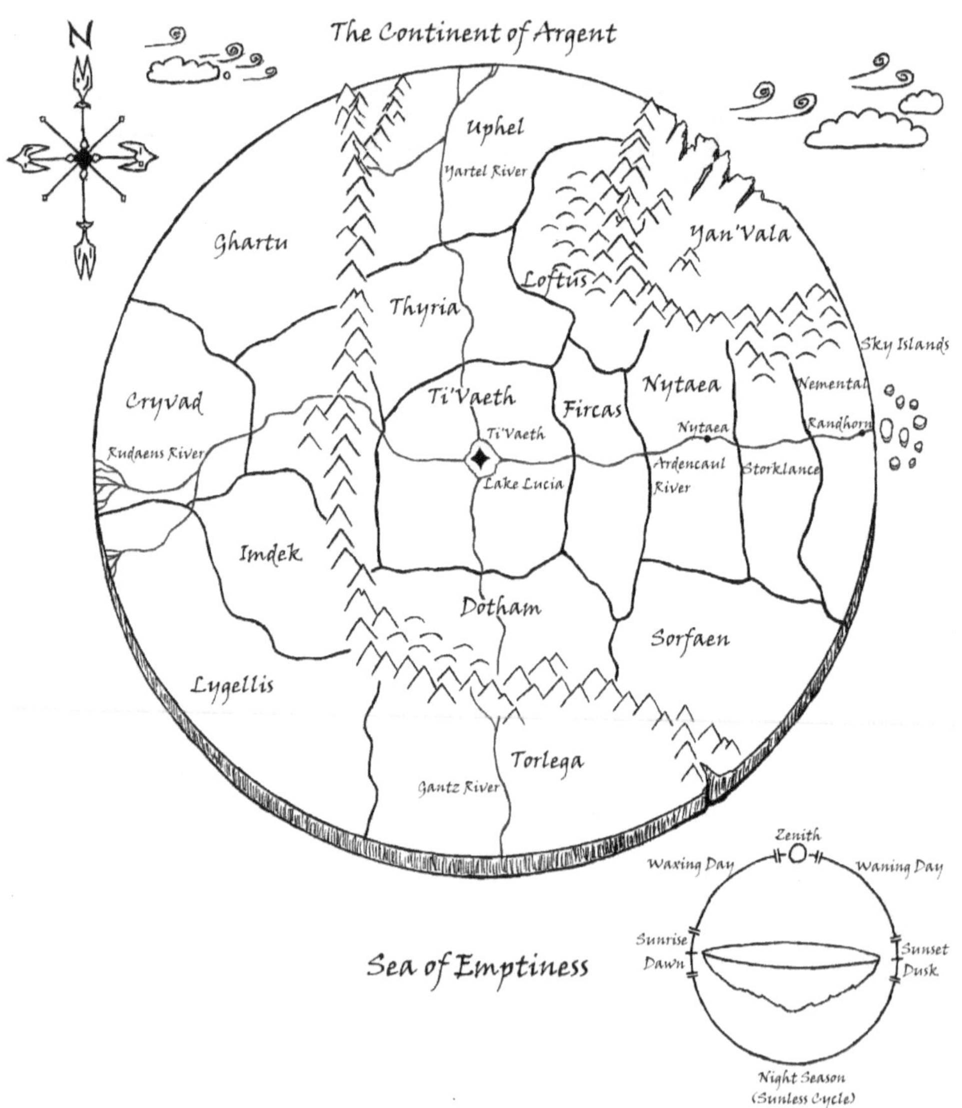

The Known World of
Mani
The Continent of Argent
N
Ghartu
Uphel
Yartel River
Yan'Vala
Loftus
Thyria
Sky Islands
Cryvad
Ti'Vaeth
Fircas
Nytaea
Nemental
Ti'Vaeth
Nytaea
Randhorn
Rudaens River
Lake Lucia
Ardencaul River
Storklance
Imdek
Dotham
Sorfaen
Lygellis
Torlega
Gantz River
Sea of Emptiness
Zenith
Waxing Day
Waning Day
Sunrise
Dawn
Sunset
Dusk
Night Season
(Sunless Cycle)

The Far Continent of
Darsor
Castanor
Ribsha
Felmani
Duchy of
Halstar
Inner Duchy
Athalar
River
Redufiel
Mannet
Land of
Storms
Eastern
Wilds
Lor'Hav
Mogdael
Eltar
Soul River
Kalatar

Gaea

GAEA
The Nine Cities of Man

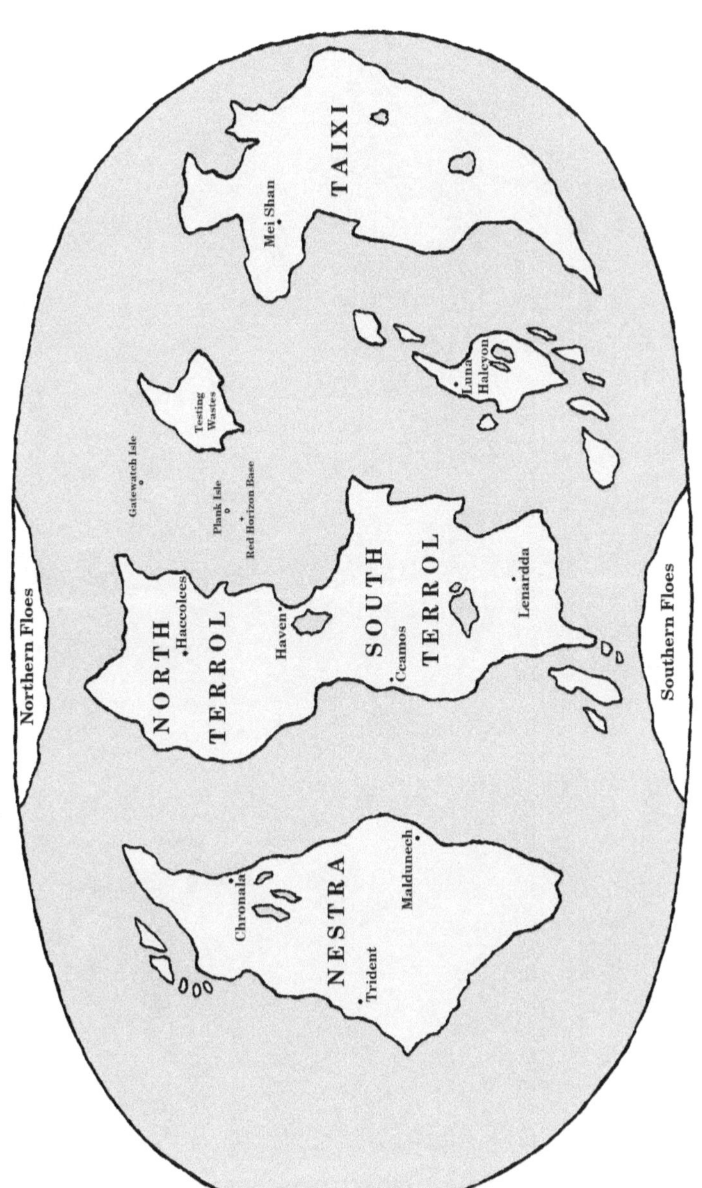

Provided by the Senatorial
Cartography Board, c. A.E. 1526

Gaea

Gaea

For Lydia

Gaea

CONTENTS

Gaea

ACKNOWLEDGMENTS

Thank God for the opportunity and freedom to write this series and publish it, for the modern technology that enables stories to get out from an insignificant corner of the world to all over the globe, and for the manifold sources of inspiration and encouragement all around me. Thank God for my loving family and supportive friends.

Thanks to Ferdinand Ladera for yet another gorgeous cover, this time showcasing the wild Sci-Fi side of the series. And thank you, alpha and beta readers who helped solidify this book. Particular thanks go to Rick Sipes and Rebekah Cochran for their efforts on the front lines; Jeremiah and Joanna, my siblings and creative peers; and of course my mother, who suffered through a 700-page Sci-Fi novel just for my sake. Fortunately, my drafting and editing methods have improved drastically since *Mani,* so these subjects suffered less in beta reader purgatory.

Quick note: I wrote this novel under the assumption that the reader has read Lyn's previous adventures, but I included a synopsis to catch you up in case you skipped it. Also, as with *Mani,* there's an appendix at the back with glossaries for characters, terms, places, worldbuilding details, etc., possibly containing minor spoilers. Pronunciations are included unless deemed self-explanatory by the Linguistics Department (aka me).

— Jacob G.

THE STORY SO FAR

Once again, I don't know who will be reading this, only that you speak the Hellebes tongue. Probably far more of you this time, as I've learned how to store my Vault digitally. So if you have not read of my journey on Mani, I'll get you up to speed.

My name is Lynchazel; Lyn for short. Mani, which you know as the silver moon, is my home. Mani turns on its axis with the lunar cycle, so our days are twenty-eight Gaea days long. An Energy Field protecting Mani creates auroras and clouds to keep a regular twenty-four-hour day–night cycle, along with rotating constellations that appear in the clouds. On Mani, magic makes the world go round, or more accurately, gives that illusion.

My people, the Legaleians, live on the circular continent of Argent, roughly three thousand miles in diameter, long thought to be our entire world. Nytaea, easternmost of the thirteen city-states of the Kystrean Empire, was run by a tyrant named Lord Kalceron. There, I was raised an orphan by the kind Lentha, who took care of my friends and me until our teenage years, when thieves suddenly came and burned it down. They killed Lentha, leaving only four of us alive. We fled, but were soon apprehended by Lord Kalceron's Mage Guard, who'd been tracking me by my unusual white hair for unknown reasons.

They ambushed us, and in the ensuing fight my beastly strength manifested, a secret I'd kept all my life. Ever stronger than a normal Legaleian, I could call on a hidden strength to make my body move at incredible speeds or kick like a horse. Captain Hespian and Lieutenant Lorta fled using teleportation magic, taking my friends Mandrie and Phoebe and leaving only Kaen by my side. Rather than give me up to Lord Kalceron—the demanded ransom—we snuck into the Palace as servants to try to find and free our imprisoned friends.

Gaea

Our efforts turned up nothing, yet I inexplicably befriended Princess Mydia, who was a secret supporter of the Underground movement and resented her father's harsh rule (his own laws forbid citizenship to orphans like me and allowed for the murder and enslavement of many). Soon, I became Mydia's new handmaiden, and subsequently met the most renowned mage scholar in the world: Rhidea, the Wandering Mage. Rhidea found out my secrets through cunning and questioning, and even became an ally, promising to help me search for my friends. Somehow, I fit into a long search that mirrored Kalceron's.

Mydia herself was a water mage gifted with plants, but also had a Perception-based illusion ability inherited from her father. She told me of her brother, a fire-based High Mage who'd long been missing.

The story sparked a discovery: I possessed dormant fire magic—Coaction, the lesser of the two arts. But I could work up to full Authority, which the greatest magi wielded. Magic is subdivided into eight branches [see Appendix C].

In my dreams, a young girl showed me visions of my mother.

Including Kaen, Mydia and even the Underground into our plans, we at last located the girls and planned a breakout on the upcoming festival day, when two recently-exposed rebel leaders would be hanged. Soon as Kaen and I sprang our friends from prison, I realized Mydia was missing. Lady Lieda, Mydia's stepmother, tried to stop me, but Rhidea came in and bound her in stone before barging into the throne room, where Lord Kalceron was questioning his daughter on my identity and whereabouts.

At the Wandering Mage's defiance, Kalceron challenged her to a duel, and I fought Lorta and Hespian of the Mage Guard. When I had bested them with my savage strength and newfound ability to cast firebolts from my hands, a beaten Lord Kalceron retreated to his throne. His rage switched to Mydia and he almost slew her before Rhidea reached out with a streaking blade of silver and . . . Nytaea was without her governor.

Rhidea managed to secure a standstill between rebels and soldiers, mediating a bargain that saw Mydia as Queen Regent and Bart and Gaela of the Underground as her two secondary leaders. Following this coup came relative peace and tense deliberation between representatives noble and common.

Rhidea announced she would take a delegation to her lord, King Fenwel of Nemental, including the new queen, me and my friends. We crossed Storklance into Nemental, which borders the Sea of Emptiness on the east. Here, we negotiated with King Fenwel for military aid for our fledgling kingdom. More pertinently to me, we discussed Rhidea's goal: A cure for our world.

Mani's magic comes from the Wellspring of Life at the heart of the continent, deep under the capital city of Ti'Vaeth. Via the Four Rivers, it supplies water to the world as well as the very breath of life and magic. Magic had long been dwindling, mirroring a heightening disparity between male and female births (far more girls), and Rhidea sought a solution.

Rhidea and her lord suspected that I came from another world (Gaea), and believed that we needed to locate it to piece together Mani's problem. The Wellspring held the key, or so we hoped.

Archlord Domon [see Appendix A] had sent threats to Nytaea. We regrouped with the council, deciding to leave for Ti'Vaeth soon to explain our purpose to Domon.

Mydia and her Queensguard accompanied us to Ti'Vaeth [see Appendix B].

There, we sought an audience at the palace. Rhidea was rejected immediately by the Archlord, so we resorted to studying the Hall of Eternity—the palace surrounding the Wellspring. Using a teleportation stone of Rhidea's, we ascended to the highest wall that looks upon the great Sky Funnel where the water gushes out of a great pit.

Using her gravity Authority, we descended to the bottom and explored a labyrinth of tunnels. The next day, we returned to pinpoint the Wellspring's entrance while Kaen and the soldiers made a distraction. They only led Domon's soldiers right to us, who pursued us into the Well's chamber. We fought in close quarters, descending a dark staircase, and I slipped and fell all the way to a dark pool. That pool was the Wellspring itself, now coated in black grime.

When the others reached me, they seemed to have made a truce. We inspected pillars carved with writing, caked in black grime, and a mural running the chamber's circumference, telling a strange story of Mani's past. We cleaned it and pieced together what we could:

Our people came from another world—Gaea—in some manner of pilgrimage, fleeing a force shown as a dragon. They brought the Wellspring from Gaea, granting Mani its elemental magic. A poem read:

> *To take the bait a world away,*
> *A Wellspring hid amongst the grey,*
> *We wait, remember, for the day,*
> *For one millennium we stay.*

This all posed more questions than answers. We needed to see the Archlord.

Corporal Harold and his men led us out, acting the dutiful captors, to his master. We got our audience, but he denied our treaty, threatening to end us all with his magic. Rhidea made a desperate gamble: An arm-wrestling match.

Intrigued, he accepted, and I won despite all his Authority working against me. Shocked, Domon agreed to a frank discussion, where we explained our goal: Gaea. Domon had made his infamous Dark Magic by corrupting the Wellspring in an attempt to protect Mani from a threat he foresaw. Deducing my Gaean descent from my uncanny strength, he vowed to help us reach Gaea, halting his invasion of Nytaea.

We left on a riverboat for Nytaea with three orbs of his making and an assassin bodyguard named Kymhar. Back in Nytaea, we informed the council of our news. Our destination would be Randhorn and then the sky isle of Scathii to learn how we could cross the Sea of Emptiness.

In Nytaea, my friends and I ambushed the thieves who'd torched our orphanage. Kaen almost killed their leader, Fraid, before I begged him to stop.

In Randhorn, we discussed engineering and magics with Fenwel's mage scholars, then set off via the nearby port town. At Scathii, the village council welcomed us coldly, as is their way. We chanced upon a keen-minded boy who made wooden gliders, his kind uncle offering aid in achieving our insane dream of traversing the Sea of Emptiness. A few models later—and one near-death experience for me—we set off on gliders with the boy, Oliver, a wind mage. He utilized the updrafts to keep us aloft for hours as we sped toward the far horizon.

Miraculously, it appeared, and we landed at the edge of a giant forest. Beyond this was a plain, and above it hung a strange sight: A blue-and-green ball, like Sol but bigger. We posed as lost travelers in the distrustful villages, who directed us toward the center of their continent, Darsor. We crossed the mysterious circular Soul River, seeking the center of the Duchy of Halstar.

We bypassed the capital, entering the Land of Storms fraught with deadly lightning and rain. An orb of Domon's absorbed the lightning for us, and we came safely to the Tower of Mani, atop which stood an arch carved with runes both Legaleian and Gaean. As I tried to use the mysterious power I could *almost* access, Kymhar turned on us, using one of our gifted orbs to summon his lord.

All turned to chaos. Rhidea held the dark emperor off; Kaen fought Kymhar. At last, I sparked something, fusing a link between worlds. The empty gate came to life just as an explosion rocked the tower and I tumbled through.

As I drifted unconscious, my dream assistant White coaxed me to accept my memories as my own. I realized that all the strange dreams I'd had of my mother were in fact memories, ones I had stored all my life in a place I couldn't access while awake: my Vault. I relived the day Mother left me at Lentha's orphanage—a heartbreaking scene, for she knew her death was near.

I awoke on Gaea to rebel soldiers Zent, Ccal and Bddo on a small island. A foreign sight. Unable to bridge the language barrier, I let them take me into captivity as Gaea's heavy gravity pulled me into submission.

The rest is history.

Gaea

xx

Prologue

Ancestor

(Planet Gaea—Anier headquarters

Soldor 14, A.E. 1318, E120)

Mother Gaea felt a hand on her shoulder. She jerked, swiveling her head to see a familiar man stepping up beside her. He was tall with black hair combed neatly back, dressed tidily in a long-tailed suit, his every mannerism businesslike. "It's time," he said quietly.

She nodded. She tried to form a response, but it got stuck in her throat, so she shut her mouth and quietly followed the man. She was in the main Anier headquarters in what used to be the capital of Starklett, a grand city and one of the few places in the world the Anier had not yet abased. Well, aside from constructing their own buildings such as this. It was framed in metal and hideous to look at, with flat glass windows and no decorative style. As she followed the tall man through the hall, the electric lighting cast eerie, ominously flickering shadows on the floor.

Mother Gaea, as they called her, was not in the condition she once was. When they'd found her, she'd been but a girl of thirteen years, and she couldn't be certain how many decades had passed. One could almost mistake her youthful face for that of a girl, but for the wrinkles and the scars, and her dark hair was now streaked with grey. On one hand, she felt as though she hadn't aged a day, but on the other . . . she was beaten and worn, and her very bones told her so. How much longer could she keep living like this? How long until her body just disintegrated into dust and blew away on the wind?

"The creature is being kept under the tightest security," the man said out of nowhere, turning to look at her as he walked. "You are in no danger."

"Thanks," she mumbled. They had told her many things about these incredible life-forms that could destroy or save humanity, but she didn't know what to believe anymore. Did her beliefs matter? Her feelings? No. She couldn't save a single soul. But . . . danger to her? That was the farthest worry from her mind.

The tall man led her down one last hallway with warning signs labeling the walls, and finally through a door marked: *Test Subjects—Do not enter without armed protection.* Inside, filtered electric lights cast an unsettling blue glare around a long chamber with many large glass tanks lining one wall. At the end was a T, and as they approached it, they met up with two more of the Anier and a half-dozen armed guardsmen, who stood watching something in a cage. A big cage, some ten feet tall and spanning the width between one wall and the other.

Mother Gaea frowned, trying to get a view of the cage and the creature contained therein. A rising lump in her throat and a feeling of dread told her she didn't want to see it, yet at the same time it triggered her scientist's fascination. She glanced back at the man who had led her there, and then moved forward, maneuvering around the stout guards to get a view of the cage.

When she did, she gasped.

The two other Anier turned to look at her, and one said, "This, Mother Gaea, is a Cydenges. Look well."

She wanted to tear her eyes away from it, but she couldn't. It was terrible . . . but beautiful as well, as though designed by a skilled artist. A predator of enormous size, capable of mass-destruction.

The well-dressed man who had led her to the containment room said, "The cage is heavily reinforced and lined with copper, which has proven to be the only insulant effective at inhibiting their energy manipulation abilities. That is their most feared trait, after all."

Mother Gaea nodded with a gulp. They had already attacked multiple times, and she had seen the destruction the Cydenges could wreak upon Gaea, but never had she laid eyes on one. *Look well.* She did just that. This was the future of Gaea, after all. One way or another.

A

Heritage

α Chapter 1 α

Zent

Finhal 1, 1294:

Another terrifying dream beset me last night . . . Mother had

disappeared, and I followed a trail of blood through the house and out into

the night. It was a moonlit night, yet the groping shadows seemed darker

than usual. I was scared and sorely troubled, calling out, "Mother!"

repeatedly, to no effect. I never found her before waking up.

— From Lhinde's Diary

(From the Vault of Lyn of Nytaea, Mother Heiress

Manidor 5, 2337)

I don't like prison.

Having avoided prison all my life, I found this out when the Gaean League and their kind Emperor saw fit to throw me in jail for being a visitor from another planet. Shockingly, the feeling only grew with each passing day.

I sighed, thumping my head back against the concrete wall of my containment cell. "I've got to get out of here. I'll go crazy."

What am I thinking, I already am crazy, I thought to myself with a shake of my head.

"No, you're not, Lyn." *I mean . . . I'm not.*

Another sigh passed my lips. What a mess. Why did it have to turn out like this? Rhidea was supposed to be here. She could solve everything. Kaen, Mydia, Oliver, they all should have been here. Well, Oliver still should have been back on his home island on Mani, but that was a different story altogether. The sky islands . . . man, that seemed an eternity ago. I was starting to forget the events that had happened to us a mere few months ago.

No, you're not. You know better, Lyn. You don't forget—you just want peace when you dream.

My hair was longer now, like it or not. I distinctly remember *not* having to tie it with three separate ties, nor being able to stretch my feet all the way out and play with my toes using my ponytail from a relaxed position. I didn't have anything at my disposal to cut the silver mane with. It had been growing avidly ever since I came to Planet Gaea. It could be a tad annoying . . . and dirty, most of the time. They didn't exactly give me many opportunities to wash myself. But oh well. I didn't smell that bad anyway . . . or had I just gotten used to my own stench?

Lyn . . . you've really got to stop having conversations with yourself in your head.

I bit back a retort and resumed fiddling with my hair once more, tapping the end of it against the stone floor. Reinforced stone. I needed to get out, and deep inside I was desperate, but I tried to cover it up and not think about it. This place might look like any old cell, but the Hellebes knew well how to keep one of their own people—including half-breeds—contained. A little bit of steel mesh, little bit of cement, little bit of copper—which is supposed to weaken Hellebes—and some more cement overtop.

All this to say, I wasn't breaking out of here. I had already tried on three separate occasions, and each time they only put me in a stronger cell. A weak Hellebes half-breed like me couldn't do much more than crack the concrete. Back on Mani, I recalled twisting cell bars apart to rescue Mandrie, but here in my cell, I was fenced in by two rows of waffle-pattern steel bars, each as thick as a human bone and spaced only a hand's breadth apart. Escape was hopeless. Silver and steel are . . . not the same in strength, I've learned.

As my mind wandered, I absently tapped the floor with my index finger, harder and harder. I really didn't know why I was in such a bad mood today. Not hormones, not sickness, and every day in this cell was just like another. Once in a while, they used to take me out and run tests on me like a lab rat, but they seemed to have forgotten that their one and only female even existed at this point. It was hard to believe I was really the only woman on Gaea. If I was so important, then why did they ignore me while I rotted away in this insanity-inducing chamber?

I had just decided to lie down on my luxurious cot for a siesta when I heard it: Footsteps coming from outside in the hallway. From the left side. Not a guard—these steps were too quick, too purposeful.

I lay my head down, rolling onto my side, and pretended to be resting while actually keeping one eye partially open. I was mildly curious to know who passed through and when, if only to keep my atrophying mind busy. Soon, I saw the figure approaching. Large and powerfully built like most Hellebes, his hair was cropped short and he wore a military uniform complete with a blaster at his belt and camera and microphone on his lapel. The chevrons on his shoulder marked him as an officer. But he looked . . . familiar.

The officer stopped in front of my cell and turned his face toward me, eyeing my prone form with a calculating look. A . . . soft look, though, for a Hellebes. Softer, anyway. He had prominent features and dark eyes.

"Prisoner," he began in a deep, gruff voice. A familiar voice. Why couldn't I think of . . .

My eyes grew wide in recognition and I opened my mouth to speak, but the man coughed and made a quick *shhh* signal over his mouth before withdrawing his hand, hiding it from the overhead cameras. They were positioned to point down at my cell, and his body cam would point outward.

I leaned up, as though grumpy that I'd been disturbed from such a good nap.

"I am Captain Zent," he said, "From district twenty-two, sector five. Since it came to my attention that the Mother Heiress was transferred to this facility here in Haccolces, and considering that my sector directly borders this one, I thought it prudent to come and see for myself what kind of monster you are. To think that the next Mother would come from one of the moons, and in this sorry state. You're not half as tall as your statues."

It took me a moment to translate the captain's words in my head. The more he spoke, the more my mind grew reaccustomed to the Hellebes tongue. If I weren't kept in captivity all the time, I would have been completely fluent by now. As it was, it took me but a few moments to catch on and shift mental gears. *One of the moons . . .* another thing that was hard to wrap my mind around. Not only had the world I'd grown up in turned out to be this planet's moon, but Mani had a sister moon: Luna.

I kept my face as neutral as I could, partly because he clearly did not want to make anything of his connection to me (for reasons I didn't yet know), and partly because I wasn't sure how much I could trust him. But there was no mistaking it—this was the same Captain Zent I had met three months back when I awoke on Gatewatch Isle. The same man who taken me in, however briefly, the *only* man on the planet who had shown me any level of respect. It'd been so long that I . . . well, hadn't *forgotten* so much as just didn't remember him.

I need to keep better tabs on my memories when I dream. I stuck the note in my mental mailbox, hoping White received it. She could be quite absent-minded.

Yes, that's a joke. If you've read my previous journals, which I recorded in captivity, you'd get it.

Glancing down at the floor, I mumbled, "I'm not a monster. You Hellebes are the real monsters." I was only partly acting—that was how I felt toward my mother's race as a whole—yet I felt a small tickle of guilt at aiming that resentment toward my one possible ally in the whole world.

Speaking of, why was he here?

"I can see why you might think that," continued the captain. "But you know that it is for the good of the race that the Senate had you incarcerated. You are the last hope of the Hellebes, after all."

Zent locked eyes with me and mouthed the words, *I haven't forgotten.*

And it clicked. I recalled the last thing he had told me: "Lyn, I'm sorry it has to be this way, but I can't do anything to get you out of this. I don't have the authority or support to hide you from the Senate and keep them away. But I will return to free you."

"To think that after all this time, we found you again," he continued, stepping closer to put two hands on the bars of my cell. "Well, I hope they're not treating you too terribly in there. Oh, and here is a little something to keep you busy. A note on the test results so far. I'm not allowed to share much, of course." He bent down and slid a folded piece of paper through the bars.

I simply glanced down at it, making no move to retrieve it, biting back my curiosity. Was that really all the note was? They wouldn't feel inclined to show me results of tests done ages ago. "Is that all you have to say, Captain?" I said in a bored but careful tone.

"Yes. I may return soon. Until then." Zent gave a meaningful wink for my eyes alone, turned, and left the way he had come.

He would . . . return.

Return. To free me.

As soon as the captain was gone, I arose from my cot and swiftly retrieved the folded note. Careful to angle it away from any cameras, I unfolded it and looked at the writing inside—which was machine printed in fine print—with as little interest as I could feign. It read:

Lynchazel,
We, the Red Horizon, have been trying to get through the right officers and officials of the Gaean League to get you out of there. None of these attempts have yielded any results. However, our plan to break you out is finally coming to fruition, with the necessary support, money and suppliers to execute the plan. All that's left is for you to wait until 22:00 tonight and wait for the sparks—we will overload the circuits of all nearby cells and hallways, nullifying the prison's surveillance measures. We will send in a small team. Be ready, be watchful.
—Zent

The Red Horizon. I smiled faintly as I read it, and then crumpled up the paper and shredded it with my too-long fingernails, trying to look as though angrily tearing up a useless sheet of paper.

22:00 tonight. Boy oh boy, would I be ready.

I couldn't believe I was actually getting out of here. I tried to calm my nerves and tell myself that there was a chance they would not come through. Or the whole thing could go wrong, and it would only end up with Zent's companions killed or imprisoned like me—they wouldn't kill a valuable specimen like myself, but who knew what they would do to those bold enough to break right into a top-secret military prison?

The time ticked slowly by, from afternoon until nighttime. I was on edge, jumping at the slightest noise and looking anxiously at the clock on the opposite wall from my cell.

Why was waiting always so hard?

α Chapter 2 α

Breakout Op

Firven 11, 1294:
Today, the Starklett Knights were supposed to be holding duels at the
castle. I was so very anxious to go, but Father forbade me. Probably because
of those recent kidnappings. So here I wait for Mother to give me more
chores to do. I shall go make a cup of tea to take my mind off it.
— From Lhinde's Diary

22:00. Finally.

I waited breathlessly, eager to hear some sound of rescue . . . and there it was—the sparks. The cameras popped and crackled with electrical noises, and I knew they were out of commission. And then . . .

Fast, light footsteps echoed from the corridor on the right. Well, light for Hellebes—most of whom weighed at least twice what I did.

Soon, three Hellebes soldiers came into view, outfitted in stealth gear, heat blasters, long-barreled energy rifles, and . . . something similar but with a horseshoe-shaped end. I didn't know what that was for.

One of the men was none other than Captain Zent. He grinned at me through the cell bars and said, "Finally arrived. Thought we'd never come for you?"

"Yes," I said truthfully, standing up and stretching. Bones popped in a series of crunches through my back, shoulders and knuckles. I tilted my head from side to side and shook my legs out. It'd been a while since my body had seen any real use, and I was restless. "So . . . how are you going to break me out?"

One of Zent's men held up his horseshoe-tipped tool and pressed a trigger. Red-and-white electricity arced from between the forks, causing me to shy away.

"Oh," I said. "Okay, go ahead."

The two soldiers with Zent set about using the tools, which they called arc-blasters, to saw through the metal bars like butter. In less than a minute, they had a section two-feet-wide by four-feet-tall cut out, and the two men stepped back to let the larger Zent rip the bars off with a heave. He set them beside the hole and motioned me out. "Follow close."

I ducked through the gap in the steel bars, turning sideways to fit my wide-shouldered frame through. I was not nearly as large as the men, but I still wouldn't have fit through front-ways.

Zent introduced me briefly to his two men. "Lynchazel, this is Bddo, and this is Ccal. You might remember them from when we first met."

I hesitated briefly. On the island . . . Yes, I did recognize them. I nodded to each. "I'm Lynchazel. Thank you very much for coming to my rescue. Thought I'd lose my mind in that cell."

Zent clapped me on the shoulder with a massive hand. "We would have come sooner if we had the chance."

I nodded. "I understand. Thanks."

He removed his hand and turned. "Now, we should be going. They've surely raised the alarm by now."

Of course, I realized. *With the electricity off, there are no alarms blaring here.* "I'll follow you guys," I said. "But . . . why blow the power? Why not just jam the cameras?"

"Could've done that," said Bddo, the lankier of the two soldiers, "But either way, these chaps are going to know something is up and immediately suspect sabotage. I mean, they'd be right."

Ccal, the broader, dark-haired Hellebes, grunted as we ducked down a corridor. "They'll be coming after us pretty soon."

They took off, and I followed as quickly as I could. My legs felt sluggish, as though readjusting to the heavy gravity of Gaea, and my awkward gown they had me dressed in didn't help anything. Couldn't a body get any decent clothes around here?

Ccal conversed with someone over his radio in short bursts as we went, probably more rebels at Red Horizon headquarters, wherever that was.

Suddenly, footsteps sounded from up ahead, and a group of guards emerged from an adjoining hallway, dressed in thick, armored grey suits and armed with blasters. Zent and Bddo already had their own guns out and took out two of the men just as the first shouting began.

"Get down!" Ccal hissed to me, grabbing my arm as he fired off his own shot.

With the emergence of another guard into view, there were a total of six. As I watched, Zent took out two more with heavy blasts of his two-handed pistol. The bright shots punched straight through the enemy's armor, seeming to melt it, though there was no knockback on impact.

A few more shots, and six guards lay dead on the floor. I found myself struggling to take a breath, standing half crouched and watching the swift devastation unleashed by my rescuers' weapons. "How did . . .?"

"They're modded," Bddo said, hitting his long blaster on the side of the barrel and wincing. "Hot. We remove the heat triggers, among other things. Buggers'll overheat like the dickens, but they pack a punch."

"C'mon, let's move," Ccal said, scrambling ahead.

From here, we kept to the sides of the hallways, taking a couple more turns before hearing more shouting guardsmen. Captain Zent led us through a small door and up an access stairwell one, two, three floors above. Slowly, carefully, Zent and Bddo peeked out the door, weapons first. Bddo muttered something that might have been a curse and pulled back, yanking his captain down. "Two on the left, Cap. Comin' this way."

Ccal gave me a quick *shh* signal. I hadn't moved from my perch on the top stair.

At a nod from Zent, Bddo poked his head back out and fired off a flurry of four blasts before dropping his blaster. Once again, I didn't catch what he muttered, but it didn't sound happy. Then he said, "They're down. We're clear."

The four of us hustled out, navigating a wide room lined with shelves and a couple of desks bearing monitors and keyboards. A few more doors led us out into what appeared to be a . . . docking bay? I was a little shaky on terminology, but the wall to the right was lined with large bay doors, and more vehicles than I could name were arrayed opposite them. Many of them were flying vehicles. The ceiling had rectangular shutters whose function I was pretty sure I could guess.

And guards. None seemed to see us yet, but a few stood nervously near doors, though some may have been off trying to capture us . . . or they were dead now.

"We should be able to get to the ship without alerting anyone," Zent said, beginning to tiptoe down the flight of stairs that led from the door to the hangar floor. "Keep your eyes peeled and blasters ready."

I glanced around the cavernous hangar as I followed them, trying to be quiet. Not that I could make as much noise as the three hulking men in their armor even if I tried. I wasn't sure which ship Zent had pointed out until we got closer. Plated in a silvery metal, it was a relatively small craft bearing four compact thrusters and a sleek nose, with a glass panel reaching from side to side. It rested in a landing dock with stairs leading into the two doors on its left side. Bddo opened the back door and waved me in, following after. Zent took the control seat.

No sooner had he started the engine than a voice called out over a loudspeaker: "Halt! No craft in or out of the prison until the premises are secured."

Ccal, opposite the captain, hit a series of buttons on his radio. "Roger that. We'll stand by till the all-clear." Immediately, he switched channels and gave instructions to someone from the Red Horizon.

"Uh . . ." I glanced around nervously as guards began to gather. Something told me Ccal's response had not satisfied the prison guards.

"Don't worry 'bout them, mate," Bddo said nonchalantly. "Just buckle up and hold onto your seat."

I fumbled with my seatbelt, and he helped me to secure it. "Thanks," I said, "but what is—"

No sooner did I begin to speak than a large *crash!* sounded from above us, and an entire wall blew in. Green sparks and shrapnel flew from the ceiling as metal panels peeled inwards, creaking and snapping following the blast. Smoke gushed in from outside. Alarms wailed.

"That'd be the boys," said Bddo.

"And our cue," added Zent, engaging the thrusters.

α   Chapter 3   α

Merry Chase

We zipped out of the hangar through the new hole in the wall, passing through the billows of smoke, which gave us cover for our escape. In a few seconds, we were out of the smoke and I got my first glimpse of the city.

Haccolces was strange beyond my imagining. I had never actually seen the capital city on my way in, only glimpses of a large complex on my way into the prison. This was . . . I couldn't describe what I felt as I took it in. Structure after structure reaching high into the sky all around us. Smoke billowing from a multitude of towering stacks, lights flaring from a thousand pinpricks on other walls, and . . . metal. So much metal. Steel? They did call it the Steel City, after all. I had only learned about the alloy recently, after coming to Gaea, as we didn't have it back on Mani—only the sparest traces of iron, and they were rarer than gold. Some buildings in Haccolces were constructed mostly of concrete, while others seemed to be entirely made of steel or a similar metal.

The sky above Haccolces, nearly the full dark of night, rippled with angry clouds, roiling and churning restlessly as they stretched farther than I could see. The smoke from the stacks rose up and mixed with them to form a picture of industrialization so alien to me that I could only watch in stunned silence as Zent flew us out of the city. Above it all was one last technological marvel I couldn't explain: A gigantic, transparent red shield stretching across the entire city. A great dome that encapsulated the entire metropolis. I had heard it referenced before by men in the labs, but . . .

We were flying right for it.

"Don't worry," Bddo told me, "We'll bust right through that shield. Watch."

"We don't call her the Shieldbuster for nothing," Zent said, hitting a red button on the center console of the ship just as we approached the edge of the city. The shield wall flickered before us, visible patterns running through it.

Suddenly, the red dome pulsed, and two towers along the city's wall went out, taking a good chunk of the field with it. The towers seemed to be what supplied power to the shield. The shield faded in front of us, staticky webs reaching between the gaps.

Zent pressed another button and fired two missiles from our ship. They shot forwards and crashed into the shield wall, breaking it open before us, and we passed through the breach.

"Yeah!" Bddo shouted. To me, he added, "We spent years developing the right frequencies for a pulse to take out those towers."

Zent looked back from his pilot's seat. "That's how we take back the Mother!"

Ccal, seated opposite his captain, was paying attention to the radar screen on the dash. "Uh, Cap? Little problem."

Zent glanced down with a Hellebes curse. "Two of 'em, directly behind us. And it had to be Stormhawks . . . Are the operatives still in the city?"

Ccal shook his head. "Already gone."

"Hang on," Zent called.

Bddo looked at me and pursed his lips. He was about to say something when Zent suddenly swung the ship into a rotating barrel turn to the right.

The tumble jarred me, and I threw my hands out, tensing my whole body to brace. It felt as though my brain were spinning around in a carriage wheel. But no sooner had Zent acted than a burst of green streaks flew by the left window. They probably would have missed us anyway, but I couldn't say. When we came out of the roll, Zent rammed his steering lever forward, sending us into a sudden dive. He proceeded with another set of evasive maneuvers as more beams passed overhead.

"We don't have guns on this ship?" I asked in panic.

"Nope," Bddo replied. "Not omnidirectional ones."

Before I could work out what that word meant, Zent engaged the thrusters to full and shot forward once more, throwing me backward in my seat. "Oh, this is not comfortable," I muttered as my stomach lurched.

"They're still in pursuit," Ccal warned the captain.

Zent did not answer, continuing to grip the controls tightly and keep an eye on the dash monitor, slowly taking us down in altitude.

No beams hit us, so I took that as a good sign and cautiously looked below us, then out at the surrounding landscape. Now that Zent wasn't doing *quite* such crazy maneuvers, I had an opportunity. And . . . what a sight. It was a mountainous land this side of Haccolces—southeastward—tapering downward mile by mile in topography, with ridges of varying height sprawling outward. Some of the taller peaks, already above us, were capped in snow, below which stretched naked rock. We didn't have that much pure stone on Mani, I was sure of that. Below this layer stretched green forest, however, and finally deep valleys too misted over to make out the bottoms. As far as I could see, there was nothing but wilderness.

Green wilderness. I still wasn't used to the color. The dark of night muted it, but it remained distinctive.

We flew at a wide angle toward one of the nearby mountain peaks, taking brief cover behind the snow-laden stone before shooting for the next highest peak. Zent was taking us down to the valleys.

"Think we can shake them here?" Ccal asked.

"Don't know, but I'll try," Zent replied, navigating past rocky cliffs. As we passed, I marveled at the intricate strata making up the stone: Burnt orange, brown and white.

"Where are we?" I asked Bddo.

The lanky Hellebes shrugged. "Just southeast of Haccolces. Still smack in the midst of North Terrol. Couldn't tell you more than that."

North Terrol. One of the four major continents of Gaea, home to Haccolces and one other city . . . Haven? *Yes, that sounds right.*

"They call these the Rooting Valleys," Zent informed me. "Trying to lose our pursuers right now, but . . . ugh, those Stormhawks are just as fast as this old girl." He proceeded to weave in and out of consecutive close rock outcroppings, displaying what must have been years of skill with the flying machines.

Well, he did say he'd been with the Red Horizon for fifteen years, I recalled, trying to keep my head from whipping to either side. In fact, if what he'd told me a few months back was true, he knew my mother and father. So far, I hadn't managed to dig up any information on him in my memories of what Mother had told me as a child . . . Photographic memory had its limits when she had only given me so much information to go on, not to mention I still had trouble accessing my Memory Vault.

Looking out, I saw we were getting out of the mid-sized mountains and into the forested foothills of one of the verdant valleys. Below us lay a blanket of fog, reminding me of the day I'd flown over the Great Chasm of Mani with Oliver on his glider . . . Oh, I missed that little upstart.

"Hurray for fog," Bddo said unexcitedly.

"Not like they can't find us with their instruments," Ccal pointed out.

"I'll take what we can get," Zent said in a stressed tone. "We just—" He cut off as the ship lurched suddenly and a warning light began to flicker on the dash. "Blast! Now of all times." He quickly flipped a few sliders and switches on the dash, adjusting the ship's individual engine output.

I said nothing, only gritted my teeth and waited to hear that we were going to crash and die.

"Might be able to make it," Zent said. "The shields took most of the damage."

"Those are powerful beams, Cap."

We continued to glide through the fog at a fast clip, though I could feel the ship limping a bit. Soon, however, we took another hit amidst a volley of enemy fire, and I heard *something* explode that should not be exploding.

"Aw, this ain't good," Bddo said, hanging his head. "Kid, get ready to make a sudden, unintended collision with some stone. Maybe a tree if we're lucky."

"Shut up back there," Zent yelled, yanking on his controls. "Trying to slow her down, but we don't want to be shot again . . . It's showing a flat place up ahead; we can make a controlled crash there."

"How controlled?" I demanded. "What do I do?"

"Nothing, kid," Ccal snapped. "We're gonna use Geokinesis. Just brace yourself."

I did, stamping my feet into the metal floor and jamming my head back against the headrest. My heart beat wildly in my chest, as though trying to keep rhythm with the sputtering of our single engine. The ship began to spin uncontrollably despite Zent's best efforts, and soon . . .

BAM!

My whole body jolted, and the noise of the impact hurt my ears. I think the ship tumbled half onto its side, as I was suddenly hanging to the left. But we had stopped. Slowly, I opened my eyes to see that my companions and I seemed to be intact, and even the ship, except for a large spiderweb of cracks running across the glass.

Then I noticed the green glow around us. Ccal and Bddo both wore faces of intense concentration, only now easing up, and around them streamed green energy like a floating liquid. It dissipated quickly, seeming to sink back into the ground, running straight through the ship's hull. I wondered briefly what this phenomenon was, before Ccal looked down at me and said, "Geokinesis. Comes in handy. I assume you don't know how to use it yet?"

I shook my head, an awkward motion from this angle. I'd heard the word, but knew only vaguely what it was.

"Well, let's get out first," Zent said. "And quickly. Hopefully, they'll assume us dead, but we can't be sure. We do have the Mother Heiress, after all."

"Yeah, why would they do that?" Bddo grumbled. "Considering our cargo and all."

Zent did not reply. Instead, he proceeded to heave himself free from his seat, holding it with two heavily-muscled arms as he kicked both doors free, the ones now facing upward and accessible.

The rest of us did likewise, working our buckles free and climbing one at a time out of the ship. Bddo hauled a bag of what I assumed to be provisions out of the hull. The drop to the ground was a solid ten feet, which on Gaea felt like forty. The men took it in stride, but I would have stumbled without my mystery strength, which I now suspected to be Geokinesis, to enhance my feet.

We were deep in a forest at the bottom of the Rooting Valleys. The ship itself had lurched up against a massive tree whose top was shrouded in the misty cover. Its leaves, lit by the lights of our busted ship, were some shade of green like the others scattered around, and more than my own height in length. The vegetation on Gaea was truly something to behold. Dark green moss squelched underfoot.

Zent shut off the flickering floodlights of the ship and led us away, uphill toward . . . the way we had been heading? I wasn't sure. My sense of direction was thoroughly skewed, though I was able to walk just fine, with only minor bruises to attribute to the crash. Just shaken up a bit.

"Anyone hear them?" Ccal asked, scanning the foggy sky.

I shook my head, looking around as I followed my companions. I couldn't hear the drone of engines or the sparking noise of blaster fire colliding with the mountains anymore. All was still, save for our feet splurtching in the wet mossy valley floor and the chirping of . . . birds? Insects? Did frogs make that kind of sound? I was pretty sure they had frogs here on Gaea.

"I think the buggers're gone," Bddo said at length. "What do we do now, Cap?"

Zent stopped, turning his head both directions and listening for a moment. "For now, we're stranded."

α Chapter 4 α

In the Rooting Valleys

Firven 18, 1294:

My home. My beautiful home . . . they have burned it to the ground. I can scarce believe it. I know not the whereabouts of Mother and Father, and I'm trying my best to be strong and not panic. The Anier attacked us two days back. They shot out the windows and door with their new . . . muskets? They shot Father, and he wasn't moving, but I know he'll be all right. Mother was still there, and I know she must have gotten him out and taken him to safety and be nursing him at this moment. But the house, it's gone, burnt to cinders! They torched the whole thing after desecrating it with their horrible weapons. I feel miserable and scared because I don't know why they want me or where I am being taken.

— From Lhinde's Diary

In the end, we decided to camp for the night. In the middle of a foggy, creepy valley. (Trust me, it was creepy at night.)

Zent and Ccal tried for hours to send coded radio signals, but none seemed to be getting through. We even discussed making some smoke signals in the morning to see if the rebels' satellites would pick them up, but that was far too risky. The Gaean League knew roughly where we were; the Red Horizon did not.

So we holed up in a cavern on one side of the valley, whose roof overhung just enough to give us shelter from the rain, should it decide to pour down upon us. Zent said that it was common in this area. We sat around a fire that I'd helped Bddo to make, listening to the chirping of the bog crickets and tree frogs. Bddo had enlightened me as to their identities. And no, they were apparently not good to eat.

The sack had indeed contained food, but precious little else in regards to comfort. There was a spare suit in there that they'd brought along for me, for which I was very grateful. I took it, searching around for the best place to change despite their blank looks. Idiots. They didn't even know what a woman was, much less how to treat one modestly. Finally, I went a short hike outside the cave into the fog and put the suit on. It was composed of elastic black pants, a shirt and a long-sleeved jacket, all of which were probably made to fit the smallest of Hellebes, in other words someone bigger than me. Oh well. I stuffed my prison clothes behind a tree and walked back to the fire, frowning as I tested the fit. I'd never worn anything so stretchy in my life, let alone halfway formfitting. We'd brought sheets of moss up from the boggy areas to dry by the fire, and I plopped myself down on my own sheet. It would be comfortable enough for my tired back after this hectic day. Not to mention I was used to prison comforts, or lack thereof.

"So, mate," Bddo said at one point. "What's it like being female?"

The question took me by surprise so much that I gave a sputtering laugh. "Where did that come from?"

The lanky Hellebes shrugged. "Just thought I'd ask. Seeing as, y'know, you're the only one alive."

Oh. Right. I nodded. "I try to forget about that. I guess you've got a point, huh?" I tried to think of an answer to give him, but I couldn't come up with anything that wasn't exceedingly awkward. "I don't know. I suppose I mostly just feel like an outsider here. Like—like I'm home, but I don't belong."

Bddo looked like he wanted to say more, but he gave a pursed-lip nod that said, *Fair enough.*

He started to say something more, but Ccal grabbed his arm. "Just stop, man. She's obviously overwhelmed."

I smiled despite myself. With a grunt, I leaned back against the moss I'd dragged up. "How do you guys manage living here? With the heavy gravity?"

Three heads swiveled my way. "We're raised with it," Bddo said. "Not much we can do about it. To us, this just feels normal."

"You're from off-planet," Zent said. "It's going to take time to get used to. We'll get you acclimated eventually. As a female, you're naturally weaker, and as a half-blood, you're at an even bigger physical disadvantage. But once you learn to control your Geokinetic powers, you'll be unstoppable."

"Why is that?" I asked.

"Because female Hellebes are supposed to be crazy strong," Ccal said. "No limits."

"No limits, huh?" I raised a hand up, turning my forearm and clenching my fingers. "Sounds nice. I don't know, I feel pretty exhausted."

"Once you master Geokinesis, it will keep you going for days," Zent explained. "I'll bet you're pretty hungry already, too."

"What, you aren't?"

"Here," he said, handing me a decidedly sketchy foil-packaged snack. Not as sketchy as the ones I'd eaten in the Haccolces facility, of course, so I took it gratefully. "Now, before you eat that, I want you to focus. You already know how to use Geokinesis a little bit instinctively. Focus on that energy beneath your feet and just sort of feel it."

Instinctively? How could he know that? I eyed the captain silently, trying to do as he instructed. I could feel it like a rushing river far below, flowing in every direction. I'd sensed it in Haccolces, but I'd taken it for granted as another strange feature of Gaea. "All right, now what?"

"Pull from it. Slowly, just a bit. Don't use it; just pull."

"Ok." I . . . supposed I did know how to do that on impulse. I drew from the planetary energy of Gaea, sucking it into my body through my palms, and my skin began to glow ever so faintly with wispy green light—a phenomenon I'd never observed back on Mani. There, I had hungered for this but never truly gotten it. It felt . . . good. Comforting.

"There you go. That will tide you over for a while at a time, and if you draw just a bit all day, you can keep your metabolism going even without food."

I looked down at the pre-packaged meal in my hand. "So . . ."

"Go ahead and eat it," Ccal said. "You need whatever you can get until you're up to speed."

I unwrapped the meal and ate the hard, brown bar inside. It was dry and crunchy, but didn't taste any worse than it looked. Soon, my stomach no longer grumbled at all. I kept up the small intake of planetary energy as instructed. "So, Ccal, Bddo, what's your story?" I asked. "How'd you end up with the rebels?"

The two soldiers looked at one another. "Well," Bddo said after a moment, "We're in the Gaean Air Force, just like the captain here. Or . . . were, before that all went in the dumpster today. But we're also Red Horizon."

I nodded. I had gathered that much already.

"We joined the Red Horizon six years back after Cap took us into his confidence," Ccal added. "I'm the one that convinced this idiot to join."

"That's only 'cos I'd never been a rebel before," Bddo objected.

"Sure it was."

"They are under my command in the Air Force," Zent explained. "We all lead another life in the Red Horizon. Needless to say, we don't actually get back to HQ often. With my military rank, I was able to get the three of us on gatewatch duty very often."

"Right," Ccal said, "and Cap would just leave us there on that Mother-forsaken rock and head out for meetings with the Red Horizon."

"Doesn't the Senate keep pretty close tabs on the island?" I asked.

"You'd be surprised," Zent said. "Technically, the Senate considers it a key location, but as long as they have someone guarding it, they don't care too much. No cameras on the whole premises, no weaponry."

I frowned. Something about that seemed strange.

That night as my body slept, I retreated to my Vault.

Nobody has them back on Mani. It took me all the way up to my arrival on Gaea to come to grips with my ability. The Legaleians store memories in their brains just like us, only . . . we Hellebes don't forget them. We *never* forget.

It's just that I was the only Hellebes who couldn't access my Vault all the time. Only when asleep. I took it to be a side effect of being a half-breed.

For me, the place was a dream world shrouded in mist. It looked slightly different each time, but tonight the floor was made of craggy rocks, possibly my mind subconsciously telling me that I should be sleeping in a more comfortable location. And, as always, there she was: White, my assistant figment who kept me sane. She appeared as a young girl, maybe ten years old, dressed in white and wearing her waist-length pearly hair straight like normal.

"Hello, Lyn," she greeted me warmly.

"White, I want to know about that island, the one with the Gate of Gaea where I wound up after the explosion."

The girl looked up briefly. "Mmm, you're out of luck, then. All you've got is what the guys said last night and a few comments from the background as you were escorted between labs. Gatewatch Isle doesn't get talked about much."

I started to ask if she could play them when I suddenly heard the exact audio in my head from weeks past:

". . . That island is but a relic of the past now. More like a dead crime scene. No one expected the child to actually . . ." A snippet I'd caught from one of the doctors who had examined me on more than one occasion.

". . . Gatewatch Isle are all quarantined . . ." This one I had only caught as a tiny snippet.

There were a couple more references, but no meaningful context or information to go along with them.

"Anything else you want to see?" White asked, looking up at me patiently.

I took a dream breath and began rattling off my list to my assistant. I basically just wanted to go back through all the early memories I had from my first year of life with my mother, when she used to tell me information to reference later in life. I could not say if she had predicted my inability to access my Vault by instinct.

The first thing I did was run through all the Gaean terminology that would be useful to know, struggling through the harder words and paying close attention to the context. She had often gone out of her way to explain terms and topics, but sometimes she would get lost in her own familiarity with her world. After all, she had been almost like a . . . I really didn't know what, other than the progenitor of all Hellebes in some capacity. They kept her in a lab where they harvested her eggs somehow? And, according to Haccolces scientists, she'd been kept alive for centuries and played a key role in the Gaean Elites' control of the world. So surely she had far more knowledge than she was reasonably able to pass down to me.

There was one thing, though, relating to that exact topic. She mentioned once that she had uploaded her own Vault to a data bank in the labs below Haccolces . . . the city that I had just fled. The Steel City, capital not only of North Terrol but of the entire Gaean League—and home of Emperor Lldsaor. How had I missed that before? I'd run through most of my mother's words during the eighty-eight days spent in my cell alone.

Her entire Vault . . . uploaded to a data center. You could do that?

α Chapter 5 α

Through the Wilderness

Norven 16, 1294:

Here I sit in a prison cell, feet chained to the wall behind me and nothing but a woolen blanket to huddle in. The rags covering my body are filthy by this point. I have been here for nigh a month and only now got up the gumption to write in my journal. At least they let me keep it. Why did the Anier take me from my home, from my loving mother and father, only to dump me in this dank jail beneath the town hall? It makes no sense. All I know is that I am famished. The guards leave me food once per day. Once! I crave nothing more than to quit this cell, even if it means facing the Anier again . . .

— From Lhinde's Diary

We arose early the next morning and began discussing what to do. No one had contacted us yet, and that was a problem.

It was so strange to me that it could already be light out. Or, well, lighter—thanks to the fog blanket. Nighttime had just . . . come and gone. A whole day cycle. I was used to the lunar cycle of Mani, where each day was a month long. I could see how sleep cycles made much more sense on this planet, but . . . it was still strange. I rather missed the daily auroras, but I'd give that up in exchange for two moons. When I grew up, we never had a moon at all . . . we *were* the moon. One of them.

Strange stuff.

Ccal let out a grunting sigh as he stretched, broad back cracking with the volume of hoofbeats on stone. "Well, Cap? Your call."

Zent scratched his mustache and goatee. "There isn't much for it, boys. We'll have to strike out southward and see if we can make it to the closest shelter."

"We've got one in the Craglands?" Bddo asked skeptically.

The captain nodded. "Maybe a hundred miles south of here." He glanced at me. "Sorry, Lyn. You're just going to have to try your best to keep pace."

"A-a hundred miles," I repeated. "We're going to walk a hundred miles?"

"No, we're going to run a hundred miles." He shrugged. "Give or take. It might be a bit farther."

Ccal clapped me on the shoulder with a massive hand, causing my entire body to shudder. "You'll do fine. You're a female, remember? Infinite channeling?"

I glared at the giant man. "What do you take me for? I hardly know anything about Geokinesis, and my power is *not* infinite."

"We'll give ya some tips," Bddo said encouragingly. He looked over at Zent once more. "We, uh, we are going to run all that way?"

"Affirmative. Better start stretching."

"Okay, just checking."

"So," Ccal said, leaning forward in a runner's pose. "Remember this one thing and you'll do fine. Breathe. As slowly and regularly as you can manage. It helps to circulate that Geothermic energy. Your body is more capable than you think. You'll get out of breath far quicker than we will, but as weak as you are, you're also a fraction of our weight."

"And don't stop channeling that mean green steam," Bddo said. "Here, have another bar. We've got to go quickly."

I took the snack, but not without a bit of grumbling. "What about water?" I said between bites. "We've hardly had anything to drink all day."

"Our Hellebes bodies are very efficient at cooling, even when burning planetary energy," Zent explained. "As you exercise, you'll find this out. Your pores open up, exchanging heat while retaining most of your body's moisture. We can make do on very little water. Can't speak for Legaleian hybrids, of course."

I shook my head. "I'll . . . just hope I'm similar to you guys, then." I supposed I had never needed quite as much water as my Legaleian friends, but the idea of baking in the sun all day was not very appealing.

"We've still got some left," Bddo added, shaking the water flask. Maybe we'll get lucky and find some more fresh water."

"Let's go," Zent said, propelling himself into a run.

The other men broke into a run right behind him, and I followed as close as I could. I may not have been used to running in this world, but I could keep pace with them with effort. Following Bddo's advice, I drew upon the lifeblood of Gaea to power my legs, breathing as regularly as I could manage. I had no idea how fast we were going, but faster than I normally ran even on Mani. I doubted I could sustain it for long.

We streaked through the misty forest, weaving our way between trees, headed for the southern end of the valley. The fog was still thick overhead. Hopefully it helped to hide us. Gradually, I found myself lagging further and further behind, breaths coming in short gasps. "Wait," I panted, "Guys, I can't keep up."

Bddo slowed and looked backwards. "Come on, Lynchazel, you can do it! Don't let the earth win!"

"Easy for—you to say," I muttered between breaths. It was all I could do to follow Ccal's earlier instructions and force myself to breathe slowly. *Breathe, breathe!* It wasn't easy. Looking down, I tried to imagine myself drawing in the planetary energy like heat from a fire. That was how it had worked with my Coaction on Mani: I pictured it in my mind first, and then it became so. Never before had I needed anywhere near this much planetary energy, nor had I known I could take in so much of it. I pulled more, forcing myself onwards and catching up to the men slowly.

Finally, after an hour or more of running, Zent called a halt for a short break. Gratefully, I stumbled to a stop behind them and nearly fell to my knees as they threatened to buckle. Was this how normal Legaleians like Kaen and Mydia felt when trying to run distances? I'd never experienced the displeasure of my lungs feeling like I had accidentally set them ablaze with my own flame Coaction. I bent over, clutching my jittery knees with my hands, gasping for breath.

Zent bent down and looked me in the face. "You really aren't acclimated, are you?" he didn't even look like he was breathing hard, much less sweating. Truth be told, I wasn't sweating much either, probably because of the reasons Zent had explained already.

I shook my head, a terrible taste clinging in my throat. "I told you."

"Here." Bddo handed me the water flask. "Just a swig, mind you."

I nodded and poured myself a mouthful. A big one. Then I handed it back. "Thanks."

Looking around for the first time, I surveyed our surroundings. We were out of the valleys and into an area of foothills gently sloping this way and that. A stream flowed to our right, trickling out from the mountains, and Bddo went to fill up the flask there after we'd all drunk our fill. According to Zent, from here on out we would progress into what they called the Craglands, a parched expanse of broken, stony ground.

A few minutes later, we headed back out. Ever southward. By now, Sol had risen to well above the horizon, bathing the grassy fields beneath our feet in golden light through partial clouds. In the clear patches, I could see the radiant blue hue of the atmosphere. Yellow sun, blue sky. It couldn't be more alien to me. Before coming to Gaea, I never would have believed it had someone told me.

Fortunately, the breather had allowed my body enough respite to go on for another while. I gritted my teeth against my body's complaints and tried to keep pace with the Hellebes soldiers. *Come on, body . . .*

As I ran, my mind wandered toward my Manese friends, who had accompanied me so faithfully to the end of the world and . . . past, had things gone right. As far as I knew, the explosion killed them, and if not, I failed to see how they could survive a fall off the tallest tower on Mani. What a snake, that Domon . . . he had played us all. Why he wanted to destroy the Gate, I had no idea, but we had still accomplished one thing: I was here on Gaea. And I was going to learn what I needed here. Then I could find a way back to the silver world and finish what Rhidea had striven for. I would fix what was broken between out worlds, somehow.

But . . . I probably wouldn't ever see my friends again.

We emerged from the foothills onto the rocky ground that Zent had described. It was hard for me to pay close attention with my chest feeling like it was exploding from exertion, but I could see as we ran downhill that the grass petered out ahead, leaving only stone. Jagged cracks ran out through the stone, some appearing to be fairly wide and long. It looked dry and desolate, and . . . everything I didn't want to be near. No animals in sight, either.

Finally, blessedly, they stopped, and once more I nearly collapsed right on the ground. I panted and heaved for a moment before taking the water jug that Bddo was passing around. I noticed that the others were quite out of breath as well at this point. Their stamina was not endless, simply greater than my own. The sun was now high in the sky, and the air temperature was rising considerably.

"The Craglands get nice and toasty in the daytime," Ccal said as if reading my mind. "Just wait until we get to the volcanic parts."

I groaned. Volcanic. I knew the word only from reference, but I understood the concept enough to wish we didn't have to proceed farther.

"You'll soon see why no one ever wanted to build a city out in these parts," Zent said.

I looked up with a frown. "A city?"

"We only dwell in cities nowadays, or didn't you know?" Zent replied. "Been that way for centuries. The Nine Cities of Man."

"So I've heard. It's just . . . there aren't *any* people outside of the cities? The walls, the shield domes?"

Zent shook his head. "Only fools. And rebels like us."

"It's not safe," Bddo added.

"But . . . why? We're out here, and aside from thirst and hunger, I don't see much danger."

The soldiers looked at each other. After a moment, Bddo asked, "You don't even know about the Cydenges? Or the radiation hazards? Man, they really sheltered you."

I shook my head at each question. "No. Just mentions. Aren't the Cydenges like . . . some kind of creature that almost destroyed the world?"

"They *did* destroy the world," Zent said. "Over one thousand years ago, wiping out much of human civilization. And they've attacked on many occasions since. We never know when a strike will come."

"How long has it been since the last one? And where do they attack? Do they really come from Luna?"

Zent looked at his companions once more. "They do. Luna is their world, and we let them keep it rather than trying to invade and wipe them out. They target high energy signatures, and can be *quite* dangerous. It's been six years now since the last attack."

"Oh." I couldn't think of anything to say to that. They really told me nothing of this? Well, of course they didn't. The people at the labs were not exactly on my side, and certainly weren't forthcoming with their information. What more insane things was I going to learn about my birth world in the future?

Eventually, we got going once more, though no one ran at the pace we had earlier. We kept up a steady speed—and I tried to ignore the pain in nearly every muscle of my body—until late afternoon, as Sol's heat was just starting to abate, when Zent declared that we would stop for the night.

I immediately dropped to the stony ground, heedless of the pain it caused to my rear end. Certainly I had never felt this bad in my entire life. No one had. Humans weren't meant to feel like this, right?

Bddo crouched down beside me, placing one hand on the ground and one on my shoulder. "You're doing well," he said between gasping breaths, chest heaving up and down. "We're worn out, too. How far do you think we've gone today, Cap?"

Zent stopped stretching mid-pose. "Perhaps fifty miles." He consulted his wrist console, a device all three soldiers wore on one arm that gave them access to a suite of features I couldn't name. "We should be almost halfway there."

I felt at the skin on my forehead. It was hot and dry. "What'd you say that sickness was called? Sunburn?"

Ccal took a quick glance at me and said, "Yep, you've got it. You're a pale one. What, do you not get any sunlight on Mani? At least not much UV?"

I squinted against my pounding headache, still struggling to get my breath back. "Don't know what UV is. But we get a lot of cloud coverage back there. And Sol doesn't really shine very brightly, not like this sun—or, well, like it does here. And it's not yellow, it's white."

Bddo looked at me like I was from another world. "White? How does that even work?"

I shrugged. "Magic? Or something about the atmosphere. Everything on Mani is some shade of silver. It's made of silver. So I never questioned it."

Zent turned around. "Silver. Mani is made of silver." He said it in a questioning, almost disbelieving tone, as though I'd quoted a nursery rhyme.

I nodded tiredly. "Silver. Do you have silver here on Gaea?"

"We do, but we use it as currency because of its rarity. Or we used to, rather. It's considered a precious metal."

I scratched my head and then immediately regretted it because it irritated my scalp. "Well, I suppose I never would have believed that you guys use iron every day here on Gaea. Steel. Iron and carbon, right? My people don't know anything about science. And now I can see why, because it wouldn't do them any good on Mani."

I don't think any of the soldiers knew what to say to my ramblings. We broke out some more dry rations, after which Zent got up and motioned for me to rise as well. "Here, Lyn. We're going to do some training."

I felt my stomach sink at his words. "Some . . . what? What kind of training?"

"Geokinesis."

"What! But we just did that all day." I couldn't believe what I was hearing. I could hardly stand.

"No, we didn't. Not this kind." Zent put his fists up in front of his face like a boxer's stance.

Why do I have a bad feeling about this . . . ? I took the same pose. After

Kaen and Kymhar's training on Mani, it was comfortable, almost natural.

"Good stance," he said.

"Thanks," I mumbled, shortly before the ground rumbled and *moved* underfoot. Suddenly, what was solid stone became a shuddering, rippling surface, and I slipped, falling backward.

"Aw, now that's not a good stance," Bddo called from behind me.

I spun my head to glare at him from the ground, rubbing my bruised head, and then clenched my abdominals, looking down between my legs. The stone was solid once more, but in an altered, broken state. "That's not fair! My legs can barely move as it is."

"Hard lessons," he replied, staring smugly down at me.

Maintaining my graceful crab-stance, I asked, "How did you do that?"

Zent shrugged. "Geokinetic mastery. It's actually an elementary trick. Watch." He changed his stance, stamping his foot onto the earth and pointing with a half-tilted hand. He jerked his hand upward, and the earth cracked in a straight line, bursting forth with a spray of green planetary energy. It swirled and sputtered in the air before dissipating.

I stared in awe. "You can . . . you can just do that?"

"There's a lot you don't know," the captain said. "We need to get you up to speed as quickly as possible. As you already know, female Hellebes are famous for having virtually no limit to the energy they can draw from Gaea. And you're the last one, so this is imperative. Now get up!"

He spoke with such sharpness that I jolted to my feet with a quick, "Yessir."

"Take your stance." I did so, and he said, "Keep your footing. Feel the earth, read my movements, and respond accordingly."

Feel the earth . . . read his movements? That sounded a lot harder to do than to say, but I took my fighting stance and tried to pay attention. I kept my eyes on him, as that was what my former training told me to do in a fight. My hips ached with every rock of my body. As he swept a foot to the side, I felt the earth move underneath me and dodged to avoid it, but I misjudged and stepped into it instead of away. I lost my footing, landing hard on the rock, this time on top of multiple stones that had broken free.

A loud gasp burst from my chest. After getting my breath back, I shouted, "Are you trying to kill me?"

Zent didn't respond to my outburst, but simply motioned me back up.

I rose with a wince.

"Wider stance," Zent snapped.

I adjusted my feet shakily, trying not to slacken my stance from fatigue and pain. My body ached, not just from the all-day exertion but now from numerous bruises. Stone didn't feel good to hit so hard, with the level of gravity this planet had . . .

This time I moved in the right direction to avoid his Geokinetic trap. Almost immediately, however, I felt the earth . . . twitch, and suddenly the stone burst under my feet. I tried to move, but I was too late.

I bit back another shout of, "How did you do that!" and instead tried to understand how he did it without moving his body. But I didn't even know how he was causing the earth to move and quake. Some means of manipulating the Geothermic energy to push and pull on the stone . . .

"I don't need to make motions with my body in order for the earth to respond," Zent explained. "It can be useful for focusing and channeling the power, especially for a beginner, but it's not necessary and you can't expect your opponents to do you the kindness of tipping off their attacks with hands and feet. So, what do you do?"

I realized my mistake. I'd stopped paying attention to the most important sign every combatant gives: Eye movement. No fighter could keep from subconsciously moving his eyes before making every move. I nodded, locking eyes with him.

"That's right, watch my eyes. You were doing it for a bit."

Zent proceeded to make a few more Geokinetic attacks, leaving much of the ground around us broken or twisted, prompting me to step carefully, but I managed to avoid every one of them . . . until I tripped on the rocks left by his traps and went down. I tried to catch myself with my hands, but only banged those up as well as my palms skidded. I gritted my teeth, struggling not to snap at my tormentor.

Surprisingly, he bent down and helped me up this time. "Don't worry, Lyn," he said in a more compassionate tone. "This will take a lot of practice to get used to. Try to ignore the scrapes and bruises. We Hellebes heal quickly thanks to all the Geothermic energy we channel. Your sunburn, too—it will be gone by tomorrow."

Bddo clapped from behind me. "Good job, gal! Not a bad performance for a first-timer."

I gave him a tired smile and turned back to the captain, making a conscious effort to not fall down. I pulled on Gaea's energy to strengthen my legs. "So how do I do what you did?"

"Practice," he said. "Moving the ground, be it rock or dirt, is only one of the many tricks you'll pick up. It's all about feeling the earth and channeling its energy. You mentally command it to move and reshape, and it will do it." He raised a foot and stomped the stone, and suddenly all the broken pieces of stone and ridges that were torn up seemed to soften and reform. Within a few seconds, we stood once more upon a smooth plane of rock, albeit with the same cracks that divided the plain into pieces.

I gaped. "Wow. That . . . could come in quite handy."

"Oh, it does," Ccal said from his seated position. "You'll learn."

Zent glanced over at the shorter man. "Like you're any good at it."

"Hey! I'm not the best fighter in the world, but I'm quite passable."

"Yeah, right," Bddo said. "That's why we let you handle communications."

"No, that's because that's my specialty. Not to mention marksmanship."

"Enough!" Zent cut in. "Keep it down."

The captain proceeded to guide me in manipulating the stone as he had. I got it to move a couple of times, but it was far trickier than it looked.

"It's all about willpower," he said. "That and concentration."

"Just like Authority . . ." I said to myself.

"Hm? I mean, in a way."

"Oh." I shook my head. "No, Authority is our name for the magic we use on Mani. The elements will obey us if we possess enough Authority, like a servant his master." I was quoting my wise teacher, Rhidea of Randhorn. Auroras, I missed that woman.

Zent nodded. "So, it's true. That they are wizards."

I laughed. "I used to think that. But it's really not so different from this. Except that there are eight different elements, and some people are stronger in certain elements than in others. I am a fire mage."

"You can use this magic?" Zent sounded understandably shocked. "I had no idea. But that shouldn't surprise me."

"Wait, you can do both?" Bddo said. "That's an impressive crossbreed right there. What?" That last was directed at his companion, who had elbowed him in the side.

"About that . . ." I tried to make a flame appear in my hand, as I'd done many times since coming to Gaea, and . . . I sighed. "It doesn't work here. Mani has this special Wellspring that is said to be the source of all magic, so I guess it's just impossible here."

"We'll just take your word for it," Ccal said.

Zent grunted. "Well, as we were saying . . ." And he began his coaching once more.

Sometime later, I was finally allowed to go to bed. Which, here in the Craglands, meant curling up on some nice, comfy rocks. Bddo did me the favor of using Geokinesis to mold the stone into my vague form, making it marginally more tolerable. But I didn't care; I was asleep within a minute.

α Chapter 6 α

Shelter

Norven 25, 1294:

They finally came to let me out, claiming there'd been a misunderstanding. Something about the Prince being assassinated abruptly. I've never paid attention to such events, and even an atrocity such as that . . . well, there is always some stir, some intrigue, some horrible news. However, they say the Anier have long been opposed to the Prince and his ways, pushing for a new government. What this means for Terrolia and Starklett, I know not, but I fear it may affect me greatly. When they brought me before the important man of the Anier, Lord Teuchan, they shoved me to my knees and bade me speak when spoken to, or else taste their whips. Lord Teuchan began to rattle off a story of the origins of humanity and our inevitable demise, most of which I didn't understand because of my country education. But I got the gist of it: Our race is waning, and the Anier want to experiment with me to see if they can create a cure for our disease . . . our curse.

— From Lhinde's Diary

The next day, we rose early and resumed our high-speed journey through the wilderness. Ccal had to physically kick me out of my sleeping state, so worn out was I from the previous day's travails. I prided myself on being a light sleeper, but not today. Somehow, Zent's words proved true, and my body had healed itself overnight, leaving only a lingering exhaustion deep in my bones. As a very wise man (Bddo) once said, "That's a good feeling," despite looking somewhat under the weather himself.

The day went similarly to the previous one, including a lot of running and few breaks. Only today, we had far more limited water. The sky was still a clear blue, nearly devoid of clouds, as it had been most of the time in these dry lands, and the ground beneath our feet remained mostly grey rock etched with the distinctive webbed cracks. Stepping and leaping over those was only one more addition to the unpleasantness of the journey.

I will admit that I asked multiple times how close we were to the shelter, but Bddo, who might appear to be the fittest runner of us, also asked at least twice, so I felt a bit better.

At our second break of the day, a couple hours shy of noon, Zent remarked on the amount of volcanic activity in the nearby area. I hadn't even noticed, but now that he pointed it out, I saw the spurts of smoke from multiple small fissures in the earth, where the cracks ran deeper.

"What causes that?" I asked.

"We're on a fault line," Ccal explained. "Where Gaea's tectonic plates meet up. The cracks in the rock are partly from lack of water nearby, but also the seismic activity. I'm sure you felt the rumbling off and on all day?"

I hesitated. I hadn't been paying much attention to the ground, despite Zent's lessons the previous night, but I had felt a tremor on a few occasions. "Yes, I remember."

"That's tectonic shifting. Some of these plates of rock have ground together enough with the vibration that their cracks have opened up into the earth. Where the Geothermic energy runs stronger, it sprays up into the air, along with brimstone and lava closer to the volcanoes."

"Is that them in the distance over there?" I asked, shading my eyes against the sun to squint at vague mounds on the southeastern horizon. The heat distortion from the sunbaked stone didn't help anything.

The men followed my gaze. "Yes," Zent said. "There are more volcanoes farther south. You'll get a better view."

Soon, we resumed our running. As usual, I forced my legs to move and keep moving. Ccal and Bddo still tried to give me advice on how I should be channeling energy more efficiently, but they didn't seem to understand my struggle with the steep learning curve.

Around noon, we began to see closer volcanoes. Gouts of smoke and even lava flows scattered the surrounding countryside, and, in more than one location, the very earth had been ripped up violently. Some sprayed streams of green energy, proving Ccal correct. It was hard to gauge how tall the peaks were, but easily the size of the foothills we had left yesterday, some actively leaking bright red lava. I made counting the volcanoes into a game to keep my mind occupied while my body worked itself to keep up with the others. But the more I saw of them, the more a certain thought nagged at me.

"Hey," I said at one point, "Why are the volcanoes disconnected? Why are they smaller than the mountains around Mt. Beides if this is on a fault line?"

"So, you figured it out?" Bddo asked through heavy breaths, turning his head to look at me. "There's tectonic activity in this area, but that's only part of what created the volcanoes. Right, Cap? It's really the Elites' fault."

The larger man grunted. "That's what they say, anyway. This area is cursed to bear the weight of their sins, if you believe the tales. When the Gaean League decided to use Geothermics industrially, it wasn't long before they pulled all stops and went . . . big. They threw everything out of whack, and now the entire planet is in a state of imbalance."

"But—but don't all the Hellebes use Gaea's power every day? Geokinesis and all that?"

Zent looked back with a laugh. "This? This is nothing. You have no idea the amount of energy they siphoned—and do every day—for their own purposes. Even back at Red Horizon HQ, we use a lot. Now your mother . . . she knew. She knew exactly."

I felt the hair on the back of my neck prickle. *My mother . . .* But what *did* she know? What were the experiments she spoke of? She had mentioned the Gaean League harnessing energy, and . . . through *her*. But it made no sense. What did that have to do with her being the "Mother" of all Hellebes? I had to get to the bottom of it. I had to learn what happened to this world.

I picked up my pace, boosting a few of my strides with extra energy to catch up to Zent, who had gotten ahead. "Zent, what did they want? What were their purposes? My mother never expounded on it. I've been through all my memories of her words, but . . . I still feel like I know nothing."

He regarded me with a serious expression, saying nothing for a few strides. "I don't know it all, either, but . . . there's a lot to tell, and you're not ready for it yet."

"Not ready? When will I be ready?"

"When you've heard it from her yourself."

"From . . . so from her Vault?" After a moment, I gasped. "You know about it!"

The captain gave me a strange look and a small shake of his head. "Don't get ahead of yourself. It's more like wishful thinking right now." I opened my mouth, but he cut me off. "Don't even bother asking. We don't have any intel on it, if it even does exist. We're working on a plan . . . but we can't do anything with you until you're trained and in fighting shape. That will take some time, as you know. We can't risk taking you on a mission until we know you can defend yourself." With that, he turned his face forward and fell silent.

As I lost Zent, Bddo came up beside me. "What they wanted was protection for the Hellebes race."

Protection . . . "The Elites, you mean? From what?"

"Take a guess."

"These Cydenges guys?"

Bddo nodded. "Dead on. At least . . . that was what they said."

"And did they achieve that?"

"Depends who you ask. Ask a fellow like me, and I'd say no, since the Cydenges are still out there, biding their time on Luna, waiting to devour us all."

Late that evening, just as I thought they would make me run all through the night, we came upon the location. Zent and Ccal repeatedly checked their wrist consoles until Zent announced that we were right near the hideout.

I stirred as though awoken from sleep, giving a delayed whoop of joy. "How close?"

The men ignored me, slowing their pace and pointing around the area. We had reached a part of the rocky plains where there seemed to be actual soil and a sparse bit of strange, webby vegetation. Could there be water nearby? We had long since passed the volcanic fields, and now especially with the sun down, it wasn't so unbearably hot.

Bddo and I slowed behind them until we were all walking at a more normal speed. I was able to catch my breath, or rather try to, as I compensated for the men's longer stride with a quicker one. Zent led us to a cleft in the earth that looked a bit . . . different from the other cracks, which were quite sparse at this point. It looked almost man-made.

Zent stooped in front of the crevice and then hopped in, falling nearly up to his knees. "Bddo, Ccal, give me a hand," he said in a ragged voice, deep as ever but dry and worn out.

The two Hellebes crept into the pit beside him and bent to take hold of what appeared to be the ground, lifting it up to reveal that it was in fact a large door. Sandy soil poured down from the door's surface as they pulled it up. Perhaps a meter wide by two in length, the door cut a groove into the soil that covered it as they heaved it upward. Pressurized cylinders held it open, leaving enough headroom for the average Hellebes to descend the dark steps in a crouch.

Zent hit a button on his suit, turning on its flashlight feature. "Let's go. Come on, Lyn." He waved us inside and pulled the door shut behind us. The soldiers' chest lights lit up cement walls and a reinforced ceiling, which followed the stairwell to the bottom ten meters below surface level. Our feet tapped on the cement stairs with the forlorn echo of a long-abandoned escape tunnel. At the bottom, the tunnel extended in front of us, terminating at a steel door. Likely stainless, as I could spot no rust on it. And to think that I didn't even know what rust was before coming to Gaea. . . .

Zent opened the door and led us inside the shelter, flipping a switch to turn on a series of hanging light bars. In the unnaturally white light, we beheld a large space, perhaps twelve meters square, with various shelves lining the walls packed with supplies of all kinds. Cobwebs and dust decorated the entirety of the chamber, and multiple missing bulbs in the lights completed the look of disrepair, some blinking and twitching. There were two tables and a dozen chairs stacked against the right-hand wall, and a few doors led off into side rooms, one of which was labeled "Docking," and another, "River Access."

"There's a, uh, river near here?" I asked, confused.

Zent turned to look at the door I'd pointed out. "Yes, an underground river. More like a stream, but in these parts, that's plenty. It's the secret entry point to this base, and how the Red Horizon was able to construct a lot of similar bases across North Terrol. Even a few in South Terrol."

"Speaking of which!" Bddo interrupted, looking around. "That means water. I'll be back."

The long-legged man, bless his soul, returned a minute later with a large jug of water, giving us all a drink. Somewhat less blessedly, he began stripping off his suit immediately afterward, saying he'd found the shower room. He was just about to pull off his pants when he caught a look from Ccal and turned to me with a confused expression. "What, she's—you're one of us. I don't . . . Okay, never mind. Whoever else needs to rinse his grimy pits off, follow me."

Zent raised his hand and followed.

Ccal looked at me with a half-amused, half-apologetic look. "Sorry. I don't think he catches on very quickly. I can tell you're uneasy around us. I'll be back. Just don't . . . touch anything till we get done. Don't want Cap getting upset."

I sighed and leaned back against the wall near the door. A sigh that came from within my bones, echoed by every screaming, overworked muscle in my body. A shower sounded infinitely good right about now . . . but I could wait fifteen minutes.

α Chapter 7 α

Rivers in the Desert

Norven 25, 1294 (Continued):
It made me very nervous, this idea of experimentation. I had no idea
what all this would entail. Apparently, they captured twenty-three other
girls of childbearing age, so I was just one of many. In fact, I believe I am
the youngest. After Teuchan was done explaining these things, he gave the
guards a gentle order to unhand me and only restrain me if I tried to run.
Then he had them take me to a room where I could wash up and put on
clean — if simple and odd — clothes. After this, and some much-
appreciated food, I was sent off in another carriage to a different town. I'm
still riding in the cab, sweating and nervous of my future. I only pray that
my fortune improves and I can see my parents again soon.
— From Lhinde's Diary

I felt like a new woman after a hot shower. Not quite the same as a hot soak
at Mydia's palace, but people on Gaea weren't very fond of baths, particularly
the ones who built rebel emergency bases. I'd spent most of my life as an
orphan, anyway, somewhere between peasant and urchin as the class
structure back in Nytaea went.

Only problem was finding some clothes now.

The men were busy fiddling with computers and communication
instruments as I poked my head out of the shower room, wearing only one
of their strange, thin towels. Ccal glanced up and made the universal
shushing gesture. After another minute of trying to get Bddo's attention, I
gave up and stepped into the room barefoot, heading toward the back. There
should be a door . . . ah, there it was. I kicked open one labeled "Locker."

Inside, I found rows and rows of, well, lockers, as well as many jumpsuits
hanging on the far wall. Exactly what I was looking for. After rummaging

through multiple sections, I found what could pass for underwear and pants. Far bigger than my size, but thank the auroras for elastic technology. What kind of fiber was all this stuff, anyway? Some kind of synthetic plastic material, as far as I knew. Nothing the Hellebes made seemed to be remotely natural. After donning a shirt that was supposed to be form-fitting, I made myself a makeshift hair tie and called it good enough. There were no mirrors to check myself in, but then I wasn't Mydia . . . I could manage.

Wandering back outside, I found Bddo poring through the rations shelves whilst Ccal and the captain sent messages back and forth to HQ. "Hey, there you are!" Bddo said, coming over to take me by the shoulder. "Took you long enough. The suit fits you just fine."

It definitely did not; I was the one wearing it, so I should know. But I simply replied, "How's the communication going?"

"They got a hold of HQ and are filling them in."

"So, what's our plan?"

"Whatever Cap says it is," Bddo answered. "Here, want one?" He handed me a foil-wrapped object, long and flat.

"What is it?"

"Dunno. Some kind of protein bar. I think it's made mostly of meat."

I unwrapped the bar and sniffed it. "Is this for humans?"

He shrugged, popping his own bar in his mouth and crunching on the whole thing at once. If it was meat, why did it crunch?

I followed suit, jamming the entire bar into my mouth. It was difficult to chew, being that it was of indeterminant age and packaged to last a lifetime. The taste was less than pleasant at first, becoming still less so as I chewed and leaving an even worse aftertaste. I made a face, but Bddo simply gave me a thumbs-up as though he enjoyed his.

"Hey, you two!" Zent called from his seat at the comms table. "HQ is officially expecting us."

"When do we leave?" Bddo asked.

"ASAP."

I sighed. "That means no time for a nap, right?"

Bddo arched his back, grunting as he stretched. "'Fraid not. Believe me, I wish."

Fifteen minutes later, we filed into the docking room, which led down to the underground river. The chamber was lit by strip lights reaching out to the water's edge. Metal stairs rang out hollow tones as we descended toward the docks. The water flowed surprisingly quickly. The channel was perhaps twenty feet across. A handful of sleek, metal watercraft floated by the bank, chained to the docks. Zent approached the one nearest us, opening the door and trying the ignition. He grunted. "Dead. Ccal?"

"Told ya, Cap." Ccal handed him the spare battery he had brought, and the captain deftly removed the old one from the compartment. After this, it turned on with a hum and a whine that changed pitch before steadying out. The flick of a switch turned on the boat's powerful floodlights. "The battery is electric," Ccal explained to me. "These things run on both electric and Geothermic power. Water doesn't conduct Geothermic power very well."

We got in after stowing our supplies in the back compartment and unchaining the vessel. Zent engaged the Geoelectric engine and the boat zipped into motion. The tunnel through which the river flowed was only perhaps six feet higher than our heads, tight enough to give me a faint sense of claustrophobia. The echo of the boat's rear motors droning behind us was odd and disorienting, though not overly loud.

Bddo punched me on the shoulder lightly—for a Hellebes—and grinned. "Bet you've never ridden a speedboat underground before, have ya?"

"Uh . . . no? But there are a lot of things I've done recently that I never dreamed I would." I snorted. "Especially back on Mani. Kaen would flip if he knew I was having so much fun."

"Who's Kaen?" Bddo asked.

"My friend. We grew up together since childhood. We . . . used to live in an orphanage. A place for children who have no other home. You *do* know what children are, right?" He nodded. "The orphanage—well, it burned to the ground, and I was left with Kaen, his little sister Mandrie, and Phoebe."

"Phoebe is . . . another female name, yes?"

I nodded. "We have a lot of females on my planet. You would have quite a time looking for a . . ." I cut off with a small gasp. "Sorry. That's probably mean to tease you like that, since you guys don't have any way to find a mate on your world . . ."

An uncomfortable silence followed my words. Finally, Zent said, "Lyn, perhaps you don't know this, but most Hellebes are sterile."

"Oh." I was suddenly very glad for the poor lighting, so that Ccal and Bddo couldn't see my face redden. "So . . . like, from birth? Or do they . . . y'know . . ."

"From incubation," Ccal said, turning his head. "Hellebes can't reproduce naturally. Just the way it works."

"Oh," I repeated in a soft voice. "I'm sorry. I didn't know." Truth be told, I wasn't sure how I hadn't heard that already in the Haccolces labs amidst all the tests the doctors were running on their precious little Mother Heiress. I did, however, know that Hellebes were not exactly *born,* per se, which explained Ccal's slight hesitation when I said the word *birth.* Rather, they were formed in some sort of human production facilities in . . . Chronala? One of the nine cities. I recalled the scientists talking about it.

As I considered the matter, my significance in the world seemed to increase. *Hellebes can't reproduce naturally . . .* Suddenly, it made sense why these men were so unconcerned about my modesty. They probably couldn't even understand. What would it be like to grow up in a world where you knew you could never have a progeny to carry on your legacy? No family, no siblings?

We rode on in silence for a while, and I stared hypnotically at the black water as we cut through it, spraying up a neat wake behind us. We were heading downstream, which meant . . . a larger body of water somewhere ahead, unless we were getting off sooner. It was still hard for me to grasp the way water worked, as Mani didn't have nearly as much as Gaea. On Mani, I had been on a boat once, and only once, on one of the four rivers that ran from the single lake on my home continent. From the lake to the edge of the world.

"So where is HQ?" I asked after a while.

"Top secret," Ccal said.

"Like, the top of the top," Bddo added. "Of secret." This elicited a chuckle from Zent in front of me.

"Where do all rivers flow?" Zent asked.

"The . . . sea? Eventually?"

He nodded. "That's where HQ is. We might arrive in two or three more hours. Try to get some sleep in the meantime."

I did as he suggested, shifting to lean against the side door, propping my feet up on Bddo's tree trunk legs. Being the shortest, I had the most room, and I was going to use it. Before long, the hum of the engine and the steady rocking motion put my heavy eyes to sleep.

"Lyn?"

It was White, unsurprisingly. I blinked as I stared out over the vast pale field that was my Vault, making to stand but then realizing I already was. "Didn't . . . realize I'd fallen asleep."

"Mm-hmm. You did," she said helpfully.

This was my subconscious. This was what I had to deal with.

"And . . ."

"Well, you're obviously totally beat from all that Geokinetic training, so you need your sleep, dummy!"

I woke to Bddo poking me. "Sit up. We need to put up the canopy."

"We have a canopy on this thing?" I mumbled, pulling my legs down and my elbow off the door. A brief look around showed me that we were already out on the ocean. Not on the shore, but the ocean itself. That explained the faint spray misting my face. Water stretched infinitely in every direction. The shore was a *long* way away already. *Where are we heading . . . ?*

Zent hit a button, and a canopy slid up from its clever concealment in the rear, raising up in sections with glass plates in the front to form a windshield.

"Plus, you might want to see this," Bddo said.

Zent hit a button on the controls, and we slowly began to submerge. "Here we go."

I glanced around in equal parts nervousness and wonder as the ship dove into the water. The floodlights illuminated only a small portion of the milky blackness beneath the surface, giving an illusion of infinite depth. The captain continued to pilot us downward at a low angle. The ship's navigation panel showed that we were nearing the destination, which appeared to be both in front of and below us. Now it all made sense, how the Red Horizon's base of operations had stayed hidden for this long—they were stationed far below the ocean. Genius.

After another minute, it began to fade into view: First the lights, surrounding the base in a massive ring and blinking from towers. Then the wall and shield dome, much like that of the city of Haccolces, except that this shield was blue, not red, fitting with the underwater theme a bit better. I could only wonder how strong the shield had to be in order to keep the base safe from hundreds of feet of water pressure. Was the shield responsible for that?

"Welcome to Red Horizon HQ," Bddo said. "Didn't expect this, did you?"

I shook my head in amazement.

Zent picked up his microphone and said, "327 to base, 327 to base, this is Captain Zent, requesting permission to dock."

A moment later, a reply came: "Captain Zent, welcome back. Proceed to dock."

As we descended toward the front wall of the base, one of five bays opened, revealing a chamber just wide and deep enough to comfortably fit our vessel. Zent expertly guided us in, and as soon as we landed, the doors closed behind us and air hissed as the underwater airlock began to equalize the pressure in the room. Once it was finished, the far doors opened, and we were able to drift into a small docking bay.

Zent surfaced the vehicle and made his way over to one of the docks, letting down the canopy. After we all got out and grabbed our luggage, a mechanical arm reached down from a beam spanning the high ceiling and grabbed our boat, slotting it into one space among many along the outer wall. A convenient way to store many boats at once. The ones currently in docking ranged from smaller to larger, and some even appeared to be well armed.

"All right," Zent said, taking me by the shoulder. "You ready for this, kid?"

I shrugged. "I guess so."

We entered the main complex through a tall door that slid both ways like the airlocks. Inside, we were greeted by two Hellebes of imposing presence, wearing formal suits emblazoned with an eagle holding an axe and a spear—the symbol of the Red Horizon. One man was extraordinarily tall, close to seven feet by Legaleian standards, with close-cropped blonde hair and squinty eyes, while the more normal sized Hellebes bore a jagged beard and a disgruntled frown.

"So," said the frowny one in my direction with a similarly displeased emphasis, "You are the Mother Heiress. I am called Getts."

I wonder where he Getts all his attitude . . .

The tall man made a surprisingly polite bow and said in a more pleasant, if stuffy, tone: "And I am Vass. We are the Directors here at the Red Horizon. It's a pleasure." He stepped forward and reached out a long arm.

I took his hand and shook it, trying to ignore the fact that my slender hand was like a baby's in his. "Likewise, sir."

Vass looked up at Zent. "Good work, Captain. Corporal Ccal, Corporal Bddo."

The two men saluted their leaders sharply, but Vass dismissed them with a wave.

Getts gave a loud *harumph!* and said, "Captain Zent, we request that you meet with us at once to discuss our direction from here."

Zent gave an almost inaudible sigh. "I was expecting as much." He gave me a curt nod. "We'll be back, Lyn. Boys, want to show her to the lounge?"

Ccal and Bddo led me down a hall toward the right while Zent departed with the two Directors for the Board Room, wherever that was. I'd have to remember not to call those two Tall Tom and Skinny Sam. Although those spots were vacant for any fitting rebel leaders . . . ugh, what was wrong with my sense of humor nowadays?

α Chapter 8 α

The Red Horizon

The lounge was a long room with floor and walls paneled in the same utilitarian metal as most of the base, but also included a view of the surrounding ocean through reinforced glass paneling on the outer wall. A nice touch. The dark, murky waters were mesmerizing to look at. Seats and couches lined the room, set with a few table games unfamiliar to me. Two Hellebes occupied the room at the moment, sitting across from one another at a small table and playing a strategy game of some kind.

As we entered, the closer of the two men looked up, glancing my way briefly before doing a double-take. "Whoa! Curt, she's here!" His face was youthful and bright-eyed, a feature accentuated by his excitement.

The other man, significantly broader in shoulder and completely bald, looked up in surprise. "Well, well. So you're the Mother Heiress?" he said in a bored voice, looking me up and down. "I pictured you being bigger."

"Excuse me?" I said, indignance flaring up of its own accord. "You guys are all giant."

"Mm, I don't think so. Trust me, I've known a lot of Hellebes, and they're all twice your size. Is it a female thing?"

I rolled my eyes.

"Sorry for Curt's lousy attitude," said the youthful one. "I'm Jed, by the way." I couldn't place how old he was, yet I couldn't help but think he looked barely more than a boy. Perhaps my age. A handsome boy, if I was being honest. Then I remembered what the soldiers had told me on the way here and flushed.

"Um, what are you playing there?" I asked to cover my brief embarrassment.

"Oh, this is called Gogi," he enthused. "It's a strategic game about placing your own pieces and then capturing your opponent's pieces. These get flipped over and added to your own pool of pieces you can place." He demonstrated by taking one of the circular black pieces from his pile and placing it next to one of Curt's pieces, which already had three surrounding it, and took Curt's white piece from in between, flipping it over to its black side and placing it next to a half-dozen other black-side-up pieces on his own side of the board. This elicited a grumpy frown from Curt, until he put everything back as it was. The board, currently occupied by a dozen pieces of each color, was composed of a checkered grid outlined by steel plates set into the board. The plates each had a grain that crisscrossed diagonally, contrasting with each other orthogonally while being the same shade.

"Looks . . . complex," I said.

"If you can't tell, I'm winning," Jed said proudly, responding to his opponent's move once more. "As usual."

Curt grumbled something under his breath, scratching his bald head.

Ccal stepped up casually, surveying the board. "I'm always happy to put you in your place, kid."

Jed glanced up sharply. "No, that's okay, Ccal. I like winning."

Ccal smirked.

"Here, let's get you to the outfitter," Bddo said, dragging me away. "Later, guys."

"It was nice to meet you, Jed," I said, waving as I followed Bddo.

The long-legged corporal led me down a series of echoey steel corridors to a door labeled, "Quartermaster," stopping to knock loudly. He waited a moment, then knocked again. "Hodge! You in there?"

"What! Who is it?" came a gruff, nasally voice. Soon, a bug-eyed man with the biggest mop of frizzy hair I'd ever seen opened the door, glancing from Bddo to me. "So, you brought the Heiress. What does she need?"

"Um, hi?" I said tentatively.

The outfitter ignored me.

"She needs a new gillsuit, you idiot," Bddo said.

"Why? She looks perfectly comfortable in that."

"She *needs* a suit for combat purposes."

"One that actually fits," I added. "This is anything but comfortable."

Hodge graced me with a brief flicker of his eyes and gave a nasally grunt. "I'll see what I can find."

He made to close the door, and I protested, "You're not going to take any measurements or anything?"

The outfitter looked back at me with the utmost exasperation. "I already know we don't have your size. Do us both a favor and grow some meat on those bones." With one last wide-eyed glance at Bddo, he said, "Just send her back after they finish with all their exams and stuff, all right?" He slammed the door, somehow managing to avoid shutting his stupid hair in it.

Bddo sighed. "Sorry, Lyn. Hodge is . . . a little different. He does things his way. Come on, let's go back to the lounge and wait for the meeting to finish."

As he led me back, I asked, "So, what actually is a gillsuit?"

"Oh. That's what most of us soldiers wear." He slapped his chest. "These things are made to be form-fitting and versatile, resistant to weather and wear, and they have a breathable layer that lets Geothermic energy through both ways for when you need it. It helps keep your body cool and keeps the vapors and radiation from building up. Those can be toxic in high concentrations."

"But . . . don't you store all that inside anyway? Why doesn't it hurt us?"

"Because the properties of planetary energy change as we release it. Just like the air we breathe. That's why it can't just be recycled infinitely. It has to make its way back to the earth and be recycled, and so we have to draw more."

I nodded. *Interesting.*

Back in the lounge, we found Ccal sitting across from Jed in a game of Gogi, while Curt looked on with greater interest than he probably meant to let on. Bddo and I sat down on a nearby couch and watched the Gogi game unfold. Periodically, Bddo would make commentary explaining how little he understood about the game or complaining about how strategy took brain power, which took extra calories he didn't want to spend. I could sympathize, though right now, it was something to distract my nervous mind from waiting.

Hodge had mentioned examinations . . . I knew they were coming. No big deal, I told myself, as I had been put through a lifetime's worth already in the imperial laboratories. What was one more? Physiological, biological, neurological. I didn't know what the leaders were discussing in the meeting, but . . . it had to be about me.

At long last, I heard footsteps coming from the direction of the Board Room, and soon a whole group of important people emerged into the lounge doorway. Zent, Vass and Getts, and three others new to me.

"Lynchazel," said Vass, "This is our head researcher, Dr. Dekla." He motioned to the giant mountain of a man beside him, the first truly heavyset Hellebes I'd laid eyes on and certainly the one with the most chins. "He will conduct a quick physical analysis."

I rose reluctantly and approached the massive scientist, giving him a small head bob.

"Lady Heiress," he said in a voice so dispassionate it must have been practiced. Dry as old paper and then some. "If you'll follow me." He turned and waddled off with heavy thumps, and I followed. After a few minutes, just enough turns for me to get completely disoriented, we arrived at his lab. He propped the door open with a hand the size and shape of a ham and followed me inside.

I was greeted by the nostalgic sight of white tables and more instruments than I could count. It was like coming home, if home was a dreaded nightmare I wanted to forget about. But I did as Dr. Dekla instructed, disrobing and donning a thin, sheetlike garment far too big for me. I climbed up on the high table and the doctor proceeded to prick me with many needles, drawing blood samples and checking vitals. He took Geothermic readings, measured energy levels and pumped me full of various types of radiation for good measure. Then I laid down and he sent me into a full-body scanner. Oh, I always hated that one.

The entire time, Dekla intoned his comments and instructions in the driest monotone, putting all the doctors I'd dealt with previously to shame. Was the man even *alive?* His loud breathing was my best indicator. At long last, he allowed me to get up and change into my too-big jumpsuit, turning away only out of disinterest as he regarded his assessments and recordings. He reported none of his findings to me, but merely said, "You may go now. We will conduct another checkup in a little while."

Little while could have meant a few hours or a few weeks—hopefully closer to the latter. I wasted no time leaving the office, shutting the door behind me extra firmly and looking around, wondering for a moment which way I'd even come from. Then I had a moment of clear memory, sharper recollection than I was usually afforded while awake, and the path manifested itself in my mind. In a couple of minutes, I was back in the lobby. I met Zent first, who was speaking with one of the men who'd been in on the private meeting: A heavily muscled officer with dark skin. As I approached, the man turned to regard me, face hard and impassive. I couldn't read his expression.

"Lyn," Zent said, gesturing to his companion, "This is Musha. Master-at-arms and retired military trainer for the Elites."

Now that Zent said the word *retired*, I took another look at the man, noting that his close-cut hair was indeed greying. He had grey facial hair, cut similarly close. But I never would have taken him for old, so toned was his body and solid his stance. Even his face displayed muscles I didn't know existed.

"Good to meet you, sir," I said with a small bow. "I'm Lynchazel."

The man remained straight-backed, eyes unblinking. "I know who you are," he said gruffly. He stepped forward, taking me by both shoulders. I had to struggle to not shy away. Zent made no move to keep him away. "Weak. You're weak, and I've been tasked with turning you into a weapon."

I gulped, nodding. I thought it best not to reply to that. Why they thought that necessary . . . well, I got the impression that arguing would do me no good.

"We've decided to train you for two weeks," Zent said. "Not a long period of time. Musha is tough, but he's effective and he knows his stuff. Do everything he says without complaining, prove you've grown as a result, and the Red Horizon will let you in on our next mission."

Musha let me go.

"And . . . when do I start?" I asked.

"We'll meet in the Iron Dojang in one hour," Musha replied.

α Chapter 9 α

The Brutal Way

"All right, kid," Musha said, popping his knuckles loudly. "Forget everything Zent told you. He's too soft. We do things old school here."

We stood facing one another in the Iron Dojang, a large chamber two stories below main that was composed mostly of metal, my favorite thing in the universe. Also one of the softest. There was no padding in sight, not even on the floor. To one side of the room were weights, bricks and other training tools, most of them—you guessed it—made of metal. Even the lighting was harsh, coming from blue-white overhead lights that left a dozen shadows of my new trainer on the floor. Vents were installed in the floor and walls to allow free use of Geokinesis.

Something about this place just gave me a bad feeling. A feeling that *the old school way* meant the brutal way.

We were dressed in a traditional piece of clothing called a dobok, a simple, long-sleeved vestment belted over loose pants, used for training. I wore a youngling's size.

"Fighting stance!" Musha snapped, louder than I expected. My body moved almost of its own accord, snapping into the stance Zent had drilled into me.

I glanced down briefly to check my foot spacing, and suddenly something slammed into my chest, something hard and heavy. Before my mind could register it, I was thrown off my feet, landing on my back and rolling until my feet came up over my head and reached the ground once more. I thought my neck would snap. Slowly, painfully, I rolled onto my side and got back up. Gasping for air, I focused on my ribcage just long enough to decide nothing was broken. I would—gah!—I would be fine. Musha was still in the same stance with which he'd punched me, one fist held out and opposite foot forward. As I watched, trying to ignore my pain and retake my stance, he moved backward into a neutral stance and gestured for me to step forward.

I did, locking eyes with him and not letting go. I still didn't know how he had crossed the three meters between us and struck in the time it took me to glance downward.

With a shudder, I felt a second wave of pain slam into my chest. My abdominal muscles clenched viciously, stealing my breath, and the flesh where his fist had connected felt like it was trying to cave in, as though my breastbone were a gaping crack. But . . . no, it was . . . fine. *Breathe! Breathe, Lyn, come on.* Geothermic energy circulating in my body, the fiery pain slowly ebbed away, and I resumed breathing.

"First rule," the hulking man said. "Never take your eyes off your opponent. Surely Zent taught you that one."

I nodded with a wince, not breaking eye contact. I corrected my footing into the combat stance that Zent had taught me.

Musha took up a fighting stance as well, beginning to circle me slowly. "How do you feel? If you don't like your bones being smashed against solid steel, then pay attention and don't mess up."

I nodded again.

"And stop nodding! Just listen and do as I say." With that, he began to run me through various simple training exercises, many of which I had already done with Zent out in the Craglands. Occasionally he would throw in difficult and unexpected commands, yelling at me and dealing out one of numerous punishments when I failed. If I was close to him, he would simply shove me down onto the metal floor or strike me with his powerful fists, though not as savagely as the first time. On other occasions, he would simply shout at me, voice reverberating through the training room, and make me do fifty pushups while he stood on my back or pullups with weights strapped to my waist. Whatever it was, I had to complete the torture in full, or he would come up with something worse. My body cursed me to my face, but it obeyed.

I truly don't think I understood the limits of the Hellebes body until that day, the beating that even I could bear. At one point, he called a short break to drink water and eat some bland energy bars. "Keep that Geothermic energy flowing strong while you rest," he told me, "Otherwise your body will lose its strength and eating will replenish less energy. Also heals your injuries a bit, if you're used to it."

Easy for him to say. I couldn't even name all the places on my body that throbbed in pain. My head felt dizzy, and I think I'd have passed out if not for the steady stream of Geothermic energy I made sure to burn.

After only about five minutes, he made me get up and start my training again. He went back to the basic stances and set me to breaking cinder blocks and even black iron. He showed me how to punch and kick straight, so that the bones aligned, using the first two knuckles of my fists and the ball or heel of my foot. And my shin. That was sheer pain. Musha taught me to always commit and never pull back, an easy lesson to learn when he screamed at me like a demon and held the threat of harsh punishment over my head.

If there was a brutal way to teach me, so he did. That was the way.

By the end of the day, my muscles were pushed to exhaustion and I had more of my body covered in bruises than not, some blue and purple from it. My fists were cracked and bleeding at the knuckles, dry from gripping weights, and felt like lead weights themselves. For four hours, I had burned planetary energy taken from the floor vent, siphoned from beneath the ocean itself.

"Six o'clock sharp tomorrow," Musha grated in his harsh voice as he closed the door to the Iron Dojang behind us. "We'll start on basic hand-to-hand combat."

I felt my body groan. Not my mouth, lest he hit me again even outside of the dojang. Wordlessly, I left to find the showers. I'd go anywhere to get away from this madman, but my body needed something to relax a bit. Bddo had already shown me to my bunkroom earlier, and hopefully I could remember how to get to it in my present state.

A few minutes and one elevator later, I stumbled into the locker room nearest my bunkroom with my new set of sleepwear and a towel in hand. I fumbled with my dobok, throwing it in a heap in my locker and heading for the shower at the back. A voice in my head mumbled something about modesty, but I paid it no mind. Only a few heads turned my way. What would I tell them anyway, to go use the men's room?

The showers were all situated along one wall with narrow dividers, with two or three Hellebes currently using them. I took the closest one and soon basked in the warmth, sinking down, curling up, hugging myself, whimpering quietly. I hurt so badly . . . Would I die from this pain? Was that possible? Surely that long run from the valley to the shelter hadn't been this horrific. *You'll be okay, Lyn*, I told myself over and over. *You'll make it through. You'll make it.* My numbed mind strayed back to Mani, replaying comforting scenes from my homeland, scenes of Nytaea, of my friends. Oh, not them. Not now. I'd replayed their deaths in my head so many times already, deaths I hadn't personally seen but could easily imagine. I was past it.

Slowly, I stood up and began to rinse myself off. All the men were now gone. How long had I been there?

When I was finally finished, I put on my sleeping clothes, loose and moderately soft. Better than I'd expected, plus the fit didn't matter. I headed back to my bunkroom, where four of my seven bunkmates were already in bed. I headed straight for my bunk and climbed in, falling asleep almost immediately.

The next day was more terror.

Musha met me in the Iron Dojang at six o'clock, right on schedule. I made sure to get there a few minutes early, just in case. Sure enough, he was already there. Somehow, my body had healed miraculously fast: The benefits of Geothermic energy channeling. I still felt the lingering effects of his punishment, however.

"Come on in," he said, waving me inside as though we were about to sit down to some Nytaean Royal tea. And then more gruffly, "Let's start warming up." He ran me through some stretches and warmup exercises, and I got through the first half hour or so without messing up anything badly enough to merit punishment—for which my aching muscles were glad.

Then we got down to combat training, just as promised.

"The first and most basic weapon of a Hellebes," he said, "is his fists. Yesterday, I unleashed a small amount of that power on you, and you probably thought you were going to die, huh? Well, the truth is it takes a lot more than that to kill a Hellebes, even a little string bean like you. The more I push your body's limits, the more you'll be able to push yourself when needed. Your body can take it."

I gulped.

"Now, you're probably wondering when we're going to get to Geokinetic training, but we don't even touch that here in the Iron Dojang. We're training in the basics. I want you to be able to fight even when disconnected from the ground. On a sea ship, in a sky ship, even in a copper room where your Geokinesis has all been stripped away. For now, you need Geokinesis, so we've got access here. Now." He put his hands up in a fighting stance. "Come at me."

I hesitated.

"No hesitation! Now!" he roared.

My body leapt into action, and I crossed the space between us, readying a punch.

Musha swept me off my feet with a quick backhand fist, and I was down. My momentum threw me forward and to the left, but I caught myself with my hands and sprang back up into my stance.

"You're learning," he said. "Always get back up immediately. Your attack was too slow. Again!"

I came at him a second time, readying a kick. But Zent's training paid off as I spotted a flicker in his eyes, a twitch in his hips, and I backed off.

"Good," he said. "I was about to block your leg and shove you on your back. Now defend!"

He rushed at me, readying a punch with his right hand. I could see it coming, and I adjusted my stance and formed an X-block, taking his blow on my forearms. Still, I gritted my teeth at the pain. My arm wasn't strong enough to take his blows.

He backed off, and I lowered my guard, returning to a neutral defensive stance.

"Come on, kid, what do you do if you can't reliably block attacks? If your opponent is stronger? You're thinking like a fool."

He was right. If he could move quickly, then so could I.

He came in for another swing, and I read his movement, dodging to my right. But it was a feint, and his left fist lashed out, breaking through my guard and catching me on my right cheek. This time I did cry out in pain, as the blow knocked me all the way to the floor. The click of my teeth was less than pleasant, and I tasted blood. I didn't catch myself, and my head smacked the steel floor despite my best efforts, eliciting a shuddering gasp. One shaky breath later, I stood back up, shaking off my dizziness. He was right. I was a Hellebes. I could tough this out, headache or no.

"Don't make a move unless it's the right one," he said. "Otherwise, there's no use."

Next, he came in with a kick. I hopped backwards, and then dodged to the left as he swung with a left hook. He kept me dodging and weaving until finally he performed a quick combo and caught me in the chest, knocking me back. That same *painful* bruised spot from yesterday, directly between the ribs. I kept my footing this time, ignoring the fire in my ribcage. *Breathe, Lyn, breathe.* It had become my mantra.

Musha went on like this, teaching me one step at a time to evade attacks, and eventually how to strike back. He didn't dish out punishments anymore when I failed, he just kept putting my stamina and speed to the test through hands-on training, beating me up along the way. He taught me throws and holds and submissions, most of which involved me lying flat on my back and gasping for air at some point.

I couldn't have been gladder when noon rolled around and he let me go for lunch. We were to pick back up at four o'clock in the afternoon.

Once more, I stumbled upstairs and, after changing into my new gillsuit—Hodge had found me one that fit all right—made my way to the mess hall where lunch was being served. As beat as I was, I was famished. I encountered Ccal and Jed in passing, hardly even acknowledging them in my state. After a hot meal—yes, an actual hot meal—I was feeling much, much better.

After leaving the mess hall, I went to Hodge's office to see about getting some adjustments made to my suit, as per Bddo's helpful suggestion. My sleepwear, my training dobok, those were fine. But this . . . thing was just not going to cut it. If I ever got caught in a fight wearing my baggy gillsuit, I feared I would only trip myself. The suit itself relied on being skin tight, armored though it was on the chest area, and the breathable "gills" worked best if there was no room for wrinkles.

Upon reaching the quartermaster's office, I knocked on the door—loudly, as Bddo had—and was eventually greeted by the wide-eyed face of Hodge. "Hodge, I need you to fix my suit," I said, before he could open his mouth to complain.

"What's wrong with it?"

"You know what's wrong with it! You gave it to me." I sighed. "Look, I'm tired right now. It's just too big, and I need someone to make some alterations.”

He looked me up and down. “Yes, perhaps. And why are you asking me?”

“Because you’re the quartermaster! You’re in charge of clothing!”

“Providing it, yes, but not altering it.”

“Yeah, but surely you’re good with . . . y’know, clothing machines and stuff.”

Hodge paused. “I am, yes.”

“Oh, and I need a wrist console, apparently.”

Hodge pursed his lips, tilting his head to scratch at his frizzy mess of hair. With a long sigh, he opened the door wider. “Here. Come inside.”

Surprised at the invitation, I followed him into the office and saw that it mostly consisted of storage for clothing and other equipment. It was sorted into aisles, with standard issue apparel here, accessories there, surplus items there, and so on. He led me over to the accessories aisle and rummaged through some boxes, finally coming up with a wrist console just like the ones worn by Zent and his men: A flexible screen affixed to a band meant to integrate seamlessly with the left sleeve of a gillsuit.

“Here,” he said. “Try this on.” I did so, and he instructed me on how to put on the straps so that it fit snugly. “See? One size fits all,” he said, almost as if proving a point.

I mean, it was the last notch on the adjustable band, but . . . yeah, it did fit. I wasn’t going to complain.

I turned my arm, inspecting the device.

“Don’t ask me how to use one,” he said defensively. “Ask one of the soldiers.” Then he brought me over to his desk, where he had all manner of tailor tools such as scissors, needles, thread spools, and a few larger machines. He even had some of them out, and seemed to be working on some sort of prototype . . . boot? I wasn’t sure.

“So you do work on stuff here,” I said.

“Not for you,” Hodge answered quickly. “It’s not my job. Plus, well . . . never mind.”

“What?” I demanded.

He looked me up and down with a bug-eyed stare. "You're a female. Females are strange. Non-standard. I have just enough experience with female specs to know the differences are aggravating."

I laughed. As frustrating and lazy as he seemed to be, he was at least amusing. "What are you saying, then?"

"Nothing. Like I said, it's aggravating, and you are by extension. I won't fix your clothes for you. But if you want . . . I can show you how. You can use anything you want here."

I stared at him. "Really?"

"Yup."

I'd never heard anything so silly in my life, but it would do. I could get creative. I could be creative.

Silver

β Chapter 00 β

The Heart of Mani

(Planet Mani—Down Under

Ver'Ta 1, 997—??? Season)

Deep below the inhabited surface of Mani, beneath layers of stone and roots of oldest silver, within the great expanse of inner sky, a young man sat and listened. To what . . . he remained unsure.

It's talking again. Kaen couldn't deny it anymore. In this land of lakes below the continent of Argent, he'd come to the ancient ruins of stone and silver whence a faint call echoed now and again. For nigh on a full Sol Cycle he and his friends had been down here, and for those three weeks he'd heard the call—woken in the night to it and gone back to sleep, telling himself it was a dream.

Now he frowned, glancing down at the stream that flowed from the great waterfalls. The descending torrent was close enough that its sound was a steady din, like the whispering voice of many worlds. But over it all, the impression of just one clear voice:

Come to me.

Kaen rose, turning in the direction of the ethereal voice, which originated from farther into the ruins. He strode past tall pillars thrust into the ground and square corners jutting up from the green turf, remnants of some ancient temple. At least, that was their best guess. Rhidea would have a better idea, if she ever woke from her long coma. . . .

"All right, I'm going to find you this time," he muttered. Not to the voice, but to himself in reference to it. He didn't actually believe it existed—he just wanted to . . . well, get to the bottom of it, whatever it was.

That is right. Closer.

The hair stood up on the back of his neck. Did it have to sound *quite* this sinister? He didn't think it was a monster. That seemed unlikely, unless the crusades against the wild monsters had been achieved by simply dumping them off the edge of the world. Although . . . if that had been the case, they would have survived. And there'd be a lot more down here, gobbling all the locals whole.

So, if it was true, then they were all in for a rude awakening soon.

As he neared the falls, he poked his head around a surprisingly well-preserved wall etched in mysterious runes, scanning about for the source of the voice. Still nothing. Some stone blocks and crumbled wall fragments littered the ground.

I am here.

This time, the voice startled Kaen, causing him to jump. The falls were deafeningly close, and the voice came even louder in his head. Heart beating rapidly, he looked down at a specific piece of stone, what appeared to be a buried sheet with some two-by-one-foot rectangular section visible. Somehow, he knew that was the source.

With a small sigh, he approached it and bent down, feeling specks of water land on his head and neck. *This had better be it.* Running his hand along the exposed grey stone, he shivered at the cold feeling of it. It was hiding something, though. Whatever was speaking to him in his head seemed to impress the thought upon him.

An unsettling notion in itself.

Bracing his feet, he grabbed the underside of the stone and attempted to wedge it upwards. He got it to budge, but it wasn't easy. Grunting and pulling again, he loosened it more and was able to shift the dirt that had claimed it. But only a little.

He gave up and began kicking and digging the dirt away. Soft and loose as it was—as well as messy and wet—he was able to force the dirt out past the edge of the stone, freeing up nearly a half-foot more.

"All right, let's see about you again . . ." He pried once more, levering the flat stone up on itself and finally achieving enough space to look underneath. Something glinted—like polished metal. The light down here, green and ambient, wasn't such that it usually reflected clearly. With a great heave, he pushed the stone all the way up and tipped it backwards, giving it a low shove with his foot to ensure that it didn't slide back.

In the dark recess it had left in the soil, a round piece of metal was visible. It only took a minute of digging to reveal more—what almost seemed to be the pommel of a sword. Entirely silver and intricately worked. A solid yank freed the crossguard and then the entire blade from the earth.

"Whoa," he breathed, admiring the craftsmanship of the piece. It did not look like any modern or antique weapon he had seen. He brushed and flicked off the dirt as he inspected the sword. Its blade was long and delicate, two-edged and tapering smoothly near the tip. The hilt was crafted to look like one piece with the rest of it, silver twisting around itself. Was it . . . oh yes, he could tell that it was spell-forged. No sword buried down here at the bottom of the world would be a young blade made from cheap silver.

The sword hummed as the voice returned, resounding in his skull: *You will do. Not the soul I desired, nor the one whose presence awoke me. But you will make a sufficient Vessel.*

β Chapter 01 β

Awakening

(Two months later)

Mydia bent down to pick one more mushroom, dusting it off and placing it in her basket. "How many more do we need, Oliver?" she asked as she searched for others.

The boy immediately responded, "Twelve more."

"Then make that ten, because I found another two." Mydia groaned and stood upright, brushing fallen leaves off her skirts with her free hand. Honorary queen or not, she was far from her kingdom, therefore rummaging around in a forest for edible fungus qualified as a perfectly ladylike endeavor. Particularly since the forest in question lay far below the earth, under the thick fog of the Sea of Emptiness that was said to be a bottomless pit. Oh, how wrong those tale-spreading wives were.

"You're the queen," responded the tow-headed boy. "Or at least, y'know, queen of somewhere. A body can't go and make you look bad by outdoing ya, can he?" Some thirteen years old, Oliver had a quick tongue and a sharp wit, making him a favorite of Mydia's. But he could be most impolite in his cleverness.

"Why, you get cheekier by the minute," she said with a giggle. It was meant to sound both mature and stern, but she suspected it was neither. At twenty years old, it was still hard to know how to act her age after her sheltered upbringing.

"My good lady, the boy has a point," said Ferriman, her second companion for the morning. He was a well-mannered gentleman of middling years, though his greying hair sought to make him appear older. He had fallen into the Down Under a few years back after taking one too many a sip of fine wine on his way across the chasm to the Sky Islands.

Gaea

It was a balmy day here in the Down Under amidst the Rustle Wood, where the falltime leaves blew in the gentle breeze. The idea of seasons was strange and new here, explained to her as Mani's core trying to recreate a more "ideal" environment than the worlds above, which were ruled by the Energy Field in the heavens . . . whatever all that meant. The miniature forest was one of Mydia's favorite places down here. They were out foraging under the guidance of the esteemed Ferriman, who had in turn picked up most of his woodsman's skills from a strange old man named Toss. Now *he* was a character.

Mydia turned to Ferriman, giving a small curtsy. "You may both feel free to outdo me. Now, what about those apples?"

They continued like this for the next half hour before heading back home to Hearth. That was the name this community of misfits had chosen for their settlement, which was the metropolis of the subterranean world by default. Both alone in the world and its own closest neighbor by a few mile's walk, due to some fascinating geography. (They'd tried to explain it to her, but they couldn't prove anything without, so to speak, circular reasoning.) It sat in a shallow valley, a cluster of ramshackle buildings and somewhat more shapely homes built more recently as the village gathered more craftsmen. The mist came extra heavy in the evenings here, and was just now starting to lift.

The daylight cycles were strange down here, as the sun was never directly visible thanks to the giant plates far overhead that made up the twin continents of Mani—and of course the misty "sky" layer that clouded the air between, glowing green and faintly twinkling. Rather than the biweekly day–night cycles of the surface, the Down Under experienced a change in the twinkling of the fog, most likely caused by whatever made the auroras and the clouds to switch off every day. Every two weeks, a greater intensity of light indicated that Sol was crossing one side of the chasm.

Mydia followed Ferriman and Oliver down the path to Hearth, skipping lightly and whistling softly to herself. She really could get used to this place. "Hello, Marnie!" she called, waving as she saw Oliver's mother carrying a bundle of herbs.

The woman paused, turning to see the returning foragers. Her face broke into a warm smile. "Oliver! Mydia!"

"Mum!" Oliver ran toward the village fence and vaulted it in a swift motion, taking the quickest route to wrap his arms around his mother. She laughed, shuffling her bunch of herbs to her opposite arm to hug the boy back. Despite the woman's vibrant blonde hair and graceful aging, her most beautiful feature was her kindness, for which she was well known.

"Have you been helpful to your friends?" she asked in mock sternness.

"Oh, yes'm!"

His mother pinched his cheek, and then looked up as Mydia and Ferriman approached. "Did you hear the news?"

Mydia shook her head, bob-cut black hair swinging with it. It was just starting to get too long for her liking, curling as it fell against her shoulders. Perhaps Kaen would cut it for her.

"Your teacher is awake!"

Mydia gasped.

"Lady Rhidea's awake?" Oliver repeated in excitement. "For real?"

Marnie nodded. "Phyllis is with her now. I was just bringing these herbs to make her some tea for her energy now that she's come to."

"Can we—" Oliver began, but his mother put out her hand to physically stop him.

"No. Not until Phyllis says so. Mydia, you can come if you like."

Ferriman held onto Oliver as Mydia followed Marnie to the ward in the center of town where Rhidea was kept. Well, "ward" was a bit of a stretch, as it was Phyllis' own home, but it was what they called it. She came from the Isle of Scathii, just like Marnie and her husband Lester, and had been a physician there before taking an unexpected plunge into the Sea of emptiness to find herself in this place. Her skills came in useful from time to time, as Cae Rhidea had not been the first to fall down in less than whole condition. Indeed, the first child birthed here in decades had been born in her home shortly before Mydia and the others arrived.

Marnie knocked on the rough-hewn doorpost and announced herself and Mydia.

"Come in," came a hushed voice.

Pulling aside the cloth drapery that covered the door, the two women entered to find Phyllis busying herself in her kitchen. Grey-haired and slightly plump, the woman was dressed in her customary simple grey dress and white apron, which closely resembled Marnie's attire. She looked up, eyeing Marnie's bunch of herbs, and said, "Perfect! Bring them here. Mydia dear, you can go in and see her if you want. I know you've been waiting patiently for some time."

Mydia nodded fervently, feeling misty around the eyes, and hurried into the back room where Phyllis had two beds in addition to her own, crafted of straw and lined with white linen sheets. On the farthest sat the woman Mydia looked up to most in the whole world, sitting upright with the help of multiple pillows and rubbing her eyes sleepily. Even bedridden and dressed in a plain white gown, the High Mage was stunning, deep-red hair billowing behind her. The few extra age lines did nothing to diminish that beauty, but seemed only to highlight her distinguished regality.

"L-Lady Rhidea!" Mydia cried, voice cracking, and ran to fall at her side, heedless of how hard her knees hit the earthen floor.

The Wandering Mage turned, catching sight of Mydia as she rushed up, and smiled tiredly. "Oh, child, it's good to see you." She allowed the queen to hug her fiercely, gasping only slightly as she was squeezed.

"Apologies," Mydia mumbled. "But . . . good to see me? It's been almost three months, Rhidea! We thought you might never wake up."

Rhidea's eyebrows rose. "Three months? Goodness, that's a long time." She sat there for a moment, as though trying to recall what she remembered last. "We were . . . we failed. Correct? The Archlord betrayed us?"

Mydia nodded. "So you do remember. He came and attacked us, and Kymhar . . . well, he's here with us now, and he regrets what he did. You tried to contain the power of the Archlord's orb, but it was too strong and blew us all off the tower."

"And the others?" Rhidea demanded.

"They're all fine," Mydia said as soothingly as she could. She hesitated. "Well . . . except for Lyn. We don't know what became of her for sure, but she must have been blown through the Gate."

Rhidea nodded, relaxing a bit to Mydia's surprise. "Then we didn't fail. Not entirely. If Lyn made it to Gaea, then . . . all of our hopes ride on her. I had hoped to be there with her, but that will never happen now. She will have to get by on her own, and somehow find what she needs to save our world."

Mydia nodded gravely.

"Now," the mage muttered, reaching to throw off the right side of her sheet and uncover her leg, "*What* happened to me?" She stared at the long scars running along the outside of her shin, all the way to her knees.

"You struck the rocks as you fell down here," Mydia explained. "The rest of us somehow fell into the large holes between."

Rhidea nodded slowly. "Which leads me to my next question: Where are we, and how did we survive such a fall?"

"They call it the Down Under. A land deep beneath Argent and Darsor. Some trick of . . . well, they think it's Mani's magic, but people tend to land safely. Rhidea, it's amazing! We're actually at the center of Mani!"

Rhidea's eyes seemed to sink far away, as though in fearful surprise deadened by her exhaustion. After a pause, she said, "So you're telling me that all this time, it was possible to survive a fall into the Sea of Emptiness? That means . . ."

Just then, Phyllis walked in, bearing a tray of tea and biscuits, with Marnie following behind. "Here you are, my lady," Phyllis said in her matronly voice, approaching to set the tray on a small table beside the mage's bed. "Some herbal tea to boost your recovery."

Rhidea smiled. "Thank you. You are most kind." She reached over to grab the tea cup, wincing slightly at the movement, but hesitated upon catching sight of Marnie. "You . . . look familiar. What is your name, my dear?"

"Marnie." The blonde woman bowed politely. "We've all been awaiting your return to consciousness, madam."

"No need for formalities." Rhidea raised the cup to her lips and took a small sip. "I am Cae Rhidea, and it's a pleasure."

"Rhidea, Marnie is Oliver's mother," Mydia explained excitedly, rising to pull the blonde woman's shoulder down to hers, for she was a few inches taller. "They survived the accident two years ago, both she and Lester. They've been down here, alive, all this time!"

The flame-haired mage looked up at Marnie once more. "Remarkable. Why, that's wonderful. I'm sure he is happy to have you back again. My, you do look like him."

Marnie beamed. "I'm so proud of my little boy. We still can't get over having each other around again; he's like a wee child again. He has so many stories of you, of your many journeys along the way to the Tower of Mani."

"No doubt embellished generously."

Mydia laughed. "Just wait till he sees you. Oh, and Kaen! Where did he get to? He's been playing around with his new sword."

"New sword?" Rhidea asked.

"Yes, an old silver blade. He says it's special."

Rhidea sighed, a distinctly upset sigh. "I don't like the sound of that at all. Ladies, can you leave us for a minute?"

Marnie looked at Phyllis and nodded, motioning with her head. The two exited, leaving only Mydia and her old mentor.

"Mydia, were you in on mending my leg? How bad was it?"

Mydia hesitated. Why was she asking? "It was . . . ghastly. I couldn't look. The bones had ripped straight through your skin . . . jutting out at odd . . ." She stopped, shivering slightly and feeling sick. "I don't do well with grisly sights."

Rhidea nodded. "Find Kaen and Kymhar. I suppose Oliver as well. He is in on this now. I have some things to explain."

β Chapter 02 β

The Purest of Blades

Kaen twirled his blade. An ancient weapon. A beautiful sword. A deadly secret. The Heart of Mani, breaker of spells—or so it called itself.

The sword had not spoken to him all day, which could be taken as a good or bad sign.

Looking up into the misty green sky of the Down Under, Kaen couldn't help thinking of his sister Mandrie. Somewhere beyond that jade expanse, on the continent of Argent, she was awaiting his safe return. She had no idea that their entire mission had failed, that Rhidea had nearly died, and that Lyn was now stranded on Gaea.

Or did she? Perhaps the girl thought them all dead.

Kaen headed down the gentle slope toward Hearth. He had been practicing his swordsmanship up on the hill, away from . . . it would sound strange, but away from Rhidea. He trusted that he had done the right thing in taking the blade, but he couldn't shake the nagging feeling that the mage would strongly disapprove. What would she have said against it, though? He was certain there was no going back now.

That being said, she remained unconscious as far as he knew.

He just wanted to know her secret. Those bones . . . he had seen them. Silver bones. Not the bones of an ordinary human. He had an inkling what it might mean, but the implications were beyond him. He'd spoken with no one about it save for Kymhar, who'd had little to say on the matter. He just prayed that she awakened soon, because she was probably their last hope at ever making it up to the surface world again. The locals could say all they wanted about this not being a bad life, but there were important things going on up there. Who knew what the Archlord was up to at this very minute . . .

Mandrie had just better be safe.

Upon reaching the village, Kaen found his friend and mentor, Kymhar, standing against a tree near the gate, picking a fingernail with one of many blades he kept hidden on his person. Six feet tall and carrying his ethereal presence about him like a magic cloak, the former assassin was known to appear and disappear at will. He was also one of the most dangerous men Kaen had ever met.

"I take it you haven't heard yet?" Kymhar asked, not looking up, displaying his unexplainable sense of his surroundings.

Kaen stopped, sheathing his sword. "No."

"The lady is awake."

The man didn't have to say any more; Kaen was off at a run as soon as he heard it. To Kaen's immediate annoyance, Kymhar called after him:

"Not going to do anything with that first?"

Blast. He'd forgotten. Slowing his pace, he felt at his sword belt and sighed. "You're right," he said, stopping and looking back. Kymhar was approaching at a steady walk. "But where do I hide it?"

"That's why I primarily carry smaller blades—easier to hide, harder to steal."

Grumbling, Kaen fumbled at his sword belt, beginning to take it off. But something stopped him. A nagging feeling. He should keep it on, just in case. Perhaps he just didn't want to part with it.

Kymhar frowned, seeing his struggle. "You can't leave it, can you? Even for a minute?"

Kaen looked away. "That's not it. I . . ." He redid the clasp at his belt, fingering the scabbard. "I think I'll just leave it on."

Kymhar did not point out that he had avoided the question. Together, they walked to Phyllis' infirmary and asked admittance. Oliver's mother ushered them in at the door. Inside the infirmary room were already Oliver and Mydia, who looked up and smiled as the two men entered. Marnie made to go, but Rhidea stopped her.

"You can stay if you like, my dear."

The golden-haired woman glanced at her son, who shrugged

uncomfortably, and gave him a smile before looking back to the mage. "That's all right. Oliver is one of you now, as far as I'm concerned. I am not. Whatever you choose to do from here on out, I'll hear in time." She bowed herself out of the room and left the building, leaving only the five adventurers.

"Rhidea!" Kaen said. "It's been so long!"

"I know. I'm not going to give you a hug, if that's what you—oof!" she cut off as Kaen squeezed her in a sudden embrace. Relaxing, she returned the hug in brief and then said, "I wasn't expecting that one. *Now* I've given out enough hugs."

Kymhar stood still as a statue, not saying a word.

Kaen backed off, mumbling something even he himself did not catch.

"So," Rhidea began, settling back in her bed with pale arms relaxed at her lap. "We have a few matters to discuss. I have not been forthright with any of you regarding my past, and it is highly relevant to our situation."

Oliver perked up. "Your past? Aren't you really old?" He looked around the room as though surprised to receive glares.

Rhidea simply chuckled. "Very. I am over two hundred years old, boy. Yes, I know, quite shocking. My kind ever aged slowly, more so than other magi." She paused, as though waiting for the obvious question, before answering it herself. "I am the last of the Silversmiths—the clan of old who possessed the magical ability to work silver into any shape."

"What!" Mydia exclaimed. "All this time and you had *that?*"

Rhidea sighed. "I know. As I said, I've been lying about it for a long time. A very long time, ever since that . . . *monster* killed my family." That one word came out in a growl, almost guttural and surprising to hear out of the woman's mouth. "He took everything from me. Old wounds never heal."

"So that's why you hate the Archlord so much," Kaen said.

"Yes. He did it out of fear, fear of their terrible power. How did he manage to kill them if they were so powerful, you ask? You see, they were pacifists. They all stood by and let the mage soldiers slaughter them like unnecessary livestock. I will never understand it. From that dreadful day forward, I renounced the ways that they clung to so desperately, so pitifully. To have such power comes with a responsibility, and when one is too blind to use it as needed . . . it is truly the height of folly."

"I'm so sorry," Mydia whispered.

"It is well in the past, child. My parents hid me on the day that Domon's soldiers came to slaughter them, and I watched as they cut them down one by one before running away. For the longest time, I didn't touch my Silver magic, though I had an Aptitude for other elements as well. Eventually, I made my way back to the city of Nytaea, where I was born, and Master Gendric took me in as a daughter. I owe much to the man. For two centuries now, I have hidden my identity."

"Wait a minute . . ." Mydia said slowly. "I remember the day that you fought my father. You made blades out of the pillars in the throne room."

The High Mage nodded. "I wasn't about to take any chances with him. As I correctly guessed, he was too caught up in the moment to realize what I was doing. Edrius and I grew up together, both studying under Master Gendric for years before our falling-out. Thus, he never could have suspected that I was hiding so great a secret."

Oliver scratched his blond head. "I, uh . . . don't really know what to say to all that. Quite the story, your ladyness."

Kaen glanced over at the boy. "Ladyness? Really?"

Oliver shrugged. "She just came back from the dead, mate." He glanced at the red-haired mage. "She just . . . I just—I don't know many big words, a'right?"

Mydia giggled, catching herself and coughing instead.

"Rhidea," Kaen asked, "Why are you telling us all this now? Is it because of the . . ."

She nodded. "Mydia told me about my injuries. My silver bones were sticking out—in a reportedly ghastly fashion, no less—so I figured I might as well come clean. Especially since . . . well, that brings me to the next topic. This place, I believe it just may be the ancient home of the Silversmiths— from before my time."

She began to tell of stories she had heard as a child, of a place deep below the earth, beyond the silver roots of Mani, where her people used to dwell. According to the old lore tellers, it lay at the "Heart of Mani." She had searched for years and never found the place.

The Heart of Mani, Kaen mused. Coincidence?

At this point, she stretched her arms and said, "I will just have to see for myself. Whenever those women let me up, I will take a look around the place. Marnie said there are ruins here?"

"Yes," Kaen said. "At the foot of the Argent Falls."

She nodded. "Perhaps I will make my way there once my legs are working again. You can all go now."

Kaen and Kymhar, closest to the door, excused themselves, but Rhidea spoke before they could go, "Kaen, you stay for a minute. We have something to talk about."

Kaen's heart dropped, and he felt his throat constrict inexplicably. "Yes, milady," he said with a slight dip of the head. The others filed out, and he leaned against the doorway uncomfortably, fingering his sword scabbard.

"What do you have there?" Rhidea asked flatly.

"It's a sword," Kaen said. "I . . . found it."

"Here in this underworld."

"Yes." Kaen reluctantly pulled the silver blade free from its scabbard, inspecting the blade for the umpteenth time. Its beauty was strong, almost pulling him to look at it.

"May I see it?"

Kaen hesitated before crossing the room and holding the blade out sideways for her to see. She made to take it from him, but he pulled it back. "I'd rather keep it on me. Just—in case."

The mage's eyebrows rose. "Is that so? I'm not going to take it from you." She crossed her arms, adjusting her position on her sickbed. She looked . . . tense. "But do you know what it is?"

The Heart of Mani. "Not exactly," Kaen said. "But it seemed like it spoke to me, calling out. I had to take it. It's powerful, and I think it will help us."

"It's dangerous, you fool!" Rhidea snapped. "I know exactly what that sword is. But why? Why would it choose Kaen?" She said these last lines to herself, holding her head in her hand.

Kaen backed away and sheathed the sword. "I'm sorry, Rhidea. I didn't—you were asleep, and I didn't know for how long. I'd have asked you, but . . . I couldn't, all right?"

Rhidea nodded slowly. "And now there is no going back. To think that this was the place . . . and that the sword would choose now to speak."

When she didn't say any more, Kaen excused himself. At the door to the outside, he nodded to Marnie and Phyllis, indicating they were fine to come back inside, and headed back out to the hill. Not to practice with the blade, but just to sit and think for a while.

He couldn't say whether that whole conversation had gone well or poorly.

β Chapter 03 β

Inheritance

Rhidea limped out the door, holding onto Mydia's shoulder, gritting her teeth against the pain. The first thing that caught her attention was the glowing green sky, flecked with particles that sparkled and vanished in the steady but faint breeze. The air was warm here, just the perfect temperature. *My, but it's a cute village.* She took in the sight of the simple wooden houses, slowly taking more of her weight off of Mydia.

"I think—I think I can stand for a bit," she told the queen. Mydia slowly stepped aside, watching her carefully, and Rhidea tested her footing. It was the second day of learning to walk again, and to this point they had not allowed her even to stand unaided. Phyllis stood behind them in the house, waiting to step out and begin giving commands.

Rhidea took a hesitant step. Her right leg held, and she kept her balance as she limped forward with her left, then right again. Stopping, she took a moment to breathe. "I think this is working," she told the worried girl with a smile. "It aches, but my walking will improve."

Mydia nodded, but her worried frown did not lift. "And you're still not using your magic to walk?"

Rhidea shook her head. "I need to learn how to walk again with my feet first. Fortunately, the gravity seems lighter here for some reason. Here, walk with me. I want to see this Hearth for myself." Looking back at the grey-haired healer, she smiled and said, "We'll be fine, Phyllis. Thank you."

Mydia proceeded to show her the village, waiting as she caught her breath every little while, ready to catch her if needed. But Rhidea never stumbled. In fact, her energy seemed to return as she exercised her muscles and ligaments. "Have you wondered, child," she said during one breathing break, "why your magic was ineffective on me?"

The queen's face took on a troubled frown. "Every day. Do you know why? I tried to heal you as best I could."

"I have a theory. My memories of my past life are . . . hazy, if I'm being honest. But I recall my father explaining once how a Silversmith requires another Silversmith to mend his bones. We heal slowly in general, and elemental magic has essentially no effect on the process, as Silver is near-antonymous to the elements."

"And yet you wield both."

Rhidea pursed her lips, nodding slowly. "I do." Not wishing to continue the conversation, she rose from the bench on which she sat, prompting Mydia to do the same.

They resumed their tour.

The village was bigger than she expected. She had met a few of the inhabitants, many of which waved to her now or came over to greet her excitedly. She only wished she could return the enthusiasm in kind.

Mydia greeted each face cheerfully, and Rhidea could see that she really loved the villagers and seemed to have grown attached to them—even the less friendly ones. According to Marnie, about fifty of the ragtag wayfarers currently lived here, most of them coincidentally being the same type of strange men who had once been either sky sailors or travelers but had wound up in this place due to an unforeseen accident. Mydia introduced her to two middle-aged men with wild hair, named Barry and Toss, who could have been brothers. Their looks, their strange mannerisms and way of talking . . . it was almost enough to make Rhidea laugh, except that her leg was starting to throb more, and it was all she could do to keep her face somewhere between a mild frown and a pained grimace.

Mydia saw her teacher back to Phyllis' house, where Rhidea asked leave of the kindly woman to stay for one more night. Phyllis, unsurprisingly, answered, "As long as you need, my lady. It's no trouble to me."

Hopefully not long. We've much to do.

The next morning, Rhidea set out for the falls that Kaen and the others had spoken of. She insisted that they let her go by herself. Apparently there were four waterfalls, one for each of the great rivers of Argent, but one that they assumed to be the Ardencaul seemed to make the largest and most cohesive falls, whereas the others rain down from deltas.

So here she was on a hike through the grasslands of the Down Under, just far enough out of town that there was no turning back. Great glimmering auroras, her leg ached. Each limping footstep seemed to jar the bone, no matter what she did. Phyllis said she would never walk right again, but she would see about that.

The High Mage could not get the thought of that terrible sword out of her head. Why, *why* did it have to fall into the hands of that boy, of all the people on Mani? She knew the reason: it would have called out to her, but she'd been incapacitated at the time by the cruelest twist of fate. After all, she was a Silversmith herself. In fact, she had heard the voice before, long ago. But she would not by any means have taken such a relic, for she knew that it would only bring evil. That was why her forebears had left it behind in this ancient place. The temple couldn't be far, if the locals had their geography right.

But why was it only recently stirring? Many had fallen down here, yet only now had that cursed sword reached out. Her presence was the only explanation.

Rhidea continued along the vague path through the grassy plains of the Down Under, passing the fields where farmers tended animals. A stream flowed nearby, tracing its way down to a pond in the village. Someone had decided that this was the northern side of the place, with the falls beneath Argent being the northmost region and the opposite end—the sandlands where her group had apparently first come down—being the southmost. She had doubts about that, but wasn't about to question the cartography of more experienced adventurers.

Soon, Rhidea began to see more frothy streams streaking the hilly grasslands, running opposite to the way she was heading, as well as ponds dotting the area. Cresting the next hill, she caught her first glimpse of the falls through the far-off fog, which hung thicker in this region. The water sprayed down from the sky in a heavy white mist, no longer a smooth liquid stream at this height. It seemed to appear from nowhere out of the greenish firmament. The water fell into a small lake, which in turn flowed out into the ponds and streams. From them seemed to come the heavy mist, making its way steadily upwards, upwards . . .

It made sense, really. The water fell off the continents and into the Sea of emptiness, evaporating down here and making its way back up. Rhidea only wished to know how the Wellspring of Life managed to siphon so much of that water in order to spit it back out into the sky. If they could harness such a power, it could potentially be a way up to the surface.

Rhidea resumed her slow progress through the lake-filled lands, stopping to peer into one of the calmer pools of water. It was clear and clean, reflecting the hazy green amidst the ambient light. In it, she was surprised to see fish, and not of any species she recognized. Mydia and Marnie had talked of woodland creatures in the forested areas as well. It was fascinating to see such an ecosystem in the center of Mani. Had the creatures fallen from the surface in time past?

Rhidea could have simply used her magic to teleport all the way to the foot of the falls, but she chose to walk all this way in order to force her body to recover on its own. This limp could not be allowed to keep her bound, and she wasn't about to give in to old age.

As she approached the falls, the rushing of thousands of gallons of water grew from a steady whisper to a full-on roar. The falling water covered more than a hundred feet of area and sprayed droplets much farther. Rhidea used simple water magic to ward off the spray and limped around the side of the lake. It was difficult to see what was behind the water, but the stone pillars and other relics scattered about, as well as the lumpy hills and mounds of rock—some grass-and-moss-covered, others smooth—gave her an idea.

Sure enough, a few ancient structures stood behind the water. Or rather, used to stand. Now, they were unrecognizable for what they once were, proud buildings of solid stone. Not silver. Rhidea was beginning to think that there was no silver rooting to this place at Mani's heart, strange as that seemed. Instead, said roots held up the continents above . . . but did not extend to the core. What did it mean?

Approaching the first ruins, Rhidea inspected the sides, which were slick from the splashing water of the falls. Along multiple faces of stone, she found writing in the form of ancient characters she could not make out. They looked to be in the same High Legaleian text as what they'd found on one side of the Gate of Mani's arch. Before it was destroyed, that is. The few characters she could make out spoke of silver, water and sky.

"It can't ever be easy, can it?" she murmured, hardly able to hear her own words over the din of the waterfall.

Nevertheless, a plan began to form in her head.

Persuasion

Later that day, Oliver found the red-haired mage limping back to the village, looking exhausted. "Lady Rhidea!" he shouted, running up to meet her with a grin.

"Hello, child," she said tiredly. "I'm fine, thank you, I can—"

Oliver ignored her protest and lifted her right arm to put it over his shoulder and support her.

"Oh, all right," she groused.

Oliver smiled joyfully, just happy that she hadn't shooed him away. After all, she was like his mother, no? Second mother, at least, before he found his real mum down here in the depths of the earth. Well, third if he counted Mydia, too. She was like his really pretty mum. Or . . . if she was to be believed, Rhidea could be his thrice-great grandmother.

Oliver proceeded to walk the old lady down the gentle slope to the houses and show her to the place where she would be staying. That is, just as soon as he showed her the house where *he* was staying, which was his parents' house. She responded to this with mostly disinterested comments of, "That's very nice, boy," but Oliver knew this was only because she was so tired; otherwise she would have been more invested.

The old mage would stay with Mydia at a house the locals had constructed before they'd come, as was their habit to do in preparation for the next lost souls to fall down. Could be a few more months, could be three years. Apparently, one never knew. Oliver would have thought, of course, that people would just smarten up and stop flopping into the great abyss, but folks would be folks.

"Thank you for your help, Oliver," the lady said more politely, probably in an attempt to excuse herself from his presence.

"'Course, your ladyship!" he said in a much squeakier voice than he'd meant.

Just then, Mydia approached. "Rhidea! You're back. Oliver showed you our new house, then?"

"He did indeed. And Mydia, we'll hold another meeting once I've gotten a bit of rest." Rhidea looked pointedly at Oliver, who wilted only slightly under her gaze. "A bit of rest."

He took the hint and departed.

"Are you all clear on that?" Rhidea asked.

The others nodded. Oliver nodded with the others, though he saw a couple of things that could go wrong.

"So, when shall we talk to the villagers?" Mydia asked.

"As soon as we can," the old lady replied. "We are their only hope of a way out of this place, so they had better be certain they truly want to stay the rest of their lives."

Kaen grunted from beside Oliver. "I don't know, these folks are pretty stubborn."

"It is their choice if they do not wish to accompany us. Regardless, we will likely need the help of Hearth craftsmen, as well as your ingenuity." The High Mage gestured at Kaen and Oliver.

Oliver raised his hand. "We've actually been working on some things already. We were just waitin' for you to wake up. We weren't sure how we'd power them, though."

Kaen nodded. "We can show you the designs we've come up with."

"What about me?" Mydia asked. "I helped, too!"

"And you will be instrumental in this plan's success," Rhidea said in a reassuring tone. "Oliver, I'll want to see your ideas as soon as possible."

A short while later, they all followed Gaea Oliver to the workshop area where he'd been working on wooden contraptions with Kaen and Mydia over the past several weeks. A couple of gliders lay mostly unused, as he had not been able to find quite enough wind power to fly them down here. He could zip around on them for a few minutes, which was loads of fun, but there were no updrafts of hot air like up on the surface of the Sea, and therefore gliding was much harder. It was like all the hot air just wanted to go and stay up there.

But they had a larger prototype they'd been working on, to the passing interest of the Hearth residents. Oliver's mother and father had especially been interested to see the things that he worked on, which gave him great pride, and he could only assume they would come with them if . . . no, *when* they left. They *would* go, no matter what. But he had to reassure himself of that fact every day.

The large vessel was boat-like, some twenty feet long and mostly skeletal at this stage. Rhidea seemed to think it may work, but of course it would depend on how many were willing to come with them.

They began to talk to the villagers one at a time. Oliver and Mydia informed his parents of their plans to leave, and requested that they accompany them. The couple's answer surprised Oliver, though it shouldn't have: "We will have to get the villagers together and discuss it." So Oliver and the others began to inform the villagers that they would be meeting to discuss the possibility of leaving. Some laughed at the thought, and others outright opposed it, while still others seemed to struggle to remember what their lives on the surface had been like.

At evening time, as the glow of the nether sky was fading, they gathered around the Village Hearth, which was distinct from the village *of* Hearth. Oliver had made a game of the distinction at first. It didn't help that they were often interchangeable. It was essentially the town square, only it was circular, and at its center was a large firepit, in which there was nothing burning right now. The fifty-odd villagers sat in a ring around it.

"So," began Frath, a bald man of some seventy years dubbed the elder by the locals. "They say you upstarts think you have a way out of the Down Under?"

"Indeed," Rhidea said in her persuasive orator's voice. "But it will take cooperation on the part of many, and therefore, perhaps more importantly, we would like to ask who is in favor of returning to the surface worlds—if indeed we could achieve it."

"That's, uh, kind of a big if," called crazy old Barry. He was the one who had found Oliver and the others and shown them to Hearth three months prior.

"It is," Rhidea replied cooly. "And we will pressure no one. If we must go alone, then we shall."

"So, who is with us?" shouted Kaen from beside her, raising a hand.

Marnie mouthed something to her husband, who nodded. Lester was a tall, gangly man who spoke only on important occasions. Rising to his feet along with her, he said, "We will go. We have grown to love this place like home, and all of you as family, but we wish to return to the Sky Islands and tell of the world below."

The couple sat back down, and Oliver waved to them with a smile. His mother nodded. To that moment, Oliver hadn't been sure that his mum and dad would come. He could tell how much they loved Hearth.

After them, a few more villagers stood up, spoke, raised hands or otherwise expressed the desire to leave. Some voiced strong doubts, and a few opposed the idea with a passion, insisting that they had no interest whatsoever in returning to their previous lives. These were mostly the old codgers and the crazy ones, not at all to Oliver's surprise. However, the couple who had birthed the baby here declared that they wished to raise him in Hearth, come what may.

Finally, the fellows came to a general consensus: roughly two-thirds of the citizens—about thirty people—would join their group in getting to the surface, whilst the rest would remain behind. Oliver couldn't understand the poor blokes, but they wanted to stay, so who was he to stop them?

Rhidea directed those willing to contribute to see Oliver himself for orders on the craft they were to build. He was honored to bits, but also a tad nervous.

Over the course of a week, he got more help than he'd ever wanted, both men and women willing to cut lumber and shave the timbers with adze and saw, piecing them together to construct the best boat Oliver could dream up. He was right grateful for Kaen and Mydia, who were helping with the production.

The final test was fast approaching.

β Chapter 05 β

The Ascent

One week later, they had their ship. Kaen led the able-bodied men of the village as they pulled the ship on the cart they had made for it. Even on the path, it was a long and bumpy trek through the lake-filled lands. Whose idea had this been, dragging a boat along the ground when water lay all around?

But if it meant a way up that waterfall . . . anything was worth a try.

Allowing for breaks to rest, the transport trip took a little over an hour. When they arrived, they left the boat right next to the main lake beneath the falls, facing away. As the men sat down to rest, Kaen said, "Good work. I hope everyone back there is ready."

Oliver left to fetch the villagers, who were awaiting the completion of the trip. Within fifteen minutes, the half-dozen women came bearing packs and supplies. Kaen could have sworn he *specifically* told them not to bring extra weight, but there was no getting that through to a group of frontier women.

He could still feel the uneasiness among the group as folks murmured to each other about the safety of the ride: Would the boat hold up? Would the Magi be able to actually get it up the waterfall? No one looked more nervous than the Nytaean queen. But as though in response to these concerns, Mydia strode into the river with slow, purposeful breaths and began to wade through the water to the falls. She walked not as through water, but as though it wasn't there. Her long-skirted dress rippled around her, unhampered by the current. Kaen already admired her more than he wanted to admit, but he couldn't help but stare in wonder as she seemingly melted into the falls and rose up some forty feet. Her powers, or so she said, were far stronger the more water was around.

"Are you ready?" Rhidea asked the queen, looking up at her. Her voice held a surprising note of unsettledness, something Kaen could only pick out because he was so familiar with the woman and had never heard that little waver before. He could almost recall her saying something about not liking water once.

Mydia nodded from within the rushing falls, black hair billowing out, and said, "Go ahead." Her voice projected eerily out from the water around them.

Rhidea snapped her fingers rapidly and began striding towards the falls herself. "Let's go. Everyone in, and get the boat in the water."

Opening the doors of the boat, Kaen and Kymhar ushered the villagers in, who seemed more willing to obey after seeing the Water Authority of a mage close-up. Kaen and a few other men pushed the ship off the cart and into the river, and then got in themselves. Inside, they had seating enough for the passengers along the walls, with two magical lamps hanging from the ceiling to give light.

"Everyone brace yourselves," he said. "We're going up."

❧❧

Mydia floated in the waterfall, joined by her tutor. Heart beating madly, she looked down through the watery shower and beheld the ship launching into the water. It was beginning to drift downstream from the falls on the current. *Okay, they're all in. Calm yourself, Mydia, calm yourself. You're not afraid of a little water.*

Not the water, no. But heights?

Rhidea nodded, and together they pulled on the boat, tugging it gently upstream in defiance of the current, until it was directly underneath the great falls. Mydia merely had to trust in Oliver and Kaen's engineering skills and her own magic which she had embedded in the ship.

Taking her mentor's hands in her own, the queen began to draw the ship upwards through the water, combining their Authority as one, until the peaked roof of the vessel bumped against their feet. They continued to draw it up the water, keeping it centered. The liquid flowed around them and encompassed the large boat, continuing on down with gravity as though the two Magi were not using its own power to defy said gravity. Mydia had only to ignore her fluttering heart as the world dropped away . . . which was easier said than done. She focused on the water, and on Rhidea's face in front of her. Together, they could do this. They were finally going to leave this miniature world of the Down Under.

When in the water, Mydia seemed to be able to draw bodily energy from the water itself. She didn't even have to breathe. After all, water was the source of both life and magic on Mani, and both sprung from the same Wellspring inside Ti'Vaeth. A water mage such as herself was able to utilize that vitality to bypass some of her body's needs. With Rhidea's guidance and a bit of practice beforehand, she had overcome her doubts to realize that, together, they could get a ship up the waterfall. Rhidea should have had the harder time, being as she was the one who actually did fear water. Her face was remarkably resolute given that shortcoming.

The underworld continued to fall away around the two, until the misty sky obscured it completely, twinkling green all around them. Together, the two magi picked up speed, shooting the boat upwards in a sustained and somewhat smooth ascent.

An hour passed, and Mydia became more and more distracted by the fact that she had to use the privy. She hadn't exactly thought about just how long a trip it would be. Longer than the one over the Sea of Emptiness. Were they going as fast as they had then? Faster?

Perhaps three hours in, Mydia's entire body was beginning to shake from magical strain, but she could faintly see it, and even *feel it*. A large mass approaching them; a looming weight. She was feeling it through Rhidea, so connected were they by the dual exercise of Authority. It was the continent above, tapering outward as they rose, until its edge became visible through the fog. It crept toward the ship as it rose, a crawling mass of stone—and yes, silver—reaching steadily upward and outward.

The fog of the Sea of Emptiness changed color as they continued to rise, from green to blue to a quiet greyish color Mydia could not make out. On their way across the Sea the first time, during the sunset season, it had been purple, but now Mydia was pretty sure it was nighttime.

At last, the land of Argent came to bear against the ship, or rather the ship against the land, and the magi began to actively keep the ship from scraping against it. Still they pulled it upwards, upwards. The water around them narrowed the closer they got to the surface (as it showered out further with the long fall) but the density of the flow never changed. The light of the auroras above grew stronger until it pierced the fog completely and they rose beyond the fog layer of the Sea of Emptiness, hauling the ship through open air against the cliff. A few hundred yards, a hundred yards . . .

"Just a bit more," Rhidea said to her with a fatigued smile through the water.

Mydia nodded. They kept their hands clasped in a circle between them, and Mydia heard her voice easily through water and bone. They had slowed the ship's ascent considerably, but they had been rising at an incalculable, and utterly ridiculous, speed.

And then they were there. Mydia and Rhidea's heads broke the water's surface at the top where the River Ardencaul gushed out from the surface world and into the Sea. They stepped from the boat into the rushing water and pulled the boat up and over the precipice with a massive splash and an ensuing reverse wave. Now that it could float on the river's surface and gravity was not against them, it was far easier to pull against the current. They guided the ship a couple hundred yards upstream, just far enough that the passengers could get off without fear of the waterfall's proximity. Here Rhidea indicated they could land the boat. They brought it toward the shore until the keel ground into the pebble bank, leaving it there. Rhidea stayed to hold the boat upright using her Water Authority and probably some Silver, while Mydia tiredly climbed aboard the front and knocked on the wooden door.

Kaen opened it hesitantly at first, but upon seeing Mydia, he pulled her into a sudden and tight embrace. After a moment, someone inside the ship coughed, and a few called out, "Are we . . . there?"

"Yes," Mydia mumbled against Kaen's chest. "We made it."

Embarrassed, Kaen set her back down and held her at arm's length. "I can't believe it. You did it!"

"Just come on out, boy," came Rhidea's voice from outside.

Mydia stepped back, readying an apology for getting Kaen's clothes all wet, but then she realized she still wasn't actually wet. The water had rolled off her without a goodbye. "Um, everyone can come out now," she said instead, slipping into the shallow riverbank as gracefully as she could manage.

Kaen called the passengers out who would be returning to the Sky Islands, which was the majority of them, and Kaen and Kymhar helped the pilgrims out into the shallows. More than one stopped to personally thank Mydia and Rhidea, the former of which got more hugs and bows of thanks out of it as the latter was standing patiently in the shallows, holding the boat still with deceptive effort. Marnie embraced Mydia tightest, giving the shorter woman a peck on the forehead. "You take care of our little boy, all right?"

Mydia smiled, trying to pretend her knees didn't want to collapse from exhaustion. "Don't worry, ma'am. He'll be fine with us. We won't let him fall into any other worlds."

"Now, see," the boy spoke up. "That wasn't my idea!"

Lester clasped his shoulder, looking him in the eye. "Come back and visit us sometime, son."

Oliver hugged his father. "I will, Pa."

Mydia sent the sky dwellers off, including the gentleman Ferriman, who wanted to explore the Sky Islands at last. This left only the group of five explorers. Boarding the boat once more with the others, Rhidea and Mydia propelled them up the river once more, heading toward Randhorn, capital of Nemental. The Ardencaul flowed all the way from Ti'Vaeth, through Nytaea and directly beside Randhorn, which lay only a few miles from the cliffs.

Rhidea had to be worn out after using far more of her Authority than she had since recovery, and Mydia herself was exhausted, but fortunately they made it to Randhorn in little more than a quarter of an hour. The sturdy stone walls couldn't have appeared any more refreshing, nor more familiar. They hailed the guards at the harbor, who gaped upon recognizing Rhidea and the Nytaean queen. A few shouts later, the portcullis was raised to allow their strange vessel to pass into the harbor.

After docking the ship, Rhidea began to explain the necessary details of their strange circumstances of arrival to the guardsmen, who relayed the information onward to the palace. Meanwhile, Kaen and the others got off.

Mydia could not help but notice that the guards and castle stewards looked . . . tense. Things did not seem to be entirely in order. Upon inquiring what news had Randhorn in such a state, one mustachioed man replied hesitantly, "You mean ya haven't heard the news yet?"

They shook their heads.

"We've been a little ways . . . underground," said Kaen helpfully.

"Nytaea has been taken back by the Archlord, and it's in a terrible state," the man said in a sorrowful tone. "I'm afraid your kingdom isn't there anymore."

News

"Aye," said the grey-haired King Fenwel, "Nytaea has fallen."

Kaen bit his lip, watching from near the back of the group. They stood in the king's personal study, including Oliver, whom King Fenwel had greeted warmly and didn't seem to mind. After all, a friend of Rhidea's was a friend of the king's.

Rhidea tapped her booted foot, leaning against the stone wall opposite her king. She said nothing for a moment, simply looking at the floor. "So, Domon really did give up every pretense of honor for power," she mused. "A demon in disguise." Not to mention that disguise was a thinly veiled one.

Kaen wasn't all that good with letters, but he was pretty sure those two words were rather similar to start with. Instead of mentioning these thoughts, he cleared his throat and said, "But why did he want to destroy the Gate at all? He clearly had a plan."

King Fenwel looked him in the eye with that knowing stare of his, far more serious than his usual light demeanor would indicate. "Quite right. The man is a tyrant and rotten to the core, but he is cunning. He wouldn't have agreed to sponsor your quest across the world, all to ultimately seek and destroy a relic of the past, if he didn't have a greater goal in mind."

All eyes turned to Kymhar, the former servant of Archlord Domon. The assassin shrugged, saying in a quiet voice, "If I knew more of the Archlord's plans, I would have already shared them. The Umbra Council is secretive."

"The Umbra Council . . ." Rhidea muttered, rubbing her chin. "Don't we know someone who used to be in the Council?"

Mydia's eyebrows rose. "You mean that witch? Lady Lieda?"

"Yes, the very same." Kaen would have expected the Wandering Mage to crack a wry smile as she said it, but . . . not given the situation. Turning to

Fenwel, she said, "Please tell us everything you've heard concerning the city and the Archlord."

A female aide poked her head inside the study just then. "My lord? Pardon my intrusion, but here are your tea and biscuits."

"Not a moment late," the king replied, sitting up in his chair.

Kaen could not recall the blonde woman's name, but he did recall that she made good tea. She left two trays of steaming cups and scrumptious looking biscuits of multiple varieties on the low center table and departed. Kaen took his share after Fenwel. Or what he considered to be his share, anyway.

After taking a sip of his tea, King Fenwel said, "It began three months ago. My sources said the Archlord came upon the city in person, assaulting the palace by the front gates and taking out any opposition that stood in his way using his Dark Authority, including Marshal Lanthar and many soldiers. He left most of the leaders alive, but forced them back into subjection to the Kystrean Empire. He instated his own man, a new governor named Zama, and then . . . he announced that he was launching an expedition to the other continent. He took many a mage soldier of Nytaea, appointing them as his own mage force under Captain Hespian and Lieutenant Lorta, and departed. My sources are not sure how he planned to get to the new land.

"Nytaea is now occupied by two legions of imperial troops, under the command of the new governor. And that woman, Lieda, has been let out of prison and even—according to my spies—has married Lord Zama."

"What!" Mydia half shouted, half laughed the word. "What could he possibly want with her . . .?"

"Or is she just that desperate for any scrap of power?" Kaen asked.

Rhidea shook her head. "If I had to guess, I'd say Domon put her up to it. It wouldn't be the first time she went where he said like an obedient dog. It is indeed all about power—that vixen always has a scheme—but I believe it's usually Domon's power she craves."

"Exactly my thoughts," Fenwel said. "Though there is no way to know for certain. Now . . . I believe it's time you explained the strange manner of your arrival. I take it the mission was a failure? Did Domon have something to do with that?"

Kaen looked to Rhidea, who looked to Kymhar, who looked back at Kaen. Oliver glanced around the room as though seeking permission to speak, then said, "Well, your lordliness, there was a tower, and it blew up, and then we fell through some holes in the ground, and then we ended up in a big . . . What?"

"One thing at a time, boy," Rhidea said, before turning to her king and beginning the full story from scratch. Kaen enjoyed watching the aged man's eyes go wide multiple times.

When she had finished, Fenwel rubbed his full beard for a moment. "That is quite the adventure. My, you do get into lots of trouble for an old woman."

"You flatter me, my lord."

He cocked a smile. "Can I assume you are planning to go and surprise the illustrious Lord Zama?"

Rhidea pretended to hesitate, looking up with a finger on her chin, before giving a firm, "Yes."

Oliver grinned and pumped his fist.

Kaen took hold of the younger boy's shoulder. "Whoa, there. Don't get too excited. We won't be sightseeing."

"Aw, not that. I don't care about seeing sights; I want to see some action!"

"Oh, you'll get plenty of that," Mydia muttered.

Kaen was heading through the halls of Castle Randhorn when he heard the clack of heeled footsteps on stone. "Kaen, can we speak for a minute?" came Mydia's voice.

He stopped, turning around slowly. "What is it?" His hand absently rubbed the sword at his waist.

The princess—no, the queen—approached at a jog, stopping to breathe heavily. Despite having lost some excess weight—only furthering her innate beauty—she still had no stamina. She pointed at his silver blade. "That. That is what we need to talk about."

He gripped the hilt of the sword tighter. "What about it?" He didn't mean to use such clipped words, but anxiety mixed with his . . . whatever seemed to come between them when he saw Mydia. Together, it caused him to not act himself. But it wasn't the sword. Rhidea could say what she liked.

Mydia sighed, tucking one of her silky black locks behind her ear in a nervous gesture. Yes, nervous. He could tell because he himself fingered his sword pommel whenever . . . no, that wasn't a nervous gesture. Mydia's eyes flicked down to his hand, and he pulled it away from the sword with a jerky motion, crossing his arms instead. She gazed at him, and he saw worry in those big green eyes. He rarely looked her in the eye, perhaps because of his own discomfort.

Kaen glanced away, shifting his shoulders as if to shove his hands deeper into his armpits. "Why do you all keep looking at me like that? I'll be fine! I'm just—I'm just worried. About Mandrie."

Mydia stepped closer, causing his heart to beat just a bit faster. Or maybe it was his breathing. He struggled to keep his hands to themselves and not finger his sword. He didn't want to admit it, but he knew it was a bad habit, particularly in front of—

She reached up and touched his shoulder gently. "Kaen, why don't we sit down somewhere and talk about it? I think you're holding too much in."

Kaen let out a breath. How long had he been holding it? He nodded. "A-all right." He let the former princess lead him out of the stone corridor, through the main lobby and out a side door. Outside to where a patioed area connected to the front gardens surrounding the inner castle, with a couple of benches in front of well-trimmed hedges. Fortunately, no servants were in sight. Well, there came one now, but he wasn't looking their way . . .

Mydia took a seat on the bench to the left, smoothing her green skirts and patting the seat beside her. "Come sit."

Kaen nodded silently, adjusting his side scabbard to sit down beside her with as much room between them as possible—without looking like he disliked her. Where was Lyn when he needed her? Surely an awkward situation had never occurred with her around.

"Kaen," Mydia began, voice trembling ever so slightly, "I know it's been hard on you, not knowing if Mandrie is safe or not—she and Phoebe both."

Kaen drew in a quick breath and held it as he searched for what to say. Letting it out slowly, he said, "I'm sorry. I've been a jerk to you all lately. And Rhidea thinks—you think—that it's the sword. I . . ." He sat back, crossing his arms. "Maybe it is. Maybe she's right. I guess it's a comforting thing at the moment."

Mydia nodded, gazing at her lap-bound hands as she twiddled her fingers. "I understand. I think." She looked up at him and smiled, causing his heart to skip a few beats. Did she do that on *purpose?*

He was going to say something, but instead cleared his throat and looked at the ground. Very nice interlocking stonework. Master Harcost would have approved. Lights and glory, what had he been about to say? Words . . . the words were just gone.

Mydia made a noise in her throat, one of those sounds women make when they're trying to say too many things at once and try very hard to put it all into one easy-to-miss semi-verbal signal. He was pretty sure she was hungry. Or angry; was there a word for both at once? But then she simply said, "I, too, have been worried."

Kaen looked up. "About me?"

Confusion played on her face for a moment, and he could swear her pale skin flushed a few shades. Then she laughed. "No, about . . . well, yes, that is what I wanted to talk about, but—so many things: my kingdom, which I'm supposed to be *leading*, Lyn and whatever is transpiring on Gaea. My brother, who went missing fifteen years ago. Rhidea is . . . hiding something. It's eating at me."

Kaen shook off his discomfort. "What do you mean? About that last part?"

She shook her head. "It's just something that struck me a while back, and I didn't realize how important it might be until she announced her deception to us the other day." She made a *you see* motion with her hand, elaborating, "Claiming that she was an earth mage, when in fact she is the last Silversmith."

"But that's a good thing." Even as he said it, Kaen felt hesitant. The sword seemed to whisper that that was not necessarily a good thing, but he couldn't be certain that was actually the sword.

The queen let out a heavy, frustrated sigh. "The point is that I understand your struggle. But please, can you be a bit more open? I feel like you've been drifting apart. From the group." She bit her lip and looked down again. Perhaps she, too, was admiring the pavement.

"I'll try. Like I said, I'm sorry for the way I've been acting. My sister . . . she means the world to me. I'm sure Lyn told you how scared I was for her when she was kidnapped by Hespian."

"She did. I felt dreadful, like I was responsible, yet unable to help."

Kaen nodded. After a pause, he said, "Unable to help . . . like us now, with Lyn. Hopefully she's still alive."

"I know. All we can do is pray. But Kaen. Kaen."

"Hm?" He looked over to see her staring at him intently.

"Mandrie will be all right. I know it. We'll see them all soon." She smiled and leaned over to give him a quick kiss on the cheek.

She was gone before he could react.

He was left sitting there on the bench, warming in the sun. Had she really just . . .? He reached up to feel his left cheek, and then rubbed at it and proceeded to wipe his hand off on his sleeve. Never had he expected such behavior from a supposed queen. Only two females were allowed to touch him, and those were Lyn—practically a sister—and Mandrie, his blood sister. Well, and Phoebe, but she usually only touched him with her fists.

Now he was even more confused. But when he finally arose from the bench, he found himself in a better mood. He fingered his sword with a surer hand. It was almost a confident pose, a ready pose. Well, perhaps not—

Human interactions, spoke the sword in his head, causing him to jolt. *They are so fascinating. Your contradictions are nothing short of amusing.*

"Shush," Kaen muttered under his breath, glancing around to see if any castle stewards were watching him. A couple, but only in passing.

What do you desire? Do you seek to be with this female human?

"Which—" Kaen shut his mouth before he drew attention to himself. *Which one?* he thought, directing the mental words at the presence of the sword, which seemed to bear against his own consciousness like a gust against a house.

Hmmm. The one with the quiet soul. Strong, but weak. You fancy her appearance, though I cannot see it to judge for myself.

Excuse me?

You think her beautiful, the sword repeated more bluntly. *She is a she, yes? Or have my senses dulled so much? Like Luna to Mani, so one human soul to another. Thus I judge.*

Like Luna to Mani? Kaen hadn't the faintest idea what Luna was. A place? *Listen, sword. You think you're impressive because you can fill my head with poetic noise, but you make no sense.*

Who defines sense?

Kaen gritted his teeth, stalking faster through the halls. *Just shut up already.*

Such malice. Such hostility. The sword sounded somewhere between reproving and approving, and Kaen wasn't sure which. All he knew was he had lost his way to the place where he was supposed to meet Rhidea. And where had Mydia gotten to?

Listen, he told the sword, more forcefully this time. *I don't know who or what you are, but you had better stop talking to me out of nowhere.*

The more your emotions ripple into waves, the more I awake, came the sword's response. *You think I am a force outside of you, but I draw out what is inside your soul and feed off of it.*

Feed off of it? Kaen had never heard it say such a thing before. Was it . . .

He stopped in his tracks as someone cried out in front of him. He didn't catch the words, only the tone of voice. A young man crowned by a sideswept blond mop had stopped as well. "I say, haven't seen you in quite some time," he said after a moment, recognizing Kaen.

Kaen groaned inside. Who better to run into than Cort Flanning? "Sorry," he muttered. "Didn't see you there."

"Well, see now, neither did I." The young scholar adjusted his spectacles, tucking the book—which he held open in front of him—under his arm. "I heard about your adventures. Word is spreading all throughout the study hall."

"I'm sure it is." Kaen made a move to go. "I'm looking for Lyn. I need to—"

"Lyn! But isn't she gone? Back to her home and all that?"

Kaen growled, spinning around and grabbing Cort by his stupid, too-high collar. "Listen, I don't have time for your smart tongue!"

Cort's made a small noise in his throat, eyes wide. Either in surprise or fear.

Kaen suddenly realized that his face was twisted up in what must be a horrible expression, noting how tight he held the slimmer boy, and let go of him, backing up a step. "Sorry. I just . . . I meant Rhidea. That—that was not called for. I'm . . . a little stressed right now."

Cort adjusted his collar. "I can see that. I didn't mean anything about your friend. I'm sorry. I'll—be going now." And with that, he took off at a fast walk in the direction he'd been heading.

Kaen dropped his shoulders, breathing heavily through his nostrils. Had he really just gotten that upset over one comment? It must be the sword. It had distracted him.

Wrong, the sword said in his head, *it is your own emotions that stir me. How many times must I say it?*

Say what it wanted, Kaen knew it was affecting him. Perhaps Rhidea was right. What if he shouldn't have taken the sword?

The Soul of Silver, the sword whispered musingly. *You think you know her, and yet you acknowledge that she kept hidden the very reason for which she seeks to cast me out. She does not accept me, though she came from me.*

What was it rambling about now? Kaen knew he trusted Rhidea. Well, a bit less now . . . but that was none of its business. Rhidea had proven time and again to be faithful to her word.

And yet even Mydia was beginning to doubt her.

Kaen sighed, shook his head, and set off once more in search of Rhidea. The sword stayed quiet this time.

β Chapter 07 β

Shadows in the White City

"Here we are again," Rhidea said, pulling in her reins as they crested the last hill before the city of Nytaea. "We'd best approach with caution."

They rode on horses loaned from her lord, King Fenwel, and had been riding for a few days. They'd decided against taking their experimental craft up the river, swift though that would have been, as that would gather too much attention. Thus, it currently sat in Randhorn, being studied by Fenwel's water mage scholars.

The sun was now peeking up above the horizon, whilst the auroras had been steadily dimming in preparation for the Sunlit Cycle. The province of Storklance hadn't shown many signs of militarization, but Kaen knew that Nytaea would be crawling with soldiers.

The White City itself stood a mile away on the horizon, Sol's morning light blanketing its high walls in an unearthly glow. A quarter mile to the north, the ground sloped downward to the channel through which the Ardencaul exited the city. Oliver, sitting his horse like the beginner he was, struggled to get his mount to stand still as he gaped at the city. "It's . . . so big. And pretty."

"Like me?" Mydia asked with a self-satisfied smile.

"Well, the big part," the boy retorted, sticking out his tongue. He went to make a circular motion with his arms to go along with his insult, but almost fell off his horse in doing so.

Mydia gasped. "Why, you . . . you're lucky I'm not a queen anymore."

Kaen shook his head and whistled softly.

"He has more guards patrolling the walls." Kymhar pointed at the tops of the walls, where Kaen could just barely make out figures pacing back and forth. The assassin was right. "This Zama either runs a tight show or is exceedingly paranoid."

"I'd lean toward paranoid," said Rhidea. "We shall see what he's like for ourselves. Mydia? Some illusions?"

Mydia nodded, closing her eyes and taking on a meditative posture in her saddle. Her dual Authority in Water and Perception came in handy often, Kaen had to admit. In a minute, they all wore illusions, just enough to throw off anyone who would recognize them but not enough to confuse one another. She also changed Kaen and Kymhar's attire and equipment to look a bit less threatening.

Kaen himself had his living sword strapped by its sheath to the saddle just in front of him, and its appearance did not change at all. *Of course,* he realized. *It negates all magic. Or so it says.*

I can disappear, the sword said, almost hesitantly.

Kaen glanced around at the others briefly. Mydia frowned at him, probably wondering why her magic hadn't worked on the sword. *Do it,* he commanded the sword. *Disappear.*

And it did so. Mydia's eyes widened as she saw it, but she said nothing.

"Thank you, dear," Rhidea said to the queen. "Now, let us go."

They proceeded toward the city. The soldiers atop the wall stopped to watch their approach, signaling other men below. The group was met at the tall gates by a pair of spear-bearing guards in front of a closed portcullis. Kaen hadn't seen the bars down in a while.

"What business have ye?" asked one of the men, a wary look on his face. Kaen did not recognize their uniforms, dark grey with black highlights and a few too many buttons for functionality.

"We come from Storklance," Rhidea said in a tone she practiced to sound less important than usual. She had many, each for a different occasion, and in this case it matched her plain, brown-haired appearance.

The man grunted. "Well, I trust you know what yer doing. The city is, uh . . . tight on security right now. Lord Zama has small patience for trouble." He nodded to his companion, who made a signal, and the portcullis began to raise.

"Thank ye," Mydia said in a horrific impression of the guard's own accent as they passed by, horse hooves clacking on the cobblestones.

"What was *that?*" Kaen asked her, leaning over in his saddle as they passed out of earshot of the guards.

She snickered. "Practicing my accents. It's an important skill for a lady of the court."

"For a lady of subterfuge," he corrected. "But you should stick to what you can handle."

Mydia beamed, as though only hearing praise. Her disguise was that of a blonde-haired woman slightly older than herself, hair just a bit longer than her mid-length bob. Kaen was relatively sure it was supposed to appear plain, yet on her, it still looked pretty.

It took Kaen one look at the city before them to realize just what a sorry state it was in. Nytaea's once-proud beauty had already been fading under Lord Kalceron's mismanagement, but now . . . it was as though a war had been waged in the streets. Buildings were charred, window shutters hung loose where once they had not, and everything was in disorder. Military men marched the streets and the common people walked hunched over, as though chased by monsters or whip-bearing taskmasters. Where children had run and played in the streets, furtively looking about for mage soldiers or untrustworthy strangers, now dogs and rats prowled the thoroughfares. Thieves beat vagabonds in alleyways and robbed passersby, and not one of the soldiers stopped to do anything about it.

"It feels so . . . gloomy," Mydia whispered. "This is horrible."

"Was it, uh, always this way?" Oliver asked from behind her.

Mydia shook her head. "Not even under my father. It's like an army camp . . . or a prison."

A nameless fear began to take hold of Kaen as they rode toward the center of the city. A slow dread that made him shiver, mounting with every passing minute. The sword began to stir, though it remained invisible, and Kaen glanced down as it addressed him:

Your soul fears. For what has happened to your sister. You see destruction and oppression, and you fear.

I'm not afraid. Just worried. Now, be quiet. Kaen was worried more than he had ever been in his life, and what he felt was certainly fear, but the sword annoyed him too much to admit it.

What will you do if your sister is gone? Slain by soldiers? Crushed in the chaos? Sold off as a slave to foreigners?

Shut up! he told the sword, and belatedly realized that he had actually growled the words under his breath. Heart beating rapidly in his chest, he looked up to see Mydia and Rhidea frowning at him.

"Uh, Kaen?" Oliver asked. "You all right? Hearing voices or somethin'?"

"No," Kaen answered, more forcefully than he'd meant. "Sorry. I just— I'm all right."

Oliver said no more.

"Kaen," Rhidea said after a moment, "We are going to see what the people at the Palace have to say about the situation. But if you want to check in on your family first, that is all right."

Kaen grunted. "I'd like to."

"I can go with you," Mydia began, but he cut her off.

"No, I'll go alone. Don't want to draw too much attention." He hesitated, considering asking Kymhar to come just for some extra backup in case he was apprehended by soldiers or other hostiles, but then thought better of it. The last thing he needed was someone else along while his sword harassed him. As much as he didn't want to admit it, his worry was indeed feeding its . . . whatever caused it to stir and speak to him.

They agreed on a meetup point, and he departed in the direction of the district where Phoebe's new orphanage was, just south of the central ring where the Nytaean Palace loomed over all. All the while, the silver blade beckoned to him with its eerie voice, commenting and asking questions as though purposefully trying to get to him. He . . . attempted to ignore it.

Eventually, he reached the side street on which the orphanage lay and turned his horse to follow it. He was so upset at this point that he didn't even pay attention at first. Then he saw it: The scorch marks, the rubble. This street had been targeted by whoever had torched much of the city. Kaen's heartbeat quickened further, and he kicked his horse into a canter. In a minute, he came upon the ruined building that was once an orphanage.

The door had been knocked in, and all the wood on the white stone building burned up or charred badly, leaving the outer face of the building, once lime-white like the surrounding structures, scarred yellow and black. "Oh, hellsbreath," he muttered, surveying the situation numbly. *Surely they fled,* he told himself. *They must have gotten away.* He slowed his horse and kicked free from the saddle, not bothering to find a place to tie her. The sword hissed and sent a jumble of words through his head, but his reeling mind paid no heed.

Slowly, hesitantly, he entered the building, searching around for any sign of life, or . . . rather, death. He kicked over broken boards and searched everywhere he could, but he saw no bodies. Surely that was a good sign.

Or they have all burnt to death, whispered the sword. *We can find the souls responsible and dispense justice upon them.*

The words came clear in Kaen's head this time, and he paused, listening to it. "They can't have," he muttered. "You'll see, I'll find them."

After another minute of searching, he left, determined to track down every trace of them that he could find. He would not give up until he found Mandrie and Phoebe. Outside, he heard the snorting of his mare from the left, and looked to find a young girl petting her. When she saw him, the girl immediately froze and shrank back.

"Hey!" he called. "No, wait, please! Have you seen the children from the orphanage here? Have you . . . wait, I recognize you."

The girl frowned. She was small, perhaps five or six, and had dirty blonde hair tied back in a braid. Then her eyes grew large. "Mr. Kaen?"

He forced a smile. "Yes. I'm in disguise. What happened to the others? What about Mandrie and Phoebe?"

"They took us away when the magi came," the girl said. "It was scary. Do you want me to take you to them?"

Relief washed over Kaen like a wave of water. Months of worry, finally resolved. Yet he wouldn't be happy until he saw them with his own eyes. "Please," he said. And he gave the girl a lift on his horse. He was almost giddy with excitement, in a way he hadn't felt for a long time. He managed to pay attention to the girl's incessant chatter along the way long enough to catch her name, Loret, though she also listed every other one of the orphans' names.

At last, they came to a corner of town farther south where the girl directed him to one of the abandoned houses, untouched by the widespread destruction. Kaen recognized it immediately as one of their old hideouts, which he and his friends from Lentha's orphanage had made years back. In the good old days. Simpler days.

He tied the mare before coming to the shelter, taking only his sword and the girl, whom he carried in one arm. At the cobwebby door, he gave a triple tap, and then another triple tap after a pause, one of their old signs, and was met after a moment by a wary-looking Phoebe. Real live Phoebe, not a corpse, nor a ghost. Blast that sword and its pessimistic talk.

The young woman's face morphed from cautious curiosity to surprise to joy. Her dark hair, wavy as ever and unwashed, clung to her face, but her smile, a rarity on any day, was like a river in a desert land. "Kaen!" she exclaimed. "You're alive! Mandrie, Mandrie, come here!"

"Hey, Pheebs," he replied with a tired grin.

Soon, his curly-haired little sister appeared, stopping briefly to stare at him in disbelief, a childlike grin spreading wider and wider on her face. She pushed past Phoebe and wrapped her arms around his waist. "Oh, Kaen. We thought you might never return."

Kaen awkwardly set Loret down and pulled Mandrie up into a hug. Phoebe stepped out of the way, and he moved into the room, spinning his sister around before setting her down. "Oof, you've grown, Mandrie."

She giggled, bright eyes twinkling in the light of the room's two lamps. "Have I?" At twelve, she was just reaching her full height, some half-head shorter than Kaen, though her form was still more slender and girlish than Phoebe's.

He patted her shoulder, and then grabbed Phoebe's shoulder with his other hand, pulling her into a side-embrace. They were both like sisters to him, though Mandrie was the only blood sibling he had ever had. "Pheebs, it's good to see you guys again. And all of you," he said, gesturing at the half-dozen children who had joined Loret, standing back and watching the reunion. Then he obliged their requests to get spun around like their "big sis."

Finally, he asked Phoebe what was going on in the city now that Zama had taken over.

"Oh, it's been a living nightmare," she said, shaking her head. "Like a return to Kalceron's rule, only . . . well, quite frankly it's never been worse. And probably won't get better." This last comment sounded more like the grouchy Phoebe he knew.

"Brother, how did you get back?" Mandrie asked. "Are Lyn and Mydia with you? And the others?"

Kaen hesitated. "It's . . . a long story. The others? Yes. Lyn . . . no."

Mandrie frowned in concern. "What happened?"

"She . . . is on Gaea. She made it." Kaen smiled despite himself. "Don't worry, I'm sure she's doing just fine. She's tough. They're probably treating her like a queen right now."

Zama

"Are we all clear on the plan?" Rhidea asked. Three heads nodded, one particular blond head nodding extra profusely. "For tonight, we will simply be conducting reconnaissance on the palace defenses. I like to be cautious."

Mydia raised a pale hand. "What about Kaen, though? Should we wait for him to come back first? I'm . . . a bit concerned at this point."

"We'll wait for him," Rhidea said. "I have a strong feeling he will be back soon." She could usually feel the presence of that strange sword, even far off, and it seemed to have calmed down considerably, so she took that to be a good sign.

They sat around a table in an inn closely neighboring the stables where they had left their horses. Outside through the windows, the Palace walls loomed in the morning light. It had been an hour since Kaen departed to find his friends, and they still wore their illusions.

Mydia nudged Oliver. "You'll finally get to meet Phoebe and Mandrie!" she whispered, though Rhidea saw no reason to whisper.

"Kymhar," Rhidea said, "Keep an eye on these two while I'm gone, will you? I'm going to have a look around the walls."

The man gave a silent nod.

Rhidea left the inn and headed up the street toward the Palace wall. Looking up at the walkway thirty feet above, she thought, *If only it weren't morning . . .* Although the torches the guards kept lit all night long gave little room for cover in any case. Rhidea pulled out her teleportation amulet and, after a furtive glance around, used it to instantaneously move to the rooftops above, roughly on the level of the wall top. The first wall. The Nytaean Palace had tiers and layers. This outer wall connected to the four main towers at its corners.

One more spatial shift and Rhidea was atop the wall, near the northwestern tower that used to be Mydia's. From here, she was out of sight of most of the guardsmen and afforded a good view of the premises. Watchmen leaned over the battlements or paced to and fro along the walls, and more spearmen walked the grounds below. Men trained with the sword in a courtyard directly below, along with a surprising number of women. Usually, women were kept to the sidelines in the military or used only in the mage forces, but perhaps Lord Zama had decided he had too many expendables in his city.

Rhidea did not stay on the wall for long, but vanished before the closest guards could turn and see her, alighting on the street once more just in time to see a familiar figure exiting the stable. "There you are," she said.

"Rhidea," Kaen replied.

The boy sounded tired, but the mage could easily see that his entire countenance had lifted and he seemed to be in better spirits. Hopefully the change would last. "You found them?"

He nodded. "Phoebe and Mandrie are doing well. They've holed up in an old shelter with the orphans."

Rhidea pulled open the door to the inn and Kaen followed behind her. Upon reaching the others, Kaen explained the situation with Phoebe, Mandrie and the other orphans, adding, "I'm leaving them there for now. I don't want to draw attention to them."

"Smart move," said Kymhar.

"Oh, Kaen, I'm so happy for you!" cried Mydia, rising from her seat to embrace him, clearly surprising him judging by the reaction on his face. "I can't wait to see them again."

"First, we have to deal with . . . you know who." Rhidea glanced around the room, noting the eyes that had turned on their group, including the inkeep from behind the counter. Sitting back down at the table and motioning for Kaen to take the empty seat, Rhidea quickly filled him in on the plan to depose Zama.

That evening, they did as Rhidea had said and gathered information.

They split into two groups: Rhidea with Mydia; Kaen and Oliver with Kymhar. They spoke to guardsmen, soldiers, and citizens not cowed too much to speak to strangers. The inkeep, too, had been helpful, though they tried not to attract too much attention yet.

From the sound of it, the city was in a state of soft lockdown, with the Nytaean citizens kept to a curfew and imprisoned for breaking it or trying to leave the city without good reason. Many soldiers had been relocated from Ti'Vaeth, where the Archlord had previously kept his army in almost suspicious inactivity. Had Rhidea been more of a military strategist, she may have predicted Domon's plans in advance based on signs like that. Living for two hundred years did not make one an expert in all fields.

They learned what they could of Zama and his new government, and of Lady Lieda and her hand in matters. Though many seemed reluctant to admit it, none of the citizens seemed to like either one. Lieda was the important piece that Rhidea really wanted to corner. Zama, by all counts, was somewhat a fool. Just a harsh, oppressive, arrogant fool.

They spent the night at the inn. Rising before cloudbreak, they went to the main gate without illusions, eliciting shocked looks from the guards. "L-Lady Mydia!" stammered one of them. "How are—you're alive?" He looked nervously to his partner, who shrugged but did not lower his halberd.

"And I am Rhidea of Randhorn," Rhidea said. "You may want to let us in. We need to speak to Lord Zama."

"I-I'm not sure we can . . ." The man gulped, seeing Rhidea's expression, and amended his words. "I'm sure that can be arranged."

The two guards pulled back their weapons, waving the group inside, and Rhidea and her companions proceeded into the main Palace courtyard. White stone and silver pillars adorned the way, leading to multiple white halls with twin staircases spiraling up to the second story. Servants bearing the new grey-and-black attire met them, asking after their purpose at the Palace, and Rhidea repeated her request for an audience with Lord Zama. The servants departed with fear on their faces.

Upstairs on the second floor, it wasn't long before armed soldiers found them, filing in one after the other to surround the party. Then appeared a tall, broad-shouldered man with dark grey hair, the type that goes grey prematurely. He wore a decorative sword at his waist, and Rhidea could not tell if he looked a man who knew how to use it or not. But they had found their man, no doubt about that.

"Lady Rhidea, I presume?" the man asked in a dry, businesslike voice. "It is a pleasure to make your acquaintance." He looked to Mydia. "And you would be the lady Mydia Kalceron, heiress of House Kalceron?"

Mydia held her chin high. "I am she."

"I will admit," Zama continued in the same uninterested tone, "I thought my guards to be lying, as the Archlord personally informed me that both of you had perished at the end of the world."

"I'm afraid not," Rhidea replied dryly. "I see you are taking the finest care of the city in the queen's absence, however. Archlord Domon would be truly impressed."

"Domon himself set this in motion," Zama said, "And it was he who made the first strike on Nytaea. He is more preoccupied with conquest currently than he is with the welfare of every citizen in his expanding empire."

"A fine excuse to misuse your authority," Mydia replied. "Which is only that of an invading usurper."

Zama's eyes narrowed. "Perhaps you forget who you are speaking to, but I have these and many more at my command." He raised a hand, and the dozen guardsmen surrounding Rhidea's group raised their crossbows. Then he whistled, and silver-armored mage soldiers stepped out from the hall behind him. Blue capes, red capes . . . there were many different elemental divisions represented. Last of all came a slender, black-haired woman who should be in prison—Lady Lieda. She wore her customary black dress, slitted even further down her chest than usual.

The mage soldiers fanned out to either side, and the would-be queen slinked up to Zama, sidling up against him, her foxy face looking as though she had just eaten something bitter but wanted to pretend it was sweet. To think that this woman had acted just the same way with Mydia's father but a few months ago. . .

Eyeing up the intruders, Lieda said, "Why, Mydia dear, and the Wandering Mage, too. What should we do with them, dearest?"

Rhidea wasn't sure why she would ask such a foolish question, given that their previous confrontation had ended with Lieda strapped to the floor in shackles of stone, though there seemed to be . . . something . . . a look in her eyes as she gazed at Rhidea, something that said, *Just play the game.*

Mydia, for her part, looked like she was gritting her teeth, trying to remain calm. Rhidea knew that if she hated anyone in the world, it was her stepmother.

Kaen put his hand to his sword, but Zama said, "I wouldn't try that. Stand down. We will be taking you all into custody."

Rhidea laughed. She couldn't help it. The gap between an ordinary mage soldier and a High Mage was so great that one against a dozen was often considered even odds, yet with her Silver Magic, she had been able to defeat even the late Lord Kalceron in a few minutes. Surely Lieda must be up to something. Could it be that she wanted him to fail in capturing them? "I think you are mistaking your place, my good Lord Zama," Rhidea said. "The Archlord broke his contract with Nytaea and attacked it, setting you up as the new tyrant lord. And yet Lady Mydia here is the heir. One would think . . ." she brought her hands up in a slow gesture, as though surrendering, ". . . that you should know how to kneel."

She thrust her hands down, and the entire hall full of soldiers and Magi slumped to their knees, dragged down by a sudden weight. Gravitational magic, Rhidea's own specialty born of her innate Silver Authority. Many of the soldiers dropped their weapons as they struggled not to fall on their faces, and any who tried to raise a hand to shoot, she pulled harder and they collapsed. Zama and Lieda both lay hunched on the marble floor, struggling against the overpowering gravity. Only Rhidea and her companions were immune.

The Wandering Mage strode forward. "You see, power is a strange thing.

You think you have something, until one greater than you comes along and puts you in your place. I try not to make a habit of bullying rulers, so in this case, I am merely enforcing the respect you owe to your queen. Lord Zama, if you appeal very nicely, she may just grant you the kingdom. Mydia, what do you think?"

"Absolutely not," scoffed Mydia.

Rhidea smiled.

End of Part One

Memory

α   Chapter 10   α

Tests

Venidal 28, 1294:

Time has been passing like a breeze for me. I am excited for Soldor, as with it comes the Festival of Lights! . . . Although I shall, of course, still be stuck in this windowless building. I have learned so much that I feel like a completely different person. I wonder at our teachers' identity, and whence came their broad stores of knowledge? My companions and I have been at our new home for five moons, learning under the tutelage of our mysterious Anier masters. Increasingly, we have been studying some odder topics: Complex energy and physics studies, biological studies of plants and animals and the ecosystem, and in-depth human anatomy and physiology. This last subject scares me more than anything, because I know that their true purpose for us might have something to do with the population crisis . . . They've spoken of it on multiple occasions.

— From Lhinde's Diary

I pulled on the top piece of my gillsuit, rolling it down to my waist and fastening the clips that held the suit together. Emerging from the small closet in Hodge's workshop, I spread out my hands and spun around. "Tada! How does it look?"

I don't think he was used to the same ideas of wearing clothing for looks, and particularly the general feminine line of thought that one's look must be admired by observers. Regardless, he shrugged and said, "Not too bad. Considering you made it yourself, and I've never made a suit designed for a . . . what do they call you again? A woman?" He scratched at his massive mop of hair.

As though he had the capability to forget vocabulary. The mannequins in the closet were more poetic.

I sighed, lowering my arms. "Thanks." I didn't really care, and was simply relieved that my new combat suit ended up as comfortable as it was. With Hodge's help, I had made it from scratch with the few minutes of spare time I had every day. I had also added a few extra details, like extra elastic in the crotch area to allow as free of leg motion as possible, as well as extra support and comfort in the chest area. For another touch, I'd asked Hodge for his most heat-resistant material . . . just in case the time ever came when I might be wearing this and able to use Coaction. The chances of that, of course, were slim as starvation, but hey . . .

"For real, though," I said, approaching the quartermaster to shake his hand. "I do appreciate all your help."

He tilted his head back and forth before finally taking my hand. "Well, I guess I'm glad you got something that works in the end. Training going well? How long was it again, before they're supposed to head out?"

"Actually . . . tomorrow, if I pass Zent's test. Whatever that is." I muttered this last part, as I was not looking forward to it. It was now the evening of the fourteenth day since I'd started my training, the date I had been given for my next test and physical examination. Almost subconsciously, I rubbed my forearms, one of many parts of my body that ached dully from recent training, though I had grown used to the daily beating. Perhaps . . . resistant? I hoped. They'd also assigned me regular classes on the fundaments of Gaean science, language, mathematics and the like.

I left Hodge's office and headed back to my rooms, still wearing my new gillsuit. On my way up, I encountered Bddo and Jed, who gave approval to my new outfit. "It suits you," Jed said.

I looked down. "I should hope so." I glanced down at my wrist console. 18:41. "I have to go. I'll catch you guys later."

Ten minutes later, I was dressed in my dobok and down at the door to the Iron Dojang. Musha wasn't there, however. A minute later, Zent stepped out from the elevator, dressed much like me. "Ah, here already. I see you're learning punctuality."

"No Musha?" I asked.

"He says he is confident you'll die within ten minutes of real combat. He doesn't change opinions like those easily, so I'm simply here to see if he's right."

"Oh." I wasn't sure whether to take that as encouragement or not.

"Let's begin," Zent said briskly, motioning for me to follow him into the large, metal-lined arena. We faced each other in the center of the room, twenty feet apart. He took up a traditional ready stance, and I mirrored him. We bowed to each other, assumed more relaxed fighting stances, and then began.

The large man started off by closing the distance between us and throwing a few punches at me to test my reactions. I evaded the blows, seeing them coming easily after all of Musha's drills, despite my movement capabilities not being anywhere near on par with a male Hellebes. I may have been small and lightweight in comparison, but net physical strength and speed were everything in this game.

I ducked and weaved as he threw increasingly complex techniques at me, recognizing each one as I'd been taught. There was no ground here, so he couldn't make cheap attempts to knock me off my footing with Geokinesis. Rather, I used the power coming up from the floor vents to enhance my own speed. The earth was my equalizer, or so these Hellebes thought, if I could only learn to use it at my full potential.

So I gave it my best. I drew on the Geothermic energy to boost my bones and muscles and increase my limits. The only key function it couldn't increase was my brain, so I had to keep on my toes at all times in order to avoid Zent's attacks. Every one, until he feinted and came in with a spinning kick using the leg he had been standing on a moment before. The kick took me fully in the side, throwing my body to skid along the metal floor a few paces away.

I managed to spring back into my stance via a controlled tumble, rolling and recovering in time to catch his next attack. The man was relentless. After learning to fend off Musha, I had somehow assumed that Zent was neither as strong nor as skilled as his war machine mentor, but I couldn't be more wrong. Musha was simply more effective at teaching. I tried to fight back against Zent, but he was an overpowering force, countering my every move with ease and somehow managing to keep one step ahead.

"You've grown stronger, Lyn," he said after some ten minutes. "Faster. Musha has been doing his work well as always."

"I suppose so," I muttered.

"You're also learning to harness Geothermic energy to move, which is good to see. One day, you will excel at that." He backed away finally, making a hand gesture to stop. "That's it. I saw enough."

He returned to the ready position with feet together and hands at his sides, and I did likewise. We bowed to one another, and he said, "Well done. I will talk to the Board and we'll go from there. Dr. Dekla will want to see you now, by the way."

"Right now? After working out and getting beaten up by you?"

The captain smirked. "Especially now."

"So . . . what about tomorrow?"

Zent's expression hardened. "As I said, I'll talk to the Board and see. I can't make any promises. It's ultimately not up to me." He read my face and added, "And no, you can't be in on the meeting. Sorry, not yet."

I followed him back up the elevator and from there we parted ways. I headed straight to Dr. Dekla's office, not bothering to shower first. If research was this important, then he would just have to deal with my stench. Ugh, my whole body ached from getting thrown on that steel floor again. I was certain it wasn't made for that . . . In fact, the impact on the floor tended to hurt worse than the actual blows themselves. Perhaps that was the true purpose of the Iron Dojang, to encourage trainees to keep their footing so that they didn't have to slam into hard metal all the time.

Five minutes later, I reached the exam office, taking a breath before knocking on the door. I doubted I would ever get used to these invasive exams, but I had to get it over with. At least on this occasion I was actually curious to see the changes from last time—if they would show them to me.

The fat giant greeted me with all the warmness of one of his computers. I stepped inside, quickly going through the normal process of disrobing and putting on the loose, paper-thin medical gown. Then began the same procedures as usual: needle pricks, pressure readings and X-rays. All that good stuff. The monitors showed a variety of readings, most of which I did not understand aside from that my weight had increased by a few kilos. When Dekla was done, I asked him, "So, what changes from last time?"

Surprisingly, the man didn't ignore me, instead pointing at one of his computer screens. "Actually, the results are remarkable. Static Geothermic levels have increased by more than double, and your bone density and muscle tone have increased dramatically as well. All other vital signs are nominal." After this, he lost interest in me, and I took the cue to change back into my dobok and leave the office.

I couldn't tell if Dr. Dekla's findings would be satisfactory for the Board to give the all-clear for me to leave on the mission tomorrow, but I sincerely hoped so. I was beginning to feel cramped and suffocated in the sub-ocean base and couldn't wait to get back to the surface world. After a quick shower, I changed into more comfortable clothes and went back to the main lobby to see who was there. Curt and Jed were there playing Gogi, but I saw no sign of Bddo or Ccal. Two other men I had only met once or twice, Kidd and Orlando, were chatting over a snack. They were relatively new recruits, to my understanding, having joined the Red Horizon a little over a year ago. Both soldiers were shaved bald, which didn't help me in telling them apart, though Kidd was a hair smaller, allowing me to remember him by his rather appropriate name. I couldn't place how young they were. Age was not something I had learned to pinpoint yet when it came to Hellebes.

I took a seat across from Kidd, who looked up. "Oh, Lynchazel. This your big day?"

I nodded. "Tiring so far. Captain Zent had to go all-out in his 'test.'" I tried to refer to Zent by his title most of the time.

Orlando laughed. "Knowing him, I doubt he really went all-out on you. That man's a legend in the fighting ring."

"Well . . ." I rubbed my throbbing triceps. "I suppose you're right. Are you two going to be in on the strike tomorrow?"

Kidd shook his head. "We were out just a week ago. Small outing, nothing major. They don't give us much excitement. I think this one is by volunteer, right, Orlando?"

"Think so."

"Yep, volunteer," came Jed's voice, followed by the clack of one of his Gogi pieces on the board and a small groan from Curt. "I'm going."

"Because you're a showoff and a thrill seeker," Curt grumbled.

"Precisely! Your move, Curt."

I smiled, getting up to see how the game was going. Hovering over the two men, I saw that Jed held a distinctly better position, as usual. A few moves later, Curt resigned with a huff.

"I'll play, Jed," I said. I needed a break from all my physically taxing activities.

"All right." The young man seemed to always be in the mood for some strategy. He began setting up the board in its original position, and I took Curt's spot across from him. Jed and Ccal had been teaching me a little bit, so I knew the basic rules, though only the most basic level of strategy.

The blond man let me go first, and I started out the setup phase by placing all five of my first pieces in what I meant as an aggressive position, near the center of the board. Jed only matched some of mine at the center, placing two other pieces near the back of the ten-by-ten board. Next, I placed another black piece opposite one of his white ones, pinning it between two of mine. He simply moved it, connecting to another of his white ones beside it.

I paused in thought, trying to picture how the board would turn out. I knew he would beat me, but I wanted to delay the inevitable as much as possible. So I placed another piece, forming a wall in front of his two pieces, and so began a divide at the center of the board. From what I recalled of games I'd seen so far, this was a fairly common occurrence due to the rule prohibiting placement of pieces on the opponent's side before five of each color had been played.

Before long, Jed had multiple pieces of mine cornered and in danger, all the while building stronger defenses of his own. Every attempt I made at surrounding his pieces failed miserably, and I began to lose mine one by one, each of which stacked against me in his growing reserves.

Eventually, I gave up and shook his hand, accepting my defeat. "You'll get better with practice," he said. "You'll memorize patterns and strategies."

Right, I thought to myself, *I'll memorize them. But not like you do.* I didn't mention this to Jed, even though I had already related my struggles to Bddo and Ccal. Considering how secretive the Red Horizon was being with me, I felt it best to keep some things to myself.

Just then, my arm buzzed with a message from Captain Zent. Glancing down at my wrist console, I skimmed the message: *Come to the Board Room. The leaders have made their decision and request your presence immediately.*

α Chapter 11 α

Briefing

Soldor 21, 1294:

Here we are—the Festival of Lights is upon us! Apparently, the experiments are ready, because . . . I can't bear to think about it, but they've taken Borgha and Est. They've . . . been gone for a week now. I tell myself repeatedly that they are coming back safe and sound very soon, and that the tests were nothing harmful or anything. But I said the same of my parents, didn't I? My own naiveté is pathetic. I just . . . don't want anyone to die. The twenty-four of us are like family now, not to mention we comprise most of the female population of the Sovereignty of Starklett. We are all waiting with anticipation to find out. But the Anier just announced this morning that two more will be going away for testing today. It's got my nerves in knots. I'm going to go and take my mind off this horrible business, if I can . . .

— From Lhinde's Diary

Heart beating rapidly in my chest, I excused myself and made for the Board Room. What were they going to say? I wanted to believe that the reason I was being called to meet with them personally was that I had passed my exams and was up to their expectations. I did not want to be stuck in this underwater military base for the rest of my Gaea-bound days.

Stepping inside the room, I was struck by its austerity. We were in a privately funded military base, so what did I expect? It was perhaps ten meters square, with a circular table at its center. Standing around the table were Captain Zent, Getts, Vass, Dr. Dekla, Musha and one other man. I had seen him before but didn't know who he was.

All eyes turned toward me as I walked in, doing nothing for my anxiety.

"Ah, there you are, Heiress," said Vass. "Come join us."

I stepped up to the table with what confidence I could muster, taking the empty spot next to Zent. The table, I now saw, was in fact a digital interface, featuring a war map with markers and notes, such as what resources and weapons a given city had. It was centered over the continent I had come to recognize as North Terrol, home to Haccolces and Haven, two of the greatest of the world's nine cities. Haccolces, the Steel City, was ruled by the Emperor himself, and was where I had been imprisoned for three months. Such fond memories.

And yet I need to get there. At some point.

Getts gave a grunt, catching my attention. "Yes, well, welcome to the council. Don't get too used to the attention."

"And we're finally going to let you in on some info you've been craving," Zent added. "Right?" He looked questioningly at Vass, who nodded hesitantly. Whatever passed between them was lost on me, but the sense of deliberate doling-out of knowledge . . . that was not.

"Lynchazel," Vass said, "You are very important to the Red Horizon and all of our operations. I know you already understand much of your significance to Gaea, but you have many questions. Sadly, we cannot tell you everything just yet, but we can start."

"Then," I began, but the tall man cut me off with an upheld hand.

"No questions yet. Doctor Dekla has given us his new report, and—" He tapped the screen on the table, and it switched to an anatomical model representing my own body in discomforting complexity, showing multiple angles and layers, from simple wireframes to monochromatic breakdowns of muscle composition "—the results could not be more interesting."

I peered at the images in fascination, while everyone else looked at the screen more idly, having of course already discussed it in length. What fascinated me was the interior detail, depicting bone and muscle health, blood cells and other molecular structures . . . even a detailed comparison of my brain and its makeup before and after (I couldn't tell the difference on that one). The differences that I could see, however, were remarkable.

"Your muscle mass has grown considerably, Heiress," Vass continued, pointing out the diagrams as he went, "And your bone density as well. You are adapting to Gaea more and more, and the pressure Musha has been putting on you is working wonders."

Doubtless, I thought, *painful wonders.*

"Your chemical makeup has changed as well," Dekla said. "There are a plethora of differences in your DNA when compared with your mother's or any male Hellebes. Regarding your Legaleian side, while we only have your father's DNA to go on, we can say that yours bears much of the . . . weaknesses, shall we say, that his did, but with seemingly generous potential for adaptation toward either side. Some of the adaptation toward your moon world has been undone already."

I nodded. It sort of made sense, though genetics was not a subject I had had the opportunity to study in any detail yet. The mention of my father sparked a question in me, one that had been burning since the day I arrived on Gaea, but I simply held my breath as I waited out a few more details from the scientist.

Awaiting the verdict.

Finally, Zent cut Dekla off. "All right, back to the topic at hand. Lyn, you're coming on the mission tomorrow."

I raised my eyebrows, letting out a breath a moment later. *Whew.* They wouldn't keep me penned up in this place any longer.

Dr. Dekla looked quite annoyed, yet everyone else seemed relieved at Zent's interruption.

"Yes, this meeting is growing a bit long," said the ever-dour Getts. "Let's cut to the chase."

"Very well," said Vass, turning toward me. "Lynchazel, we are sending you out with the task force under Captain Zent. He is our very best, so he should be capable of keeping an eye on you. But first, Admiral Skye will brief you on our larger objective." He motioned toward the sixth man.

Admiral Skye possessed multiple crisscrossing scars on his face, reaching up into his short-cropped black hair. He appeared to scowl at me, though somehow it came across as less personal than Getts' ill-mannered looks. "Well, recruit, let's take a look." He tapped the table's screen, returning it to the view of North Terrol that had been previously shown, and gestured broadly with a finger. "North Terrol. You made your way across the continent to the eastern sea here, where we are. And Haccolces, where you were imprisoned, sits here at the center of the continent. That's the capital of the world, where Lldsaor rules with an iron thumb."

He used two fingers to blow up the image drastically, zooming in on the Steel City. "It's defended by a near-impenetrable shield wall, but of course you've seen how those can be circumvented. Here is the lab where they kept you, and here . . ." He angled the map in the third dimension, displaying a 3D cutout of the monstrous complex of buildings including where I had been confined, and zoomed in to show a plethora of subterranean layers. "Underneath all of that is their deeper labs, where much of the Elites' genetic research has gone on for centuries."

"It's also where they kept Mother Gaea," Dekla added, crossing his voluminous arms. "Thus the laboratories and . . . everything else."

Mother Gaea . . . my own mother. What *had* they used her for? No one ever seemed willing to elaborate on that. They always mentioned genetic research and "the good of the world," but they'd clam up when pressed. The more candid Haccolces scientists told me they used her eggs to replicate all the generations of Hellebes since the females died off, but was there more to it? And when did all that even happen? How had they developed such a miracle solution to the population crisis? It was so strange to me that Gaea had suffered the opposite of Mani's disparity: The women had died out, not the men.

"Right," continued Skye with a curt nod to the biologist. "The heart of the imperial operations. And that is our eventual target. We've been in the planning stages for a while, and we only need one more piece before it becomes achievable. That's why we're making small steps, like attacking this base three hundred miles south of here." Skye zoomed out and centered on a spot in the ocean region where our rebel base lay, zooming back in to reveal a large ocean rig in the shape of a ring. "It's a reactor that draws energy straight from beneath Gaea's crust. All we're after is two transport vehicles and some extra batteries; we're not shutting the plant down. But we do want to make a scene. Fortunately, Zent is quite adept at that, so you'll be in good hands."

The admiral directed a scowl at Zent, who shrugged, a passive expression on his face. "She will. Is that all, Admiral?"

"Yes."

"Very well," said Vass, clapping his hands. "Lynchazel, you are free to go for today. You will meet Captain Zent at first light tomorrow in the docking bay."

First light meant five o'clock regardless of the season, but I didn't care if I had to stay up all night if it meant getting to see some action. I followed Zent out of the Board Room, walking quickly to keep pace with his long legs. "Thank you."

He looked down at me. "You think that was me? Musha was the one who tipped the scales. Vass and Getts didn't want to send you out at all. I don't think they really trust you. As weird as that sounds," he added, seeing my face.

"I just don't get why they can't be honest with me," I complained. "I know they were hiding some things from me. I mean, even you won't tell me anything."

"I would if I could."

"Then at least answer this one question," I said. "Dr. Dekla mentioned my father earlier . . . who was he? He's dead now, isn't he?"

"Your mother really didn't mention him? I knew him well, if only for a short while. His . . . yes, I can tell you: His name was Kallyn."

I stopped. "You're kidding."

Zent turned around, frowning. "Why would I be? Do you recognize the name?"

"Kallyn Kalceron?"

"Yes. He came to Gaea through the Gate some fifteen years ago now."

My heart thumped a faster beat in my chest. My mind raced. *Fifteen years . . . it lines up. That would make me only fourteen, though, give or take. Maybe less.* So young. Based on our assumptions, I'd thought myself to be about fifteen, but . . . we'd never known for sure. I'd always matured quickly. Kallyn Kalceron, Mydia's long-lost brother, was my father. "I . . . can't believe it, and yet it makes so much sense. He was the son of my ruler, the governor of the city-state where I grew up. Almost like one of the Elites here on Gaea, And a powerful wielder of magic. Mydia said he went missing fifteen years ago, and Rhidea . . ." She'd hinted at some deeper meaning to the man's disappearance. Just how many secrets had the woman taken to her grave?

"I have no idea who those people are," Zent said, turning around. "But I have somewhere to be, so walk with me."

"Sorry, sir." I sprang into step behind the broad-shouldered man, following him through the steel halls of the base. "Mydia is—well, *was*—the younger sister of Kallyn. She was my close friend. I hope she's alive . . . somehow. She was with me and our teacher, Rhidea, when the Archlord came and destroyed the Gate of Mani."

Zent shook his head with a snort. "You really stirred up some trouble before you left, huh? You never know, your friends might have survived."

"I don't see how. Although . . . with Rhidea, I've come to expect the impossible."

"So, she was a . . . mage? A magician of some sort?"

"Yes, Mani's very most powerful. Aside from the Archlord, perhaps."

"Impressive. Are all women on your world powerful?"

"No. She's a . . . special case. She had some—some kind of secret she never told us." I shook my head. I'd never figured it out. "There was just something about her."

"Huh." Zent said no more, but he looked pensive. We soon split ways. I headed to the mess hall for some much-needed dinner and then hit my bunk early. I had a big day coming up.

α   Chapter 12   α

Strike

Manidor 1, 1295:

Borgha and Est have yet to return. The Anier are silent as to their whereabouts and wellbeing. I am almost certain that they are dead . . . Now my other two best friends next to Borgha—Kae and Rue—have been taken as well. It almost seems like those monsters did it on purpose. I hate the Anier, no matter all they have taught me. It has all been for their hidden motives and devious plots! I don't care that they are trying to save the world from the curse; their motives are not upright and I know it. Two more girls will be taken tomorrow if the tests on Kae and Rue do not go as expected. That is what they informed us today. At least they are being more forthright this time.

— From Lhinde's Diary

The next day, we were zipping across the ocean in a small watercraft similar to the one we had used in coming to the Red Horizon. This one was slightly larger, however, with room for six passengers. Aside from me and the captain, there were Ccal, Bddo and Jed. Jed was seated in the back, hands over the seats and conversing with Bddo and Ccal, whilst I reran our plan in my head. Simple as it was, the inaccessibility of my Vault caused me to second-guess.

As with the approach to the underwater base two weeks back, Captain Zent submerged a ways before we reached the target, though this was for a different reason: stealth. He engaged a cloaking mechanism which was supposed to hide our presence from enemy radar. Looking on the central monitor, I could see that we were approximately five miles out . . . four miles out . . . three . . .

"Everyone ready to dock?" Zent asked.

A round of assents echoed back.

Two miles . . . one . . . The murky shape of the reactor's subsea foundation came into view, and at last I could see the spiraling cables that ran down into the dark abyss, pulsing with green light that streamed ever upward toward the surface. The sight was eerily captivating.

Zent slowed the vehicle as we approached, maneuvering our craft to dock. Not at the two main docks, but rather in a warehousing bay next to one of the docks, where they stored charged vehicle batteries. He brought us up out of the water slowly after a quick scan of the surroundings and landed behind a few carrier crates. Putting on his helmet, he said over the short-wave radio, "Everyone out. Remember, Lyn, stick with me."

I nodded, getting out opposite him and moving to his side. The others, led by Ccal, nodded in our direction and headed off. I wasn't clear on what their side would be responsible for; in fact, my knowledge was mostly limited to following Zent and doing as I was told. And so I did.

Zent unclipped his blaster from his belt, and I did likewise, drawing my standard-issue weapon from my right hip. Zent had explained very clearly that these were only for emergency situations, but, well . . . I remembered how the escape from the prison had gone, with plenty of shoot-outs to go around. I would do as Musha had trained me and be ready for whatever may come.

We were on the inside of the station's outer ring. Looking through the wide bay doors past the stored containers, we could see the inner part that housed the reactor, pulsing with light, the seawater lapping at its edge. There was something . . . transfixing . . . about the light, the ethereal green radiation emanating from it. Like the Geothermic energy I had dealt with already, but stronger, deeper.

"Lyn!" Zent hissed over the comm. "We don't have time for lollygagging. Stick close!"

I nodded, as though he could see me. He hadn't even turned around, and was now coming out of his low crouch to sidle up against the far wall to the left of where we had come in, looking from the center of the station. I followed him after glancing both ways. *If only the visibility spread was better in these helmets.*

Zent peered in through the doorway to the next room, one hand cocked at his side, the other holding his blaster. He waved for me to follow, and I snuck in behind him. The lights in the hall were bright enough that I didn't need my suit's built-in thermal vision. No guards were in sight—of course they were not, as Zent was experienced enough not to have missed a guard patrolling the corridor . . .

Zent crossed the hallway with stealthy speed, and I followed. We took a right turn, followed by a left, which brought us into a control room. Here, Zent immediately stopped, putting up a hand to stall me. The reason was two guards occupying the room, one at a computer and the other standing up. Fortunately, neither had seen us yet, but I knew Zent wouldn't take chances. He looked at me with a soft, "Well?"

I kicked my body into action, moving swiftly but softly toward the standing guard to drive the heel of my hand into the back of his neck. Just where Musha had taught me, saying that enough pressure should drop most men instantly. Either I didn't put enough force behind the blow, or I missed the nerves, as I only elicited a curse, causing the man to spin on me. I pulled back, leveling my blaster on him, but Zent was quicker, piercing the man's temple with a blast, and then another only two inches away, before the man could even drop. I caught him before he fell, trying to ignore the two gaping holes burned into his skull. Burned in, seared black and smoking, stinking like charred meat.

The other guard rose, shouting, "Ccam!" before attempting to signal his comrades via his headset. But Zent was already piling his weight into the guard, having crossed the room in a blink, and put him into a tight sleeper hold. Ten seconds and he was out. Zent laid the guard out on the floor, next to where I'd dropped the dead man, and began binding and gagging him. "Sloppy, Lyn. You just got a man killed."

"I didn't—" I cut off before my captain could rebuke me. It felt unfair, but he was right. We could have taken them both out without lethal force had I done my job right.

Zent proceeded to take the second guard's spot at the computer, switching off the mic and typing in a few lines on the screen. When I inquired, he answered, "It might not do any good, but it should stall the reinforcements for a—" He cut off, looking at the blinking dots moving on the digital map. "Okay, never mind. Let's run."

We scrambled out a side door, from which the least number of guardsmen were immediately coming, and headed for the docking chamber where we would steal the craft we needed.

"The boys are almost ready," Zent said out of nowhere.

I had forgotten that Ccal and the others were on another channel most of this time. I didn't bother switching now, as Zent would inform me of anything important and I certainly wouldn't be of any value in their conversation.

Presently, a door slammed shut in front of us, a red light flashing above it. Zent cursed, and I looked to see the door on the right closing as well. Footsteps and shouting sounded from behind us.

"We'll have to blast through!" Zent shouted into the comm, drawing his blasters and firing at the device above the door as well as the locks on either side. I shot the center of it twice, producing a vibrating hum and consequent flash of heat with each shot. After the second, the door shuddered open an inch, and Zent hurried to wrench them apart just as soldiers began to swarm in behind us.

"Lyn!" Zent hissed, holding the door with one hand and taking a shot at the enemy with his other.

I dashed through the doors, ducking to avoid a blast from a soldier's pistol, and made it through a moment before Zent slammed the door shut. We bolted down the hall and took the first turnoff, Zent on the left and me on the right. We sidled up against the walls, just out of sight, and nodded to each other as the soldiers approached.

"We saw you hide," said one in a deep voice. They wore no helmets, so we could easily make out their words.

"Tret, just don't let 'em trap you. Remember, one of 'em is the . . . the . . . you know . . ." He spoke the last words in a hushed whisper, and I realized they feared me. They didn't know what I could do.

"Yeah, and you're the numbskull who opened fire!" The reply brought a round of low grumbling.

Zent pulled an explosive from his belt, a small, round bomb. He rolled it at an angle down the hall, keeping his hands back from firing range. A curse came, followed by a loud explosion and a scurry of movement. From the sound of it, it hadn't done much to hurt the men, and was more of a distraction. Zent immediately whipped his guns around the corner and fired into the center of the hall. Peeking around my corner, I did the same. Cries answered from the clearing smoke, along with the sound of falling bodies.

Shots came back at us as the remaining men got their bearings back, but it was too late. Zent picked off the last two before shoving his blasters back into their holsters to cool. "Hot!" he muttered through the mic. "That could have gone better."

I already had mine holstered. Auroras, these blasters did get hot. Not that my Coaction-numbed hands felt it much. "Where were we heading?"

He glanced down at his wrist console, then pointed down the hall behind me. "That way. Let's go. There will be more. They have over twenty soldiers stationed here, besides guards."

I remembered that much from the briefing, but I made no comment. I dashed after him, and doors opened before us as though not just on automatic but on cue. Before long, we came out into the docking bay, and I saw Jed piloting an omnicraft—a ship that traversed air or water with equal ease—while Bddo guarded the place and Ccal played with some kind of device—likely what they had used to hack the system.

"Oh, hey!" Jed waved at us from inside the omnicraft, whose glass shell was still down.

Ccal tapped a couple of buttons as we approached, and the large bay doors began to open behind him with a dull *thrum*. Looking up, he said, "About time. Looked like you two were having some trouble there."

Zent looked down at me as he stopped his run. He said nothing, clearly refraining from speaking his mind.

"We still need those batteries," Ccal said. "Captain?"

"On it," said Zent.

He waved for me to follow, and we headed to the left, where batteries of various sizes were kept. We grabbed two, took them to a new omnicraft, and were just about to start it up when Bddo cursed and said, "We've got company! They've gotten around my override!"

"Great," Zent muttered. Looking at me, he said, "This might be where you show your stuff, Lyn." He started the motor, and I nodded and headed off in the direction of Bddo.

"Where from?" I asked the large man.

He pointed toward two exits. As I watched, the doors opened, and two soldiers barreled out of the one on the right. I rushed for the left one as Bddo took the right, opening fire on the two soldiers. Ccal downed one of them with a shot from the hip as he ran to back me up.

A soldier was at the door by the time I got there, but Ccal picked him off with dead aim. Behind him came two more, however, who opened fire. Ccal and I dodged to either side, and I came in with a kick as they stepped out, taking one man in the shin. He went down with a shout, and his companion turned to me, raising his gun, but Ccal took him straight through the helmet with a shot. I put an energy charge in the back of the downed man, and another to make certain. Still more soldiers poured out of the door.

"Need some backup?" Jed said over the comm. We backed away as he steered his omnicraft in front of the door and opened fire with the ship's medium guns. I looked away as bodies were thrown back by the blasts.

"Okay, time to go," Ccal said, backing up toward Zent's ship with gun still trained on the doorway.

I nodded, retreating in the same manner.

"Roger that," Jed said. "You guys go ahead. I'll get ours."

We got in the ship with Jed and he immediately sped off through the still-open bay door. To my surprise, he turned immediately and hovered beside one more bay door that Ccal had opened. I was about to ask what we were doing when I realized that this was where we had originally docked. "See you guys at the base," Bddo said, jumping out.

Jed turned our craft to face the inside door, guns ready, but within thirty seconds Ccal was steering our original omnicraft for us. "Okay, now we can go," Jed said.

He took us into the water, and I saw Zent's and Bddo's vehicles just ahead. Together, we streaked back to base, chatting along the way. I didn't pay attention to much of it, instead replaying in my head the soldier's death at my hands. The first Hellebes I'd killed. It felt . . . strange. I'd killed before, but those were my other cousins, the Legaleians. These were my long-lost kin, no more or less related. And then there was the man whose death Zent had blamed me for. Would we really have been able to make it the whole way on stealth? Was all that killing my fault?

One way or another, time could not be reversed. I could only hope that they would let me on the mission to Haccolces.

α Chapter 13 α

Secrets

Manidor 3, 1295:

We got them back . . . Not Borgha and Est—they are dead—but Kae and Rue . . . They were not the same. I do not know about their vital organs and reproductive systems, but there was something wrong in their brains. I was horrified to watch, but the guards kept us there as the Anier walked them down the corridor to us, hands cuffed behind their backs, mouths gagged. Their eyes were afraid, but not enough . . . There was nothing behind them. From underneath the gags foamed a purple froth, like blood mixed with something blue. I won't recount everything else that happened today, because it was horrific, but they announced that the experiments had failed and then proceeded to force us to watch a live examination of what had gone wrong, including seeing my friends cut open while their failing life energy ebbed away. I couldn't look at first, but then my medical training from the Anier kicked in along with the shock and I began to pay attention. We'd performed surgery before this point. The actual operation was something to do with implanting a blue stone into the heart and neck of the subject — there was nothing to do with the reproductive organs at all. The stones were meant to change the chemical makeup of the women into something different. The other two had died very shortly afterwards. These two had survived, but were not able to cope with the energy from the crystals.

— From Lhinde's Diary

"Lyn, don't be so down," said White. The little girl stood on a hill of white flowers, misty skies rolling down around us with a faint breeze that rustled the girl's hair. She was like a miniature version of myself.

I said nothing. My dream cognition tried too hard to be helpful sometimes, particularly in the way of useless advice.

"Come *on*," she said, dragging out the word. "Don't be like that. The fights weren't that bad. You've killed lots of guys before!" She said it almost brightly.

I sighed, crouched amongst the flowers. "That's not true. And it's not even that. I don't think. It's what's coming. I want to get my memories back. But I just . . . have a feeling the Board's going to come up with a reason to not let me come."

"Because . . . you didn't kill enough people?" She tilted her head to one side, as though this was my logic and she were trying to make sense of it. Maybe it was my logic.

I thought about it. "I was mostly useless weight, so . . ." With a flash of annoyance, I snapped out of it. How had she gotten me talking? "Look, you're supposed to be fetching my memories! Now shut up."

She shut up. I had her pull up some memories of my fights at the Nytaean Palace alongside Kaen, taking out guardsmen on our way to rescue Mandrie and Phoebe. I almost cringed as I watched in detail. I'd known almost nothing about combat. I simply counted on my overpowering strength to carry me through. And that was on a world with far less gravity. Granted, no Geokinetic boosting, either.

I flipped through memories of my bout with Harold, a corporal of the Archlord's guard retinue back in the Wellspring chamber underneath the Hall of Eternity. Ti'Vaeth. Man, that was so long ago . . .

A short while later—or what passed for a while in the Vault within my mind—I dismissed the girl and went back to sleep, letting my mind wander into random dreams.

In the morning, I forgot all but the memories I'd relived with White in my Vault. Even those faded a little bit. I really needed to learn how to access that at any time, as all my Hellebes compatriots could. Few of them knew, and if they did, they must think it extremely strange that I could not. But, well, they *were* self-admittedly ignorant of what being a female Hellebes was like, especially a half-blood.

I got out of my bunk and headed to the locker room to change. There, I ran into Bddo, who was already up. He informed me that I would be asked to the conference room soon, which I'd been expecting (Okay, hoping). I couldn't help a tightening in my stomach at the thought of it, though. I thanked him, finished dressing as soon as he was out of sight, and messaged Zent using my wrist console:

When is this meeting?

6:30, so you've got time, he responded.

You think they're going to let me go on the big mission?

Doubtful. We'll see.

I ground my teeth in frustration. Did they still not trust me? Or did they just think me too defenseless to stay alive? I supposed I was a pretty valuable asset, whether I liked it or not. Valuable in the wrong way.

Jed messaged me shortly thereafter, asking if I'd heard anything from the bigwigs yet. I replied saying that I had not, and he asked if I had time to meet in the north wing dojang. It was one of the smaller dojangs, situated on the main level.

A minute later, I met him there. He was the only one using it at the moment. Despite his youthful appearance, Jed was a half head taller than me and built like the superhuman a drooling Legaleian woman might dream of. Not me, of course. I didn't dream like that. He was shirtless and currently laying into a heavy bag with far too much gusto for six o'clock in the morning. Sweat dripped down his back, and he wiped sweat up into his sandy hair as he heard me approach. "Oh, there you are. Up for some training?"

I shrugged. "I guess. Is that another way of rubbing my weakness in my face?"

Fortunately, the young man detected my light-hearted tone and grinned. "'Course. Let's see your moves." He stepped back and gestured at the tall bag hanging from the ten-foot ceiling, still shuddering from his last strike. It was of the usual variety: one hundred kilos, filled with sand and fine stones.

I approached the bag and threw a couple of light punches, pulling just short of shaking the bag too much—even with my relatively small frame, I could knock it around well enough if I tried—and followed up with an elbow and spinning back elbow. I bounced back and forth and threw in a few more combos while Jed said, "Not too bad. You're picking things up."

I said nothing, merely glanced over at him while I practiced some scissor kicks and spinning kicks. Eventually, he said, "So, you did pretty all right yesterday. I don't know if Cap is going to say it, so I will."

I gave a brief smile, stepping back from the bag.

Jed bounced lightly on his heels before pivoting smoothly, driving a heel into the bag with terrible speed. He hit it at the exact right height to cause it to swing without simply shuddering violently, though it did that enough. I took an involuntary step backward. Before the bag could swing fully backwards, he spun and hook-kicked it with his other leg—his right—sending it rotating toward me.

I took the cue and roundhouse kicked it from a posting position on my right leg, clattering the chain and sending it jerking back toward Jed. Far from a perfect kick, and it sent me off-balance, but I was not as practiced as he.

Jed grinned and one-two punched it to relieve momentum before elbow bashing the bag harder than either of our kicks. The bag arced wide, and I took a half step back before sending it around full circle with another kick.

"So anyway," he said, "You're probably wondering why we even bothered with that little outing?"

"Mm-hmm." We still kept the bag moving between us.

"Truth is," he said with a kick to the bag, "I don't know. Can't figure it out. We didn't need those craft. We draw power from our own subsea wells, in addition to sneaking power from the grid all over the place."

"So we don't rely on raids like that?"

"Well, we raid the League all the time," he answered, "But they made it sound like such a big deal."

"Zent seems to think it was a test to see how capable I've become."

Jed stopped and nodded. "So he told you, too. Thing is, the higher-ups are . . . fickle. They won't even—" he cut himself off and looked away.

"There are things you're not allowed to tell me. I know."

He nodded again. "It's frustrating. I like you, Lyn. I'm not the only one who considers you one of us by now. And yet . . ." He suddenly smashed the heavy bag with his full force, startling me. It flew up, shuddering like crazy, and I thought for sure the bag was going to rip.

I had never seen a Hellebes so upset. Well, Zent had gotten pretty fumed on a couple occasions, and Musha had pretended displeasure and anger, but only in the training dojang.

"Sorry," Jed said, steadying the bag with a large hand. "I think you know what I'm saying. The Board is just using you. And it ain't right."

"They want to keep me in the dark so I have no choice but to follow them."

Jed tilted his head from side to side. "Sort of."

"Then, if you're on my side . . ." I stepped forward and took hold of his freakishly-oversized arm. "Then why don't you just tell me? What are they hiding from me?"

He looked down at me with an expression I couldn't read: pity, sadness, guilt, agony. It could have been any or all. Okay, maybe not agony; I imagined that one. "Look . . ." He gently removed my comparatively small hand with his own. "It's not that simple. I'm sorry, but I can't betray my superiors' confidence."

"Then why bother telling me about all this?" I demanded. "If, as you claim, you understand, then what's the point in telling me so if you can't give me any more to go on?"

For the first time, annoyance crossed Jed's face, annoyance at me. "Sorry I said anything. Just forget it. Believe what you want to believe. I told you how it was because I wasn't expressly commanded not to."

I almost made another retort, and I'd like to say I managed to see through my emotions and choose the rational way out, but it was something else that took the words from my lips. Something he had just said . . . and I couldn't place what it was. After a moment, I said, "Sorry about that. I don't—I need to go. Thanks for the workout session."

Jed said something in reply, but I was already making my way out of the gym and he didn't bother to raise his voice after me. On my way to the conference room, one thought rolled around in my head: Commands . . . Jed had been expressly commanded not to tell me about . . . whatever secrets the Hellebes were keeping from me. Not top-secret information, but information that every Red Horizon soldier somehow knew. Every one. How was that possible? Would they truly go to such extensive lengths just to keep me in the dark?

What did they have to hide?

α Chapter 14 α

Disorganized Organization

Aidor 5, 1295:

Two of the test subjects have killed themselves since the last tests. It was horrible . . . First, Viktali slit her own wrists, bleeding herself to death, and the next day Keth drank bioloctate, a deadly poison, during class. Our captors and teachers tried to stop both of them, but after it was hopeless, they quickly gave up, and then proceeded to make a live-body science spectacle out of it. Both times, I felt my stomach want to cough up everything I'd ever eaten in my life. If nothing else . . . I think none of us are going to try it again. Who would want to do that to her peers?
— From Lhinde's Diary

The meeting was much like the last one. The same group gathered around the same high-tech table. Vass and Getts stood at the back, looking regal and displeased respectively. Admiral Skye was arguing with Musha about something, both looking up briefly as I walked in.

"Lyn." Zent dipped his head toward me. I could tell he seemed . . . on edge, just as much as I felt.

Dr. Dekla arrived a few minutes after me, shuffling his weight through the door like that much extra baggage.

"Very well, let's get down to it," Vass said, and thus began my second meeting with the Board.

"Are we just going to tell her what we've decided?" the heavy doctor asked.

"We haven't *decided* anything," Zent snapped.

"Do excuse me; I must have forgotten that both the Heiress and her loyal supporter were here," Dekla replied, voice dry as ever but words cutting.

I looked from one man to the other, surprised at the dispute.

"Calm yourselves, gentlemen," Vass said. "We're here to talk about Haccolces and our plan to infiltrate it." He reached out and tapped the table's screen, bringing up a holographic image of the Steel City. "Lynchazel, we need you in on this as well, just in case." He waved me forward with a pointed look at Zent.

Zent began to go through some of the details of their planned operation, zooming in on various parts of the city as he did so.

Admiral Skye spoke up. "Haccolces was not our original target. We were planning to invade Trident, but we lacked the resources necessary to do so."

"Trident is known for weapons manufacturing," Zent said. "So it was a logical place to invade first."

"But . . ." I prompted. No one tried to shut me up.

"But that's an insane task!" Getts finished, playing with his mustache. "We couldn't have pulled it off."

"Precisely," said Vass. "We can't take a city. That's why we called it off. We eventually switched our sights to Haccolces."

"But . . ." I glanced around, expecting to be cut off. ". . . That's an even bigger city, right?"

Vass nodded. "But in Haccolces, one strike could mean much more. You see, Heiress, *you* were the missing key. When we discovered you four months ago, we immediately began work on a new plan. But it hinges largely on your capacity to do as your mother did. As the Mother did."

A chill ran down my spine. Those words just sounded too ominous. At the same time . . . was he talking about the goal that I had in mind? Or about Hellebes reproduction? There was no way they were simply after information.

"The Mother had the capacity to channel energy through her body like a human conduit," Dr. Dekla clarified. "On a macro scale. If you can produce the same results, Heiress, then we can use you against the Empire to bring down not just one city but their entire grid."

I let out a small breath in relief. They weren't trying to use me as breeding stock. But what was this about . . . ? Zent and his men had explained about females possessing greater limits for Geokinetic transfer. That must be what he was referring to.

"*If,*" Getts said with annoyance, "you are confident in her abilities, Doctor. What have your studies shown?"

Dekla held up a meaty hand. "Nothing is conclusive yet. And it never will be until we test it." He glanced dispassionately at me, making me swallow nervously, and continued, "I'll have to run at least one more biological test before we can confirm that her cells possess the Omega trait. Beyond that, yes, she has the genes we're looking for."

"Which we expected," said Vass. "What you are saying is that you are not sure whether she can act as a stand-in for the Mother *yet.*"

I do not like where this is going . . .

"And that's the crux of the issue," Getts said, poking the table rhythmically for emphasis. "Uncertainty. I'm against this fool plan."

"I am confident—" Zent began, but he was quickly cut off by Dr. Dekla.

"Enough with the rubbish, Zent. We understand. You waited for fifteen years—and so did we. But in your case, like a lost puppy waiting for a friend." The fat man's voice held no more emotion than usual, and yet this time I could feel the personal note in his words.

"And as I recall, *Doctor,* you were not a part of the Red Horizon when we lost Lynchazel and Kallyn."

"And you are bragging?"

"Enough!" shouted Admiral Skye, cutting between them. "I am against it as well. Too much is at risk. We should let the Heiress develop and continue our experiments while focusing on finding the labs and replicating the Empire's facilities. Imagine we march in and lose her, then what?"

"Hey, I'm right here!" I said hotly. "I can fight, and—"

Zent reached out and clamped a hand on my shoulder. "Hold your peace, recruit."

I withered under his admonishment. To hear it from the captain was only more embarrassing.

"She did perform well enough at the reactor facility," he said to the admiral.

"We're not looking for adequacy, Captain," Skye replied. "I saw the footage. She can barely hold her own, and she is supposed to be the most powerful Geokinetic channeler on the planet. We can't throw our most potent tool at the enemy to be destroyed unforged. Or worse . . . captured."

Zent did not respond. I got the impression that he had nothing more to back up his position.

"I'm inclined to move forward with the plan using the Heiress," Vass said with resignation, "but I myself am uncertain and the majority vote seems to be against it. So we should prepare for Plan B as soon as possible."

"Agreed," Getts echoed his sentiment.

Indignation boiled up within me alongside numerous objections. But I knew they wouldn't listen to a single one. The least they could do was explain what this "Plan B" entailed. If I wouldn't be included . . . then what were they after in Haccolces? After this point, I paid little attention to the meeting. Zent did not try to stick up for me anymore, and I knew anything I said would only gain me another reprimand.

After the meeting, I could have sworn that Zent did not follow me out of the meeting room, and yet before I knew it, he had caught up to me. "Lyn, I'm sorry," he said quietly as he came up beside me. "I said what I had to. Dekla is not the only one who thinks I'm getting too close to you."

"Well, you sure helped me out," I mumbled.

"If I can find a way to show them that we need you, then there's a possibility I could change their minds."

I snorted. "So I'm not the only one who thinks their plan won't work without me?"

"They've another goal in mind. They don't want to waste all the preparations, but they especially do not want to lose you. As you can see, the Red Horizon leadership is . . . disorganized," he said. "It's hard enough to get them to agree on anything, much less anything *logical*. Or perhaps they're too logical. In any case, I'm trying. But I have to go now."

He took his leave, striding quickly with those long legs. For creatures of such bulk, these men could move so *fast*. I sighed as I walked, no particular destination in mind. Today's classes—biology—were at 9:00, but that wasn't for another two hours. I ended up at the door to the gym where I had been training with Jed only an hour before. I pulled myself away from stewing about the Board's decision only to realize I had been a complete jerk to him. What was I so up-tight about? *Oh, right, the meeting . . .*

I made a snap decision and ducked into the dojang. Perhaps some more exercise could take my mind off of things.

Two hours later, my mind was still very much occupied. My biology instructor, Dr. Phreska, was just letting me out of our one-on-one tutoring session, and I suspected he wasn't impressed with my level of attention. In truth, I had been listening once he began explaining the Hellebes mind and its workings: Memory Vaults and the Hellebes ability to convert stored memories to digital data . . . Of course, it was only fuel for my wandering mind, as it got me thinking: What if there was a way for me to prove, with my own memories, the necessity of my going to Haccolces? After all, surely Mother had left me some sort of clue . . .

The problem was that it would necessitate me divulging my own secrets to these rebels. That was like backing down in a fight. But surely, if there was one person I could trust with my secrets, someone who would listen but could also get the Board's attention . . .

With a sigh, I tapped my wrist console and called Zent.

"Make it quick, Lyn," he responded.

"I need to talk to you. Privately. Sir."

A brief pause. "You think you have something for me?"

"Mm-hmm."

"Meet me in ten in the secondary maintenance room."

"Where is—" I began, but he had already hung up. I checked my screen to see a set of coordinates, presumably for the location. Why such an out-of-the-way place, though? I was pretty sure he had his own quarters.

I pulled up a map, quickly locating the old maintenance room using the coordinates, and made my way there. It lay at the dark end of the westernmost hall, where an overhead light flickered and the rusted door read, *Authorized Personnel Only.* Before long, Zent showed up, wearing a training dobok without the top, and opened the door. It wasn't even locked. I followed him inside, and lights kicked on automatically. There was no one here.

"If you're wondering," he said, "This is the first place I could think of where we wouldn't be disturbed, and more importantly, where we're not being watched 24/7."

"They watch you in your own quarters?"

He looked at me like I'd said something strange. "Lyn, they watch you while you sleep. All the bunk houses. Every restroom."

"Oh." That was . . . a distinctly uncomfortable thought.

"Well, all right, maybe not every single one, but . . . you get the point. The only guy who cares about this place back here would be old Tanner the maintenance man. Maybe one of his apprentices." He appropriated an old air compressor for a seat, heedless of the coating of dust. "So, let's talk."

I followed him, taking up a leaning position against a support post and breathing out slowly. "I trust you, Zent. I don't know how many of you I can, since everyone is keeping things from me. I've . . . been keeping my own secrets. I tried to hold out until this blasted organization would give me some answers . . ."

Zent cocked a smile. "Trying to barter, huh?"

"I know, it's not going to work. I tried on Jed already."

He spread his hands. "As long as you understand. Shoot."

I took a breath, then said, "I can't access my Vault unless I'm sleeping."

He frowned. "Unless . . . you're sleeping. That's not how that works."

"I know. But it's the truth. I've tried to bluff my way by as though I could. Sometimes I get a flash, a quick recollection. Otherwise, I'm just like every normal Legaleian. I think it's a half-blood thing."

Zent nodded slowly. "It's not too surprising, really. I just wouldn't have thought it would work like that. I wasn't even sure if it was possible to inherit the ability genetically, except that Lynchazel possessed it."

"What?"

The captain shook his head. "Never mind. Not important. You'll eventually overcome this handicap. I assume it's only one of many differences you've noticed in yourself and neglected to mention?"

I nodded. "There are others. But . . . see, my mother left me her Memory Vault. I only recently dug up the memory of her telling me about it. I think . . . she didn't predict how my mixed blood would affect me. But she said her Vault is stored in the labs beneath Haccolces, where they kept her, and that only she had the key."

Zent rubbed his goatee. "Organic memory data is a tricky thing. Being the Mother, it might just be different for you. If she was able to do such a thing, then you would likely be the only person alive who could extract it. I like it."

"I don't have much more than that to go on," I admitted. "Do you think they would listen if you tell them?"

"Quite frankly, no. But there is one who may."

A Secret for a Secret

Dirhal 4, 1295:
There remain sixteen of us.
— From Lhinde's Diary

"What is it now, Zent?" Vass asked, looking up from his desk, shortly before I followed and he added, "Oh, and you brought a visitor. I'm a little busy."

"You said you had a few minutes. Are you willing to listen to something she has to say?"

Vass eyed me with a calm but tired gaze. "Very well. Lynchazel?"

"Sir, I have information that I believe is relevant to the upcoming mission. My mother left me notes on the world of Gaea, instructions and explanations, and . . . not all of it made sense. I was barely more than a baby when she died, and I only recently got my memory back."

"And the point of this?"

I related to him all that I had told Zent a few minutes prior, including the part about my lacking access to my own memories. I finished with, "Please don't leave me out of the Haccolces mission. I really feel it's necessary for me to go along."

Vass pursed his lips. "You're asking me to sway the minds of the other leaders?"

"No," Zent interjected. "I'm asking. I know the others think I'm being sentimental, but I'm only trying to work with this girl as a fellow Hellebes, one who happens to be a great asset to us."

I considered speaking up about how unfair it felt to be continually treated as unworthy of fundamental details of the Red Horizon, but I discarded it as unwise. I badly needed to find the data storage left by my mother, but they didn't need to know just how badly.

"Look," Vass began, "I . . . I want to believe her, and you know I respect you, Captain. But she is also our most valuable weapon, and we can't just throw her away." He stopped, as though waiting for an interruption that did not come, and continued, "But we have a week. Let's get her trained to the best we can. I will talk to the others."

I couldn't stop a grin from breaking out across my face. "Thank you very much, sir. You won't regret it."

Vass folded his arms. "I believe we can trust you. Now, Lynchazel, do you think that you are ever going to recover full access to your Vault? Did your mother know about your irregularity in this regard?"

"I don't know. But I'm hoping that I will gain that ability once I retrieve her Vault."

Vass nodded. "It seems plausible. And are you prepared to answer some questions before the Board? It will be necessary to hear from your own mouth, if they are willing to listen."

"I can do that."

"That's the spirit!" Zent clapped me on the shoulder. While I was more used to it now, I still didn't understand why they all had to do that to me.

Vass called the meeting the next day, presumably after talking to the other military leaders and Dr. Dekla. As he had said, they pestered me with questions, but I had already made up my mind to spill everything. If it meant going on the Haccolces raid, I would do almost anything.

In the end, only the ever-dour Getts disagreed with sending me. Even Dekla was swayed by the prospect of digging into the depths of my mental faculties and seeing what made me tick. His direct, almost morbid obsession over biological studies made me want to vomit. Surely even oversized, lab-raised men were supposed to have emotions. And . . . respect for human dignity? That one certainly didn't seem to be a popular trait here.

Musha came over to shake my hand and give me another thunderclap on the back. "Kid . . . I guess I have to say welcome aboard now."

"Aboard?" I asked, mildly confused. "Are you leading the mission?"

A scowl appeared on his dark face. "Of course I am! Along with this scoundrel. Might be my last, and I'll make it a damn fine farewell."

Zent punched him in the shoulder. "Don't say that, you old bear."

Musha, unmoving as a brick wall, turned an uglier scowl on his former student. "Ain't afraid to admit it. Now, Lynchanthrope, you know what this means, right?" Seeing my blank face, he said, "We're heading out in eight days, on the tenth of Soldor. Back to hell camp for you."

I groaned.

Just as he said, it was back to the Iron Dojang. However, Musha did not have enough time to dedicate to my training, so he bullied me for a couple hours per day while others, such as Ccal and Bddo and Zent, took turns. I was relieved when Musha called an end before lunch on the first day back. Immediately afterward, however, Zent swung by to take up his slack.

The following day, after Musha ran me through nearly non-stop rigorous workouts, it was weapons training with Ccal. He took me to the gun range, a long gymnasium-style room featuring multiple lanes with heat-absorbent targets at the end, a high ceiling to allow for hanging and moving targets, and only one rule: Don't shoot anybody.

"All right," Ccal said, setting down the guns he'd brought. "What did Musha give you?"

I pulled out my two pistols. The first was a standard issue thermal blaster that spat globs of pure heat energy fueled by Geokinesis. Its battery lasted for five shots, after which the user had to channel each blast himself, and consecutive shots tended to make it overheat. Particularly these ones, which the soldiers liked to modify to shoot hotter.

The other was a custom-made revolver with eight battery charges which could be fired off individually or rapidly. She was dubbed the Octobug, and was a gift from Hodge the quartermaster. By clicking it into burst mode, one could simply hold the trigger and spin through a few or even all eight shots in a hot stream of destruction. But that invariably caused overheating and was inaccurate and wasteful to boot. Those charges were not cheap, though

Musha said they could be reliably recharged within a few minutes in battle if one had the opportunity, at least up to a few times.

"Well, well," Ccal said as he inspected my Octobug. "That's a beauty. Hodge did say he was making you something nice."

I hefted the revolver. "I don't really know how to use it well, though."

"Then we'll have to remedy that."

"Well, I didn't mean—" I cut off as he ripped it out of my hands.

Turning it over, he pulled his lips downward in a satisfied expression and brought the gun up to a shooting position. He tried a couple shots single, and then clicked it into auto and discharged the remaining chambers, causing them to rotate quickly. A green burst of light came from the barrel with each shot, accompanied by a heat distortion in the air and faint green smoke which spread to the rest of the gun as he set off each charge. By the end, he quickly put the gun down. "Ouch, that's hot."

I grinned. He didn't know my secret. "Now you've wasted all my ammo," I complained.

Ccal rummaged in his jacket pockets and pulled out a bag containing more of the same type of charge that the revolver took. "I've got a little bit of everything here. I'm not above wasting a bit of the Red Horizon's budget if they give it to me for training purposes."

So that's how it is, I mused.

For the next two hours, Ccal helped me to waste a whole lot of ammo, or rather, to blow it in a constructive manner, giving me pointers on how to aim, the professional way to draw and holster a pistol quickly, and how to shoot them akimbo as well (a pistol in each hand), which was . . . horribly inaccurate and rarely a good idea. It was during this instruction that he realized I didn't seem to be bothered by the heat from the guns. It was something I hadn't noticed immediately when Musha began my weapon training.

My going explanation was my Fire Coaction from Mani. Even though I was now on a planet with no Wellspring of Magic, the affinity for the element seemed to have ingrained into my body a permanent tolerability for heat, though eventually even I reached my limit. But this was only after unloading so many consecutive pistol rounds into the target (or near it—let's be honest here) that my arms were numb. My "Heiress" abilities seemed to already allow me to channel energy into batteries to recharge them quite efficiently compared to most Hellebes like Ccal, so I could manually recharge my Octobug in less than a minute.

My target accuracy was improving—slowly—and Ccal's tips should help me improve further. He instructed me to practice down here in the range every day. (Great . . . more to add to my list.) At least gun practice wasn't physically intensive like most of my training, which continued to make every muscle in my body feel like giving up the ghost.

After Ccal let me go, I went back to the mess hall for some food, showered, and retreated to my bunk quarters for a nap. Two of my bunkmates whom I had hardly even met—their names were Plato and Task—sat around the small central table playing a game of cards. When I arose a half hour later, they were gone. And I could have sworn I didn't even close my eyes . . .

I laid my head back on my stiff pillow. *What am I even doing here?* Deep under the sea on my dead mother's planet, trying everything I could to recover lost memories while hulking muscleheads beat the tar out of me. My bones felt heavy, my back sore. With a sigh, I arose to hit the gym. *Don't want to get soft.*

α Chapter 16 α

To Haccolces

Norven 10, 1295:

I fear myself. I fear who I am becoming. A monster. An unfeeling, all-knowing passive observer and scientist. I've watched them dissect my fellow inmates alive with . . . fascination. I sicken myself. But it is times like these when I must remind myself that it is not I who am to blame . . . but my captors. Someday, they will pay the ultimate price for their cruel actions and all their sins, either in this life or the one to come.

— From Lhinde's Diary

The week ticked by, day by grueling day, and at long last the day came for us to embark on the mission. At four o'clock in the morning, Zent called us to a briefing room adjacent to the Board Room. It was nearly unfurnished save for a screen on the far wall. No chairs, as the Hellebes weren't too big on those inventions.

The team members filed in one after another: Ccal, Bddo, Jed, and six others, not including Zent and Musha. Twelve in all. Zent gave a nod to Musha, who grunted and clapped his heavy hands. "All right, young'uns. You're probably wondering why I'm in charge here, and I don't care. Just gonna say it right now, I don't give a sea squid's backside. That'll answer most of your questions."

We looked at one another, and I saw no surprise in anyone's reactions.

"Your favorite captain, Zent, is going to take half the crew," Musha said. "Six each. We'll arrive together at Haccolces at oh-seven hours and split at the five-mile range. Ccal, Bddo, Lyn, Task and Janus, you're with Zent. Everyone else is playing backup with me. We're Team B."

I made a small fist-pumping motion—hoping Musha did not see it—

upon hearing I was assigned to Zent's squad. Unfortunately, Jed couldn't come with our crew, otherwise it would be a perfect team. I barely knew Task, and I had never met Janus before, but how bad could they be? If they were being assigned to this mission in the first place, it spoke to their tactical and combat skills. I was the only greenie in the group.

Zent brought up some images on the wall screen, and he and Musha proceeded to lay out the infiltration plan step-by-step. It all seemed a tad risky, a sentiment uttered by a few team members under their breath. But that was because the Red Horizon was betting everything on it—no going halfway at this point. They needed to retrieve the power of the Mother for . . . well, I couldn't speak to their purpose, but as for me, I needed to retrieve her memories. I didn't even know what this "power of the Mother" was.

"As Musha explained," Zent said, "Team B will be handling distraction and support while Team A gets in and finds the data cache. I'll pull the few military strings I have left to get us into the city, and from there we'll take transit vehicles to the main laboratory complex. Memorize these maps, because they'll come in handy as we progress, particularly if everything goes haywire. Musha's men, you'll be in the eastern part of the city for the most part, so take a careful look at these sectors . . ."

He continued like this for a few more minutes. Specific instructions were given to certain men, such as one called Seidrake, apparently a trusted sniper on Team B, who would be taking up a position within view of the complex to give backup. Team B would be taking heat camouflage gear, capable of hiding heat signatures for greater stealth. Shortly after the presentation, we set about getting ready. Zent barked orders to his crew of five, telling me to stay put.

The captain took my shoulder as the others left. "Remember, Lyn. A lot is riding on this, and you are our most important asset. Not me, not Musha. If we all die, and you alone escape with the data, that's all that matters. Just remember that."

I gulped. Surely he didn't mean that as bluntly as he said it. *That's . . . a lot to shoulder. And my shoulders are pretty small.* "Yes, sir."

"We're not expecting things to go wrong. I, for one, think we can pull it off. But be ready for anything. We will fight to protect you at all costs, so don't let that go to waste."

I nodded hesitantly. "Yes, sir."

He pulled me into a hug and sent me off with a firm pat on the shoulder. "Go help Ccal and Bddo with the omnicraft."

An hour later, the six of us were on our way, speeding through the ocean in a midsize omnicraft. We all wore mock Haccolces uniforms fabricated by the one and only Hodge. Team B followed a short distance behind. Along the way, Zent gave instructions and reminders similar to the ones he had given me: "This may be the most important mission we've ever attempted, and one of the most dangerous. I trust each one of you, and I ask that you lay down your very lives in order to protect Mother Gaea."

I shivered. *Mother Gaea.* This wasn't the first time I'd been called that, but I never wanted to be again. *Auroras.* I didn't understand the full meaning of the phrase, only that it was a nickname given to my mother back when she was alive. Or . . . before she was alive? I knew nothing about the previous Hellebes Mothers, nor, especially, what life had been like before this Mother Project had culminated in their creation. My own mother, Lynchazel, had referred to that once or twice. It was all one big, dark mystery to me. Perhaps a web of mysteries.

"Lynchazel," Bddo said from beside me, nudging me with a dark-skinned arm. "You listen to any of that?"

"Huh? Oh. Um, a little bit."

"Well, it wasn't much," said Task from my other side. His voice was rough and deep. "Stuff we know already. You know, I've never really gotten to talk to you before now. The mysterious female."

I snorted. Mysterious female. That was a little better. He meant it so seriously, and yet on my world, it would have been tongue-in-cheek.

"What? What did I say?"

I shook my head. "It's nothing. Back on Mani, there were so many females that, well . . . it's just strange to be the only one."

Task grunted. "Really? Guess that would be strange. Janus! You still buying a Haccolces dinner when this is all done?"

Zent turned his head. "Say that in my good ear?"

"Nothing," said Janus. So far, he seemed one of the quieter Hellebes I'd met, speaking with a calming voice when he did so. The man, though tall like all the soldiers, had a thin frame and angular face that somehow matched his personality.

"Well, just remember we've got a few steps to focus on before you lads can be making any illicit food stops in the Empire," Zent said. "Besides, if we all make it out of this, *I'm* buying the food."

Ccal, seated in the front right, was busily polishing one of his pistols. Looking up at the monitor, he said, "One hundred leagues away, guys." He switched channels to speak with our operatives in the city, and then said, "Cap, when should we radio the city patrol?"

"Let's say in five minutes."

We rode in silence, watching the fish and dark underwater scenery that sprang to life under the omnicraft's floodlights, before Ccal radioed the Haccolces military: "Come in, Sector Seven. Sector Seven, this is Sergeant Fisk ten-forty-seven. Yes, we have the cargo, and are approaching the city from the south, one hour off. Yes, sir, over." He looked over at the rest of us. "Yes! We're in the clear."

Ccal reported the security update to Team B, and we soon surfaced to traverse the open air. Not long after, we came upon the mountains, and eventually Haccolces became visible on the northeastern horizon, its ominous red shield wall looming high above. Did the engineers behind these cities somehow *not* intend them to look evil? If this was a story from back on Mani, we would totally be flying into the Dark Lord's stronghold.

Musha's ship split off from ours as we approached, heading for the eastern city gate, and Ccal radioed Haccolces one more time.

"All right, Cap," he said. "Let's take her in. Can't let the cargo wait."

α Chapter 17 α

Infiltration

Norven 12, 1295:

They did two more tests today. They . . . had us perform them ourselves. We willingly complied, numb to our emotions. I was in charge of my peer Lueth, who lay on the table, sweating beads and breathing heavily. I told her that it would all be well and I would make sure the experiment succeeded on her, and bent over to kiss her forehead before sinking a soporific syringe into her shoulder. We then began to make incisions and cut her open, working with quick but careful efficiency.

— From Lhinde's Diary

We passed through the shield wall at the southern city gate, a massive metal structure like a rigid mouth with heavy, locking doors. The shield surrounded the gate on both sides and above, and not far to the left and right were two of the towers that supplied power to the shield wall. It all stemmed outward from those twelve towers along Haccolces' perimeter, weaving into an electrical web that repelled nearly anything—except, of course, when the rebel-designed Shieldbusters knocked them out, as we had done previously. But those were only for when stealth was not needed.

Inside the entry bay, an array of screens and flashing lights guided us inward, leading to a scan station that would do a pass of the interior of the omnicraft. Zent had said the "cargo" was supposed to be some sort of highly specialized piece of technology, but our craft was an overhauled stealth model with linings that hid our heat signatures and created an image of a piece of machinery being hauled in the cabin instead of four extra passengers. The guard at the station gave the all-clear, waving for Zent to pull through and dock the vehicle. He did so, passing more guards in armored uniforms, and landed us in a tall bay next to other vehicles of varying size.

Two guards came over immediately, bearing hefty energy rifles and protective armor, asking that all personnel step out of the vehicle for the examination. Zent made a signal with his right hand telling us to stand down, whilst opening his door to step out. A moment later, I heard two thuds in quick succession, and Zent called the all-clear.

We exited the omnicraft, and I saw both guards lying on the ground before our captain, who was binding their hands in copper behind their backs. I briefly wondered how he had been able to take out two soldiers so quickly, but, well . . . he did have a reputation as one of the best fighters in the Red Horizon. "Can't have them going anywhere too soon," he said. Ccal approached, stooping down to disable their wrist consoles.

Then we were off. I followed close behind Zent and Ccal, who led the way toward where a public transit vehicle was supposed to be waiting for us, making sure to stay out of the way of patrols and in as many camera blind spots as possible. I couldn't recall any details of the layout of the city, so I was trusting those who did. Ccal spoke with Team B over the radio as we went. "Everyone in place? All right, all right. Yes, he should have. We'll just—hey, Cap. Did you get confirmation from Zibbs?"

"You were handling that, remember?"

Ccal tapped his headset. "We'll confirm in just a . . ." He cut off with a curse as we came within sight of what must have been the designated location. No transit vehicles were in sight, only a small squad of armed guardsmen. "Team B, we've got a situation."

"Hold," Zent hissed, throwing out his hands. We took cover behind the nearest wall dividing hangers and bays.

"They seen us?" Bddo asked, gripping his pistol in both hands at the ready.

"Judging by the shouting, I'd say yes," Ccal shot back.

Zent peered around the corner briefly and ducked his head back in time to avoid two successive Geokinetic bolts.

"Move and we shoot!" shouted one of the guards.

Zent growled. "Don't make a move yet." Tapping his earpiece, he said, "Team B, now would be a good time for that backup!"

A moment later, multiple lights clicked off in our bay of the building, and then the rest. "Wrong bay," Zent hissed.

All the lights went out in the adjoining bay where the enemy was, followed by the hum of a blaster and a cry of pain.

"That's our cue," Zent said, ducking around the corner and firing off a couple of blasts. "Thermal."

"Oh." I fumbled at my headset, remembering about the thermal lens feature. I clicked it on and a screen flickered into place between the two prongs that jutted forward from the left earpiece and those on the right. It showed a hazy black-and-green image of the rooms we were in, the floor glowing dully—brighter where Geothermic conduit ran. The forms of my teammates and the enemy stood out as slightly blurry human shapes, brighter whenever they channeled extra planetary energy.

There were too many of them. As I watched, the members of my own team traded shots with the security force, the blasts creating sharp streaks of white light on my screen, almost like lightning. I couldn't make out who had come in to help us, but he was on the far side of the bay. Our men had thermal dampening tech in their suits, so their signatures were duller. The guardsmen must have been equipped with infrared as well, as they seemed perfectly able to see us, although they were clearly outmatched. By the time I pulled out my standard blaster and took aim at one of the enemies on the far right, most of them were already down. I thrummed off one shot, and then another. Both charges missed my target, yet he fell to a beam from someone on my left as I watched.

"Lights!" I heard someone snap, and soon felt a tap on my shoulder as the world became very bright.

"Forget about the thermal, Heiress," came the soldier's gravelly voice.

I clicked it off, blinking as the world snapped back to normal. The light had conflicted with my thermal vision to create multiple light sources. No wonder that was so disorienting. I saw that the one who had taken my shoulder was Task.

"We're good now?" I asked, looking around and not seeing any guards.

"All goo—" Task's large frame shuddered and fell to the ground, a hole burned into his upper left chest.

I shrieked, jolting and then ducking for cover behind some unknown machinery. Ccal and Bddo immediately raised their pistols, scanning for the target as one more shot was fired. The two rebels fired back, and a cry of pain announced their hitting the target.

"There's more up there!" Bddo shouted, moving to stoop beside task. "Aw, Task." He felt his neck and brushed back his shirt to inspect the wound. "He's gone for sure. This armor ain't plus grade. C'mon, Lyn, let's go."

"Where!" I said more loudly than I meant.

"This way!" called Zent from the other side of the room. Amidst the chaos, I wasn't sure if he was shouting to us or at the other four on the far side of the room.

Bddo pulled me up and towed me toward where Zent, Janus and Ccal were retreating, firing off shots at the catwalks above where guards were attacking our position. On the floor was a light-haired man with two holes melted through his chest: Jed. A soft, horrifying hiss escaped his lips, surely the last sound he would ever make.

He was the backup member they'd sent.

"Jed!" I cried, running to him. "No, no." I made to stoop down at his side, but Bddo scooped me up in his long arms as he ran by. Green bolts continued to rain down from above, returned by Zent and the others at the doorway. *Not Jed . . .*

"No time for that, Heiress," Bddo said. "Gotta keep you alive. He . . . made a gamble by rushing in like that from the backup squad. Poor kid."

"But—" I began in protest.

"Get to safety now!" Zent roared. "Whoever falls stays behind."

I didn't ask where. I wasn't going anywhere, as Bddo was still carrying me. He and the other three men dashed through the doorway, headed for one of the exits. "It'd better be there," I heard Ccal say from behind me. Then,

"Okay, guys, blow the system now."

Sparks rained from the ceiling as every light cut out once more. Not flipped off this time: some major circuiting blew.

"You guys have the place in full lockdown?" Zent demanded over the radio, and then grunted in satisfaction.

The squad kept running. I didn't bother trying to switch my thermal vision on, partly because Bddo had my arms bundled together with his left arm. Soon, we came upon it: An armored truck with six heavy rubber tires that came up to my chest, that is to say Bddo's midsection. Zent hopped into the driver's seat and Bddo threw me into the backseat and climbed in after. Bddo, Ccal, Janus, me and Zent. That was all who were left. I couldn't believe that Jed was just . . . gone. Dead. Murdered by a security officer who was merely doing his job.

I hadn't even gotten to apologize for how I'd treated him last.

With a roar, the truck's engine started, and Zent threw it into gear, taking us out not by the main bay door but a smaller one our operatives had already opened. The sun was just coming up, casting the first light of dawn over the Steel City as we pulled out. The black-paved streets were lined with glaring lights of a sort I'd never seen before, along with a multitude of fluorescent and neon lights dotting the buildings that towered high above the streets. I had only seen the city on two occasions: one when Lldsaor's men shipped me into the city to go to celebrity prison, and another when Zent and his right-hand team had broken me back out.

Today we were back. And only two casualties so far.

Only two. That felt so wrong to even think. These were real men's lives.

The truck's radio came to life, and a gruff officer's voice demanded, "One-one-thirty-nine, do you have permission to leave the premises? Reports state that an incident has occurred at the south gate."

"This is sergeant Gibbs," Zent said through his mic as Ccal called up Team B. "We have the high-priority cargo and managed to get away. The intruders are still in the building."

He snapped his fingers, Ccal sent the message, and a well-timed charge detonated from within the building we'd just left. Looking back, I saw smoke pouring out of the doorway.

"—And we're going to have a lot more on our tail soon," Zent was saying over his radio. "We might have a minute tops before we've got aerial pursuit."

"We need to know what's in that truck, then," came the voice over the radio. "State your purpose. We are sending units to the south gate hangars, and we will take out that truck if you don't—"

The transmission cut off, and Zent gave a cold grin. "Looks like Seidrake tracked down his signal already."

"The sniper guy?" I asked. "He must be really good with a rifle."

"Oh, he doesn't use a rifle," Zent said. "Usually prefers his bow."

His bow . . . I tried to picture the capabilities of a Hellebes-tailored bow, recalling that I had indeed seen such a weapon back in the range in the undersea base, featuring massive steel limbs. I hadn't even known what it was until Ccal told me.

Bddo nudged me with a long elbow. "Hey, uh . . . I'm sorry about back there. Not easy to lose any soldier, and you weren't the only one who liked Jed. And Task—he was one of your bunkmates, no?"

"Yeah." I shook my head. I never even talked to the man. Jed . . . him I knew. He didn't deserve this. Neither one did.

"Just try to keep a cool head, yeah? We ain't seen nothin' yet, and you can count on that."

α   Chapter 18   α

Laboratories

Norven 14, 1295:
Lueth did not make it . . . just as I feared.
— From Lhinde's Diary

The distractions began with a large plume of smoke coming from the eastern side of the city, where Sol's morning light tickled the skyline. Two explosions rocked the earth, and Bddo grinned from beside me. "Sounds like they're getting up to some trouble."

"Hopefully enough to buy us some time," Zent said from the front. He reached over and disabled the vehicle's built-in radio features. "That's not going to do us any more good."

Sure enough, it wasn't long before the sirens caught up to us, and we saw vehicles approaching from behind with guns mounted on top. Ccal pulled a mid-length energy rifle from his shoulder and cracked the back window open far enough to point the muzzle behind us. Then he opened fire on the vehicles, which were already blasting our truck with fully automatic fire. As I watched, the vehicle on the right jolted, spinning out on a blown tire and slamming into the other.

"Whoa," I breathed, watching as the two assault vehicles rolled. "Did you do that, Ccal?"

He pulled back from his aiming position. "You kidding? From here? That was Seidrake." He pointed out one of the tall buildings we were passing, but I couldn't make out the sniper's location.

"More in front," called Janus from the front passenger seat.

"Great." Ccal tapped his earpiece. "Seidrake? Got a visual?"

The sniper responded by loosing two shots into the half-dozen assault vehicles coming our way, strategically placed to cause the front ones to skid into the others. I couldn't even see the arrows, just the magnificent impact of each one on the multi-ton vehicles. The gunfire ceased as their vehicles spun into disarray, and Zent steered us straight through a break in the trucks. Looking behind me, I witnessed two more arrows streak down from the sky to pierce the windshields of the remaining vehicles that were in working order. To my amazement, I realized that some of the shafts had pierced all the way through and were jutting out of the pavement a full meter.

"Great Auroras," I muttered.

"We're getting close to the complex," Zent said.

"Here come the Stormhawks," Bddo said, pointing out the left window with his blaster. "Hope Musha's got a backup plan."

We rode in tense silence until another armored truck roared out of a side street and merged with us. "That's them," Ccal said, and I caught a thumbs-up through one of the heavy glass windows of the approaching vehicle. The two Stormhawk ships flew our way, tracking us ominously before opening fire. I was thankful for the heatsink armor and energy-repellant plating, which caused the first beams to glance off or be absorbed. Haccolces had good tech, including these transport vehicles. With another backwards glance, I saw one of the gunships pinwheel and explode just before we crossed out of the line of sight.

"Yes!" I said, making a fist.

"He got one?" Zent asked. "We're not in the clear yet. We're entering the old sector now."

"The high security sector . . ." Bddo mumbled.

Indeed, the cityscape changed drastically, and we entered a decline. The buildings looked older, darker, wider and shorter. Up ahead was a scan station at the entrance to the main lab complex, where dozens of guards were gathering, taking aim at our trucks. As I watched, an arrow slammed into the right side of the gate and detonated, throwing multiple men to the side. Seidrake once again. And then . . .

Zent hit the brakes while the other truck accelerated. Suddenly all four

Hellebes soldiers jumped out of the other truck, rolling as they hit the pavement. Musha must have jammed the accelerator somehow, seeing as the truck kept moving. Team B rolled to either side of the truck, and another explosive arrow struck underneath of it, lifting the giant vehicle to soar through the air, spinning end over end, straight at the gate.

Zent stopped our truck near the members of Team B who had bailed from the moving truck, just as their former ride struck the shielded door . . . and exploded in a burst of fire. I felt our own truck shake as the entire front wall of the building was devasted, the Geoelectric shield tearing away and all personnel guarding it devastated by the blast.

Musha and the three others approached at a run as Ccal waved them in, hopping into the bed of our truck. Zent peeled away, and we drove straight through what was once a heavily-shielded security gate.

"Wow," I said, trying to make sense of the scene. "Did they plan that?"

Bddo opened the back window of the cab. "Yo. You fellas plan that stunt or what?"

Musha snorted. "'Course we did. You think we got lucky?"

"Just glad it worked," mumbled one of the crew members beside him.

In a moment, we were inside the building, leaving behind the smoking scene of carnage and scrap metal. It was dark inside the complex, with long rows of dim lights running across the ceiling. We wasted no time in ripping through the building, making our way toward the nearest entrance to the subterranean levels. Alarms rang out everywhere as we careened past storage bays, complex machinery and wall after wall of quantum computers. The team in the back kept their guns out, seemingly unheeding of the jolty trip as they scanned for pursuers and reinforcements. They used their crouched legs as shock absorbers. I really wasn't sure how many armed personnel were stationed in this laboratory complex, or rather I couldn't recall from the briefing. There were signs of hasty evacuation in some offices along the way.

The first wave of interceptors came from our right, and Team B traded gunfire with them from the truck bed. Three, six . . . maybe almost a dozen men dressed in strange white uniforms with sharply-pointed helmets. The enemy had the advantage of not being in a moving vehicle, of course. I heard a curse from behind me and looked back to see one of our men clutching his shoulder where a beam had grazed it. Amidst all the shouting, blaster fire and crazy truck driving, it was hard for me to focus on anything.

"Here we go!" Zent shouted, swinging us into another sharp turn. Suddenly, we were going downhill at a low grade, headed for the lower floors.

"'Bout time," Bddo muttered from my left. "You ready for your big moment, sunshine?"

I started as I realized he meant me. "Um, I hope so?" I said honestly. "Are the labs really down here?"

"Sure as the sun is yellow," he replied.

Suddenly, I had an instant of clarity as I recalled images of a laboratory scene from the early briefing, or . . . no, not that. Not from any briefing. I glimpsed a dark room lit by an eerie glow, with many cables running outward from a green-tinted tank, an unearthly jade light emanating from it and pulsing through the cables.

Then the image was gone, and I was left holding my head. *What was . . . that?* I had never experienced anything like it. In that instant, I felt a pulse, a heartbeat, a . . . signal? Coming from below us. It was regular, as though coming from a living creature.

I gulped, my throat feeling dry, and glanced around to see both Bddo and Ccal looking at me with concern.

"Don't scare us like that, Heiress," Ccal said. "You sure you're all right?"

"I just had a . . ." I cut off. "I'm fine."

Janus gave us a sidelong glance from the front, not saying a word. He simply gripped his pistol, ready for when we would inevitably have to fight again.

Zent crashed through a wide set of doors, ripping them down and trampling over the metal with the truck's heavy tires. The height clearance was close. "We'll have to ditch this thing soon," the captain said. "Team B! Get ready for ground deployment." Looking back at us, he said, "You all remember the layout down here? We're looking for the deepest labs, but it's quite the maze."

We were in a large room with a relatively low, paneled ceiling and more dim lighting. Zent proceeded to drive past or over tables dotting the area, whichever was most convenient. Two rooms later, we came upon the elevator down to the next level, and he ground the brakes, stopping the large truck with less than the gentlest amount of shuddering, shaking and screeching. We clambered out just as the shouts began to catch up to us from behind.

"C'mon, team!" shouted Musha in his rough voice, waving toward the elevator. He slugged Zent on the shoulder as he passed him. "Nice driving, son."

I followed close on their heels, while Ccal and one of the Team B members kept their guns trained behind us. Sure enough, as I reached the elevator, I saw men approaching from the opposite direction. Ccal and his companion picked the first two off with their pistols before retreating into the elevator, which was now filling past the max capacity. Zent and Bddo, the last to cram in, slammed the doors shut manually as Janus shot the ceiling brackets off, and suddenly we were freefalling.

"Brace yourselves," the slim man said, almost tongue-in-cheek. A moment later, we *slammed* into the floor, causing my head to rattle along with the entire elevator. Channeling Geothermic energy helped to soften the fall a bit. Musha kicked the doors out, and we piled out of the elevator.

Before us stretched a long hallway lit by flickering light bars placed every twenty or thirty feet. There was only this one passage, a single direction to go. As we stepped out of the elevator and into the hallway, I noticed the different . . . energy down here. The same warm feeling of Gaea's planetary energy that could be felt anywhere on the surface, but deeper. More powerful. And the heartbeat I had felt was stronger down here, pulsing at a steady rhythm like the blood of a living creature. Or of the planet itself. Running up and down the hallway were cables much like the ones I had seen in that brief vision, throbbing with green light.

"You guys feel that?" Zent asked.

"We're close," Musha growled. "Comin' up on the lab where it all began."

They set off at a run, and the rest of us followed.

"Wait!" I shouted, trying to catch up to Zent. "What . . . what's in there right now? Why are all these cables still running Geothermic energy?"

He hesitated, as did a few other men, turning to glance at me. "No time, Lyn. It'll become clear soon enough. Now let's hurry!"

I shut up and followed.

Before long, we came upon another intersecting hall. We didn't stop at it, though I did hear unsettling shouts and stomps coming from the right. Our pursuers had alternate ways of getting to us, it would seem.

"Janus, Ccal, guard this exit once we're in," Zent said as we ran.

They gave an affirmative, and I heard a distinctive grim tone in their voices. They knew well that it might cost them their lives, as this mission already had for two others.

And then I saw it up ahead. A light that grew more distinct as we neared the door. As we approached, I saw that it was a heavily reinforced glass door, armored enough to prevent even a trained Hellebes soldier from simply bashing it in. Zent took out a key and inserted it into the card slot, punching in a few numbers and leaving the key in. The door beeped and slid swiftly to both sides, unlacing its forked metal workings at the middle.

"We're in," Zent said. "It's showtime, Heiress."

He and Bddo, along with Musha and his men, moved out ahead of me into the final room, the main laboratory. It was a massive, circular chamber with thick conduits streaking out from the center in all directions. They traced the floor and ceiling, intertwining and twisting, each one pulsating with one heartbeat, originating from a tall chamber of glass in the center—just like in my memory flash. Inside that chamber, the indistinct form of . . . something . . . floated. It didn't appear to be female, nor Hellebes at all, but rather a twisted, mutant creature. I was glad that the thick green liquid in the cell obscured its form, as what I could see was truly hideous.

Did this . . . thing . . . fill the spot that my mother once had? Was this her replacement? The substitute they'd been using all these years? If so . . .

then how?

"Lyn, come on!" Zent called, waving me on. "Don't bother staring."

"The computer ought to be around here somewhere," muttered one of Musha's men. Multiple of our soldiers were already scanning the room for the control module we needed. Various equipment cluttered the area, computers and monitors that I didn't recognize, but apparently one in specific guarded the access we needed to . . . What were they even trying to retrieve? I wasn't completely sure, only that I needed to find the Memory Vault.

"Lynchazel," Bddo said, approaching me. "Any clues on this Vault?"

I shook my head, sweeping the room with my gaze. I tried to remember if there were more details, tried to *feel* the heavy pulse in the room for something unique, but the planetary energy down here was so immense that it clouded my whole head. All I felt was pure, raw power. Enticing power. "I . . . I don't know," I said truthfully.

"Well, keep trying," he said. "I think they found the energy flux control."

"'Think' ain't enough!" barked Musha.

Energy . . . flux control? Something to do with their other objective? It sounded dangerous.

I approached Zent and two of the others, who hovered around a screen some thirty feet from the containment cell, while Bddo went back to looking out toward the multiple exits, scanning for danger.

"What is it?" I asked them as I approached.

Zent looked up, face grim. "First things first, any leads on the Vault? Griggs, start running a scan for it."

"But Captain—I wouldn't know where to—" The man cut off as Zent gave him a glare. But before Zent could respond, Ccal shouted from the doorway:

"We've got company!"

I glanced behind to see him and Janus opening fire on a security force, the first to follow us all the way down here. There would be many more before long.

"Captain," I said, "I don't have anything to go on. My mother—she didn't give me any clues, just that it was down here somewhere."

"Then start looking!" Musha roared from the other side of the room. "More soldiers are coming from this direction, and we need to get out of here ASAP."

"All right, forget the Vault," Zent said sharply. "Griggs, back up your captain. Bddo . . . start the energy siphon." With that, he moved off to the first door, shouting, "Ccal! Get back, I'll—Ccal!"

I jerked, turning to look, but Bddo grabbed my shoulder in a vise-like grip. "Focus." Touching a couple buttons and adjusting a sliding lever, he said quickly, "Here's the deal, Heiress. You're gonna tap right into the Geothermic stream, got it?"

"What! That wasn't part of the . . ."

"Oh, yes it was. Whole time. C'mon, hands right here." He motioned to a terminal that looked like a palm scanner. Only it was steaming and glowing green, intensifying as Bddo adjusted the lever until it was a jet of green light streaming upwards, distorting the air around it. Ignoring the hum of blasters and cries of pain around me, I did as he instructed and hastily placed my hands over it, widening my eyes at the sudden influx of energy in my system.

"What is this supposed to be doing?" I asked through gritted teeth.

"Tripping your Geokinetic block and opening up your full potential. If this doesn't work, then . . . just—feel anything yet?"

"Like . . . a tremendous amount of energy? Fire in my bloodstream?" I asked with gritted teeth.

"Maybe." He motioned for me to withdraw from the stream, but at a shrug from me, he swore and said, "Not enough energy. You're going to have to make direct contact with the transfer chamber. Yes, that's the one."

I gulped, staring at the creature in the large cell. Seeing the way the situation was going, and the lives at stake for my protection, I did exactly as ordered, running to the tall cell. At least five feet wide, it was imposing on multiple levels, and as I approached, I got the closer glimpse I hadn't wanted at the abomination that occupied it. The thing's frame was twisted, its skin dark and pocked with small protrusions and growths. Its face was long, jaw offset and sprouting ghastly teeth, some looking almost human but others like a predator's.

Gritting my teeth, squeezing my eyes shut, I touched the glass with one hand and felt an electric jolt go through my arm and down my spine. It held my hand in place like a direct current. My jaw clenched tight, and my throat tightened. My forehead felt warm, my hair staticky, as pure energy siphoned into me.

A vision flashed through my mind like the one I'd had on the way in, but in the quickest of flashes. A cell like this, but housing a feminine form with flowing white hair. A scene of shattered glass and broken computers, and a dark-haired Legaleian man standing before the containment unit. A dark sky with flashing lightning. A raging ocean.

The images passed by as quickly as they'd come, but my vision remained dark. I heard blaster fire and chaos, shouts from every direction, but it was all distant, as though I couldn't wake up from a deep dream. Dimly, I heard Bddo shouting at me. What was he saying? Something about enough, enough energy? Step away?

And then suddenly I was jerked away from the tank. It was Bddo. My vision came back into focus and the noise around me returned with a roar. As though a switch had been flipped, I heard him:

"Did it work? Do you feel different?"

I shook my head, feeling dizzy. "I don't know . . . I don't—" I cut off as I realized that I could sense something underground, beneath all the planetary energy flowing from the tank. The tank only provided a trickle. Beneath the earth was a well, a great, roiling sea of Geothermic energy, *life* itself, untapped.

I began to draw on it. Not through the cables, the technology, nor even the tank of pure energy behind me, but directly up through the ground. It streamed into my hands as I shuddered with unexpected ecstasy. Bddo watched me, wide-eyed, and then turned with a grin and began to back up his comrades.

I continued to draw on the current, slipping into a different visual landscape where everything was white. Amidst the noise of battle, I heard a deep voice over the speakers: "This is Emperor Lldsaor. Stand down or die. The Mother is ours."

But it seemed so distant. What was the voice even talking about? The power was right here, the power to obliterate all in our way, to wipe out all attackers. The power of Gaea, pure and undefiled. On this plane of whiteness, I looked down and beheld a deep wellspring of green energy, twisting and curling and streaming up toward me, and I could *feel* it in my body now, building up like a hot inferno. It was life and death itself, indistinguishable, a primal power without limit or end.

Eventually, even in my dearth of sensory logic, I knew I'd reached my max. The power yearned to be set free from my mortal flesh. I looked about me, seeing only dark shapes on the plane of white: my foes. I reached out a hand and released a bolt like lightning. It leapt from my palm and crashed into the shapes, and I turned, seeking for more. One was right in front of me, but I wasn't certain it was an enemy, so I turned farther, seeing more hostile shapes, and reached out my hands. Another bolt, and then a continuous stream, came forth from me, drawn from the depths of Gaea. I swept it to the side, incinerating those in its path.

I stalked toward the largest group of enemies, drawing more energy. Somewhere in my mind, I knew I couldn't handle more, nor could I control what I had, yet I did not stop drawing more. I inhaled, breathing the life energy deep into my lungs, and opened my mouth in a scream, releasing a Geothermic wave of devastation that ripped across the white room. I couldn't see details in this state, but I had a sense of machinery being ripped apart and bodies melting before the fury of Gaea, their life energy scattered by the green gale.

Suddenly, a mass slammed into me, and I turned to obliterate this threat as well, but . . . my body gave out, tumbling to the ground, slipping out of whatever white world had sucked me in. Power rushed out of me and back into the earth with a sensation like a rushing waterfall pouring over me. My vision returned as I slammed into the metal floor, shuddering, and perceived a pool of blood nearly soaking me. Blood . . . whose . . . ?

I gasped, trying to scramble away, but I had no energy to do any more than sit up on knees and elbows. "Bddo . . ." I rasped in a dry voice, a voice I hardly recognized.

His form lay mangled on the floor, ripped nearly in half. Rather, half remained while the rest was gone entirely. I couldn't even bear to look at it.

"Lynchazel, snap out of it!" a familiar voice shouted from behind me. Zent. He lifted me off the floor, and I got a glimpse of the room. Half of the wall was eaten away and on fire, smoldering and sparking, leaking Geothermic energy at a rapid rate. Cables were torn open and bodies lay strewn about. There was Griggs . . . I couldn't tell if it was me or the enemy who had killed him. The smell of charred flesh and blood gnawed at my tongue.

"Lyn!" Zent repeated, shaking my shoulders and turning me around to face him. "We have to get out of here. Everyone is dead, and the Emperor will be here any second. You don't want to—"

He cut off, seeing the dazed look on my face. My lips moved as though trying to form words, yet I didn't recall telling them to do that. I couldn't believe I had done this. I never meant to. My body had moved of its own will, its own volition, as though another will had seized hold of me. I tried to tell him this, but my lips still would not obey, babbling incoherently. I could feel my body going limp, my consciousness slipping.

Zent slapped me, and I jerked awake. "Stay with me, Lyn!" He hoisted me up onto his shoulders and sought an exit. "I'm going to get you out of here."

α Chapter 19 α

The Pain of Gaea

Norven 21, 1295:

I'm starting to see it. I feel so cold and callous as I write this, but . . . I think I will be the only one left. I don't know why, but I feel that if any of us make it, it will be Rena or me. And she's . . . well, no. I don't know, I just hope, deep down, that I will not die as all the others. It is horrible, and I realize that. It's what they've done to me, to all of us. The Anier are truly demons. I still wonder what their true goal is. A modern world. Unity. Stability. These are the things they preach, but in such dispassionate, uncaring voices. And I still know nothing about them.

— From Lhinde's Diary

Zent hauled me away, dodging flaming conduit, debris and dead bodies. I felt helpless, strength of bone and mind having abandoned me. I had just used an incomprehensible power to murder dozens of men, including my own companions. *They must have died already to the League's soldiers,* I tried to tell myself, but it was no consolation—a weak lie. All I could see was Bddo's broken corpse, shorn asunder at my own hand. My own doing. I had killed my friends.

I couldn't see where the captain was taking me, as I was slung over his shoulder, but he ducked through a hallway, one of the multiple exits—the back exit, I thought?—that led out of the giant laboratory. It wasn't long, however, before sounds of further opposition could be heard from farther along, joining the blaring alarms.

"This could get hairy," Zent muttered, though I thought that was quite the understatement. With his free hand, he held his blaster out. Ducking down a side hallway, he set me down gently. "Can you stand?"

He let me go, and I held myself up with shaky knees, leaning heavily against the wall. "Yeah. I think."

"Okay, stay right here." He aimed out past the wall into the main hallway, firing off a Geothermic blast. It hit its target, apparently, as I heard a gurgling cry that cut off shortly. Two beams came in response from other soldiers, and Zent ducked back to avoid them. After waiting a moment, he dashed out, leaping off the wall to engage in melee combat, and I heard grunts accompanied by heavy thuds against the walls.

Trusting my commanding officer's combat skills, I focused on trying to regain my strength by taking deep breaths and shaking out my legs. My whole body tingled frantically. But I could stand. I could—I could walk, yes. Peering out past the corner of the wall, I saw Zent ramming his blaster into the temple of the last of four security guards, knocking him out. The others were either dead or out cold.

"Lyn," he said, rising to his feet and turning to face me. "Glad to see you can walk. Think you can keep up?"

I nodded uncertainly, and he turned to stalk down the hallway, energy gun held out before him. "Just keep an ear out behind us. I don't know if the Emperor was bluffing or if he's actually here already, but we need to move as fast as we can."

Something about his tone made it sound as though this Emperor Lldsaor was someone to be feared. *What am I saying? Of course he is—he rules the world.*

But perhaps a bit more . . . personally.

I tried my best to keep up with Zent, but he had to keep stopping to wait as I caught up, breathing hard. I couldn't even place what was wrong with me, other than the fact that I had channeled beyond my body's limits . . . or perhaps I was testing them. It must have messed up my body somehow. Zent was ever vigilant, looking carefully down any side halls we came across. Finally, the hall turned, and Zent ran ahead, calling, "The elevator, finally!"

I caught up to the corner and stopped, watching as he approached the metal elevator doors and punched in some buttons. Nothing was happening, apparently, as he seemed frustrated. Hearing a noise from behind us, I turned to look. Nothing yet, but . . . "Enemies are coming from behind, Zent," I said worriedly.

"Expected as much. Now we're caught, since this elevator doesn't seem to be . . . Oh, no."

As he said it, I felt a weighty presence from above us, descending to our level. "What is that?" I asked.

"It's him."

I didn't have to ask who. A moment later as pounding footfalls sounded from behind me, the elevator doors opened, revealing a man so tall that his head barely cleared the door as he stepped out. His frame was impossibly large, and the finely-tailored uniform he wore only accentuated his powerful physique. His waist was the width of my shoulders, and his torso tapered upward to the biggest shoulders I'd ever seen. His arms, bulging at the sleeves of his uniform, were crossed over his chest. A thick neck led to a square jaw and a hard-featured, scowling face with jet-black hair slicked back over his head.

"Well, well," said the Emperor in a voice that matched his stature, striding forward leisurely. "The girl we've been hunting all this time has returned to be taken in once more. Perhaps we got off on the wrong foot, madam? And Captain Zent, the rogue officer. It's been some time."

"Lyn, run!" Zent shouted, shortly before the gargantuan man sprang into action.

I ran. Or at least, I tried to, before turning the corner only to come face-to-face with half a dozen guardsmen.

"Hands in the air!" one of the soldiers shouted. I could see the fear on their faces. I tried to summon the power I had just minutes ago, but I felt nothing. Only a greater trembling in my joints. *Probably a bad sign.*

"Don't even try to run, miss Lynchazel," Lldsaor said from behind me. "Just come here like a good girl, or I'll kill this rebel insect like he deserves."

I froze, trying to think of a way out. But there was none. Slowly, I slinked back to the Emperor in defeat, seeing him pinning Zent down with one hand, thumb and forefinger squeezing his neck against the floor so that he couldn't speak. The captain didn't even try to fight back.

"That's right," Lldsaor said, looking up at me. "You see you can't win. Looks like you can hardly stand up. What's the matter? Finally exceed your capacity?"

I nodded numbly, not listening. The man had an . . . aura . . . to him. An atmosphere of palpable energy. This was no ordinary Hellebes. He seemed to radiate a feeling of power and terror, such that I could imagine him soaking up all of the energy I had released earlier, absorbing it as the ocean does a heavy rainfall. Even if I could manage the same feat, would it suffice to defeat him?

The Emperor rose from Zent's limp body and nodded. Suddenly, someone behind me rammed a cold object into the back of my skull, and I lost consciousness.

⁂

I swam in a sea of molten lead. Or thick oil. Something dark. I couldn't breathe, and my eyes refused to open. I tried, but something heavy kept them shut. I had a distinct sense of drowning, despite never having experienced it in my life. A primal terror enveloped me, and I opened my mouth to scream.

Before I could utter a sound, my dream changed, and I stood on a mountaintop above the clouds, in the dead of night. No stars shone above. Far below me crashed the waves of an endless, roiling ocean. Lightning flashed in the enveloping clouds, and thunder roared in my ears with every flash.

As I watched, a moon rose on the horizon unnaturally quickly. The yellow moon called Luna, who gave her light once per night. But in this dark night, she shone with a gold halo that turned to red, and as I watched, the halo overtook the moon, turning her surface an otherworldly crimson. A streak came forth from it, lighting the path to Gaea in a blazing red pillar of light which quickly subsided. Below me, I saw a flash of red light and heard a great crash as something landed on a continent I couldn't see. An unearthly shriek followed, piercing the air and causing the spire upon which I stood to quake. Its sound was terrifying beyond anything I'd ever heard.

Suddenly, a great wind arose and carried me off the peak, and I was falling, falling, until I hit a cold metal surface. I gasped, looking around me. Not in pain, but in shock. Where was I? The metal felt slick, and as I tried to stand, I slipped, falling on hands and knees. And there before me, I saw his face: Bddo, whom I had killed. His face was fixed in a half-smile, half-grimace—I couldn't tell which—and his body was torn open and burnt, with blood oozing out, never stopping.

Looking down, I realized in horror that it was not water that I had slipped on, but blood. Glancing around from side to side, I saw more men similarly slain, some with heads twisted unnaturally, some cut open, dismembered or burnt beyond recognition: Ccal, Musha, Janus, Griggs and more. All of the Haccolces assault team lay dead, adding to the blood pool that threatened to overtake whatever surface I stood on. Task, Jed, Seidrake—whom I had not killed . . . or had I? I stood and tried to flee from the scene, but only encountered more—even my friends from Mani: Rhidea, Mydia, Kaen, Oliver . . . Kymhar, who had betrayed us all.

No, I wanted to shout, *I didn't do this! I don't deserve this!* But another Lyn stood in accusation, blaming me and refusing to quit. I had killed my friends, I had left them to die and fled to Gaea. I alone had survived.

I gripped my skull, trying to block out the scene and the voices of the dead. One voice rose above them all, a quiet woman's voice saying, *Make them pay.*

This voice caused me to look up, shaking me from my despair. "Who . . . ?"

This injustice belongs to the ones who chained me, the ones who corrupted me, who made me their slave. I am the voice of Gaea, the widow in the darkness, the mourning virgin, cursed of the ancient ones. They shall know my pain.

The voice sent a shiver through me. Who . . . what was it? "Who are you?" I asked. "Show yourself!"

But the female voice had retreated into the darkness, and all else faded into blackness. The void around me became heavy, bearing down on me, and I crouched, hugging myself, whispering, "Mother . . . I'm scared."

Suddenly, the nightmare began to crack at the seams and pull apart. The darkness seemed to fall from above like thin glass, shattering around me, giving way to a starlit sky. The black ground pulled away, revealing a familiar field of white grass. A breeze began to blow, and a feeling of warmth sprang up in my chest. A feeling of safety, familiarity, home.

And there she was, just like normal. "White!" I cried in delight, running toward the female shape. She stood on a slight hill an indeterminant distance off. The girl had grown a lot taller somehow.

As she turned, my breath caught. It was not White, but . . . my mother. She stood tall in a white gown, hair spilling down her back and gleaming in the starlight. It flowed out onto the grass behind her like a wedding train. She smiled at me, and I ran all the faster to see her.

"Mother!" I tackled her in an embrace, and she hugged me back. Her arms were smooth but strong, her grip firm as iron.

She pulled back, staring into my eyes, and I gazed into her face. So beautiful, a face I only wished I could have someday. Her white eyebrows were thin and tapered ever so slightly inward, her smile folding her cheeks in the warmest, most motherly way. Perhaps it was just the way I saw her, like my mind accounting for never having had a mother. But this was how she looked in every memory. Only . . . this was a dream, so my mind was simply pulling from my own memories.

I looked down, face falling a bit.

"What is wrong, Lynchazel?" she asked. Her voice was like liquid silk, flowing from syllable to syllable in the smoothest Hellebes speech. Old and familiar.

"I . . . it's nothing, Mother." I felt silly talking to my own mind's maternal conjuration.

She reached out and touched my face with a soft palm. She was nearly a half head taller than me, so she didn't have to reach up at all. "Lynchazel, you've nothing to fear. What has you so troubled?"

I found myself answering her despite myself. "I . . . just discovered my powers. That I got from you. I destroyed the lab and . . . and killed a lot of people. Enemies and friends. I'm ashamed and—and so terrified. Now Emperor Lldsaor has captured us, and I'll have to go back to prison. Maybe a lab."

Mother Lynchazel simply listened, a concerned look on her face. "I'm sorry, daughter. But it's not your fault, remember that. You didn't choose your heritage, nor your enemies, and neither did you mean to kill your friends."

I shook my head. "I know. But . . . it's just so terrible. I've never experienced anything like today. I couldn't even control myself. It was like . . . like another's will was trying to take me over."

My mother's brow furrowed. "Another's will? That sounds like her . . ."
"Who?"

She looked pensive. "I'm not sure. Lynchazel, there are many things I couldn't tell you before."

"I know, I know." I couldn't help a slight eye roll. I had heard her words multiple times over, so I knew full well that a lot of things were missing.

She took hold of my shoulders and gave me a small but firm shake. "Lynchazel. I know. But listen to what I'm saying now."

I froze. What she was saying now? Something about that just felt . . . different. "But you're a figment of my own mind."

She shook her head. "You don't get it? This is me." She gestured at herself. "Me. Based on my own memories, not yours."

My eyes widened. "You mean . . . but I never found the Vault!"

She smiled. "Yes, you did. When you touched the containment cell. I can't tell you exactly how it will work for you, since you can't fully access your memories—correct?"

I nodded. "Only when I dream."

"Perfect. I think you'll find you have full access now. At least to your own Vault. I can tell this place seems special to you."

"Normally, I have an assistant called White," I said.

"An assistant." She looked at me with a curious expression before bursting into laughter. "I'm sorry, that's just . . . it's amusing."

Feeling embarrassed, I said, "I suppose . . . I'm just glad to have my mother back. Even if it's not for real."

She smiled again. "It's good to hear you say that. Even though you're right."

α Chapter 20 α

Lldsaor

Verda 24, 1295:

As I expected, Rena and I are left. The others are dead or mutated beyond recognition into something inhuman, growing silvery spines and acting with animalistic aggression. Rena is strong, but she is taking it so much harder than I. Have I progressed farther from human to unfeeling rock than she, or have I just learned to shove my feelings deeper? I don't know. The Anier, however, have made it clear to us that this will be the last experiment session. I get the feeling that they have all the data they need, and have only been doing this to us because . . . let's be honest, because they only ever wanted one of us. Those that they saw to be slightly less desirable or holding up less well than the others were usually the next test subjects. Rena and I are to play a game of Drachi to decide who it will be. At this point, though we love one another, we both know that we will try our hardest.

— From Lhinde's Diary

When I awoke, I was in shackles. I blinked, sitting up on a plain prison cot. I quickly took in a familiar scene: A square cell with no windows, featuring heavy bars at the front. But I realized that what I thought were chains and shackles were simple copper bangles fastened around my wrists and ankles. Copper, the one metal that could suppress Geokinesis and keep our Hellebes abilities at bay.

As my mind cleared, it all rushed back to me. We had gotten cornered in the lab, I'd tapped into the power of the Mother, and . . . I didn't want to rehash the rest of it; I'd already been doing that in my sleep.

Sleep. Dreams. I'd had a terrible nightmare, and then . . . my mother. I met her for the first time since childhood in the form of memories. Recalling my conversation with her, I tentatively reached for the Vault in my mind and opened the door with ease. My memories called from within, a deep pool reaching back as far as I wanted. Nothing was missing, nothing was hidden. It was like having White with me all day long.

Ah, what a relief. Just . . . not enough of a relief to keep me from agonizing about what would happen to me now. And Zent—what had become of him? He too was captured, unless . . . I didn't want to think about the alternative. With everyone else on the strike force dead—save for Seidrake, or at least I hoped—Zent was the only one left, and possibly the sole rebel I'd ever see again. The prospect of getting out of here seemed entirely impossible. Would the Red Horizon even try to get me out at this point?

Suddenly, I heard footsteps coming from the hallway outside my cell. A stout Hellebes in a crisp military suit strode up, hands clasped behind his back. The stars on his shoulder distinguished him as a general. His entire face was downturned in a droopy expression of distaste. He stood in front of my door, as though teasing me with the possibility of escape, before saying, "Mother Heiress, it is good to see you safe and in custody once more. My lord the Emperor is most pleased."

"So I've gathered," I muttered, turning on my cot to face the general.

"I am Third General Chimeth," he continued. "You should know that your compatriot, ex-captain Zent, is in safe accommodations as well. And he will remain so for as long as you cooperate with us. Do you understand?"

I glared, gritting my teeth, trying to force myself to stay calm. "Perfectly. Sir."

"Excellent." The general pulled his drooping cheeks into a pleased expression resembling a smile. "His imperial greatness has commanded that you be brought before him, so I will let you out of here." He reached down to unlock the door with a key card but stopped. "Just to be clear, Heiress, you are in no wise capable of escape, and any attempt will be met with immediate and harsh repercussions. So I suggest you come quietly and not cause a stir."

He unlocked the door and motioned for me to step out.

I obeyed without delay. I didn't snap to my feet, but neither did I drag them as I came to the door and followed him. Despite being so well-spoken and mild-mannered, I could sense a wrath lurking below the surface, as though he eagerly waited for me to act out so that he could swat me down like a fly in my weakened state.

General Chimeth led me down the hallway, which was decorated in strictly utilitarian fashion, much like my previous prison. I didn't know where this one was located, but I assumed it to be somewhere in the Steel City. We stopped at a door that stood ajar, and Chimeth announced, "The Heiress is here, sir."

"Have her step inside," came the bass voice of the Emperor from within. Chimeth gestured for me to enter, and I did so. The general himself waited outside.

The room was small and square, drab as the rest of the prison, with two chairs and a round table in the center. Emperor Lldsaor stood to the left of the table, more massive than I remembered. He was at least a head taller than any Hellebes I'd met, dwarfing my feminine frame. "Sit down, Lynchazel."

I did so, taking the closer seat. I wasn't sure why he insisted on calling me by my name, since he clearly viewed me as no more than an animal.

Lldsaor sat down across from me and folded his hands with palms and elbows on the table, leaning toward me. "Perhaps I ignored you for too long," he said. "Long enough for your new friends to plan a way to break you out. We kept you locked up, only experimenting from time to time and studying your slow adjustment to Gaea—do you know why?"

I shook my head.

"Because we couldn't decide how to use you," he said matter-of-factly. "The Senate seemed to all have different ideas of what to do with the new Mother everyone feared we would never find. We grew lax, and suddenly you were taken from our grasp. We have yet to agree on a permanent course of action, but regardless, I'm not going to make the same mistake with you."

"Meaning?" I prompted. I didn't want to rankle the Emperor of all of

Gaea, but this story was showing neither an end nor a purpose. Was it simply a fact of nature that tyrannical overlords liked to give long speeches? I thought they only did that in stories. Then again, if what he said was true and this senate required convincing, perhaps he didn't have all the power that I thought he did.

"Meaning I will be keeping a close eye on you, Little Gaea." Lldsaor gave a self-satisfied smirk.

Little Gaea . . . I should be used to strange names by now. In fact, perhaps they were all making them up as they went along? "What about Zent?" I asked. "Will I at least be able to see him?"

"Perhaps. He's being kept here in the jail." Seeing the curious look on my face, he elaborated. "This is the western city jail, which borders the Capitol Building here in Haccolces."

I nodded. That information was useless to me.

Rising from his seat, the Emperor said, "We will see about you getting to visit the captain. I do not wish to make your life overly miserable in that cell, and it's not as though you can get up to any trouble. But you will be under guard at all times, naturally. General!"

Chimeth entered immediately. "Sir?"

"Take her away. Ensure that someone is ready to answer any . . . reasonable requests she may have."

Oh, sure. I felt a lot better at that. What a magnanimous man, this Emperor, bordering on hospitable. But I rose quietly, dipping my head slightly to Emperor Lldsaor before following Chimeth out the door and back to my cell.

It was just too familiar. Concrete and steel. Perhaps I could get them to give me a more comfortable bed? They sure as Sol weren't going to give me any privacy.

Plunking myself down on the hard cot, I leaned over my knees and closed my eyes, placing my fingertips to my temples. *Think, Lyn, think. The Senate is fighting, I'm stuck here in copper, and Zent is the Emperor's hostage.* I would rip right out of these cuffs if I could, but the copper was too thick and banded with high-carbon steel. I would need Geokinesis to break them, and that was exactly what they prevented me from accessing. These imperials knew what they were doing.

White, I said in my head, concentrating to access my Vault. In a mental realm of my own making, like a waking daydream, she appeared, a small girl in a snow-white dress.

Yes? she asked.

You know what, I said impatiently. *You have access to my memories anytime now. How can we get out of this predicament?*

She took up a thoughtful pose. *So do you, Lyn. At least you seem to be holding your horror at bay following your brush with the Mother's power.*

Forget about that.

She crossed her thin arms. *Well, then in that case, you're stuck. Your only chance is to manipulate this Senate somehow. Find out more about them. Lldsaor indicated that they are at odds with each other and need a majority vote to decide anything, and he clearly hinted toward trying to sway you to help him win them over.*

Huh. True.

Yeah, it was obvious. That general is also a boot-licking dog, so his loyalty could potentially be manipulated against Lldsaor to get you free, but that's a long shot. There's also the off chance that the Red Horizon might come for you. But . . . even if they tried, Haccolces will be ready for them.

Yeah, we can't count on them, I agreed. *I need to talk to Zent. Perhaps he could help me figure out something.*

She held up her hands. *Whatever you say, Lyn. Just make sure—hey! Don't just—*

I opened my eyes and stood up. I couldn't handle that little girl for long anyways.

α Chapter 21 α

Whispers of War

The next day, they came to take me to my first examination. I'd been dreading this. I still wore my blood-stained custom gillsuit. Two Hellebes soldiers approached, unlocked the cell door and led me away to a nearby laboratory. There, they had me strip down and even removed my copper bracers. This last they did only with great trepidation.

"Do we have to?" one of the men whined.

"Of course. Look at her, she's as weak as a mouse. These clowns need them off for their scans." They unlocked the wrist cuffs and stood by as the doctors began checking my body up and down, taking all sorts of notes on their pads and cross-checking data with grunts of surprise. Then came the dreaded scanners.

As horrible as the scan machines (one was not enough) may be, it felt nice to have my wrists free. Not that I could do anything . . . yet. But it was something to go on.

On went the cuffs once more.

Not long afterward, when I was back in my cell wearing a fresh and flattering jumpsuit brought by the prison guards, a man came to take me to see Zent. My hidden knives were still nestled comfortably in my gillsuit, which I had discarded in the corner where—hopefully—no one would retrieve them.

I made sure to note the path we took to get to his cell, which was only a two-minute walk, along with all the side doors and hallways. The layout could come in very handy if all went well, and my memories were readily retrievable now.

His cell was similar to mine, faced with steel bars and lacking in space. A cot and a small excuse for a toilet. He rose to his feet quickly, looking worse for wear in his dirty gillsuit. Had they beaten him? "Lyn!" he said in a relieved voice. "You're all right."

"And you too. They're treating you well?"

He laughed. "I've seen far worse. A day in jail could've been less pleasant."

The guard who had escorted me shifted on his feet, looking mildly displeased. He probably wanted nothing to do with the notorious traitor.

"Can we talk privately at all?" I asked the guard in my most convincing voice. Sweet-talking was not, of course, my best skill.

He huffed. "You think? No."

I shrugged, turning to Zent. "Well, at least I got to meet the Emperor. Again."

"Did you, now? And what did he have to say?" He kept a bored tone, but I could tell he was eager to know if I'd found out anything worthwhile.

I shook my head. "Not much. He's holding you hostage to try to get me to cooperate. I guess the Senate doesn't really know what to make of me yet. And they were pretty upset when you guys stole me away." I held up my bronze bangles. "These things are fun to wear, of course."

"Oh, I love mine." He had his own thick copper bracelets and anklets, clamped right on over his suit.

"Yeah, they shipped me off to the labs today and I only got to take them off for five minutes." I flashed my eyebrows in emphasis on the phrase, *take them off*. "Then back on they went, of course. Can't have me replicating whatever I managed to do yesterday. Or . . . two days ago? I don't know how long I was out."

"Two days," Zent said. "Not surprising that they're taking such precautions. They don't want you taking them unawares and blowing up the place or something."

The prison guard shifted, looking noticeably uncomfortable at that notion.

"Relax," I told the guard. "Trust me, I still feel like garbage. And these bracelets keep me from doing anything." I gave Zent a meaningful look, and he met my eyes, nodding ever so slightly.

"So, Lyn," he said a bit more seriously than his previous words. "You hear the rumors? About the Mani invasion?"

"No." There'd been similar whispers back at Red Horizon HQ, but I'd dismissed them as baseless mutterings.

"I heard one of the guards talking about it today," he said. "Supposedly they've been making some experimental starships with the express purpose of breaking through Mani's energy shield and attacking the planet."

I felt a flutter in my chest, a twinge of worry that superseded all my worries here on Gaea. Mani was my beloved home. They couldn't just . . . why would they even want to invade the moon? *I'll have to check this out.*

Then a thought came to me: The Archlord had feared this exact thing happening. Had he somehow known the Gaeans would attack? How could he possibly have predicted it? Even Reality Authority didn't give one the power to see the future, did it? Maybe he wasn't such a fool after all, just . . . insane?

"Huh," was all the response I could think of. "I'll ask the Emperor if he calls me in again."

I said goodbye to my friend and allowed the guard to escort me back to my cell. I had been watching the guard patrols and their rotations, trying to take note of weaknesses in the system as well as where the cameras were located. That one was a bit harder. Zent was officially on board with the escape plan, though I knew he must be worried about leaving it in my hands.

I had to find out about the Senate's assault plan first, though.

Who knew? Maybe I would get lucky and the power of the Mother would somehow return. If I regained whatever connection I had that allowed me to draw Geothermic energy straight from the pool under the lab, then would I be able to break through the copper bands' inhibition? I doubted even the scientists here at Haccolces fully understood that phenomenon. But if I could get them off, then that would be a different story.

The next morning, I was summoned to meet with Llsdsaor once more. The same general, Chimeth, came to get me, droopy face and all. He led me down a different path through the halls. I didn't ask where we were headed, but simply followed quietly. My newfound photographic memory wouldn't miss so much as a glimpse.

A short elevator ride down, we arrived on the ground floor, according to the lift controls. From there, we headed through a door into another building. This one was immediately recognizable as higher-class, perhaps part of the main Capitol Building, the heart of the superstructure. It actually had windows, and through them I could see the layout of the surrounding city, as well as the towering forms of the Capitol complex. This must be one of the offices.

A clerk checked Chimeth and me in, making a note on his desk console with a nod to the general. He eyed me warily, as though someone had brought a lion to a family gathering. A few turns later, we rode an elevator up to the fourth floor and soon arrived at an imposing set of wooden doors. Not metal, but carved wood. That clearly indicated class over function, as Hellebes did not lightly make anything decorative. An attendant standing by opened the door for us, and just as he did so, I realized whom I was being taken to see. Not just the Emperor, but . . .

The Senate.

Sure enough, inside was a grand council chamber, with nine men standing around a large globe of Gaea. No—eight men. Each had a wooden podium before him, complete with a touchscreen and microphone, but an additional podium stood empty. I assumed one leader had something keeping him from meeting here. Each Senator was nearly as massive as Lldsaor. A couple were even larger. I'd wondered if his size was just a fluke, as no one back at HQ had ever talked much about the Senate, but it seemed they all shared at least this one trait. Genetic modding?

Lldsaor looked our way, waving us in. "Chimeth, just in time. Bring the Heiress and take a seat."

There were chairs between the door and the closest two podiums, and I took a seat beside Third General Chimeth. The stares of eight titans of the world, not only politically but physically, unnerved me.

"So, the Mother reborn," said one of the Senators in a grand voice that spoke of love for self and all things fine. He wore a golden sash over a uniform somewhat gaudier than the others. His thick blond hair, styled and gelled, reached down nearly to his shoulders. "How long would you have kept us from seeing her, good Emperor, had these little . . . occurrences not come up?"

"Oh, spare us the gibberish, Brant," said one of the Senators across from him. "You know full well you're not going to blandish an answer out of him." This man's voice was higher pitched with a superior tone, and he sported well-trimmed facial hair tipped by a dark goatee. His thin eyebrows gave the impression of craftiness, and his stance showed comfortable cockiness, like a man who doesn't just think but *knows* full well that he is a cut better than the rest. Smarter, certainly.

"Thank you, Vladimir," said Lldsaor, crossing his arms. "As that is the very reason I've called you all here. Bringing her was what is called an act of good faith. We can't ignore her any longer, leaving everything to our imbecilic scientists."

"Your imbecilic scientists," Vladimir corrected. He crossed his arms, mimicking the Emperor. But on him it looked more smug than intimidating. Just watching this man was infuriating, and I wasn't rooting for anyone here.

"General," said another Senator, dressed in a sharp military uniform. "Care to introduce us?" Everything about him, from his stiff stance to his mustache, indicated a military man to the core.

General Chimeth stood from his seat quickly, giving a salute. "Certainly, sir. My good Senators of Gaea, this is Lynchazel, daughter of Her Gr . . . um, Mother Gaea." Beginning with Lldsaor and quickly moving on to the uniformed Senator, he named them off, pointing: "Lynchazel, you've already met Emperor Lldsaor, chief of the Gaean Senate and ruler of Haccolces. This is Strongs, Senator of Haven. Brant, Senator of Maldunech. Holman, Senator of Luna Halcyon. Sylleo of Ccamos. Vladimir of Trident, Daedalus of Chronala, and DeWitt of Lenardda."

I nodded along with the general. It was strange, but for the first time in my life, I actually had the memory capability to glance back at any one of the eight and immediately remember his name. *Oh, this is going to come in so useful.* I found it more than a little odd, however, how naturally General Chimeth skipped right over the empty podium, as though it was a usual occurrence. After all . . . there were supposed to be nine cities, right?

"Now that that's out of the way," said Daedalus in an upbeat tone, "Are we still going through with the invasion of Mani?" His voice was high-pitched and bright, contrasting with his bull-like bulk.

"The *reconnaissance* of Mani," Sylleo corrected. Clean-shaven and athletic, this Senator was younger in appearance than most of the others, despite his silver hair. His suit was simple, dark-colored with a relaxed cut and high collar. His mannerisms spoke of quiet calculation and tact, of patience and mental agility. "I'm still against the whole idea," he added as an aside.

"Reconnaissance in preparation for invasion," said Strongs, hands still clasped behind his back in a rigid stance. "We are not about to back down after hundreds of years of preparation."

I couldn't believe my luck, not even having to prompt anyone to get info on the plans. If Lldsaor or any of the others were bothered by my being present for any of the discussion, they did not show it. Maybe they'd already forgotten I was here?

"The latest starship models have been flight tested and cleared?" asked the Emperor, addressing Chimeth.

"Yes, sir. A whole squad's worth."

I held up a hand, ignoring a glare from the general beside me. "May I . . . ask a question?"

The tall men looked at me one by one. None silenced me, which was a step up from the leaders of the Red Horizon.

"Go ahead, Heiress," said Holman, who had kept silent until now. Wide-shouldered, wearing a square-cut beard and a strange, flat-topped hat, he had the distinctive look of a man who wished he were anywhere but this meeting. He might as well have added, *I'm sick of hearing these blabbermouths, anyway.*

I cleared my throat. "Why do you want to attack my people? What have they done to you?"

I held my breath, waiting for one of the Senators to snap at me or order Chimeth to hogtie me, but more than one of them simply laughed. Strongs did not laugh, but instead stared coldly at me.

"Your people?" asked Emperor Lldsaor. "You say that as though you've already chosen a side."

"She was raised there," Sylleo said. "Surely we can cut her that much slack."

Brant scratched his blond mane. "You do realize, missy, what happened a thousand years ago, right? Why the Legaleians were banished?"

I said nothing. I had no clue, and I hungered to know.

"Because their 'magic' posed a threat to all of Gaea," he continued. "All this time, they've been only gaining power."

Oh. Was he saying what I thought he was saying? What a preposterous assumption—based neither in history nor facts. "That's not true," I said, taking a risk. "My people are dying. Mani is dying, just like Gaea is. Why do you really want to conquer another world?"

I mean, they might as well walk up to a bunch of pigs and say, "We want to eat you all, not because you're tasty but because we know you're secretly plotting to take over the world."

I got momentary silence in return this time. Chimeth looked ready to either faint or slug me. His expression and pallor seemed to suggest both. Many of the faces around the circle exchanged glances with one another, as though calculating how to answer. *Which lies to tell . . .* Finally, Lldsaor said, "We will discuss this matter another time, Lynchazel; the fate of one world or another is not your concern right now." Turning back to the others, he said, "Now, what do you all think, having seen her in person? Does she live up to your expectations?"

"Could you be more . . . specific about these expectations?" Vladimir asked, itching his facial hair with a disturbingly predatory gaze on me.

"Vlad," said Sylleo in a low but sharp tone.

"I think there are numerous uses we could have for her," said Daeadalus, cracking his giant knuckles. "Just bring her to Chronala; we'll start up some cloning sequences and gene replicators. Or we could just try breeding her the old-fashioned way." He looked around at the room. "Right? It's an idea. Seems like the only way to get a fresh female. It worked last time."

I kept my mouth shut, but it took effort. *A fresh female . . .* The man said it so casually. He could have been kidding, and yet, judging by the other Senators' reactions, he was entirely serious. There was something about these men that just seemed . . . different . . . from the Red Horizon soldiers like Zent and Bddo. They reminded me of so many predators, lunatics, criminals, someone I'd be afraid to meet in person.

Yet here I was.

Finally, Emperor Lldsaor cleared his throat and said what was really on his mind. "I would like to propose that Lynchazel be trained to become the new Mother Gaea. It will take time, as well as further research and some biological conditioning, but I think her performance could be even greater than her mother's. Her test results from yesterday are quite something. The current Zeta Beasts can only do so much, even if we do . . ." his eyes rolled my way in an ugly yet absent-minded look ". . . get things back together soon."

He was met with multiple different responses. It was five minutes or more before the chaos of back-and-forth argument subsided, soon after which they adjourned the meeting. As far as I could tell, nothing had been decided. Lldsaor looked displeased as he stalked away from his podium, stopping briefly to give Chimeth the order to take me back to my cell. The general took me away before the eager Senators could smother me in questions.

Well, it hadn't gone as I'd expected, but I'd learned something of their plans regarding the strike on Mani. Or . . . *reconnaissance*, as Senator Sylleo had put it. It had to be stopped. But more importantly, someone must warn them. Someone had to get word back to Mani. And that someone was being escorted back to her cell by a lab-raised general—in copper, pathetic and docile.

As I followed Third General Chimeth back to my cell, I began to put together the pieces for my escape plan.

α Chapter 22 α

Transferrable Skills

Hersta 3, 1295:

I can't believe it. Rena actually pulled it off. She's amazing. A genius. Truly deserving of whatever reward they have for the first successful student to master their experimental techniques. Deep down, I think the Anier didn't even expect the experiments to work. It's now a week from the last procedure, and I am a new woman. No, am I even still a woman—still human? I haven't grown any metallic scales yet, so that's a good sign, but this ability to feel the earth itself . . . it is both uncanny and extraordinary. They call it a breakthrough in human evolution. I've already had to be very careful. I've never had this force, this energy, running through my body. My vitality is unprecedented, my vigor and dexterity only increasing every day. And my mind . . . it continues to change in uncomfortable ways, clawing its way into my past against my will to retrieve memories I'd rather keep buried. But . . . I just wonder what they will do with Rena now. And . . . what will become of me?

— From Lhinde's Diary

The next day, I put the escape plan into action. I made sure to have my gillsuit on when they came to get me; the guards didn't seem to find it strange. They led me down to the same lab as the other day, standing guard at the door while two scientists in lab coats had me strip down and don my comfy medical gown. After examining me and checking my vitals, they called the guards in to remove my four bracelets.

One, two, three, four . . .

Distantly, I could feel it. Oh blessed auroras, I could feel it coursing through the Geothermic conduit, the quantum computers, the cables in the hallway outside: The life energy of Gaea. I bent down and rubbed my ankles, which were quite sore from having that stupid metal on all the time, though I made an extra wincing motion for the drama. I was stalling to prepare my body for what I had to do.

Breathing in, I drew upon the planetary energy around me, more and more. Once I had siphoned past the cap that had previously limited me, I stood up and spun on one heel, taking one of the guards in the chin with a hook kick. Geokinesis gave me the speed and precision to do it, but also the power to knock the man right out. Indeed, he tumbled to the floor even as the three other men stared.

My opening lasted but a moment; the other guard quickly recovered and took up a defensive stance, reaching for his blaster with his off hand. But I moved quicker, getting inside his weak guard and ramming an uppercut into his chin. I heard and felt his teeth snap together. Hardly able to believe my luck, I turned around to face the two scientists, who were backing up to their equipment desk, trying to contact security for help.

"Come on, come on!" cried one to the other.

"I'm trying!"

I leaped over the chair that lay between me and the man who had gotten to the radio, sending it clattering with one knee, and drove a knife-hand strike into the side of his neck. He slumped over, and I set upon the last man, taking him out with an elbow to the head. That one hit hard enough that I felt bone give way, but I didn't stop to assess the damage. Breathing quickly from adrenaline, I tore off the rest of my gown, which had already ripped laughably with my kick to the first guard's chin. Fortunately, my victims hadn't the opportunity to notice, let alone laugh . . . though I couldn't say how long they'd be down for. So I hurriedly retrieved my gillsuit and donned it, then grabbed the electronic keys and both blasters off the guards.

I dashed out into the hallway, headed for Zent's cell. I got there in under a minute, running faster than I ever had. Hopefully, I could get us out of here before the guards could arrive, but I knew that was overly optimistic.

"Lyn!" the rebel leader exclaimed upon seeing me. "It worked?"

I nodded, aiming one of my blasters and firing one, two, three shots into the bars of his cell, near the top. "Look out." With swift kicks, I ripped the bars apart, bending them inward at a harsh angle. "Come on!"

Zent wasted no time in wrenching the bars down enough to slip through. I handed him one of my blasters and set about unlocking his bonds with the keys I'd stolen. "Where to, Lady?" he asked.

"That way!" I pointed down the hall toward the nearest elevator that would take us downward. As we both broke into a sprint, I said, "I have a crazy idea, and it all depends on how quickly we can track down those experimental starships."

Zent grinned. "Now that's more like it."

The alarms began to ring just as we made it to the elevator. "You sure we can take 'em on?" Zent asked as he punched the first-floor button. "How are your energy levels?"

"Never better." I got in after him, and we began to descend. "Guess I just needed a day to recover. I don't think they expected me to reach into the floor for Geothermic juice."

At the bottom, I led him through the first floor of the prison toward an E-exit. Before we made it, guards began to swarm in from all over, brandishing blasters and shouting for us to freeze.

I swiveled, feeling at the energy beneath our feet. I could feel it so much more clearly than ever. I pulled at it and heaved with my mind, ripping up the floor in a Geokinetic wave that traveled toward our enemies, crashing into them. "Come on, Zent!" I hissed.

"Roger that," he said, turning back to the door. For an emergency exit, it was well sealed. This was a prison, after all. Zent shot the locks and rammed his shoulder into it to force it open. "There we are."

Outside, we scanned the cityscape in the morning light. Military craft buzzed out of the southmost area of the Senatorial complex, headed for us. Zent pointed toward their origin. "There! Those must have come from the military hangars. We'll start there."

We hurried over the paved lot, reaching the closest building just as the ships above began opening fire with stun charges. We were still in the Capitol complex, which sprawled over tens of thousands of acres. We ducked around the corner, headed for the hangars.

Soon, we were being chased by gunner vehicles. As they opened fire, we dodged down an alley behind the nearest building. "Here!" Zent shouted, pointing at a door that looked less heavily armored than others. With a mighty kick, he bashed the door in, and we scrambled inside.

We found ourselves in a warehouse. I couldn't tell what precisely was stored here, but there was a lot of it. Alarms blared in here as well. I followed Zent as he picked his way through to the next room, which was less cluttered but also had more exits—one of which was already teeming with guards. We made a break for the far exit, which, according to the sign, led to the aircraft hangars.

The hangars, large and well-lit, housed dozens of aircraft and omnicraft docked near their own Geothermic power supplies. There were also soldiers, who quickly came after us with their stun guns. No lethal weapons were to be used on the Mother . . . although, from what I'd heard, I didn't want to be shot with one.

"You sure you don't just want to take one of these?" Zent asked. "I could hotwire any of them."

"Will they get us to Mani?" I asked sharply.

"No," he said with a shake of his head. Shooting yet another guard with his blaster, he said, "I think the experimental designs department can't be far. Let's find those ships."

We stopped briefly to scavenge more energy weapons off the guards' corpses, and then searched about for the doors that would lead to the ships we sought. Just as the soldiers began to pin us down with large numbers, we found it. A dozen starships were docked in a comparatively small bay, each bearing a long, sleek design with powerful omnidirectional thrusters.

"I'll try to start one!" Zent shouted as he ran for one of the ships. "But we're going to need a distraction, Lyn."

"Yes, sir." I spun around, seeking out the power of the earth underfoot.

It was strong here. I pulled upward, causing the earth to rip up through the floor and crush the soldiers in the hallway, effectively sealing it. "Wow," I muttered, surprised at the ferocity of Gaea's response. It was almost like Authority back on Mani.

Then I rushed over to the ship Zent had commandeered. He had the back hatch open for me—there were only two seats, front and back—so I jumped in and shut the glass hatch, sealing it seamlessly into the frame and the rest of the glass canopy.

"All right," Zent said, hitting a button on the control console to raise the bay door in front of us. "I've never flown one of these before, but I think the skill is somewhat transferrable from a regular aircraft."

He lifted the ship into a hovering position using the anti-grav features, and as the door rose high enough to get under, he engaged the thrusters. Sure enough, there were vehicles already waiting outside in a perimeter, but we blasted past them, accelerating at an incredible rate. The force of the acceleration was enough to throw me back in my seat. Zent jerked the ship upward, just clearing the nearby buildings before roaring straight upward at full power.

"Um, Zent? How are we going to get through the shield?"

"Well, I haven't exactly tested it yet . . . It seems these things have a built-in stealth feature designed to get past energy barriers. I've heard whisperings of the tech. After all, that's what protects Mani—an energy barrier." He continued to take us higher, rapidly closing the distance to the red web of staticky energy that enclosed Haccolces. A single button engaged the stealth mode.

I gritted my teeth, closing my eyes as we passed through the shield. I swear I could feel it somehow, but when I opened my eyes, we were past it. With a glance out the cockpit window, I caught a dizzying view of the city below me, the energy field stretching out red and angry over the grey metropolis. I leaned forward again, struggling against the surprising G-force. We were traveling nearly straight upward into the cloud layer. Haccolces was afflicted with near-constant thick cloud coverage, compounded by the smog and smoke from numerous industrial facilities. The clouds obscured our view as we ascended, until finally . . .

We passed out of the clouds and into the middle atmosphere. The sun hit us sidelong, nearly blinding as it filtered through a misty cirrus layer to create a glowing morning halo. Mani, on the other hand, was nowhere in sight. Luna peered like a watchful eye from the far horizon, so that meant that Mani must be directly opposite.

"Into the sun it is," Zent said, turning to head straight for the eastern horizon. The sudden change of direction threw me to the side, causing blood to rush to my head and darken my vision uncomfortably, almost painfully. The ship picked up terrific speed until Zent said, "This is probably the safe limit for Gaea's atmosphere. Once we're out, I can open her up and see how fast we can get to your homeworld."

"Okay. And . . . what about the batteries?"

He glanced down. "We've used two percent so far, so I'd say we're good. Huh, that is impressive. Now . . ." He browsed the radio settings, then spoke into his headset. "Agent 327 to base, Agent 327 to base."

Some static, and then, "Zent?"

"The one and only."

"How in the nine hells . . . how did you make it out of there? I want a full report, STAT." The voice sounded like Admiral Skye.

"I'm afraid there's no time, sir," Zent replied. "It's a long story. Only Lyn and I made it out. The mission was a partial success, but we've gotten . . . sidetracked by a plan of the Senate to raid Mani. We were captured, imprisoned—we just escaped in an experimental starship."

"A starship."

"Affirmative. We're heading to Mani. We will return before long. Please hold off on any plan of action until we get back."

Mani coalesced on the horizon like a silver sunrise. Sol was now overhead, shining from above. Zent took us out of the atmosphere in a straight shot toward the silver moon. Admiral Skye's next response was staticky, cutting in and out until we had no more communications.

"Well, no turning back now," Zent said. "Oh, and good work back there, kid. Your plan worked." He reached out a fist, and I bumped it with my own smaller fist. "Now we'll just see how far behind they are."

"Do you think they'll come after us immediately?" I asked.

He glanced back, smiling grimly. "No doubt about it."

α Chapter 23 α

Homecoming

Hersta 22, 1295:

Still alive. Oh, Mother . . . Father . . . sisters of experimentation,

sacrifices of progress . . . you are not, but I am. I am alive.

— From Lhinde's Diary

The trip to Mani was eerie and dreamlike, truly an alien experience. Stars swam around us in a black sea as we left the earth behind. Soon, Gaea was nothing more than a giant ball of blue and green swirled with white clouds, its atmosphere glowing in the sidelong light of Sol as it slowly shrank. It was strange beyond words to see with my own eyes a phenomenon such as the day cycle in such presentation: A world dark on one side, daylit on the other. It made so much sense, yet in all my days on Mani, I'd never questioned it. Since Mani orbited Gaea once per day, tracking along with each planetary rotation, the sun seemed to stand in place, each day cycle passing only once in four weeks.

The universe had never felt larger, and yet . . . at the same time, never so small.

Our starship picked up speed as we traveled through the vacuum of space, with no air resistance to pull against the ship. "So, um . . . is this *actually* the first space-faring vessel they've made?" The thought made me more than a little nervous to be riding in the cockpit.

"Who knows?" Zent replied. "The first made to carry Hellebes? Far as I know. But they've sent out many probes and drones to Mani and Luna, and none of them ever came back. The Energy Field that surrounds the moon renders most technologies useless. I've been in the air force for a while, but I never specialized in the tech development department, so I only know rumors of their experiments."

"But it should be all right? Passing through the field?"

Zent shrugged. "We can only hope. Yeah, let's say we will."

I gripped my seat harder. Mani drew slowly nearer, a gleaming silver gibbous growing from the size of my outstretched fist to twice that size in the space of an hour. Then larger, larger, until it filled half of the cockpit's view. Slowly, I began to make out what I was really seeing, a dark, swirling atmospheric field that reacted to the sun's light, glowing in response. Nothing was visible through it. The layer did not block the light, otherwise it would never be able to get through.

It was almost like its very own advanced shield wall. The thought sent a shudder down my spine.

"We're getting close," Zent said, looking back at me. "Get ready for a wild ride."

The Energy Field drew closer, crackling with what appeared to be lightning. It spread weblike over the surface of the globe, flickering like Gaea's shield domes. Soon, Zent engaged the stealth feature, and we passed right through the layer. Now *this* one I know I felt. A ripple of liquid energy tugged on the ship like it wanted to have us, almost like the feeling of breaking out of the ocean in a Hellebes omnicraft.

But we were alive and unharmed.

Zent engaged the brakes, rotating the ship's thrusters to slow our descent. Below us swarmed thick, dark clouds. The Land of Storms. "Zent, take us farther on," I said. "This region is incredibly stormy, but it's only a few miles in diameter." He'd taken us dead center using the built-in AI. I could have had him head for the outer rim of Mani, but then how would we get our bearings?

"Roger that." He took us over the thickest of the clouds, descending past the angry storms to soar over the hole-pocked fields of grey stone where greenish light glowed from the cracks. Farther out over the horizon, I could see vast reaches of the Duchy of Halstar on the Light Side of Mani, as the Gaeans referred to it. There was the River Soul, twisting out in its ouroboros path that inexplicably returned upon itself.

"Wow," Zent said, surveying the countryside from our high vantage point. "So this is what your world looks like."

We were still sweeping along at well over five hundred kilometers per hour, already long past the Land of Storms and the surrounding land. I tried to recall the landmarks we'd passed on our way, in order to get my bearings, but nothing seemed familiar. We must not be following the same latitudinal path. "I suppose," I said. "Though I'm not used to this side of Mani."

"This side?"

I grimaced. I hadn't exactly briefed him on Mani's geography before we came. "There are two halves," I explained. "This half, which you call the Light Side, is separated from the other half of the world, where my people live. There's a great chasm we call the Sea of Emptiness that spans the gap between. You'll see."

"And we're going all the way to the far side?" he asked.

"Yes. To Nytaea. Oh, that's . . . wait, that's Redufiel," I said. "Inside the River Soul. And . . . it's at war!" On the far right horizon was the city, and I could see the small shapes of burnt buildings, smoke and army encampments around it. What could possibly be going on? I didn't remember any rumors of war from when we came through just a few months back.

"Do you want to stop and find out what's happened? Sounds like you weren't aware of this."

"No, just keep going. We don't know where they'll strike, but we need to warn the magi in Nytaea and see what the Archlord is up to."

"The one who killed your friends," Zent said evenly.

I clenched my teeth. "The very same." Just thinking about him brought back memories of my loving friends, friends I would never see again. And Rhidea . . . Mani lost its strongest mage that day. But what disturbed me most was the fear of what Domon had gone on to do after sealing the Gate shut. In his naïveté, he thought that that would keep the Gaeans out of Mani . . . Had he already reclaimed Nytaea?

We passed over the Soul, coming in sight of the chasm's edge as we reached the coastal grasslands. Then the enormous Darsorian forests, and then . . .

"Oh, *that* sea of emptiness," Zent said in awe as we came upon it. As per my instructions, he veered to the right as we zipped over the misty sea of nothingness. Sol was far to the left, nearly on the opposite side of the planet, and the chasm glowed dimly with golden light on that side. We angled toward the kingdom of Nemental, reaching the shore just south of the Sky Islands, and continued westward until a familiar sight came into view: The white walls of Nytaea.

"All right, Zent," I said. "This is the place."

He immediately engaged the brakes, which were quite efficient at our relatively low speed as we had neared our destination. We coasted over the alabaster walls, garnering many looks and gestures from the guardsmen. I think they were too confused to even bother shooting at us, not that their crossbow bolts would have done anything to the hardened steel plating and tempered glass of our vessel.

And then I saw it—the damage, the destruction. Domon had nearly laid waste to the city. Houses were burned, streets in disarray. Nytaea looked to be in worse condition than when the tyrant Lord Kalceron had ruled it. Anger welled up within me as I surveyed the scene.

"Has it always looked this . . . bad?" Zent asked from the pilot's seat.

"No," I said, my emotions clear through my tone. "This . . . this is despicable. Domon is going to pay for what he's done."

I guided Zent over the city to the Palace, deeming it best to present ourselves directly to the local officials—whoever was running this debacle in Domon's name—instead of waiting for them to hunt down the unidentified flying machine. An insidious detail caught my eye: Banners bearing the black and gold of Ti'Vaeth, though others featured Mydia's stork over a blue-and-white field. Guards could be spotted in hideous black and grey, though again the colors were intermixed.

Guardsmen rushed to and fro along the walls of the Palace and through the courtyards, shouting orders and warnings as we approached. *Good. Let them sweat a little.* If Rhidea and the others had still been here, they alone might be able to guess who it was, or at least where we were—

Wait. There she was.

How?

"Rhidea!" I shouted, causing Zent to jump. "That's her down there! And . . . and Kaen!" Indeed, they were rushing out of the front doors of the Palace to meet us, looking up into the sky as Zent brought the starcraft to a standstill in the air some fifty feet above the Palace. The anti-grav features, developed for Gaea's weighty pull, laughed at Mani's gravity. Rhidea seemed to be giving orders for the soldiers to stand down, holding out her hands in a wary but steady stance.

"Well?" Zent said. "Want to give them a welcome speech?"

He switched the radio to an external broadcast setting, and suddenly my voice channel was projected out from the ship's speakers. I cleared my throat. "Citizens of Nytaea, this is Lyn. I am returning from Gaea in peace. Please allow us to land."

Rhidea and Kaen hugged each other and smiled, waving toward our ship. I waved back through the glass. They shooed the guardsmen away from the courtyard below us, and Zent took us down to land. A minute later, I was embracing my old friends and breathlessly introducing Zent, who looked on with bemused interest at our alien language. I tried to interpret for him as best I could.

I can't properly describe the shock I felt upon discovering that my friends had made it out alive. And not only alive, but here in Nytaea! Mydia came out wearing a crown of gold, rushing to embrace me as well. "Oh, Lyn! It's been so long. We never thought you would make it back."

I shook my head in wonder. "I . . . I can't believe you're all still alive. That's even more amazing. But there isn't time. Who's in charge here?"

Mydia looked to Rhidea with a wry smile. "I am. We had to take it back forcibly. That dastard the Archlord destroyed Nytaea and marched off to—"

Zent nudged me.

"I'm sorry," I interrupted, "there's really no time. Call your strongest

Magi, and prepare. Because . . . we may have been followed. The Gaean League is sending out a strike force to invade Mani very soon."

"How large, child?" Rhidea asked in a cutting voice. "What means of weaponry do they have?"

"Quite advanced," I said, hesitating before deciding against further elaboration. "Half a dozen ships like these, armed with explosives and weapons with similar power to a High Mage."

The red-haired scholar nodded. "Then we can handle it. How do you know they are coming here? Did they track you somehow?"

"We don't know for certain. They might very well have." I struck my thigh in frustration. "I didn't even think of . . ." Turning to Zent, I asked in the Hellebes tongue, "Do you think they have trackers installed in all these ships?"

"Without a doubt. Would they be able to use them on Mani? No idea."

I turned back to my friends, who listened to our strange language with fascination. "It's very possible. If so, they'll be here soon."

"Understood," said Mydia.

α Chapter 24 α

Attack on Nytaea

Soldor 1, 1295:

Another dream . . . This one puzzles me, because I am certain that the "me" in the dream was someone from long ago. I tread a long-forgotten townscape full of architecture that I've never seen in real life and didn't recognize. Everything was foreign, and yet I am convinced that it was a real period in time. No one was in sight as I walked through the street, and I could tell that this was unusual. I was Khor, a raven-haired young woman of some twenty years. My clothing was odd, one narrow, richly embroidered piece which wrapped around me multiple times and pinned together to form a wavy dress. My head was adorned with gold. My hands were thin and pale. These details were vivid, as were my surroundings, but my role in life and my purpose for being in this place were beyond my recollection. I came across other citizens of the forgotten town dressed similarly to me, but just as I made to speak to them, to ask them where I was and what this town was called . . . it all blurred and faded away.
— From Lhinde's Diary

It wasn't long before the fleet arrived in Nytaea. They dove from the sky like birds of prey, swooping down from the horizon upon the White City. The evacuation had already been ordered, and as many citizens as possible were corralled into the safest buildings, where Magi would do their best to shelter them. All others were being assembled at the Palace and stationed on the city walls.

"Of course they found us," I muttered to my team members as I saw the starcraft. The "team" included Zent, blaster in hand and at the ready, and Kaen, who held his strange silver sword. I wasn't entirely sure what he planned to do with it, but I didn't argue. We'd left the ship where we landed it, setting up lightning, wind and fire magi around it to use its beacon as a trap. We stood on the southern side of the Palace, where I hoped that my presence would ensure safety for those around me, for surely the enemy's goal was to recapture me alive.

Unless . . . Senator Strongs had been vocal about the invasion plan, and he was also the one most eager to be rid of me. He couldn't have been the one who sent these . . . no, that wouldn't make sense. They'd come from Haccolces, just like us.

Foolish girl, I chided myself. *Focus!*

"What?" Kaen asked from beside me, and I realized I'd spoken the words aloud in Hellebes.

I ignored him, however, as the fleet descended, slowing to hover high above the city of Nytaea. Over one of the ships' radios came the order, "Surrender yourself, Heiress, or we will open fire and take you back by force."

"They're holding the city hostage!" I shouted to the others around me. "They want me to go back with them peacefully or they'll open fire on the city."

"Tell them they can try!" shouted Mydia from the Palace doors, where her guards were holding her back from danger. Many voices echoed the sentiment.

"Then let's show them what Mani is capable of!" I shouted.

The magi surrounding the Palace let loose a torrent of lightning, firebolts and cyclones, and the pilots immediately responded by dropping bombs on the city and opening gunfire on the citadel. Soon, all of Nytaea erupted in chaos, smoke rising from multiple locations as blasts detonated and walls crumbled. Most of the magic the mage soldiers hurled at the enemy did little more than harry them, but one of the ships' engines was taken out, and it spiraled from the sky, trailing smoke.

Zent and I took aim and attempted to hit the moving targets with our blasters—which were limited to their batteries here on Mani—but were largely ineffective against the strong shielding. Heat shielding was standard on Gaea, along with conductive fuselages and static wicking to withstand the powerful lightning of Gaea.

The only one who seemed able to achieve anything of note against the fleet was Rhidea, who used her gravity Authority to pull the starcraft toward the earth, bending their flight trajectories as they tried to maneuver. Since they were airborne, the effect was not as deadly as it would have been closer to the ground, but as I watched, she pulled out another trick . . .

I'd seen it before, in the fight with Lord Kalceron last year: She drew pale metal from nearby buildings, even up from the very *ground*, which morphed into glittering blades of silver, hovering in the air around her in a sharp-bladed weapons array. She launched them, homing in on the flying machines and spearing them through. She took down one in this manner and damaged another, and then knelt, putting a hand to the ground, and ripped a hole in the earth. Out of it shot a savage spear of pure silver, growing larger and longer, which chased down one of the ships that ventured too close. The massive metal horn impaled it, screeching and grinding horribly as it bent under the ship's momentum. The silver held, and the gunship hung in the air, raining sparks.

I gaped. Never had I seen such an ability. That was like . . . Silver Authority. A lost art. An impossibility. But soon I noticed a far more pressing issue: Two of the surviving pilots had bailed and dropped to Mani's surface, and were now coming after me. The mage soldiers attempted to stop them, but the Hellebes were too quick, hopping and darting through the streets and off of building walls, stun blasters in hand.

"Zent!" I shouted.

"On it."

We leapt into action, closing the distance and engaging the Gaean soldiers hand-to-hand. It was strange for all of us off-worlders to be able to move so freely on Mani, but I had the advantage of being used to it, albeit from when I was much weaker. My opponent was strong and swift but tended to overshoot in his movements, and I caught him off guard with a gut punch, following up with an intense blast of heat directly to his chest—

achieved by my Fire Authority. At long last, it was back.

Becoming aware of Kaen shouting from behind me, I turned to see him engaging with a third pilot, fending him off with his long silver blade. Where had he gotten that thing? His skill and the man's own misjudgment of Mani's gravity difference seemed to make the fight almost even.

"Kaen!" I called. "Hold on!" I scanned our surroundings, checking for more Hellebes on foot. Seeing none, I made to approach. But as I ran to interrupt the fight, I saw the Hellebes soldier trip Kaen and knock the blade out of his hand while pinning him down to the ground by the throat, just as I'd seen the Emperor do to Zent a few days back. "No!" I shouted in dismay.

The soldier looked up at me, saying, "You know this man? All you had to do was give yourself up, Heiress. It was that easy!"

I started to reply, but cut off as a small girl ran out from the Palace, shouting, "Kaen! Let him go, you monster!"

Kaen tried to twist his head, shouting harshly, "Mandrie, stay back! Get away!"

Suddenly, the last of the Gaean ships spun down from the sky, twisting madly before crashing into the white walls of the Palace. It detonated, sending chunks of metal and white stone flying all around, showering the area in dust.

"*MANDRIE!*" Kaen screamed, voice choked and breaking under his Gaean attacker's grip.

When the smoke cleared, a silver spear protruded from the Hellebes soldier's midsection, its red-haired originator standing fifty feet back with a shocked look on her face. I watched numbly as she jerked the spear out with a bloody spatter and Kaen shoved the great corpse off him. His silver sword streaked right into his hand, glowing and pulsing with a terrible light and humming like an overheating energy blaster. With an uncontrolled roar, Kaen rose and attacked the rubble that had crushed his sister, sending sparks off the steel carapace of her grave. And despite the sparks, it was . . . it was *cutting*. How was that possible? The Hellebes pilot inside was already dead, and from beneath the wreckage ran a rivulet of blood where a small hand stuck out.

Many others had been injured or killed as well. All around me, soldiers and civilians rushed to and fro, shouting for help and support, but I could only stare at the sight of Mandrie, crushed beneath tons of stone and metal, and Kaen, seemingly pushed past his breaking point. Rhidea made her way over to him, shouting orders to the mage soldiers as men and women moved to gather the dead and wounded.

Zent took my shoulder, arresting my attention, and I broke from my daze to see that there were no more Hellebes living. The one I had torched was slowly bleeding out, a hole melted through his uniform and into his chest. Did I really do that? *Oh.* No, I'd put a blaster charge through him immediately afterward. Already, my training was becoming instinct. Zent had apparently put his own opponent down with the final shot of his blaster at close range.

All of this to repel a flight of six starcraft—just one handful of Gaean invaders. Five destroyed, while the last had escaped. I was starting to see why Domon had considered them so grave a threat. If only we had a whole army of Rhidea clones . . . What *had* she used to destroy those ships? Could it really be Silver magic? That shouldn't be possible, even for her . . .

But Mandrie was gone. One more of my childhood friends from the orphanage. Kaen's pride and joy, his beloved sister. Just . . . gone.

"Thank you, Zent," I murmured, brushing off his hand and walking over to my longtime friend. "Kaen. Kaen, look at me." I reached for his shoulder, but he turned even as I did so, a crazed look in his eye, teeth gritted in an ugly snarl.

"What!" he snapped, sword raised and pulsing with eerie light. A moment later, he seemed to recognize my face, relaxing a bit. "Lyn? How . . . how did . . . my sister. She's dead."

"I know, Kaen." I pulled him into a hug. "I'm so sorry. I tried to protect her—and everyone. We all tried. I-I'm sorry."

He clutched my shoulders, leaning against my greater weight like a post, and thumped his fist against my collarbone. "I can't believe it." He struck me again and again, and I absorbed each blow without moving, not saying a word. My frame was no thicker than his, but my muscle and bone density was far higher. Still, I was unused to being a physical support for anyone.

When he pulled back, I saw more than raw sorrow and grief in his eyes. I saw a hint of resentment . . . and a deep, burning anger. I wasn't certain whom it was directed against. Softly, so low that I almost couldn't hear it, he said, "Vengeance . . . vengeance."

β PART TWO β

B

Sorrow

Gaea

A Somber Reunion

Phoebe turned away from Mandrie's grave, wiping tears from her eyes with a handkerchief. The burial service was just too much for her. Queen Mydia, seeing her distress, came over and laid a hand on her shoulder—ignoring, of course, the guards which insistently followed her. "I'm sorry, Phoebe," she said in her soft voice. The words were clearly meant to be comforting, but mere words were of little value against the torrent of emotions.

Around her, the others who'd been close to Mandrie looked solemn, some shedding their own tears—even Lyn, that seemingly impenetrable rock. But it wasn't just Mandrie being mourned. Nearly two dozen graves lined the small hill-turned-cemetery, which lay just south of the eastern city gate. Many among the nobles and the common folk of Nytaea had gathered here to mourn the loss of family, friends and neighbors. Master Gendric, the heavyset old headmaster of the Nytaean Mage Academy, was just finishing up his speech, including some words for the dead Gaeans, whom he referred to as, "foreign invaders."

A bit generous.

Zent, the man whom Lyn had brought back with her, stood near her, looking awkward. After all, he didn't even understand their language. He was enormous, a half head taller than most men present, and impossibly sculpted like the statues and paintings of ancient heroes in the Palace. She had observed from afar what these Gaeans, these . . . Hellebes . . . were capable of, treating the laws of Mani like a child's sandbox. Even Lyn herself had moved like a different creature upon returning from Gaea, as though she had learned to swim and everyone else was simply dog-paddling.

But he was so . . . well, no matter. Right now, she couldn't do much more than thank Mydia and pretend she hadn't been sobbing her eyes out, but she did steal a couple more glances at the man. Just a couple. How could she help it?

Kaen stood behind them all, distancing himself from as many people as possible. Phoebe knew better than to think it was for any lack of compassion for his sister, for he had loved Mandrie with all his heart. Rather, he didn't trust himself to be controlled around so many people. She could almost understand, although . . . he really worried her lately. That horrible sword seemed to be taking a hold on him, and no one knew what it might do to him.

Soon, citizens began to trickle away from the gravesite, many bringing flowers to lay on the graves before leaving. Phoebe brought her own flower, a simple daisy, the perfect remembrance for Mandrie's simple cheerfulness in life, and laid it on her grave. Tears threatened to surface once more, and Phoebe ignored them by reaching up and brushing back her dark hair. When she turned to go, Kaen was nowhere in sight.

Lyn stepped forward and took Phoebe's hand. "Come on. Let's go find him."

Phoebe gave up on finding Kaen back at the Palace, heading down to the orphanage with Lyn instead. Lyn said she wanted to see the children. It wasn't far from the Nytaean Palace, tucked into a small alley—meant as a covert hideaway from the regent Zama in his short reign of terror. Fortunately, he had been put away by Rhidea and Mydia, but they hadn't moved the orphanage yet. The queen and her retainers were busy cleaning up the city, as well as preparing for the eventual return of the Archlord and his forces.

The female mage soldier, Lanna, was still guarding the front door to the orphanage just as Mydia had ordered. The queen liked to keep soldiers on watch from time to time at all the orphanages in town, and had stationed the blond woman here to guard the children following Mandrie's death, as the girl had been Phoebe's right-hand assistant. The woman wore her hair bundled up in a bun, no helmet on her head but otherwise a full set of elegant silver armor. Phoebe wasn't sure if it was the authentic ancient silver armor crafted by the Silversmiths, or the newer type made from mundane silver. She had no idea how mage soldier stations worked, or who got to wear the hallowed sets.

"Ma'am. Lady Lyn." Lanna dipped her head as the young women approached. "Did everything go . . . well?"

Phoebe gave her a tired smile. "We're not the only ones who lost a loved one. You can go back to the Palace, Lanna."

"With all due respect, ma'am, Queen Mydia has ordered me to stay here until you find more help."

Phoebe scoffed, a muted bark that would have been a laugh under better circumstances. "That's what I've got Lyn for." She gave her friend a rap on the shoulder.

Lyn looked down at her, face somber, shaking her head. "No, I'll have to return to Gaea with Zent before long."

Lanna opened her mouth as though to ask for clarification, but seemed to decide it wasn't her place. Like most of Nytaea, she knew nothing about the other world besides rumors that had been circulating ever since Lyn and her group had set out to find Gaea.

Phoebe frowned. "You're really just going to . . ." She glanced at Lanna. "All right, then, I guess you can stay." She said it more harshly than intended, ending with a subconscious sniff brought on by crying. Approaching the tattered front door of the orphanage, she knocked, calling, "Children, I'm back!"

A moment later, a black-haired girl appeared in the doorway, carrying a toddler. Annie was the oldest girl at ten years. "Phoebe! And you're . . . Lyn, right?" She looked up at Lyn, who stood behind Phoebe, three inches taller and broad-shouldered, silver hair twinkling in the light of the auroras.

"May we come in?" Phoebe asked, and the girl moved aside, allowing Phoebe and her friend to step in. Inside, a tallow candle was burning on a table, and smaller children watched with big eyes from another candlelit room farther in.

Phoebe picked up the toddler, Jess, and held her up with a grunt. The other children slowly trickled out and began to swarm Lyn like kittens to their mother. "Hi, Miss Lanna!" Annie said cheerily through the doorway. Lanna waved at the girls from outside before shutting the door for Phoebe.

Lyn seemed to tread carefully around the children, as though afraid of crushing one, but a smile sprang to her face as she began to play with them. They tried to tickle her to death, but Phoebe knew from experience that that didn't work on the girl. *Auroras, but 'girl' hardly describes her anymore.* She was . . . somewhere around two years Phoebe's junior—they'd never been sure—and yet she looked a full-grown woman, not to mention a traveler of worlds and . . . apparently not even entirely Legaleian? No, not just that; her mother was from Gaea, while her father had been the queen's brother. A nigh-unbelievable, not to mention ironic, revelation.

Phoebe set about making supper while Annie kept the rest of the kids entertained with some help from Lyn. "So, Lyn," Phoebe finally said, "What was this Gaea like?" She hesitated as she said it, unsure of how to even broach the subject to her old friend.

Lyn looked up. "Well, it's—it's a long, crazy story. I don't know if you'd even believe it."

Phoebe looked back, seeing a haunted expression on the girl's face. The ache of recent trauma, not unlike Kaen's expression after losing Mandrie. "Oh. Was it that bad?"

Lyn was quiet for a while, causing some of the children to back away in boredom and others to complain all the louder. After a few light words to them, she turned to face Phoebe. "Gaea is an alien world unlike anything we know here. The similarities are so few. The men there—there are only men, no women in the entire world, and they're all huge brutes like Zent and the invaders. And it's all militarized, highly technologically advanced and . . . brutal."

Phoebe snorted. "If they're all men, how do they have babies? That's ridiculous."

"Is it? We have so many more women than men here on Mani, and yet nobody questions it because it's normal." She paused, as though seeing the inconsistency of that argument. "Well, quite frankly, I'm not sure how they reproduce, but it's all orchestrated by the Gaean League and done in large-scale laboratories. Like big places where you manufacture things, only they make people. I don't think you'd want to know any more details even if I had them."

Phoebe shook her head, feeling slightly nauseous in her throat. "No, probably not. What did they do to you when you first arrived?"

Lyn drew in a deep breath and began to relate to her a story of metal and machines, prison cells and advanced weaponry, rebels and friendship. And finally . . . death. Surely it was the abbreviated version, yet . . . *What a tale.*

"I'm sorry," was all Phoebe could think of to say upon hearing of the rebel Hellebes who had given their lives for Lyn's sake. There were things she'd clearly left out, particularly having to do with this whole "Mother" thing she mentioned once or twice, but Phoebe didn't press. There was only so much strange she could take in one day. "And you're really going back there?" she asked with trepidation.

"Yes," Lyn said in response. "I have to."

β Chapter 010 β

Ethereal Voices

Kaen stalked the streets of Nytaea, taking a roundabout route toward the Palace, avoiding most of the traffic headed to and from the main gate and the workers buzzing around the largest damage sites from the previous day's attack. He didn't bother to command his sword to turn invisible, as his thoughts were elsewhere.

Vengeance, the sword whispered to him. *Your soul craves to return the blood of your sister on those who caused her death.*

He tried to ignore the voice, but as usual of late, he was unsuccessful, finding himself replying, "And who is responsible? What if I don't know?"

Of course you do not know. Did you think me unaware?

No, he returned, this time in his head instead of under his breath. *Just annoying as an ass with a sore throat.*

Somewhere deep down, Kaen knew he should be shedding tears, not sinking into misery. But the pain of losing his only beloved family was more than he could have imagined, despite all his paranoia and fears. Worse than all his nightmares, so great that he wanted to crawl into a hole in the earth and die. He'd dreaded this day for a long time, and in retrospect it seemed as though her death had been an inevitable thing that he couldn't keep away; a boulder intent on rolling down a hill. He knew that was just his grieving, irrational mind embellishing his memories, but . . . the notion nagged at him nonetheless.

He needed a good place to sulk. Looking up from his reverie, he found himself standing near the west gate of the Palace, where four men were busily clearing debris from the sky attack yesterday. Kaen could only wonder what these poor people thought of the attack, those who knew nothing about Gaea, only a sudden warning that strange invaders were coming from above.

He himself did not understand the technology they had, of course, nor anything of what Gaea was like. They had dragged the wrecked ships, five in total, to an off-limits area where scholars from the Palace were examining them. He had a feeling the ignoramuses wouldn't find anything to work from.

Gaea, my mother's land, the sword whispered in his mind. *An evil place. Full of evil beings, though not as dangerous as those who dwell on Luna.*

"Luna?" Kaen muttered. He'd never heard that word before . . . no, perhaps the sword had mentioned it once. It said it as though this Luna was another world, a third world.

He must have said the name louder than he meant, because two of the workers looked up at him with quizzical expressions. Seeing the glowing silver sword, and perhaps Kaen's dark expression, they hastily returned to their work.

Yes, the sword replied, *She is my sister, my oldest foe. Luna hungers endlessly, and has since her creation. She drinks the blood of worlds and gives nothing back. Her children pillage Gaea to this day, but they cannot come here. The ancient contract forbids them.*

Kaen felt the hairs on his neck stiffen. So there was more to deal with than just another world? Two? More? Shuddering, he continued down the street with an uncomfortable glance at the workers. Of all the sword's eerie words, these were some of the most disturbing he'd heard yet. *So, who created you?* he asked, lips moving along with the words but creating no sound.

That is . . . a complicated question, Vessel.

Typical. A direct question, and an evasive answer. *'Her children,' huh?*

"Kaen, we need to talk," came a feminine voice from behind him. He started as though waking from a dream. Lifting his chin from the heel of his hand, he turned to see Lyn approaching from behind. How had she found him here? He was at the back of the eastern Palace gardens, sitting on a low bench. Somewhere he'd neither expected nor wanted to be found.

"What is it, Lyn?" he asked tiredly.

"What do you mean, 'what?'" She came over and plunked herself down beside him, causing the wood-and-silver bench to shudder and creak. "Oops. Look, you've been avoiding me since the battle yesterday. We haven't gotten to talk at all, and . . . I need to at least offer you a sincere apology."

"For what?" He knew full well, but didn't feel like being terribly agreeable right now.

"For getting Mandrie killed," she said frankly. "I allowed that attack to happen. I drew the enemy to Nytaea. And I-I'm sorry for being so reckless." She bit her lip, blinking more than usual. However blunt, the words hadn't been easy for her.

Kaen nodded absently. "Thanks." He meant it, even if it might not sound like it. Her apology seemed heartfelt, and should have made him feel a bit better. It just . . . didn't. A few words couldn't bring back his sister's smiling face. "It's good to see you again, Lyn. I'm glad. That you returned." He really meant the words to sound a bit more enthusiastic. But there was only so much effort he could muster.

"Kaen. Please look at me."

Why did people keep saying that to him lately? He jerked his gaze up to meet hers, taking in her worried expression, her pale skin tinged a shade darker since her trip to Gaea; her straight, silver hair, tied back into a longer ponytail than ever. It reached past her waist now. And he certainly didn't recall her body looking so mature, her shoulders so well-muscled, nor the complex spiderweb of veins bulging at the skin of her arms and neck. She lacked Mydia's quiet beauty and refined elegance, yet Kaen had never felt more . . . attracted to her. In a way. It felt wrong to admit it to himself.

"Kaen?" she asked.

He glanced down once more, cheeks feeling hot. He never blushed. Well, rarely. *Stupid man, stupid boy!* he scolded himself. *She's practically your sister!*

Desire, whispered the sword. *Embarrassment. Indecision. You are struggling, Vessel.*

He gritted his teeth and turned farther away from Lyn, crossing his arms.

In his mind, he cursed the sword and its stubborn persistence. It cursed right back, but in its own serene, implacable manner.

"Hey!" Lyn reached out and punched his shoulder. She probably meant it as only a light tap, but it hurt, causing him to jump and snarl at her. "What is going on with you right now?" she demanded.

He glared, rubbing his shoulder. He could swear her fist weighed as much as a coppersmith's anvil. "Nothing," he hedged. "I'm fine! Why can't anyone just leave me alone?"

"Kaen, you're being ridiculous. We haven't seen each other in months. I almost died on Gaea, and the whole time I thought for sure you were all dead. I was so relieved to see you were still alive."

Something seemed to twist in Kaen's stomach, and he couldn't tell if it was a good or bad sign. "And then Mandrie died."

"I just said I'm sorry. I really am!" Her face was a mask of convincing pain. Her sincerity was obvious, and it made him feel weak for not accepting it. "Is it the sword?" she asked. "Mydia said it talks to you. Is that true?"

"It's not the sword!" he growled, gripping the hilt tighter in his left palm. It was pointed blade-first into the ground, and now pulsed with white light as he made his objection.

Lyn's eyes widened. "Easy, Kaen. Look, I don't know how you came upon it, nor what it is . . . but I think I can understand. I-I have voices that talk to me as well."

He relaxed, giving her a skeptical stare. "You do. You have voices that talk to you."

She nodded, giving a brief, uncertain smile. "Did I ever tell you about the dreams I used to have back on Mani?"

He shook his head. "Only a couple; nothing too strange." How much had she kept from him, anyway?

"Whenever I would use a lot of my strength, I would dream of a girl who showed me these visions. Eventually, I realized they were memories. It's actually a Hellebes trait I inherited from my mother."

Curiosity got the better of Kaen, and he found himself sitting up, listening to her intently. "So you can't forget."

She nodded. "Mm-hmm. But I didn't know it at the time. Anyway, I joined a rebel militia called the Red Horizon. They broke me out of prison and . . . it's a long story, but I came to realize my goal would be to try to retrieve my mother's memories. It's complicated, but Hellebes keep their memories in a personal Vault, a special part of their mind. From there, all information they—we—take in can be retrieved and even passed on directly in the right circumstances. It's the reason I was able to master their language so quickly."

Kaen nodded pensively, a nod that did not reflect his struggle to make sense of the words. A special place in the mind? It sounded ridiculous. "So your mother was someone special."

"She was . . . yes, quite important. We ended up finding the laboratory where she had left her memories, and I was able to retrieve them. At a heavy cost." She paused, for reasons he couldn't place other than the haunted look that crossed her face. "Now . . . I have her knowledge and experiences in the back of my mind. I can't access them all the time, and I don't know if I can at all on this world, but it's like—like I'm actually talking to her!"

Kaen gave a low, thoughtful grunt. "That sounds . . . interesting. Not very similar, though. This sword is more like an annoying pest. It says it draws from my emotions, but I swear it's the other way around—it effects them."

Lyn frowned. "I see. That makes a lot more sense. What is it called?"

He hesitated. "It calls itself the Heart of Mani."

She stared at the blade, mouthing the words. "And you said you found this where?"

City of Magic

Lady Lieda picked at her fingernails. "So, let me get this straight—that white-haired ratling came back to Mani in a flying vehicle, and then some other flying vehicles swooped down from the sky, killed some citizens, and destroyed the city? That's all?"

"Not . . . the whole city," Zama said from his cell across from hers. His was two doors down, situated so that they could only see one another if they both came to the front of their cells—but of course she didn't want to see his hideous face ever again if she could help it. Rather, she sat on her cot, leg crossed in her brown bedsheet of a dress they'd given her. It was humiliating, being cooped up in here, but she could bide her time, and she could look like a lady while doing it.

If what the buffoon had heard from the guards was the true, then it would certainly explain yesterday's tumult of voices and explosions in the city. Ordinary townsfolk didn't make that kind of disturbance. Today, beyond the drip-drip of water in the back corner of her cell and the coughing of an unknown prisoner far down the hallway, she could make out the chipping of hammers on stone from outside. Perhaps the sound of men laboring to repair the city. Had the Palace itself been struck? She wouldn't have minded a heavy blow to, say, the back wall of her cell.

"Personally," the once-regent continued from his cell, as though she was still listening, "I don't know what to think. If this girl is truly back in the flesh, then Archlord Domon will be back before long to deal with her, along with the rest of these insurgents."

Lieda could swear the man's voice only got more boring with each passing day in jail. She'd hate to see what he looked like now. Playing along as his seductive wife had barely been worth the energy. She certainly wouldn't bat an eye when Domon came back and decapitated him. Well, she wouldn't *watch*, of course, but she'd keep her tears in check.

She did not grace Zama with a response. He would either carry on or shut up, with or without a response from her. She picked at her right thumbnail, dislodging a particularly stubborn grain of Sol knew what and flicking it away. It was hard to keep a level of grime from getting on her in this murky, filthy dungeon. She could feel it building up on her skin, powerless to wash it. Truth be told, this was almost a forgotten place nowadays, as her last husband, Edrius Kalceron, had made it more and more a practice to either ignore crime or punish it with swift death. (Zama, of course, had leaned heavily toward the former.)

Crime, that is, or whatever Edrius saw fit to label as such. She had done her fair share of the dirty work, although in her case it was always clean and tidy. She liked to kill with a single jolt, usually in as unexpected a way as possible. She detested blood, but watching the expression left on a face as her prey died in pain-laced shock was truly delectable.

Switching to her other hand, Lieda contemplated how many more men she would have to go through to get what she wanted. Domon still kept her on the Umbra Council, so he hadn't lost faith in her. From his favorite mistress, to his useful, cunning assassin, to his gift to Kalceron, and now to being Zama's fluff-headed seductress, she'd played all the parts. Oh, there was the matter of that vile Eivael, whom she'd had to kill off. That had been a personal vendetta. Now . . .

If she was being honest, which was something she tried not to do, she still had two goals. One of those was to kill Mydia Kalceron in the most painful way possible, and the other . . . Well, the next Umbra meeting should be soon. She'd see how that one was coming along.

⁂

Captain Zent paced the stone halls of the Nytaean Palace, head bowed and hands clasped behind his back. Servants and noblemen who passed by—mostly women, actually—gave him curious glances, and he tried to be courteous by dipping his head, not saying a word. All their speech was like a madman's babbling. He might as well be a child let out of the biomanufactories in the fourth or fifth stage—unable to decipher the words. He had picked up a few key words from Lyn, but only insofar as the Hellebes tongue did not have a counterpart, such as Nytaea, magic or mage, or words whose equivalents she didn't yet know. Slowly, he'd build an index in his Vault until he could speak half-fluently. Lyn said the grammar was similar.

All that to say he'd never been so uncomfortable in his life. Was this how Kallyn had felt on Gaea fifteen years ago? Lyn had possessed a basis to work from, using memories of her mother's speech from her childhood.

A door creaked open, and Zent turned to see Lyn striding into the foyer, from which stretched the hallway he was pacing. "Ah, Lyn!" He tried not to let on *quite* how relieved he was to see her.

She began to respond, and then stopped herself, apparently having started out with a common Legaleian greeting. "Hey, Zent," she said in Hellebes. "I think Rhidea is ready to meet with us."

"Then I'll follow you." He allowed her to lead the way, and they ascended a large, curved staircase to the second floor. As they walked, he remarked, "This architecture really is something. I never expected to see such marvelous work from a culture so . . . ancient." He almost said *backward,* but he caught himself.

The Heiress laughed. "Ancient. I've never thought of it that way. These halls were built some few hundred years before my time, and yet, growing up here in Nytaea . . . all right, I was an orphan off the street, so this was extravagant to me. But not ancient."

Zent nodded absently, and then in approval as they passed a tall set of ornate silver armor standing up along the wall, matching a set two meters to its right. Such exquisite workmanship. He supposed if one had magical powers, perhaps it was easier to create such works of art. Still, it baffled him. No engineering department, no computer design programs, no power tools, no heavy machinery . . . yet this entire palace, a silver-and-alabaster marvel, stood tall. The blasts from the invading fleet had only effected minor external damages, save for the large doorway near the front gate where an entire vessel had crashed into it.

He had seen the magics of these magi firsthand the day before, when they struck out at the invading fleet with lightning and large fireballs. With instruction on the weaknesses of Gaean military craft, they could be more effective, but that one woman, that single, flame-haired woman Rhidea . . . Lyn had been telling the truth when she boasted of her powers. Seeing those pillars of silver snake forth from the earth and spear ships out of the sky had been nothing short of jaw-dropping. She was like Mani's equivalent of the Mother.

Soon, they came to a set of ornately-carved oaken doors. Lyn knocked, announced herself, and was admitted into the meeting room by a royal attendant, the woman he had seen briefly yesterday. Keuda? Apparently, she was an official who had stayed on since the administration of the dreaded Lord Kalceron, whom Lyn had described as a monster and a tyrant. A . . . familiar description.

A long meeting table was overlooked by windows on either side. Ornate curtains and crown molding surrounded the windows, which let in the rippling light of the unearthly auroras. Around the table sat the mage Rhidea, Queen Mydia—her two bodyguards leaning against the back wall behind her protectively—the young man named Kaen who possessed that queer silver sword, and a few others Zent did not recognize. One was a small boy with sandy hair, who sat kicking his feet back and forth next to a quiet man in a multilayered cloak and leggings, silent as a bird of prey. Had Zent not been far larger than the man, he would have found him intimidating. Rhidea greeted Lyn and Zent in that strange, rolling tongue of the Legaleians, and Lyn gestured to an open seat, taking the one beside it.

Zent inspected the chair dubiously before sitting down. The frame was molded from pure silver, and held his great weight with only a slight creak. Nothing seemed to weigh much here on this world anyway, not even him. "You are to be the interpreter, yes?" he asked Lyn as he sat down.

She nodded and spoke something to the queen, who raised her voice over the murmur of small talk and spoke. Lyn translated the words for Zent: "Please welcome our honored guest, Captain Zent of Gaea."

The introduction brought on various responses from the room's occupants, some less than pleased. Lyn came to his defense with a sharp rebuttal, repeating to him, "I told them you came with me, and you helped fend off the enemy forces."

Rhidea asked a question, and Lyn repeated in Hellebes, "Zent, do you swear that you mean us no harm?"

He nodded. "I swear."

Lyn repeated his words, adding something that included the name Kallyn Kalceron. Presumably, that the two had known each other on Gaea.

The room hushed. Evidently, this was news for some of them. The looks exchanged by the ring of faces, followed by a swarm of questions, showed that they were coming to grips with the fact that Lyn was Queen Mydia's niece. The queen did not look shaken by the revelation, so she must have already known.

After the ensuing question-and-answer session, Rhidea said, "As fascinating as this introduction has been, we must move on. What of these flying ships from Gaea? You say they are newly invented, and there are not yet many of them?"

Zent tipped his head from side to side. "Most of the technology has been around for long enough. The leaders of Gaea, called the Senate, could have invaded Mani already had it not been for the powerful Energy Field that surrounds the planet. They recently discovered a way to bypass it, and now that one ship has returned and reported the news of the attack, the senate can begin to replicate their space-faring design for a large-scale invasion."

Lyn repeated his words easily after he was done, using her newfound memory capability, apparently adding in necessary details for the rulers. He couldn't say what terminology they may or may not understand on Mani. From here, the meeting centered on the capabilities of the attack ships and how Mani could defend against them. Zent and Lyn explained that most or all Hellebes machinery would never be sustainable on Mani, and that, just as

Mani had its own magical energy that could be manipulated to great effect via Coaction, Gaea's planetary energy fueled almost everything the Hellebes did. Away from Gaea, they were limited to what their batteries could hold.

Through Lyn's interpretation, Zent began to understand a bit more about the workings of this small country of Nytaea. The people were not primitive so much as old-fashioned and lacking in technological impetus. As much as they did not understand the workings of Gaea, he found it hard to wrap his mind around the same number of details about Mani and the workings thereof—even with the use of his Memory Vault.

By the end of the meeting, he was mentally exhausted, though grateful to Lyn for acting as mediator and translator. She was no longer merely the only female with Hellebes blood—she was the sole living person, Gaean or Manese, who could speak both languages and thus interpret. He would have to find some way to get her to share her knowledge of the language directly, or better yet, upload it to a database back at HQ for future knowledge. If she was willing.

Before anyone left the meeting, Zent was personally introduced to all present, including Oliver and Kymhar, the two that had stuck out to him as odd. They were apparently a part of Lyn's original team of six who had traversed the entire broken globe of Mani to get her to Gaea. Though he needed an explanation of what this "Down Under" place was. The way Lyn translated the name, it sounded almost silly.

Then a few of the minor dignitaries headed out, those who were there for the strategic discussion only, and Mydia even made her guardsmen leave. They hung around right outside the doors, however. He smiled at their loyalty.

Left were Rhidea, Mydia, Lyn, Oliver and Kymhar. The young man Kaen tried to leave, but they insisted he stay. "Now," said Rhidea to the Mother Heiress, "I'd like to hear what actually happened to you after the Gate was destroyed, and I'm sure the two of you are eager to hear of the Down Under as well."

Gaea

β Chapter 012 β

From the Vixen's Mouth

Mydia watched the towering man leave, filing out the door behind Lyn and seeming to duck on instinct in the doorway despite having enough headroom. A giant, a monster, and yet . . . why was he so handsome? It didn't seem fair, particularly not to Kaen, who . . . oh, he was already gone. Teli and Julia could poke her all they wanted about the boy, but this foreign mountain of a man was *far* out of the question. Soon, Mydia was alone save for Cae Rhidea. Her friend, tutor and advisor. She tried not to let the strange emotions bleed through from her mind to her face. She wasn't really so concerned with the way men looked, was she?

Besides, she vaguely recalled something in the story from Gaea about it being a world of all men, men who were incapable of reproducing. *Oh, Mydia, you fool*, she chided herself.

"Dear, what are you reminiscing about?" Rhidea asked in a light voice.

Mydia gave a small squeak—a very small one—and turned to face the tall woman, who had risen from her chair and begun to stretch her arms. "Nothing in particular. I was enjoying my small reprieve from the watchful eye of my guards." She said the words loud enough to be certain they heard it from outside the doors, eliciting a chuckle from her mentor.

"Forget I said anything, then," the mage said.

"Oh, now we need to go and make copies of those missives, do we not?" Mydia said with a sigh. Rhidea nodded in response. They had decided to send out letters to all the villages of Nytaea, as well as riskier letters to the bordering city-states who still belonged to the empire of Kystrea—letters explaining the attack on Nytaea and the necessity of banding together to prepare to counter the Gaean threat. King Fenwel was first on the list, and if she recalled correctly, the Wandering Mage had already contacted the scholars at Randhorn castle. When the Hellebes came again, they would not strike Nytaea first. They would swoop down upon the unpredicting nations and capture or level them in a blink. Furthermore . . .

"What of the new world?" Mydia asked, referring to the far continent of Darsor. Archlord Domon had marched to the Sky Islands and demanded passage for his troops to the far side, taking control of the port city that stood on the near shore. Though Nytaea was still a fledgling nation recovering from Domon's black grip, it would be necessary to get word out somehow to the new world.

"Darsor is the most likely first target of the Hellebes," Rhidea said. "None can say for certain when they will attack again, but more than likely Domon will be in for a large surprise as his new kingdom is swept from his grasp."

"Assuming he has a kingdom over there," Mydia mumbled. The man was insane, and had shown extreme recklessness in his recent exploits. However, he likely had some manner of intelligence stationed in Nytaea and the surrounding lands with a way to funnel information back to him via Reality magi.

Nytaea, Mydia's beloved city-state, was the largest weight bearing down on her mind ever since they came and wrested power back from Mydia's stepmother and her newest husband two months back. It had been better under her father's rule, as much as it pained her to admit it. Since then, she'd worked tirelessly with staff both new and old—most of whom accepted her willingly as their ruler—to right the wrongs in this city and get it back on course. It was no quick process, and now they had one more source of damage to fix—not to mention an impending war of worlds to prepare for.

Bart and Gaela, the government representatives of the people appointed following the fall of her father's regime, had been the first in Zama's culling. He'd left Ethas Gandel, Mydia's regent, as a sign to the commoners that noblemen were superior. Mydia had quickly sprung him from the dungeons and appointed him permanently as her second.

One thing Mydia kept in place that Zama had started was an effort to double down on military and train women fighters in addition to men. Of course, the first thing they had done was command all troops to bow the knee to the queen or flee the kingdom. She wasn't about to kill Domon's loyal troops just for being too afraid to disobey him. But they did need soldiers. Mage soldier training had continued as well, in conjunction with Master Gendric's famed Mage Academy, though they had entirely removed the conscription system set in place originally by her father.

They would have to meet again soon to decide what immediate actions to take, since Zent and Lyn both had to return to Gaea before long. Mydia knew her friend would not be willing to stay no matter how much they insisted. With a sigh, the queen got up from her seat and left the council room, greeting her guards at the door and checking with Keuda, who stood dutifully by, waiting to ensure the letters would be written up and sent out promptly.

Being a queen was exhausting work.

A quarter of an hour later, Mydia found herself down in the dungeon with her two guards and Kaen, whom she had coaxed to come with her. Not only would his presence help to ease the anxiety she felt around her old stepmother, but it would do him good to stay occupied in these times following his sister's death.

They passed right by Zama's cell. He sat up, calling out to them, but received only a rude reply from one of her guards. Mydia didn't bother to reprimand the soldier. Stopping at Lieda's cell, Mydia looked in on the wretched feline. She sat lazily upon her cot, arms crossed, black hair in knots, bearing the distinctive look of a woman trying to ignore her humiliation using the fine art of delusion. Such behavior defined the woman to her core. Mydia's disgust for the woman was less than hatred—yet also far more—but she could palpably feel the malice that poured from her.

Lieda looked up with something between a smirk and a disgusted grimace on her foxy face. "Why, hello there, darling," she said in a mocking voice.

"Hold your tongue, witch!" Kaen snarled, stepping toward the bars with a hand at his sword belt, where his silver sword was sheathed for a change.

Mydia laid a hand on his shoulder. "Don't let her get to you, Kaen. Lieda, I need some answers. I know you still have a connection to the Archlord."

The woman twitched as she said it, showing that she'd struck a dissonant chord. She recovered immediately, transitioning smoothly to sit cross-legged facing the party, probably to try and show as much leg as possible to the men present. Mydia couldn't help but notice with faint amusement how much leg hair was growing back now that she had no access to a razor. Her face was missing its usual multilayered makeup as well, and Mydia couldn't say if that helped or hurt her looks. Probably hurt.

"Domon and I have not spoken for years, my dear." Lieda's voice dripped with condescension. Never in a thousand years would the woman refer to her stepdaughter by her true title, as that meant admitting that Mydia had made it all the way to the throne despite her best efforts.

"And I should believe you because . . . why?" Mydia asked in her best impression of Rhidea.

Lieda smiled. "Because I have nothing to gain here in this drippy, grungy old cell."

"And nothing to lose. Except your life, of course. I'm sure Kaen would be more than happy to put you out of your misery if I let you out of that cell." Despite her quickly-beating heart and the slight tremor in her voice, Mydia was surprised at how cold and level she was able to be with this woman. Of course, she could not let him do that, as that would contradict the law. When dealing with dangerous animals, one had to respond in the appropriate manner.

Kaen fingered his sword's hilt. "More than happy," he affirmed.

Lieda said nothing, only stared at Kaen's sword with pursed lips. "That blade. Where did you get it, boy?"

"This?" Kaen made to draw the sword, probably to intimidate the ex-queen, but Mydia stopped him.

"Don't," she said. "Don't play her games. Lieda, you really are a hair's breadth from execution. Don't make me bring a bad report back to those who'd like to see you dead."

"As though you weren't chief among them?" the woman retorted with a chuckle.

Mydia tilted her head to one side. "I wouldn't say that. I'm not a killer like you, but I do find you distasteful and sickening, and I know full well that you deserve to hang. So yes, I'd feel a lot better if you were dead."

Lieda's eyes widened as though hurt by the harsh words. "My, my. And that from Eivael's precious little girl."

Mydia waited a moment, composing her thoughts and breathing deeply, slowly, before saying, "I know about the Umbra Council."

Lieda froze, flicking her eyes back and forth between the queen and Kaen. Making a small, likely subconscious lip-chewing motion, she said, "And?"

"And I know you must have some usefulness to Domon, or else he wouldn't have kept you around so long. What if I began penning some stories to put into the hands of the common people, exposing a bit of your history?" It was mostly a bluff, as all Mydia knew was that Lieda had been on the Umbra Council at some point, along with her own father Edrius, and had worked for Domon before that. That she remained on the Council had been a lucky guess.

"What do you want to know?" Lieda asked coldly. All pretense of guile and mockery was gone.

Mydia smiled. If there was one thing she knew about the fox, it was that her self-image was perhaps the most important thing in the world to her. "I want to know what Domon's plans are."

A Call to Action

Following the meeting, Cae Rhidea waited for an opportune moment to catch up with Kaen. She reached out with her Silver magic, slowing his walk just enough to tip him off to something strange. He turned with a frown, and she strode up, face neutral. She'd made it out here to the front gate of the Palace just in time to catch him up, and the lack of foot traffic made it all the better.

"What?" he demanded.

"Relax, child. I haven't gotten a chance to talk to you since the funeral. How fare you?"

"I don't need your sympathy. Enough people have already given me their condolences, and none of them are going to bring back Mandrie from the dead."

"No, they're not." Rhidea stopped beside him. "But how *are* you?"

"Managing. The sword says you annoy him."

She raised her eyebrows. *Him?* "Oh? Well, tell it the feeling is mutual." Clapping the boy on the shoulder, she said, "Chin up, child. We're all in this together. It will be a long and jagged road from here on out, and there's no telling who you may lose along the way when the war comes. Do not lose sight of what remains to you. Lyn won't be here much longer. And neither, perhaps, will you."

He looked down, Adam's apple bobbing. With a sigh, he said, "I know. I don't mean to treat everyone like garbage, it just . . . comes out. I want to run away and leave all this nonsense behind. And yet . . . I feel restless. Like I need to do something to help, but I don't know what."

Rhidea nodded slowly. "Good. That's a good sign. Soon, we will have to put together our plan of action. Until then, do some thinking. Do not forget that you have friends around you."

She left him to himself, heading back to her study to plan. As necessary as discussion was, she needed time to personally assemble the information she had and plot the next step for the people she needed to keep alive . . . alive, afloat and one step ahead. Right now, it was Nytaea . . . and the world. That fool Domon could not be allowed to let it slip in his efforts to avoid that exact thing.

Arrogant? Perhaps. But much was at stake.

Small steps.

She reached the ornate oaken door to her study and entered, lighting the wall lamps with a small snap of her fingers. She didn't need the motion; it was merely a physical sign to go along with her Authority's direction, but she had done such things since time out of mind. The lamps lit up a familiar, cozy den kept for her since before Kalceron ever took office. No ruler had dared touch it, not even Domon and his little henchman, Zama . . . she really wasn't sure why, but they had left it well enough alone. All the better, as few places in the world felt more like home to her.

Rhidea had many homes, and she had none.

Sitting down at her desk, she brushed back her long crimson hair and took a deep breath. She would meet with the leaders of Nytaea tomorrow morning to discuss their next move. The people were already growing restless and needed an answer, not to mention the surrounding leaders who would actually listen—they'd demand to know what Nytaea would do about the alien forces.

Speaking of which . . . pulling out a stack of parchment and dipping her quill pen in ink, she got to work. She began skimming through notes she'd taken since their arrival in the city, mostly on the plans of Domon and the movements of his forces. They had multiple avenues of intelligence lined up in nearby countries, keeping tabs on political shiftings and opinions regarding Domon—his insane conquest, and his lengthy leave of absence from the continent of Argent.

As she went to jot down a new note, however, something stopped her: A shudder, a tremor. She immediately froze and listened, glancing around the room, trying to ascertain whether it had come from her own self or something around her. It felt . . . odd.

A voice breathed out of nowhere, speaking directly into her mind: *Soul of Silver.*

She didn't move, only waited to see if the voice would persist.

Awake, Soul of Silver. Answer, daughter.

Rhidea narrowed her eyes. *Mani?*

She received an impression of quiet pleasure, like a smile. *The very same. Long has it been, my daughter. How long, since the blood of silver was left to you alone? Since the black soul attempted to cut off my touch from mankind forever?*

Two centuries. Why come to me now? You already chose your Vessel.

Only because you have pushed me away indefinitely, Soul of Silver. You know that. But time grows short . . . and now a greater threat arises.

Gaea?

Nay. I fear not Gaea, nor her legions, but the one who seeks to bind me and use me as a shield. The black soul.

Domon. What *was* that imp up to? *You are truly frightened of him?* she asked Mani.

There was a slight hesitation, and then, *In a way. He seeks to bind me into an agreement and take my power as his own. I fear that I may have no choice.*

Rhidea shivered. *What are you saying, then?*

You must do your part to right the balance he has thrown askew, and to turn back the abominations he has set in motion. Already, he has destroyed the bridge between worlds, and he will go farther, running blindly to a cliff, expecting me to give him the power to fix it.

I am already working on it, she replied. *If need be, I will personally see to him. What about the boy, Kaen? So far, all you have been doing is tormenting him. How will that lead to anything good?*

We are done with this conversation, daughter. Know that if you do not deal with the black soul, I will take measures in order to protect the power vested in me.

The voice left. Rhidea could tell that Mani had not simply stopped speaking, but had withdrawn from her consciousness altogether. She breathed out a sigh of relief. She wouldn't have expected the exchange to be quite so . . . stressful. Over the last two centuries, she had nearly forgotten the voice of Mani, until awakening from her coma a month back to find that the Heart of Mani, that cursed sword, had sought out Kaen in her place. Would she have had the strength of will to resist its call? Now, it seemed that the spirit of Silver itself had somehow found a way to sneak inside her mind.

The boy made out the voice inhabiting his sword to be an almost mindless will, though he seemed to hold increasingly in-depth silent conversations with Mani. Was the entity growing more sentient? What was he scheming?

Later that night, Rhidea was working in her study when a knock came at her door—originating from none other than Lyn.

"Hello, child," she greeted the tall girl with a brief glance upward. "Enjoying your visit to Mani?"

There was a short but uncomfortable silence, then Lyn cleared her throat. "Yes, yes, it's good to be back. Just . . . troubling."

The High Mage looked up, face softening. Perhaps she hadn't realized how stressed she was. No need to push that stress onto others. "You have something on your mind. Please, sit down." The High Mage gestured to a seat, and Lyn took it gingerly.

After a long breath in, the silver-haired maiden began: "Rhidea, you knew my father. Prince Kallyn. You two were close, right?"

"Indeed. Eivael too was a good friend."

"And—and that's not all. You knew my mother as well. Or at least you met."

Rhidea eyed the white-haired girl. "That I did. Once, and briefly. Perhaps I should have told you. When she stumbled into this city fourteen years ago, clutching that baby, I didn't know what to think. I tried to talk with her, of course, but—" she laughed suddenly "—well, you can imagine how that went. So instead, I tried to show her to the Palace, to get her to talk to Eivael. I had only a sneaking suspicion of who this otherworldly woman was, but . . . she wouldn't listen. But then she said his name: Kallyn. And Nytaea. When she saw I recognized his name, she handed me a letter that I still keep in my desk. Here."

Rhidea fished around in a drawer and took out her prized note, fingering it briefly before handing it to Lyn. "You can have it. In the end . . . I wasn't able to get through to her, and she took off, spooked by the Palace guards."

"She brought me to Lentha's orphanage," Lyn said softly. "I remembered it when I started getting my memories back. I must . . . I must have been asleep until then. Thank you, Rhidea." She looked down at the note, eyes roving it hungrily.

Rhidea watched her face, awaiting her reaction. She saw the tears glisten in those implacable eyes. The girl kept staring at the paper as though it would speak to her, and then she lurched up from her chair, rushing over to put her arms around Rhidea.

"There, there." Rhidea stroked her mane of hair. "Pull yourself together, child."

After a long moment, the girl did, retracting from the embrace. "Thank you," she said again. "I . . . I think I'll be going."

Rhidea nodded and watched her leave. Then a smile sprung to her face, one that lingered throughout the evening.

β Chapter 014 β

Farewells

Phoebe waited in the Palace courtyard, pacing back and forth. Soon, she saw Lyn, Zent and Kaen emerging from the Palace, and grinned in relief. A fleeting expression, more instinctive than genuine. Lyn would be leaving, and Kaen as well, one way or another.

"Sorry we took so long," Lyn said.

"So, this is goodbye?" Phoebe asked. "Who's going with you?"

"Well . . ." Lyn glanced behind her, as though expecting someone. "More than we can carry in our vessel. It only seats two, but we can cram in three since I'm not as large as most Hellebes. Oliver will come with us, and we'll take a Reality Stone for Rhidea and Kaen to follow."

"And Kymhar," said Kaen. "We've all got a score to settle with the Archlord."

"Oliver wanted to come with us to Gaea," Lyn added to Phoebe. "But Rhidea said no. Mydia, of course, has to run the kingdom, so she stays. Oh, here she comes now."

Zent simply watched the conversation in mild fascination, as Lyn did not interpret it. How was the man *so* tall?

Phoebe looked and saw the queen coming with a procession of guardsmen and well-wishers, as well as Rhidea, Kymhar and Oliver. Hugs, handshakes and much sappiness followed, with Phoebe staying out of the latter as much as possible.

"I'll miss you, Lyn," Mydia said as she embraced her friend.

Zent surprised them by bowing to Mydia and saying in the Legaleian tongue, "Goodbye."

Before Phoebe's eyebrows had a chance to lower, he turned to her and laid a massive hand on her shoulder. "Goodbye." Looking into his eyes, she saw a moment of connection, but he briskly turned away and started toward the metal vessel with Lyn and Oliver. The blond boy looked perhaps more excited than Phoebe had ever seen him. She certainly saw no reason to be so enthused, and flying in a strange vessel across the open air didn't appeal to her, but she supposed when one's whole life revolved around flying, such a prospect appeared far grander.

And then they departed in the ship. Its propulsion devices rotated and began to blast hot air at the ground, propelling it into the air. Phoebe had to take a few steps back, along with other onlookers. Soon, the ship streaked across the sky and was gone over the city wall. Just like a bird.

Phoebe looked to Kaen. "I guess you'll be leaving soon as well?"

He nodded and pulled her into a side embrace. "I'll be back, Pheebs. We all will at some point."

"But let me guess, you can't say when."

He shook his head.

Phoebe sighed. *More waiting, then.*

⁂

Oliver could remember flying on another occasion with Lyn. Once again, they were smushed closely together. Why did he always get stuck with a smelly girl? Perhaps it was fate. They barely fit, crammed between the walls and glass canopy of the shuttle, ignoring the safety straps entirely.

This time was far different from the glider, however—they were *flying*. He couldn't stop staring out the glass, watching the land far below as it streamed past in a blur. When that got boring—well, slightly so—he stared around the cabin, trying to guess what all the instruments did. If only he got to go all the way to Gaea . . . He could only dream. One day, one day he would.

He'd tried to get them to let him at least go back to Darsor, but they hadn't even batted an eye as they swatted him down. The Sky Islands would suffice, and it wasn't without a purpose that he was returning. It had been a while since he'd seen his Uncle Ben, not to mention he would get to be with his mum and dad again. Maybe they would talk Rhidea back to her senses.

Lyn and the big man, Zent, conversed back and forth in that funny language of his as they flew. How had she picked it up so fast? He still couldn't picture this other world at all, despite having heard snippets here and there describing it. And she was some kind of . . . goddess there? Or something? He could picture that, but not really any of the other stuff. He would like to watch the giant, burly men spar and throw one another around with superhuman strength, however. Lyn had fascinated him with her stories of their martial arts. That would be great fun. Right swell.

"Well, kid," Lyn said as they neared the shore of the Sea of Emptiness. Randhorn Castle was visible through the window. "We're almost there. Let's make this quick and get going before too many townsfolk gather to gawk."

❧ ❦

"They reached Redufiel already?" Kaen asked.

"Quite so. Let us be on our way." The Wandering Mage held out her hands.

Kaen took one hand while Kymhar held onto her other. Mydia gave him one last smile, saying, "See you all again."

"We'll contact you as soon as we can," Rhidea said, working her Reality Authority. A wave pulsed through Kaen and the air around them, once, twice, and then . . .

They were standing on the far continent. Kaen couldn't recognize the location specifically, but the grass and foliage looked familiar. They were on a hill surrounded by trees, and there on the southern horizon stood the city that must be Redufiel, square and walled in wood. The Darsorians liked their wood, and they had plenty to build with.

"You made it!" Lyn's voice came from behind them, and Kaen turned to see both her and Zent standing in the grey grass. The ship was farther down the hill. "Have to say, I had my doubts that it would work so simply."

"You should know better than to doubt the lady," said Kaen.

Lyn laughed as though remembering an old joke, but Kaen couldn't see what was so funny.

"Now, let's see what we're up against," Rhidea said, surveying the distant city. "Oh dear, that is a mess."

"Are you sure you can—" Lyn began, but Rhidea held up a hand, cutting her off.

"Fear not, we can manage. Kymhar and I, that is."

Kaen stiffened at the assassin's name. "But you said—"

"I said Domon must be stopped. I think you know as well as I that you are simply not a good fit, not in this vengeful state. I can't let you near Domon, lest you compromise the entire mission. Did you not say you wished to see Gaea?"

Kaen glared down at the ground. He'd known that she wished to send him with Lyn, but she had given no definite answer. Looking down at the sword at his belt, he thought of what the journey to another planet might do to it—to his connection with it. Something clicked into place, and he realized that she probably counted on it losing connection with Mani. She was trying to help, just like the others. Grinding his teeth in frustration, he resorted to a curt nod. He wasn't going to get his way, and she had a point. He would . . . go with Lyn.

Glaring at his friend, he asked, "How much room is in that ship?"

She glanced sidelong at the vessel. "Ah . . ."

❧⋆☙

End of Part Two

α   PART THREE   α

A

Factions

Gaea

α   Chapter 25   α

A Tactical Retreat

Aidor 4, 1296:

I don't know why I still keep this diary. But today . . . today, I especially felt like making an entry, for it seems I have forgotten my past, as though I awoke only today from a dream. A nightmare it was, of proportions so unimaginable that I fell into a trance and pretended it was a mere dream that would pass when I woke. But I shall never wake until the day I die. The Anier took everything from me, and now they are stealing the world out from under the entire human race. If they carry through with their plan . . . I can but imagine what human existence will look like. Of course . . . first, one must define human.

— From Lhinde's Diary

We arrived back on Gaea after another strange flight through that sea of emptiness—the true one called space, where infinite stars watched us. Kaen, for his part, was distracted from his moodiness by the jaw-dropping sights. The only thing hampering the flight was that it was even more cramped than with Oliver beside me.

No sooner did we pierce Gaea's atmosphere than Zent radioed HQ, trying multiple times before getting the signal to speak with them. I had my own headset—not Kaen, who wouldn't have been able to understand a word anyway—so I was able to hear the conversation:

"We're back in the atmosphere," Zent told them. "We should be arriving at base in a half hour." He'd taken us down nearer the base than where we had exited last time.

"And I trust you'll explain your adventures on Mani and why you had to go rushing over there in your shiny spacecraft?" The voice sounded like Getts.

"Yes, sir."

"Then you probably haven't heard—they called off the attack."

"It didn't exactly go as they planned," I muttered. At a confused look from Kaen, I repeated the same in Legaleian.

Zent gave a similar response to mine, receiving a chuckle in reply. "No, that's not it at all. The Cydenges have decided to come out to play."

I felt the hair rise on the back of my neck. *The Cydenges . . .* The mysterious menace about which I still knew next to nothing. Getts made it sound like a significant event. I'd never heard detailed reports of when or why the aliens attacked Gaea. In fact, I'd been denied any details about them save for basic descriptions, and of course that they were frightening and dangerous.

"I see," was all Zent said in reply. He hung up soon after. "You catch all that, Lyn?"

"Mm-hmm."

"It's good for us," he said, "because it will create a distraction we can use, plus it gets the Senate off our backs for a while. Any Cydenges raid usually puts the entirety of Gaea in an emergency state."

"Really? They're that dangerous?"

"Well . . . let's just say, when it snows, it's a blizzard. You never know how many will follow the first ones. They've probably already landed. It's hard to predict a Cydenges invasion. Usually, the first warning you get is the red lights."

"Red . . . lights."

"That's when they land. You'll see them at some point if the raids keep up for a while. Hopefully not too close to HQ, or we'll have to take action. The cities are well protected, but our little base is somewhat more at risk. They're quite nimble in the water. Land or sea, a run-in with a Cydenges is a bad day."

Well, didn't that just make me feel all warm and fuzzy inside?

"What's he going on about, Lyn?" Kaen asked from beside me.

I looked over at him, shifting my weight for the umpteenth time as I tried not to crush him. "Uh . . . neighbor problems. Just an alien race that lives on Luna."

"Lives on where?"

"The other moon. There's Mani and there's Luna, remember?"

Recollection dawned on his face, and he nodded. "But I don't remember you saying anything about people living on it."

"They're not people—they're monsters. I don't know much about them. But apparently, they're attacking Gaea right now, which is good for us, since that draws the Senate's attention away from Mani."

Kaen gave a worried nod. "That's . . . reassuring."

"Lyn," said Zent, catching my attention. "We may have some pursuit before long. Depends how distracted they really are with this Cydenges breakout, but I'd think they were expecting us."

"Roger that." I turned back to Kaen. "You feeling it yet?"

"What's that?"

"Gaea's heavy gravity."

"I . . . uh . . . don't think," he grunted as Zent took us into a dive at Mach speed. "Can't really feel anything past this horrible feeling of getting the guts sucked right out of me."

"That's called G-force," I said. "It's good for you."

We submerged into the ocean, or rather split its surface so quickly that the world suddenly turned a different shade of blue around us, and we were speeding past fish and whales and forests of kelp. Kaen gasped as we broke the ocean's surface, gritting his teeth and squeezing his eyes shut the whole way down, and finally opened them and gaped at the ocean scenery around us.

"So this . . . this is the ocean," he said breathlessly. "So much water. We're *underwater*."

"Yep. Just wait till we get to base."

It wasn't long before Zent put on the brakes, and shortly thereafter, the form of the Red Horizon complex and its shield dome came into view through the murky depths of the sea.

"Oh, no way . . ." Kaen breathed, craning his neck to look past Zent's shoulder. "It's underwater?" As we slowed, however, I could see him beginning to feel the effects of Gaea's powerful gravity as the net pull on his body began to recenter downwards. "Oh, now I see. Ugh, that is . . . heavy."

"You didn't believe me," I said with raised eyebrows.

Presently, Zent took us into the airlock, and we waited as the doors closed and the water was partially pumped out. The engines required to perform the task hummed loudly until the pressure equalized. With a hiss, the pumps released and the far doors opened, revealing the docking bay. We went through the same docking procedures as last time, landing the ship and getting out before an automated crane swung out to take the craft and slot it into an empty bay in the wall.

Kaen struggled to stand, and I reached out a hand to hold him up. He let me, shoving down his pride with a glare that almost seemed embarrassed. "It's going to be rough adjusting," I said. "I honestly can't say if you'll ever be able to handle it."

"Oh, cut it," he snapped. "You're half Legaleian, and a girl to boot, so I can do it too. But . . . great, blithering auroras, this is stronger than I thought."

Zent looked down at the smaller man with a pitying expression. "He's going to have trouble here. His people are weak. But I think I have an idea."

As the first guards arrived, Zent asked for Admiral Skye and Vass, whilst explaining the situation in brief. "Any updates on the Cydenges situation that I need to know about?"

The guard shook his head after a short pause. "None that I've heard, sir. Nice ship, by the way."

Zent grunted. "Thanks."

"And . . . who's this?"

Zent looked down at Kaen. "He's our guest."

"So, you brought a Manese man," Vass said. "I trust you have a good explanation?"

We were standing in the main war council chamber: Vass, Getts, Skye,

Zent and me. Kaen had been sent off to a variable-G room designed for underwater training. I had never spent time there, but apparently some Red Horizon soldiers were trained to use diving gear for various purposes. I hoped the Hellebes soldiers were treating him all right, given that he was unable to speak their language.

"A few reasons," Zent replied to his superior. "I wished to bring back a trusted Manese compatriot of Lynchazel's in order to teach him our language, since we had no time to stay there, and they have no data-recording tech as we have. He is a long-time friend of the Heiress who grew up in the same city, and he also bears a very distinct weapon capable of absorbing energy both magical and Geokinetic."

A few eyebrows went up at that.

"So we're going to use him against the Senate?" Getts asked.

"If we can train him to walk first," Skye muttered. "Better to just take it, maybe see if Dekla can replicate it somehow."

"No," Zent said firmly. "We must observe its effects in the hands of its owner. It is . . . well, I couldn't understand a word anyone was saying on Mani, but Lyn says it is supposedly alive. Made with Mani's oldest magic. I don't think it's a weapon that can be replicated, certainly not with any materials on Gaea, and only he is capable of using it. We will see how quickly and how well we can acclimate Kaen to the gravity and atmospheric pressure here, after which we will go from there."

Admiral Skye crossed his arms with a huff. Vass looked pensive, lips pressed to a thin line.

All this talk made me a bit nervous. Zent was leaving out one big issue: Kaen's unstable temperament of late, and the sword's negative influences in that regard. Not to mention, would it even work here on Gaea? Part of the reason for Kaen's coming here had been to see if the sword's influence would persist or not. If not, then it would likely lose its power as well, but if it did remain even between worlds . . . then I couldn't say where it all might lead. I wasn't sure if his anger would burn hotter against Domon, a world away, or toward the leaders of Gaea—the Senate who ruled from the shadows.

"Very well," Vass said hesitantly. "That is likely the best course of action. Now, regarding the Cydenges attack, I'm sure you know what this means, right?"

"Let me guess, we are going to seize the opportunity and make another aggressive move," Zent said with a sigh. "Even though Musha and nine others of our best soldiers died in the last one."

"Exactly," said Skye. "Because we have no other choice. What else can we do, wait for the Senate to set their sights on Mani once again? I know you don't wish for that."

Nor I . . . But of course, he didn't mention me or my wishes. These rebel leaders hardly wasted a flick of their eyes on me.

Zent said nothing.

"We won't strike immediately," Vass said. "But we've been planning since yesterday, when the Cydenges first struck south of Haven. They are still coming in waves, and will most likely continue to invade for days or weeks to come. So we have time."

Zent nodded slowly, and I could tell that seemed to ease his mind a bit. Just a bit. "So let's hear some details. Where are we hitting, what's our goal, and who's going to lead this attack?"

All three leaders stared at him.

"All right, so I'm leading the attack. Where? Haven is too close to the battle, right? And knowing Strongs, he'll have that city under a tight thumb no matter the circumstances. He's no fool."

"Of course we won't attack there!" Getts said. "Maldunech."

"Maldunech," Zent repeated slowly. "I can see it. Remote, feels safe. Brant was probably one of the first to deploy heavily against the Cydenges?"

Admiral Skye nodded. "He's a cocky showoff."

"That leaves only the goal," Zent said. "What does Maldunech have that we need?"

"I wanted to hit Daedalus instead," said a throaty voice from behind us, and I turned to see Dr. Dekla shuffling his massive form into the room. "But none of you would listen."

"Yes, because you're an obsessed lunkhead," Getts retorted.

"Obsessed, yes. But science could win this war if we could get our hands on his biomanufactories."

"You mean . . . take the whole city?" I asked incredulously.

The fat man shrugged. "Why not?"

"Because it's insane," Vass said flatly. "Though the walrus is right—if we could somehow steal the Hellebes production facilities and hack into their incubation programs, we could theoretically overwhelm their armies in time."

"If we could hold them at bay until then," Skye growled. "Which is impossible."

Zent seemed contemplative, saying nothing as the other leaders bickered back and forth. I nudged his shoulder. "Zent, isn't the main laboratory unit underneath Haccolces necessary for the biomanufactories to function? Isn't it all useless without that?"

He nodded, and then paused, either in confusion or epiphany. Then he addressed the others. "The Mother has a point. What about the laboratories—you know she destroyed the main power facility, right? Have they gotten it back online already?"

Vass looked at Getts and then Skye. "Somehow, they've managed. I think it has been spotty. That's one more reason why right now is the optimal time to make a move. I'm sure it won't take them long to rework the infrastructure and connections. After all, it's not their first time. I think they have backups in place already."

I frowned. This idea of a biological energy conduit was new to me, and not a little upsetting. Coming face-to-face with the monstrosity that had taken the place of my mother, the 'Zeta Beast' . . . I wouldn't ever forget that experience even if I were a normal Legaleian. So I asked, "What was that power facility even for? Why do they need a . . ."

Zent silenced me with a look. Then he said, "Come on, Vass. You know she has a point."

Vass cleared his throat. "We can arrange for some . . . further explanation regarding this topic, Heiress. But for now—"

"For now, it doesn't matter," Getts cut in gruffly. "We need to plan. She doesn't have any tactical experience."

"However, she does have one thing now," Dekla said with an unsettling level of enthusiasm. "Right, Zent? You said her Geothermic thresholds have finally been unlocked? I can't wait to run some tests."

I groaned. Not this again. He was right, too. All this talk about Kaen's sword, as though they were completely forgetting the whole point of our last mission in Haccolces. The prize for which a dozen men had given their lives. Perhaps they all wanted to forget the giant losses we . . . well, *they* had suffered to get it.

I looked to Zent for sympathy, but he only shrugged apologetically.

Of Father and Fire

*Of one thing and one only am I sure: I hate them. All the Anier . . .
everything to do with them. They may be nine, but to me they represent
the entire forces of hell.*
— From Lhinde's Vault

"How are you managing, Kaen?" I asked as I entered the compression-locked chamber. Just stepping in, I felt lighter. Not as light as on Mani, but close.

"Well, the guards could be a little gentler," my friend grumbled. "Other than that, it's not bad, I suppose. But . . . this is pretty zany. I feel more claustrophobic than ever before, cooped up in a metal cell deep under . . . what is it called again?"

"The ocean," I said. "That's Hellebes for a vast body of water. You'd better get used to it, because you're going to be learning their tongue as fast as they can teach it to you. For now, I'll act as your interpreter. Zent wants me to go over basic words with you every day until the mission."

". . . Mission?"

"There's a lot to catch you up on. I'm really not sure what they're expecting to do with you, but they want to see how you adjust to the planetary differences. I've got Hodge working on a special suit for you." At a blank look from my friend, I explained, "He's the quartermaster. The . . . how do you say that in Manese? He makes and distributes equipment. Anyway, it should help you out a lot once you get used to it."

"If you say so."

For the next while, I filled him in on as many details as I thought they would allow me, using Gaean words for non-interchangeable terminology and whenever I could slip one in. My encyclopedic memory pool allowed me to pick and choose what words would be most relevant for him to know, as well as those most commonly used by the Red Horizon soldiers who worked with him. It was more than a simple memory stash. Certainly an overload, but he was a quick learner—quicker than me—and I knew that he would pick up most of it in time.

A Hellebes soldier came in with a bag of weights and laid them out, proceeding to show him some training exercises to strengthen key leg, back and core muscles. I translated his instructions as needed.

They ended up bunking Kaen in a room with other Hellebes soldiers, one of them being the ever-brooding Curt, at the end of the day. I was thankful, as, while I had gotten somewhat comfortable with being around these strange, oversized males, the idea of bunking with my longtime male friend was distinctly uncomfortable. Hopefully, the massive Gaeans would not intimidate him too much.

I retired to my bunkroom, which was one soldier emptier with Task gone. Just like the absence of Bddo, Ccal or Jed in the lobby, it was one more blow that stung, reminding me of that fateful day when friends and allies fell before my eyes, at my own hands . . . I crawled into my bunk and squeezed my eyes shut, trying vainly to blot out the horrors from my mind.

⁂

I had another nightmare that night. I stood on a shifting sea of black stone that rippled and twisted as though trying to swallow me up. The sky above was heavy, like a sheet of dark metal pressing down against me. No wind blew, yet I struggled to keep my footing, my white hair whirling about me while an invisible force pressed against my chest and shoulders.

My foot slid, and suddenly I was tumbling down waves of stone, sliding, sliding . . .

I hit the bottom, or at least a hard surface, hard enough to hurt. It was darker than night here as well, and my eyes could not pierce it despite my best efforts. "Hello?" I said hesitantly. My half-conscious mind wasn't sure why I said it. It was that dreamlike instinct that drives one to say and do ludicrous things, which was not a common experience for me.

A voice answered from out of the darkness, low and distant yet omnipresent, and distinctly feminine: *The world comes to an end. Nations at war, kings slain in their beds while a great threat looms above all. Humanity must survive, humanity must endure.*

The words vibrated through the very air, through my own skull. The unannounced, mysterious voice that had spoken to me in my last dream. "Who are you?" I demanded, looking up at the darkness around me.

All this and more they promised me. They bound me in chains of iron, copper and gold, they trapped me in a coffin and made me their slave. Me, mother of the earth and goddess of mankind. And yet a slave, a corrupted tool of evil and desolation. Hear the voice of Gaea, and do not let me die a slow death in obscurity.

"What do you want from me?" I shouted into the void. But the voice did not return. She, or . . . it . . . was gone once more.

One lingering phrase remained, echoing through the darkness: *Avenge me.*

From here, the dream transitioned to a brighter scene, and suddenly my mother was there. "Mother!" I cried, rushing up to her. "Where have you been?"

She smiled at me. "Hello, my daughter. Evidently, wherever your consciousness was not. Is all well?"

I nodded, then stopped to consider. "Actually . . . I'm very worried. We flew back to Mani in this experimental ship, and then we stopped a small-scale invasion sent from Haccolces. But my friend Mandrie was killed."

Her face grew sad. "That is unfortunate. It seems you were very close."

I nodded again. "She was my best friend Kaen's little sister. She was his whole world, and now that she's gone, he's sworn to avenge her, but we don't even know who to blame most. I don't . . . I don't want him to lose himself to revenge."

"I see. And he is . . . here with you now on Gaea?"

I paused. "So, you can read my thoughts?"

She shook her head. "I can only see impressions on your consciousness, not the whole thing. Few specifics. If you show me, I can help you better."

I furrowed my brow, looking down at the swaying grass in thought. "White, come here."

The girl appeared instantly. "Yes?"

"Get me a monitor. No, a few. Yes, that's good." She worked as I said the words, bringing a simulation of Hellebes tech to life in my dream, a slanted wall of computer screens with an intuitive menu on them. Even as I went to touch one, the software shifted and changed into an array of images, slanted at an angle like an extended desk. *Ah . . . that's better.* Why couldn't the Hellebes operating systems be this simple? Not that I really had much experience with them.

Mother approached curiously. "Yes . . . fabulous." She began flipping through thumbnails abbreviating specific dates and hotspots in my memories as well as various bits of organized information I'd collected. In what felt like a minute (time worked strangely in my dream, of course), she nodded and said, "I think I have a good grasp of what you've been going through. My, what a journey. Mani sounds more wondrous than I ever could have imagined!"

Wrinkling her brow, she continued, "The matter of Kaen and his silver sword is troubling, isn't it? It seems to have taken a certain hold on him. But why . . .? Ah, that woman Rhidea. She is the one who . . ." She frowned. "So I have met her. Or . . . I did after taking you to Mani. That is most interesting."

"Yeah," I said, shaking my head. "Still hard to believe that the reason she was watching for me in the first place was because she met you."

"And this woman . . . she knew your grandmother Eivael well, according to these memories of yours. They studied the Manese magic along with Kallyn. Oh, Kallyn . . ."

"Can you tell me more about him?" I asked excitedly. "I know so little about my father."

Lynchazel nodded. "A bit. There's so much to say, and yet I don't have much. He was an amazing man, strong and brave despite being . . . well, you know, a Legaleian trying to cope with Gaea's planetary strength. He was a genius, yet humble and not given to bragging, but he said he was quite the accomplished mage on Mani, one of the strongest."

I nodded. "That's what they say. But . . . why did he come to Gaea? Why on Gaea would he try to rescue you from Lldsaor?"

She smiled, as though at a strange, fond memory. "It's a long story. And I was never completely certain myself."

"I wish I could just pick your brain," I said idly, and quickly realized something. "Wait a second, why can't I just comb through your own Vault like this?" I gestured to the computers White had conjured for me.

She looked suddenly uncomfortable. "That . . . that's not a good idea. I would gladly share with you all of the knowledge in my Vault, but there are dark corners that you would be wise to avoid, and I don't trust myself to control the one buried deep inside."

I frowned. "That doesn't make any sense. I already have your Vault with me; I just apparently can't access it freely. Is it the knowledge itself that's dangerous?"

She shook her head. "It's not that. It's . . . her. You heard her voice last time—you probably heard it again tonight?"

I nodded slowly. "She called herself the voice of Gaea, mother of the earth and goddess of mankind. What does that even mean? Who is that?"

Lynchazel went from uncomfortable to fearful, glancing around furtively as though a monster were about to jump out at us. "Don't speak of her here. But yes, that is her. T-the first Mother Gaea, the original. I do not know her full intentions, but she cannot be trusted."

"Okay," I said quietly. That didn't give me much to go on, and certainly wasn't very encouraging, but I was not going to press for further details. I would have to trust this dream apparition and take in what information she was willing to give in this spoken manner. "Then is there anything else you can tell me about my father?"

She thought for a moment. "Well, there is one thing he did while on Gaea—he used his magic. He could create large flames for light and heat, and put them to good use in his raid on the laboratory. When he . . . rescued me."

As she said these last words, she hugged her arms around herself like a widow speaking fondly of her lost lover—at least a shadow of her.

Which was exactly what she was, in a way. They were both long lost. I was not an overly emotional or sentimental woman, like Mydia, but it was enough to bring tears to my eyes, threatening to spill out. But . . . my father, could he really use his Authority on Gaea? Or perhaps only Coaction, the lesser elemental manipulation. Zent had mentioned the same thing. "I'll have to figure out how he did that," I said thoughtfully.

My mother spread her hands. "I can't speak in any depth on the matter, as I'm not from Mani. But he was smart. Extremely so. As I said, Kallyn was a true genius if ever there was one."

I looked down at my palms. Genius he may have been, but I wished I'd inherited that intelligence. Of course, if I could actually see into my mother's memories, then certainly she had some words from him in there that could reveal how he'd done it. As well as the secret to how he, and later Lynchazel herself, had gotten across the Sea of Emptiness on Mani. That one still baffled me.

I wanted to talk to her more, but I could feel the dream slipping away. Even as I looked up, the woman once called Mother Gaea was fading from my sight. "Goodbye for now, Mother," I said.

α Chapter 27 α

Thresholds

Terrified, I watch as a world is born—afraid not of the awesome sight before my eyes, nor of the power that worked it, but because I have already seen this world die.
— From Lhinde's Vault

The next day, I arose early and went to do some training until Dr. Dekla contacted me. He'd be running some manner of tests on me today, and I was not looking forward to it. I found myself in the small gym in which Jed and I had trained just before the disastrous Haccolces raid that had taken his life. I slammed my bones into a heavy bag in practiced rhythms: one, two. One, two. One, two, elbow strike. One, two, knee kick. Pretending the bag was the face of my enemies did nothing to assuage my guilt, of course.

Because the real enemy was me.

Or at least, that was what one of the many voices in my head whispered to me. I couldn't tell if it was my instincts, my rationality or my emotions talking. Perhaps just the voice of insanity.

Or could it be that awful voice of Gaea? Whoever she really was. I knew it couldn't be her. That voice, according to my mother, belonged to the original Mother Gaea, but what did that even mean? The way the Hellebes all talked, Lynchazel I had been ancient.

This injustice belongs to the ones who chained me, the ones who corrupted me, who made me their slave.

The words returned to my mind, echoing like the day I heard them in my nightmare.

I am the voice of Gaea, the widow in the darkness, the mourning virgin, cursed of the ancient ones. They shall know my pain.

I struck the bag, mulling on the strange words whilst wishing I'd never heard them.

They bound me in chains of iron, copper and gold, they trapped me in a coffin and made me their slave.

"Who are you?" I muttered as I spun and kicked the bag once, twice, a third time, sending it rocking with each impact, jingling its chain. "Mother Gaea." The name felt like a curse in my mouth. Some said it with respectful reverence, some out of straightforward duty, others mockingly, and still others with religious fervor. Indeed, I'd heard that there was a religion that still worshipped the Mother. Did the followers even know that their goddess had vanished fifteen years ago, destined to die on Mani? That she'd been reborn as a half-breed, useless and incapable of saving her friends?

No, they probably didn't.

I hesitated and dropped my leg short, landing on the ball of my foot. What an idiot I was—I completely forgot to ask her how she had died. But . . . no, the memories stored in her Vault were from before she ever left for Gaea. She wouldn't be able to tell me that. No, I *should* have asked about her origins.

Before I could go down that rabbit trail, my wrist console notified me of an incoming message from Zent: *Where are you? I've got some tests in mind.*

Great . . . more tests. Likely separate from what Dr. Dekla already had in store. *Where and when?*

I like your gusto! Meet me in the Geo Labs in fifteen. And you'll want your gillsuit.

"The Geo Labs?" I muttered. I'd heard the name, but I knew little about the place or where it was. Helpfully, he sent coordinates almost immediately, and I traced them on my map to find they lay on the southern side of the base, on the lowest floor. The description read:

Authorized personnel only.

[Geothermic Harvesting]

[Energy Conflux]

[Power Storage]

[Geokinetic Experimentation]

I raised my eyebrows. That sounded awfully interesting. Perhaps there was more to this base than they let on. And now I would get to see some of the more fun—potentially confidential—side. Or so I hoped.

Fifteen minutes later, I arrived at a set of heavy steel doors glowing from a complex web of Geoelectric locks. Wires, cables and heavy conduit ran through the walls around the doors, pulsing with light almost like back in the underground labs at Haccolces. For a moment, a feeling of uneasiness swam in my belly, morbid nostalgia, but then it was gone.

"Right on time," said Zent, who stood in front of the door, hand poised to open it with a key card. He did so, and the lock beeped, retracting with smooth *ssshk-ssshk* noises to allow the thick doors to slide inwards toward either wall. From inside, a wave of cool air and faint mist came.

I followed him into a chamber lined with . . . generators? They were mounted to each wall, pulsing with light and each displaying complex readings in script too small for me to read. We walked right through, lights snapping on overhead as we went. The metal floor, paneled in a textured array of square tiles, clanked under our thin-heeled boots.

The next room, adjoined to it by more pulsing cables, was long with an indented floor leading to an eerily-glowing pit. The room was large, the recess railed off with hazard warnings as though too dangerous to approach, which I could totally believe. Four rooms branched off, two on the left, two on the right.

"This," Zent said with a sweeping gesture, "is where we harvest our own Geothermic energy directly from Gaea's mantle. Beneath the ocean."

"So that's a . . ." I searched for the right word. "Well? A rig?"

"That is indeed the well," he said, and then pointed at the room behind us. "That is where it is processed into Geoelectric energy. That room there is where it gets refined for Geokinetics and power. We don't, of course, have our own Mother, so it's a process of refinement. Those two rooms are entirely for battery storage. And here—" he gestured toward the far left, walking in that direction as he said it "—is the Geokinetic Experiments lab. You'll love this."

"Am I actually allowed in here?" I asked, surprised that he was showing me all of this.

"Oh yes, I got clearance from the rest of the Board. They're a bit more willing to trust you now, after what we've put you through. They just don't want to show it openly."

Or in the case of Getts, I thought, *he doesn't like to show it, period.*

He opened another steel door, and we stepped into the lab. Lab was clearly a code word for yet another mess of rooms, each with their own equipment, including a large gallery with experimental machines built for . . . well, war, by the looks of them. And mounted guns, also probably experimental, some with Geothermic cables running to them and others with their own batteries.

Zent led me into the gallery, announcing, "This is the place. We'll have to move some of this junk, as this is where the boys test out all their new weaponry. We don't just steal from the empire—we innovate." He began moving the wheeled machines off the floor, pushing them into an adjoining storage room. "How else are we going to one day take them on?"

"You mean . . . in an actual war?" I asked flatly.

"Precisely. For years, we've harried them in small raids, nothing organized since the time we, uh, stole the Mother and wrecked the Elites' entire power grid. The Catastrophe of 2322, as they call it. They caught us then, but we rebuilt and they haven't since, although lately we've been getting bolder. And . . . we're starting to take some losses." He frowned, and I wasn't certain whether it was because he was troubled to reflect on such things, or simply displeased at how many more objects lay out on the floor. "Big losses," he added.

I snapped into motion, helping him undo brakes on gun-mount carts and roll them away, until the range was free. "So, what am I supposed to be doing exactly?" I asked.

Zent stretched, rotating the top half of his body clockwise and then counter-clockwise. "I'm going to test out the strength of Mother Gaea."

I flinched as he said it, a reflex born from the haunting memory of the cataclysm I'd unleashed the last time I'd tested my limits. But . . . I'd used it on multiple occasions since to rip up the earth and trap my enemies. Perhaps there was a way to temper it like that? "Are you sure that's a good idea?"

"With moderation," he said, gesturing with palms held outward. "Don't go too crazy. But don't worry, this room is heavily reinforced and all the conduit has breakers and disconnects in place in case anything gets out of hand. We'll start with some strength exercises to see how much you can enhance your body."

He took me over to a machine that measured force and torque, where I pushed or pulled against stout bars and pedals, running results on a built-in screen that displayed foot-pounds and a long list of measurement units I was not familiar with. I drew on the nearby Geothermic vents to increase my body's abilities while Zent made notes on his wrist console. He made it clear that I must not draw upon the Mother's power, that is that I not go beyond my normal threshold. I was relatively certain where that was, so I didn't push any further.

After a few more exercises, he declared that to be enough. He took me to another machine, where he measured my ability to manually transfer energy from one source to a recipient feed. (Which he called Geokinetic conversion efficiency.) I didn't have much experience with it, so I gave it my best shot. Feeling the energy course into my right hand, through my body and out my left was one of the strangest sensations I'd ever felt. Judging by Zent's expression when I looked up, I must have been performing all right. "How's that?" I asked in a tight, focused voice.

"Is that your limit? Keep going until you don't think you can reasonably draw any more. Don't worry, you're not going to draw too much any time soon. Well . . . probably not, anyway."

I increased the flow, shutting my eyes to concentrate on the influx and outflow of Geothermic energy, feeling it like a rushing, rippling current of water, a hot, fiery vein of lava, and an electric current all at once. My body shuddered involuntarily as I drew more, more, until Zent said, "All right, that's enough."

I didn't hear him, or didn't immediately register his words. In my mind,

I was experiencing the flow of Gaea's life force on a personal, close-up level. He said something else and touched my shoulder, but immediately pulled back with a curse. "Lyn! That's enough!"

A buzzer beeped somewhere, and the flow of power vanished. I snapped out of it, opening my eyes to see the metal orifices beneath my hands glowing with a green so bright that it had developed a golden hue, seeming to shimmer and burn with it. I gasped, releasing my hands at once, and the planetary energy left inside me seemed to snap as the flow was cut off. Shaking, I nearly fell to the floor before catching myself.

Zent reached out and steadied me, not pulling back this time. "The heat coming from your gillsuit was so strong it almost burnt me," he said. "I'm surprised it didn't trip the breaker sooner. So . . . *very* good results there. We'll just assume you can draw a lot more than that, and . . . efficiency seemed to be quite high, especially considering you're a newbie at energy transfer. Now for the fun part."

"I get to go crazy?"

"You get to go crazy," he confirmed. "Just not . . . completely crazy." He pointed at the Geothermic vents scattered about the floor. "Those don't have limiters, and the floor from here to the targets on the far wall is constructed of multilayered reinforced steel with advanced heatsinks. Let's see what you can do with raw Geothermic power."

Way to get the chills running down my spine.

He instructed me to draw power until I tapped into the Mother's abilities, breaking my old limits, and then see if I could funnel it into an energy stream like back at the labs under Haccolces. With a nod and a deep inhale, I began to draw. Zent backed away as I absorbed more and more of Gaea's energy, until I felt my eyes go wide and my breath catch involuntarily. Blood pulsed heavily in my temples and my vision began to blur slightly around the edges. "Okay, I think I'm there," I tried to say, but I couldn't tell if the words came out right or not. My hearing was fuzzy. How was he going to stop me in this state if I *did* go on a rampage again? The thought would have struck fear deep into my heart, but in this state, I was distanced from such worries and it was more an absent pondering.

I released the energy, pouring a stream of liquid heat from my hands which converged into one beam aimed at the far wall. The metal smoked, warped, and began to burn and melt, peeling off by the layer. I aimed the stream downwards, eating orange lines into the hardened steel and leaving black streaks. With effort, I stopped, cutting off the release of energy but not the influx that I was drawing from the vents. I tried to channel my thoughts to focus on what I should be doing with this power, but it was difficult to think at all, or even to remember what was going on minutes prior to the surging life that had poured into me. The green tsunami built and built.

With a scream and a lurch, I slammed a foot into the floor, pouring Geokinetic power into it and blasting upwards in a straightforward line. The metal plates ripped and tore as Gaea's fire surged underneath, tearing upwards in a line like the spine of a mountain range until the blast hit the far wall and exploded with green light, golden particles and a shower of sparks.

Dimly, I heard a shout from behind me, and I turned quickly, trying to pinpoint this interloper. But no sooner did I turn than the power cut off from the grates, and I was left with a roiling sea of energy inside me, a still lake behind a broken dam. Breathing heavily, I felt my mind return to me, and I opened my palms to release a short burst of hot plasma into the floor in front of my feet, eyes widening as I beheld the destructive force of it. That used up the excess, and suddenly I was just . . . plain old me. Exhausted, empty, gasping, head foggy and aching.

But just me. Plain old Lyn.

"Well done," Zent said from the far wall, opposite of where the devastation had just taken place. His hand held a lever, which he had thrown to cut the power to the entire floor. Even the light in the room had diminished with the loss of the Geothermic energy spouting from the vents, though the seam and craters I had ripped into the floor still smoldered green, glowing as the metal slowly cooled. "You've definitely done a number on the weapons range."

"Wow," I breathed between gasps, one hand to my chest feeling the breakneck beat of my heart. "I-I did that. *I* did? That was . . . exhilarating. I couldn't . . . it was just like the last time—I couldn't think, couldn't see, couldn't hear you speaking to me. My mind was in another world, focused on the power of Gaea."

Zent approached and laid a hand on my shoulder. It shook slightly, and I noted a faint tremor of nervousness in his voice as he said, "It's okay. I was careful. I told you there was no limit, but I was ready to cut the power whenever I deemed necessary. But I trust you, and I think you'll learn to control this ability with time. You can do it, Lyn."

I looked down at my hands, feeling almost sickened by my own power. Nodding slowly, I gulped and said, "I hope."

$$\alpha \quad \text{Chapter 28} \quad \alpha$$

The Catalyst

Today I, Lhinde, became a goddess. I couldn't be more frightened of it. The ones who want to rule Gaea . . . the Anier . . . they have finally succeeded. Their last specimen, their final attempt . . . they say I might already be the only female on the planet. That they will use me to save the world, although I don't understand how.
— From Lhinde's Vault

An hour later, I had cooled down and my headache seemed to have mostly abated. It was time to meet Dr. Dekla for the day's tests. With a groan, I arose from a moderately comfy chair in the lounge, where I had been scrolling through a nifty thing the Hellebes called the Net, and grabbed my shirt. I had changed out of my gillsuit and into more comfortable clothes.

I arrived at his office dressed in only a loose pair of pants and a black camisole—why put my shirt back on yet?—and went to knock only to find the door already partially ajar. Curiously, I peeked inside to find Dr. Dekla moving away from a small sitting man, holding a tablet and taking notes. No, not a small Hellebes, but Kaen.

"Lynchazel," Dekla greeted me in his signature dry tone. "Perfect timing. I was just finishing with your Legaleian friend here. Come in."

I gulped, backing up as Kaen turned to glare at me, wearing one of those stupid, oversized medical gowns. "No, I'll-I'll wait," I said, hastening to shut the door.

A few minutes later, Kaen emerged, wearing the suit I'd had Hodge make for him. Sturdy but with a wide range of motion, it was made of two pieces that fit together seamlessly, much like the gillsuits, and had built-in Geokinetic body enhancements that powered his limbs and back, moving as he did, giving him far more support and strength in his fight against Gaea's harsh gravity. The tech had been around for ages, but the Hellebes simply had never had much use for a super suit. Hodge said it would have worked far better if he was making it for a Hellebes, but I wasn't quite sure if he meant because we were able to manually power Geokinetics and channel planetary energy, or because of the way our brains were wired, giving the suit's nerve sensors a better read. That seemed strange but possible.

"Hello, Lyn," my friend said in Legaleian. "I mean . . ." he struggled to find the correct greeting in Gaean, and I reminded him. "Ah, right. Ugh, I've never felt so overwhelmed in my life."

"How'd the, uh, checkup go?" I asked.

Kaen scowled in reply. "That fat doctor creeps me out. Is he even *alive?*"

I laughed, but before I could reply, Dr. Dekla beckoned from inside, sounding more impatient than usual, and I excused myself. Inside, I took the gown handed to me and proceeded to put it on under the robotic gaze of the gigantic scientist. He didn't give any sign of looking away, but was rather waiting with calm mock-patience to get on with the examination. I was long used to being humiliated in front of Hellebes scientists, and could suffer this man just the same . . . What made my skin crawl was simply how robotic he was, like a data-gathering machine whose only hunger was for more data.

"Just the usual?" I asked as he began to poke and prod at my neck, heart, nose and ears, taking measurements and checking readings on his tablet. I already knew the answer.

"Not quite. I've a few extra things in mind today, some tests I've been wanting to conduct for a while now."

"And what about Kaen?" I asked as he checked my blood pressure and pulse. "What kind of tests were you running on him?"

"Very basic ones," he said in a bored tone. "Vitals, signs of health, plus a few blood samples. Turns out your blood type is the same. I'll be comparing them to yours to see the genetic similarities and adaptive potential. Please lie down now."

I did as instructed, and he ran through the rest of the motions before putting me through the scanners. This time, however, he had another torture instrument ready after the scanner, a syringe filled with white liquid. "This is a solution that will track the short-term changes to your blood cells as they interact with Geothermic energy."

He set me on a table unceremoniously with one and a half hands, and then pricked me with the syringe, emptying the white liquid into my veins. "Don't worry, Heiress, it's quite harmless. It only causes the chemical changes to stand out when I scan you in a bit. This—" he held up another syringe "—is what we call a catalyst, which will induce Geokinetic pulling. It's important that it be reactive, not conscious."

I tensed, breathing faster, eyeing the syringe with a fearful expression.

"There's no cause for concern," he assured me, "as the effects won't last long, and you will be back to normal. And I won't give it to you yet." He tapped his tablet a few times before turning. "Follow me."

I sat up, suddenly curious, watching as he approached a door at the back of his office, one I'd hardly noticed before. It was sealed by electronic means, disengaging as he slid a card across the lock. The door flicked back into the wall, revealing a passage that ended in an elevator. I followed the large man, and we got in the elevator, descending two floors.

When we emerged, I recognized the place immediately. "This is the Geokinetic Experiments lab," I said.

Dekla shuffled out of the elevator, and I trailed behind. "Close," he said after a moment. "It's the Bioresearch division." He said nothing more as he waddled to a computer desk and began making a few adjustments to a complex settings menu. I stood by, awaiting his instructions anxiously. Was he really going to make me go through the same exact thing Zent had, in the space of a couple hours? I hadn't had time to rest or recharge, let alone recover from that.

Finally, he glanced over at me. "If you will." He pressed a button and gestured toward a narrow but heavy door—no a *series* of doors—that opened up to his right. "You'll be heading in there. Only thing left is this." He caught my arm as I approached the door and jammed the second syringe into my flesh. I gasped, but before the catalyst could take effect, he roughly shoved me through the doors and slammed them shut with a hiss of air and a triple *boom.*

The room was small, made of solid, cold metal. I couldn't tell how tight the space was exactly, as it was completely dark. The only light came from Geothermic vents set in the wall by the floor. My shoulder throbbed from where he had poked me twice now, and my body shivered from whatever drug he'd used, my teeth set on edge and clicking together. My head felt . . . fuzzy . . . but I was still in control. Breathing hard, fearful of the dark, hands groping the walls desperately as though I'd find a way out, but my mental faculties were still working. Given how tired I was, I didn't think I'd be able to go into that special state even if I wanted to.

Then the first wave hit me. My stomach lurched, and I doubled over, coughing and retching dryly. My arms tingled, as though my veins swarmed with itchy bugs seeking release. The swarm seemed to reach out, settling on the Geothermic energy flowing into the room, only I knew it was my own mind. Under the catalyst's effects, I suddenly needed that energy, *craved* that energy, and found myself jerking my arms outward, drawing in Gaea's warmth.

In my mind, I screamed, *No! This is too much too soon. I can't do this! Let me out!* But I had less and less control over my mind, and soon I was drawing in as much Geothermic energy as earlier in the morning, breaking my threshold and going into that frenzied, terrible state. I could feel my own frantic pulse in my eyeballs.

Yet . . . it was different. I possessed a sliver of my own mind, watching and feeling as my entire body stretched itself to the seams to inhale this energy like a hungry monster, whimpering and then screaming at the close walls. It was like watching someone else run my body, and it was horrible. Was that what I became? At the same time, I was aware that it elicited pain while being powerless to stop it.

Throwing back my head, I screeched with a ringing cry that hurt my own ears, and opened my mouth to blast pure heat energy from it, throwing my head wildly from side to side and lighting up the steel walls in orange streaks, pouring out the energy while continuing to suck it in from the vents at the same rate.

My legs trembled and my muscles spasmed, but still I kept on. I couldn't control it. Inside, I was fighting and clawing, trying to get a grip on myself, but my body was like a vehicle that had been thrown into gear and the throttle jammed open, speeding away from me. The panic grew, until finally a thought made it through, and I heard myself shout, *"Dekla!"*

Not just a shout, but an ear-splitting shriek that didn't sound like me.

Turning toward the doors, I blasted them with heat and kicked, denting them outward, shouting the doctor's name multiple times. I could tell I was getting more control over my own mind, yet I was still in rage mode and could only think aggressively. I blasted the door with even more heat, until finally . . . it ran out. The streams of green energy dissipated in my hands, and my mind returned to me. It was like a switch was thrown inside me, turning off the overwhelming power of the Mother. I was left feeling empty and drained, shaking uncontrollably as I dropped to my knees. I pounded the floor with a weak fist, sobbing at the pain that I was left with. My arms, my shoulders, my head, every muscle in my body and all flesh between seemed to smolder with the leftovers of an uncontained blaze. It had consumed my body like kindling when I thought I was too dry to channel any energy, and now I suffered the aftereffects.

Light flooded the small chamber as Dekla opened the doors, but I didn't look up. I didn't want to do anything. I hated the man, but not with the passion that had consumed me in my rage. I felt like I couldn't even rise from my slumped position on the steel floor. The superheated metal was burning my skin through my medical gown, and indeed the insufficient apparel was smoldering, but I didn't care. Dimly, I wondered if he thought at all that I would—and indeed should, if I weren't a fire mage—be burnt by my own doing in that metal prison.

"Heiress. Get up." The doctor kicked me—not roughly, but as a simple means of getting me moving, like starting an engine. All it accomplished was tipping me over into more burning metal, though. I looked at him and tried to say something, but I couldn't. With an annoyed growl, the huge man bent down and lifted me up with one arm, inspecting me like a dead rat he'd caught in his kitchen. "Well, I suppose the tests are over for today," he said idly.

"De . . . kla," I murmured, too low and slurred for him to even make out. I tried to reach a hand up to his shoulder, or perhaps his neck—yes, his neck—but only made it to his upper arm. My fingers would only tighten so much, and I held onto his fat-insulated arm with all the grip of a child, as though it would give me consolation. Perhaps revenge.

Then I passed out on his shoulder.

Gaea's Bane

They've explained it all to me by now; no sense hiding it. The bid for a Cydenges Queen is as dead as my sisters. They have expanded their imagination far beyond that, and intend to use me as a conduit, now that my blood has merged with the Cydenges core and I have successfully manipulated direct Geothermic streams at high intensity. I will power the world, enabling the utopia they envision: Neo Gaea.
— From Lhinde's Vault

I awoke on an operating table. Or . . . hopefully a simple exam table. For some reason, I had a recollection of being on fire. I tried to sit up, but I got my head only high enough to realize I was naked. A thin sheet had been pulled over my body, but it didn't even come up past my stomach. I laid my head back with a thump and a small grunt that didn't leave my throat. I would have groaned, but I stopped myself as soon as I saw Dr. Dekla at his desk, typing away at a keyboard with his chubby fingers as he spoke into a microphone.

". . . Yes, the same. Results are a bit higher than I expected on that front." A pause, and then he continued. "It's contained. I wouldn't let her rampage through the entire facility and destroy all my research."

He didn't look my way, but rather seemed to assume me to still be sleeping. I rested my head to one side, simply watching him. I didn't want to rustle the covers or make a sound, lest I alert him, but I also didn't have the energy yet.

Maybe I could learn something? All these secrets, all these things they were only now beginning to let me in on . . . I was sick of being ignorant.

I couldn't clearly see the computer screen behind his head, but what I could see was a mass of gibberish, numbers and text forming some kind of complex statistics report. He must have been speaking with Zent or Getts. If I got lucky, I'd get to hear some important inside information.

"I can't say how long it will take for her to reach that state," he said in reply to an unheard question. Whoever was speaking on the other end, I could hear nothing of his words from my perch on the bed. "No, I can't say when they're heading out, but she is still in a phase where she cannot control her powers at all, and is a harm to both friend and enemy."

I coughed involuntarily, and Dr. Dekla's thick neck swiveled, fat rolling as he looked at me. "Well, well. Hmm. I need to go." He ended the transmission and clicked a couple buttons, switching displays on his screen before rising to approach me.

By reflex, I immediately pulled the sheets up over my chest. I didn't have much to show, but I felt vulnerable lying here on this medical table, uncertain how long I'd been here or what kind of experiments he may have done on me in the meantime. At least my arms worked.

"Good to see you awake," he said, his croaking voice implying nothing of the sort.

I glared up at him. "How long has it been? What else did you do to me?"

Dekla's calm face showed no disturbance. "Nothing major. I surveyed your results and made sure all your vital signs were positive. I've been running the data while the rehabilitation drugs work."

Rehabilitation drugs. Lovely. "I don't trust you," I growled, trying to make it sound like more than a passing comment. Looking around, I realized I was on one of the operating tables at the very back of his office. I'd never been back here before. "Can I have my clothes back?"

To my surprise, he actually fetched them for me, dumping them in a pile unceremoniously on my stomach. Then he turned back to his desk and resumed his work, leaving me to don my clothes as fast as I possibly could. Which was . . . not fast, but at least I got my legs to comply in tandem with my arms. The sleep seemed to have temporarily recharged my batteries, though I could feel a deep shakiness in my bones, warning me against doing anything too strenuous. I felt I would wear out in a matter of minutes with any activity.

Standing, I stretched and approached his desk, trying to look nonchalant as I surveyed the various statistics displays, as well as the document he was writing up—some sort of scientific communications? And on one screen . . . a 3D image of Kaen's silver sword, with boxes of text attached. With a huff that sounded almost exasperated, he turned to me. "May I help you?"

"Just looking," I mumbled defensively. "What is all this research for? Why do you have to study my Geokinetic powers?"

"You are an idiot." He said it matter-of-factly, almost as though that were the answer, and turned back to his computer. "It should be obvious. You are the largest asset we have here, and it would be foolish not to explore the scientific possibilities and ramifications of one such as you. You may go; I'm done with you for now. Don't worry, I have more experiments planned."

"Not today, you don't." I slammed the door shut behind me as I stalked out.

You sadistic creep.

After freshening up in the nearest restroom, I sought out my friend—the one whose planet I'd actually grown up on, not the sadistic creep—reaching out to him via his wrist console's communication features. He responded with a comical jumble of text, and I called by voice instead. "Kaen? Where are you at?" I asked it in Legaleian.

"They've got me in this . . . training facility. Dojang or whatever. Not the low-G room; another one."

I instructed him on how to share his coordinates, and quickly found the location. Upon reaching the dojang, I saw a few soldiers sparring hand-to-hand and another Hellebes standing to one side. It was Curt. He was trying to talk to Kaen, who crouched on his heels in his power suit, looking overwhelmed and a couple cakes shy of comprehension.

"Lyn!" he said in relief as I walked up.

Curt turned as well. "Oh, it's you. I really don't know how they expect any of us to communicate with your friend when his Hellebes is about as fluent as a first-stage youngling. Maybe a rat."

"How are you doing, Kaen?" I asked in the Hellebes tongue.

He gave me a brief, annoyed eyeroll, which quickly changed to an upward-looking expression of mental searching. The eyes swiveled to the right, then the left, then at me.

I repeated the phrase in clearer, more simple language, and he understood.

"Doing . . . well," he said, struggling with each word. "Doctor . . . Dekla, Dekla . . . don't like? Hate his . . ." He made a gesture at his own midsection, trying to come up with the word for guts.

I laughed. "Well, Curt, what are you trying to teach him?"

"Just running him through basic exercises," he said. "Getting him used to moving like a proper Hellebes in that suit."

I helped the soldier out by showing Kaen with gestures what Curt was trying to teach him and supplying Legaleian translations as needed. Kaen's sword was leaning against the wall behind him, and his training seemed to keep his mind off of it. He continued to obsess over his sword, but I couldn't tell if it was because it still spoke to him or if it was simply an outlet for him to keep his anxiety at bay. Kaen was a quick learner and enjoyed a challenge, so he took to the moves quickly.

Afterward, I walked with him down to the main restroom and shower station, as he especially needed the latter, being a Legaleian. The power suit was effective at enhancing his body, and somewhat effective at ventilation and keeping him cool, but he still sweated far more easily than any Hellebes. I was just about to follow him in when I remembered this was my Manese friend, not another Hellebes. Blushing, I said, "You, uh, go ahead. I'll use another restroom."

I left him looking somewhere between bemused and relieved, and headed to another restroom to use the showers. It had small dividers between stations, but it wasn't like they gave much privacy. I was well used to it, not to mention quick, and simply picked less busy times like these—but I didn't want Kaen to know.

Afterwards, I met Curt in the lobby and challenged him to a game of

Gogi to cool my mind. We were just finishing the opening five moves when Kaen walked in, wearing a loose pair of training pants with his sword belted on around his bare waist. The look on his face hinted at both the refreshing feel of being clean and the constant weight that came with taking off his custom suit. But he couldn't wear it all the time.

Plopping himself down on a nearby seat with a thud, Kaen leaned back with arms behind his dark-haired head, surveying our game. "What's that?" he asked me in Legaleian.

I glanced at him. "It's called Gogi." I spoke in the Hellebes language, repeating the name when he gave me a questioning look. With a sigh, I switched languages and explained the objective of the game and a few basic rules while trading moves with Curt.

Curt, for his part, was rubbing his lower lip with a thumb, focusing intently on the game. Certainly, he was better than me. Perhaps I'd gotten good enough to finally pose a challenge for him, or he was just taking it extra seriously since both Ccal and Jed, who had normally gone out of their way to beat him whenever they had the chance, were both . . . well, deceased. Maybe him beating me would do something for his mood.

But that didn't mean I would roll over.

Kaen watched for another minute before sighing and saying, "Please, Lyn, can you . . . not talk to me in Hellebes when we're supposed to be relaxing?"

I looked up at him, pulling my attention away from the game. His face showed a serious expression . . . one I couldn't discern. Pain? He was being sincere, not idly complaining.

"I'm sorry," I said in our mother tongue. "You're right, it's a lot. I had a large advantage in learning, yet it took even me a while." Turning my attention back to the game, I frowned in thought. I didn't like the way Curt's pieces were encroaching from the flanks, even though I had somewhat of a straight shot through the middle. His style of play was less obscure tactically than Jed's and less brutal than Ccal's, but was deceptively clever. He gave up ground in order to gain more, and in the process had gotten a piece up on me.

"I'll bet you think you've already won," I muttered, despite having no effective plan of my own.

Curt looked up in confusion. "Huh? Was that to me?"

I realized I'd said the words in Legaleian. It was confusing, juggling two languages while Kaen was around. "Sorry," I said with an uncomfortable laugh. "Nothing important." Shaking my head, I tried to focus on the game. However, at this point, it was hopeless. I was too distracted. One by one, I lost more pieces as he surrounded them with superior placement, and I soon resigned.

"I'll get you next time," I promised.

Curt smiled as he rose from the table. An actual smile.

"Care to try?" I asked Kaen, careful to use our mutual tongue.

He shook his head with a wide-eyed expression that said, "I'm staying out of this insanity," even though I was sure that, under different circumstances, he would have loved the challenge. Right now . . . well, he was under many different weights, physical, mental and emotional.

I looked at the young man and smiled a forced smile that felt almost disingenuous. Now that Curt was gone from the room, I said, "I'm sorry, Kaen. I know this isn't what you wanted, and I know . . . well, I know it's still hard."

He nodded tiredly before laying his head back on his chair's headrest, closing his eyes. "It's actually working, at least in part. Taking my mind off of Mandrie, off of Domon . . . even this cursed thing." He indicated the sword, though he soon replaced his hand on it, rubbing a thumb along the scabbard, which was cocked outward to allow his sitting position. The pommel was nearly digging into his side.

I glanced down at the sword, and then up and down the long lobby. Two soldiers whom I didn't know stood at the far end of the room, discussing something with loud words and the occasional belch, but the setting was as close to private as we were likely to get. "Kaen," I said, looking him in the eye. I waited for him to open them, revealing those dark, stormy irises, before continuing. "Does it still talk to you?"

He eyed me for a long moment, shifting focus between my two eyes. I held his gaze, not to be intimidating but as a signal of accountability between friends. Slowly, he nodded. "It does. He spoke to me twice this morning. Once shortly after I woke up, and again when Dekla tried to steal it for research."

I sat up straighter. "Say what?"

He snorted angrily, eyes flashing as though recalling a strong, murderous urge to kill the fat doctor. "That blubbery creep tried to take the sword without even asking. When I tried to tell him he couldn't, he laughed. It was . . . I didn't like that laugh. He told me they needed data on it for research, and that he'd give it right back."

"And did he?"

"Well . . . yes. But—" He jiggled his head side to side. "There's just something about that man that makes me want to run Mani's blade right through his fat gut. Do you think it could even reach anything vital?" His tone heavily implied that he was contemplating the thought as he spoke.

I rolled my eyes, sucking in a long, contained breath. "Look, you can't just . . ." I stopped as I realized we shared the same view of the man. "Well, okay, I agree, he's infuriating and makes my skin crawl. And possibly up to something shady." I shrugged.

Kaen gave an ironic laugh. Falling silent, he rubbed his sword with longer strokes. "No, it hasn't gone away," he said finally. "The anger, the whispers of Mani . . . I thought maybe he couldn't reach me way out here. He seemed . . . distracted at first, but then I realized it was only uneasiness. Can a planet be uneasy? Can a god be fearful?"

He? A god?

I swallowed, eyes flicking from my friend's hand to his face, which stared intently at his sword. I didn't know anything about gods, but his words struck far too close to home for comfort. I hadn't realized back on Mani, when I'd opened up and told him about the voice of my mother, how similar our recent experiences were. It was uncanny, and more than a little coincidental, and yet . . . it was only that. Coincidence. My mother was a human, exploited and abused by other humans for the purpose of technological advancement, my predecessor the same, and Gaea . . . Well, I preferred not to think about her voice. If indeed that was her.

Was . . . was it truly Mani, the moon itself, speaking to Kaen? Inhabiting his mystical sword? Could it be? If so . . . what of Luna? Did she have a will, a voice? Gaean legend held that the two were twins, born of the sun goddess Sol. Male and female, twin guardians of Gaea. It was a silly story that came from an indeterminant age in North Terrol's past, but it rang oddly true in the case of these voices.

I opened my mouth to speak, then quickly shut it, clearing my throat. I didn't trust my voice not to crack. "Kaen, I don't know. I wonder the same exact thing. I have . . ." I glanced furtively around the room. It didn't matter if anyone was listening in, as we were talking in Legaleian, and the leaders had ears everywhere in the form of hidden microphones anyway. And if their quantum computers could somehow translate language from scratch based on audio . . .

Oh, well.

"Kaen . . . Gaea speaks to me." I said the words slowly, letting them sink in. *Remember? I did tell you this already, sort of.*

He glanced up with a dubious expression. "Gaea. Do you mean another god, or this "Mother Gaea" they talk about, your mother who died fourteen years ago?"

I shook my head. "Both. My mother talks to me in the form of collected memories. They call it a Vault. They form a depiction of her that speaks to me in my dreams. But . . . sometimes I hear another voice, a woman calling out from the darkness, claiming to be the planet herself. She scares me."

He nodded grimly. I couldn't tell what he made of it, whether it reassured him or only served to further his feeling of alienation in this harsh world. "Maybe we're both just insane." His tone said that it was a very real possibility, just . . . not likely.

"Well, we don't have much time to spare, so get some rest." I reached over and slapped him on the shoulder, not intending to hit hard but still causing his body to jolt. He caught himself with one hand on the armrest beside him.

I gasped, and he glared up at me with pain in his eyes, pushing himself back up into a sitting position.

"I'm sorry," I said hurriedly. "I didn't mean to—"

"It's fine," he growled through gritted teeth. Rising with a low grunt, he stalked off in the direction of his bunkroom.

I gazed down at the Gogi board, feeling terrible for him. "I'm sorry," I whispered to the pieces.

They didn't respond.

α Chapter 30 α

Final Preparations

Aidor 4, 1296:
This may be my last journal entry. I have experimented sufficiently
with my new memory storage, which the Anier are calling a Vault. I'm sure
they think they have total access to it, or will one day, but I think I can
keep them out, for I am the first to explore this power. The pioneer, the . . .
owner, in a way. In any case, this diary is almost entirely useless now.
Just . . . hard to let go, despite the fact that I've committed it all to memory
in my Vault already.
— From Lhinde's Diary

Later that afternoon, Zent informed me that I was expected to attend a meeting at eighteen-thirty to discuss strategy. Over the course of the remaining afternoon, I helped Kaen as much as I could without making him feel too helpless. He said almost nothing to me, merely nodding when affirmation was needed and shaking his head most other times.

The hours passed with no messages from our evil scientist, so it was with some relief that I headed to the Board Room, meeting Getts along the way. The mustachioed man didn't say a word, acknowledging me with only a dip of his head and a scowl that could have meant a dozen different things, most of them negative.

I entered the circular chamber, approaching the table to see what kind of info they had up. Vass was pinching and dragging at a map of Maldunech, to no surprise of mine, and talking with Skye and Zent, who looked up distractedly as I entered. I tried to ignore Dekla, despite the impossibility of such a thing, pretending he simply couldn't see me and wasn't at this very moment plotting his next diabolical experiment.

Looking up from the map, Vass clapped his hands together and said,

"Very well, everyone is here. As we've discussed, this is a somewhat desperate operation, so we're throwing whatever we can possibly spare at it."

"Which means we need to know the power of our secret weapon," Skye said, eyeing Zent and then Dekla. "Captain? Doctor?"

"I'm sure you got the data," Zent told him. "Right, Dekla?" He turned a pointed look, almost a glare, at the biologist.

The fat man held up his hands. "I have no conclusive evidence yet. I need more time to experiment—"

"On your lab rat," Zent said. "*Without* killing her."

"As I recall, you were the first to purposely trip her Geokinetic limits."

The two stared each other down. Meanwhile, I shifted slowly away from the biologist.

Getts gave a great *harrumph!* Blowing down his mustache, he said, "Time isn't cheap. We need results. We don't have much longer."

"No indeed," Vass agreed. "We've got multiple intelligence crews working to crack Maldunech. We'll have to go within the next couple days."

"We'll make it one, then," Skye said.

Dekla tried to object, but Getts cut him off. "Shut it, lab coat. We need results, and if you can't get us any, then we'll have to go in without 'em."

"And what about the Legaleian boy, Kaen?" Zent asked.

Multiple sets of eyes flickered between me and Dekla. He cleared his throat and said, "I have . . . no actual data on his sword yet, but—"

"You were supposed to be studying its composition and capabilities!" Vass said, sounding vexed.

"I had very *little* opportunity," Dekla replied.

Sounds like a lie to me, I growled silently to myself. *White—take a note.*

The girl wasn't doing anything right now anyway.

From here on out, the meeting turned toward the specifics for Operation: Maldunech, which reminded me of the last briefing we had received, shortly before everything hit the fan. The plan this time around was similar, our goal to sabotage production and cripple their power gird—which would be far easier while the entire League was recovering from the Haccolces disaster.

This time, we would have more backup support. But that backup had less time than even the Haccolces mission had.

Three teams would be sent from the base this time. Maldunech was a port city set on the southern edge of the continent of Nestra, which lay far to the west of Terrol, across the Cynnith Ocean. Nestra was home to three cities in total. An advance party would be sneaking in ahead of us. All in all, the plan sounded quite possible, and considering Maldunech was the largest processing center of consumable goods in the world, we might just hamstring the Gaean League's supply chain.

I would be going with Zent and his team, while Kaen would stay here at the base. While I didn't like the idea of leaving him alone with Dekla and whoever else was left, I had to admit that he just didn't seem acclimated enough to Gaea to be in combat, power suit or no.

Shortly thereafter, Kaen messaged me, fumbling with Hellebes text before simply voice calling me. "How did the meeting go?" he asked.

"Oh. We'll be leaving tomorrow night. Admiral Skye and Captain Zent will be leading two teams, with Major Stenek leading an advance squad to get in position. We'll be . . . well, I won't bore you with the details, but I'm going with Zent and apparently you're staying here."

He let out a traditional Legaleian curse. "I knew it. Those fools. Don't they know how useful the Heart of Mani could be?"

"I had a feeling you would want to come."

"Of course I do! They're letting you have all the action while I sit here idle. I can use this power suit, and you know I can fight."

I hesitated. He was right, he could fight . . . but he was still new to Gaean martial arts and energy weapons. "I don't know Kaen . . . how powerful do you really think that sword is?"

He snorted. "Who cares? They've hardly let me use it at all."

"Let me talk to Zent," I said. "Maybe we can arrange a little demo."

A pause, and then: "All right."

"So you really think he's combat ready?" Zent asked skeptically, eying up my friend.

I gave a small shrug. "We should test it. What do you say, Kaen?"

Kaen nodded, understanding the gist of the captain's question.

"Then let's experiment," Zent said.

We stood in the energy lab, equipment laid out around us. The engineers had been hard at work on readying experimental weapons for the upcoming assault—not to mention mending the scars of our earlier tests—and a few of the men were still present, working on weapons in a side room and stealing glances our way.

Zent had Kaen try the sword's blade on various materials, and it proved to be keen enough to cut through most metals—even hardened steel, provided it was not thick enough to impair the blade's movement due to the angle of its edge. It was as though the alien magic of the sword enabled it to break the rules of the planet, and yet I had seen the blade absorb magic just as well. Any type of energy, it would seem.

We tried that next, carefully releasing blaster charges into the outstretched blade of the sword. Each one was not only absorbed but sucked in as though by a magnet. The silver pulled the energy from the air, curving its very streak. Indeed, it did not allow a single shot by as Zent, aiming with precision, fired above and below the outstretched blade.

Next, Zent had him hand the sword over, taking it by the hilt and turning it over in his hand. The sword's glow faded immediately, though it had not been particularly strong at the moment. Swinging it into the floor, he found it still bit into steel easily. Close examination showed the blade to be fine. We tried the same experiment with blaster fire on it, and the energy glanced off or swirled around it in the case of the flames. The absorption effect did not work for Zent.

We added pure Geothermic energy to the mix, though I never touched my heightened state of energy absorption, and this too had no special effects on the blade, neither harming nor energizing it, yet in Kaen's hand, it was able to redirect the energy elsewhere like a lightning rod grounded into the earth.

"Well, I'll be," Zent said, calling a halt. Our time was already up. "I'm impressed. Lyn, I think he could be quite useful."

"So . . ." Kaen looked questioningly from me to Zent.

With a sigh, Zent said, "I think I can convince them. Maybe."

When Kaen looked at me, there was relief but no warmth in his expression. He looked motivated and eager to prove himself, perhaps a little bit obsessed. Obsessed with vengeance. The look softened, but it was there long enough for me to recognize that he had set his sights on a new, more specific target of vengeance for Mandrie: The Gaean Elites.

Oh, Kaen, when will you rest? When will you be satisfied?

Maldunech

I believe this Memory Vault is far more secretive than they wish. But that is not the only miscalculation they have made throughout all this. Yes, I grow more certain each day that I will see vengeance visited upon the Anier. I care not if I die first—in fact, I most certainly shall—because my bloodline will continue. My will shall carry on, through blood and bone and every cell of my progeny.
— From Lhinde's Vault

They were poking me with hot irons. Each jab blazed with pain, eliciting screams my body was too tired to give. Who were they? Was there a name or a face behind the torture? I couldn't tell. I just knelt, taking the pain. Like unpleasant medicine. Surely it was good for me. I deserved it.

Medication. That was it. I lay on a medical table, awaiting more torture. "Medicine time," said a raspy, freakish voice, and a blurry figure held up a massive syringe filled with something black. "Don't worry; if it kills you, all the better. But it won't; you'll just wish it did. You'll turn into a monster for a bit. A dragon. Maybe go on a rampage, kill a few loved ones."

"No," I tried to moan, but nothing came out. No sound at all. My lips opened, but my throat was locked, as though I was choking silently on something. *Help,* I thought desperately. *I don't . . . I don't want to . . .*

The dream cut again, becoming a familiar scene of death in a laboratory, blood and sparks and bodies everywhere. The male voice was replaced by a female one, equally evil or more: "Relax, girl. Bask in it. Accept it. Admit to your own brutal nature."

Again, I could not speak. Every time I tried, accompanying pain throbbed deep in my chest. Cold pain.

At last I awoke, sweaty and gasping. *Just a dream.*

The next day came and went, comprised mostly of training, preparation, communication and a final briefing. Kaen was introduced to Zent's group, which was made up of ten Hellebes plus me and Kaen. Kaen and I were to stick together as much as possible for better communication, not to mention we knew each other well and could trust one another to guard our backs.

Or at least . . . that was the idea. Deep down, I worried how well that would work. Kaen and I had been growing more and more distant from one another, and the sword's continued hold on him worried me. Or was it his own uncontrolled emotions that gave it that power? No, that was silly. He couldn't be the one giving it the ability to absorb magic. Somehow, Mani's consciousness and power extended all the way to Gaea.

I would just have to make sure he didn't do anything stupid.

The briefing was at 22:00. We left shortly thereafter. Stenek's advance party had already left at twenty, and would arrive in a few hours. It was supposed to be a five-hour flight to Maldunech. We left at 22:30, taking two vessels per party. They were heavy vessels, larger than the typical omnicraft and more heavily armed, not to mention packing weapons that were only recently let out of classified research. Admiral Skye's group had another two vessels, similarly armed, and would be attacking from another sea gate.

The ride was tense, and Kaen spent most of it sitting silently next to me, rubbing his sword with a vengeance (no pun intended). The vessel we rode in, piloted by Zent—the other being piloted by one Sergeant Kidd—had windows we could look out, so at least that gave me something to do to keep my nerves at bay. I watched as the bubbles and schools of fish passed by amidst the darkness of the deep ocean. We had to rise nearly to the surface to pass through the sound that separated North Terrol from South Terrol, as that was the route we were taking.

After that, we submerged even deeper, to the point where we would be entirely blind without the vessel's powerful floodlights—although infrared and thermal technology gave Zent easy access to alternative visuals. These would come into use should we run across any nearby vessels. The scanners, however, did not pick any up. The Cynnith ocean was massive, according to the globes I'd seen, so much so that it was impossible for me to wrap my head around just how much water it contained, not to mention the fact that the twin continents of Mani could easily be crammed together in the space between Gaean continents.

Gaea's face was largely covered in water, something I never would have thought possible back in my homeland. A planet . . . covered in water. The thought had crossed my mind that perhaps these continents themselves floated on the water, much as the silver continents of Argent and Darsor floated in open air. But apparently modern science had long ago determined that to be false. The oceans only scratched the very surface of Gaea's sphere, like puddles on the ground.

Soon, the sea view lulled me to sleep, and I got perhaps two hours of sleep before Plato, who sat in front of me, turned around to wake me. "Psst! Almost there, moon dwellers."

"How far off are we?" I asked sleepily. My wrist console said 3:00.

"Fifty miles," Zent replied from the pilot's seat. "Everyone look sharp." A minute later, he radioed the other vessels to coordinate. Admiral Skye's crew seemed to have already deviated from the course we took, and were running parallel to us some hundred meters away. I wasn't sure exactly how big Maldunech was, but our intel said the gates were roughly a half mile apart. As I watched, our sister ships cut their lights, as did Zent, piloting by infrared and radar in the dark sea.

Eventually, just as we were slowing down and beginning to rise with the shallower waters, I saw the deep red glow of the city's undersea lights. One by one, they appeared out of the murky reaches of the sea. It was slightly less black up here, where we were perhaps one hundred feet from the surface and rising. As we came closer to Maldunech, I observed thick, sturdy walls reaching from the sea floor to the surface, and I knew they also extended upward. From there, the shield wall covered the city just like the other eight. I'd seen diagrams of the city, but experiencing this from underwater was another thing entirely.

"And there's our gate," Zent said, pointing ahead to where the eerie red guiding lights distinguished a heavy steel gate, much like the airlock doors back at the rebel base. Guns were mounted beside the doors but seemed inactive at the moment, unless our stealth was working exceptionally well. I knew that the advance team was supposed to have hacked into Maldunech's systems to drop security alarms around the two infiltration gates. Our operatives weren't able to actually open them, but we had a solution ready for that. A wondrous thing called . . . experimental weaponry.

A blast of energy issued from Sergeant Kidd's ship, a green-gold beam of pure Geothermic energy not unlike what I had produced in the energy labs while testing my powers with Zent. It split the doors down the middle, shearing in two the heavy locks, and with a few standard energy charges, the gates broke open. A missile blast sent them hurtling to either side, revealing the water-filled chamber of an airlock inside.

They repeated the same heavy laser blast on the inside doors, and a shiver ran down my spine as I realized what was about to happen. I could only hope no one was inside those doors, because . . .

Sure enough, the second barrier soon cracked open and, with a terrible *boom* that was palpable even through the insulation of our ship's hull, the doors burst inward under the sheer pressure of thousands . . . no, millions? Perhaps billions of tons of water bore down on it, creating a massive influx of water through the gaping hole. While the engineering it must have taken to build those doors was impressive, it seemed like a distinct weak spot.

The men in our ship cheered, and Zent cautioned Kidd over the radio before heading in through the busted gate, riding the current. I could feel the water wrestling the ship around as we went through, and I feared our hull would strike the sides, but Zent's experienced hand at the wheel kept us from doing so. Inside, we entered a flooded docking bay, similar to the one back at headquarters—aside from the too-high water everywhere, bursting at the doors. I could see where the Red Horizon had gotten the inspiration.

Dimly, through the hull of our omnicraft and the water rushing throughout, I could hear the sound of pressurized water breaking glass and ship hulls alongside a dissonant harmony of blaring alarms. I couldn't see any guards . . . had they evacuated? We broke through the far doors with torpedoes and rode the current through, rising toward the tall ceiling of a chamber I couldn't identify until we finally reached the level past which the seawater could not go. We broke above it, and I saw through my window the rushing, churning water, thrashing about as though frustrated at having to stop here. Random bits of debris floated here and there.

Here, we met our first real opposition in the form of mounted turrets which opened fire on our ships. Zent turned our vessel, maneuvering to land on the upper floor while Zig, who sat in the passenger seat and controlled our weaponry, took aim with our energy cannons and put the mounted guns out of commission. Kaen, who'd watched all this with a mixture of wide-eyed excitement and seat-gripping suspense, turned to me and asked, "Is the ship all right?"

I asked Plato, and shortly replied to Kaen, "Mostly intact. Eighty percent hull integrity. Kidd's ship is mostly fine as well."

As soon as both vessels landed, we piled out, weapons in hand. Kaen had a rather straightforward energy rifle, powerful and accurate but slow-firing and not a large heat producer, and I had the same blaster Musha had given me along with a replacement Octobug revolver cannon. Good old Hodge . . . Ever since I'd learned to exploit my new Geokinetic limits, I was able to charge my weapons almost infinitely as long as I had a good connection to the ground, with my elemental fire affinity from Mani providing extended resistance to the weapon's heat.

The alarms continued to blare as our party of twelve set off down a hallway. Apparently, Team C was not able to silence them once they'd begun. We were on the surface level, and had bypassed the main gatehouse in favor of the underwater one while creating a huge distraction, but now we needed to move. It wasn't long before guards intercepted us. Our heavily-armed squad gunned each group down without hesitation.

Kaen stuck close to me near the center of the squad, rifle half-raised, ready to fire but not wishing to harm any allies at the front. He said nothing, looking as tense as I felt. His suit afforded him the strength to keep right up with us. The metal-lined hallways we traversed were very similar to those back in Haccolces, evidently a staple across the nine cities, and clanked loudly with the tread of our boots. Periodically, Zent and Kidd radioed Team B—the admiral's group—and seemed to be growing increasingly frustrated as Team C did not respond.

"Stenek!" Zent hissed into his microphone. "Team C, come in!" Halting the party, he said, "Looks like Major Stenek's force has been compromised, so we'll be lacking backup. And no, that doesn't mean the mission is off," he said sharply in response to a budding question from Plato.

"Team C is not responding," I said quietly to Kaen. "Look out and stay close."

We proceeded onward, reaching the transport sector of the complex, and found what we were looking for: A subway leading straight into the manufacturing district. Team B would be headed toward the freight district. We boarded the underground tram and began a speedy commute to the manufacturing sector. Perhaps now I would actually get to see some of the city. As of yet, I'd only gotten underwater and indoor glimpses.

No sooner did we arrive, however, than the power cut out. Zent and Kidd kicked the tram doors open, ripping them off their tracks, as they refused to move. The overhead lights had cut out, leaving only the faintest lighting running along the bottom of the walls of the subway center. We emerged cautiously from the transport car, clicking on our thermal vision. Sure enough, a troop of soldiers appeared on my thermal visor from multiple doorways, showing up as simple but crisp humanoid forms.

"Halt!" called a digitally amplified voice. "Proceed no further, agents of the Red Horizon, in the name of Senator Strongs."

Senator Strongs . . . of Haven. What were they doing here? Was he bluffing? More and more men poured out of the doorways, walling us off with overwhelming numbers. Zent said quietly over the group channel, "Hold," before calling out into the darkness, "That's an awfully bold lie."

"I can assure you, I am telling the truth," the voice replied. "Senator

Strongs sent us on the basis of information received from a source in your organization. We already took out your advance party and pinpointed your location."

"Lyn," Zent said over a private channel. "We need a wide energy burst. Do you have enough Geothermic energy underground?"

I felt at the earth below me, far beneath the floor and other sub-surface levels. "Yes, sir."

"Wait for my cue."

Zent addressed the officer. "I take it you want the Mother?"

"Lay down your weapons and surrender. Have her come forward."

My companions parted to let me forward, and suddenly the lights snapped on, one at a time. I immediately put away my thermal visor, blinking at the sudden source of light, and beheld some forty to fifty soldiers blocking our way, weapons at the ready. Chief among them was a captain standing wary but confident, eying me up. He must have given the order for the power to be brought back on.

"Now, Lyn," came Zent's voice in my earphone.

"Roger that." Now that the enemy could not see heat readings, I drew steadily on Gaea's power, filling my lungs with it, my veins, my bones, every blood cell. Then I released it in a verdant wave, issuing from my mouth like a pressurized torrent. At the same time, I stomped with my foot, ripping up the floor in a wave that slammed into the troop of soldiers. They tried to fire back, and some tried to flee, but the surprise element of the Geokinetic blast guaranteed their quick demise, tearing through armor and slamming them against the far wall. The wall itself crumbled and collapsed.

Around me, my companions gasped, particularly Kaen. But they recovered quickly as I forged ahead, trampling over and past the dozens of bodies and mangled metal.

"Great work, Lyn," Zent said, slapping me on the shoulder as he caught up. "But I already ordered the evacuation for Team B. Those were Strongs' men, no mistaking it. We need to get out of here."

I stopped. He was right. Had the power of Gaea clouded my mind? I turned, looking at the faces of my comrades. Sirens from overhead vehicles—possibly land pursuit as well—came from outside. "Then let's go," I said.

"One problem," said Plato, gesturing at the broken tram behind him. "We're, uh . . . not getting back this way."

That was when the explosions sounded.

α Chapter 32 α

Sylleo

I'll give them a son . . . or a daughter! Oh, the thought . . . and I'll do so
gladly. Gladly, I say, for even a chance . . . just one chance.
— From Lhinde's Vault

They came from outside the building, rattling the already-damaged wall and blasting us with bits of rubble. I held my hands up to shield my face as floodlights poured in through the gaping hole in the wall.

"Come out of the transport building now!" came an amplified voice from overhead. "Or we'll level the whole thing."

Zent cursed. "If he's brought out the big guns, we're in trouble."

"Orders, sir?" asked Sergeant Kidd, scanning the visible city through the breach.

"Don't engage directly. They won't destroy the building from the air without knowing exactly where the Mother is. This is Brant's city. Let's see if we can't thin their forces while we find a means of escape."

Kidd and others of our group scattered for strategic cover while taking aim at the ships above. "Ground vehicles on the right!" someone shouted. Return fire came from snipers on the trucks and ground troops stationed across the wide street from us. Meanwhile, Zent, Kaen and I looked for a good way out, nearly walking into an ambush as we did. Zent's quick reflexes saved him from a blast to the face, and he immediately put down the two soldiers who'd been waiting there, listening in on us.

We walked the halls more carefully now, and Zent called out to his men to follow us. A couple more kept pace with Zent, surveying the situation before proceeding. Soon, we encountered more guards pouring in from outside. A full-out firefight ensued in the twisting hallways, and two of our men fell wounded. More soldiers poured in from behind, and I replicated my feat of Geokinesis—not quite as impressively—ripping up the floor to send it crashing through the hallway, effectively blocking the way.

Eventually, they began to bomb the building after all, and we were forced out into the open, trying to pick off the attack ships on our tail. "Zent!" I hissed into my mic. "What about Team C? Are they coming back?"

"Not sure, but I wouldn't count on it."

"Why are they attacking so recklessly, though?" I demanded.

He didn't have an answer. Our men took out one of the Stormhawk ships just before the other landed a hit with a missile, launching a half-dozen of our men aside in a blaze of fire. We took cover across the street beneath the pillared overhang of a sturdy industrial complex. I fired my Octobug into the enemy, trying to save the last of my Geokinetic strength for when it would count most.

"Lyn, this is insane!" Kaen said as he took aim with his energy rifle. "We can't possibly fight off all these troops."

"I know," I muttered back. "Hopefully, Zent has some secret plan."

Just then, a sleek, armored vehicle roared up behind us, followed by a half-dozen smaller ones, bearing a foreign design distinct from Strongs' forces and Maldunech's, plated in blue and chrome. As they approached, their mounted guns began firing at the remaining Stormhawk and the ground troops around us. The vehicle in front stopped, and the side door opened for a tall man—no, a *huge* man—bearing silvery hair and a pair of dark spectacles. My mind instantly recognized him, despite having only met him for a few minutes:

Sylleo, Senator of Ccamos. An Elite had arrived.

I tried to say something, but my mouth wouldn't quite work. Zent put a protective hand in front of me and said, "Lord Sylleo, what are you doing here?"

The titan made no reply, instead looking skyward, where the Stormhawk spiraled to its detonation. Before he looked back, he was gone. I thought I glimpsed a blur, a streak . . .

Something slammed into me, and suddenly I was held tight to someone's chest—Sylleo's chest. He stood with his back against the industrial building behind where I'd stood, one arm in an adamantine chokehold around my throat. My feet dangled over the ground, kicking weakly at iron legs. His grip was so stern that my vision fuzzed and my strength seemed to fade. He had moved like lightning . . . how?

Zent had barely turned before Sylleo said, "Give up. I won't kill any of you if you surrender and come with us. Unlike Strongs, I'm not here to kill her."

The words sent a chill down my spine.

Zent's eyes narrowed. "We'll take you at your word."

"Excellent." Sylleo squeezed harder around my neck, and before I knew it, I was unconscious.

I awoke disoriented, lying on a plush bed in a well-kept room. I would almost call it fancy—was that a thing on Gaea? Yes, when it came to the Elites. For a moment, I couldn't recall why I might be here. My brain seemed too busy trying to limp its way to my Vault to ascertain where I was.

Then it clicked. I'd been captured—again. Only . . . the cushy room didn't match my experience of Gaean incarceration. This didn't look like a prison. And I'd been with a full party, minus those who'd died along the way. I got choked out—must have been a blood choke, as that was far too quick for asphyxiation—and then . . . next thing I knew, here I was. And that Elite, Sylleo, how had he moved so *fast?* There was Musha speed, and there was impossible speed.

I sat up slowly, squinting my eyes at the dull hangover that seemed to follow any time I got knocked out. Looking around the room, I saw that it was not large or overly decorated, but everything just seemed lavish compared to what I was used to. First off, I had a soft bed with covers. The walls were not bare metal, but rather plaster. Woodworked windows were framed into one wall, inviting a stream of morning sunlight, and an unfamiliar potted plant sat on one of the sills. A rug twice my height in length, mottled with two shades of red, adorned the floor. On the far side of the room from my bed was an adjoining room with a door that stood ajar, a personal bathroom.

Hos . . . pitality?

How long had I been out? It couldn't' have been long. I still wore my gillsuit, which smelled faintly of the spicy, smoky scent of planetary energy in addition to gunpowder and dust from the excitement in Maldunech.

I groaned, leaning back on my pillow and holding up my hands. I felt so tired after using my powers every time. Every single time. But just then, I realized something: I hadn't been shackled in copper. Sitting bolt upright, I surveyed the room suspiciously to find copper lines etched into the walls, running parallel to the floor. A quick test confirmed this. I should have known. Sylleo was no fool, and was not going to let the Mother break herself right out of prison. It added a generous helping of cold reality to the surprise of this inviting room.

Still, why so nice?

Rising from the bed, I stretched and inspected the door, which was of ordinary Hellebes size, somewhere between eight and nine feet in height— almost three meters. A practical door crafted of solid steel and clearly built well. The lock was heavy and sealed electronically. One thing they had taken from me was my wrist console. I supposed that was simpler than just blocking the signal, as Lldsaor had done back in Haccolces.

What is with all these Elites trying to capture me for themselves? I wondered, shaking my head. Or . . . no, if my captor was to be believed, then Strongs had actually been out to kill, not capture, me. But I knew better than to think that Sylleo was going to be any better, no matter how comfortable a room I'd been given.

I took a quick step back from the door as distinctive clicks announced the disengaging of the lock. *Shk-shk-click!* I held my breath as the door slid open to reveal . . . not a guard, but the Senator himself: Sylleo. He paused in the doorway, looking me up and down. The man was as tall as Lldsaor, perhaps taller, but had a narrower, trimmer look, as opposed to Lldsaor's hulking shoulders and bulging musculature. Sylleo was like a professional athlete sized up one or two notches on photo-editing software. He wore a shirt and belted slacks that looked expensive, comfortable and less formal than the military uniforms I was used to. His silver hair was a shade darker than mine, yet his face, devoid of facial hair, had a quality of eternal youthfulness. I didn't know how old any of these Elites were, but something told me he was older than late-twenties.

"Lynchazel," he said after a moment. "That is your name, correct?"

I eyed him warily, giving a small nod. He had the same signature aura of power as Lldsaor and the other Elites. My instincts told me to keep backing up and find a place to hide, but I forced myself to stand my ground under his cool gaze.

"Good, good," he said. "May I come in?"

I glanced around the room as though searching for a reason he might not want to. Then my frightened-gazelle brain realized he was just being mock-polite. He waited in the doorway, however, apparently expecting an answer, so I gave a minimal shrug and said, "I'm not going to stop you."

Sylleo surprised me by laughing. It was one of those laughs distinctive of an individual person, not scripted but almost awkward as it came out. It didn't fit his clean-cut aesthetic. "I'll take that as a yes." His voice had a smooth richness to it that spoke of refinement beyond what I would ever expect from a Hellebes. He entered, and the door shut smoothly behind him. I didn't miss the fact that, as casual as he might seem, he happened to block just enough of the doorway that I could not possibly escape past him, not to mention the fact that he could instantly stop me with a single hand. He knew there was no possible chance of escape for me.

He pulled out the one chair that stood in the room, made of sturdy wood, and sat down. He gestured at the bed from which I'd risen minutes ago. "Please, sit."

I did so, plopping myself down on the springy mattress and using my hands to triangulate my balance. The mattress creaked ever so slightly with my weight. Though a half-dozen questions were brimming at my lips, I kept them back, playing along with Sylleo's cool approach to conversation.

The Senator leaned forward, broad hands engulfing the ends of his armrests. "Do you know what happened earlier?"

I hesitated. *Might as well be direct.* "How much earlier? How long was I out?"

"You were knocked out for a mere minute or so before we gave you an anesthetic. I won't lie to you. That was two hours ago. Didn't want you waking up and trying to replicate your feats of energy manipulation out of panic while we flew you back here."

"To . . . Ccamos?" The city Sylleo ruled.

He nodded. "Indeed. Allow me to explain: The rebel organization who keeps trying to use you—the Red Horizon—decided to strike Maldunech while Brant and most of the other Elites were busy responding to the recent Cydenges front. Which makes sense, as Brant is just the sort of ignoramus to forget about his city's defenses and the obvious logic of Maldunech as their next target—the Red Horizon's, that is. Strongs, however, is cunning and experienced in military strategy, though I suspect that he had inside knowledge of the Red Horizon's plans." He eyed me strangely. "One of your friends is a traitor."

"There aren't many I'd call friends," I said truthfully. Particularly on the council, though I didn't say that part. Of course, I recalled the words of Strongs' own captain, who had admitted they'd had inside intel.

"Well, in any case, I've also been tracking your movements, as well as those of the Red Horizon. I knew they were likely to make a move soon, taking advantage of the Cydenges attack. And I know Strongs. I have eyes in all eight cities, and he was acting more than suspiciously. So I tracked his forces to Maldunech and intervened. And what I said is true: He does intend to kill you, Lynchazel. Strongs believes that we would be better off without the Mother's bloodline, that the . . . current methods we have are sufficient. He's also a blind fool."

That last line was more cutting than I expected, spoken with true animosity toward his peer. "You Elites really don't like each other, huh?" It was all I could think to say, as there wasn't much difference to me between enemies who wanted to capture me for experimentation and those who just wanted me dead.

Sylleo snorted. "Not all of us. There are factions, alliances . . . I'm a nationalist, but a smart one. I don't have many friends, but I don't have many enemies either. I'm not particularly fond of Lldsaor and his party, but Strongs' growing campaign against the Mother and all she stands for makes me especially angry. He and Lldsaor are both slaves to progress, but their methods differ."

I almost asked, *And you?* But I realized that now might be an opportune time for some questions of more personal relevance. "Where are my friends? Are they alive?"

Sylleo tilted his head, giving me a *How much should I tell you?* look. "They are indeed. We took them all with us, and my medics are trying to save as many of the men as possible. A few will not make it, and others have been injured quite severely. We left ten, however, who were already dead."

I looked down at the floor in dismay. More men dead because of me. Only . . . it wasn't for my sake this time, was it? Still I felt a sense of responsibility. I mouthed the words, *I'm sorry,* as I thought of their sacrifice. Why did everyone around me have to die?

Then I looked up sharply. "Zent and Kaen are still okay, right?" They had been when I lost consciousness, but . . .

"The former captain is fine," he replied calmly. "And if you are referring to the Legaleian man with the silver sword, then yes, he is all right as well. Feisty little guy. It took some convincing to get him to cooperate. Is he . . . all right up here?" He made an amusing circular gesture with his finger pointing at his head.

I laughed despite myself. "Yes. I think. He's . . . I'm just glad he's okay. But why did you save them all? Are you holding them hostage to get me to cooperate?"

Sylleo raised his grey eyebrows. "Hostage? Yes, I'd say so. But it's more a matter of principal. You can't trust me yet, so I can't trust you to not try anything drastic. I respect you, both as a human being and as an important piece in the future of Gaea, so I ordered you be brought to this room. But the copper is necessary for security."

"You say that like you're a nice person," I accused.

Another laugh from the tall man. "And am I?"

I narrowed my eyes. "I don't know. But you Elites are all the same, trying to control Gaea like a machine that works for you, treating Hellebes like slaves, like mindless animals."

"And did you ever think that there might be a reason for that? An explanation?"

The question surprised me. I wasn't sure why, because it was such an obvious imperialist line to disparage the masses and justify their treatment as a necessary role in society. Taking my hands off the mattress, I leaned forward on my knees, causing the bed to creak once again. "I'm not that stupid. I don't trust you, and no amount of nice things is going to change that. The Emperor tried the same thing, coaxing me to support him."

His eyebrows went up again. "Did he? And here I thought he kept you in a concrete dungeon with iron bars."

I hesitated. He had a point. *No, forget these distractions, you fool.* "That's . . . not what I mean. You could feed me strawberries and ice cream, and I still wouldn't trust you, because you're just trying to manipulate me. Everyone is."

Sylleo steepled his fingers, producing a wooden creak like a cry for help as he leaned back in his chair. "Even the Red Horizon," he said.

The words stung. Not because they were unfair, but because they were true. The rebels were just like the Senate in that regard, using me as a tool to further their agenda. I looked down at the floor again. On his face, I pictured a smug smirk, as he'd squarely won that exchange.

Instead, he rose from the chair. "I'll leave you to your thoughts for now. But know that your friends are safe, and will continue to be. I will not harm them. I'll return before long to discuss more important matters."

With that, he turned to leave. I watched him go, chin held in the heel of my hand, which was propped up by my elbow. The door opened seemingly on automatic for him, and he passed through the doorway, head a mere six inches from the top. It shut behind him, sealing off all sound from the outside world.

Except the windows, that is. Exhaling, I rose and approached the nearer of the two. It was perhaps a meter square, with two reinforced crosspieces as thick as the wall itself, studded deep into the walls. There was no fitting through the holes, and no breaking through without the use of Geokinesis. No, sir. As fine as this room looked, it was an effective cell.

But I wasn't expecting to get out of here.

Leaning on the sill, I was granted a breathtaking view of the city of Ccamos. It was different from the heavy industry and manufacturing that I'd seen in my limited glimpses of Maldunech, in that most of the buildings were smaller, cleaner, neater. Many districts were entirely made up of what appeared to be residential buildings two stories tall, some painted in light colors. The roofs were either of tin or polished stainless plating, reflecting the morning light in a dazzling array. Only one or two districts had high-rises, and most of these appeared to be office buildings of a sort. Looking back at my earlier instruction on world economics, I recalled that Ccamos was the largest in population, and was also a large center of engineering, communications, software design and administrative tech development, so most of the work done here was on the cyber level. Powerful signal towers enabled the workers' connection around the world, although of course AI and quantum computing did much of the heavy lifting in that regard.

I just . . . hadn't expected the city to be this orderly—even beautiful. Sure, if I looked up at the red force field seemingly bearing down on the city, it ruined some of the effect. But perhaps one of the things that made the view more agreeable was the lack of thick smog and industrial smoke clouds that overshadowed Haccolces and Maldunech, billowing high into the sky.

What if Sylleo wasn't that bad after all? What if he was telling the truth? Maybe he was doing some things right? As unlikely as that seemed, the thought that at least one of the Elites was not a power-hungry maniac was an enticing dream indeed. The question, then, remained:

What *were* his motives?

α   Chapter 33   α

A Strange Prison

How many years has it been since Starklett? Since the Anier murdered Mother and Father? Did that really happen? It is already mid-Firvaen of 1302, and seven moons have turned this year. I can recall such dates and details with ease thanks to my new Cydenges—or . . . Hellebes—mind, and yet my previous life seems so distant, like a memory glimpsed in a foggy mirror. I have crossed that mirror and no longer reside in that world. That middle-age world of princes and knights is passing away.
— From Lhinde's Vault

Over the course of that day, I slept off my eventful night. Servants came periodically to bring me meals. Actual servants, not uniformed guardsmen. They bore crisp non-military uniforms, complete with shiny black shoes and long-tailed vests. They weren't overly talkative but were respectful and polite. The food was not half bad, including even meat and . . . I think some fruit? Something sweet. Neither was something I was used to back at Red Horizon HQ.

According to the analog clock hanging above the door, it was thirteen o'clock when Sylleo returned. I actually breathed out a sigh of relief upon seeing him, not because he was a friendly sight but because it meant one more small way he was holding to his word. He paused in the doorway. "Hello again," he greeted me with a small nod.

I nodded back. I wasn't sure why; it just felt right. His manners compelled me to respond in kind.

He stepped inside, and the door slid shut behind him. "I'd like to discuss a few matters if you don't mind."

"All right." I watched as he took a seat in the same chair, once again making it look small and weak holding up his oversized frame.

"Let's be frank," he said. "I'm imprisoning you in this room because I can't trust you, because you can't trust me. I realize it can't come immediately, but I'd like to get past that. So let's talk for a bit, and I'll let you in on some secrets."

"I just want out of here," I said on impulse, unsure why, as that was not all I wanted. I wasn't desperate to get out. Perhaps his direct words triggered a rebellious impulse in me.

He chuckled. "I know. Tell you what, I'll let you out of here if you hear me out and we can come to a personal agreement."

I narrowed my eyes. *Did I hear that right? He wouldn't actually . . . just . . .* "You're not going to let me out of here."

"I am." He said it as a matter of fact. "If, as I said, we can come to an accord."

"And what about my friends? Zent and Kaen and the others?"

"Those not currently held in the medical ward are being kept in the same accommodations as you," he replied.

I raised my eyebrows. I believed him, or I thought I did, it was just . . . surprising. I assumed he had them locked in some dark, subterranean dungeon since their title didn't start with M and end with "other." "And you'll release them too?"

"Yes."

I took a deep breath. His frankness and apparent generosity caught me off-guard, and I had to recover. "Then . . . what is your proposal?"

"I don't think we're ready for that quite yet. You and I both know you'd run off at the first good chance of escape."

I rolled my eyes. This conversation was starting to sound circular.

"We need to establish a level of familiarity," he continued. "You and I. I'm aware of a lot more than you think regarding your relationship to these rebels. Most factions on Gaea know a fair bit about the Red Horizon, and, as I already said . . . I think at least one has a plant directly in their group. Personally, I have no reason to go after them. Strongs . . . well, now that you escaped his grasp, I really can't say. At some point, I'd like to establish a connection with them to exchange information and perhaps even work together. Surprised?"

I didn't say anything, but I'm sure my face gave it away all too well.

"You see," he explained, "Strongs wants to be rid of you forever, if possible. Hopefully, that will be harder now that you are in the custody of another Senator, provided he doesn't go as far as starting a civil war . . . Lldsaor, on the other hand, wishes to re-implement you as Mother Gaea. Brant would like to add to that by ushering in a new era of Mother-worship . . . you probably don't even know about that, do you?"

"I've heard that there are some who worship the Mother as an actual goddess."

"Yes, well, it's worse than you might imagine. In any case, my goal is to establish a peaceful alternative that doesn't rely on taking advantage of the one . . ." He made a strange grimace, retracting both lips in a thin line. "The one real human left on this planet." He eyed me. "I can tell from your face that you don't know what *that* means. Just take my word for it."

I looked aside, making an effort not to roll my eyes at the statement. Did he think I didn't know about the artificial breeding program? I wasn't that out of touch. I mean . . . I didn't know many details, but I knew full well that my mother giving birth to me through natural means was an unheard-of thing nowadays.

"So what do you want from me?" I asked finally.

He smiled, as though I'd lit upon the correct question. "I'd like you to come with me, and I'll show you some things."

"Come with you, like . . . you're just going to let me out of here."

Sylleo took a small breath, appearing to consider my words. "Yes." He said that one word with a calm confidence that implied there was no reason he couldn't handle me should I act up. Could it be that all these precautions were only a ruse? That he wasn't scared of my powers at all?

Or, I realized, *he's not scared—but he also doesn't want me killing his servants. Ruining his property.*

Somehow that felt like giving him too much credit.

I looked the tall man in the eye, and it seemed he dared me to question him further. We shared a silent understanding. His almost imperceptible nod seemed to say, *Yes, I could easily put you down.* Or maybe I was jumping to conclusions.

"All right," I said.

We both stood, and he led me out of the room. We passed a pair of armed guardsmen at the door, who looked askance at me with brief fear, but Sylleo waved them away, saying, "We are leaving for a bit, and you don't have to attend me."

No copper handcuffs, no bracelets.

The hallway stretched nearly fifty feet in front of us after branching off to either side, lined with red carpeting. The plastered walls were hung with classical paintings, and molded wooden trim adorned the bottom and top of the walls. Doors matching that of my room were spaced at intervals of twenty feet or so. Once more, I wondered where we were.

At the end of the hall, Sylleo opened another tall steel door. He scanned his hand over the lock and it whooshed open. After waving me in front of him, the Elite stepped through and we continued, descending a long flight of stairs, broken by no less than three landings. We arrived in a large room bustling with activity, spanning dozens of feet in every direction and bearing multiple walkways and exits. A closet was tucked in here, another stairway there, tables for eating over there, and . . . something smelled really good, coming from my left. Yes, there it was, an open kitchen laid out on one side of the room, staffed by Hellebes cooks preparing something delicious.

"Is this . . . your house?" I asked, beginning to catch on.

"Of a sort," he responded, moving down one aisle toward another room. Every servant and guard we passed simply gave the Senator a respectful nod, while others farther back pointed and whispered, either at the sight of their ruler or of the mysterious Mother Gaea in the flesh. I wished we were heading toward the food to try a bite, but alas, he took me out a door into yet another room, which appeared to be an office of some sort.

"We check in visitors here," he said to me, as though that explained something. Approaching one of the desks, he told the clerk, "Checking the Mother out for a little while to see the city."

The man nodded professionally, stealing only a small glance at me. "You . . . don't need me to call for some accompaniment, sir?" he asked skeptically.

"None needed."

The clerk said nothing more, though his face betrayed the same concern that the guards outside my door had, that of one seeing a man walking a dangerous predator on a leash. He stamped something on a pad and clacked some keys on his keyboard as Sylleo led me out into yet another room.

This one was an entryway outfitted with magnetic and thermal scanners and a pair of straight-backed guardsmen, rifles held at the ready. Their posture was quickly made even more formal as we approached, though these did not echo the sentiment of skepticism toward their Senator's judgment.

They opened the door, which slid to both sides from the middle, and I got my first closeup view of Ccamos: Sunlight streaming sideways over two rows of trees, which lined an immaculate quarter-mile lane ending in a tall, black iron fence. Beyond lay houses and other buildings, although most in this district looked to be administrative. Inside the fence to either side spread a landscaped lawn peppered with artful stones and statues and birds, most of which I could not tell real from fake. Overhead waved silver-and-red flags bearing a flying heron with a crown and an arrow over its head—the insignia of Ccamos.

"So . . . where is this?" I asked, following him out a few paces. "Your own private mansion? Or is this the Capitol Building?"

"No, the Capitol is to the south of here. This is my estate. Basically a mansion, as you say." He stopped some thirty feet from the building and turned around, gesturing at it.

I followed his gaze, turning to take in the majestic view of a mansion easily the size of the entire Nytaean Palace. It was built like a brick cube that had met another cube, settled down and had some baby cubes. The entry room, for instance, was one of these square babies. The roof of each segment slanted downward gently, growing steeper toward the edges, tapering toward lower roofs in a subtle attempt at elegance. It was . . . not hideous. In fact, it had character—just too much of the modern Hellebes design for my taste. "Nice place," I said. "So you just . . . live here? And have hundreds of servants to do whatever you want?"

Sylleo glanced at me, combed silver hair catching the sunlight. "Yes," he said simply, pretending that hadn't been an accusation. "That is what they are for. They all live a good life, along with the guardsmen. I provide for their needs and pay them a stipend on top of it; they live a meaningful existence."

For all of his friendly demeanor, these last words felt oddly cold. Not simply because he was speaking frankly about his servants, but because of the long familiarity that accompanied his words. He spoke of facts of life, the same as he might about gravity or weather changes. But . . . that was no different from Lord Kalceron, or Archlord Domon. What bothered me most was the way he said *meaningful existence* with neither derogation nor sympathy.

"So, what do you think?" he asked.

"Of what?"

"The manor," he said.

I looked once more at the soaring rooftops and considerable girth of the building, and then frowned. "It's . . . not bad. Wait—why are you keeping me in this building? Why do you check prisoners in and out of here if it's just a residence?"

A small tilt touched the edges of his lips, seemingly in approval. "Now you ask. It doubles as many things. It contains many guest rooms and amenities, in addition to no less than two infirmaries, a surgical center and a lab."

I frowned. "I think you're confusing guest rooms with prison cells."

He shook his head. "No. We have some higher security rooms than others, but any that you would actually call a cell are back in the jail at the capitol. I consider you a guest."

"And my companions?"

"Also guests. And hostages. For that reason, they have to be detained securely, but as I said, they've been kept in the same accommodations as you. Come, walk with me and I'll show you around."

I canceled my next response as he set off with long strides, radial to the manor house. He showed me elaborate gardens and a fruit orchard, a large training grounds where shirtless guardsmen and trainees sparred with polycarbonate weapons, and a luxurious swimming area, which seemed to be reserved for Sylleo and his most distinguished guests. It was so strange to think that, wherever family had a place back on Mani . . . there was nothing on Gaea. I didn't even know who these VIPs would be—perhaps League officials or high-ranking military officers. Considering all his words about hospitality, perhaps foreign dignitaries from other cities.

I said little as he showed me around. He seemed to get a bit caught up in showing off his many possessions and property, as well as his accomplishments that supposedly bettered the lives of all those at the estate. Sylleo had a flare for boasting.

At one point, he asked, "Are you hungry, Heiress? We could get a bite to eat from the resident cooks. They should have all manner of culinary delights on hand."

Having been listening to my own stomach as much as to Sylleo for the past fifteen minutes, I was immediately on board. "That sounds amazing. I'm . . . really hungry right now." I was *always* hungry. Back on Mani, they'd teased me for having the appetite of a large man; now having become a stranger, almost alien, creature, my appetite continued to outstrip most other Hellebes. Either it was the fact that I was half Legaleian and thus had a different metabolism, or it had something to do with my abilities as the Mother . . . whatever that truly meant. Seeing as it had only increased after I unlocked my new traits, the latter seemed pretty likely.

He led me inside by another entrance, checking me in at the desk, and we reentered the open, multipurpose room where the kitchen was set up. The cooks, seeing the Senator approach, looked up and asked, "How may we assist, sir?"

"We'll take a couple of those sweet-and-salty biscuits, and . . ." he looked at me. "Anything you see that you'd like, ask away." He gestured at the glass display case where a long tangle of burners kept various pastries, rolls and desserts warm, as well as other foods I did not recognize.

My stomach grumbled. I glanced from the pastries to the cooks, and then back to Sylleo, who was taking the two biscuits handed to him by one of the cooks. I asked for four different pastries I'd never had the luxury to try. No one turned me down; Sylleo merely raised his eyebrows as the cook grabbed all four and handed them to me on a light metal plate. Tin, perhaps.

"Quite the appetite you have." Sylleo handed one of his biscuits to me as he took a bite of his own. "Here, try this first. Ccamos sweet-and-salty biscuits are famous."

I did so, balancing my plate of goodies on my left hand. I tried not to be a pig, but somehow the crisp, flaky pastry was gone in a mere few seconds. I hammered my chest, trying to choke down the last bits wedged in my throat. It was a bit dry, but . . . the taste was just as heavenly as the Senator had made it out to be.

A stocky Hellebes cook swiftly produced a cup of water and silently held it out for me to take. I nodded in thanks and took a swig. After swallowing, I said, "Thank you," and looked sheepishly at Sylleo. "That was good."

He gave a wry smile. "Anything else you'd like to eat?"

I glanced down at my plate of golden, chocolate and frosted goodness. "Mm, this'll probably do me for now." I took the chocolate pastry and bit deeply into it. It melted in my mouth, crackling as I crushed the crispy inner layer. Where did they get these *recipes?* Here I'd thought all Hellebes ate pre-packaged emergency food and dry, bland military rations . . . Sylleo may have been buttering me up to trust him, but his bakers were doing a fine job of the buttering as well.

Sylleo grabbed one more baked good, which he called a pretzel, and took me upstairs to a formal dining area, or perhaps a conference room—though it wasn't as sparsely decorated as I'd expect something like that to be—where he sat me down to eat and chat. Neither servant nor guard bothered us here, save for the quiet guard who stood outside the door, just out of earshot.

"I thought this room might make for a more private place to converse," he said as he crunched into his pretzel.

I nodded vaguely, scarfing down my pastries. Between Hellebes-sized bites, I asked, "How come the other Senators are out fighting the Cydenges, and you're, y'know . . ."

"Sitting idly at home with my men?" he finished. "A very good question. We'll just say I find ways around such obligations. In case you're not aware, I suppose I ought to explain the League's agreement regarding Cydenges raids: All cities have instruments tracking Luna around the clock for disturbances, plus a number of satellites orbiting Gaea and taking frequent readings. But . . . it's hard to tell anything until it's already begun. By then, it's almost as easy to simply look for the red lights in the sky."

"Red lights," I repeated uneasily. "That's what Captain Zent said, too. How do they get *here?* From the moon?"

He took another bite of his pretzel. "That's not the only thing about the Cydenges that defies basic physics. The simplest explanation is that they jump from one world to another. We've studied it as closely as possible since long ago. For centuries. They crouch and the red light that glows from inside of them intensifies, and suddenly they are gone in a pillar of red light, landing on the surface of the other world. We've replicated many of the Cydenges traits through experimentation, but whatever power they use to teleport, that we've never discovered."

Cydenges experiments, huh? Wait . . . centuries? I'd heard similar wording back at the Senate assembly. One thing at a time. "So, uh, they can go back and forth between Gaea and Luna?"

He nodded.

"Then . . . why haven't they attacked Mani yet?"

"Another excellent question." Sylleo tapped a finger on the dark wooden table between us. "You know about the energy barrier that surrounds Mani, yes? It has proven more powerful than you might think. Generations of Lldsaor's engineers have struggled to come up with a way to bypass it.

Apparently, it is capable of repelling even a determined Cydenges. Or at least . . . that is our going theory. Another states that there is some reason the Cydenges are only interested in Gaea. A grudge, some say."

Something didn't quite add up. If these Cydenges were so powerful that they could bridge worlds at will, then surely they could get to Mani? The teleportation Gates worked, or at least *used* to work before the Archlord destroyed the Gate of Mani . . . and how different was the Cydenges' ability? But regardless, the question remained: "What did you mean by *centuries?*"

Sylleo paused. An accidental slip of the tongue? If so, he'd done it twice. "The Gaean League has existed for the better part of a millennium, Lynchazel."

"But you said 'generations of Lldsaor's engineers,'" I pressed.

His eyes traced an imaginary shape on the wall behind me. "That's complex. I think we'll have to dig into that answer another time. Suffice it to say Lldsaor is far older than he appears. I am as well. We've technology on our side the likes of which you can only dream, and technology can achieve wonders. Wonders and horrors."

I started to object, then sighed and dropped the question. I'd get to the bottom of it, but I had enough questions for now. "So, what if the Cydenges really did have some . . . vendetta against Gaea?" I asked. "What if they suddenly decided they wanted to wreck my world instead? I don't know how you guys deal with them here, but Manese magic may be ineffective."

Sylleo frowned. "Remember that this is your world as much as Mani. You may be right, however. There's no way to know for sure. The creatures certainly have enormous strength, greater than any Hellebes, as well as the ability to siphon energy, so it's possible that they would simply overpower the unsuspecting Manese and overrun the silver moon." My immediate reaction was to balk at his words, but he held up a forestalling hand. "I'm not saying they will attack Mani. There has been no sign of such a thing. That said, we have discussed the possibility before; remember that there was no way to know how humans had adapted in exile until you came back to Gaea."

"In . . . exile?"

Sylleo paused for a moment, and I realized that had been an accidental slip. "You wouldn't know about any of that," he said with a small sigh. "The Red Horizon probably tried to hide information from you—in fact, I know they did, and they had to."

"Everyone keeps saying that," I muttered. "It's a convenient excuse not to tell me anything."

"Then we can remedy that. How about I give you some answers? I'd be willing to bet that will open the door more than anything else for some mutual trust."

I nodded. "Okay."

"Then let's start with the exile, or as some call it, the Great Pilgrimage: Your people came from Gaea—specifically, a region known as Legaleia, or Mani Halcyon. There are multiple stories floating around today, some saying that they committed a great sin and their god took them away to another world, others claiming that they were kidnapped by moon-dwelling aliens . . . But the ancient archives state that the Legaleians indirectly caused the first Cydenges attack, drawing their attention to our world, and thus brought about a massive slaughter. Eventually, the ancients found ways to combat them and drive them away, but it was agreed that the world would be better without their magic."

"So they shipped everyone off to the moon?" I asked. "Just like that? What about the Wellspring—was that when that was placed on Mani?"

"I assume you speak of the Ancient Fount, the source of their magic? Yes, the magicians found a way to construct the Gates and transport the Fount to Mani. Without some . . . pressure from the nations around them, they would not have willingly gone. But they made an accord, agreeing to leave for a thousand years. But . . ."

"It didn't work," I guessed.

He nodded. "The Cydenges came back anyway. It was a foolish plan. The Legaleians were so enraged with the other peoples at that point that nothing would have swayed them from going. They were determined to turn a disgraceful exile into a fresh start in a new world."

"So how did they do it?" I asked. "How did they just . . . uproot this Wellspring, this . . . Ancient Fount, and take all the world's magic to Mani?"

He shrugged. "I know little about it. Your guess is better than mine. Personally, I would say the Ancient Fount was an important object or relic that allowed magic to thrive, without which Gaea could not sustain it."

"They didn't take the magic with them," I mused. "It died out when they left. That makes sense." And it corroborated the story told by the mural deep beneath Ti'Vaeth. I was going to say more when I suddenly realized I might be giving this man more information than I should. Sure, he already knew about the Wellspring and the Exile, but any information on what Mani was like now, after the Wellspring and the Great Pilgrimage, could go directly toward the invasion of my homeland. Although he had been one of the few to oppose the initial offensive.

"What else would you like to know about?" he asked, resting his chin on his thumb and forefinger. "I have a vast array of historical knowledge, both in my Vault and at my fingertips here in the city."

It was a tempting offer, and even seemed genuine. But I knew, despite his criticism of the Red Horizon, that he wasn't going to tell me *everything* I wanted to know. Just the harmless info. He'd already brushed off one query, and right now there was something far more pressing.

"I'd like to see my friends," I said. "I can learn things later." I also could use the time to let my head clear. My thoughts were starting to jumble like crowds in a narrow street.

"I can arrange that. Would you like to go now?"

I nodded.

α Chapter 34 α

Animosity

I am defective.
— From Lhinde's Vault

"So that's where you've been," Kaen grumbled. "Playing around with the Senator. Why am I surprised?"

Apparently, he couldn't think of a more polite way to greet me as I walked in, tailed by Sylleo. Both Kaen and Zent numbered among the room's occupants, along with Plato. Three more were held in a nearby room, those not still in the hospital. Sylleo had informed me that the surviving injured would be sent here as soon as they were well enough.

Once again, the guards waited at the door. No copper lined this room, either. Zent eyed Sylleo and me, eyes darting between us, but said nothing beyond a relieved nod to acknowledge my presence. The Senator seemed to make him uneasy.

"Zent, Plato, Kaen," Sylleo said, dipping his head to each respectively. I was impressed that he'd actually taken the time to learn all their names. Not that it took long for a Hellebes.

"Come here, Kaen," I said, approaching and embracing him like a dog might a familiar but unfriendly cat. He didn't push me away. I moved on to Zent, shaking his hand and moving in for the one-handed shoulder clasp I was used to. I made sure to hit him as hard as he hit me.

"It's good to see you safe, Lyn," the captain said. "You did well out there. No one could have expected that op to go so far off the rails." Letting go of my hand, he looked up at Sylleo. "Thank you, sir, for treating her as well as you promised. How are my men? And the admiral?"

"Your men are recovering, all except for Skye and Dim. I promised I would take care of them. Criminals you may all be, but not under my

"

jurisdiction. Strongs is upset, and the Mother is alive, so I call that a win."

"Skye . . ." Zent's voice betrayed more emotion than usual. "They're that bad, Senator?"

Sylleo nodded.

"Lyn," Kaen said quietly, drawing my attention. Sylleo also glanced at him, but of course was unable to understand. "You know you can't trust this monster."

His words caused an involuntary shudder inside me. In them I read a question, a statement, animosity . . . and an implication that I was one of the monsters—Sylleo simply the greater one.

"Kaen, I don't know yet. I don't know that."

He glared at me. "Don't be a fool. If you don't know, it means you can't trust him. Yet you look all buddy-buddy to me."

I was going to respond when Sylleo spoke again, withdrawing his curious stare from Kaen and addressing all of us: "I plan to set you all free in time. Mark my words."

"Why would you do that?" Zent asked bluntly, folding his arms. "You already went to all the bother to lock us up—why let us escape?"

"Because I wish to work with the Red Horizon. I believe we can find a common goal and further each other's pursuits. Naturally, I can't achieve that without some mutual understanding between you and me, and I can't let you go until I'm certain, particularly since there is a spy in your midst."

Zent's shocked expression did not escape me. "So you know about that? I've suspected a traitor ever since Strongs' army showed up so quickly . . . but then how did you know?"

"I have ears everywhere," Sylleo answered. "I was just telling Lynchazel what I think of the Haven Senator and his philosophy . . . not very highly, that is to say, but he is cunning, and I believe he has an agent or two in the Red Horizon. I tracked him down to Maldunech and stepped in to foil his plans."

Zent shook his head in wonder. "I don't know what to make of any of this, sir." He glanced at me, then flicked his eyes back to the Senator. "Would

I be allowed to speak with her in private for a minute?"

The request seemed almost silly, given that this room was not copper-lined and the Ccamos Senator would be allowing three Hellebes, one the Mother, alone in the room. To the surprise of all, he merely nodded thoughtfully and made to step out of the room. "A couple minutes," he said before opening the door and shutting it behind him.

Kaen gave me a sidelong glare. "What's going on now?"

"Sylleo wants to make a deal," I explained. "He wants to work with the rebels, and he claims there's a traitor in our midst who gave intel to Strongs. The one who sent those men after us. I'm going to talk with Zent." I repeated this last in Hellebes.

He nodded, and Zent said, "Lyn, are you sure you know what you're getting yourself into?"

He obviously understood that Sylleo was targeting me as both his bargaining chip and spokesperson with the Red Horizon. "I think so," I said. "I can't say for certain about him, but I think trusting him is by far our best option. He could be just putting on an act, waiting to turn me over to some other Senators as soon as I agree to join him, but . . ."

"But he wouldn't bother asking for your consent in that case," Plato chimed in.

Zent nodded. "Just so. He seems a sharp, calculating man who knows what he's doing. If his intentions were to kill you or imprison you like the others, he wouldn't be trying to sway you this hard."

"I mean . . . Lldsaor tried the same thing," I reasoned. "But poorly—he treated me like garbage, less than human. He only cared about getting the Senate to go along with his plans."

When Sylleo opened the door once more, we were ready. "Well?" he asked. "Come to any conclusions?"

"We will abide by your wishes," Zent said.

Sylleo clapped his hands. "Excellent." Looking at me, he said, "I'm glad you made the wiser choice. There are just a few more things to arrange first. I will be taking Lyn again for today, but we shall reconvene soon."

He neither gestured nor called for me; he merely glanced my way, nodded at Zent, and took his leave. I followed wordlessly. For all his casual demeanor, the Senator's mannerisms brooked no argument. His uniform rippled across his muscular back as he glanced from one guard to the other—two armed Hellebes guarded the door—and proceeded to descend the steps, as these rooms were also on the upper floor of the prison building. The man was a living, breathing mystery, a titan of the modern world whose age and origin I did not know. Hellebes were not supposed to live very long, right? Could he have been serious about living centuries thanks to technology? Those were Legaleian High Mage years and more. How was a Senator even chosen in the first place?

At the top of the stairs, as soon as I thought we were out of earshot of the guardsmen, I asked Sylleo, "How come you treat them all so nicely?"

He paused, turning his head to look at me. "Your friends from the Red Horizon?"

I nodded.

"Kaen is the only full-blooded Legaleian present on this planet, and thus poses an intriguing opportunity in multiple ways, and Zent is a leader among the Red Horizon, with whom I wish to establish contact. The least I can do is be courteous, as it serves my purposes."

I followed the Senator as he resumed his descent. "And Plato? You even went to the bother to learn everyone's names."

"Ah, but that could simply be to win your favor, no?" He chuckled to indicate that it was a joke. "Or perhaps I enjoy common courtesy, both given and taken."

We reached the bottom, and he began to take me back outside. "If you wish to continue this, I can show you another desirable place," he offered.

I said nothing, assuming he would take the silence as consent. But before we'd reached the check-in room, I asked, "Then do you treat your own servants and guardsmen the same way? They're just . . ." I paused as he went through the same process of checking me out of the building, until we were outside and out of earshot of anyone else. He led me around to the right and toward the taller cluster of buildings he'd pointed out as his personal residence before. Though connected to the main complex, it was distinct. "They're pretty much robots, right?"

He glanced sharply at me, though he kept walking. Indignation? A sore spot?

"I mean—the obedience gene," I hurried to add. "It keeps them from ever disobeying you, right? I wasn't trying to say—"

He waved away my apology, nodding hesitantly. "True. It does. But that doesn't mean I see them any less as people just because we the Gaean League have figured out a way to control genetics. Their will remains entirely free in all other regards, and there are less in the way of programmed predispositions than you might think—predispositions to do only and exactly as demanded, that is. I pay them a wage for their services and allow them to purchase and sell goods on the free market, make goals, chase hobbies, et cetera."

I frowned. That still sounded a lot like slavery to me. I didn't bother to mention that these men were conditioned from artificial birth to love and obey the Senate via a strict training regimen that dictated their entire lives. Nor the fact that none of them could ever have families, no progeny to carry on their work or family line. Did they even have any connection to one another? Friendships? What kind of hobbies would they keep?

I stewed on these thoughts, getting a bit distracted by the landscaping and architecture of the manse, where Sylleo led me inside the front door. We came into a massive foyer with a light interior and intricately tiled floor. Much of the theming and decoration was similar to the rest of the complex, but this foyer was noticeably more extravagant and classical.

A butler met us at the door mere seconds upon entering. Bowing, he asked, "How may I be of service today, master Sylleo?" He bowed to me second with a polite, "Mother Lynchazel."

"Greetings, Margill," Sylleo said, removing his shoes and leaving them at the door.

I glanced down at my own feet, covered by the built-in boots of my dirty grey gillsuit. "Should I . . .?"

Sylleo waved a hand. "No need. Margill, we will be meeting in the west parlor. Perhaps some tea?"

"Right away, sir." The butler hurried toward what I assumed to be the kitchen area.

I followed Sylleo to the left through an ornate door made of thick hardwood, down a wood-paneled hallway and into the parlor. It was long and furnished with comfy-looking leather reclining chairs and two paintings of astonishing workmanship, one of a tree dotted with pink blossoms and the other of a medieval-era castle, much like one might see on Mani. *Lilta Castle, Starklett*, read the inscription.

Sylleo took a chair near the long far wall in front of a broad bay window, gesturing in front of him. I took the indicated chair, but neglected to cross my legs as he did. Then he spoke: "Lynchazel, you seem to be under the impression that I am just like the other Senators. Despite me going out of my way to show you that I am not."

"That's not—" I began to protest, and then considered my words. ". . . exactly . . . what I was saying." His defense was unfair and basically flawed. I took a breath. "I just feel like I'm still in the dark, missing all the important details while everyone hides them from me. Who are you? Where did you Senators come from? Why did you mess with human genes? What's . . . real? And what's a lie?" I was not trying to be accusatory, just getting the questions off my chest.

Sylleo let me rant, watching me with an unreadable expression, fingers laced in front of his raised chin. When I was done, he said, "What if I told you I would give you all those answers?"

"What if the truth is only more horrifying?" I countered. "And you really are a demon in disguise?"

"Then . . ." He made a gesture of open hands, as if to say the answer was obvious.

It was. "Then there's nothing I can do about it anyway," I grumbled. With a small sigh, I laid my head back against the upholstered headrest of my recliner, rocking back and gazing at the ceiling. The chair was comfortable, more so than it even looked.

"Lyn," Sylleo said suddenly, drawing my swift attention. "Is that the name you prefer? I noticed Zent calls you that, as well as your Legaleian friend."

I narrowed my eyes before considering it and relaxing my face. *Of course he was paying attention when I talked to Kaen. He's not stupid.* "I do prefer that, yes." Here on Gaea, I was used to people referring to me either as simply "Mother" or "Heiress," or my full name, Lynchazel. But Lyn was my nickname back on Mani, where my full name came off sounding outlandish and strange, so it was comfortable, even calming, to hear.

"Well, then, Lyn, I . . . we committed grave sins in the past. Long in the past. And . . . I wish to move on from that. I like to think I've changed in recent decades, and I've taken a new approach to life and toward my people. I've seen the difference it can make. You really don't know the half of what we've done to humanity, to Gaea . . . to our creator. But I want you to understand that I regret what we did."

I stared with mouth half open, unsure of what to make of his speech. It certainly sounded sincere, as did much of his words. Not enough to bring any pity out of me, mind you. But he had some explaining to do before I could even understand the meaning behind those words. Clearing my throat, I said, "You . . . mentioned a deal."

Sylleo inhaled, puffing out his chest before letting out a long breath. "Yes. I'll just tell you: If you agree to stay here with me, and you help me to convince all your friends to do the same, I will set you free."

"You'll set me free if I agree to stay? How does that even make sense?"

He smirked. "We'll call it mutual trust. I will not restrict your comings and goings between these buildings, nor will I prevent you from leaving the city. However, I do not believe that would be wise. If you but ask, I'll provide whatever supplies, housing and transportation you require. In return, I ask for your cooperation. Oh, and one more thing, which is silence. No radioing your rebel friends from the city before we can arrange a plan to meet with them."

I scoffed, an expression of what I can only assume was amusement on my face. I should have been used to his strangeness, yet it struck me all over again. "You're really serious?" I asked, belatedly adding, "Sir?"

The tall man nodded. "Entirely."

I opened my mouth to accept his proposal. I'd already agreed with Zent that going along with the Senator was the wisest option, and I knew it to be my only real course of action. There was just . . . something holding me back.

So I shrugged it off. "Sounds good to me," I said.

Sylleo smiled, a genuine, trustworthy smile. "That's my girl. The other Senators don't know what they're missing out on. They can't even see you for what you truly are."

"Which is?"

He gestured toward me. "A beautiful young woman! You've got your mother's best features. Not to mention you're from Mani and are thus a treasure-trove of knowledge from a world completely unknown to us."

All that registered in my brain was the first part of those words, and they stirred a discomfort deep within me, something I hadn't felt since coming to Gaea for the first time. No Hellebes had ever spoken to me like that. Not even creepy old Dekla, in all his scientific obsession, had ever come off as having any sort of . . . attraction? Attraction to me.

Seeing my discomfort, Sylleo began to explain himself, though he seemed to trip over his own words. "The rest of the senate, they see a test experiment, a battery or—or a dangerous weapon. Well, except for Vladimir—he obviously wants you as his concubine—of which he has multiple, I might add. Don't worry, I won't let that happen. He's not pulling you from my grasp, not if . . ." He cut off, as though realizing his rambling was not helping me to feel any more at ease. "Sorry, forget I said anything."

I couldn't forget it, not even if I lacked the Vault I had been born with. But I realized two odd things at once. The first was that he seemed genuinely uncomfortable, like Kaen did when he talked of his relationship with Mydia and, more recently, with me as well . . . The second was that Sylleo was obviously, well, not like the other Hellebes. There could only be one reason he would be saying such things about me, not to mention Vladimir's rather lascivious comments about me, and it was obvious now.

"You're . . ." I said the words quietly, trailing off with a small shake of my head. I felt my face heating up, and I suddenly felt very self-conscious.

Sylleo didn't question my implication. Instead, he cleared his throat and removed his crossed leg from the other, composing himself. "If there are any other questions you have for me at the moment, go ahead," he said.

I shook my head. "I think that's enough for now. Sir," I added belatedly. *I have to get away from this man.* "Should I just—are you going to escort me back to my room at the prison?"

"No, I'll let the guards know that you are now allowed free access to all sectors of the complex. I'll also give you free use of your computer, with which you may message me anytime, along with your friends."

I raised my eyebrows. "Thank you. I guess I'll . . . see you in a while?"

"It won't be long. Farewell, Lyn. And enjoy your stay." The giant had recovered himself remarkably quickly and showed no outward signs of discomfort, but it did nothing to erase the awkwardness of that moment. Hellebes men fighting over me . . . possessively. That thought was uniquely disturbing. And . . . what was that about Vladimir having concubines? I didn't even want to think what that could possibly mean. Some secrets were not worth finding out.

α Chapter 35 α

Cydenges

Data Re-encryption Date: 1/20/2333:
The word Cydenges means "Shining One," and of course can be
singular or plural. The implication is clear just to look at one, yet I've oft
wondered at the innocence of it. None can say who first coined the term,
just as their origin is a mystery. Were they once allies of mankind? Or were
they at first taken to be some form of majestic angels?

The next day, Sylleo messaged me with an unusual offer. He wanted to take me to see the Cydenges battle site northwest across the ocean: in the vicinity of Trident, city of Senator Vladimir. I stared at my wrist console, trying to parse why he would suddenly ask such a thing. All I could conclude was that going with him would be the wisest move. (Was there another?) After messaging Zent to tell him of Sylleo's request, I arose from my bed and stretched my stiff limbs.

I still wore the comfortable set of clothes—cotton, I thought—that the servants had brought for me. Sylleo must have custom ordered them for me, as they fit nearly perfectly, right down to the undergarments. I wasn't going to question where they had gotten the know-how to make those. It wasn't like there were female Hellebes around.

The servants, bless their hearts, had washed my gillsuit. I put this on, since I would most likely be needing it today. I didn't really know what to expect from the excursion, but safety favored the prepared. I used my same dirty hair ties to pin up my white hair in a practical bun.

Time to pay my host a visit.

Margill awaited me atop the flight of introductory steps to Sylleo's residential suite. The aging butler informed me that the Senator would be with me shortly, and led me inside to a waiting room. Within five minutes,

Sylleo came out flanked by two high-ranking Hellebes officers from his military, whom he introduced as General Frauss and General Inecc. "We'll be taking a force of two dozen soldiers, hand-picked by these two," he explained. "We're going to put down the Cydenges before they cross into our territory."

A comment came to mind, centering on how he only now bothered to fight off the terrors when it became more personal, but I thought better of it. Somehow these two ordinary Hellebes intimidated me more than the Elite himself. It must have been my growing familiarity with the man, or else the generals' gruffer demeanor.

They led me down to a ship that transported us to Ccamos military headquarters, situated a half mile eastward. Sylleo himself flew us. The HQ complex sort of blended in, as though it had been designed to look like the more peaceful sectors of the city, bearing less of the harsh metal design and obviously-mounted weaponry visible in other, more militaristic cities.

The twenty-four warriors were all ready when we arrived at the barracks, along with two large military aircraft outfitted with heavy weaponry for use against the Cydenges. I specifically noticed how none of those weapons were energy-based.

General Frauss and General Inecc piloted the two large aircraft while Senator Sylleo took me in a smaller vessel, an omnicraft. I climbed in next to him and we took off, followed by the other two. Nervous jitters coursed through my body, more than I'd felt since Haccolces, perhaps even since first coming to Red Horizon HQ with Zent and his men. Auroras, but I missed those guys . . .

But was it being alone with this man again that made me feel that way, in a ship that he was piloting? Or was it the prospect of meeting one of these feared Cydenges face-to-face? My head said it could be either one, but my gut said it was the latter.

"So . . ." I said hesitantly, trying to sound nonchalant. "What exactly should I be expecting? Are we going to be, like . . . fighting these things from the air? Or head-on?"

He looked over at me, face unreadable. "We're lazy cowards, remember? We sit back in safety and fight only if we have to."

I nodded slowly, waiting for him to continue.

"Gotcha," he said with a devilish grin. "We'll be taking them head-on. But you'll be watching. First we'll bombard them from the air. We'll have to watch out for Lldsaor and Vladimir's forces, because they're both there right now. After unloading everything we've got into them, we'll land and take it to the ground to finish them off."

"And . . . do you know how many there are?"

"Around seventy-five," he replied. "So enough to be deadly. Hence the reason you'll be staying back for most of it. If you have to defend yourself, then I recommend trying to trap your enemy in stone. Don't fire any energy projectiles its way, or it will simply absorb it. Am I clear on that?"

I nodded. I hadn't even thought of how the Cydenges' ability to feed off of energy would affect combat with them, but it made sense.

"Good. When we get to the ground, just stick close to me and don't make any moves without my orders."

I harbored no intentions of acting out or disobeying, as I knew he was likely as great a threat to me as any Cydenges ever would be—not to mention the other Elites—and I didn't want to get on his bad side.

In a little over an hour, we arrived. I knew by the ominous scarlet streaks in the sky and pulsing red lights beneath the clouds as we flew. "Whoa," I breathed as Sylleo took us down and we broke through the grey clouds. The sight that greeted me was surreal. The land here was a jagged and broken plain of grass, upon which Hellebes fought with creatures of great length and speed, who darted around the battlefield graceful as snakes and quick as lightning. The Hellebes forces were beating them back with heavy ballistic weapons and even massive swords.

Cydenges . . . whispered my mother's voice, and I could feel her sudder inside my mind. *Not a sight I've wanted to see again.*

You've seen them before? I asked her, realizing it was a foolish question. She had been privy to most of the data in the world over a long period of time.

But she was already gone.

"All right, Frauss, Inecc," Sylleo said. "Let it rip."

The ground forces looked up and began to retreat in coordination, perhaps having been notified of our arrival.

The Cydenges themselves, for all the brief glances I caught of them as they leapt about the plain, were four-legged with pointy joints similar to species such as dogs or horses, though these were far larger than either of those. Their necks were long, and from their skulls sprouted one or more sets of various types of horns: Jutting, twisting, curling, bifurcated. Their entire bodies were sheathed in glittering metal plates, light in color and highly reflective, and between them shone red light that flashed as they moved, creating dizzying displays of mirrored light. Their whiplike tails ended in various spikes, fins and barbs, matching rows of spikes on their backs and dagger-like claws and fangs.

As Sylleo's generals opened fire, the Cydenges turned their malevolent gaze upon us, quickly pinpointing where the assault was coming from. I was almost afraid that they would find a way to attack us up here, such as sprouting wings and flying, but they only shied back. Ones not currently engaged by other Hellebes forces were bombarded with missiles, whilst the others were sniped by men on our ships.

"Ballistic weapons are effective against them," Sylleo explained through my headset, "Bullets, arrows and the like. Explosives are only somewhat effective, as direct, focused contact is better for piercing their plates. We'll be letting the archers down shortly."

As I watched, Inecc and Frauss swung their ships lower to the ground, letting out a group of snipers with giant bows and steel arrows, before landing their ships. Sylleo took us down farther to the left, close to where I could make out Emperor Lldsaor and his forces.

"Listen carefully," said Sylleo. "Our arrival made all the difference here, and they're on the run. A few may escape, but we'll get most of them. I just want you to gain some experience, so stick close and don't try anything stupid."

I was about to ask what he meant by "escape," but I thought better of it. He was already getting out, taking out a two-meter sword and handing me another, perhaps two feet shorter. I took it by the long hilt, unsure of what to do with it. The thing was heavy, with a thick ridge running down the center of the blade and a tapering design that made the lower part of the blade several inches wider than near the tip.

"Always aim for the neck or the center of their chests," he said. "Only use it if you have to. And you won't."

I nodded and stepped out onto hard stone—which comprised the majority of the ground where the tall grass was absent, making for an odd landscape—and watched uncomfortably as Sylleo waved to Lldsaor and his men with a charming smile.

"Finally decided to show up!" growled the Emperor.

Sylleo nodded. "And in the most esteemed company, too." This elicited a dark scowl from Lldsaor.

The metallic clatter of metal crashing against Cydenges scales, accompanied by the chorus of gunfire, drew my attention—and a pained grimace at the decibels—and I turned to see many of the Cydenges taking bullets and arrows in the shoulder, chest and neck. To my surprise, this largely only slowed the draconic creatures, though some crumpled to the ground after a direct shot to the neck or multiple to the chest. The arrows had the most effect, driving them backward and slamming the metal predators into the ground.

I glanced dubiously down at my greatsword. How effective could a cutting . . . no, more a battering weapon . . . be against one of these monstrosities?

Hellebes still fought with the ones closest to their ranks, using bows and ballistic weaponry along with swords at closer range, singling them out in coordinated maneuvers. Lldsaor and Sylleo teamed up to take out multiple with their own swords, and I watched in fascination as they blocked the Cydenges' attacks whilst striking in between to cleave through their opponent's neck or stab into its heart. The steel greatswords held their integrity, piercing through the metallic scales and releasing bursts of red light as they felled the silvery titans. When a fatal blow was struck, the beast would collapse and the glowing red essence that powered it would release, absorbed into the ground like Geokinetic diffusion. This phenomenon was not lost on me, though I didn't understand its meaning.

I did as Sylleo had instructed, moving behind him, though I didn't want to come too close to the Emperor, as my previous experience with him had been less than pleasant. I held my oversized sword in two hands at an upward angle, a generic wary stance, not because I knew how to use it but precisely because I didn't. *Don't want to poke anybody with this thing . . .*

The Emperor and Senator made quick work of the Cydenges in their path, laying into the alien creatures like a living storm. Their assault, almost choreographed, spoke of a long history of combat together. To the north, I finally spotted Senator Vladimir, who looked distinctly out of place in his surprisingly functional armor, a steep change from the last time I'd seen him. His fighting was ferocious and feral.

A couple of the Cydenges, however, did not crumple and die from Sylleo and Lldsaor's onslaught, instead shying back, appearing to realize that their companions were dead or dying. Spewing red light and sparks from their wounds, they crouched and made a leaping motion, creating a pillar of red light and disappearing. It was as though they became an elongated blur and for a moment *were* the ruby sunbeams. Each pillar lasted for only a few seconds, then no trace was left.

So that's how they do it, I thought to myself in wonder. I immediately felt silly for it, realizing that I didn't at all know how they were able to teleport, just what it *looked* like. It was certainly fascinating to watch.

Whether by death or retreat, the number of Cydenges left alive on the ground dwindled to zero in the next few minutes, and the booms and clash of metal on metal ceased to be, leaving a deathly silence. This was promptly broken by Hellebes commanders shouting the order for their men to put away their weapons and withdraw to their appropriate vehicles. Those that were still alive, that is. The Cydenges had torn, maimed and killed a good number of Hellebes, which were rushed back to waiting vessels on stretchers. In fact, they seemed to have brought extra vehicles for the express purpose of transporting the wounded and dead.

I couldn't help but wonder what they did with dead comrades here on Gaea. We had had to leave a few men behind on missions—no, *many* men, I reminded myself—as there'd been no time to retrieve them, so I had yet to actually witness what a burial ceremony looked like. Did they even bury their dead?

Unsure of what to do in the aftermath of the battle, I hung close to Sylleo, trying to stay out of sight of the Emperor. I watched the broken remains of the Cydenges, which sparked and sputtered and even fell apart scale-by-scale. It was hard to tell in the light . . . but it was as though the scaly exoskeleton *was* their body. If there was anything else inside, it seemed to fall apart, burn or otherwise vanish upon death. Vladimir, meanwhile, ignored his men entirely and came over to converse with the two Elites.

"Sylleo!" he called in a cheery voice. "Why, it sure is nice to see you. You know, finally and all." His face was that of a happy friend, but he was clearly less than pleased to see him.

The reverse was certain. Sylleo turned a controlled but annoyed glare on the tall man, jamming his sword into the stone at his own side. "Hello, Vlad," he said in an even voice. "At least we made it in time to save your sorry hides."

"True. And I see you've brought your new pet, no less." Vladimir turned his eyes on me, looking me up and down with approval. "You always were a slimy one, no?"

"Me?" Sylleo said with a hint of amusement in his voice. "I merely know how to take opportunities when they come. I'm sure you understand that she is under my care as an honored guest, and thus is not up for grabs."

Up for grabs . . . I hated the way these men talked about me.

Lldsaor cleared his throat. "That's questionable, at the very least. But we should be clearing out of here for the time being. I trust you will bring her to the next meeting?"

"Which will be?"

Lldsaor gave a predatory grin. "Quite soon."

"Very well," Sylleo answered. "But know that I picked Lynchazel up in defense of her own life, as she was about to be killed by a certain party. More on that later."

Vladimir simply looked annoyed, but Lldsaor seemed to take this information seriously, nodding slowly. "In three days," he said. "At the Haccolces Capitol. Be there, or we will decide on a suitable course of action."

α   Chapter 36   α

The Council's Decision

They never told me how the Prince died. He was simply assassinated and was no more. Turmoil engulfed the Sovereignty, and the Anier ended up ruling. But I am no longer innocent; I know better.
— From Lhinde's Vault

For the next hour, I hung close to Sylleo as he gave orders to his men and coordinated cleanup with Vladimir and the Emperor. Neither one went out of their way to so much as question me, apparently saving that for this upcoming meeting. Oh, what a joyous time that would be.

Then we were off, bound for Ccamos. We followed Inecc and Frauss, who flew their heavy gunships at a less reckless speed for the return trip. The entire way there, I wanted nothing more than to pester Sylleo with questions, yet all of them died on my lips: *Will you be able to protect me from the Senate? Will they try to take me? What if they all band together?* Surely then there would be nothing even Sylleo could do to stop them. But if he was right, it wouldn't come to that . . .

For his part, Sylleo called the deployment a success. Stopping the Cydenges today had never been much of a question. Even without Sylleo's intervention, they would have been able to eradicate or scare away the predators, albeit with greater losses, but it was important for relations. Ccamos had to keep up some appearance of support, else the Senate would have boundless political ammunition.

When we arrived in the city, I was allowed to go and report the goings-on to Kaen and the others. The sun was just breaking here in Ccamos, peeking over the modern buildings like creeping gilt dew. I quickly navigated to the apartments where Kaen, Zent and the others were being housed, not bothering to even knock. The guards were no longer there. The door opened for me, probably via facial recognition, and I paused as I saw Plato sitting down, looking at me with a strange expression.

I swiveled my head, searching for the others. "Where are Kaen and Zent?"

He jerked a thumb. "They went to find the bath house. Apparently, they have one. They didn't message you?"

"No." I was pretty sure I knew the place he meant, which was more of an elaborate shower room than the fancy bath houses back in Nytaea. "I guess that means you all heard that you're free now."

"*Relatively,*" Plato said with an exaggerated hand motion. "That's the way I heard it. So kind of like being under arrest but with a long leash."

"The League doesn't use leashes when they arrest people."

"In a manner of speaking, then."

I turned to go, opting not to respond further. I typed out a message on my wrist console as I descended to the lower level of the complex. Was that . . . what were those called, stench fries? They smelled good.

You know that's not it, you idiot, White said in my head mockingly.

Yeah, yeah. It's an old word for tasty, I know.

I stopped by the cook station on my way to the bath house and came away with a basket of fresh potato fries, a fine delicacy only found here in Ccamos. Or at least they hadn't served them back at the undersea base. Before I could cram even a dozen of the warm, crispy fries in my mouth, Zent called me.

"Hmph?" I asked over my mic as I walked, trying to wolf them down. An ordinary person would probably have burned herself.

"I said, where are you now? Where did you go?"

"Uh, mmph, Phrident? We're back now."

I heard Zent curse under his breath, following it up with, "Lovely. So that Cydenges raid alert was coming from Trident?"

"Mm-hmm." I licked my fingers before nodding to the security guard on my way out. He didn't try to stop me, only gave me that same wary stare as I passed through the metal detectors. "You guys all done yet?"

"Me and the other soldiers, yes. Your friend Kaen was searching for somewhere more private and settled on the handicapped shower for the injured. I don't think he knows that's what it is. He should be done soon."

I laughed. Not because Kaen was being silly, but simply the way he told it. "All right, I'll be there in about thirty seconds, so tell him to hurry up."

I still felt like I was going to get caught for something, like I'd flown my cage, as I walked the rest of the way to the bathhouse, trying not to go too fast. I could only assume that Zent and the others felt the same in Ccamos now that they were allowed to walk around unsupervised—although I was pretty sure that location trackers on their suits, perhaps even in their bodies, kept the local authorities apprised of their whereabouts. Anything too suspicious, like trying to leave the city, and Sylleo would be notified. Not to mention audio recording and data tracking on all communications, of course.

Zent and two of his men, already dressed in casual military attire, met me outside the building—which was little more than a collection of stone and cement pillars, some interconnected by walls, which shaded parts of a pool area directly outside the main complex on the western side, giving little in the way of privacy. There were multiple baths, some heated, others salted or jetted, and shower stalls lining both outer walls. A few crew-cut Hellebes heads turned to look at me as I approached, and most quickly turned away; likely in uneasiness at the presence of "her."

"So, how'd it go?" Zent asked, folding his beefy arms.

I approached the front wall, positioning myself so that as much stone and as few windows as possible were between me and the inside. "Well, I didn't have to do any fighting. Senator Sylleo just asked me this morning if I wanted to accompany them. He took two of his generals out there, south of Trident, and I tagged along while they obliterated some Cydenges. They're . . ." I paused as a half-clad Kaen walked out, a scowl on his face and holding a folded-up towel in his hands. "Hi, Kaen."

"Hi."

I turned back to Zent. "They're frightening. Not quite what I pictured." In truth, the descriptions I'd heard had been accurate; they simply didn't do the alien creatures justice.

Kaen looked from me to Zent. His scowl made for an amusing expression as he craned his neck upward to look the man in the eye. Then, carefully, he said in Hellebes, "Cydenges? You went . . . to fight?"

I nodded.

My friend sighed and relaxed his face, as though giving up on being angry because it was too much work—which I took as a compliment. He opened his mouth to say something and paused, calculating his words. "You do . . . trust? Trust this man? This . . . Senator?"

Zent shrugged his giant shoulders. Then he slapped Kaen's shoulder in a playful, backhanded gesture, pointing at me. "*She* does. I don't know about me."

I started to object, then thought better of it. "He's . . . weird. But I do trust him. I think I do."

Kaen simply nodded.

"So, what do you plan to do now that you've struck a deal with Sylleo?" Zent asked. "Or rather, what is he planning?"

I grimaced. "I don't know. We talked to the Emperor, and he wants him to bring me to their next Senate meeting, which is in three days. So I have to go to that. They'll try to capture me or sway me to join one of their sides. They might even try to sue Sylleo or something."

Zent snorted. "Sounds like a legal battleground. Just be careful, all right? I doubt any of us will be allowed to go." He paused and looked at Kaen. "Although . . . did he mention anything about your friend?"

I shook my head slowly, then paused. "He did a couple of times. But he never made it sound like he would try to bring him before the Gaean Senate."

Zent nodded.

"I'll keep in touch with both of you," I said with a nod to Kaen. As I turned to go, he made a noise that implied discontent with that ending, and I turned my head to glance at him but did not slow down. I knew what he wanted right now; more time with me. Time away from these tall freaks. But I had a whole world's worth of secrets to unravel.

I tapped out a message to Sylleo: *Are you busy at the moment, sir?*

A bit, but you can come on up.

I assumed this meant to the manse, so I made my way there as quickly as I could without looking like I was in a hurry to see him. I ascended the polished marble steps and approached the door. Before I was there, Margill the butler opened one of the heavy oak doors and asked, "My lady Heiress?"

"I'd like to see the Senator."

Margill gave a curt nod. "Most definitely. Right this way. He is in a meeting currently, but instructed me that I should allow you in should you make an appearance."

The greying butler led me to an upstairs office and cracked the door just far enough to poke his head in and announce, "The Mother Heiress has come to see you, sir." With brief head-bobs toward the individuals in the room, he ducked back, opened the door a bit further, and shooed me in, closing it promptly behind me.

I immediately saw what he was so leery of disturbing, as Sylleo stood accompanied by two important-looking Hellebes and others watching via two-way camera. The room was ornately trimmed, a far cry from the usual Hellebes meeting rooms. Sylleo stood on the left before a digital blackboard.

All heads looked to me as I arrived, though the two I didn't recognize only glanced at me long enough to communicate clear distaste with a bit of annoyance sprinkled in before looking away. That didn't do anything for my opinion of them, nor did it calm the cabbage moths in my stomach.

"Ah, good of you to join us, Lynchazel," Sylleo said briskly, glancing at his companions to see if they would offer any further greetings. "These are two of my advisors, along with a few operatives we have in other provinces." He waved at the screens, giving brief introductions, and I gave a nervous smile as the eyes of three more Hellebes displayed thereon turned to me.

Sylleo waved me over discreetly, and I jerkily moved to stand beside him like a loyal dog, unsure of whether to stare up at him or face the others in the room. I felt my face slowly heating up. Fortunately for me, he quickly resumed from where they were.

"Gucchin, repeat the last part of your report," the Senator ordered. He spoke with authority but not overbearingly.

The black-haired officer on the leftmost screen nodded, parted his large lips and said, "Senator Vladimir's judicial officers have cited dramatic increases in insubordination and have been handing out more punishments, including multiple death sentences. It's uncertain whether political motivations may be behind it, or if there is some cause for rising insubordination in his jurisdiction—such as breakdowns in the programming."

Sylleo gave me a quick glance, as though gauging how much of that I had processed, before nodding to the next agent, a bald Hellebes with an accent I didn't recognize who quickly identified himself as an operative in Haven. He reported that Senator Strongs had made no public announcements regarding his ambush of the Mother Heiress in Maldunech, nor any statements at all regarding her. According to him, Strongs already had operatives in Ccamos—which Sylleo confirmed under his breath—and displayed many signs in his interior government of making strides toward eliminating the Mother.

I said nothing throughout this, being once again the newbie who didn't belong. This time, not among some group of rebels, but the council of one of the nine most important people in the world. Or . . . eight.

"Sir," said one of the two generals in the room with us. His name was Fors, while the other was Inecc. "It seems reasonable to assume he would not attack her before the meeting is called, especially here in the city."

"Not directly, no," Sylleo said. "Nor indirectly, I think. But we should be prepared in any case."

The discussion went on like this for some time, eventually losing me in unfamiliar terminology, and I found my mind wandering toward thoughts of my mother. Perhaps it was what they'd said about Strongs hunting me down and trying to eliminate me. Absently, I backed up until I felt the door at my back and jumped slightly, rousing from my thoughts. General Inecc and Sylleo both turned inquisitive eyes on me.

"A little jumpy, Heiress?" Inecc asked.

I shook my head sharply, staring at Sylleo's feet, and mumbled an excuse. Fortunately, they ignored me. What was wrong with me? I'd been in the Gaean Senate with eight Senators present, all staring down at me, and I couldn't handle this?

Why did Sylleo include me in this? He kept glancing at me almost like he was expecting me to chime in . . . did he just want to keep me up to date? Surely he wouldn't let me in on just any confidential communications. So was this one of particular importance to me? If so, he would have called for me, yet I had been the one to invite myself—in a way.

Eventually, Sylleo dismissed his advisors. General Fors only gave me a grunt as he walked past, though of course he saluted his commander-in-chief. One of the agents, Lieutenant Ccatros, actually gave me a word of farewell before signing off. General Inecc clapped me on the shoulder and said, "Good luck, kid."

I watched him go with a frown. Then I was alone with Sylleo once more, something I hadn't exactly wanted but knew was necessary. "Sir, about the meeting—"

The giant held up his hand, cutting me off. "My turn first—What did you think?"

I shut my mouth in annoyance, trying not to glare. My first reaction after he finished interrupting was, "Hmm?" before I thought about it and said, "Oh. Um . . . why did you want me to hear it all?"

Sylleo stared at me until my cheeks burned. "It was your idea."

"But you clearly wanted me here . . ." I trailed off. My objection was not only silly but juvenile. "Sorry, sir. It's just, I tried my best to understand, but I have little context concerning world events. I have a lot to learn."

"How much did the Red Horizon teach you?"

I paused, tapping into my Vault. I had learned a lot by now; about Gaea's natural sphere, science, mathematics, modern military tactics, and the current structure of the Gaean League. Not much history, nor Hellebes anatomy or mass reproduction methods. And then there was what I'd learned from memories of my mother. If only she would just let me . . .

No. With a brief shake of my head, I said, "They . . . just taught me basic stuff. Things Hellebes know by the time they're out of school."

"Hellebes haven't attended school for well over two hundred years," Sylleo said flatly.

"They . . . what? Oh, I guess I didn't realize . . . Oh, wait." *That one was from Mother.* "Well . . . then let's just say there's a lot they kept back."

"On purpose. As I told you."

I nodded hesitantly. "So, what are you saying I should do?"

Sylleo crossed his arms. "I'll leave that up to you. But you may want to ask your friend Zent if he can fill you in on what happened with your mother and father. Now that he's . . . distanced, you might say, from your rebel friends."

I started to nod once more when I realized his implication: He knew that I didn't have access to all my mother's memories. But then . . . of course I didn't. It wasn't magic—she just left the memory bank before running away with Kallyn. And yet she still seemed to control access to that Vault somehow. Did he know that? Could he? It didn't seem possible.

At last, I said, "I'll talk to Zent. But I hope you'll give me some answers as well, sir."

"In time."

"And what is the plan for Wednesday?"

Sylleo shrugged. "There isn't much. We will take you to Haccolces, and you and I will attend the council. From there, we'll play it by ear."

"Yes, sir. Thank you, Senator."

I left.

α Chapter 37 α

Biodigital Convergence

Hellebes . . . to think they would name them so. It is Carthinian for "future sons." From the late speech helle *(yet to be, to come) and* -ebes *(offspring, son of), the term would seem almost innocuous except for the setting. It is eerily fitting.*
— From Lhinde's Vault

That night, I tried to get more information out of my mother's Vault. I felt her once more, fighting me. What had she said about . . . Mother Gaea, the original Mother Gaea, trying to escape the depths of her Vault and wreak destruction? Supposedly, she was guarding against her, but I wasn't completely sure if I could trust Lynchazel. As much as it hurt to say it.

The next morning, I cornered Zent as Sylleo suggested, asking to speak with him privately. We found one of the upstairs rooms not far from his own, and sat down across from one another. He looked uncharacteristically nervous, as though he knew what it was about. I didn't want to have to translate everything for Kaen, so I hadn't bothered inviting him; I'd relay the info to him later.

"I want to know about . . ." I hesitated briefly. "I was—I was thinking on the whole laboratory thing with my mother, and who she really was."

"You want to know about fifteen years ago."

Oh. Yeah, he saw right through that.

Zent sighed, sitting back on his bench and brushing his short-cropped hair with his fingers. "I suppose I can't—shouldn't—hold it back from you any longer. I thought . . . well, I almost hoped you'd be able to remember it via the Vault. But there was no way to know how up-to-date that data was. What is the last thing you were able to retrieve from it?"

I opened my mouth to answer. "Ah . . ." Looking down at the floor, I finally said, "I don't know. She won't let me in. The Vault was guarded. Maybe . . . double-guarded."

"That doesn't even make sense. Lyn, a Vault is a Vault. Unless . . . does it have something to do with her genetic memories? I recall her saying something about genetic memory kept by the line of Mother Gaea."

I nodded. "Yes. She says that the 'first' Mother Gaea attempts to influence me through the Vault, and so she needs to keep a lock on most of it to keep her at bay."

Zent blew out a breath in amazement. "That sounds pretty intense. Does that have anything to do with the day that you . . . the day the power contained in that laboratory killed all those men?"

I winced. "I . . . think so. Because she spoke to me—Gaea. I didn't know who she was, but her voice was unforgettable. Dark and sinister, full of long-held bitterness and revenge. '*Make them pay. This injustice belongs to the ones who chained me, the ones who corrupted me, who made me their slave. I am the voice of Gaea, the widow in the darkness, the mourning virgin, cursed of the ancient ones. They shall know my pain.*'"

I made sure to drag out the last sentence for dramatic effect, and maybe a bit of mockery.

Zent raised his eyebrows. "Oh. That is a little creepy. 'Who corrupted me and made me their slave' . . . huh. And who are . . . ? Never mind. I don't even know what to say, other than to be on your guard in the future. She may try to get in your mind."

She's already in my mind, I thought, half expecting to trigger a response.

When I didn't reply, Zent cleared his throat and said, "Okay, so I assume you want the whole story. This will take some time. First, there are some things you need to understand about Mother Gaea, and who she really was to us. Growing up in the developmental guidance facilities, I heard about her nonstop. She was our hope, our goddess, the shining beacon for all humanity to see. All . . . Hellebes, that is. Not exactly humanity."

He glanced at me, as if to see if I would interrupt there, but I didn't. I wanted this information—I needed it. So he continued: "Mother Gaea has multiple religious sects worshipping her still today, one of which in particular was set up by the Elites some three hundred years back. There are monuments to her around the world, as I'm sure you've seen, and shrines made in dedication to her. The immortal queen, who gives birth to all human life. Well, only the zealots truly believe that part, as it makes no sense. But even if we were descended from her in any way, that wouldn't make us any more human.

"Mother Gaea, as I'm sure you're aware, was an experimental human given extraordinary powers through the most unnatural means. I'm still unclear on many of the details, but the experiments began many centuries ago, nearly all the way back in the time of the Great Pilgrimage, by some records. The tank she was held in lengthened her lifespan, slowing her aging to almost nothing. Scientists didn't even know if she had any reproductive capabilities left at that point, and were fearful of ever removing her from the laboratory. No, she was simply a battery."

"I know . . . most of that," I said. "But, um . . ." *Battery?*

"I'm getting there, Lyn." Zent took another deep breath. "The Senators, known at that time as the Anier, had moved so far away from natural human reproduction that our entire society was centered around artificial repopulation. Supposedly, every female died out centuries ago, and humanity long since abandoned hope regarding that. Many experiments were made involving advanced robotics and AI, cloning and stem cell research, and even the creation of an entirely new species—each of which was a dead end on its own. And, of course, one of the main focuses of modern research became . . . the search for immortality."

I nodded along, an uncertain frown creasing my brows. I saw the threads, and I saw where they were leading. During his pause, I asked, "So, you're saying they made their own new humans somehow? But that's impossible. . . . Wait—even if they did, why are all Hellebes male? Or . . . most of them, anyway."

"That . . . might be a better question for someone else. Some lines of research went nowhere while others bore unexpected fruit. Once again, I don't know all the specifics and history behind the creation of Mother Gaea or the Hellebes, but what I did learn blew my mind. Fifteen years ago, we discovered the truth. It's all thanks to your father, Kallyn, no less. Basically . . . it's as you say, the Hellebes are not human at all. I am not human. We are what you call biomachines—the result of centuries worth of research and perfecting. We are living machines, made of fabricated cells cultivated from artificial birth using cellular engineering and gene-splicing and enhanced with Geothermic energy—finally, implanted with digital coding that runs our bodies and is easily tuned and tracked by the Gaean League. When we say they keep tabs on us, it goes far deeper than simple surveillance.

"The Elites, on the other hand, are ancient—all nine of them. We don't know for certain how old, but they were alive back when all this was in the early stages, and obtained a sort of immortality through scientific means. They created new bodies for themselves and transferred their consciousnesses to those through neurodigital data conversion, near as we can tell. Most likely, these titanic bodies of theirs are sustained by frequent "repairs", along with massive amounts of Geothermic energy."

I interrupted him at this point. "Zent, Zent, hold on. I can't . . . this is a lot for me to process, okay?" I scratched frantically at my silver hair—which was down right now—causing the waist-length strands to whirl about and threaten to tangle. As I attempted to rearrange it, I said, "So . . . Sylleo, Lldsaor, they're all giant versions of the Hellebes, biomachines that feed on planetary energy?"

"No. We think they are very different. I mean, they may just be enhanced versions of the Hellebes that have found a way to keep their bodies going for far longer than the average forty-year Hellebes lifespan, but I believe they've managed to integrate remnants of their old DNA into their new bodies, and thus are the first and only beings of their kind."

I gave a deep nod, trying to wrap my head around the concept. "And what about me, then? How do you know I'm human at all?"

"Well, how about you let me tell you the actual story now?"

"Oh. Yes, sorry."

"So, with all that said," Zent continued, looking relieved to have gotten this far, "I came in contact with a Hellebes doctor named Rissius some eighteen years ago. I was a captain in the Haccolces air force at that time, and had recently come back from active duty, which in my case meant sitting around and waiting for the next Cydenges strike. This man, Rissius, also worked for the military, but he was in an accident that nearly killed him. It left his body with certain neurodigital features permanently offline. They were going to kill him as soon as they realized it—since that's the protocol—but he happened to be one of the smartest Hellebes in the last generation. He staged an escape, stealing equipment and supplies and hijacking a military vehicle.

"As you can guess, he was the founder of the Red Horizon. But his passion was to be a doctor. And so he quietly, carefully got in contact with friends among the military like myself and offered to do what had accidentally been done to him: Wipe us clean of the loyalty programming. You see, the way it works . . . we could speak with one another, plan, and do virtually whatever we wanted; there were just certain things that we could never do, or else our minds would wipe the data from the last few minutes. It nudges you, walls you off from certain branches of thinking . . . The code is complex, but quite simple at its core. He talked his way around it, and when he was sure that one of us would listen to him and join him when he was done, he made quick work of it and spirited us away into hiding.

"When he did so for me, he explained everything he did and why. I was like an animal let out of a cage, exploring a new world for the first time. Musha was one of the first he freed, along with Vass and Getts. They had a small group by the time I came along, at which point we set in motion a long-term plan to reclaim and reform the League, taking it back from the corrupt hands of the ancient Elites. We conducted as much research as possible into the background of the Elites and the current government system. Science, mathematics, everything. Getts oversaw military engineering in our fledgling organization, while Musha and I focused on recruiting and training new fighters. I remained on in the Gaean military, however, as an inside operative. Two years later . . . your father entered the scene.

"We found him more by chance than anything. I happened to be assigned to Gatewatch Isle for the first time in my career, and was there when he stumbled through that Gate. It was a new scenario, an anomaly that no one knew how to handle, but I had to report it to my superiors. While he was still struggling to hold himself up on the island, I took him into custody and flew him back to Haccolces. On the way, I radioed Red Horizon headquarters, which was in the Beides mountains at that time, and tried to get support before having to hand Kallyn over to the authorities. In the end, I arranged for him to be intercepted in the hands of other soldiers, who lost their lives as punishment for their negligence. The Gaean military is unforgiving.

"So . . . we studied this newcomer. He warmed up to us over time and caught on to our language extraordinarily quickly. Your father was the most intelligent man I've ever known. Together with Doctor Rissius, he formulated a plan to take control of the laboratories beneath Haccolces. Kallyn also discovered a way to regain his magic abilities from Mani, like I said before, but I couldn't tell you how he did it. He could juggle fireballs, and even incinerate a building with the wave of his hand. Eventually, we initiated our assault on the labs. Kallyn led the assault himself, navigating the mazelike ventilation passages throughout the complex in a power suit while our soldiers flanked it from both sides. Our plan was to recreate her containment lab back at our headquarters and use her as a bargaining chip to barter with the Senate.

"But Kallyn outsmarted us all. He called the Elites' bluff about the Mother being so important and implemented his own plan. He snuck into the lab early, hacked the scientists' computer systems and extracted your mother himself. At that point, we could do nothing but back him up with support. He calculated that she would be able to survive outside the cell given enough time, whereas the bargaining plan would have failed on ones such as Lldsaor and his corrupt Senators. So we took her back to headquarters and nursed her to health with much medical aid and constant caution. He was right; she did recover from semi-stasis quite quickly, and with a heavy diet of planetary energy we got her to serviceable health. Her organs had shrunk and adapted, and she was nearly unable to eat any solid foods. She grew stronger and stronger, and ate up more and more geothermic energy, forcing us to find new ways to harvest it beneath the radar of the Elites.

"Lynchazel proved to retain some memories from the old days, but something we thought to be old trauma seemed to hold her back from most of them. I now know that that must be the "first Mother Gaea" that you mentioned. But something strange happened. As soon as she was lucid enough to speak and move, she seemed to imprint on Kallyn and cling to him like family. It took some adjusting for her to come to grips with what the world was like, but it appeared that she had absorbed some information during her imprisonment in the laboratory, as she quickly caught on. Despite seeming to care . . . the more she learned about Gaea's plight, the more fearful she grew. I don't know how to explain it, other than paranoia. She would only open up to Kallyn, and my companions in the Red Horizon all thought he was taking advantage of this to convince her to side against them, but I . . . don't think that was his intention. Everything Kallyn did, he did for the good of Gaea and Mani both. Well, perhaps she seduced him a little bit. Quite frankly, I wouldn't know."

He paused to cough uncomfortably, and I couldn't help but chuckle at his face as he caught his breath. He had been talking for a while. I'd expected a story, but this was turning into a full-on epic. An engrossing one, too.

"And then they fell in love," he continued. "Kallyn decided he was going to try and take her with him into hiding until she was better, so I helped them escape from the Red Horizon. They took up hiding in the wilderness near Helstrom—on the eastern coast of North Terrol. Of course my colleagues were peeved with me. Next I knew, the unthinkable had happened: She was pregnant. We got Doctor Rissius out to see her, and she seemed to be doing well. I got to see her only once during her pregnancy, and it was surreal for me. But . . . her mind. She was convinced that the whole world was out to get her. Kallyn wanted to take her to Mani, but Rissius insisted they stay until the baby was born.

"So they did. And . . . during that time, the Gaean League located our headquarters and bombed it. Many of our men died. Lldsaor's men caught traces of Lynchazel's trail and realized we were the ones who'd taken her. They tracked down the Red Horizon hideout and flushed them out of there. Lynchazel gave birth to you while on the run, while the doctor was there, but shortly thereafter he was killed in another raid. The birth was very hard on your mother, as her body had changed so much from what it was naturally.

"Finally, fearful of all the fighting, she took you and hid again. When I heard from Kallyn, it was only to say, 'meet us at the Gate in three hours.' As soon as we arrived, so did the enemy, and we battled them on the beach of Helstrom as Kallyn distracted them with walls of flame—and one of our best pilots carried you and your mother to the island. If the Elites didn't know before what was going on, they knew now—though I think they only knew we were sheltering your mother. I don't think they knew about you. When at last she got through, they attempted to follow, but she had destroyed it behind her. At long last, their precious Mother was gone."

"So that's why they keep such a close watch on Gatewatch Isle now," I commented.

The captain nodded. "Indeed."

"And . . . how did my father die?"

Zent looked down at his feet. "Bravely. Very bravely. He was a good friend to me, one of the best I've ever had. You might say he went out in a blaze of glory."

I snorted, a smile tugging at my lips as I wiped my eyes. Humor from this guy? "That's the stupidest comfort I've ever heard, but . . . thanks. It's good to finally know." If my father had met Zent in the early days of the Red Horizon, then Kallyn was practically a founder . . . I knew he had died, but never the details behind it, and especially not the virtues that drove him try to break my mother out of her confinement. Part of the story still did not add up, but I knew Zent lacked some details, as he'd said.

"I'm sorry," Zent said softly.

I looked up to see him eying my face, and suddenly realized I was still crying. "I-It's nothing," I mumbled, wiping more fiercely at my eyes. What was wrong with me? I never cried.

Zent rose from his seat and came and sat beside me, his massive left shoulder a few inches from my right. He looked at the ground and occasionally at me, until I turned away, pulling one knee up to my chest and resting my foot on the bench. "This is supposed to be comforting, right?" he blurted. "To someone in time of emotional weakness?"

I rolled my eyes at an angle he couldn't see. "Where did you hear that?"

"I . . . don't remember," he said.

"Liar." I turned back, and sure enough, he was still sitting in the same exact position. I scooted over to him and slowly, tentatively rested my head on his shoulder. Then I hugged my arms around his thick torso, or tried my best. My fingers just barely touched on the other side. I didn't sob or anything, and I don't think I cried anymore, but it was indeed comforting to have someone to hug. "Is this all right?" I asked.

"Yes," he said simply. "A bit awkward, but I'm trying. I couldn't be there for your mother. Perhaps if I had been, she would have stayed more stable. So . . . well, if letting you cry on my shoulder is any penance, that's fine with me."

I nodded into his unyielding shoulder, smearing my tears onto his uniform. I knew I had to get out of this pathetic position before somebody saw me, but I didn't want to. "Thanks," I said, slowly letting go with my arms. Zent made for a good comfort, better than he should, since he was incapable of romantic attachment. Whereas I never knew what was going to pop out of Kaen or Sylleo's mouth.

"You done?"

"Yes!" I said with some exasperation. "You know, you really have to work on your woman-comforting skills."

"I suppose so. Though you're one of a handful of women I've met so far in my life, and the only one who happens to be present on my planet."

I smiled despite myself. Taking a deep breath, I said, "I'm sorry, Zent.

Thank you for all the answers. I'll have to try to get the rest out of Sylleo sometime. And . . ." I sighed. "You think you could tell Kaen all that stuff you just told me? I don't want to have to do that."

"Uh . . . with his fluency? That would take a while."

"Oh. Fair point."

α Chapter 38 α

The Gaean Senate

Transmission Date: 1/20/2333:
TN: 92867312879

The rebel faction known as the Red Horizon continues to be a thorn in
the side of progress. We are still looking into just how this rebellion began.
Disobedience of the gene that denies such rights is puzzling at best and
troublesome at worst. One or more of their leaders, clearly, was formerly an
upper minister or similar rank, but that explains only the tip of the iceberg.
— Minister Sefron to the Haccolces Military Board, ID: 1134-35794-28

"Is that Haccolces on the horizon?" I asked, though I knew the answer.

Sylleo, who rode beside me in the passenger seat of our official aircraft, nodded. "That'd be the shield dome. And . . . there's the skyline. What did you think of the city during your time spent there?"

The question caught me off-guard. "Are you serious? I spent most of my time in prison, and then running for my life, and then more prison, then running for my life again."

Sylleo quirked a smile. "But this time you're not. Take notice of what you see, as I'd like to hear about it later."

"I mean, I could look up all sorts of images and guided tours online, right?"

"Yes, of course. Have you?"

"Um, no. What I saw didn't impress me much anyway. Too much smog, too many ugly, square government offices. Too much concrete."

Sylleo raised an eyebrow. "And steel, I assume?"

I laughed. "And steel. All right, it was way uglier than Ccamos, that's for sure. It felt industrial and man-made, and too . . ." I searched for the right word and couldn't come up with it.

"I understand what you mean," he said. "And I would take no offense even if it was my city. Haccolces is a monument to the absolute power of world domination, shown in realistic ways, not glorified or romanticized. Lldsaor is not the type to waste resources on meaningless things."

Feeling the ship's powerful brakes, I looked out once more and suddenly the shield wall loomed before us, vaster than my full range of sight. As I watched, we descended and entered through one of the gate portals in the shield, which closed back up seamlessly after us. Another large League aircraft, probably one of the other Senators, was coming in just behind us from the east. We landed in an official docking bay and were escorted to a transport tram that would take us toward central command.

We got a private car, of course, though our guards occupied either tram car before and behind us. "You remember what I taught you about the Senators and their factions?" Sylleo asked. He'd been grilling me on it for most of the flight, while the previous day had been spent mostly learning about the different factions among the Elites. Apparently, he didn't trust my fledgling Vault abilities.

"Lldsaor, Brant and Vladimir are imperialists," I said immediately. "Strongs opposes them and you. He's a militarist. You are a nationalist, while Daedalus, Holman and DeWitt are non-conformists. But Daedalus leans toward Strongs' position. And you still haven't told me anything about this ninth guy."

"Very good. And I don't need to. Not yet. You can basically pretend he doesn't exist. But hopefully you understand enough about those terms for now. Just remember that things can change, sometimes more quickly than I can keep up with. Be on your guard."

I took special note of the phrase, *pretend he doesn't exist,* which hinted that he did indeed exist—everyone just wanted to forget about him. I nodded, observing the Steel City through the tram's slitted windows. It felt like being in prison again every time I had to ride on one of these things. Perhaps because it was the only way they'd ever transported me around the city. And yes . . . I would make Sylleo tell me about this ninth Senator, among other things, soon—the sequel to my conversation with Zent. I still hadn't gotten the chance. My mind was still in recovery from that.

Presently, we arrived at the Capitol complex and got off at the station. Our guards accompanied us most of the way to the twentieth-floor conference room. They kept watch from a distance within sight of the conference room doors, spacing themselves from other Senators' guards. *Biomachines all* . . . they were not even human. How was that possible? I spotted a few trying to pretend nonchalance while keeping a vigilant eye on things. What was the point? Such a ridiculous redundancy. Who in the world could these guys need protection from? What if they all just started having an all-out brawl instead? That would be way more entertaining. I wondered if they all knew each other by now, and just pretended not to.

One Senator, Daedalus, was still waiting outside the doors when we got there, and brightened up when he spotted Sylleo and me. With an even thicker neck than the rest of the Elites, Daedalus was an imposing man in every way except his bright, high-pitched voice. "There you are, Sylleo," he said almost cheerily. "And her excellence the Mother Heiress." He took my hand as we approached, as though about to kiss it.

Thankfully, he didn't.

"Mr. Daedalus," I said politely. "It's a pleasure."

The bull-like man turned to Sylleo. "You've taught her well! Anything interesting to report? Any discoveries on her?"

It wasn't lost on me how his attention immediately shifted from me as a person to me as a scientific object to explore. It made my skin crawl as much as Dr. Dekla's attention ever had.

"None so far," Sylleo said more curtly than usual, turning to walk away.

"Well!" Daedalus huffed as Sylleo turned his back on him. Staring at me instead, he slowly closed his mouth, eyeing me up dispassionately. It was like he had an outgoing side and a robotic side, ever at odds with one another. "My girl, I would so like to have you come out and help our scientists with their research . . ."

He droned on, but I wasn't listening. I looked up and down the hall, trying to decide whether I should simply follow after Sylleo instead of talking to this creep, but I was saved by the arrival of yet another Senator: Brant. I wasn't convinced he'd be any better company, of course.

"Well, well, well!" he exclaimed, voice growing louder with each repetition of the word. "If it isn't the lady of the hour!" He strode up animatedly and shook my hand. I tried to squeeze back as hard as I could, simply to not have my bones crushed. Squeeze or be squeezed. "This is quite the reunion. Quite . . ." he glanced at Sylleo, who was trying to cover up his possessive glare, ". . . the reunion indeed." He made the uncomfortable pause into a sort of show.

I couldn't quite tell, but the two didn't appear to get along too well. "Brant," Sylleo said, making a small, forced nod. "It's good to see you."

"Indeed, indeed," Brant said, voice regaining most of its bluster. He was nothing if not charismatic, the type whose hobby was entertaining people and capturing their attention. He probably practiced on his pet Hellebes. This time his attire was almost showier than before, if perhaps not as gaudy: A black suit with maroon and white highlights, complete with a white tie and fedora. He doffed it at me. "And how are you today, my lady? Oh, hello, Daedalus."

"Hi," Daedalus said, glancing between Brant, Sylleo and me as though waiting for two fellow vultures to step away from the carcass.

Brant lifted my hand and actually did kiss it. I tried to keep from recoiling, and just hoped this wouldn't be a recurring thing. He must have smelled fear, however, because he didn't stop there. "Fair maiden," he said grandly, "forgive these boors for not offering you the courtesy, but if you would allow me . . ." he held out an elbow for me to take and prepared a smarmy, raised-eyebrow smile for the other two Senators, and when I made no move to take his arm, his eyes rotated back comically. I was relatively sure he did this all for the effect, but I couldn't be certain.

"I'm all right, sir, but thank you," I said with a small curtsy. Did women . . . use to curtsy on Gaea?

Brant seemed genuinely impressed for some reason. "Now, that was a proper curtsy! Right, Sylleo?"

"I believe that is what it's called," Sylleo said simply. "Your vocabulary continues to astound. Now you've met some of my colleagues, Lyn. Only four more to go."

"But what about the Emperor!" Daedalus chipped in, as though he'd thought of something clever. "After all, he's . . ."

"He's the one who imprisoned me twice, remember?" I said cheerfully.

"Careful," Brant started, "Just because you have your mother's looks doesn't mean . . ." He trailed off as Sylleo started toward the oversized double doors and I followed close on his heels. I didn't hear whatever Brant muttered after that, but it didn't sound quite as pretty as most of his words.

"Here we go," Sylleo muttered. "Remember, just endure it and be on your best behavior."

I said nothing as the guard opened the door for us and I followed Sylleo. Brant and Daedalus trailed behind. The conference chamber was just as I remembered it, massive with high-reaching walls that met in the middle, framed by a great curved I-beam skeleton. Sure enough, five Senators stood around the circle by their podiums, including Emperor Lldsaor.

One of them coughed as we walked in, and I wasn't sure who it was. "And here they are," the Emperor said in a supremely unexcited voice. "Lynchazel, we will do things a bit differently today by having you take this ninth podium, as our ninth Senator will not be joining us." He motioned to the empty one.

I tried to look neither stiff nor overly excited to be here as I approached it, not too fast and not too slow. *Ugh, all these eyes, these raptor eyes . . .* Did they really think I wouldn't question the absence? Or that I didn't already know what was up with that Senator? I mean, I didn't, so Lldsaor was right to assume, and no one here was about to explain. As I took my place, Sylleo gave me a barely perceptible nod from behind his podium.

Once we were all ready, Emperor Lldsaor said, "Now. We have some . . . topics to discuss tonight, and they all happen to center around this female monster you see before you."

Thanks, Mr. Emperor. You think?

He didn't bother to gesture toward me, merely flicked his eyes in my direction. There were nine monsters here, but only one female. "And of course, we all know that our friend Sylleo has been harboring the Mother ever since he rescued her and some of her rebel friends from within Maldunech. Right, Brant?"

"Hm?" Brant adjusted his collar, looking uncharacteristically uncomfortable to be here. I supposed Lldsaor's words were basically a direct assault on his image, as Maldunech was under his leadership. He stole a glance first at Sylleo and then at Strongs. "We're still repairing the massive damages, so we're not sure what happened there."

Strongs, for his part, stood rigid as a statue, chin held high, hands clasped behind his back. His posture projected strength, while his facial expressions always seemed to display . . . distaste for the entire world? Surely that wasn't the case, though. Deep inside, he was just a nice guy who wanted to kill me.

"Now, let's not all start fighting here," Vladimir said with purposeful inflection. "Wouldn't want to get off on the wrong foot just because of some squabbles."

The Emperor gave him a pointed look but said nothing.

About half the eyes in the room were on me, and had been since I arrived. I tried to ignore them, difficult though it was. I struggled to keep from looking to Sylleo for support. Despite my distrust of the man, he was my anchor here, my only lifeline to freedom.

Sylleo spoke up now. "Emperor Lldsaor, you called this meeting, so why don't you explain what you'd like to discuss first. That way, we can proceed in an orderly fashion."

"Hear, hear," Holman said from his spot directly to my left.

"Very well. Let's be frank, Senator Sylleo," Lldsaor said, tapping two fingers on his podium. "You crossed a line. But you're clever, and realized that you could recruit her as an ally and a guest instead of imprisoning her."

Yeah, which of course would have been the natural thing to do, I thought sarcastically.

"You essentially are holding her hostage against us," the Emperor continued. "We cannot make a move to take her from you without breaking our old agreement. What have you to say about this?"

Sylleo took a breath, and I could see him thinking, *Here we go.* "I believe that Lynchazel should be treated as a human being, an ally," he said evenly. "Whatever we may have done to her mother in the past, and for whatever reasons, I feel we wronged her on a personal level. We have proven with the first—and now second—successful Zeta Beast that we can get along without using a human conduit."

"Not as efficiently," Lldsaor was quick to put in, "But yes, it suffices."

Sylleo paused for an extra second before answering, subtly implying that Lldsaor was rude to interrupt. Or perhaps that he only accentuated Sylleo's point. "As I said, this is a personal matter involving a human being, the last of her kind. I have come to feel strongly about this. Lynchazel is not another lab-raised Hellebes robot—she is the last true human we have."

"Except this other human you're keeping," Vladimir said accusingly. "You did take him into custody, correct? You're not stupid enough to kill off such an interesting creature."

Creature. Did these men purposefully try to creep me out? And belittle my kind, all at the same time?

"Correct," Sylleo confirmed. "I am not. Your deductions are as sharp as ever, Vlad. Now, I believe that Lynchazel's unique abilities can be used for the good of our world, and that she is far more useful as a partner than a prisoner."

DeWitt, usually one of the quietest of the Senators and more than willing to let the others do the talking, was nodding along with him. "I see the wisdom in that. Though there are other ways we can make use of her without sending her back to the Haccolces labs."

"That's right," Daedalus spoke up. "We can—"

"Use her as a breeding experiment, we know," Brant finished.

"No," said DeWitt, leaving Daedalus to simply shut his mouth. "She can offer further insight into the origin of the Cydenges. Think about it, my good men."

That seemed to give all the Senators pause. Strongs didn't want to look overly bloodthirsty, while Sylleo was probably trying to think of a way to refute such a good argument. For my part . . . well, I just wanted to know what I really had to do with the Cydenges in the first place. I knew I supposedly had Cydenges DNA in me, if indeed that could be passed down through human genetics. And if the other abilities I possessed were any indication, then that was the case. Zent hadn't said much on that part.

Lldsaor was the first to speak. "I never said we would be putting her straight into the containment units. Experiments would be wise. But . . ." He looked at me more directly this time, as though gauging how to best act like he saw me as a person. "I can also understand wishing to work with her—with you, Lynchazel."

"I don't," Strongs said. "The Emperor himself said it—she's a monster made by the hands of scientists working for the good of humanity, not one individual human hybrid."

That one almost made my jaw drop. Even from a man like him, those were unexpected words. Perhaps he was just ticked at being brushed off every time he spoke up, which was something I could relate to. From the looks of it, the other Senators had a similar reaction to his words.

"Now, see," Vladimir said with a patient tone, raising a pointed finger in front of his angular face. "That's not quite what we're going for here, Doc. Of course, the more you scare her away, the greater the chance she'll come running into my arms."

Holman pretended to cover a snort. "Right, your arms. What arms?" Holman himself was a veritable mountain of a man, built like a brick wall and topped by a wide, square-bearded face—and of course his wide-brimmed hat. Vladimir was much thinner by comparison, but . . . well, to be fair, I wouldn't want to have to wrestle any of these titans. Each was more than a match for any Hellebes.

Vladimir spared him no more than a passing glare.

"Next," Lldsaor cut in, "we must discuss the Cydenges raid that is currently in full force. You may not realize, Sylleo, as you like to stay out of important things like this, but they are still coming in force near Maldunech and Chronala."

"If I may," Strongs' harsh voice cut in, "This is the perfect opportunity to test out the Mother's combat capabilities. One Cydenges monster against another. What say you? Sylleo already took it upon himself to bring her to the front lines—might as well give her a weapon and let her at them. As we've all seen, she's already developed destructive capabilities even with tectonic Geokinesis."

Multiple Senators looked at each other dubiously, and I glanced knowingly at Sylleo. *He's trying to kill me,* I tried to convey to him telepathically.

I don't have telepathic abilities, but I think he understood.

"I have reservations about that," Lldsaor said. "As you well know, manipulation of energy cannot defeat a Cydenges, no matter how strong the user, and the Mother is simply too valuable a specimen to endanger without good reason. She's already a genetic miracle."

"A volatile freak of nature," Strongs corrected him.

"Why, friend," Brant said with exaggerated shock, "You sound almost like you want her dead. You should be more careful with your words."

Ooh, I thought to myself. *I suddenly like this guy.* Well, slightly more. He still didn't understand how to treat a woman.

Strongs gave no reply. I assumed that meant he knew when to give up in an argument like this. I didn't know how the others felt about his extreme philosophies, other than that Daedalus of Chronala supposedly tended to side with him. But Daedalus had his own plans, by the sound of it. I wasn't looking forward to having these Senators fight over me after the meeting. I knew full well that they wouldn't let me go this time without at least a solid shot at persuading me to join them.

"So, are you going to try to take her back?" Sylleo asked at one point.

A cough from Holman.

I tried not to jerk my head as I turned to stare at Sylleo. Was he trying to start something? *Hope he knows what he's doing.*

The Emperor looked at Brant and Vladimir in turn. "That would be the next point on my list. Sylleo, we feel strongly that you have crossed a line and should give the Mother over to imperial keeping once more."

Sylleo nodded slowly. "Or? Are you threatening invasive military actions, or perhaps a lawsuit?"

"I want to know who constitutes 'we' first," Strongs interjected. "Lldsaor, you sound as though something has been predetermined, yet the Senate has yet to make a decision."

"And that would be why we are meeting now," said the Emperor. "I didn't have time to confer with everyone except my inner circle. And I'm threatening lawful action, nothing more, Sylleo." He looked around the room and raised his voice. "Brothers, leaders worldwide! This man seeks to harbor the rightful property of the imperial laboratories and keep her for himself! He has taken her through devious and unlawful actions. What say you? Should we act or sit back and let him be?"

At this, murmuring rippled all across the chamber, some hotter and some more whiny, like Daedalus. The Emperor let them be for a minute, and slowly, one by one, the Senators voiced their opinions on whether to wrest me from the safety of Ccamos. Sylleo, of course, remained silent and composed.

"I say no," Strongs said, surprising me.

"Most definitely," Brant said, eying Sylleo with a purposeful expression.

"Yes," Vladimir said.

Daedalus raised a hand, eyeing Strongs. "I say . . . no."

"No," Holman said, crossing his arms.

DeWitt licked his lips, looking uncertainly between Senators, as though gauging who would try get back at him more for picking the other side. "I'm against it," he said finally. "I'm saying no."

I breathed out a sigh of relief. *Safe for now.*

Emperor Lldsaor leaned on his podium with two hands, lips pressed tight together, studying the room. "Very well, then; It's settled. We will take no further action against Sylleo and the Mother . . . for now." He said these last words pointedly, staring straight at me.

α Chapter 39 α

Politics

The Mother stares unwavering, her watchful eye unchanging. The Mother knows me, and at this awareness I tremble both with excitement and fear. She is ancient and beyond mortal ken, and a part of me yearns for her favor. The daughter of Cybele . . .
— From Lhinde's Vault

As expected, I didn't make it out of the conference room before the first Senator accosted me: Vladimir. He sidled up to me, placed a palm on my opposite shoulder, and pulled me close, whispering in my ear: "You might have lucked out a bit, honey. I almost had you."

I glared up at him. He was tall, freakishly so just like the other Senators, but his face was more angled and far creepier, not to mention his sugary voice. "Sir, please unhand me," I said tightly.

"In a moment, darling." He bent down even closer. "He would have let me have you. See, one of these days, he's going to get his wish. But he won't lock you up immediately, perhaps never. You're far too valuable."

I said nothing. The man seemed to get exponentially creepier the longer he held me close. Finally, I was saved by none other than the Emperor. He came over and placed a massive hand on Vladimir's shoulder. His were twice the size of Vlad's, and he easily pulled him away. "Vlad, give her some space. He's not as bad as he seems, Lynchazel. He just hasn't seen a real woman in a thousand years."

"Ouch," I said with perhaps a bit too much emphasis. Vladimir gave a small *hmmph!* in reply and backed off.

"Now, Heiress," Lldsaor said, "I hope I did not give an . . . unsavory impression. I rather like Sylleo, and we've been friends and colleagues since time out of mind, but he can be a bit stuck in his ways and likes to take the moral high ground. In this matter, I simply can't let him use you as a political weapon against the rest of the world, which is what he's doing. Surely you see that."

Indeed. "More like you want to run your experiments on me and stuff me in a cell, but yeah, I hear you. Sir."

Lldsaor's face tightened, as though he had spoken to me only on a dare and was now having his objections proven right. "No, once again, I did not wish to convey the wrong idea. That is not our plan, as Vladimir knows full well." He threw the lanky man a pointed look and continued. "I would give you very similar rights to what Sylleo has, but you would be under the authority of the empire."

"You're trying to convince me you're not as bad as Sylleo," I said, "But you're not going to make me leave Ccamos. I like it there." It was the truth, albeit spun as though I'd freely chosen the place for my home.

"Now, honey," Vladimir began once more, but Lldsaor silenced him with a small shake of his head.

Not now, he seemed to be saying. *We'll try again later.* Something told me that Team Imperial had not counted on losing to a vote. But Sylleo had been right: The council was divided, and few of the Senators wanted to give absolute power over to Lldsaor. Rather, they'd let Sylleo keep me until they could figure out a better plan.

Strongs was the first one out, brushing only inches past my shoulder with no acknowledgment whatsoever, while the other Senators hung around, waiting their turn to persuade me to their side. After Team Imperial, it was Daedalus' turn. I could have sworn I saw him watching Strongs as he left. Perhaps he didn't want him to know he was communicating with me.

"Heiress," he said in his high voice. "Heiress, I haven't—haven't gotten a proper chance to talk to you." He sounded downright nervous, and was still looking around to see who was listening, although of course the other Senators were pretending not to see or listen in on our conversation. "But how opposed are you to experiments? Surely you are not against scientific progress. I know not what the Emperor means to do, but you could help me advance the cause of science in Chronala—for the future of humanity!"

I swallowed uncertainly. "Um . . . yeah, science. What would be the difference in these experiments?"

"Well . . . like I said, I don't know the Emperor's plans, but I'm sure you're aware that most of the Hellebes biomanufactories are in Chronala, yes? It's been my passion, ever since . . . since we came up with the idea. Centuries ago, now."

So Zent hadn't been making that up. It was hard not to stare as he admitted it to me, but . . . wait, what if I could keep him talking? "So it was really that long ago? That must have been quite an undertaking." *Little bit of interest, little bit of flattery . . .*

"Oh, it was!" His nervous excitement confirmed my success, simmering down slightly as he took a furtive glance around the room. "Can we go somewhere a bit more private? I'll tell you whatever you want to know. I'll bet Sylleo hasn't said a thing about the biomanufacturing process."

It was true—he hadn't yet. "Sure," I said tentatively, and followed him out of the room. Brant, who was just heading out, looked our way curiously, and Sylleo made sure to keep track of me. "I'll be back in a few minutes," I called to my chaperone. "I've a few questions for Senator Daedalus." The last part was for the prying ears. Daedalus opened a hallway door and led me into a smaller conference room, likely for less important personages.

"Have a seat." Daedalus pointed toward a chair behind one table while taking the opposite one, brushing off the dust carefully before sitting down. He very intentionally did not touch the table's surface, but rather laced his hands and leaned his massive elbows on the tabletop. Come to think of it, he had made no move to shake my hand as the others had. Or kiss it.

"So," he began. "How much do you know about the Hellebes mass-production process?"

"Not too much," I said. "The Hellebes aren't human, right? They're a man-made species?"

"Of a sort. We created them as a means of continuing the human race without the necessity of sexual reproduction. Because of a rampant disease that had spread throughout the world one thousand years ago and was slowly but surely killing off the world's female population."

A disease, eh? "So you had declining female birth rates? Or were all birth rates going down as well?'"

"Ah, both happened, but it was because of the lack of female births. Two-to-one, four-to-one, ten-to-one . . . all the way down the line. It didn't happen all at once. But the . . . an organization rose up to create a solution to the problem. Many were discussed, and a few were even implemented. One of those was a long-term plan to create a method of reproduction that could be copied, like cloning. So . . . we tried that. Didn't work so well, not to mention you'll never have a race of people, only an army of perfect clones. Like worker bees."

"But there were other scientific breakthroughs that led to the Hellebes, right?"

He nodded fervently. "Indeed. Seven hundred years ago, the first computers were made, and they advanced rapidly in technology. Later, alternative computing methods competed with the established tech, and the modern quantum computer came out on top. AI, or artificial intelligence, was a booming field at that time, and we experimented with using it to recreate a human mind. After all, if you can put a mind inside a robot and give it a personality, it's essentially a human, right?"

"Not really," I said. "It's still a robot."

"Precisely! That was my philosophy too. Artificial intelligence wasn't good enough. It was around this time that our scientists were making breakthroughs in gene-splicing and genetic engineering. And . . . we'd better make this quick, yes?" He took a deep breath before continuing on, speaking even faster than before. "Genetic engineering led to the discovery of genetic coding, which led to genetic digitalization: In other words, the ability to store the data from nucleic acids in a computer and print it out in the form of a living creature. The next key was discovering how to write information directly to and from the brain, and it followed in due time. We called this point the Biodigital Convergence, and from there it only rolled downhill.

"I decided that we needed to combine these ideas to see if we could transfer an entire mind to a new, fabricated body. The body, created from the ground up using not cloned but constructed DNA. Digitally synthesized. The mind, an exact digital copy of the host's. It took . . . some experimentation, but we successfully made a complete transfer and revolutionized the world. The first-ever Hellebes mind used artificial intelligence to recreate a human brain."

Whoa. That was some high-speed information. *Good thing I have my Vault now.* I frowned as I parsed the info, thinking for an extended moment. "So . . . then does each Hellebes have the brain data of a human from long ago?"

"No, no. We're long past that. We combined ideas, remember? First it was transfer, but now it is generation. Genetic data governing all bodily components and systems is combined in a way that makes sense according to the supercomputers back at the biomanufactories, which store the data of all successful Hellebes, along with that of thousands of olden-days humans. Sad to say, the first few generations had a lot of problems, but the computers have since learned what works and what doesn't. But they individualize each one, so that no Hellebes has ever been the same. Just like humans, but without most of their weaknesses and with far stronger bodies—not to mention Geokinetic ability."

I tried to wrap my head around this information. "Then I . . ." I cut off, realizing that I was so engrossed in the conversation that I was beginning to let my guard down. "What were the first experiments like? I mean, I know you wouldn't be doing the same things to me; I'm just curious." I knew nothing of the sort.

Daedalus gave a little grin, one that looked a bit out of place and forced on his massive, square-jawed face, as if to say he understood me. *That's right, little piggy, of course I won't turn you into sausage.* "Right, of course. What were they like? It started shortly after the Great Pilgrimage. You know about that?"

"Somewhat," I said in an uncertain tone, implying a desire to know.

"Well . . . we don't have time to talk about that," he said quickly. "But the Anier wanted to create a . . ." He paused again, as though realizing he had let something slip, before rolling with it. "They wanted to further humanity—well, to preserve it—and so they set a plan in motion to revolutionize the world."

"And . . . this was still back in medieval times, right?"

He made a *sort of* gesture. "Renaissance. But they were visionaries who found clever people, the skilled and the gifted—geniuses who wasted their talents on art and music—and began to study the laws of nature, advance written language, and further the fields of mathematics, engineering and natural philosophy—which we now call science. Eventually, they began researching secrets of immortality, cures for impossible disease, and of course a forever cure for the greatest plague ever to face humanity—the population crisis."

"And did they? Or was that not until later?"

"They did," he said excitedly. "Over time. In their later years, the Anier experimented on women and . . . well, they were trying to create what would eventually become the Mother."

"But . . . like an actual mother of human kind. Like what I was supposed to be."

"You were . . . well, yes, we'll go with that. Yes, they were searching for a way to turn one woman into a factory for human reproduction. Or multiple women. You see, the Cydenges themselves have a sort of "queen bee", according to our research. Of course, it didn't work out. A human female is too limited by nature: The fixed number of egg cells over a lifetime, infrequent egg cycles, and a host of other issues. Attributes that cannot be altered while maintaining a stable specimen. What they discovered instead— and far more importantly—was how to acclimate a human body to Cydenges DNA. This in turn led to the discovery of Geokinetic powers, one of the greatest and most important revolutions in Gaea's history. From there, we took over, as that corresponded with the construction of the nine cities."

I nodded. "And that was when?"

"About eight hundred years ago."

I raised my eyebrows. "Wow. I knew the Senators were ancient, but I didn't know you'd been around that long."

"Yes, yes. It has been a long journey. But the Cydenges don't sleep for long, and many advances in technology have come along. As I said, I was most instrumental in the creation of the Hellebes species from humans."

"Hmm. Would . . . would we be able to talk more at some point? I'd love to know more about the Hellebes, and the Red Horizon held all that stuff very close to their chests, like—I might side with you guys if I knew more."

Daedalus huffed. "I can understand that. You are a dream specimen born of thousands of experiments, while they are ants in an army. They think themselves free, but they're still not *quite* human." He grinned like he'd won some kind of existential fight against them.

"Yeah," I said with a fake laugh. "They're really just like robots anyway."

He nodded. "Exceedingly complex robots, of course. Para-robots. Meta-humans. They make me proud. But . . ." He ground his fist on the table, causing it to creak in pain. After a moment, he looked up, eyeing the door. Rising, he said, "Well, I will get in touch with Sylleo. If you ever want to tour the biomanufactories, I'd be more than happy to show you. I . . . hope I didn't sound over-eager with any of my talk of science and research. You see, it's a passion of mine. In fact, I hope we could be partners of a sort. The first Mother was a scientist in her own right, did you know? Before she . . . Well, in any case, I'd be careful of Sylleo if I were you. He's the best liar of us all."

I dipped my head in his direction. "Thank you, sir. We shall talk later." With that, I left the room, emerging into a hallway full of nonchalant but observant spectators and their bodyguards waiting to talk to me. Actually, the only ones still waiting were DeWitt and Holman. Brant must have given up on waiting. I didn't know anything about DeWitt, but Holman seemed like a decent fellow despite his intimidating appearance. I recalled a very old video program, some horror story about a large, square-headed creature who looked just like him. Well, except for the stitches and bolts, which Holman lacked.

Holman lumbered over, followed by the smaller DeWitt—who still towered over me. DeWitt was built like a Hellebes. If I didn't know, I would have thought he was a sandy-haired, well-dressed Hellebes coming home from a long day at the office. Holman contrasted with him, an oversized bull of a man with impossibly thick shoulders and a massive square beard, topped by the hat he loved so much.

"Lady Heiress," Holman said, the politeness falling flat in his gruff voice. "If you'd be so kind as to give me a minute to explain my case to you." He shifted uncomfortably, as though nervous to speak to me.

"And I as well, fairest Heiress." DeWitt said comically fast, taking a short bow from beside his colleague. After watching Daedalus slink out, the two looked at one another and seemed to forcibly avoid glaring after the hulking Senator. I got the idea these two often cooperated simply because no one else took them seriously.

"We both happen to be non-conformists politically," Holman said. "Though we are separated by large geographical distance. In the island nation of Luna Halcyon, my people innovate in cultural and architectural design, among other things—and it's also the home of the largest church of the Mother. People there sing your name all day long, and you would be loved and worshipped."

"Oh," I said, a bit disappointed. "But do you?"

"Well, of course not. I just thought it might . . ."

"I'm not interested in being worshipped," I said indignantly. "They're being lied to, and you're letting it happen!"

"But it's necessary—" He cut off as DeWitt interrupted.

"My lady, you also may like to come live in Lenardda. We have a strong agricultural tradition in the area, and the land is among the most fertile on Gaea. We also process and package a majority of the world's food supply, among other things, and I like to think it's one of the healthiest environments on the planet."

"For the people or the planet?" I asked.

DeWitt hesitated only a brief moment. "For both. We take steps to ensure our carbon footprint is less each decade and to recycle whatever we can and put back into the earth as many resources as we're taking out. We've brought down radiation levels in the vicinity by over two percent in as many decades, and forests are regrowing at unprecedented rates."

I nodded. "That's good. Or at least I assume so. I wouldn't really know. You said you're both non-conformists? Like Daedalus?" They had already said as much, minus the minotaur's name, but it was all I could think of to get them talking about something different. Something besides this transparent publicity rhetoric.

At the mention of the Chronala Senator's name, they shared gestures of uncertainty and a look of annoyance. I'd struck a chord here.

"Daedalus does his own thing," Holman said. "But he's also notoriously close with Strongs. It's commonly thought that he makes experimental Hellebes for Strongs to try out in the military, thus why they get along so well. I'd advise trusting neither of them."

"And what about Sylleo?"

Holman stole a glance at the tall Senator, who was leaning against the hallway wall some fifty feet away, near his bodyguards.

"He's mostly harmless," DeWitt said. "But he's a nationalist, which is not a popular opinion these days and for good reason. The world has changed, and we exist in a globalized world whether we like it or not. Nationalism is not a feasible worldview. We don't like to pick sides quite as much.

"He seems to find fun in defying the Emperor and the council at large," he added. "To Sylleo, the world is black and white, almost as much so as Lldsaor. The two really aren't so different, other than that Sylleo is more friendly and reasonable."

"And doesn't, you know, want to conquer my whole planet," I said. "Or put me in prison. Or experiment on my body."

"That too," DeWitt said with a nervous laugh. "That too."

"I would advise caution with him, Heiress," Holman reiterated. "You might think him just a kind old uncle who wants to give you presents, but you don't know his history. He used to be . . . extreme."

"As I said, black and white. That's the world to him," DeWitt said.

I pursed my lips. Their description of him didn't add up with what I'd seen so far. I didn't completely trust the man, certainly not, but I couldn't picture him being anywhere near as bad as Lldsaor. On a whim, I asked, "So what do you think of Strongs?"

DeWitt raised an eyebrow. "General Strongs, now called Senator Strongs, is and has always been a military man. In the early days of the Senate's control, when the nine cities were being constructed, he was the one who marshaled Lldsaor's forces and defended our projects. He kept the peace and opposed those who would stop us. He spearheaded the great purging and fought off the Cydenges many times. Strongs has never lost a battle. Still today, his generals train the troops for the whole world. War . . . war is his world."

War is his world, I mused. So what war was there to fight today? The League defended Gaea from the Cydenges whenever they invaded, but that was no war. No, Lldsaor's war was with the people of Mani, for whatever reason. "Do you think Lldsaor and Strongs agree as much now as they used to?" I asked. "Lldsaor is very firm on invading and conquering Mani, but is Strongs as well?"

Holman shook his head. "Hard to know with that one. But you saw how Strongs opposed him to his face in the meeting. I think if it came down to it, Strongs would wage war against the Emperor himself if it meant getting his way."

A chill ran down my spine. War . . . why was everything about conflict? I couldn't even imagine what a full-scale civil war between Senators and cities on modern Gaea would look like.

Eventually, I managed to convince the two Senators that I wasn't interested, and we exchanged farewells. At least I could be pretty certain that they wouldn't try to give Sylleo trouble about me. Daedalus probably wouldn't either, although . . . ugh, had I really agreed to communications with him? It was a distasteful thought, for sure, and yet . . . I wanted to know more about the Hellebes and their origins, and he was the expert of experts in that regard. If nothing else, I could use it as leverage to get Sylleo to tell me a bit more too. The man talked of openness between us but had yet to divulge much . . .

That thought appealed surprisingly well.

"Ready to go, Lynchazel?" Sylleo asked as I approached. There was no hint of resentment in his voice.

I nodded, and we left the building, chatting about the meeting along the way. I hadn't learned much, but it was certainly not pointless, especially since Lldsaor's vote got turned down. It seemed a weight had been lifted from my chest, allowing me to breathe more easily. I realized belatedly that I forgot to thank Holman and DeWitt for voting against the Emperor. Had either one of them gone the other way, it would have been a near tie, and who knew how that would have gone?

The Tour

When I got back, I felt emotionally exhausted from all the politics and shenanigans at the Senate that day, but I made a point to go straight to Zent and the others and explain the situation, at least for the most part. I left out a few details that I didn't think they needed to know. Kaen was trying to avoid me, as he didn't show up until I was almost done. Was it that sword again? I wished I could just get rid of it . . . but it was too valuable.

It wasn't long after our little debriefing session that a steward came, informing me that I had a transmission from Senator Daedalus. Kaen's face displayed surprise, then a distrusting scowl, but what was he expecting? I'd just been to a meeting with eight of these Elites fighting over me, going at it like tomcats.

"Mother Heiress?" said Daedalus over the screen as I entered the comms room, where Sylleo already was. "It is good to speak with you."

"Hello, Senator."

"I wanted to thank you for being willing to converse with me earlier. And also to formally invite you to come tour the laboratories here at Chronala this Saturday, unless you have plans already."

Awfully eloquent all of a sudden. I looked to Sylleo, who said nothing. "Um, no, th-that's fine. I . . . would appreciate that. Thank you, Senator."

"Excellent," Daedalus said, steamrolling on. "Sylleo will be giving you my contact information so that you can get a hold of me directly at any time. Oh, but I must ask one favor in return. Nothing major or long-term . . . but I'm requesting that you allow us to run two small laboratory examinations.

Nothing more, no further obligations."

"I'd . . . really rather just take a tour," I said honestly.

"I understand, Heiress. But these are my stipulations. Think it over. Sylleo." He nodded in Sylleo's direction.

Sylleo bobbed his head. "Senator."

The transmission cut, and we were alone in the room together. I sighed. "I should have known he wasn't that generous." I'd already related most of our private conversation to Sylleo.

"I did warn you, Lyn; there's no such thing as a free meal. That being said, if you want to go, I won't stop you. It would be good for you to get some firsthand knowledge of how this world truly works. While I don't entirely trust Daedalus, I doubt he would break a promise so easily."

"But doesn't he have ties to Strongs?" I asked worriedly.

"He . . . does. I am not certain how close. The thing is, the last time Strongs attacked was in Maldunech, Brant's city, and Brant is allied with Lldsaor as far as we know. So there's not necessarily any safe place, even here, yet I think Strongs is bound a bit tighter at the moment and will have to be a lot more creative—or patient—if he wants to get to you."

How comforting, I thought. *He'll have to be more creative if he wants to murder me.*

"Then let's go," I said. "I think I should. I . . ." Auroras, it was hard to say. The last thing I wanted was to let another possibly-deranged scientist run exams on me—the very one responsible for creating my mother and grandmother, no less. And the Hellebes race. But . . . I nodded. "Yes."

"Very well." Sylleo typed something out on his wrist console. "There. And here is Daedalus' contact information."

A notification popped up: *Senator Daedalus added to contacts.* "And you don't have a problem with this, Senator? You don't think I'm trying to double-cross you or anything?"

"I do not. If I didn't trust you this far—and if I didn't believe trust to be essential in our partnership—then I would never have informed you of the transmission from Daedalus. You would never know, even if you tried to hack into our systems and find out for yourself."

Well . . . we might have to see about that, I thought to myself. Somebody back at Red Horizon HQ might just have the skills to do that. Like . . . *Auroras above.* Like Ccal. And Janus. Images of their bodies, along with Bddo and the others, lying bloodied and broken on a hard metal floor, charred skin smoking, flashed through my mind. I couldn't even pick out the real from the fake memories, or . . . no, I just didn't want to.

I teetered to one side and caught my balance with a jolt.

"Lyn!" Sylleo reached out a hand with lightning speed. But I had already restabilized. "You sure?" he responded to my protests.

I nodded wearily. "Just . . . spaced out. I was recalling the . . . the time I . . ." I bit my lip and turned my head away from the towering Senator, mortified by the burgeoning tears in my eyes.

"The day you inherited your mother's powers in the Haccolces labs," he finished.

"Mm-hmm." I didn't quite trust myself to speak. My lips and eyes wouldn't hold still. *How does he even know about that?* I thought dimly.

Some things you think you're over until they slam into you out of nowhere. Perhaps now I could see why the Hellebes had such trouble understanding my emotions and feelings—they weren't human at all, but biomachines operating on programmed thoughts, programmed emotions, programmed . . . *genetics.* But Sylleo, what about him? Daedalus made them out to be something more, something greater. Did that extend to emotions?

I was just seeing myself out of the comms room when I got a message from Kaen, asking to meet and talk. This cheered me up a little bit, as it seemed a good sign from him. Wiping my nose self-consciously, I recommended we walk through the western estate gardens.

He was already there when I arrived, wearing clothing provided by Sylleo's servants, most likely to build his physical strength and endurance outside of the power suit. His adjustment to the steeply harsher gravity was quite impressive, and he was never one to show outward signs of weakness. In this case, though . . . He looked tired in a different way. And of course he was rubbing the hilt of that horrible sword.

"Hi, Kaen," I greeted him as I came to the gardens.

He turned, seeing me for the first time. "Lyn. Thanks for coming."

I approached him and gave him a quick hug. He'd spoken to me in Hellebes, but I responded in Legaleian. "Of course. You look like you're having a rough day. Come on, let's walk."

He nodded as I led him down a path through the impressively arranged botanical gardens. I wondered if he thought the same as I had, that they reminded him of the Palace gardens back in Nytaea. Finally, my friend said, "I feel like we're growing apart. I think . . . it's not just us, it's . . . me. I'm tearing apart. I think it's this—" His hand twitched, and he seemed to forcibly avoid looking down at it, neck muscles bulging. "It's not as bad as it seems. But I'm starting to realize I might have made a huge mistake."

I nodded. "And?"

He took a heavy breath. "And . . . I don't know what's causing it, but I feel like I'm being split in two, and I'm fighting myself. One half says I like it here, the other half says I'm dying. One half says I should be angry, the other says I should feel guilty. One half says I-I love you, and . . . the other half says I hate you." He said the last three words in a near-whisper, looking down at the ground as he walked beside me.

I opened my mouth to say something. A hot-headed response, most likely, or an expression of my incredulity and utter confusion. I'll admit, I wanted to grill him on this supposed love for me, but I knew he wasn't in a right state of mind. He needed help, a solution, and I didn't have one. "Kaen, I don't know what to say. What do you want me to say?"

"I . . ." he began, but trailed off with a disquieted frown. After a pause, he asked, "Does your mother really speak to you?"

"Yes. Not as often now."

"And . . . what kind of stuff does she say? Does she tell you to kill me? To murder everyone you love?"

"Kaen! No, of course not! My mother loved me. She wouldn't . . . No. But the other voice I heard, the one I mentioned back at HQ . . . I think she was evil, very evil."

He nodded.

"Kaen, why are you asking me all these questions? What's going on with you? Is it getting worse?"

He scoffed. "Why, are you going to put me down like a sick dog? Or a dog who bites?"

I stopped, taking him by the arm. "Why would I do that?" I tried to stare him in the eye, but he avoided my gaze. When he finally did look at me, it was with an expression I didn't recognize. Hostility? Uncertainty?

"Because that's what—" He cut off, biting his lip with either a snarl or a grimace; again, I couldn't tell which. "Never mind."

"Okay." I thought for sure he was angry with me, but then his next words surprised me:

"Is it all right if I come with you to Chronala tomorrow?"

I frowned at him. "That's an odd request. I mean, sure. That's fine with me. I think . . . Daedalus wouldn't mind. I'll ask him."

He nodded absently.

Daedalus sent aircraft the next day to pick me and Kaen up. We boarded a large vessel with multiple armed personnel, along with a small retinue of protectors for her most esteemed Motherly Heiressness. I was pretty sure I could threaten to drop the ship in the ocean—draining all its energy and sending everyone down with me—if they tried anything. Hopefully they didn't, because I didn't want to have to do that.

After an awkward ride with my troubled friend, complete with gorgeous aerial vistas as ever, we had crossed part of the Cynnith Ocean and landed in Chronala, which occupied a coastal region of northern Nestra. The place was just as high-tech as I'd imagined, that is to say it was a Hellebes city. But this one in particular was a veritable maze of laboratories and gargantuan facilities where countless thousands of Hellebes were brought up from incubation to adolescence.

One of Daedalus' aides met us with professional cordiality at the airport and explained that we would be getting a guided tour, courtesy of Lord Daedalus. When I messaged the Senator to ask where he was, he explained that he sadly was not able to make it yet due to administrative concerns. This was followed by a hasty apology. I shrugged it off and set myself on trying to enjoy the tour and pay attention. Afterward would come the less pleasant part, where they ran yet another round of (hopefully) pointless exams on my body. He'd probably show up for that.

The aide, a shorter Hellebes with a thick mustache and an accent I couldn't place, introduced himself as Minister Cortez, and apparently held a fairly high rank in the city's hierarchy. Meanwhile, we headed to our first destination: The incubation laboratories. These proved to be inside one of the massive, square complexes. We rode right inside on our tram, heading through the first floor of a multilevel laboratory. Here, we gazed upon row after row of glass incubation chambers with Hellebes fetuses being nurtured by machines, a monitor capping each row and nervous interns cycling between aisles and marking down numbers on a pad. Above us, glass ceilings allowed glimpses of one-to-two stories up, which were near-duplicates of the first floor, itself a large space.

"This is unreal," I muttered to Kaen, who continued to stare wordlessly. He didn't seem to show much interest in the tour so far.

Minister Cortez rattled off some history and statistics surrounding the laboratory. Next, we transitioned into the lab that housed Hellebes in the next phase of development—essentially babies. These were kept in glass cells barely larger than the incubators, each replete with speakers and multiple robotic arms that rotated in nearly every direction to administer whatever the babies needed at the moment. Instead of diapers, they were situated on machines that took care of all waste simply and efficiently. This lab was far bigger than the first, due to the less efficient space usage.

It got more interesting, but also sadder in a way, as we went through the plethora of nursery and educative centers that raised the younglings from toddler to adolescence, training them to walk, talk, read and write—all manner of educational programs. There was also physical training and even, in the later stages, Geokinetic training and some rudimentary martial arts. Each stage apparently took around a year of development. In one of the final labs, I asked about an intriguing sight: Separate biodevelopment units for younglings in the seventh and eighth stages of development—nearing adulthood—who looked different from the others. Their movements, their gazes . . .

Cortez assured us that they were ordinary Hellebes, but he did say that they were a prized achievement of the Senator, a new type that could revolutionize the industry, yada yada. He just didn't elaborate on *what* was different about them. Likely, I wouldn't want to know.

Then it was testing time. The aide took us to the outskirts of the biolab district, where another research lab stood, and sure enough, Daedalus met us here. "Lynchazel!" he said brightly. He introduced us, grinning like a child, to a Hellebes doctor who would see me for the testing. He blustered right through any questions I could've asked and simply handed me over, saying we'd talk soon. It was as though he was too excited for the grand pursuit of science to even remember our agreement. *So much for our chat.*

Nervous though I was and more than a little irritated, I followed the doctor calmly, and . . . well, everything went just as expected. I was done in ten minutes, and then Daedalus' stream of bubbly biochemistry chatter turned into the audience I'd been waiting for. He gave me time to speak as I followed him out to a domed cafeteria. I started out awkwardly, having been a bit off-put by the huge Senator's unpredictable mannerisms.

I wasted little time, however, in having Daedalus order me a tall burger. When it came to food, I didn't mess around, and Sylleo had spoiled me to the secret that Hellebes were fully capable of cooking terrific food.

Over the next half hour, I questioned him on things in the tour that had caught my attention but hadn't been explained well by the guide. Most of what I asked was relatively unimportant, points of curiosity that the Senator obliged with answers, each filling in another small piece of Gaea's background in my Vault. I wanted to know more about these biomachines and just how human they really were. Slowly, he grew more impatient, something I don't believe was intentional on his part. I didn't get the sense that he wanted to cover anything up or mislead me.

I thanked him for his time, and he led me back to the others. Daedalus encouraged me to visit anytime, saying that he'd be happy to show me more if I let him run some further tests.

I tried to answer politely without making any commitments. Then we said farewell, and the same transport shuttle loaded us up to take us back to Ccamos. The visit could have gone worse, yet somehow I felt exhausted.

We hadn't gone a hundred miles when an alarm sounded from the cockpit, soon followed by a curse. "We're going to have to make an emergency landing, guys," said the captain over the loudspeaker. "Hopefully we can fix this quickly, but I'll call Ccamos just in case."

Kaen and I exchanged dubious frowns. *At least this didn't happen over sea . . . whatever it is.*

We landed in a grassland some hundred miles south of Chronala, past the outskirts bases. Orders came to sit tight until help arrived from the city to sort out what went wrong in the shuttle. At least they'd let Kaen wear his power suit for the flight . . .

The attack came without warning.

The first I knew was when the missiles struck the side of our craft, nearly knocking the whole thing on its side. Kaen and I flew from our seats, flinging out our hands for something to hold on to. The second blast took out our shields, sending the vessel into a full tumble. By the time we stopped, I could hear soldiers gathering all around. After some loud noises, someone ripped the back doors right off our craft and shouted, "Bring her out! Or you all die here." It was a helmeted Hellebes packing a heavy energy cannon, backed up by a squad of soldiers.

Our own men, to their credit, reacted quickly and opened fire. A firefight ensued, during which I searched the ground beneath us for Geothermic hotspots. There were none, just the ordinary residual stuff—this far from a city, I should have expected as much—so I drew on the ship's batteries first, draining the power and shutting everything in the ship off. I released it in spurts, blasting pure energy out the door and peeling up the ground, hurling it at our attackers.

With a cry, our team surged out the door and engaged the enemy in earnest. Only now could I see that we were heavily outnumbered. Mother or no, we could not win this. I pressed the distress button on my wrist console that would call Sylleo for reinforcements. It would take them over two hours to get here, however.

I tried to process in my head who might have attacked us and why now, but I couldn't think amidst the battle. So I carved an alternate exit in the ship and looked out to make sure the way was clear. "Kaen!" I called, looking back. "Let's—"

But he wasn't there.

I circled around to the front of the ship to see enemy soldiers boarding us, apparently trampling the bodies of the brave Hellebes who had fought for me. And Kaen . . . there he was, slowly stalking toward his opponents, sword held out. He slashed at the soldiers as they passed him, the blade tearing through armor and coming out bloodied, and killed those who tried to subdue him. No one could land a shot on him because the sword pulled Geothermic energy out of the air like a powerful vacuum suction. It occurred to me that one would have to fight him like he would a Cydenges.

"Kaen!" I shouted, ducking back immediately as the enemy pinpointed my location. So they were trying to capture us? They clearly weren't out to kill Kaen. Soldiers came at me from inside and about the ship, shouting for me to put my hands up, and I blew them off their feet with Geokinesis. I collected a couple of pistols and tried to make a break for Kaen.

The soldiers kept coming. They had multiple vehicles, which seemed to have been kept nearby for the ambush. When I finally caught a glimpse of my friend, I saw that they had already subdued him and wrested the sword from his hands. As I watched, one of the enemy aircraft pulled up to his captors, landing and opening a ramp for them to load him up. Confused shouts seemed to indicate they wanted me as well.

Angrily, I burst out all around me with Geokinesis, encasing my remaining assailants in stone. Then I took aim with my blasters, trying to pick off the men who had Kaen. I managed to hit one, but that only gave them a bead on me, and soldiers began firing back. They threw Kaen in the ship and it immediately lifted off. At that point, it was clear that he was gone. I had to hold out here until Sylleo arrived. I could do nothing more.

And so I ran.

α Chapter 41 α

The Way Forward

He is strong, handsome in a way. Maybe even the type of man I'd have started a family with. Not that either of us had a choice. No, in the Anier's new world of progressive ideals and freedom for all . . . somehow, they left those key things out. Of course, how am I to trust that the human I met so briefly was the father? All they feed me is lies. Where is he now? Dead, surely, like all the others.

— From Lhinde's Vault

Sylleo's men arrived in less time than I thought possible, but they were still an hour and a half too late to save my friend. Two flight crews took me back to Ccamos, while another three stayed behind to scout the enemy's trail, examine the battle site and collect data.

Daedalus' men had never arrived. Either someone was jamming the signal or the trap was more elaborately set up than I thought.

Back at Ccamos, we met up with Sylleo and some of his trusted tacticians in the military base, where I explained what had happened. Of the crew that had flown us to Chronala and back, none were left alive to give a report. Zent arrived shortly thereafter, looking concerned. The news of Kaen's capture by the enemy—whoever they were—had disturbed both Sylleo and Zent.

Suddenly, we received an urgent transmission from an unknown caller. Sylleo took it there in the command room, allowing most of us to see it, and the screen popped up with a poorly lit scene in what appeared to be a solid steel containment room. Kaen, bound and stripped of his power suit, knelt on the floor. Then the camera cut to reveal an unidentifiable Hellebes in a full, black-armored combat suit and a mask Sylleo did not recognize. His suit reminded me of the soldiers who had come to capture us, however.

"Hello, Mother Gaea. And hello, Senator Sylleo," the Hellebes said in an altered voice with several layers of filters. "We have your friend, of course. I am ordered to instruct you on what you are to do. Stay out of our business, and do not interfere with the political workings of Gaea. To our understanding, this man was considered to be a potentially formidable weapon to you. But to show you how serious we are . . ." he made a gesture, and the camera cut back to Kaen.

"No," I moaned as I saw it coming. Sure enough, as we watched, they shot him through the back. Once, twice, three times, and then proceeded to shear his head from his shoulders with a gleaming sword. I would have screamed had my gag reflexes not kicked in, and I turned to one side, coughing. I looked back, just to make sure, but his attackers only ran him through the back, stomped his dead form onto the floor, and ran him through again, leaving the blade to stick in his back. Only then did I recognize it as his own special silver sword, its glow faint and sputtering, marred with new stains along its length.

The camera feed showed color very clearly, displaying the head and the blood leaking from his body, more blood streaking the silver blade of the sword . . . The camera cut again, and the masked Hellebes said, "That is what will happen to the Mother if she interferes with our workings again. If she rejoins the rebels, or you send her to fight your battles for you, we will know, and we will hunt her down and kill her. This world has no need of her."

The transmission ended, and we were all left speechless. All I could do was mouth the word *no* over and over. Sylleo took hold of my shoulder and pulled me to his side. I ground my forehead into his shoulder and mumbled, "Why? Why would they do such a thing? Who are they?"

Sylleo took a breath. "I can only conclude that Strongs is behind this, just as last time. It's surprising to think that he would throw away such a valuable tool, but . . . his ways are extreme. There's always an order to them, it just might not make sense."

"Senator," Zent said, "Do you really believe that video was not faked?"

Sylleo looked at one of his generals. "We will have to go over it again with an expert, but . . . yes, I believe that footage was real. They can only fake so much on a transmission like this; it was verifiably live."

I pulled away from Sylleo, nodding numbly and feeling stupid. My enemy had just taken the person I loved most in both worlds, and he would pay. If it wasn't personal before, it was now.

"Sir," I said shakily to the Senator, trying to ignore my twisting guts, "I will not cower just because that *demon* is set on killing me. I'm not afraid of him. I'll fight."

"And you are also emotional right now. It's not a good time to be making decisions."

I ground my teeth, biting back a response. He was right. Zent voiced it too, just in case I didn't realize.

"Please excuse me," I said curtly, and left.

Later that day, after a time of mourning and a bit of rest, I went back to Sylleo and restated my resolution, which had not wavered. I would *not* cower in the dark and let more of my friends die on my behalf, and I wouldn't let Strongs or Lldsaor destroy Gaea or Mani. I wouldn't play their games.

"Very well," he said with a sigh. "I knew I wouldn't be able to change your mind. I suppose that horrible video only served the opposite purpose, huh?" After a pause, he said, "I'm sorry, that was insensitive."

"It-it's okay," I said, clenching my teeth to keep my jaw from quivering. My throat still had that swollen feeling like I needed to swallow something but couldn't.

Sylleo cleared his throat. "Lyn, there's . . . something I should tell you."

"You want to marry me. Yes, I know."

The tall Senator looked like he'd gotten slapped from the shadows. "What? I—no. I mean . . . no. Different. I know of a place that you could go if you want to become stronger. Strong enough to challenge Elites and win."

Now he had my attention.

"You asked about the ninth city, and the ninth Senator," he went on. "The truth is that we consider that city to be lost, as it was destroyed in the only civil war ever fought since the founding of the Gaean League. Known as Mei Shan, it lay in the far eastern continent of Tai'Xi. Its Senator, Long, was known as the Earth Sage. He believed very differently from the others, and when he opposed our ideals, it was decided that we would cut him off from the senate. But Strongs convinced the Senate to bomb the entire city.

"He knew a secret that most of the others didn't—what the Sage was keeping in Mei Shan, and what it meant for mankind. Long and I got along well, sharing many aspirations. I wasn't always the man I am today. He had a large influence on me. But . . . I could do nothing to override the vote, and bomb it they did. To this day, Mei Shan lies bleak and desolate . . . or so everyone thinks. However, I can assure you that Long is still alive, and leads a small but flourishing society there. I've been in contact with him regularly for decades now."

"So . . . you're saying I should go see him?"

Sylleo nodded. "Precisely. I wasn't going to suggest it, but now I think it would be a good way for you to disappear for a while. I'll make some excuses to the Senate for your absence, and that will appear to be a sign of compliance to Strongs, so hopefully he will relax his aggression for a while. I still worry what and when his next move will be, but I'll handle that. You need to see the Earth Sage."

"A-all right," I said. "This should be . . . a good diversion. But, can you do something for me? Can you let Zent and the others go? Back to the Red Horizon?"

Sylleo inhaled slowly. "Yes. I think I can do that now. I will talk to him. I think we have a good enough mutual understanding. My only concern would be the spy in their midst, because there most definitely is one. But perhaps I can use that to my advantage."

I thought about what had transpired these last few weeks, the lives lost in my name and the political power struggles going on, most of which centered around me. If only I were strong enough to forge my own way and fight back against the Elites and their plans. What would this Earth Sage be like, and what kind of secrets could he hold that Sylleo thought so important?

There was only one way to find out.

Gaea

β PART THREE β

B

Domon

Gaea

β Chapter 015 β

Penumbra

Ex-queen Lieda opened her eyes. It was time; she could feel it. The jail was dark, and rat lord Zama was snoring ever so softly two cells down. She didn't know where her teleportation crystal was, but she called its name now through the magic gag, a murmur in the dark. Sure enough, it came to her, appearing in her right hand. That had been such an ingenious idea on Domon's part: Including a trigger that depended on voice, not Coaction. Whatever she thought of the man, he was truly intelligent.

Taking a breath, she whispered the activation words and the crystal transported her instantly with a small hum. After a disorienting eyeblink, she was sitting in a corner of the Umbra Council's octagonal room where they met every Sol Cycle. She rose to her feet with what was supposed to resemble dignity and grace, and realized she had four pairs of eyes on her already. Of course she did . . . why couldn't she ever be on time lately? Shrugging off her discomfort, she strode over to the heavy stone table, rolling her hips, meeting the eyes of the others only briefly but bowing to Domon, who stood across from her.

I'm not late. I'm not wearing a sack. I'm not late. I'm not wearing a sack.

Kyal, Lord of Imdek and Lhiard, Lord of Uphel, stood to her right, whilst on her left was Tyiv, a landholder of Dotham. Lhiard, in his high-pitched voice, said, "My wives would be most jealous of your apparel, Lieda."

"The magic seal is a lovely touch as well," Kyal added. "I see your new queenship is going well."

Her face flushed, though no one would be able to see it in the dim light cast by the reddish flame in the center of the table. She fought with the band behind her head before giving up. It culminated in a black mouth mask that did not prevent speech but did have a profound—and negative—effect on one's Coactive abilities. Gendric's High Magi had never been persuaded to spill their secrets on the things. "I would have changed, my lord," she said sulkily, "had I the chance in the dungeon. As soon as my lord the Archlord chooses, I will be free of this gag as well."

"Zama knows nothing of your visit tonight?" Domon asked sharply, ignoring her second comment.

She nodded hastily. "Nothing. I hardly tell him anything, of course. Why bother? No one saw me go."

He nodded in satisfaction, but offered no further acknowledgements to her. It was gracious of him not to make mention of her failure in Nytaea. As she watched, Lieda saw another woman appear in the far left of the room, wearing a sleeveless gown that billowed from top to bottom, over which she wore a red stole that stretched from one shoulder to the opposite hip. The loose getup would have looked hideous had the woman wearing it not been stunning of form and face. She had her sunset-red hair pulled back in a complex bun and pinned in two places, with earrings of silver and gold and fine jewels adorning her ears. Her features were delicate, her eyebrows sharp. As she walked toward the table, Lieda saw her go from uncertain to confident in the space of a second, taking control of the situation and sashaying with grace and purpose, calm and authority.

Who is this? Lieda wondered with a rising sense of loathing. She usually only hated things she envied. The woman sidled up to the Archlord and looked up at him like a . . . Lieda wasn't certain. Either a lover or a proud student, or perhaps a she-bear. Yes, Lieda liked that. She looked uglier the more Lieda stared at her.

"Good day," the woman said with a strange, clipped accent.

"Brethren," Domon said, placing a hand on the she-bear's slim shoulder, "this is Solomiya, our newest member. She works in intelligence here in Redufiel."

Yes, intelligence, Lieda thought wryly. *I can see that.*

"I am happy to serve however I best can for the glory of the empire," Solomiya said in her sharp accent. Lieda couldn't tell if she spoke a different language over on the far continent or merely a different dialect. There were no separate languages on Argent, although it was said that before the thousand years spent in Argent—which was now being called the Great Exile—humans had many languages. Domon claimed that the people had only brought one—Legaleian—to Mani with them.

Kyal glanced at Lhiard with a distinctly sleazy look. "She is certainly easy on the eyes."

Lieda snorted. The woman herself paid them no attention, merely glancing from Domon to the group at large. When she did look at anyone individually, it was as though she stared right through them, not at them.

"Is this everyone?" Solomiya asked, looking up into the blond Archlord's face.

Lieda interpreted these words as: *Is this my only competition for your favor, O Most Glorious Domon?* It was written all over her face.

The blond conqueror merely nodded, looking around the room. "Let's begin. Updates from the continent?"

They went around the room, sharing what was happening in the various regions of Kystrea and the small neighboring countries. After patiently waiting her turn, Lieda told them of the recent events in Nytaea, as best she knew of them from her location in the dungeon. Only Domon and his new feline seemed to pay much attention, while the others clearly didn't believe her.

"I saw these vehicles passing overhead myself," Domon said. "Had they been any closer, I would have shot them out of the sky. But now I am glad in a way that the Gaeans have attacked Nytaea, since that will distract Rhidea and her little posse for a while. I'd rather keep her out of my hair."

And that wretched ratling Mydia . . .

"Yes, these vehicles, they are strange," Solomiya added. "I have been compiling all accessible stories from our side of the world—the Light Side, as my lord calls it—but none of them refer to flying metal machines. Methinks they did not exist when our ancestors came to this world. However, there are many things that I have uncovered, particularly about what historians refer to as the Great Pilgrimage. They say that our ancestors came to Mani to flee aggressors on Gaea. This new world was to be a free place, one where . . ." she trailed off, eyeing the Emperor, and seemed to change her course. "But Mani was never meant to be a permanent home. They say we were supposed to go back after one thousand years. Which is fast approaching.

"But some ventured to the far side of Mani," she continued, "and built kingdoms there, and eventually an empire. Now, it would appear we stand at a crossroads."

"So what made you join our leader?" Tyiv asked, voicing the question no one wanted to ask.

She shrugged. "He compelled me. But it was the wise choice. We may have other side arrangements, but my specialty has always been in procuring information, no matter how difficult. I seek it out, I break through the lies, I dig up graves—whatever is necessary to obtain the needed information."

So you're a spy, Lieda mused. No wonder she'd felt an instant rivalry with the woman.

"In other words," Domon concluded, "Gaea is our enemy, and we need to learn everything we can of this enemy."

"Then why did we destroy the Gate?" Lhiard asked. "Especially if it did no good?"

Domon's eyes flashed. "To stall them. We could not know that they had flying ships capable of crossing worlds, but it was likely enough that they would figure out some way to find us here eventually. You heard what Solomiya said: Mani was meant as a temporary home, but we have built an empire here, and that empire is only becoming greater. Gaea does not want us back; they want to crush us. The attack on Nytaea only confirms my suspicions in that regard. Our empire was fated to be. Together, we will unite Mani to stand against the threat of invaders."

Lieda nodded slowly along with the others. That was actually an impressive plan. Before, she hadn't seen the reasoning behind it, but it would appear that the Archlord's predictions had indeed been prescient. "How long, then, until they return?" she asked. "How long do we have to prepare?"

Domon set his jaw. It must have irked him to hear that Rhidea's group had once again ousted his governance in Nytaea, because he seemed irritated with her. "That is hard to determine, but I doubt it will be soon, as the attack obviously did not go as planned."

"And in the meantime?" asked Kyal. "Should we assemble to conquer Nytaea?"

"No," Domon said to everyone's surprise. "If they strike Nytaea again, that will only be to our benefit. Let us focus on bolstering our defenses around the world, lest the next invasion begin where our empire is weakest. I am still working to secure and strengthen the new empire in Darsor and establish systems of communication, trade and transportation between continents."

"And what about this whole matter of those rebels climbing up from the Great Chasm?" Lieda added. "Do you believe that is worth looking into, my lord?"

"It was indeed a shocking turn. But now that they are back, what's done is done. We have more important work here."

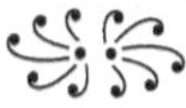

β Chapter 016 β

Redufiel

Rhidea had gotten used to the smoke here by now. Something was always burning. Three days back, when they had glimpsed Redufiel on the horizon, the first thing they'd noticed was the smoke. The scent seemed ubiquitous. Even houses and farmland surrounding the capital city of Halstar had been charred by Coaction or torch. In the city, everything was more controlled, but . . . barely.

It reminded her of Nytaea, when they'd returned to the White City two months back. Houses charred and listing, homeless sighted all over the place. The only difference was that order had been established here in the city of Redufiel, oppressive though it was. Domon was efficient; he unleashed only the necessary amount of chaos and destruction to serve his purposes, then moved in with his mage soldiers and built a new regime from the dust. The established officials, of course, were either brought to heel or ousted.

Now, she walked the streets with a slight shuffle and tediously uneven gait, practicing her commoner look. It helped that her leg wasn't *quite* healed, though it was getting there. She had dyed her long hair mouse-brown using Perception Coaction and put it in a simple bun, and wore a plain flax dress and a popular squarish hat. Many of the women who passed her by on the street looked nearly identical. With the brim of the hat tucked ever so slightly downward and posture diminishing, she blended right in and no one could tell the difference.

She was looking for a certain shop . . . there it was. It was a spinning shop that sold many varieties of thread and yarn for clothing. Certainly not the most elaborate or attractive establishment, but quaint. Clopping on the paving stones with her wooden shoes, Rhidea reached the door just as the first drippings of rain were falling from the overcast sky. Opening the door triggered a small bell to go, *Ding!* An elderly woman looked up from behind a counter, running a single-treadle spinning wheel. Tuck-chinned and quite obese, she was muttering to herself but stopped long enough to smile and give an unintelligible greeting to her newest customer. Her non-pedaling foot was making an odd half-peddle motion in time with the active one.

"I'm looking for the scarlet thread used to bind a red dress," Rhidea announced, taking off her slightly-damp hat and looking the old woman in the eye.

The woman met her gaze and held it briefly. "Very well, dear. You're sure that's what you need?"

"Quite, madam."

"Then follow me." Her accent was thick and she spoke into her heavy chest instead of projecting. She got off her stool and waddled over to a cellar staircase, waving Rhidea onward. They descended a set of creaky wooden stairs before coming to a door hung with a blanket. Before brushing it aside to enter, the old woman looked back up at Rhidea, who was two steps behind her. "You're certain, dear? You know what you're getting yourself into?"

"I'm aware," Rhidea replied.

The woman inspected her a bit longer, then brushed the blanket aside and held it for Rhidea to enter. "Go ahead, then."

"Thank you, madam." Rhidea stepped through the door and into a basement filled with curious trappings like tables, chairs, bookshelves, and a few candles kept burning on candleholders mounted into the wall. Rhidea's original plan had been to come as traveling merchants seeking stock to buy and sell, but Kymhar had insisted that it was better if he pretend to be a soldier looking for work, and she a lower lady of the local nobility. Renting just one room at a mid-grade inn called the Lucky Kettle, they'd quietly encouraged people to assume them married. After three days of digging around, Rhidea had located a political faction that met in this very basement, one that opposed Domon and sought to undermine his authority.

Two members were here now. Both were women, one petite and the other a few inches taller and rather stocky, both with dark brown hair. They turned a suspicious glare on her from their table as she entered. The basement, while a bit cluttered, had plenty enough space to navigate to where one needed to go, and just enough light to see well.

"Hello, madam, madam," Rhidea greeted them both as she approached. "I was informed of your group by someone I will not name. I, too, value anonymity."

"You speak as a foreigner," said the small lady. She had a voice that was slightly too nasal to call pretty, but still managed to match her form.

Rhidea winced, hopefully not noticeably. Was it that easy to tell? She'd been working on her accent. "I am from a neighboring country, it is true."

"Which one? Felmani? Castanor?" the same woman asked.

"No, the accent isn't right," the larger woman mumbled nearly inaudibly, more an idle comment than an expression of disbelief.

"The one where privacy and anonymity are kept in high regard," Rhidea returned.

The small woman narrowed her squint, but the bigger one merely nodded as though that was a fair response. She motioned for Rhidea to take a seat beside her, and the mage did so, smoothing her grey skirts as she sat. She managed to click one of her wooden shoes on a table leg loudly, and winced again. What possessed the locals to wear these things? Clearing her throat, she tentatively placed her hat on the table, where the two women already had theirs sitting.

"What brings you here, then, traveler?" asked the large-boned woman in her gravelly voice.

"I want to know the political state here in Redufiel since this . . . Archlord took over," Rhidea replied. "I never cared too much for what happened here in the capital, but I see the writing on the walls and I know he's going to try to invade lands around Halstar as well. Thus, I came here with my husband to learn how to fit into this new empire."

The little woman seemed almost impressed at that. Surely, she still didn't believe Rhidea, but probably just appreciated the sense that her explanation made. "Well, you're here now, so we might as well fill you in on our group. We are the Preservation faction, and our goal is to wait out Domon's rule and ensure that a leader is instated next who is favorable toward the people and particularly toward historical Redufiel. I am called Nora, and this is Helena."

Helena gave Rhidea a wide-chinned smile. One of those warm but extremely brief ones.

"You can call me Ridda," Rhidea said. "And I assure you I want no trouble in any circles here in the city. Nothing leaves this room, and I ask that you in turn do not tell anyone of my arrival. I fear my family's house being targeted if I was deemed a political enemy of the current regime. Surely you understand. My husband has no other wives yet, and it would likely destroy him as well."

"We understand," Nora assured her. "I am from a middle-class merchant family who's been in the city for generations, and we do not want Domon's rule to push us out. Helena here, believe it or not, is related to the shopkeeper, Miss Hetty. And she also married into the nobility."

Rhidea could not help but wonder how they hoped to have political influence of any import in Redufiel and Halstar at large, but she didn't voice it. They might not be helping much, but they were almost certainly harmless. "What I am most interested in, ladies, is what this Domon has been doing in the city lately, how the people feel about him, things like that. Obviously, I've done some searching around, but everyone seems too fearful of prying ears."

"Fair enough, Miss Ridda," Helena said in her rough voice. "As you say, people are scared. Uncertain. He swept in over two months ago, burned some farms and showed the Duke's army that he meant business. He marched on the city with his army of . . . what do they call them? Magi? The strong magic wielders from Argent. He killed as many men and women as he had to to get the Duke to listen, and then a lot more before old Dudley gave in and surrendered the city."

"But he didn't stop there, did he?"

Helena shook her head. "Heavens, no. He seized power and strung up dozens of nobles and citizens who opposed him in any way, Dudley first of all. He made a proclamation that the killings would end there as long as the people took him seriously and gave their allegiance to him. After that, he got an official declaration from all the noble houses, swearing fealty to him. But he's obviously cunning, not just evil, because he made connections in the houses very quickly, and set up a new military commander, new minister of trade, et cetera."

"With command of the military," Nora explained, "he set about conquering the surrounding lands, forcing the provinces of Halstar into submission one by one. Any governor who refused to swear fealty was killed on the spot and replaced. Now, as you said, he's reportedly set his sights on surrounding kingdoms outside the Dutchy, all the way to Darsor's edges."

"Is he going to instate a new Duke and move back to the far continent?" Rhidea asked. "I heard he's an emperor already over there."

"Well, hopefully his empire back home is already crumbling," Helena grumbled, "I've never seen a more power-hungry man, nor heard of one. We don't have rulers like him over here."

"Do you believe he can be reasoned with?" Rhidea asked. "Has he shown any signs of listening to the nobility here in Redufiel, or does he refuse any and all requests?"

Nora tilted her head from side to side. "He . . . has made some accommodations. Mostly in the trade department. But of course, there are hosts of outraged farmers and merchants complaining about the farmland that he wantonly burned, and most cannot even voice their concerns without fearing for their life and that of their household."

While the women spoke, Rhidea tried to take note of their peculiarities of speech to later improve her accent. She asked many more questions, backing off when particular matters seemed too sensitive to the two women. She gathered that there were some half-dozen others who met here in the shop basement, usually only a few at a time and not on any particular days or patterns of days. While they had some influence among the people, none were terribly high in the nobility, though they did have many ties to the general public.

Frankly, Rhidea didn't care about their troubles, as merciless as that may seem. She cared about Nytaea and Randhorn above all else, and after that came the world at large. Domon was a threat to all of Mani, and she needed to discover his plans and formulate a strategy to counteract them. First, she needed information; second, to act on that and confront Domon face-to-face. Hopefully, she could force him into an accord, but that might not be possible. Kymhar was seeking out information from soldiers at this moment and trying to get as close to Domon as he could without getting caught or recognized as the traitor that he was. That could not end well.

Rhidea thanked the two members of the Preservation faction and left for the day, thanking old Hetty on her way out.

β Chapter 017 β

Disappearance

Mydia sipped her tea, contemplating the end of the world.

"Milady, you have a visitor," Teli announced, performing a flawless curtsy.

Mydia sat up from her upholstered seat, tucking back a lock of obsidian hair. Mydia could often be found in this formal sitting room by any wishing an audience with her, and indeed she welcomed them. "Tell her to come in."

Teli hesitated before nodding fervently. "Yes, Milady."

She exited the way she'd come before returning with a tall man of some thirty years. Mydia recognized him as one of the upper-rank guardsmen of the interior palace. "My Queen. Lieutenant Mant," he introduced himself with a bow. "My Lady, I wanted to inform you that we're doing everything in our power at the moment, but . . . we can't find Lady Lieda anywhere."

Mydia felt a chill creeping up her spine. "Are you telling me she's escaped? What about Zama?"

"Just her. All other prisoners are in their cells. But we have no leads at present. I apologize for this blunder, Milady, but there was no sign of an escape. The door has been locked the whole time, and other prisoners we interviewed corroborated the fact. The guards saw no one come or go."

"Then someone is lying." *Unless . . .*

"Y-yes, Milady," Mant said, taking another small bow. "But . . . I know this sounds ridiculous, but the circumstances surrounding her disappearance are more than strange. You may want to look into it for yourself, along with some experienced mage soldiers."

Mydia frowned, setting her tea down on the end table next to her chair. "If she indeed vanished without anyone noticing, then you're right; it must have been using magic. Thank you, Mant."

Teli watched the tall lieutenant go, only glancing back when the queen called her name, rising from her seat. "Teli, I'm going to check out this matter. Stay here and answer any requests in the usual manner.

"Of course, Milady." They had a system; depending on the request, Teli was at liberty to give an appropriate response out of a set of predetermined ones.

Mydia gathered her skirts and left the room in a hurry. She soon found Straif, the new captain of the Mage Guard. A shorter woman with blonde hair and a stout frame, she was far more capable than she looked, and had the vital skill of keeping a calm temperament in any situation and solving problems with rational thought. Her ornate captain's cape was red, symbolizing the element she was strong in: Fire, just like Lyn. "Straif, have you investigated Lieda's disappearance yet?"

"Not quite, my lady," Straif replied. "I was notified a few minutes ago by the guardsmen."

"Then gather a small force and . . . never mind that, just come with me and we'll inspect the jail before the trail goes completely cold."

"Are you certain that's wise, Milady?"

"I've been down there to talk with her while she was contained. Come now, let's hurry."

Straif nodded and followed her queen. As they descended to the dungeons, Mydia tried to mentally prepare herself. She had already gotten used to putting on the mind of a queen and dealing with the needs of her kingdom, but once in a while something grim or especially dangerous happened, and it called for a mind of its own. Hopefully it was not, but . . . this could be one of those times. She knew she had to be on her guard.

Mydia readied her water Authority as they descended the dungeon steps. She knew that Lieda was only dangerous up close, and all she would have to do is stop her in her tracks with ice. As they strode through the dungeon, the only thing that suggested something had gone amiss was the guardsmen swarming every inch, examining the largely empty cells and conversing in low tones. Men turned and saluted as Mydia and Straif passed by, but Mydia only stopped to talk to one of them.

The dungeon was linear, a single hallway with cells on the left and right and no exit on the far side. The only way Lieda could have gotten out was through her cell door and then the main entrance, which had multiple guards posted at it. Finally, they came to the cell where Lieda had been incarcerated. Zama watched silently from two cells down, looking as though he wanted to disappear to wherever his former queen had gone. Mydia briefly locked eyes with him, but only for intimidation.

"Well?" she asked Straif.

The blonde captain took hold of the bars of the cell door and shook it, feeling the chunky *click-click* of bronze on bronze. "It's like Mant said."

Mydia nodded, raising a palm over one of the lateral gaps between cell bars. She focused and envisioned the air from wall to wall in the cells—more specifically, one-third of the water in the air—suddenly turning into snow. *Change now*, she told it. *And then you can revert.*

It did so, heeding her call and dropping in temperature, coalescing into flakes of snow that fell, blanketing the floor in a perfect white coating. Zama's eyes bulged at the sight. Mydia had hoped to find that Lieda simply had gifting in Perception that she didn't know about, and had bypassed her seal, camouflaging herself in the corner of her cell to await a chance to attack.

But no, she had indeed vanished. There could only be one explanation.

"Reality," Straif said, voicing her thoughts. "It's the only way she could have gotten out."

"Except for one thing," Mydia said. "I want to know how she got that magic seal off. Zama? Got some information for us?"

He gave her a distrusting stare that seemed to say, *Why? You won't set me free if I tell you.*

Mydia sighed. "If you tell me, I'll shorten your sentence by one year."

He raised his eyebrows. At this point, that was nearly cutting his term in half. "Why would you do that over one woman?"

"Because she's a lot more dangerous than you," Mydia said coldly. It was the truth.

He cleared his throat. "I . . . tried to communicate with her from this cell, but she treated me like a rejected piece of garbage, acting like she was still a queen. Like she was waiting for something. Then she just . . . vanished earlier today. She blinked out and was gone."

"When?" Straif asked harshly, stepping over to Zama's cell.

"A-a half hour ago. Maybe an hour."

"And you're sure there's nothing else you need to tell us about her disappearance?" Mydia demanded. "If we found out you were withholding information, your amnesty would be revoked very quickly and another five years tacked on."

Zama opened his mouth, either in surprise or protest, and then seemed to think better of it. "Nothing. Your grace. She kept to herself, and mostly only spoke to me to make sport."

Mydia nodded and turned to go. There was nothing more to discover here. As she made to leave, however, the former regent called out in a pitiful voice.

"Wait, My Lady! You haven't . . . you don't . . . can you say when he's coming back? If he's coming back?"

She turned only her head to look at him. "You really are pathetic, aren't you?" With that, she left, Straif on her heels. To think that Lieda had been so tight-lipped, refusing to tell her much of any value despite threats of harsher punishment, while this sobbing wretch was desperate already. Desperate but largely useless. . . and now she had to lighten his sentence. Of course, Lieda's restraint made sense now, since Lieda had an escape plan lined up the whole time.

"My lady," Straif asked quietly. "Shouldn't we stick around a bit longer?"

Mydia hesitated. "You can, if you think you'll find anything."

"You doubt that we will?"

Mydia nodded. "I have a feeling her trail leads far away, and is not a trail at all. I think Zama makes a good point: We should be ready for when the Archlord returns. Somehow, I know this all has to do with him."

❧ ❧

β Chapter 018 β

Vessels

Soul of Silver, wake. A terrible event has befallen us.

Rhidea bolted upright in her bed, producing a twinge in her leg. The low plank ceiling and plain walls of their room at the Lucky Kettle Inn greeted her, insisting that everything was as normal as Redufiel's new Archlord allowed. She almost wondered if the whispered warning had come from within a dream, but her mind could not so perfectly recreate that ethereal whisper: The voice of Mani. No matter how hard she might try, never that fell whisper. Briefly collecting her wits, she replied, *What is it?*

The soul you sent to my mother with the soul of Gaea. My Vessel. He is now dead.

Her breath caught. It couldn't be. Kaen? Dead? *Are you certain? How can you know that? How could you even sense him over there?*

Do you mean to say you thought I would not be able to reach my Vessel from a planet away, daughter? The Vessel was unchanged aside from extra stress, and my connection with him did not wane. I have spoken to him on multiple occasions, but now . . . I have spoken with him for the last time.

Rhidea ground her teeth, swallowing down a lumpy sense of foreboding. *Just get to the point! How did he die, and are you truly certain?*

The enemy laid an ambush for your friends. He was captured—held against his will, it seemed. I may have misinterpreted his bloodlust when he rushed to protect his friend, sending him headlong into the enemy. I felt my blade sever many souls before they subdued him, but alas . . . for this error, I offer apology. He is no more. His essence blinked out and was gone. There can be no mistake.

Protecting his friend . . . Lyn and Kaen ran into trouble with their enemies. Somehow, the Gaean soldier Zent had not been able to protect him.

Anger at the being that was Mani welled up in her, but she suppressed it in pursuit of answers. *What about Lyn?* she demanded. *Is she safe?*

I cannot say, being now blind on Gaea. But I believe I would have felt a shift in Gaea's aura were that the case. She has a deep connection with my mother. There are powerful beings who rule Gaea . . . I believe they call them Elites. One of these was present when the Vessel—when Kaen was killed; I could feel his aura.

Elites. Zent had mentioned such a name. He claimed there were nine who ruled Gaea, one for each city. Every time she heard that planet described, it sounded only stranger. Larger than both continents of Mani put together, yet populated by only nine walled cities? And only men? What she wouldn't give to go there and explore it for herself . . . but no, there were more important things to think on right now. More disturbing things.

I should mention an occurrence that coincided with the death of your friend, Mani said after a pause. *Regarding the reservoir of my power that was the sword. Still is the sword. There was . . . another soul created. A copy, you might say. I cannot say what it is or how it was created, but created it was, not born. It mirrors the soul of Kaen, yet I believe it to be a copy, a shadow— not the same.*

Rhidea gulped. It was rare these days that she heard something that truly made her blood run cold, but this news was more disturbing than any she could have dreamt up. *How do you know it's not him? Can you tell me anything about this 'shadow?'*

I cannot, other than that it has a different, preexisting body, and yet an indistinguishable replica of the aura that Kaen possessed, as though it stole his signature. I sensed it as soon as his soul was severed from his body, but faintly, distantly. I believe they soon transferred the sword I inhabited to this new body's control, for I now sense his presence closely. The clone was made in order to give them access of my sword, and control this replicant has achieved.

And have you spoken to him since then? To this replicant? Rhidea asked, holding her head. She wished she had never woken up, because this was simply too much to deal with right now.

That is the concerning part, and also why I say he is not the same soul: I cannot access my own sword, nor can I access his mind. I can feel it, but only inasmuch as I could feel any human soul that grabbed hold of my sword. Even one cut by its blade.

So in other words, the sword is lost to us, likely forever. Does it still contain any power?

I am afraid it does. Terrible power. Someone on Gaea, this Elite perhaps, knows about me, and the power that boy possessed, and conceived an insane plan to take possession of it . . . and it worked, so far as I can tell. They seem to be calling this creation "the Hunter." I shall keep you apprised, Soul of Silver, but I am afraid there is nothing more to be done. I am cut off forever from my Vessel.

A creation. Such talk of living things being made by mortals was disconcerting, to say the least. To create a human, or even a close approximation, one that moved and talked and had any sort of soul . . . was such an abomination truly possible to make?

Rhidea sighed. *Let me guess . . . you want me to be your new Vessel. Is that even possible?*

. . . Yes. It is, and now is our only option. I cannot tell you how dangerous this new soul that bears my blade is. And, awakened as I am now, I require a replacement Vessel. It could be the only way to contain, to limit, the power that resides in that sword, and to do what must be done to protect your people. Your own body is of silver, and thus you would act as both Vessel and Heart.

I . . . I need to think on this, Rhidea responded. *This is all very sudden, and I have work to accomplish here in Halstar.*

Think about it you may. But these events run deeper, Soul of Silver. You have heard of the Silver Beast? The prophesied destroyer? I believe the worlds have just witnessed, or rather are about to witness, the birth of the Silver Beast.

The Silver Beast . . . it was a legend that Rhidea had decided must refer to these Cydenges creatures, the metallic creatures that had plagued Gaea for centuries—or millennia? Beasts, not just one. But could it really be . . . ? *What makes you so certain?* Rhidea asked Mani. *How could one Hellebes with a powerful sword be greater than these Cydenges? A race of metal devils bent on destroying entire worlds?*

Trust me when I say that this creation, this . . . Hellebes . . . is able to destroy a Cydenges with ease. They are many, but they do not possess that sword. There is only one like it, and there will only ever be one. And I just lost dominion over it. Do you even understand the potential power it has, now that my limits have been removed from it?

Limits . . . Rhidea tried to imagine, as the Heart of Mani said. It was a bit abstract . . . and the night was also very late. With a groan and an accompanying creak from her bed, she rose and adjusted her night gown's silken belt, tiptoeing over to the southern window on bare feet. Kymhar was probably awake already, pretending he didn't hear her and quietly waiting to see if he was needed. She wouldn't be surprised if the mere change in her breathing had alerted the Dalim mid-sleep.

The High Mage pulled back the curtain and looked up at the heavy, larger-than-life form of Gaea, which now shone from directly overhead. It gazed down upon the Light Side of Mani with an intensity never glimpsed from the Dark Side. Gaea . . . a foreign world with strange threats. And a new threat, just feeling out his newborn strengths. Could Mani be right?

Mani, she said in her head. *If all this is true, then how much danger is Lyn in? This is vital; I need to know if there is a way that I can help her.*

The voice of the moon was silent for a minute. *I really cannot say. I know she is in much danger on Gaea, but she also has the blessing of the earth mother and grows only stronger by the day.*

So why are you not afraid of her, then?

She is not of me. She is of my mother and magic. Magic is not of Mani by nature, and will one day pass from my surface. This is the destiny of Mani. The soul of Gaea, whom you call Lyn, fights Gaea's battles. She wars with powerful tyrants who have seized Gaea's power for themselves. And she wars with Luna, my sister. What troubles me most is the sword, because its rogue presence spells danger for me. It could one day be used to destroy this entire lunar shell of mine. We must reclaim it at all costs.

Rhidea sighed, watching the sunlit atmosphere of Gaea in all its swirling glory. Outside, the wind continued to beat the inn with small droplets of rain. The weather seemed entirely indifferent to the momentous decision being waged in the High Mage's mind. The fate of worlds could very well rest on her answer.

Breathe, Rhidea, breathe. In and out. With her third extended exhale, she said, *Very well. Mani, I will be your Vessel. But we will have some rules to this arrangement.*

⁂

Mydia awoke early to the buzzing of her communication stone. She started awake and scrambled out of bed, dressed only in her green silk shift. Fumbling on her dresser, she found the stone and activated it. "Rhidea? What is it?"

"Mydia, I have some news to share with you. I am afraid it isn't good news, either."

Mydia brushed repeatedly at her black hair with a hand, something she did subconsciously when nervous, all while trying to shake the tingling of sleep from her numb foot. "Um . . . All right? Does it have to do with Lyn?"

"In a way. It's . . . it's Kaen."

Mydia tensed, gritting her teeth and rocking back onto her mattress. In her head, she heard half a dozen continuations of Rhidea's words, none of them ending well.

"He's dead," Rhidea finished, confirming the worst.

No, a voice whispered in the queen's head. *No, that's not right. He can't . . . How could . . . He's not even . . .* The objections ran on and on, some logical and others less so, but she couldn't bring herself to voice any of them. She only listened as Rhidea went on to explain that Mani itself had informed her of it. Mydia tried to listen, but the ringing in her ears stemmed from more than simple tiredness. She could deal with being woken up early. It had happened before and it would happen again. But . . . it was like Rhidea was spouting nonsense, or recounting a dream. Telling a story. It couldn't be about Kaen, the actual Kaen, the one with the charming smile and the moody air of masculinity. The one who had just lost his only sister. The one who had followed Lyn to another world to act as ambassador in Mydia's place. The one she'd cried for when that terrible sword began to infect his mind.

Yes, that Kaen. He was dead. He was dead.

"Mydia, are you still there?" came the Wandering Mage's voice from the stone.

Mydia shook herself back to the present, back to her royal bedchambers. "Yes, I'm—I'm here. Are you . . . you're quite sure the sword was telling the truth? I mean, Mani. That Mani was telling the truth?"

"I'm afraid I am, child. I'm so sorry. I know you loved him. I promise I'll find more details for you soon. I'm sure Lyn is all right."

Mydia tried to form a response, but her voice choked out like a quenched flame. She blinked back the tears and forced her jaws not to tremble. She couldn't quell that terrible lump in her throat, nor the rising feeling of nausea. She hadn't realized until this moment just how much she loved that young man. He was everything to her. Just watching him go off, knowing he was following Lyn to an unknown world alone, with no guarantee of when they would be back . . . that had been hard enough. And now this.

Now this.

Oh, dear auroras, he can't be gone.

❧

Kymhar dropped catlike into the abandoned alleyway, boots hissing softly on the rain-coated cobbles. It was a perfect day for sneaking around without detection. Despite the sun being at its zenith this day, storm clouds pelted the world in angry bursts of rain and wind that obscured his sounds. The rain had slowed to a drizzle, but his layered cloak, soaked completely through, told of the downpour that had followed him out of the citadel.

He'd seen a lot today. Not just talked with soldiers here and there, but actually been inside the enemy headquarters. It was strange to think of it as that, because it should have been merely a foreign city he didn't know, now taken over by his master. That was a simple situation. But no, Domon was now his enemy. His invasion of these lands was not a mere extension of his empire, but war. Ravaged farmland. Senseless killing, fear spread far and wide, and all for nothing. Kymhar would have served the man till he died, regardless of any of it, had the Emperor not thrown him away—essentially stabbed him blind, all for simply carrying out a mission to completion. He had left Kymhar for dead, and the assassin had risen a free man, contract voided. Kaen and the others had convinced him to make his life his own this time.

And he was seeing the world for what it was. His former master, for the monster he truly was. If all of mankind had an enemy, perhaps it was Domon. He was still unsure how he felt about Rhidea's plan to join forces with the conqueror, the originator of Dark Magic.

Kymhar dashed across the paving stones, headed for the Lucky Kettle. Hopefully, the Silver mage was not there, because he would most likely strip out of his wet clothes and find somewhere to hang them immediately. Even his inner clothes had gotten damp this time. Not that he couldn't simply wait it out outside. But . . . he ought to keep at the top of his health in preparation for what lay ahead. It wouldn't be long before they were ready to act.

When he reached the inn, he slipped inside and took note of the four faces in the common room. Even as he headed straight upstairs for his room, he memorized each face and compared it to ones he'd seen. The heads that were turned still gave themselves away by their ears and jawline and posture. He had long since learned to identify people. Today, no people he'd seen.

He knew immediately upon reaching the door that Rhidea was within, due to the way it was shut but not quite *all* the way shut. This door had multiple stages of closing, and creaked at the second. This was the third stage, which appeared upon cursory examination to be shut, but Kymhar knew the difference. He knocked four times in quick succession and then opened the door, swiftly closing it to that fourth and final stage.

He ignored her presence, though his peripheral vision showed the mage sitting at the room's single desk, which they had moved to the immediate right of the southern window, out of sight from the road. They wouldn't have had to share a room were it not in their interest to look like a married couple. He slept on the floor. Beginning with his three-layered cloak, he threw his clothes at the foot of the fireplace, which the mage had going.

"Stop, you fool," the mage said from her desk as he'd almost gotten his inner shirt off.

With an indiscernible shrug, he pulled it off anyway, and then looked her way as she strode over to him. She was barefoot, and she must have washed her feet, because those horrid wooden shoes she insisted on wearing trapped mud like a vase whenever it rained. The crimson-haired woman took the black shirt from his hands before he could throw it on the floor, looking surprisingly upset for a mystical 200-year-old.

"What are you doing?" she demanded. "Do you realize how simple it is for me to dry clothes?" She waved a hand, and he felt the oddest sensation as the moisture and water droplets were wrung out of his hair, off his skin, and through the remaining clothes he had on, as though he were a damp rag and she the washwoman wringing and wringing.

He shivered despite himself but made no mention of the discomfort. Rhidea proceeded to pick up his other clothing and magically wring the water from it as well, sending additional water vapor into the air. This she channeled to waft up the chimney. She handed him all the clothes and said, "There. Now keep them on this time."

He stared at his garments for a moment, expressionless, before taking them. He wasn't surprised that she could do that, but neither did he feel foolish for what he'd done. Perhaps a bit, but he wouldn't give her the satisfaction of knowing. "Thank you," he said finally. It came out as almost a growl, but he meant it. Magi were useful, and he wouldn't begrudge an offer of Coactive help.

"My pleasure." She walked back to her desk as he re-donned most of his layers and sat down. She didn't sound pleased. Taking up her quill pen, which she had set down a moment before, she asked, "How did it go out there?"

"Well enough. The rain hid me, so I was able to map out most of the interior of the citadel. What leads on your end?"

She didn't answer immediately. When she did, it was in a lower voice. "Some. But not on my end, but Lyn's. Kaen is . . . dead. Her Gaean enemies killed him."

He nodded. That was . . . a great pity, to say the least. He'd liked that boy and had spent many hours training him. "And what of the sword?"

"That's the upsetting part."

β Chapter 019 β

Of Water and Falls

"Of course, of course you can!" Fenwel said encouragingly, patting the young woman on the back. "Come, my dear Syneria, don't be modest! Modesty is for boring folk."

The blonde turned to stare suspiciously with pouty lips. Always those sharp reactions . . . "I'm just going to assume you don't mean that a certain way, your majesty."

The elderly king spread his hands, doing his best to look hurt. "What do you take me for, dear child? Hmm, but you have a point; that does sound moderately scandalous. Forget that—I trust you to see this mission through safely. You'll do fine."

Now she smiled. Not only that, but she turned and embraced him. "Thank you, your majesty. I'll do my best. But remember, we're not leaving until tomorrow."

"I know. That is why you must prepare. Now go." He pushed her away and watched as she strode off, silken grey skirts swishing with the spring in her step. Sometimes life wasn't so bad, getting to smile and spur on his faithful teams of scholars and researchers, along with the occasional important Nementali officials and of course the common people. It was only a lucky bonus that most of all of those were pretty young ladies who liked to hug him. Did he feel a little guilty? Just a little? Perhaps, but . . . well, no. Guilt was for the boring. And miscreants. And he was too old to be either.

King Fenwel was left standing on the stairway overlooking the western courtyard of Randhorn Castle. Overhead, far above the reaching rows of stone pillars, clouds streamed across a daylit sky. It had been full day for three days now, being a total of five days into the Sol Cycle. Birds chirped on the pillars, finches and robins and some other bird he couldn't see. That one was slightly annoying, sounding like a hoarse cat. Perhaps . . . more than slightly annoying.

Erren! Erren! Nyerren! Yerren! Yerrrrrrren!

With a breath in, Fenwel turned and performed what once would have been a proud stride as he attempted to climb the steps back to the castle—but was now a shuffling, slightly limping walk. He wasn't infirm, but at eighty-five years of age, he was well over the hump of a normal Legaleian's life. Some lived to be a hundred, and strong magi lived far longer, but he was the weakest of Magi, so perhaps 120 was the longest he could expect to live. Magic sustained them all, but it didn't favor everyone equally. Now that Rhidea . . . she was something special, blessed by whatever god had created Mani. Of course, Fenwel was one of the few in the world—up until recently—who knew how unique that blessing really was.

Young Syneria was to lead a group of mage explorers, the first of their kind, down to the depths beneath the falls. Each skilled Water Magi, the team of young scholars planned to descend the waterfall similarly to how Rhidea and Queen Mydia had ascended two months prior. But the descent should be easier than the ascent, and Fenwel had the utmost faith in his scholars. Their goal: To seek out clues about the ancient Silversmiths and their place of heritage. Were Rhidea here, she might have disapproved, but she had already given something similar to consent when the plan was first presented to her after the flying boat incident.

The woman didn't like others doing dangerous work for her.

Inside the castle, Fenwel walked the tapestry-hung halls, treading crimson carpets past hanging plants of all different kinds. His family had long enjoyed fine taste in decorations, somewhat reserved except for the potted plants. Upon reaching the Coactive studies ward, he nearly bumped right into his quarry—Cort Flanning, the thunder mage. The young man's shaggy blond hair jostled as he stopped. Hastily adjusting his spectacles, he said, "Your Majesty! My apologies."

"None needed, my boy. Now, how are your studies going on the silver?"

"We . . ." Cort reached up as though to adjust his spectacles once more, and then thought better of it. "We haven't gotten anywhere far. Had Lady Rhidea made known to us sooner her profound connection to Mani's roots, we could perhaps have made some breakthroughs, but . . . we're really waiting on Syneria's expedition. Hopefully they can learn something from these runes that are supposed to be down there."

Fenwel nodded. He had expected a similar response. He was about to dismiss the young man when he suddenly resumed his verbal torrent.

"Your Majesty, if I may . . . Lady Rhidea has not been particularly honest with us—her students—nor with Queen Mydia and the others who recently accompanied her. I wonder sometimes if she might have other loyalties and motivations unbeknownst to us. I do not mean to doubt her, and I know it's not my place, I simply . . . as a scholar, I should hate to think that all my efforts are in vain. So to speak."

The king widened his eyes bit by bit as the stream of words went on, finally scratching his itchy grey beard as he let out a long sigh. These curious types, they were fine until they started asking questions. After a bit, he said softly, "Look, son. I like to think of that woman as my daughter. But . . . the truth is, she could be my grandmother. She's seen many things, and I'm sure you've heard of her vendetta against the Archlord by now, since word seems to be getting out. But I've known her long enough to say that she has her reasons. She's not *always* right, but she's never given me reason to doubt her character. I have the deepest respect for her, and we trust one another."

Cort nodded, and Fenwel wondered for a moment if he was going to realize that he'd given him no information of actual substance. But the boy simply said, "You're right. I'm sorry for doubting her. Sometimes I just get a bit frustrated in my studies when I start to feel stagnant."

"Well." The king sighed once more. "If it's any consolation, my boy, she'll be back soon. Hopefully. Then you can get her help directly."

Cort nodded absently before excusing himself.

β   Chapter 020   β

Knowledge

"Do not speak," Kymhar whispered in the soldier's ear. He pulled the man to the ground as he did so, dragging him to the side through a trapdoor, emerging into a secret room he had discovered in the barracks. His captive was one of the middle rank of infantry commanders.

This room—dank and floored with rough wood planks like the rest of the barracks—had a stairwell leading downward, and Kymhar walked the commander down the steps at knifepoint. The long hall at the bottom had no other purpose that Kymhar could discern than as a secret passage into a sector that Domon had nearly completely torched.

They stopped in the midst of the pitch-dark hallway, lit only vaguely by a ray of light from the far end. "Far enough," he grunted. "Cooperate and I will let you go. I'm not interested in your life, nor those of your men or your family."

The officer coughed and slowly straightened as Kymhar let him go. "Who . . . are you?" he wheezed.

"I represent the Rising Moon faction," Kymhar said roughly. It was a lie, as he had made up the faction. "We are interested in dethroning Domon and nothing more, so do not fear needless deaths, though I cannot promise that we will keep any soldiers in particular alive."

The man barked a laugh. "Rising Moon . . . you're insane! Nothing like that is possible. Do you think we *willingly* joined—" he cut off abruptly with a growl, clearly realizing he should say no more on that track. "You know nothing!"

"Then enlighten me," Kymhar said, keeping his voice even. "I'm looking for information on your military structure."

The man said nothing, merely turned and bolted suddenly. He got only a few inches before Kymhar's foot tripped him. He was on him immediately, knee pressing down on his back even as the commander's hands caught the ground. Kymhar slammed him into the ground and drove a long knife into the earthen floor a fraction of an inch from his neck.

The officer grunted, then yelped at the knife. Kymhar waited long enough for him to realize he didn't mean to kill him. "Escape is pointless," he said in his same monotone. "If you value your life, tell me what I want to know."

"Then you can just . . . kill me," the man grunted. "You're not going to get anything . . ." he grunted again as Kymhar lifted him bodily off the ground and slammed him back-first against the wall of the shaft. He glared at the assassin, who stared with cool intensity back into his eyes. Eventually, he seemed to give in. "All right, I-I'll talk. What do you want to know? We all hate Domon, you already know that. He's a monster and a tyrant and listens to no one."

"I know. I want to know what he's doing in the military here. How does he maintain control? Who are his most loyal adherents?"

The man took a breath, winced, and then licked at a cracked lip. "He's got four generals under him. There used to be five, but he killed one as an example. That's been his pattern, starting with the Duke. He's one of those . . . magi, as you call them, an incredibly powerful one. He could kill most of his commanders immediately if he wanted to, so they say. No one under him wants to mess with him, not to mention the battalion of mage soldiers he brought with him. They're a whole branch of the military now."

"But who is actually loyal to him?"

"That's . . . a bit harder to say. I can give you a few names."

Kymhar smiled to himself. A Kymhar smile, faint enough that the officer couldn't see it even had this dank tunnel been lit. *That's better.*

⁓ ⁂ ⁓

"Mani, I will make you bow."

Archlord Domon did not so much utter it as mouth it along with a forceful thought aimed at his . . . prospective ally.

He glanced up, sending his gaze out through the artfully framed stone window of the high castle of Redufiel, the very fortress that had once housed Duke Dudley of Halstar. That fool lay six feet beneath the soil north of the city in a more honorable grave than had been given the other nobility who'd stood up to Domon.

If he had any regret about the matter, it was that Dudley had not died for his evil, nor for his willful stand against the invading empire . . . his death had been simply political; inevitable and necessary. But it was a small regret.

Fifteen noble leaders of Halstar, to Domon's count. Fifteen had perished so far, and hopefully he would not have to purge too many more, lest more paperwork be created and less suitable men and women be instated in their places. Not to mention the inevitable progression from paperwork to economic crisis.

Domon sighed and crossed his arms, surveying the city full of square wooden buildings. Everything here was orderly, neatly packed into a metropolis without getting too chaotic. The chaos that still persisted was of his own doing, a fact of which he was well aware. The people feared and distrusted him, and rightly so. Meanwhile, his more loyal officials worked to bring the surrounding lands to heel in a timely fashion, one after the other, without needless risk of losing his grip immediately. But these people were still afraid of what his mage armies could do. Darsorian magi were weak with the exception of one—and she worked for him—so they looked at Domon and his mage soldiers as near-gods. He theorized that it had to do with their distance from the Wellspring.

But no, his real work was going on in his study, in the well-preserved archives—on pain of death, his orders had been clear to keep that building from harm—and in meetings with the best scholars and lorekeepers in the area. He had summoned more from nearby lands. So far, the information yield had been little. Now, he would have Lieda working here as well. She would get only one more chance. But sufficient for some progress. He needed to know more about Gaea, and more about Mani. Darsor was one half of a whole, the complement to Argent, offering less magic but more history. So far, the best lead he had was that there was something below Darsor, in the Sea of Emptiness. Too many myths and superstitions about this "Silver Beast" that lurked below to be all lies. Intuition told him that it might be the key to tapping Mani's power and finally realizing his dream.

The truth was that Mani was a dying world. Doomed to blink out and cease one day, a day that encroached with each Sol Cycle. Plus the threat of Gaea, which he had overplayed in Ti'Vaeth to High Mage Rhidea to get her to bite on their bargain. Oh, how neatly that had gone—minus the fact that they'd somehow lived, that is. The gnawing doubt about his ploy's effectiveness could stay under the bed where it presently lay.

Some were certain—many indeed—to mistake the reasoning behind his actions: Tapping the power of the wellspring, siphoning and twisting it into its dark twin in order to further Mani's technological and defensive capabilities, but his plan had not yet been put into full motion. He had silenced some dissenters in the past, who had claimed as Rhidea did that Dark Magic would kill Mani sooner than the magical drain would ever have. Did they not realize he knew that already? If one lay on the ground wounded, wondering whether he should rise lest he expend vital energy, he must soon realize that it is necessary nonetheless. He cannot live, cannot stay, on the ground, but must rise to a position whence he can right his situation, mend his wounds, seek help, bolster his body.

Whatever is necessary. That was Domon's mantra.

"My Lord Emperor," a silky feminine voice said from behind him. He turned to see the slim aide in the doorway, dull of hair and wit but good with statistics and not bad to look at.

"What is it, Vyss?" he asked, trying to keep the exasperation from his tone. He couldn't very well respond in such a manner with every Halstarian.

The thin woman withdrew one hand from the doorpost and gave a quick, prim bow. Not a curtsy, not here in Redufiel. "There is word from Eltar, Lord Emperor. The governor has agreed to your proposal and accepted the occupation of your forces."

Domon nodded. "Very good."

"Shall I . . . arrange for a missive to be sent back?" she asked, tucking a lock of mousy hair behind her ear. A nervous habit of most aides, perhaps women in general.

"Yes. Send word that he is to transfer two dozen of his most capable magi for training here in Redufiel. Half shall be sent back after six months' time, while half shall remain in my army."

"That is the whole message?" she asked.

The Archlord stifled a sigh. "Phrase it in your most tactful way, I suppose. But no creative fluff. That is it for now."

"Yes, My Lord." She bowed once more, even deeper this time but just as swiftly, turned on her heeled sandals, and departed with that implacable *clip, clip, clip*. How had he not noticed the woman sneaking up on him before she spoke?

He turned back to his window. Now he had to get his brain going again. Despite hardly aging, he swore his mind grew duller with each passing year.

Mani . . . the power of Mani. The purest power: Silver.

He wondered how Solomiya was faring on her little quest now.

❧ ❧

Rhidea stood from her crouch atop the southeasternmost tower of Redufiel. A square wooden structure that matched the city's architecture, the tower just barely came to the level of the main castle's roof. Situated near the outer wall of the city, there was perhaps a half mile between her and the administrative superstructure. It was impressive what these Darsorians could do with wood and grit.

She surveyed the square city, eyeing the castle without always looking directly at it. In truth, she was trying to get up the determination to do what she was already prepared to. It would be just like in Ti'Vaeth, only he had yet to develop nearly as tight security here, not to mention the split loyalties and grudging obedience among the natives.

By now, she and Kymhar had scouted five different rebel factions who opposed Domon in some way, and each one was either too afraid or too clueless about the foreign emperor to take any stand against him. That was well, because her goal here had never been to stage a rebellion and kill or oust Domon. It would only throw these lands into further chaos and get more innocent people killed. What she had to do now was force Domon into a position where she could speak privately with the man. She had to understand why he was doing this, and she had to make sure *he* understood what was really going on with the Gaean invasion. Somehow, he hadn't made any preparations for an attack, at least not any obvious ones . . .

If he would not listen to reason this time, then that would require some more desperate action. She hoped he would listen, and even expected it.

Her new trump card, Mani, would enable a direct approach.

No sense in waiting any longer.

The Depths of the Sea

Syneria Tolruin took a deep, steadying breath, then let it back out. Another one . . . another . . .

"You ready, Neer?" asked Hetta.

Syneria started; imperceptibly, she hoped. "Wh—Ah, yes, Hetta. I think we all are. Just . . . calming my nerves."

The black-haired girl gave her a tight smile that betrayed her own nervousness. She was as sharp-nosed as she was short, nearly half a head below Syneria despite being four years her senior and far more mature. The two others in their group stood to either side of Syneria, Viktor Amma and Stessa Valiant, Hetta's fellow magi employed at the castle by King Fenwel.

Syneria gave a nod to the two beefy attendants who stood silently to one side. "We're ready to board."

"Very well," said the one. "May luck favor you, madam. Though I think the machinery will, too." The way he said it indicated that *think* might be a euphemism for *hope* in this case.

Either way . . . not as reassuring as it was meant to be.

The sun was busily beating against Syneria's back, and she was grateful to step closer to the cliff, fitting herself into one of four standing harnesses in their descent contraption. It was four-sided and made of heavy wood, reinforced with silver and tied to a large bracket at the top, where a heavy rope connected it to the large winch they had rigged. The winch itself was buried, bolted and tied down to the stone shore of the River Ardencaul. The two attendants began operating the boom, lifting all four scholars up and swinging the end to take them out over the cliff so that their feet swung over the misty abyss.

Syneria shut her eyes violently, suppressing a scream of terror as the rushing river washed over her back, and tentatively blinked them open to see the attendants, who tried to look reassuring, slowly winding the winch to give them more rope. Magi and servants were ready to back them up at a moment's notice, or to hold the rope and splice on more if the explorers needed extra length. They had nearly a mile's worth, but no one knew how much it would actually take.

But the truth was that Syneria and her team were all trained Water Magi who could easily guide their contraption down the falls. Everyone else was insurance. They were simply . . . testing the waters, so to speak, and would eventually give a signal before cutting the rope. Rhidea and Mydia had managed a similar trip up. Some of the scholars theorized that space was distorted between the surface and the Down Under, but if Rhidea was right, it was a thousand miles or so down. Not all the rope in the world would be sufficient to span that gap.

Hetta nudged Syneria. "You're supposed to be the leader, remember?"

For whatever reason, Syneria felt like adding. Opening her eyes all the way, she grinned, for the first time feeling genuinely excited. Hesitantly, she glanced downward, watching the murky mists slowly rise to meet them. Fine mist from the river was spraying out onto them, wetting her neck, but it felt comfortable to her, as water magi tended to not experience sudden cold when exposed to water. "It's not quite as bad as I feared," she admitted.

"I was most scared of the boom malfunctioning, not the river," Viktor said, his words perfectly encapsulating what Syneria had been thinking.

As they descended, the pull of the rope seemed to drag them into the river, or else the rushing water was expanding outward as it fell, flicking onto and lashing against the car's occupants. "Very well," said Syneria, gathering her courage. "Let's try it out."

Together, they used their Coaction to pull the carrier into the falls, submerging them all. Hetta's specialty alone allowed them all to breathe, pulling oxygen into the water and allowing it to flow freely into their lungs, but no water. They had practiced dozens of times in the river, and she was a true master of the art. Stessa and Viktor handled the general manipulation of the water, pulling and guiding it to flow around their vehicle and support it from beneath, while Syneria used her Ice Authority to freeze the water beneath them, making a platform that fused with the rushing liquid of the falls to hold them in place.

The tension of the rope stopped altogether. The attendants and gathering magi could tell, as evidenced by the winch slowly winding back upwards—until it pulled taught once more. This would assure the operators that the rope had not somehow broken.

"Ready, set . . ." Syneria unleashed a bolt of ice that zipped upwards through the falls, angled just outward from the cliff so as not to hit anyone above. She had set it to shatter in a small spectacle upon reaching the surface world, and within ten seconds the group felt two firm tugs on the rope. Their signal to cut.

"Here we go," Syneria muttered. "Brace yourselves."

With a blade of persistent, undulling ice, she cut the rope.

❧ ❧

Oliver tapped his leg and danced nervously from side to side, as though to a tune that nobody else heard, or perhaps as though he had to pee. He kind of did.

It was late in the day, the clouds rushing to cover the waning sun as he stood before the Scathii Council hall. Uncle Ben had promised him a chance to propose his plan; it was a good one, so they'd better listen. He knew how they were, though, not just with young folk but anyone who didn't fit their stuffy ideas in general. But after he'd helped return half the missing people of the last twenty years, things had changed.

Finally, the door to the hall opened, and the face of Uncle Itoll welcomed him, with Uncle Maximus right behind him. Well, the Uncle part was Oliver's addition. It helped him to familiarize the old men in his mind to think of them all as brothers of Uncle Ben.

"Come in, Oliver," said Uncle Itoll smoothly. "Let us hear this proposition you have." There was the slightest delay before the word "proposition," as though he were going just a bit out of his way to humor this wee boy.

Oliver tried not to get upset. *They're your uncles, Oliver. Just remember they mean ya well.* As he walked into the long log hall, he noted Uncle Ben standing off to the right, clearly trying not to look too personally invested in what Oliver had to say. Sighing inwardly, he reckoned he understood. There was a crowd of some dozen people total, which was a crowd to Oliver.

The blond boy stopped between elders Itoll and Maximus, who stood amidst a semicircle of onlookers, hesitant to go further. When prompted, he came up and stood on the far side of the main room, in front of two wall-mounted animals and an antique coat of arms, where old people typically stood to address fellow old people. Nervously, he cleared his throat. He glanced at Uncle Ben and started to ask, *I can speak now?* but then thought better of it.

Hesitantly, he began to lay out his plans for the new fleet of ferries to and from the continent of Darsor, and what kind of ships he thought would work best for it. He knew Uncle Ben had already told them some of his ideas, such as establishing ferries like those, but he built on that, not to mention his specific plans for the designs. He told them how he thought they could work with King Fenwel to train men from shore to pilot some of the ships, keeping them going round the clock to ferry across travelers and traders to meet the people on the other side, or to negotiate alliances. With the world going the way it was, national governments were only more interested in banding together to stop these incoming invaders.

Oliver also related his plans for the defense of the Sky Islands, which he had run by Rhidea and Mydia. Mostly, these centered around swapping out magi of different elements with the mainland, training potential Wind Magi in Argent in return for bringing skilled mage soldiers back to the Sky Islands to bolster their defenses. He made sure to add that Queen Mydia of Nytaea was personally for this idea.

Lastly of all, he had plans to construct towers on the Sky Islands to use the expanse around them to their magical advantage. Rhidea seemed to think that with enough Coactive power, one could build a resonant device to amplify magic for use in extremely long range. Across the Sea of Emptiness and circumferentially about the empty ring, one could theoretically detect and attack invading air forces, with magi from each linked location lending aid where needed. It would take a large number of Reality magi to pull it off.

With each idea, he unrolled a sheet of parchment scrawled with diagrams over its face to show his plans. He knew this last one would get shot down quicker than most of the others, and was not surprised to see that exact outcome, but he wouldn't stop trying. He'd get them to see reason. Overall, he got fewer funny looks and more pensive ones than could have been hoped for, and had warmed up in his oratory skills over the course of his presentation enough to not miss too many important details. There were questions, of course, and some rebuttals to his ideas, a few of which he lacked answers for entirely.

The elders thanked him for his input and dismissed him, and he reluctantly left, feeling somewhere between abashed and relieved to be done with it. He caught a look from Uncle Ben, however: An approving one. That made it all worth it.

He couldn't keep the satisfied grin from spreading across his face. Time to go see what Mother was cooking.

⁕

King Fenwel gazed up at the sky, pondering a world he had neither known nor seen.

Yet the leaders of this hidden world, Gaea, had attacked . . . and they would again. Perhaps a dozen more times; who could say? Somewhere beyond these thick clouds of daylit night, hidden among the stars . . .

No. He glanced down at the cobbles of his castle garden path, trying to stare into the earth below, into its silver roots. Below that spanned the abyssal reaches of Mani, with a core at its center, and then another continent on the far side of the great expanse. Beyond *that* . . . his enemies conspired against his very world.

The old king sighed. Why enemies? Did they really hate the Legaleians that much? Or perhaps fear them? He laughed at the thought. There was little to fear from a people not only stranded in exile for one thousand years but entirely oblivious to the fact. It was worth a few laughs, but he gave it but one.

β Chapter 022 β

Power

"Name?" said the mousy-haired female aide.

"Rhidea of Randhorn."

The woman nodded. "And . . . how do you spell that?"

Rhidea rolled her eyes a quarter turn and then listed off the letters.

The woman thanked her and started off, but Rhidea stopped her. "Make sure he doesn't blow you off. And return quickly. I'm not accustomed to being made to wait." After all, Domon didn't have to know she had been in the city a month now.

"Y-yes, madam!" The woman dipped a half bow that almost resembled a curtsy, and then scampered off through the red-carpeted hardwood halls.

Rhidea sighed and took a seat in a stiff, hand-carved chair. Not too uncomfortable given its looks, not that she'd have minded.

Finally are you speaking with this Archlord, came the hissing voice of Mani in her head.

Indeed, she answered. *I was not about to rush such a confrontation.*

Yet time is short, Soul of Silver. One would think you enjoy wasting it.

Something in that comment irked the High Mage. *And that is coming from a thousand-year-old entity tied to the very planet?*

Humor has the Vessel. Your words ring true. Had I not a sense both of what my mother's keepers are doing across the void of space and what this black emperor plans to do . . . then perhaps there would be no need of haste.

By void, you refer to the domain of the stars? How far away is Gaea?

Mani hesitated a moment. *I cannot say in any precise measurement, much less in a way a human soul could understand, but were you to glimpse the distance between Gaea and her moons in scale. . . my sister and I, who orbit Gaea, are separated by countless thousands of miles, many times the span of a world—far enough that moons and planets would be like insects to your eye, small islands of light and life amidst the blackness of space.*

Rhidea shivered. Mani's brief explanation revealed the universe's layout in a way she had never known. She had only a few seconds to ponder it, however, before the wooden heels of the aide *clip-clipped* through the hall and she was back.

"My good lady," she said with a jerky bow, "my lord the Emperor accepts your request for an audience. If you will follow me."

Rhidea rose smoothly and started after her. Despite the aide's loud heels, she was a good two inches shorter than the red-haired mage, her unruly brown hair bobbing with each step. Two flights of stairs later, they arrived at a stately single door, which the aide opened, announcing, "Your guest, My Lord."

Rhidea entered at a wave of the woman's hand, eyeing the blond Archlord seated at the far end of the room behind a desk. The room was large but not overly imposing. Decorated with good taste—and familiar, she thought, noting the decorations that looked to have come straight from Ti'Vaeth—the room had a tall ceiling and a crystal chandelier with at least two dozen lit candles.

Domon looked as imperious as ever, seated on a high-backed chair behind a heavy desk, firmly entrenched in his new role as conqueror. The look he gave her said, *I'm half surprised to see you, but I'm also both too busy and too annoyed to talk.*

"Thank you, Vyss," was all he said, but the accompanying wave of his hand seemed a clear enough dismissal for the woman. After a few seconds, the heavy door thumped shut behind her. "Now," he said, lacing his fingers, "Would you like to tell me why you are here?"

Rhidea took a step forward and crossed her arms, a small smile touching her lips. "Really? That is what you have to say to me, after you broke our bargain and turned on us, attempting to murder my friends and me? After you betrayed your pact with Nytaea?"

He frowned. "I *am* curious how you made it back alive. Though I exited the stage before I could see precisely what happened." He watched her for a minute, almost as though expecting her to laugh like it was all a joke, and then sighed. "Fine, I'm not just curious, I'm frankly dumbfounded. And I'm . . . sorry for what happened. I'm sure you can guess I did not do any of that on a whim, nor out of a grudge. My goal was to destroy the Gate to stop any from going to and from our world."

Rhidea took one hand from below her armpit and rubbed her chin, a nonplussed look on her face, and then replaced the arm, resuming her stance. "That was all obvious. I will not tell you how we came to survive the explosion, not yet. We need to have a serious . . . *discussion*, Domon. And no, I didn't come here to kill you, if you were fearing that."

He laughed, almost casually but for an undertone of nervousness. "You would have already tried. I know you, High Mage."

"Indeed. I have been back in Nytaea, attempting to help Queen Mydia and her retainers restore order to the White City following the dreadful state you left it in. Lord Zama was the best you could do?"

The blond Archlord rolled his eyes. "Clearly not. As I already made clear, I didn't expect any of you to live, so I instituted a government that could stand until I got back."

"And killed Marshal Lanthar and others without cause?" Rhidea challenged with metal in her tone.

Domon slid back his chair and rose deliberately from his desk. "This discussion is becoming tiresome," he said with a warning tone. "Your rebellious attitude wears on me, High Mage."

"I agree on the tiresome part. But we're far from finished. Before you let your imperial pomp take over, Domon, know that I have vital information regarding the Gaeans who invaded Nytaea recently."

The Archlord glared at her, then slowly lowered himself back down. He gestured at a guest chair. "Very well. This sounds more like you. So it's true, then? They struck Nytaea and limped off to their homeworld?"

Rhidea neglected to comment on the fact that he knew. Somehow, she reasoned, Lieda must have told him. *Or he's still in communication with spies on the mainland.* A distinct possibility. "Indeed. Domon, it's worse than you ever could have imagined. Allow me to explain."

When she had finished recounting the attempted invasion, along with answering some intermittent questions from the Archlord, he said nothing. Rather, he stared into a corner of the room miles away, lost in thought. Then his keen eyes swiveled to catch hers, and she thought she detected suspicion in them. Only for the briefest moment.

"I admit," he said at last, "I had not heard most of the details. But you seem to think this will change my mind."

Rhidea crossed her arms and smirked. "No, I'm not such a fool. I know you better than ever, Domon. I had . . . hoped, perhaps. Tell me, why does the attack not convince you that we must work together to save Mani? Your trick with the Gate did nothing, because they have other means of transportation between worlds."

"And we must gather the strength of Mani to fight against them. I think we agree on that part, Cae. But I still aim to harness the full potential of Mani. Not mere elemental magic, nor Dark Magic, but the true—"

Rhidea held up a forestalling hand. "Too late." The Archlord glared at her in a mixture of mild surprise and annoyance, but she went on, "You see, I have one last tidbit for you, Domon. Mani is working with me."

The glare simmered down to a distrustful stare. "With you."

She nodded. "The Heart of Mani. It's no myth, as I have spoken with it over the last weeks multiple times. We . . . Very well; we survived the fall from the Tower of Mani by falling through the rifts in the earth, underneath the entire continent of Darsor, which I believe is quite thin there. Long story short, we ended up in a world far below, at the center of Mani. And there . . . we found the Heart of Mani."

No need to tell him that it was Kaen who found it first, nor that said heart had inhabited a sword that was transported to Gaea and subsequently lost to the hands of their enemies.

Details.

The Archlord sat back in his seat, chin high and musing, looking as though finally having received all the pieces to a puzzle—which indeed he had. Or at least most of them. "Now, that . . . that puts a new perspective on everything. You found the Heart of Mani." He sat up straight and looked into her eyes with a new intensity. "And you are not lying to me about any of this? You are truly in communication with Mani?"

"I am not lying. And yes, I am indeed. I am his Vessel. We have made a deal together." The best outcome of this would be if he listened to her and understood that she had fearsome powers of silver, yet never caught on to the fact that she was always a Silversmith. The best kind of underestimation.

Domon nodded, a new look crossing his face, one she neither recognized nor knew how to interpret. "Then send Mani a message. Tell him my goal is his protection, and that I am willing to strike an accord with the both of you."

She paused, relaying the message. Mani muttered in her head, either curious or displeased, and seemed to have already gotten the gist of their conversation from listening in the back of her mind. An unsettling thought, certainly.

"He says, 'That will do, Black Soul.'"

Domon raised his eyebrows at that name, as though asking whether that was her invention, and she merely raised her own in response. It seemed to amuse him. "Well. That is most excellent. I require time to plan, Cae."

"Very well," she answered, both for herself and Mani. "We both know how short time is. Do you intend to make this alliance openly known?"

He eyed her thoughtfully. "No. My alliance is with you and our planet. Neither are a relation I wish to openly acknowledge."

"Then what about your advisors?"

"You will . . . be privy to a few councils, no doubt. My inner circle. And . . ." he sighed. "I will bring you to the next Umbra Council. Does that satisfy you?"

She smiled slightly. "It does, Archlord."

She rose, bowed, and left. At the doorway, however, she lingered and turned half around. "One more thing, Domon. Do not make the mistake of crossing me or testing the limits of our agreement, lest I show you the power that Mani has granted me."

He gave her a silent, calculating glare. "A threat."

"Indeed."

Rhidea used the travel stone and changed location. After a split second of dizziness, she rose and found herself in a stone chamber. This felt like . . . yes, somehow she could discern that she was on Argent. Near . . . Ti'Vaeth? Mani's consciousness inside her indicated agreement, as he could feel the Wellspring close by.

The room was octagonal, with small closet-like protrusions at each side and a tall stone table in the center, lit by red light from overhead. As she approached the table, she glanced at the occupants of the room: Domon and two other men, who looked at her with mild shock and not a bit of curiosity.

"My Lord . . . ?" mumbled the one in a nasally, high-pitched voice, turning to the Archlord. She recognized him as Lord Lhiard of the city-state of Uphel. The other man was Lord Tyiv, a noble mage of Dotham.

Domon waved away the question with a small gesture, clearly waiting for others to arrive. Shortly, a slightly portly man arrived whom Rhidea did not recognize, muttering an apology before realizing that he too was not the last one. A look of familiar annoyance crossed his face at that.

Tyiv greeted him as Lord Kyal. *Ah, Kyal, Lord of Imdek.* So they must all be magi.

And then she arrived. Rhidea forced down a smile as she watched the sorceress materialize, waiting with hands clasped behind her back as Lieda smoothed her black dress and sauntered up to the table. She froze upon seeing Rhidea.

Rhidea smiled and tipped her head in reply.

Lieda whipped her gaze over to meet her lord's. "What is *she* doing here, My Lord?" she hissed in a less than supplicatory manner.

Domon eyed her, not deigning to give a reply, then flicked his eyes between the other occupants of the room. Six in all. Rhidea suspected the stone Domon had given her to have been Kalceron's. "Very well," he said eventually. "We are all here. Solomiya is busy as we speak. As you can see, we have a new guest present tonight: Rhidea of Randhorn."

Solomiya, Rhidea thought to herself. *Sounds like a woman's name, and not one I've met.*

All eyes—all glares, more like—were upon her, distrusting and wary. Sighing inwardly, she gave an honored bow. She was afraid of none of these magi, least of all Lieda, but it would be a tiring night. She closed her eyes briefly, focusing her Silver Authority to send out her consciousness like feelers through the silver roots beneath their chamber. Mani enhanced her reach without any cognitive exchange between them. Yes, this was in Domon's palace within the Ti'Vaeth citadel. It appeared to be . . . directly adjoining his personal chambers.

She opened her eyes, revealing no hint of duplicity. She wasn't trying to break into the Archlord's palace—but the information could come in useful later.

⚜

End of Part Three

α PART FOUR α

Hunter

Gaea

α Chapter 42 α

Departure

They kept some humans; the scouring was not complete. But I don't know where, or for how long, they kept them. To my understanding, they were a sort of insurance policy in case anything went greatly wrong with me . . . or rather, with my daughter.
— From Lhinde's Vault

It was not easily that I left Ccamos, but with determination. I didn't want to run away—I wanted to fight. To light into whatever Senator had ordered Kaen's capture and brutal death. Whoever had devised that scheme to torment my mind and break my spirit must pay . . . but not yet. Sylleo was right; I needed to go. It was strange to think that Ccamos, a high-tech city run by a man who should be my enemy, would ever feel this much like . . .

Home.

"Write us some letters about the weather," Plato said with his typical humor, waving a hand as I boarded the subterranean shuttle that would send me underneath the ocean. "I've heard it's great, except for the typhoons."

I gave him a bemused snort, and Zent threw him an admonishing scowl before closing in to give me a hug. A big, awkward-but-earnest hug. "Take care, Lyn. We're going to miss having you around."

I pulled away, trying to smile. It wasn't easy right now. "I'll miss you too, big guy. Tell the Red Horizon boys I said hi. Oh, and tell Dekla and Getts I said they're jerks."

"Will do."

Sylleo gave me a nod, opening his mouth to say something, and then coughed and reached out a hand instead.

I shook it, squeezing his long fingers with all the grip strength I could muster. Never mind that our arms nearly made a right angle parallel with the ground, so much taller was he. "Thank you, Senator Sylleo," I said honestly, "For all you've done for me and my friends. Thank you for letting us go."

"It was my pleasure to aid the lady Heiress in her cause," he said, giving a small but formal bow. "We'll come for you in a month, Lyn."

A crowd of some dozen Hellebes had accompanied Sylleo to see me off. They stood at the entrance of the subterranean tunnel that would take me to Mei Shan. With one last attempt at a smile, putting all the joy into it that I could muster given the circumstances, I boarded the car and let the door shut automatically behind me. No soldiers went with me. It was a simple track, but long—a straight shot from South Terrol to Tai'Xi—and had been constructed for secretive purposes, having fallen largely out of use for the last century. Sylleo assured me it was safe, however.

The lighting was sparse in the railcar, which was some six feet square. Buttons flashed on a dated monitor, and I pressed the one that read "Tai'Xi" and sat back on a nice, comfy solid steel bench. Slowly, the car ground forward on the tracks until I was descending into the tunnel, deeper and deeper, picking up speed. I clutched the hand rails on my bench, wondering if I was supposed to be strapped in. Perhaps this was made in the days before safety harnesses, back before quantum computing.

Readings on my wrist console showed a max of three hundred kilometers per hour, shortly after which the Geoelectric motors kicked in with a hum, keeping the pace at just under that. Not the fastest way to travel nowadays, but Sylleo assured me that this tunnel was long since forgotten and far beneath the surface, insulated from any satellites and radar. My suit's computer lost signal some hundred feet below the surface, and it was one thousand feet below sea level at the bottom. I felt suffocated and claustrophobic down here, jolting with every minor curve and bump in the tracks and wondering if I would crash into some unfortunate rockfall at any moment.

Slowly, I laid my head back against the car's wall and tried to relax. Through the pressing gloom of my friend's death, I tried to dwell on happier thoughts, but I couldn't stop the flashes of memory from the video feed of his brutal murder. Each one stabbed a painful knife into me. Blinking away tears, I listened to the high-pitched, echoey rush of my passage through the tunnel.

I was reminded of the time I had ventured beneath Mani's surface with Rhidea months ago, underneath the Kystrean capital of Ti'Vaeth, where I'd observed the deep veins of silver called the roots of Mani. I now knew that they were the opposite of roots, tendrils reaching up from the depths of each continent that floated over the core, continents comprised mostly of silver. The idea was fantastical. All my life I had lived on the strangest planet—a moon, no less—and never had a clue. The Legaleians as a whole still knew so little about their homeworld . . .

And Lldsaor wanted to conquer it. To crush it beneath his iron fist. Surely there was more to being a world leader than making war?

I must have drifted off, because I awoke with a start as the car slowed to a stop. No . . . it was still moving; we were just moving uphill finally. The tunnel must have already passed underneath the ocean. I had directions and coordinates to go on, and would be deposited some three hundred miles southwest of the Gyutan mountains, my goal.

Sure enough, I was deposited within a few minutes in a deserted site in a sandy wilderness. Sparse trees, weak and scruffy, dotted the mostly flat landscape, while giant rock formations made for impressive landmarks. Almost no vegetation could be seen.

Great, I thought, *this really is a desert.* With a sigh, I hoisted my pack over my shoulder and stepped out of the railcar, shielding my eyes with one hand against the harsh sunlight that reflected off the sand. At least I was alone and it was quiet. I needed a chance to just . . . unwind and let out my emotional pressure. Although I had been alone the other day when in hiding, waiting for Sylleo's soldiers to arrive, that was . . . different. Here, nobody knew where I was. The enemy who sought me didn't have my signal, my coordinates, nor any indication that I'd left.

Tears came unbidden to my eyes, dripping onto my cheeks. Perhaps it would finally come out. *Oh, Kaen,* I whispered to myself.

There was only one thing to do: Keep moving forward. So I began my journey.

α   Chapter 43   α

Mei Shan

*Already, I look back and it all seems a dream. My home in Starklett,
my family, Rena and the other experiments . . . Sometimes I even forget I'm
having a child—a girl, no less. From my own body shall come another. She
will carry on after me.*
— *From Lhinde's Vault*

The trip was long, but my training with the Red Horizon had prepared me
for it, and my rations were packed to last at least three days. I followed the
directions and landmarks I'd memorized from Sylleo, avoiding the use of my
computer as much as possible. Didn't want to accidentally send a signal to
my enemies from the middle of a wasteland.

I camped underneath one of the large rock outcroppings for the first
night, using my pack as a pillow, and let the strange, steadily-clicking bug
noises sing me to sleep. By the second day, I began to see the mountains called
Gyutan peeking up over the northeastern horizon. I increased my pace,
coming out of the wasteland into more fertile ground, where grass carpeted
the terrain and the trees were more prominent. The world seemed that much
more alive and less eager to consume me.

Just as the sun was beginning to creep from its zenith to the horizon at
my back, I started to ascend the foothills. It reminded me of my time in the
Beides mountains south of Haccolces, where I first fled from the League with
Zent, Ccal and Bddo. *Auroras, that seems like an age ago.* As I ascended, the
flora grew ever more robust, the trees greener and taller, and I began to spot
animals rustling leaves and branches behind trees. The smell of pine-needle
mulch and dry leaves couldn't have been more refreshing as my body tired
from the second day in a row of near-constant running. I stopped only to eat
and for calls of nature.

My second night was spent at the base of the first mountains. I picked a good mossy spot with some nice-looking rocks, pulled one over to lean my pack on, and fell fast asleep before long.

Day three saw me up even earlier, long before the sun. Some stick was poking me in the back as usual, or perhaps it was the more biting chill of the night's wind that awoke me. I set off in less of a hurry, following the path through the mountains that Sylleo had set me on. I say path, but I had yet to see signs of human life in the mountain pass. Only the odd remnants of old structures—nothing that looked even relatively recent or lived-in, except by squirrels and hairy spiders. Was there really a Senator living up here?

The sun chased me up the Gyutan mountain slopes and all through the pass as I followed the landmarks. As ever, my newfound Hellebes memory came in handy. Each new hill I saw, each mountain slope I passed, each turn I took, all got added to the unforgettable compendium in my head that I could rely on if I got lost. The tricky part was seeing through all the trees, so sometimes I had to do a bit of climbing to reach a higher vantage point, like Kymhar used to do back on the Light Side of Mani.

As noon approached, I finally saw it: A gigantic crater carved out of the earth, shearing mountains in half and devastating the landscape. The plant life and trees had grown up all through it, proving that Sylleo was right in saying it was no longer a desolate waste, yet its form was unmistakable. Somewhere in there lay the ruins of Mei Shan. To my understanding, Sylleo had ways both of communicating and traveling easily between Ccamos and Mei Shan; he had simply wanted to ensure the total privacy of my visit.

I made my way down the slope, avoiding the unnaturally sharp terrain created long ago by the blast. Once again, I relied on Sylleo's directions. It was nearly an hour before I neared the heart of the crater, where I encountered the first pair of Hellebes men. Farmers by the looks of them, some apparent twenty to thirty in age and a bit smaller than most Hellebes— around my height. They stood up straight as they spotted me. Then one nudged the other and pointed. "Hey, Kol, that's not . . ."

He trailed off as I approached, slowing from my run to a long-strided walk, and the other man asked me, "You're not the Mother, are you?"

"I am," I said through heavy breaths. *Must be detectives to figure that out . . .*

Their eyes went wide, and both men bowed to me with palms outstretched together, fingers pointing toward the sky. "Forgive our rudeness, Lady Gaea."

I sighed, rolling my eyes. "Stop that, please. I'm looking for the Earth Sage. Do you know where I can find him?"

"Lady Gaea," said the first man, "The great Earth Sage keeps to himself for the most part, but he's usually on the hill just north of the lake." He turned and pointed down the path beside the sloping field they currently worked. "Follow that path till you get to the town, then hang a left."

"Thank you," I said, blowing a greasy stray hair out of my mouth. I wasn't about to try to do anything about the tangles in my hair. Seriously, who would try to worship a goddess who'd spent the night in the woods?

I proceeded on my way, jogging down the path in the direction of this town. I didn't know what to expect from this place, as Sylleo hadn't elaborated on it. Supposedly, there was some secret here, one that could change the world should they choose to share it, but so far all I'd observed was that these Hellebes seemed a bit smaller in stature than most. Also a bit less robotic than League Hellebes in their greetings toward me—they must have been "unlocked" already, as Zent called it. I only hoped this wasn't a hotspot of fanatical Mother worshippers.

I soon came upon the lake, to which most of the small streams in the crater valley seemed to run. It was so beautiful that I would have assumed it to be completely natural had I not known its history. A few small islands dotted its surface. Men and women sat fishing near one shore, wearing wide-brimmed straw hats. I hadn't seen that look since . . .

I skidded to a halt, nearly tripping myself as I stared. Was I seeing things? No, those were definitely women. There were two, one with black hair in a ponytail and the other with a greying bun, garbed in simple dresses and laughing as they talked with the men.

But . . . what are they doing here? Did the Elites send their leftover mistakes to this place to get rid of them? I knew even as it came to mind that the thought was preposterous. If they were so rare, and accidentally so, then the League would not throw them away. And given the exactness of modern Gaean science and what I had seen in the labs . . .

I tried to shake it off for the moment, continuing along the lakeside path, when two children ran in front of me. One of them, a girl with blonde braids, looked at me as I passed with a big-eyed expression of excitement and began talking animatedly with the other, a boy of some six years. Or . . . no, whatever six human years equivalated to in Hellebes growth.

I gawked at the two children, nearly stopping in my tracks once more. This time, however, I kept going. Just a couple children; we had them all over back on Mani. Just not . . . Hellebes children. The younglings in the training centers back in Chronala could hardly even be called children. I tried to stuff away my confusion. I had to find this sage, the supposed ninth Senator.

Because I had some questions for him.

At last, I came upon the hill, which stretched upwards toward a lone tree. As I climbed the incline, I made out a figure sitting beneath the tree. But . . . he was no Elite. His body was withered and old, his form unimposing. He sat in a meditative posture with knees crossed, facing the sunset. He also wore almost nothing, just a white sash and a raggedy cloth tied at the waist. He was completely bald, but had considerable hair on his beard, chest and armpits.

"Hello? Where's the sage?" I called.

The old man looked up, giving me a long stare. "Who wants to know?"

"I was sent by . . . um, I'm not sure if I should say."

"Give me a moment," the man muttered, rising slowly to his feet with a long sound somewhere between a groan and a grunt. "If you can't tell me who you are, then I have no business with you."

He was perhaps an inch or two shorter than me, though I didn't know how much a Hellebes shrunk over his lifetime. Zent was getting up there in years, yet I wouldn't know it to look at him. Why was this old fogey acting so differently from the men who had greeted me with bowing and scraping back in the periphery of the village? Then it hit me, and I let out a short gasp. "You're him, aren't you? *You're* the Earth Sage?"

He stared silently into my eyes, still waiting for my answer.

"I'm sorry, sir" I said, tripping over my words. "I didn't mean to be rude. My name is Lynchazel, and I'm the previous Mother's daughter."

The old man crossed his arms. "That is a bit better. 'Tis good to finally meet you, dear. Sylleo told me you'd be coming, that he did. He and I have a long kinship, one which goes back to before this place was . . ." He gestured all around him. "Mei Shan's come a long way, though, and I trust you'll enjoy your stay."

I nodded distractedly, following his gaze and taking in the scenery around me. "But . . . what is going on here? Am I going crazy, or are there real humans here?"

"Define human." He said the words slowly, calculatedly.

The response caught me off-guard, and I stopped with mouth agape. "I don't follow, sir. Are they Hellebes or not?"

"What is humanity?" he asked. "And what does it mean to be human? What separates humans from animals?"

I thought about it. "Our sentient intelligence. Social structures, languages, tools. And . . . our souls?"

"And how can you prove whether a Hellebes or a 'real' human possesses those things or not? What is the difference?" The sage rolled his shoulder and shifted his neck from side to side. "Oh, that was a most needed stretch. If only you hadn't interrupted it, young Lynchazel."

Stretch? He was stretching? "I thought you were meditating or something spiritual. I mean, you are supposed to be a sage."

He laughed. "No, my girl, not really. That is merely a nickname from long ago. The people here respect me a great deal, and I treat them as children and grandchildren. Few others in the world know of me, nor our little community, and that is for the best."

"Then what's with the apple tree of inner peace here?" I asked, gesturing at the tree.

"That would be a pear tree, my dear," he said patiently. "And—to forestall further comment—no, it bears no fruit. I believe one of the youths a couple generations ago planted it, some decade or two after the bombing."

I paused, thinking for a moment. "And . . . are you going to explain the humans? Or Hellebes, whatever they are."

The Sage pursed his lips, nodding along with my words. "Walk with me, Lynchazel. There is much you are unaware of."

And so I did. The old man took me by the shoulder and led me down the other side of the hill, to my right. A rough path led into the trees. He strode confidently for one so wizened, so much so that I wondered if the whole "old" thing might simply be an act or disguise meant to fool me.

"My girl," he said as we walked, "How much *do* you know?"

"A lot, but apparently not nearly enough. I know about the Elites and how you set up the Hellebes mass reproduction system, about the nine cities, and how the Hellebes are all biomachines."

The sage nodded. "And of course you know about the Cydenges. Did he tell you that you yourself possess Cydenges DNA?"

I nodded. "I know that, too. Something about the first experiments with the original Mother, that that was how they first discovered Geokinesis."

"Indeed. I know scant about all that myself. Sylleo, Brant or especially Daedalus would know far more than me. Especially since I've been out of touch for nigh a hundred years now." The old man chuckled and then sighed, glancing at me. "And I cared naught even before that. I've long followed pacifistic beliefs. I only went along with the other eight because I saw no choice—and potential benefit for humanity. As I said, though . . . what is humanity? If we could preserve the human race by turning them into living machines, then wasn't that a noble goal?"

He shook his head regretfully. "So spoke the old me. I realized over time the great pride and folly of it. We should never have tried to play God as we did. Something was bound to go wrong eventually." He held up a withered arm, whose bones and musculature were still quite solid but whose skin sagged like a ninety-year-old Legaleian's. "See, when we each picked our new bodies to create, I was already weary of the charades. I chose to look the same as my fellow Hellebes, and I turned down the special 'powers' that accompany each of the Elites—special coding that gives their bodies unique Goekinetic abilities. I hesitated to distance myself from my fellow man, an illusive ideal that my guilt compelled me to seek.

"As you surely know by now, our so-called 'Elite' bodies have to be regularly maintained. So . . . this is what has happened to me over the last one hundred years. A millennium of Geothermic energy has turned my body into an enduring machine, almost like it did for your mother before you, but it can only go so far, and I may not have many years left."

"I'm sorry," I said.

He shook his bald head. "Don't be, young one. I've lived many times the life I should have. Wasting most of it was my choice. But I'm glad I became friends with Sylleo, for he has helped me to rebuild the remnants of my city here in the mountains. And yes, those are indeed humans you see. Ye olde, standard-issue, vanilla humans. My city was tasked with keeping a remnant of the human population alive in the early stages of our plan, in case the Mother Project fell through once and for all."

I frowned. That didn't explain how they dealt with the population skewing. "But what were you supposed to do with them? Kill them off eventually?"

"Quite so. That was the plan. It's not in my nature to harm, so of course I preserved them. At first as captives, placating the Senate with excuses. And then . . . as a hidden fledgling people, the last hope for humanity on Gaea. At times, I still wish something would go terribly wrong, and the Gaean League—their entire civilization—could just collapse, so that my people could live freely and repopulate the earth. Did you know that in the wilds, the earth is destroying itself? It is depleted. The mountains heave in pain. Disease runs rampant among the wildlife. Meanwhile, our humans are thriving and population balance has been mysteriously returning."

As we walked, we came back within sight of the lake, emerging from the trees. I tried to process Long's words, seeing the irony in them. "What did you do to anger the Senate so?"

"I'm sure you can guess. They found out that I was still keeping humans here in Mei Shan, and Lldsaor tried to make me swear to exterminate them for good, sparing none. I refused, and he threatened to bomb the entire city. Sylleo tried to step in, and Holman also did not approve, but the vote was six to three—six to two, really. So I warned the people of Mei Shan and evacuated as many as I could into underground bunkers. We had already been preparing for decades, since it was only a matter of time before Lldsaor decided to do something about them. Since the bombing, we've lived in obscurity, letting the rest of the world think us dead. Slowly, as life began to bloom once more in the valley, we moved back in, as it seemed the most unlikely place to think that refugees from the past might live.

"Modern science predicted that this place would still be a waste today. The earth tears itself apart elsewhere, yet here where we have tended the earth in simple fashion, Gaea thrives—despite horrific poisoning by the weapons of man. Progress dictates rules. Progress is an idol and a ravenous creature, Lynchazel, always claiming to be just a few steps away from achieving something great for mother nature."

I shook my head, taking in the beauty surrounding me. "Huh." Frankly, I didn't have the interest to delve too deeply into his philosophical implications, but his words did strike a chord. I couldn't help but wonder if the rest of the Elites knew about the place and just didn't care yet. It was a disquieting and hollowly sad thought.

"Wait," I said, thoughts coalescing into something more solid. "Senator Long, you said the population has rebalanced itself . . . but how? I don't understand. Mani never got as bad as Gaea, but our birth rates are still four to one, favoring females instead of males."

He raised an eyebrow at me. "Is that right? Females . . . Well, that certainly wasn't the case for them at the time of the exile. Let's just say the Anier—which was us, and our predecessors—may have had a hand or two in that. At the last . . ." He shook his head. "You wouldn't believe the number of girls that were slaughtered, and that was before the purging of humanity. It was ghastly, unconscionable. All that to say, the crisis was never as bad as League propaganda made it out to be. But also . . . ever since the Wellspring was moved to Mani and the Legaleians exiled, the birth rates have changed only slightly. And yet, inexplicably, they have begun to shift toward normal."

"Oh. That's . . ." *A far cry from what I've been hearing.* This man actually lived with humans, so he should know. I felt like my whole world—this one, anyway—was flipping upside down around me.

"Come, lass." Long waved a hand, seeing that I had fallen behind distractedly, "I'll introduce you to some of the folks."

α Chapter 44 α

Hope for Humanity

Perhaps the greatest irony in human history is that I get to contribute to the human race when it is the most pointless. What I do, I do for a soulless machine run by meta-human monsters . . . the murderers of mankind.
— From Lhinde's Vault

Over the course of the next hour, Long took me around and introduced me to a host of new faces. Most recognized me or guessed who I was, yet he always introduced me as Lynchazel, which I appreciated. There were many different human ethnicities represented, which I recognized only from my classes on the human gene pool. Most were intermixed, bearing various skin shades and eye color, facial features, body types . . . It was hard to believe the human race was this diverse. Hellebes, too, possessed widely varying traits, purposely created using complex cocktails of recorded genes, but they shared a few characteristics like unnaturally large skeletons and heavy musculature.

Mani, on the other hand, seemed to come from largely one population, the Legaleians, who had light skin and dark hair predominantly. To see real humans, all so distinct from one another, was surprisingly refreshing. Features I'd seen only on huge, brutish men looked shockingly delicate and beautiful on women of similar genetic origin. (Not exactly origin, in the case of Hellebes, as that was more like . . . genetic plagiarizing?)

Some of the residents were bubbly and friendly, while others were a bit less social. Most of the locals spoke a dialect of the Hellebes tongue—which supposedly came from a western nation back in the middle ages—and it took me a bit to get used to it. Different accents had formed even back on Mani, admittedly. It was especially precious to get to meet the children here, boys and girls ranging from babies all the way to young adults. They all appeared stockier than the children back on Mani, and I deduced that that would have been a genetic trait developed over the course of countless centuries to adapt to the harsh gravity of Gaea, whereas the Manese would have lost much strength since coming to their weak planet.

Lastly, Long took me to a well-built house, introducing me to a blond woman of some thirty-five years with a few streaks of grey in her hair. I thought she just seemed moody until Long quietly explained her story. Greta was recently widowed, left with her only son. Presumably, Long wanted me to stay with them and help her out.

"It's good to meet you, Greta," I said with a small bow. "And Hans." The boy, some fourteen years old, shared his mother's face.

"A pleasure." The woman's face and tone of voice did not corroborate her statement, but I chalked that up to her situation.

I turned to Long. "Am I . . . ?"

"You'll be staying here tonight," he answered. "As well as the rest of your visit. I'm going to leave you three to get acquainted, and I'll come by in the morning to pick you up."

"For?"

"Training. It's why you're here, after all. Good night, girl." With that, the old man left, and I couldn't help but wonder what kind of training he could possibly give me. Earth sage they may call him, but he looked cut out for no more than . . . maybe paper-folding training?

The ex-Senator took his leave, and I cleared my throat, unsure of what to say. "Miss Greta, is there anything I can do to help out? I'm very good at chores."

Greta showed mild surprise, the first hint of emotion I'd seen from her. "Well, ah, sure. I suppose. Hans dear, show her how to split wood."

"Sure, Mama!" He took me by the hand and led me out back of the house, where a messy pile of large sticks lay, including one mid-size tree trunk. The boy showed me a two-wheeled cart that he used to fetch the wood, as well as a stump on which to chop it. Also a large saw which he said his late father had used to cut up logs that were too long.

He watched in shock as I took most of the sticks, large and small, and snapped them right over my knee. I began making a pile of them, separating out the ones that needed to be split, and finally tried out the axe on the large logs, wielding it in one hand and rapidly chopping circularly at the former trees. I was able to trim each to snapping width within about ten seconds and moved on to the next section. After all of those, I took the axe to each segment using the stump. Set, chop. Turn, chop. Grab, chop. Set, chop. It was a therapeutic rhythm.

Only when Hans called me by name did I realize that I had split all the wood. I stood up, exhaling and wiping my brow. "Sorry, got a bit carried away," I said.

"Sorry?" He grinned. "That was amazing! Mama will be thrilled. How do you work like that?"

I shrugged. "I've always been strong, so I'm used to helping people out with physical projects." I didn't tell him that his mama would not cheer up just because I split a lot of wood for her.

"Yeah, but . . . you're a girl! I mean, a big girl, but still."

I smiled. He was just like Oliver, excitable and unapologetically awkward. If only the two could meet . . . wait, no. I snorted, realizing the language barrier would make that a bit difficult.

"What is it, miss Lynchazel?" Hans asked. "Wait, was it what I said?"

I shook my head. "No, silly. I was just remembering something. A friend from . . . where I come from."

"Oh. That's right. Don't you guys have, like, perfect memory or something? I mean, the Hellebes. Uh, that is . . . aren't you sort of a Hellebes?"

I nodded. "Similar. And I do, just like the Hellebes. But it didn't come as easy for me. A lot of people died before I got the power I have now."

Hans, seeing he had made me sad, seemed at a loss for what to do. "I met a Hellebes once," he said after a long pause. "A real old one!"

I turned, frowning at him. "Did you?"

"Yeah! He was one of the last ones alive from before the bombing, and Master Long said he lived way longer than most Hellebes do. We used to have Hellebes and humans living with us, but all the Hellebes died out years ago."

"Interesting . . ." Look at that, I was learning history from a kid. "That's actually pretty neat." I tried to picture what that would look like—Hellebes living alongside men and women. I couldn't imagine the emptiness one of them would feel, watching human children grow up, marry and start a family, knowing they could never reproduce. To my observation, they seemed incapable of the same feelings of attraction that we experienced. It seemed such a lonely existence.

"Oh," I said, realizing I was just sitting on a log, not doing anything. "Is there anything else I can do for your mother? I don't want to look unhelpful."

Hans laughed, scratching his mop of mousy brown hair. "Unhelpful? That's a joke, right?"

I shook my head. "I want to do as much as I can to help her. She looks like she deserves it."

"Well . . . let me go ask." The youth ran off to talk to Greta, and soon I had a list of other things to do for the evening. I worked on their roof, using Hans' guidance to replace some weakened thatch, then set myself on a handful of other jobs. When I'd finished with that, I had him take me out to the woods in search of some logs to carry back. I helped load up his cart and then picked up two long deadfalls after hacking off the thin limbs, and carried them back to the house yard. Hans glanced at my two tree trunks frequently, both in wonder and nervousness, and some of the neighbors gawked.

I'd have thought them used to superhuman feats after living with Hellebes for generations, but of course it was probably my looks that made them underestimate me. Or they simply hadn't thought the Mother, eater of figs and worker of miracles, would be—in essence—a Hellebes.

The next morning, Long came so early to get me that I thought it was still nighttime. He gave some excuse about dawn coming deceptively early in the valley. I checked to make sure Hans was still asleep next to his mother before getting dressed and following the old man outside. I did not put on my gillsuit, however, but a garment the local seamstress had made for me, similar to Long's but slightly more appropriate for a woman. I opened the door and followed him out through the dewy grass in my bare feet, trying to adjust the chest wrap—the reason I said slightly more appropriate—while Long said almost nothing.

We headed out to the hill with the tree on it. I could hardly see through the heavy morning fog, which dampened and diffused what little light there was. I could swear it was moonlight, not any dawn at all. My feet were drenched in dew by the time we arrived, and I was feeling a bit chilled. Ah, but the crisp morning air did smell lovely. The fog coming off the lake carried a slightly fishy scent, along with an earthy but clean scent I couldn't place.

I waited for him to speak first, and finally he did, just as we arrived. "I mentioned that I was going to train you. But know that this is only on personal, emphatic request of my old friend Sylleo. I wouldn't train you just because you're the next 'Mother,' so called, nor so that you can go to war against your enemies in the Senate. I don't even want to know what you require the training for, but . . . I'll turn you into an unstoppable force, as that is what he asked."

I nodded slowly, still questioning in my mind what this puny old man could teach me.

"But remember," he added, "As a pacifist, I do things my own way, and I don't believe in any killing that can be avoided. Hence, I will teach you principles you can use either for good or for evil, to help or to destroy, to save or to kill. First . . . stretching."

He led me through a half-hour exercise to loosen up the body and get the blood flowing, which seemed to be counteracted by the chill that made all my joints want to tighten up. But Long almost appeared to be waiting for me to complain, so I refused to give him the satisfaction.

After the stretching, he had me do other warmup exercises, simple katas most of which I knew from Zent and Musha's training back at the submarine base. Then he got down to the real lesson. He taught me how to breathe and draw Geothermic energy in sync, with the same motions and also opposite—

breathing in as energy flowed out, and vice versa—which created different rhythms in the body. It reminded me a lot of Musha's training, but was more focused on reading the earth's energy—or breath, as he called it—and flowing with it, unlike Musha's more intensely practical focus.

The breathing exercises got trickier and more complex, and he had to repeat lessons over and over—not so much to drill them into my brain as into my body. He explained the breathing styles, parallel and opposite, as melody and harmony versus counterpoint. Not that I knew much about music. The second of these was the most difficult, following every breath with a Geokinetic pulse. Not a blast, nothing released, but a pulsing tide within. He even tried to teach me to match all of these with my heartbeat, at which point I was simply unable to follow along. So we focused on other disciplines for the morning.

The sun rose, driving away the morning mist, and we continued practicing on the hill. Long explained that the whole area harbored an enormous pool of Geothermic energy since the city no longer used any, but the hill represented nothing special in that regard. Simply a good place to train, since the weeds grew low to the ground and it was peaceful.

Be that as it may, I was famished. Long didn't allow any breaks for food, however, until I had gotten the most basic of his grueling breathing styles down. It was around noon when we stopped for lunch. All that Geothermic circulation could only do so much to sustain a body. He opened up a sack and pulled out a pair of hard biscuits. I thought the old man was joking when he handed one to me and began chewing the other one apart.

He was not. This was all I got for now. He refused to let me go back to the village until we were "done for the day," whenever that would be. When I had to go, he pointed toward the woods and waited till I got back.

After our satisfying lunch, we did some more stretching and more energetic katas, and then he began applying his lessons to combat training. For an old man who was literally falling apart, I couldn't believe how agile and strong he was. In fact, I couldn't touch him. Musha and Zent were incredible fighters, but Long was on a different level. When Sylleo had said this man was a warrior in his prime, the best of the best, I hadn't known what to think—particularly after seeing him. But now . . . try though I might, I could never land a blow. At first I held back, but he gave me a beating for that . . .

When at last he called an end to the combat training, he allowed me to ask questions. "So, how do you do it?" I asked as we stretched for the third time that day. "How can you still fight when your body is falling apart?"

The old man looked up from his seated stretch. "I don't exactly do it often, girl," he grumbled. "But you aren't going to match centuries of practice with your sloppy work."

"But . . . I mean how do you physically hold up? Don't your Elite bodies need repair constantly?"

"I was always able to get away with far less since I chose a simpler design much closer to a normal human's. And I found ways to rely less on the maintenance and more on Geothermic energy. However, I don't see myself being around for much longer."

"And what about your tribe here? The humans? What's going to happen to them?"

"They will wait for deliverance to come," he said, he said, rising from his position. "Tyranny cannot last forever."

"But you're not going to do anything about it."

Long's old eyes flashed. "I protect these people. I've taught them everything they need to know to survive and live happily until such time as they are able to come out of hiding."

"Then what about the Cydenges? Don't they ever attack here? What would you do?"

He was silent for a moment. "I have safeguards. For now, I am prepared to deal with any myself, should they show up. Then I would take the humans and flee to avoid being found. There are more prominent hot spots for Geothermic energy than here, so it has not been a target in the last century. The hot spots currently tapped by the Elites are the ones that attract their attention, because they pull it to the surface, where the Cydenges sense it more easily from Luna."

"Then what about when they do attack?" I demanded. "What if you're dead by then, and every human you tried to save, all their children and grandchildren, are wiped out in one night?"

"I have a deal with Sylleo," he began. "Should I die—"

"Then what, he'll step in and do what you wouldn't?"

Long shut his mouth, glaring in anger, chin trembling slightly. I knew I had overstepped now. "Young lady, I wouldn't advise you to try my patience like this. I have thought on these things for decades longer than you've been alive, and I've discussed them with the people. I have given up on war, as I said, but if I hadn't . . . what would I do? All my Hellebes, faithful though they were, have died off now. The eldest died ten years ago, and he was an abnormality.

"Senator Sylleo has promised to post guards here when I pass, and I trust him to keep that promise. As I said, he and I go way back. As much as violence turns my stomach, I do think you have a good chance in turning the tide of this world, Lynchazel. That is why I agreed to train you. I will turn you into the monster that I could never be, someone who can stand against one of the Elites and be victorious. But there is a greater evil to be dealt with, as every Senator knows: The Cydenges. I'm sure you've heard that if they ever come in force, they could wipe every trace of humanity from the face of Gaea.

"One day, they will need to be dealt with for good. Everything Lldsaor, Strongs, all those idiots, even your rebel friends . . . everything they do is one way of trying to reach that goal—the power to destroy the Cydenges."

"But . . . don't they already have the technology? Why couldn't they just nuke Luna's surface and blow them all up?" I was aware of how stupid those words sounded coming out of my mouth, but it seemed an obvious solution.

Long only laughed. "That would be the end of Gaea. The Cydenges can teleport in the blink of an eye. As soon as we tried something like that, they would come here and wipe us out—either preemptively, or in response. We don't even know where they live on the golden moon. We know nothing about Luna. Every probe we send ends up dead, all communication lost. The same would happen with a guided missile."

"What about telescopes?" I asked. "Surely they could at least scan the near side of the planet and see what's there?"

He shook his head, reaching over his shoulders to stretch both hands. A series of cracks accompanied the movement. "Nothing. They can never see anything, just like with Mani."

Just like with Mani . . . So it was a magical planet? Did it have its own Wellspring? I stopped pestering the former Senator with questions, instead departing for Greta's house in hopes of getting something to eat. My stomach was not happy with me for neglecting it today.

The sun was just about to pass below the western mountains, creating a vibrant orange sunset as I walked, filtering through the trees and attempting to blind me. Hans met me before I reached the house, crying, "Lady Gaea!"

"It's Lyn," I said tiredly. "How many times do I have to tell you, kid?" Nevertheless, I gave him an affectionate pat on the back. Greta came over then, saying she had some soup waiting for me. I gratefully thanked her and followed them inside to eat. It was a vegetable stew made with potatoes, rutabagas and parsnips, but also had some rabbit meat in it. Apparently, Hans had been busy with his bow.

"So, were you really out there doing meditation and martial arts with Master Long?" Hans asked excitedly through a mouthful of stew.

"Hans!" his mother chided. "Let the lady eat. And close your mouth while you chew."

"Mmph. Phorry, Mahm," he replied, putting another spoonful in his mouth.

"It's all right, Greta," I said. "Yes, Hans. Kind of. He's a lot rougher than you'd think."

"So are you going to go fight some Cydenges?" he asked.

I paused with my spoon halfway to my mouth. "Cydenges? I've seen them once, but never fought them."

"Wow," Hans breathed. "That's amazing. Dad used to tell me stories about them. Do they really have that many eyes?"

"Uh, the ones I saw just had two each. But they glow red. Their bodies are made of metal, and they have horns and long tails like dragons. Sharp claws, metal scales . . ."

I stopped when I saw his mother's look of horror. Was it the descriptions or the hand motions? "Sorry, ma'am," I mumbled.

She shook her head, pretending it was fine. She stared down at the table, glancing up only briefly at me. "No apologies necessary, milady."

"It's . . ." I trailed off before saying, *It's Lyn, not milady.* I didn't want to give her a hard time, though. So instead I said, "I want you to know, ma'am, I'm deeply grateful to you for opening your home to me."

"Of course," she said. "It's nothing."

α Chapter 45 α

Prepare for War

My new memories begin a good while after the experiments, and even heretofore it's not as perfect as they claim. It skips and fails on rare occasions.

— From Lhinde's Vault

For the next two days, I trained just the same with Long. We never did too much of the actual combat training at one time, because his old body tired out. Combat was only in the afternoons, and the rest of the day was spent doing breathing exercises. Why were they so tough? He fed me almost nothing, not to mention getting me up before breakfast each morning. Something about learning to attune to the flow of Geothermic energy by consuming it instead of food.

From time to time, Long would share anecdotes about Gaea or even allow for a small discussion. When I say that, I mean I would ask a question and he wouldn't shut me down. He explained more of his past, how he became more pacifistic only after Lldsaor began to show his true colors. He and Sylleo bonded, though they took their displeasure with the Senate's ways in different directions. Sylleo was more of an independent thinker who didn't hold to one ideal. To Long, pacifism was his penance.

I also learned that the lands around the ninth city were once home to some of the most diverse and dedicated of martial artists, from whom Long learned before becoming a Senator. Many of these arts were now lost forever, along with much of the culture, lore and ways of Gaea's people. Long also told me more of the Anier, the organization that had predated the Gaean Senate. The Anier rebranded themselves as the Senate after they came up with their plan to condense the whole world into nine cities. The original Mother, whose name was Lhinde, was chosen by the Anier for their experiments, but she ultimately failed despite them getting their formula pretty close.

Therefore, they had to restart with Lynchazel I, her daughter, and genetically mold her into the perfect Mother. The Anier had existed over generations, the nine roles of leadership changing hands with them, but it was the final group who became the Senators of the new Gaean League, with Lldsaor at the helm. Strongs, their general. Sylleo, head of tech development. Systematically and thoroughly, they wiped out all the female population, keeping only a few for careful breeding in Mei Shan, for purposes Long had already described.

Of the surviving population, many were . . . eliminated.

It was a lot to think on.

During my free time, I was allowed to explore Mei Shan a bit and meet the residents. I tried to explain to them that I didn't want to be called a goddess, but eventually realized the effort was greater than the bother it saved. They wanted to worship me, and that was their choice. They would figure it out some day: That I was a woman, not a myth. A person, not a symbol.

Right?

Among the locals I met were the two women I'd seen when I first walked in, Lana and Cora. They were friends, and enjoyed fishing. Lana was married to a man named Flint, whom I also met. They took me out in a boat, and I made an unsuccessful attempt at fishing. It hadn't really occurred to me that such a task would involve skill.

It was strange to interact with humans at all after spending so much time around the Hellebes. Hellebes and . . . Kaen. Oh, Kaen. I tried not to think about him, but it was not so easy. My heart still ached for him. What would I tell Mydia? No matter what, someday . . . I would have to bear the news, and it would break her heart all over again. But I didn't want to tell it like it was, because my last conversation with Kaen was one of our most miserable ever. That sword had consumed him till the end, and even caused it.

Or had I caused it? That doubt nagged at me relentlessly.

That night, I dreamed.

"Lynchazel, hello again," came my mother's voice from behind me.

I spun to face her, half expecting to see White's familiar slender frame. But no, this was my mother, tall and stunning as I could never hope to be. So strong, yet distinctly feminine. Did my desire to have a mother somehow color all memories of her, including this dream projection? She exuded a certain aura of power like an earthy scent—almost artificial and shocking in its intensity, yet familiar.

"Mother," I whispered. "Huh, where is she . . . ? Never mind. You've seen what I know now? You've been following along, right?"

She nodded cooly. "In a way." She breathed in, glancing around as though beholding the rich valleys of Mei Shan instead of the misty dreamscape. "I did not expect you to find such . . . peace . . . in this place of historic tragedy. Such tranquility. It is unlike anything I could picture in my—our—current-day world. I remember well the day it was bombed. The chaos and pain and fear it struck all across the world. In a way, I felt the loss—both the devastation of the earth and the deaths of those who didn't make it to safety."

I wasn't certain whether she referenced the modern technological advancements of the Hellebes or the broken natural state of Gaea. "It is peaceful here. Long is a bit harsh, though I'm learning the ways of Gaea—and a lot of history. When . . . when will I see you again, Mother?"

She hesitated. "I cannot say. Hopefully soon, but my own mother stirs deep within your memories, trying to break in. In this place, she is farther from you. For now, just . . . be careful. I have a bad feeling."

What a farewell, I grumbled to myself. As she turned away, however, I said, "Wait! I-I've been meaning to ask . . . did you love him?"

She turned her head, smiling in amusement. "Of course, Lynchazel."

"But—I mean . . ."

"I know what you're asking. Was I in my right mind? Or influenced by uncontrollable desires born of a lifetime in captivity and the panic of being set free in a mad world? I . . . may never know. But I know I loved him deeply. In return for what he did for me, I'd have done anything for him—I'd have been his slave forever. But he wasn't that type of man. I hope you take after him, Lynchazel. Goodbye for now."

She was gone once again.

❧

The fourth day in Mei Shan, Long had me do all the exercises he'd taught me on my own. He said he just wanted to observe me, but I felt certain that the last few days had tired him out more and more. It was also a shorter session. He let me off early to spend time with the villagers. On the way back, a spark of inspiration bid me test my Fire Authority once more. *Perhaps in this place,* I reasoned . . .

It was to no avail. I searched for the flame that used to listen for my voice and come when called, but it eluded me as expected.

The week carried on, soon blending into the next, and I grew in physical confidence and in restlessness. I tried the flame-calling again every day with no success, feeling an unexplainable yearning for the return of its warmth. At one point, I could have sworn I felt something, a familiar tickle of the Wellspring's touch, but . . . it was nothing. No magic could take flight on Gaea. My father was either a genius to put all others to shame, or . . . well, who could say? My mother least of all.

Before I knew it, I was consulting my suit's computer to check what day it was, just to make sure my memory wasn't at last failing me. No, I'd really been here nearly a month. Sylleo would be back to pick me up before long. Were Zent and the others still okay? Were they with the Red Horizon right now? Had the Cydenges stopped their invasion yet? And of course, the most important question: What was the Senate planning now? Had Sylleo pacified them?

When I finally asked Long, he said that Sylleo's last communication indicated everything was fine with the Senate, and that they showed no immediate signs of continuing their raid on Mani, but the Cydenges raid was most likely over. Which, of course, I knew meant Operation: Raze Mani would be back in the works soon. And that left me wondering how long I should continue to train with Long. I was beginning to master all the techniques he had thrown at me so far, and could hold my own against him in hand-to-hand combat.

How much stronger did I need to be to face the Senate? Or was there only one way to find out?

α Chapter 46 α

Hunted

They never told me how the Prince died. He was simply assassinated and was no more. Turmoil engulfed the Sovereignty, and the Anier ended up in power. But I am no longer innocent; I know better.
— *From Lhinde's Vault*

It wasn't much longer before I was left without a choice.

It was a crisp autumn morning, cooler than the last few had been, when things began to go haywire. I knew because I was waiting out in the field underneath the pear tree, doing some hand stands, and Long was late. He was never late.

First came the sirens. I didn't even know they had sirens here. Then Long came, hurrying as much as his failing body would allow, and shouted hoarsely, "Lynchazel, come quickly! There's no time to lose."

In a blink, I launched myself with one hand into a run and caught up to the old man. "What's wrong? What's with the sirens?"

"The Elites have sent a military force. We don't know who, but they'll be arriving from the east. Sylleo messaged me just ten minutes ago with the news, and I've already begun evacuating the populace underground. Can you help with that?"

"Yes, sir." I took off for the nearest houses and began banging on doors, breathlessly warning any occupants who had yet to evacuate. I knew where the nearest bunkers were, the same ones the inhabitants had used a century ago. I helped to carry some of the young ones, transporting them three times as fast as any adult human could. I'd said I wanted to help save people, and this might be my best chance. But how long until the soldiers would arrive?

When I was certain of the eastern inhabitants' safety, I began to hear the far-off drone of military aircraft. I made a break for Greta's house, wrenched the door half off its hinges and shouted, "Greta! Hans, are you—" I cut off, realizing the house was empty. Thankful of the fact, I grabbed my gillsuit, threw off my garb and changed as fast as possible. My wrist computer was already processing time of arrival, and I realized I had two messages from Sylleo.

Forget that, Lyn, read the more recent one. *Just run. Get out of there.*

I gulped, looking out at the sky. The first ship was braking, circling and looking for a landing spot, while . . . no, maybe that was the only ship. *Just one? That can't be right.* After sending a distress signal to both Sylleo and Zent, I stepped out and looked around, realizing I could hear someone crying. I circled around back and found Greta hunched up against the cabin, weeping.

"Greta!" I shouted. "What are you doing? Hurry and get to shelter."

She looked at me with tear-streaked eyes, no expression on her face. "Hans is safe. That's all I care about. He is safe, right?"

"He's . . ." I nodded. "He's safe. Now come on, there isn't much time."

She shook her head sadly. "No, I don't belong in those shelters. I'd rather see my husband."

"Your husband is dead! You need to live for Hans."

"He doesn't need me. If I die, I die."

I glanced back up at the airship, which hovered some two hundred feet up in the air, then back at Greta. Why was she being so stubborn? So defeatist? Her face, tired and dully miserable, was that of a woman too inundated with pain and despair to keep caring about anything. And yet . . . how was that fair to her son?

"Greta!" I pleaded in a last attempt. "How could you just give up on your only s—"

My words were drowned out as a harsh, amplified voice boomed out: "Where is the Mother? Bring her out, and I will not destroy your place of refuge. Refuse, and I will raze this place and return it to its desolate state. I am the Hunter, sent for this exact purpose, and I will not return empty-handed."

It came from overhead, issued from a loudspeaker on the ship. When no answer came, the ship began raining down explosive fire at random. Jets of smoke trailed out from the heavily armed craft, each one tracing to a subsequent explosion around the village. Greta's house, some hundred meters from the place over which the ship hovered, was hit by one such blast, and I jumped aside to avoid raining rubble. *No . . . Greta . . .*

My heart hurt for the woman, but I couldn't go back to check on her. There were many others in danger. More explosions were erupting all around the lake, and they would only destroy more. Someone needed to stop them.

As I neared the ship, I saw Long running up to it, waving his hands. "Stop!" he shouted. "Cease at once! You will never get the Mother unless you come down and show your face."

"So you live, former Senator," the Hunter replied. "Very well, produce the Mother and we will cease fire."

"What then?" Long shouted back.

"I will take her back with me."

Long crossed his arms and shook his head, calling, "Come down and show your face, or I cannot comply."

In answer, the Hunter rained down a trio of bombs directly atop the Elite. "No!" I shouted, running out into the open. "Hey, stop! I'm right here." *Long! Long! Please be all right.* And yet, how could he . . .

As I watched, however, Long walked right out of the explosions unscathed. "You!" he growled at me. "I told you to stay hidden." With a swift motion and a roar, he spun and swept up a skyward kick, tearing up the surrounding earth with a Geokinetic attack unlike any I'd witnessed. The earth rent itself, thrusting upward in a spire of stone hundreds of feet into the air. It just missed the ship, which moved away in a hurry. Had it not, he'd have smashed directly into it. White was fascinated by the similarity to Rhidea's Silver spear that had pierced the enemy ship back in Nytaea.

Gathering energy from deep underground, I focused, watching the ship as it circled again. When I felt Gaea's energy bursting in my veins, I let loose a torrent of white energy upward, sweeping in an arc that followed the ship. My aim was not perfect, but I clipped a wing. The burning plasma melted straight through, piercing the hull and shearing the wing off, and the entire ship began to spiral toward the ground.

Yes! It worked. Yet even as I exulted in that small victory, I saw behind the falling, flaming wreckage another few vessels approaching on the horizon.

A thump came from directly behind me, and someone grabbed me from behind before I could turn. I was thrown to the ground in a backwards twisting motion, landing heavily on my face. My attacker held my arm in a near-breaking position with a foot on the small of my back. "That was an impressive move, Mother Gaea," he said in a harsh, heavily filtered voice, as though his helmet was electronically altering it. "Now you die."

I couldn't get a glimpse of the Hunter's face, but I did see a familiar silver blade in front of my eyes as he pointed it down near my right side. I would have gasped if I had the air. *I'd recognize that sword anywhere.* "How did you . . . get that—"

The ground rippled where I lay—Long's intervention—shaking the Hunter's footing enough to relax his grip, and I rolled to the side, sweeping a kick at his legs. My first look at the Hunter revealed a Hellebes soldier armored heavily in all black, bearing an intimidating mask and strange markings on his chest. Upon his shoulder was emblazoned a rank symbol I didn't recognize, along with the Hellebes word for *Hunter.*

While Long kept the ground moving, trying to trap our attacker, I fired another white laser at him. However, he used the sword to absorb every bit of it. At this, even Long gasped in shock. The black-suited Hellebes just laughed, lashing out at me with his sword while keeping up good enough footwork to evade Long's Geokinetic earth attacks.

So it still works. The blade's power had not been severed when Kaen died. Rage boiled up inside me at the thought.

The Hunter closed in, forcing me to retreat toward the lake to avoid being sliced open. I knew better than to think I could withstand the cut of that evil blade. But how had this monster been able to use it? Not only did it work on Gaea, but another could steal it? One who wasn't even human? We were clearly wrong about its potential all along. More than anything, it made me furious that these Elites—whichever was behind this Hunter—would stoop so low as to steal my friend's weapon and use it against me.

Long dashed in and fought the Hunter alongside me, but the silver weapon closed the power gap to a surprisingly fair fight. When Long got in close and attempted to wrest the sword away, his attack seemed to be diverted even before the Hunter made a move, as though repelled by the sword. I wasn't sure why that happened, and the battle was too fast-paced for me to worry much about it. Before long, however, I was able to get a hold on his suit from behind and restrict his movement.

Presently, the Hunter's reinforcements showered the ground before us with bombs, interrupting our fight with good old concussive blasts, and one of the newly arrived ships swooped down into the water. When I found my footing and looked around for the attacking ships, they were flying off with the black knight in tow. The silver blade still glittered in his grasp as he glared down at us from the open hatch, the only remnant I would ever see of my best friend. I knew that the anger pounding in my skull was fueled by sadness, but it was hot nonetheless.

"Lynchazel," Long said to me as the ships vacated the area, "Do you know anything of this new model?"

I shook my head, holding my hip where the tip of the Hunter's stolen sword had sliced right through my gillsuit. "No. Though, come to think of it, I saw an area in the Hellebes development labs where a new line of warrior Hellebes was being created. Perhaps he's one of those? And that sword . . . it belonged to my friend Kaen, who was killed by Strongs a month ago. It was a special blade from Mani, one of a kind, able to absorb any and all energy."

"I see. So your friend was targeted for his power just like you. Strongs . . ."

"I don't technically know it was him. But we're pretty sure."

Long sighed, stretching his back. "It would make sense for him to do something like this. This is exactly his style. And, despite what he said, this Hunter clearly intended to kill you. Come, let's see how the village has fared."

I winced as I recalled Greta's house getting blown to bits. I didn't want to look, but I had to know what became of her. It pained me to know that I abandoned her to save Long . . . but I already knew what I would find.

It was confirmed when we dug through the rubble and found Greta's body, crushed, splinters of board piercing her neck and chest. Her head lay at an unnatural angle, and there was no breath in her. "Oh, Greta," I whispered, feeling the same tears I had cried for Lentha, back when I beheld her broken body and watched her die a year ago. My longtime caretaker had been beaten to death by greedy bandits, all for the crime of having no money to give them. This woman, who had taken me in and fed me, had forfeited her life for lack of will to live. Just the same, it was the cruelty of that Hellebes assassin, the so-called Hunter, that had taken her life. What would her son think? I determined to tell him that she couldn't get away, despite the fact that I knew he already knew: She'd given up.

Fortunately, there were few other victims of the wanton destruction, as most of the Mei Shan residents were already in the bunkers. "Long," I asked. "How long will it be till they return? If I depart, will they leave this place alone?"

He shook his head. "I cannot say. We may have to move. I will try to find another safe place for the humans to stay."

I nodded, looking around at the beautiful vale that had been torn by military might for no purpose at all. Hopefully the League having found me would prove enough of a distraction. "Sylleo's soldiers should be here soon. I'll go back with them or the Red Horizon, whichever show up first."

"Then go in peace, lass. We will manage."

Sylleo's soldiers, a full squad of ship's, arrived within a few hours. They had orders to stay for a week if no more attacks came. When Zent's reinforcements arrived soon after, hailing from the ocean to the southeast, I informed the Ccamos forces that I would be returning with the rebels. The captain radioed Sylleo, making sure that was authorized, then grudgingly agreed, giving a terse farewell.

I made sure to find Hans and give him a sincere apology and a hug before I left. "Come on, miss Lyn," he complained, blinking away tears. "I'll be fine.

My mother was a fool, and that's why she died. I won't be like her."

I shook the boy's shoulders gently. "Don't say that, Hans. Don't disgrace your mother like that. Just do better. I . . . I have to go."

I gave Long an embrace as well before departing with the soldiers. "Don't be starting any fights, young'un," he chided. "Especially ones you can't win. I won't be around for much longer, so I'm counting on you to be the one to make things right, to change the world for the better."

"Thanks," I said. "I'll try. I have good help." With that, I boarded the rebel aircraft and we set off for HQ. Sylleo would have to wait to see me again, heartache or no.

Shelter Beneath the Sea

The Anier have been ruthless and cutthroat in all their dealings, and not only regionally. Their fingers are in all countries of the world, causing the turmoil we hear of, upsetting nations, pulling strings to remove kings… but it's what comes next that I truly dread. Yet I'm too dead inside for it to keep me up at night.

— From Lhinde's Vault

"Lyn, you made it!" Zent said in relief, coming in for one of those awkward hugs, ending in a heavy shoulder pat. "How did it go at the ninth city? The Board will want a big debriefing ASAP."

I groaned, glancing at the growing crowd of Red Horizon soldiers in the hallway who were eager to see if Mother Gaea really was back in the flesh. Vass and Getts were among them, and I knew it was a matter of time before that fat scientist showed his face as well. "Hopefully it can wait a few minutes."

"I'm afraid not, my lady," Vass said as he approached. "Along with many of the soldiers, the Board has begun to question whether your loyalty still lies with our forces at all. Ascertaining your motives in coming here is our top priority." He looked pointedly at Zent. "*Despite* Captain Zent's rash decision to send men to retrieve you from the ninth city, of all places."

"This isn't the place for this discussion," Zent said.

"Indeed," Getts said from directly behind his taller colleague, stroking his beard. "Chop-chop, now."

Stifling a growl, I followed behind the two directors, nodding at awkwardly-spectating soldiers who just wanted to see me. Some I recognized, others I did not. I only knew a few of them well, like Curtis the Gogi player. I didn't even have time to stop by the bathroom as they funneled me directly to the Board Room.

Inside, I found Dr. Dekla already waiting. I wondered briefly why he was here so punctually, before realizing that he was probably the one who'd insisted on the meeting in the first place. I looked around for Musha before remembering that he was no more. Skye, too, I expected to see, yet I knew he was not coming. His wounds had killed him in Ccamos. Perfect memory, and I still . . . wanted to forget things.

"Welcome, Heiress," Dekla said in his nasally voice. I thought it would be at least a few minutes till I'd want to punch him, but no. As soon as he opened his fat mouth . . .

"Well, I think that's everyone," Getts growled. "Our numbers seem to dwindle every day, aside from when idiots come stumbling back from the grave now and then."

"Thanks," Zent said with a stoic nod.

"You all want to know if I'm Sylleo's spy now, right?" I asked, raising my voice.

Four heads turned to look at me. *Check that out,* I thought, *Now they give me their attention.*

"Well, I'd think you would suspect Zent as well," I continued. "You seem to trust him."

"We've had a month to acclimate to his bad puns again," Getts said with a wave of his hand. He glanced at Zent. "No, seriously."

"Lyn," Zent said in a low voice. "Now is not the time . . ."

"Right," I said, plowing over his warning. "You want to know what happened. You all heard Zent's report, right?"

Two and a half nods.

"Sylleo let me go after we lost my friend Kaen, and he let Zent come back here to HQ to try to establish trust. How's that going, by the way?" I felt they owed me that much.

"We've been in communication with him back and forth," Vass said. "Nothing more. We don't have as much faith in him as Zent does, but he has made no moves against us and has given no demonstrably false information."

"That we know of," Dekla added.

Ignoring him, I went on, "Anyway, when I said I wanted to be able to protect people instead of just being used and fought over, Sylleo suggested that I go to the ninth city to meet the hidden Senator. You guys knew that already, right?"

Three nods. *Remember that, White. Before the Hunter's attack came out of nowhere, these men knew where I was.*

"And so I met him. He's still alive and kicking, and he agreed to train me as Sylleo requested. The two have a history together, apparently."

"What did he teach you?" Vass asked.

I crossed my arms with a defiant snort. "Why should I tell you?"

The tall man's jaw tightened. "You refuse to give us information?"

"I've given you plenty, and it's not your concern. You don't have anything to threaten me with. I could blow this entire place up before any of you could put a scratch on me."

Dr. Dekla seemed to flinch when I said that. *Heh. You bet he would, having seen my power in action in the testing chamber.* But he recovered quickly, blubber-laden face taking on that look of fascination. "So you've unlocked new genetic abilities, then?" Apparently seeing that this wasn't the time for such questions, he changed tack. "Then what about the rumors of non-Hellebes refugees hiding in the ninth city?"

I shrugged. "Nothing to report about that. The ninth senator told me about those same rumors. There used to be lots of Hellebes, and humans too, but the Senate decided to bomb the whole place and now it's . . . you know."

Dekla's eye began twitching. He saw I was hiding something.

"So let me get this straight, Lady Heiress," Vass said slowly. "You called for help, and after picking you up and bringing you back here for a meeting—"

"Questioning," I corrected him.

"*Questioning,* then . . . You refuse to work with us? If so, what is the point of this discussion at all?"

"You're the ones that insisted I give you a debriefing. There really wasn't much to tell. A new type of Hellebes soldier, suited in black and calling himself the Hunter, tried to kill me. Sylleo wants to partner with you guys, since you have valuable info about how to unlock the Hellebes minds and stuff—oh yes, I know—and how to bypass security in multiple sectors of the world. You also have the surprise factor. Zent has to have told you all this. All I want is to see some people finally start working together to get Lldsaor out of power and stop Strongs from obsessively trying to kill me."

I glanced down at my wrist console, scanning a notification that had come in just a moment ago. It was from Sylleo: *Tell your friends to watch out. An attack may be coming imminently.* "Hey, guys—"

Getts cut me off. "Now, Heiress, we are already working with Senator Sylleo, but it's just going to take some time."

"I want to know about this Hunter—" Vass began.

Zent held up a hand, looking at me. "What was that, Lyn?"

"Sylleo says to expect an attack imminently."

Vass looked at Getts, who looked at Dr. Dekla, who said, "Let's not jump to any conclusions at *his* word."

"No!" Zent roared. "Sound the alarm now! We won't take any chances." He began typing something in on his wrist console, and soon the alarms were blaring full-blast.

The other three Board members sprang into action. Getts gave me a withering glare as he stalked past, which seemed to say, *You'd better be right about this, girl.*

"Should we evacuate?" I shouted to Zent over the whooping sirens.

He shook his head. "Not just yet. It's all hands on deck right now, though."

Vass stayed in the Board room, poring over the screen on the central table, flipping through menus in the radar features. I came over to look at it as well, and he glanced up only briefly. "If this really is an attack," he said solemnly, "then there's no more doubt. We have a traitor in our midst."

You think? I didn't say it aloud, but the idea that we had a double agent was old news. Naturally, my mind would jump to Dr. Dekla or Getts, but well . . . Vass was being awfully pushy today as well. It could be anyone, except perhaps Zent. I trusted him.

Vass pinched the radar screen and zoomed out, revealing a blue gradient surrounding our facility, red hostiles encroaching at the edge. With a curse, he flicked his wrist up to his mouth and barked out a few commands. Then, over the intercom, he said, "Hostile forces confirmed on the western front. Twenty klicks out and fast approaching."

On another portion of the large screen, I saw three-dimensional maps of our base with lights representing ships being deployed defensively from the main airlock. We had four guns stationed on each side of the base as well, and a couple up top. Most fired on automatic, but I didn't know how well their targeting systems worked against incoming missiles.

"What do you want me to do, Director?" I asked.

"Get ready to evacuate," he said seriously. "This may get messy."

α   Chapter 48   α

Implosion

Am I a monster? Am I . . . the monster?
— From Lhinde's Vault

I defied Vass' command, instead hurrying to the base's western lookout, where a few other rebels watched, zipping up their suits and checking their weapons. "Get ready to evac, guys," I called.

I briefly watched the underwater horizon, seeing if I could spot any enemy vehicles, but all I could see were streams of bubbles and the green glow of Geoelectric engines as our own forces took off to meet them or stand by defensively. I could only guess who had sent the armada, but . . . the real question was who had given out our location? Our enemy had not stumbled upon such information. Even if they'd tortured Kaen before killing him, he couldn't have given them anything substantial to go on if he understood neither the Hellebes language nor their coordinate system.

So I went in search of my first suspect, serenaded by a chorus of alarms as I ran. I tried to pretend it was hypnotic and soothing, rather than abrasive. I traced my inner map and soon ended up at Dekla's office. Nobody. I proceeded down two floors, entering the high energy labs. The door was locked, of course, but I broke in anyway after shearing off the lock with a thermal blast. I opened the door as quietly as I could and stepped inside, running the layout through my mind. No sign of the giant yet, though I did see some papers strewn about in the first lab.

Then the biologist himself shuffled back through one of the doorways in a hurry, stopping short as he saw me. His beady eyes narrowed even further. "What do you want? If you've come for a few more experiments, I'm afraid you'll have to wait. We're in emergency mode, thanks to you." He tried to push past me, but I blocked his way.

"What's the hurry?" I asked him. "What is that you're taking with you?"

"With me? I'm not going anywhere until we have to evacuate."

"Uh-huh. Sure. Listen, can you take me with you?"

"Why, looking to escape your doom in Haven?" His eyes widened as soon as he said it, but he tried to blink it off.

I smiled knowingly. "So you were working for Strongs the whole time."

"Strongs? I-I don't know what you're talking about. Now move. I have places to be!"

He tried once more to push me aside, but I'd grabbed hold of the doorway and wouldn't be budged. The veins on my left arm rippled, layered muscles scrunching up as I gripped tighter. With my right hand, I wrenched him back, throwing the sea lion onto the floor. His weight was immense, but now that I could bench a thousand kilos with Geokinesis . . .

He gasped in pain as his skull rang off the metal tiling. "You insolent b—"

"Don't try to fight me, Dekla," I said in my harshest possible tone. "How long were you working for Strongs?"

"I wasn't! I never had anything to do with him, I swear!" Suddenly, his voice was a pitiful whimper, all hint of superiority gone.

"Well, then—" An explosion rocked the base, causing the floor to shudder and the walls to vibrate.

"Come on, we need to evacuate!" he whined, struggling to get up.

I vacillated, torn for a moment. With a growl, I turned and sprinted for the stairs. I needed to see what was going on. If the base's structural integrity was compromised, we all had to evacuate ASAP. Even as I ran, Zent called my computer.

"Lyn, where are you? We need to go now!"

"Is it going to blow?"

"It's not certain yet. Only that one missile got through, but they've already taken out multiple of our vanguard subs. You're number one priority, though, or have you forgotten?"

I sighed through my teeth, taking the stairs landing by landing. One bound per corner. He was right, too. What was I doing, chasing down this lousy traitor . . . *Speaking of, where did he get to?* "Zent, Dekla is a traitor. I confirmed it."

"What? You found where he was hiding?"

"Yep. But—he's gotten away already."

"Forget him."

In a moment, I reached the dock where Zent was waiting. I nearly lost my footing as the entire dock lurched beneath another missile explosion. No cracks appeared across the long glass windows, however, so that was a good sign. Far outside, I could see our ships shooting down incoming torpedoes and exchanging fire with enemy craft, who had made it to our proximity.

"Come on, Lyn," he said, waving toward the waiting omnicraft as he climbed in.

I wasted no time in following him. I wanted to stay, but . . . seeing the barrage of missiles swarming about us, I was relieved to be getting out. But what about Hodge? Curtis? What about that slimy, treacherous Dekla?

"Zent," I said as we waited in the airlock, "You heard what I said about Dekla. I don't know what he's planning to do now, but I'm certain it was him that gave away our coordinates. And probably a bunch of other information already."

"You got a confession out of him?"

I started to answer, and then amended my response. "Not exactly. But his reaction made it clear."

"That's not good enough. But I believe you, Lyn. All right, you take the guns." The thick metal doors opened vertically, and Zent thrust the omnicraft into full acceleration, zipping out and downward, away from the conflict. A few enemy beams shot after us as we exited, but none connected. I wasn't sure how strong this machine's shields were, but I knew Zent was a good enough pilot to dodge most enemy fire.

For my part, I sighted through the scope of our top-mounted gun, using the monitor and steering mechanism equipped in the passenger seat. These things were fun to use, but I didn't exactly have much experience with mounted weaponry.

Won't stop me from trying.

The battle around us was mostly chaos, but I used the AI-assisted sights to easily determine which ships belonged to us and attempt to pick them off. The artificial intelligence could assist with that too, but I didn't trust it any more than my own aim. Our batteries had enough charge for up to twenty blasts, so I tried to conserve them. I let off a couple of shots only when Zent took us within good range of an opposing ship and I could gauge the velocities of both ships. When he matched one speed for speed, I was able to pick it off with three shots, two to wear down the shield and one more to detonate the engines.

Watching the explosion—more an implosion—of that watercraft sent a deep chill through me. There was a flash of brilliant green as the Geothermic battery detonated, and a vortex of bubbles erupted from the hull as the crushing force of a high-pressure ocean met with the battery's explosive energy. Ripped and crushed shrapnel curled away from the wreckage, and a smeary trail of red was the only indication that it had been piloted by a Hellebes.

"Nice shooting," Zent said.

"Yeah. Not, uh, completely used to that. Too bad they keep coming." I swiveled the sights back toward the base, seeing that the glass-and-steel structure was holding for now. "Man, that's quite the work of architecture if it can withstand all that in this high pressure."

"Oh yes," Zent said with a hint of pride. "Dr. Rissius was a true genius. He designed it with the help of a few other engineers, and we built it as we got the resources."

I wondered if my father was in on it as well. But I didn't voice this question, as our omnicraft was hit by an enemy beam. Zent cursed, pulling into a complex loop that made my stomach turn and threw off my aiming.

"There are just too many of them," he said. "The base's shields are under fifty percent, and only more ships keep coming." He pressed a button on the computer. "Vass! What's the status? This says shields are at forty-six percent."

"Correct. We can't hold out for much longer. Should I order the full evacuation?"

"Yes."

A pause. "Very well."

No sooner had Vass gotten off the line than another wave of missiles streaked toward the base. Where did they get all these weapon-loaded assault ships? At least three of the missiles struck the base as the last of the shield blinked out, and Zent's display flashed with a critical error from the station.

"Okay, time to leave," he said, taking us up and away from the base. Looking back through my sights, I beheld a terrible sight: The entire station quivered and suddenly *snapped* like a balloon. It compressed inwardly from top to bottom like a box being folded up, ripping up the foundation and crushing the upper canopy to meet it. Green light flowered from it, and a huge shockwave blew aside nearby vessels, rushing out to meet us.

I could only stare numbly at it. Home of over one hundred Red Horizon soldiers. A large chunk of them were already deployed, but most wouldn't make it, and I doubted any were able to safely evacuate yet. No one could have predicted the shield would give way so soon.

And great auroras . . . the shockwave really was going to catch up to us. "Uh, a little faster?" I suggested.

"Going as fast as she'll let me," he replied. "But we'll be all right. The force will die down the farther out it gets. It would have to be on the tectonic level to cause a real tsunami effect."

I could only hope he was right. "And what about the others out there fighting?"

"Looks like the attacking forces are retreating, now that their mission was accomplished. Plus, nobody wants to get caught in that blast. The remaining men will rendezvous at Plank Isle."

That was an island south of here, I recalled, equipped with a smaller base which the Red Horizon had converted from an abandoned military outpost. I typed out a message to Sylleo upon realizing I had four missed ones from him. Another was from Vass. *Goodbye, Lynchazel,* it read. *Keep fighting.*

I hung my head, thinking about all the lives lost today. He must have sent it as soon as the shield gave out. Surely some had gotten to safety? Why hadn't he called the evac sooner? Sylleo's words rang in my head, telling me that the Hellebes were mere worker bees, drones to be used, tools of society . . . but I had met them. Laughed with them. Lost Gogi games to them. I knew better.

No sooner had those thoughts sprung to mind than Sylleo called me. "Lyn? Are you safe?"

Oops. Guess I forgot to respond to him. "Yes, I'm safe. Zent is taking me to an island base, where we'll meet up with any Red Horizon survivors."

"So your entire base was destroyed?"

"Yes."

"I see. I am sorry to hear that. Tell Zent as well. I'll send men to pick you up and bring you to Ccamos. It will be safer. You don't know who your spy was, do you?"

"I do," I replied. "It was our biologist, Dr. Dekla. He was working for Strongs all that time. Probably sending him all kinds of data. He even slipped up and asked if I wanted to escape to Haven with him."

Zent glanced at me with a raised eyebrow.

"Then assume the island base is compromised as well," said Sylleo. "Don't take any chances." He left the line, and I relayed his words of caution to Zent.

The old captain nodded. "He certainly has a point. First, I need to see if Vass or Getts are still alive."

"There's no way Vass is. Getts . . . maybe. But Sylleo could probably house all our refugees and put them to work in his city, right?"

Zent grimaced. "Not going to lie . . . That feels way too much like giving in, but you might be right. What's the point in pride if it gets all your friends killed?" He glanced over at me. "All those men in that base . . . they were my friends. I knew every one of them, even the newbies. A lot of them I helped recruit over the years. Each time my friends die on missions, it's hard. But that . . . that was fifteen years. Almost half my life."

I gulped, trying to quell my rising nausea. The closest I could come to understanding his sorrow was the feeling I'd had when Nytaea got attacked by the Hellebes ships. "I'm sorry, Zent. I wish this could have been avoided."

Within a few more minutes, we arrived at Plank Isle and entered an underwater bay. A smart idea, hiding the bay from the eyes of satellites and aircraft. We surfaced in the docking bay and got out, allowing the mechanical arm to slot the ship for us. From here, we went through a set of doors into a main lobby. Much like the underground shelter back in the Craglands, I could see the entire layout of the base just from here. But it was large enough to house all the Red Horizon men we had left, and I was certain it was stocked with enough weapons and rations to go around.

Slowly, more rebel soldiers showed up, looking as bedraggled as I felt. Zent met each one with a shake of hands and a clap on the shoulder. The eventual count was thirty-one persons, including myself. Neither Vass nor Getts ever showed up or responded when called. Addressing everyone, Zent said, "Men, thank you all for your participation in defending the base. I apologize for what happened. That was a lack of foresight on our part. We knew for a while now that a traitor existed among us, one with access to a lot of sensitive information, yet I failed to act on that knowledge before it was too late. But we do have the Mother back. With the help of our ally Sylleo, we can continue to make strides toward the freedom of the Hellebes race."

A weak cheer rose from the Hellebes gathered in the lobby, though a few remained quiet in the face of what had happened. It was hard to be upbeat at a time like this.

"You've probably heard of this Hunter by now," Zent continued. "We can't be sure, but he was probably involved in the attack earlier, and he won't stop there. He is an assassin, sent presumably by Senator Strongs, with a mission to kill Lyn, and he won't stop until he does. So I want each of you to be on the lookout and ready to defend her at all costs. We can't give the enemy what he wants."

But how much will we give up before there's nothing left for them to take? I asked in my head. *When is a cost too high?*

α Chapter 49 α

Promises

I have heard of this religion that worships me. Supposedly, the Anier did not start it, but that seems impossible given their systematic culling of humans from the earth. I suppose I can congratulate them on being the first proper Hellebes religion; I just wish they had a different goddess. If ever I do accept their worship, then that would be proof that my vengeance against the Anier has been successfully undermined.

— From Lhinde's Vault

"White, you've got to have more than that."

"I'm trying," she whined, sparing me a small glare as she rummaged through my memories, which manifested as assorted scraps of reality, images that faded, even mere audio clips recorded by my brain over my lifespan. "You realize you can do this anytime now, right?"

"And I haven't had a chance," I said, emphasizing each word. We were searching the obscure corners of my memory and recollected details for anything that could help me in my struggle against the Hunter.

Then my mother appeared. One moment she was not there, and then she was, materializing in my dream for the first time in a while. She seemed to glide from the air to land at my side, white dress fluttering in a nonexistent breeze. "Hello, dear one."

"Mother! Where have you been?" I paused what I was doing to turn and hug her tall frame. As always, physical touch was not in this imagined realm what it was in the corporeal world . . . because, of course, she wasn't really there.

"As I explained, daughter, I have tried to stay away. Never mind that this conscious of mine you see is only assembled by your own mind from my memories."

"No, that's not right," I said slowly. "You . . . you think and act as your own self!"

"I know. But again, that is only the personality taken from my memory pool—which I have kept hidden from you for security reasons. Already you feel her."

I paused, listening, and shuddered. "I do. Very well, then; what can you offer?"

"Hope. Lynchazel, listen very carefully, for I may never show myself to you like this again, though I will try. You must return to my Vault in Haccolces and retrieve my security key to unlock my data. It is more important to you now than safety from Lhinde."

White nodded slowly from my other side. "She's right, Lyn. You could use those memories. Now git, shoo!"

⁂

I awoke from my nap with a jerk. It took me a few moments to recall where I was, but thanks to my Hellebes mind, I could recall my dreams perfectly now. I'd lain down for a nap . . . yes, I conversed with my mother's dream phantom, and now I was back in a cramped bunk in the Plank Isle base. With a groan, I rose from my bunk and redid my ponytail. One, two, three hair ties and it was good.

I need to find Zent.

The captain was conferring with a few other officers in the old director's room. When I walked in, they got quiet.

"Lyn, glad you're up," Zent greeted me. "We were just discussing how to respond to Sylleo."

I took one of the vacant seats around the hard steel table. "Why, what did he say?"

"He made a proposition. He offered to take us in and incorporate the Red Horizon into Ccamos as a military team, thus granting us safety from the rest of the Senate. He also promised to help us attain the goal of freeing all Hellebes."

My eyebrows shot up. "And? In return?"

"He said all he asks is one personal favor from you. Which leads me to think he's up to something. He wants to capture you, experiment on you, or perhaps demand something that only the Mother is capable of. He said he must speak to you about it, however, and only in person."

I frowned. In person? This didn't sound very promising. I mean, the deal sounded great, but . . . why all this formality? It didn't sit right with me. *A personal favor . . .* Oh, great auroras, it couldn't possibly be . . .

I cleared my throat. "I'll go. Are his soldiers here?"

"They just arrived, I believe," Zent said. "You're sure about this?"

A mere ten minutes later, I was being shipped off to meet Sylleo once more. Just me and a contingent of four rebel soldiers. I almost wished they were a bit more talkative, as it was a long flight back to Ccamos. Sylleo's men and the Red Horizon soldiers seemed to hold an uncomfortable standoff the entire ride, outdoing one another in awkwardness like some kind of sport. I didn't want to think of Sylleo and what his request might be. Worst of all, could I be walking into a trap? I knew that line of thinking didn't make much sense, given the circumstances under which I'd met him. He could have done whatever he wanted with me and my friends at any point.

Frankly, I missed Sylleo already. I didn't know if I could ever return his unsettling affection for me, but I could at least call him a friend. An ally. He was the only one on the Gaean Senate who showed actual human emotions— good ones, anyway. And he was tall, handsome, and even gentlemanly when he wanted to be. Not that those were any consideration.

When we finally arrived, I shook awake to realize I'd dozed off again in the aircraft. I must have really exhausted myself during the past day. Fighting the Hunter, all the travel, and then a high-stress evacuation procedure had left me drained. Or perhaps I was simply recovering from the month-long training I'd undergone with former Senator Long.

I don't know, Lyn, that vacation should have been relaxing as all-get-out.

Shut up, White.

We landed at the executive airport in Ccamos, whence the soldiers quickly shipped me off to see Sylleo. They left me at the doors to his manse and departed, bowing to Sylleo, who himself stood at the door to greet me. The rebel and Ccamos soldiers resumed their vigil of awkwardness.

"Come in, Lyn," Sylleo said cordially.

"Thank you, sir," I replied, stepping in as he held the door for me. An unexplainable relief flooded me at his greeting, perhaps because it seemed a positive sign that things remained as they'd been. The relief itself annoyed me, and I felt a tinge of heat in my ears, a moistening in my armpits. What was *wrong* with me? I distracted myself by searching the entryway for Margill the butler, but I didn't see him.

"Margill is busy with dinner preparations," he said, as though reading my mind.

I nodded. "Dinner preparations. That does sound pretty good." My stomach was already complaining about having eaten nothing but one round of rations for the day.

"If you need to freshen up, one of the servants can show you to the nearest bathroom. I'll have a change of clothes brought to you as well, and you can feel free to take a nap if you need it. You look exhausted. Dinner will be served at six o'clock."

"Um . . . thank you," I said awkwardly, unsure of how to respond. Even for buttering me up, this was going a bit far, especially considering that I already had rooms back at the main mansion. "But . . . are you sure we have time to waste like this?"

"It's an important occasion." Sylleo didn't offer much more in explanation, and seemed to be in no hurry to talk further about the situation with the Red Horizon and the Senate. What was going through his head right now?

I did as he suggested, though. He was too powerful an ally to offend right now. The servants prepared a hot bath and I had the best soak I'd had in . . . well, a long while. Swimming in the crater lake in Mei Shan didn't quite count. Despite my inhibitions and anxiety, the warm water, bubbles and relaxing scents gave my muscles a good lesson in relaxation.

After the bath came a shock I should have been expecting, but somehow wasn't. Let's just say the servants who came to bring me my dress and do my hair were not male Hellebes.

They were women. Hellebes women.

"Hello, Mother Gaea," said the slightly shorter one, blonde and dressed in a skirt and jacket that fit her just a hair too snugly. Or was it the Hellebes muscle-toning that made it appear so?

I was far too busy gaping to tell. "Are you . . . you're—um . . . who are you?" I asked, tripping over my words, the last one coming out high as a shrew.

The female servant stifled a laugh that seemed amused and embarrassed. Her companion, who stood a few inches taller than me with short black hair and a prominent jaw—though not at all ugly—took over: "We represent the female staff here at the manse. We're quite rare, I know, but you could say that not all Hellebes from the biomanufactories turn out male. The Senate finds places for us to serve."

She said it with a straight face, yet my mind immediately jumped to specific ways that would make the most obvious sense. *I'll bet most of them end up in Vladimir's house. Or palace, or whatever it is.* Feeling far too self-conscious, I said, "I assume you're here to dress me and make me look pretty?" That was how princesses were treated back in Nytaea, and they looked too much like handmaidens for me to help the comment.

The blonde-haired woman looked to her partner with a shrug. "Yes? That is the idea."

The taller attendant unrolled the towel she was holding and held it up for me to see. "Feeling shy, My Lady?" She raised it up over both their heads. It was a massive, fuzzy towel.

I instinctively crossed my arms over my chest. "No."

The woman made no move to lower the towel. After a moment's hesitation, I sighed and got out of the tub. I was starting to feel like a child, and besides, I'd left my modesty on Mani.

As they helped me into a lovely sky-blue dress and brushed my hair, they introduced themselves. The blonde was Iselda, while her taller companion was Taressa. They were the only female Hellebes in Sylleo's employ, but they made no mention of their relationship to him. I wasn't that stupid, but I didn't press. What did I care if he had concubines or wives he hadn't told me about? Back on Mani, polygamy was an everyday thing.

Lyn . . .

I mean . . . maybe it bothered me a little. But these two seemed like pretty genuine folk as Hellebes servants went. Iselda even mentioned that Margill was like a father to them, which was the most touching thing I'd ever heard from a Hellebes.

Iselda and Taressa offered me a guest room where I could take a quick nap, but I politely refused. There wasn't a chance on Gaea I'd be able to sleep right now.

Finally, I sat down to a fancy meal across a giant table from Sylleo, who was dressed sharply in a red suit with a ruffled white collar and long sleeves. It had an air of antiquity to it. "Lyn," he said politely as I entered, gesturing at the chair opposite him. Margill pulled it out for me to sit and retreated for the time being. "Thank you for joining me."

I gulped and nodded, reaching up to fiddle with Taressa's hair clip that held my hair up in two folds, with twin sweeping strands hanging just below my ears. They'd assured me it was a good idea. I wasn't concerned with how I looked or anything, just . . . this felt like a royal date back at the Nytaean Palace. I didn't want to look slobbish or something. Supposedly Margill himself had tailored the blue dress, which almost didn't surprise me. It fit impressively well and wasn't awfully gaudy.

The first course of food was some manner of battered and fried shellfish, which seemed odd to me before I tried it. I pretended to be ladylike as I wolfed the gooey meat down, but . . . it was hard to. This man had some seriously good cooks. Margill and the other servants brought in more courses as we went, taking plates that weren't even half eaten. My eyes followed each one longingly as it departed for the void. It was like they were only letting me taste-test the food, not actually eat. . . . What was wrong with these servants?

We made small-talk as we ate, but Sylleo seemed a bit extra fidgety, like there was something he really wanted to talk about but just hadn't felt it was the right time yet.

So I prompted him: "Sylleo, what was it you wanted to discuss tonight?"

He coughed, seeming to almost choke. "Oh. Well, I—I thought we could finish our dinner first."

"Then why is it just the two of us?"

Sylleo took a breath, held it for a couple seconds, and then slowly let it back out. "Very well, it's like this: You and your Red Horizon allies have goals. I can help you reach those goals, if it is in my power to do so, and I can shelter the Red Horizon as well. I will give you as much freedom as you like, and whatever resources I have, to help you achieve your dreams here on Gaea."

"And in return?"

"In return, I ask that you marry me."

There it was. Bam. The breath he let out at the end indicated it had all been a pre-prepared string, more of a miniature rant than a proposal. I'd been hoping that wouldn't be it, but what else was he going to ask for? My autograph? My shoe size? I opened my mouth to speak, but the tall Senator held up a hand.

"I know it's a big thing to ask, but hear me out. I had an entire month to think about this, while the Senate pressured me. I care for you and feel attracted to you in ways I thought I may never feel again, but there are also political reasons I believe it would benefit Ccamos and the world at large. It would be a bond not easily broken. The Senate would take both of us more seriously, and the Hellebes could see that you are a human, not some goddess to be worshipped."

He must have stolen that last line from me. I remained silent, but only with effort. My lips were especially hard to stop from quivering and twitching in anger. I didn't want to respond rashly, because . . . I knew I might have to make a difficult decision here. He wasn't just proposing; he was offering an ultimatum. Despite his calculatedly pleasant words, I knew he was taking this seriously. "I . . ." I swallowed and tried again. *Don't quiver, voice. Don't quiver.* "I don't know quite what to say, Sylleo."

"That's quite all right. I understand it's a lot. I wouldn't want to put you in a tight spot where you can't—"

This time, I couldn't hold it in. "Don't lie to me!" I shouted, standing up and screeching my chair back. "This was all about forcing my answer. You planned this whole conversation, and you're not going to take no for an answer."

Whoops. There it was on the table.

Now it was Sylleo's turn to pretend calmness. "Please sit back down, my lady," he said quietly, gesturing at my seat.

My lady. With a flare of my nostrils, I did as commanded and gathered my skirts, pulling my chair back in as I resumed my seat. "I'm sorry. But really, if you want me to be your wife, the least you could do is be honest with me. Maybe tell me about your mini-harem in advance, or the way you program your entire population of happy people." I prepped a hand gesture and opened my mouth for more ranting, but I judiciously—miraculously— cut off before I could dig myself too deep a hole. If my lips had quivered before, now my whole jaw felt like it was experiencing a magnitude seven.

Calm down, Lyn. Keep it together. Don't ruin this.

Sylleo stared into my eyes, saying nothing for a moment. "Very well. Let us be honest. Many Senators would like to have you, but most of them not as a bride—you would only be added to their harem. In my case, I promise to treat you very well, and to protect you. It's not a bad deal. You can't keep running with the rebels anymore. Most of the Senate voted to destroy the Red Horizon base. Did you know that? Strongs convinced them that you weren't there, and got them to go along with him. Lldsaor was the one who gave the order. And if you turn down my offer, I cannot guarantee your friends' safety, because quite frankly, you matter far more to me than they."

So in other words . . . that's a threat. Now he was being a little more honest. He had bargaining chips, lots of them. He had lost the emotional battle, and now he would win the reasoning battle. I knew what Kaen would say if he were here, but . . . he wasn't. He was gone. The one man I could ever say I loved, yet I hadn't gotten the chance to do so. Now I had the chance to trade my love for a contract—in exchange for people's lives. Staring down at the varnished wood tabletop, I thought of Rhidea and Mydia and what their advice would be. I thought of all the things I'd do to make it back home to them, and especially to stop the invasion of their world. I thought of my old friends at the Nytaean orphanage, and what I would do to protect them if I could go back and do it all over again. I fought with my emotions, trying to wrestle them into submission. If I could have married a king to save my friends and build them a future . . . would I have? Would I now?

Yes. Yes, I would.

"All right, I'll do it," I said, looking up into Sylleo's eyes. I couldn't believe what I was saying, but I was saying it anyway. "I'll marry you. But on one condition."

He eyed me, waiting.

"A favor."

α Chapter 50 α

To Break a Limb

I can't let my hatred fall. Not for me, or so I insist to myself . . . No, but I am the last who can feel this seething hatred in my chest, who can remember and avenge humanity. This isn't for me: This is for the countless millions sacrificed for the new world order.

— From Lhinde's Vault

So there we were, readying to go out on another mission. This time, the Red Horizon and Ccamos military would be working together. Officially, it was just the Red Horizon. And me.

Sol dripped steadily beyond the horizon as we approached Haccolces. I rode with a squad of five rebel soldiers, all outfitted in gillsuits and traveling in a Red Horizon (that is to say, stolen) aircraft. It was an old design, operating on a propeller system, though it still trailed green smoke from the engines.

Five other teams were bound for the same destination, but Sylleo's soldiers should be waiting there already. They would be our key to success.

"How close are we?" I asked Captain Balfour of the Red Horizon, our squad leader.

He turned his head, shoulder-length brown hair sweeping with it. "Five minutes. Better get ready, men." He eyed me, as though challenging me to object, but I wasn't about to split hairs on semantics.

Se-man-tics, White chuckled in my head. *Oh, you've gotten funny, Lyn.*

Curtis, who was one of my squad mates this time, looked over at me. "So, you excited to be getting married?"

I glared at him. "Take a guess."

He shrugged. "I wouldn't know. Is it something people normally get excited for?"

"Yeah. Normally." I was nervous, but I didn't think that qualified as 'excited.' Curtis was probably just trying to get under my skin before the mission. I could think with a clear head, even on the fly. Just . . . just had to breathe. *Only another mission.* It must be fun to see a girl squirm. What had I been doing for a month now? Learning to breathe.

I could breathe.

We approached Haccolces from a low altitude, nearly level with the tall south gate, skimming the topography of the surrounding land. Balfour radioed in to the other squads, and I responded through my earpiece when Zent called my name.

A ship darted in from our right and opened fire on us, letting loose a chain of three-round bursts. Balfour cursed and took us into a barrel roll, shortly before executing a nosedive dodge maneuver that nearly took us straight into the ground. "Easy," I growled. How did that thing get so close without our instruments picking it up?

"Sorry, Heiress. Hang on to your seats."

I had to admit, he wasn't a bad pilot. This enemy, though . . . I saw him circling, coming back in for us. His flying was tight and skillful, not to mention familiar. "That might be the Hunter," I said, breath quickening. I'd half expected him to show up out of nowhere like this, but how had he picked out my exact ship? Could it be that he could track my signature? Did it mean the enemy was on to our whole assault force? Including Sylleo's troops? Strongs must have had men staking out Haccolces just in case, because there was no traitor around to leak our intel anymore. But we couldn't know for certain.

"Uh, he says, 'This is the Hunter. Hand over the Mother immediately,'" Balfour relayed, not looking away from his controls.

Yeah, it was him. And somehow, he was a better pilot than Balfour, because he was blocking us off from our goal with one ship. Balfour took us into the surrounding hills and valleys, trying to find cover, but the Hunter only pursued and resumed fire.

I couldn't help but wonder why he would even bother to make demands if he intended to kill me anyway. I was certain that this Hunter would watch us plummet to our deaths and not blink. Balfour tried to dodge the fire, but we took a hit to our shields before he was able to duck around one of the hills. The Hunter closed in even further in pursuit.

"Zent? Kinneson?" Balfour asked in a hurry. "A little help here?"

"Already on our way," Zent said.

We took another hit to the shields, triggering an alarm. "Get ready to bail," Balfour warned, "Because we're not going to make it until they arrive."

"Let's go, then," I said. "I can take out his ship. Trust me, I've done it once."

I wasn't one hundred percent confident, but I didn't mention that.

In response, Balfour swerved around the next hill, braked like mad, and shouted, "Go!" He released the canopy, and we all jumped out, falling for a second before slamming into the grassy hillside. No parachutes necessary, only Geokinetic strengthening and a roll to break our heavy fall. As soon as I was on my feet, I turned, drawing all the planetary energy I could, and unleashed a beam of destruction into the sky, tendrils of blazing light tracking the Hunter's ship.

In anticipation of this, the black-suited figure did not attempt to dodge but instead ejected from his own ship, falling to land a hundred paces away from us. *He remembers our last encounter.* "You are mine," he said through that harsh voice filter. Or was that just his natural, upbeat voice? He dashed up the hill toward us, holding the silver sword of Mani—my *friend's* sword—in front of him to absorb my companions' blaster fire. The very sight of the Heart of Mani drew hot anger from deep in my chest, burning with raw emotion. The very demon blade that had been Kaen's demise . . .

When my squad mates realized the impotence of their blaster barrage, they turned to flee but were two late. I tried to warn them, but the Hunter was faster. He took two of them out in the blink of an eye with lunging sweeps of the sword, slicing right through gillsuit, flesh and bone and leaving behind bloody corpses.

He flicked the blade one more time, flinging threads of blood as he turned on me.

"Get back!" I shouted to my two remaining companions, stamping my foot onto the ground to unleash a massive Geokinetic quake that shattered the hillside underneath the Hunter. He was caught for only a moment before dashing at me, sword held ready, ignoring my two remaining companions.

Balfour uttered a short complaint to the effect that it was their job to keep me safe, but I ignored him. I had trained for a whole month to be able to protect people, and already I was failing. I would not let others die on my behalf.

As the Hunter closed in, feet a blur of speed, I breathed in, feeling Gaea's blood pulse through me, the same energy I'd just spent to deflagrate my enemy's ship. It roared like flames, seethed like magma, waiting to be released. I let out my breath, and with the same outward motion I cocked one foot and spun, dropping to one hand as I kicked out the Hunter's feet. I kept moving, closing in further as he caught his balance with catlike reflexes. I grabbed for his wrist, attempting to twist the sword from his grasp, but the Hunter was too quick, slipping out of my reach. In a split second, we were apart again, and I managed to get out without a scratch. I had to separate him from that sword, though, because it alone posed a threat to me and my squad.

When he jumped back again, I sent a spiral of stone from the ground to trap his feet, moving my limbs as I did. The motions always seemed to help me focus. He dodged my attack, but I didn't let up, growing only more aggressive with my attempts. *Seize him! Bind him!* I commanded the earth, much like a Manese mage would exercise her Authority. All I managed to do was clip one of his legs as he dodged again, despite my efforts. He was *fast.*

The Hunter threw out Geokinetic attacks in response as soon as I let up, but only as distractions so that he could close in with his sword again. He was *highly* intent on bisecting me. Breathing in, I used his own ferocity to my advantage by aiming a lightning kick where I knew his sword would be in a split second.

It worked. The silver blade flashed in the sunlight as it whirled out of his grasp. His left hand snaked out to grab it, but I shot back with my same foot—a heel kick that nearly clipped his chin—forcing him back half a step. We exchanged blows for a few more seconds until I had him pinned against the ground, left arm in a submission. He was a good ten feet from the silver blade, with no way to grab it. My breathing had risen to a pant, but Long's training was the only reason I'd gotten the better of him, focusing my body and enhancing my Geokinetic control.

"Just give up," I growled. "What is your obsession with killing me? How did you even find me?"

"Like I'd tell you," he scoffed. Up close, I could better make out his voice through the black mask's grating filter: Deep and crackly, not all too different from Lldsaor's but lacking his command. His tone implied a single-minded fixation on the hunt. A chill ran down my spine as I realized that he had likely been created for only one thing—to track and slay me like a wild animal. What kind of life was that?

I pulled tighter on the Hunter's arm, but he only chuckled hollowly.

"Fine, then," I said in frustration. "Balfour, want to do the honors?"

Before Balfour could take his aim, the black-armored assassin suddenly jerked his entire body away from me, snapping his own arm in my hold with a loud crack. In shock, I slackened my grip and he threw me off. Was he modified to not feel pain? Calling in his ship—no, another, as I'd destroyed his—the Hunter reached out his off hand and summoned the sword like a recalled hawk. Then he leaped upward, using the blade itself to pull his body in through the ship's open door as it flew overhead.

"He just . . ." Balfour made a snapping motion with his hands.

"Yep," I said with a sigh. "But I have a feeling I'll see him again. Not to mention . . . Zent? Where are you?"

"Just arriving. Hang tight." A moment later, his ship swung into view along with Captain Kinneson's, and they swooped low to pick us up before racing back to Haccolces. "I take it he got away again before you could finish him?" Zent asked, apparently taking for granted my ability to beat him in a fight.

"Yes . . . because of my stupidity," I grumbled, taking an empty seat in the fast-moving vehicle. I rolled my shoulder with a grimace. "I had him pinned, and he broke his own arm to escape. But I have this feeling they'll find a way to patch him up in record time. He might even have enhanced healing abilities. He's no normal Hellebes." *I wonder how many of these Hunters they have by now.*

"Can't say. But we have to act fast, before Strongs can warn Haccolces of our presence."

"He doesn't know about our plans, though," I reminded him. "The Hunter couldn't have known about Sylleo's men waiting in the city . . . unless that's how he knew to come after me. I didn't even think of that."

"Too late to second-guess ourselves," said Zent. "Sylleo knows what he's doing, and I'm confident in his men's ability to turn the odds in our favor."

"As long as things don't go awry like last time," I said, feeling a cold lump in my throat. Oh, please, please . . . not like that again. I couldn't be certain which was worse: Seeing my longtime friend get hacked apart by Strongs' soldiers . . . or coming to my senses back in the lab after my powers awakened, realizing I'd annihilated my own comrades. Both were nightmares I never wished to repeat. Then there was Mandrie . . . And now I'd just let two more men die in my name. Soldiers who were there to support and protect me. When was this going to end? When could I be free of this guilt?

I knew the answer to that question. A quiet voice whispered it in the back of my head: *Never.*

Never, echoed Lhinde, almost a cackle. *Never.*

α Chapter 51 α

A Key

A new Anier joined a few years back, named Vladimir, and most of the others are also younger than Lldsaor. Lldsaor is the worst of them. He is the mastermind, a mentor to tyrants. Soon, they shall put their plan in effect to immortalize themselves through science. I am not privy to all the details— in fact, I mostly have guesses—but it will mark a new age. No longer will man rule over man, but meta-men over biomachina. Had mankind known that the alternative to their manifold oppressions would look like this— extinction and replacement—would they have done something to stop it? Could they?

— From Lhinde's Vault

Sylleo's operatives let us in at the city gate, pretending to scan our ship briefly, before waving us on. From there, we rode the trams deep into Haccolces, eventually arriving at the old sector where the labs were kept. I couldn't say what my mother's memory data would reveal, but what fascinated me most was the hideous creature they were using in place of her. The . . . Zeta Beast? Of course, I could just ask Sylleo, but he would be too busy planning that trip he said the ancients used to take shortly after getting married—a honeymoon, he called it? I wondered if that was named after Luna. She was, after all, a bit more honey-colored than the silver Mani.

We managed to get all the way inside the labs without setting off alarms or having rockets shot at us, so that was a good sign. Everything inside was just as I remembered, with dated computers and laboratory equipment everywhere, a large portion of it unused. To my understanding, the majority of these above-ground labs served as a cover for what went on underneath.

As we neared the subterranean lab, my mother's voice sounded in my head: *Where are you . . .? Why have you come back here, Lyn?*

What do you mean? You told me to come here.

Yes. Yes, I did. But . . . I don't know why. You have to find the memory key, and you must do so quickly. Before she takes over.

Who? Lhinde? I knew the name only from talking to Long.

. . . Yes. She wanted this. She comes. I will try to—

Lynchazel's voice vanished in my mind, and I was left shaking my head to clear it. It was always disorienting. What would it be like once I finally had all her memories back? No more guessing, no more being out of the loop on the Senate's history and motives. Hopefully, I could pressure Sylleo to tell me more secrets if I knew more. He always encouraged me to ask questions, but if I didn't know the right questions to ask . . . he didn't have to give the right answers. Somehow, I always ended up getting them out of others.

She wanted this . . . my mother's voice echoed in my thoughts. When I finally got the data back, would Lhinde become a problem? As she had been for my mother? That was the part that scared me. It was like those ghost stories I'd heard as a child of a girl's discontent grandmother coming back to haunt her and similar nonsense.

Somewhere in the meantime, Haccolces workers had repaired the elevator that we broke. As we stepped out of it at the bottom floor, I realized that they had redone everything in here: Walls repaneled, new conduit pulsing with green light, running along the walls and ceilings toward the inner sanctum that was the massive lab. One final checkpoint . . . clear. We were good to go. The door slid back after Zent scanned his keycard—a fake imprinted with an authorized scientist's number, as his own no longer worked anywhere in the League—and we filed out of the hallway.

I stopped, blocking my companions as I stared from ceiling to walls, taking in the all-new cables and computers. They had been busy indeed. *This is new . . .* whispered my mother's voice.

Will the data still be here? I asked.

I don't know. I think it should. Start checking the computers.

"All right, guys," I said. "I think it should be in the computers here."

"You don't say," Balfour said with a snort.

I felt my cheeks grow hot. He was right; that was the whole reason we had come here anyway. But I didn't voice my mother's skepticism that the data was here at all. I stopped at the nearest computer and began clicking through menus, trying to find how to hack into it without tripping every alarm system they had. After a minute, one of the Red Horizon men politely scooted me aside, saying, "I'll take over this one. I'm trained in hacking."

Right. I . . . kind of wasn't. I stepped back, staring at the keyboard and screen as he typed bewilderingly fast. As I watched his large fingers race, I mulled over what my mother had said. A file . . . not memory data, but rather a key that would give me full access, much like how it worked for administrator accounts on computers like these. If we couldn't convince it we were the administrator, there was no getting at any data.

With a gasp, I realized what I was missing. I pushed the hacker away with a mumbled apology and placed my hand on the palm reader. These scanners were activated not by handprints, but by reading unique geothermic signatures. I focused on my mother's memory storage inside my brain, drawing out her signature from deep inside. The computer only beeped at me negatively, and I moved on to the next computer, repeating the same thing until finally . . .

There. I got a response on the fourth computer, informing me that my identity had been verified and access would now be granted. The next screen showed a menu largely made up of hundreds of pages that outlined her memory storage. Dates, times . . . *Whoa.* Scrolling down to the bottom showed ones from E201, which was roughly eight hundred years ago.

I whistled. "E201 . . . E208 . . ."

Zent and the others crowded around me, all who weren't actively watching the exits or looking at their wrist console radar. "Whoa," he agreed. "Well, now you're in—so what's next?"

"I apparently already have all this data, so . . ." I scrolled back to the top, looking for another menu, but I couldn't find one. *It had better not be hidden among all these files,* I thought glumly. That would be impossible.

No. No, she wouldn't have made it like that. But it would be hidden, so that not just anyone could gain access. I already had her digital signature to access the key, I just needed to *find* it. Where would she hide it?

I don't know, she said sadly in my head. *I cannot say.*

"That can mean two different things, Mother," I muttered through clenched teeth, drawing confused looks from the Hellebes.

Finally, it came to me: What could no Hellebes think of? I began madly typing in keywords related to Mani, ones she could only have learned from my father Kallyn. Finally, a result came up under "Kalceron." It was my family name, after all, as uncomfortable as the thought was. I clicked on it and proceeded to place my hand on the scanner, downloading the data organically. Instantly, I felt something shift in my mind, and I knew it had worked. I had the data key. "All right, we're good," I said, turning to look at the others.

Most of them were already back to waiting at the door. "What . . ." I began, but my vision went black and my consciousness blinked out.

⁂

I was in a different place. That field of pale mist on which I spoke with White and my mother's dream phantom. Lynchazel was there this time too, standing tall in that white dress. But even as I watched, those clothes vanished, replaced by a skintight white suit with strange ports placed in it at the upper back, neck, breastbone, hips and elbows. From these issued streams of bright white Geokinetic energy as she floated in a liquid tank. Slowly, a scene took shape:

My mother, Lynchazel I, was suspended in a contained sea of green liquid, glowing white. At the top of her tank, cables ran outward in all directions, thick and pulsating with eerie, green-white light. The heartbeat of a machine world, powered by a one-woman machine.

Lynchazel, she said to me. I gazed upon the woman in the tank, stared hard at her face, but her face was downcast, eyes closed, lips unmoving. This was just a vision of her, perhaps shown as a summary for what she saw her life to be. *My daughter,* the voice continued, *I am so glad that you made it here safely and alive. I don't know how everything worked out for you, nor even how you came about this key. I would have made it more readily accessible for you, but I didn't want Lhinde's control to influence you before you had time to acclimate to Gaea's climate, our history, and the powers that you inherited from me.*

I realized now that this was a narration left by Lynchazel, unlike the phantom dream version of her. This was a story she had left to explain what happened to her daughter, and the legacy she'd left me.

Listen and remember, child. I will hold nothing back.

<h1 style="text-align:center">α Chapter 52 α</h1>

Bad Memories

I'm out. I'm back. Oh, Lord of all stars . . . I'm still trying to catch up. "What did they do to me?" I ask myself repeatedly. Yet I know exactly what they did to me. My veins feel as though still carrying fire in them. I look down at my arms, expecting to see cracks pouring molten lava.

— From Lhinde's Vault

It began with a vision of a woman of some apparent twenty years of age, bearing black hair streaked with white that came down to her waist. Her face was sharp and angular, but bore some resemblance to . . . my own. Her frame, while not small for a human's, was slight compared to mine or my mother's. The form of a human.

This is the woman once known as Lhinde. She was a poor girl, barely grown, from a lower caste in a medieval country called the Sovereignty of Starklett. This nation fell in the year E106, when an organization called the Anier forced their advanced technology upon the world through a show of deceptive military might. It is now known as Luna Halcyon. The Anier predate the Great Exile and are the architects of the Mother Project.

A series of scenes went along with this, mostly still shots of a kingdom that looked not too different from present-day Mani, which must have come from Lhinde's own memory. Among these were flashes of dimly lit men in strange outfits, who I assumed to be the original Anier.

Lhinde was taken by force, one of twenty-four young women kidnapped by the Anier for their experiments. At that time, the population and birth rates were already leaning heavily in favor of males, and a massive war had left Starklett and the surrounding countries in a desolate state with decimated population and even less females. That is to say the Anier took a large chunk of them, and all in the name of preserving the human race.

The Mother Project was all about power, from start to . . . well, it's not finished yet. It all began shortly before the Exile, when the Legaleians discovered the first Cydenges. It had come to our world seemingly lost, as though looking for a way back home. Upon witnessing its powers through the loss of many lives, mankind feared the creature. But the Anier began looking for a way to use its power. Being already well into planning their first war, the Anier were elated to potentially revolutionize war itself . . .

But it couldn't happen. Not with their technology. This idea was kept on the back burner, though they focused on creating new technologies and weaponry over the years. Generations passed, and their leaders changed, and before they knew it, the Cydenges had returned. The "moon dragons," as they were then called, wiped out entire cities before being driven back by the Legaleians' magic.

The Anier plotted against the Legaleians and blamed them for the invasion, claiming they instigated the monster attacks. In the end, the Legaleians were all but forced to make the trip to Mani to find a new home, which was theorized after one of them discovered a way to make a portal to Mani. They called it . . . Reality Authority. First, the Anier wanted them to make a similar door that would lead to Luna, but that was found to be impossible for reasons unexplained.

The Legaleians took their Wellspring of Magic, which gave abundant life to their corner of the world—Mani Halcyon—and moved away to live on Mani. Meanwhile, the Anier developed stronger weapons like cannon and muskets, which could penetrate the hard metal scales of the Cydenges.

Another couple of generations passed, and the Anier prospered in the shadows, making money from war with which to cause more wars, all in the name of advancement for humanity. And now we come to Lhinde's time. The disproportion between male and female humans—a phenomenon still unexplained today—had become not only distinct but drastic by her time, so that she was one of a few left. The average woman was expected to birth nearly a dozen children, and one girl out of those was considered good odds. Humanity truly seemed to be dying out.

Lhinde became the first test subject for the Anier's Mother Project. They had captured a Cydenges during the last raid and studied it closely, speculating that all Cydenges were male except for one, that there must be a mother, a queen. They speculated that they could fuse Cydenges DNA with humans to create a queen bee of humanity to allow our kind to remain on the earth without dying out.

This failed miserably, although the Cydenges fusion was indeed proven to work on Lhinde, the final experiment. This marked the first discovery of Geokinesis, the power used by the moon dragons. At first, she destroyed many with her new powers, but the Anier learned to tame her. They developed new ways of tracking and altering her physiology and abilities, and eventually realized that she was simply incapable of doing what they wanted—and never could. Through blood tests and surgery, they found that her entire cellular makeup was changed, though her reproductive system was not.

However, she not only possessed these new powers, but she was like a conduit for Gaea's energy—which was only recently discovered and thus untapped by man. To explain briefly: Bioforms with the power of Geokinesis can tap Gaea's energy one hundred times more efficiently than any machinery ever developed by human or Hellebes. . . and the reverse is also true: Only from a bioform like Lhinde could they draw nigh unlimited planetary energy, and a Cydenges is much too wild to contain for these purposes.

They used this planetary essence to develop new weapons, new tech, and it only grew from there, thrusting Gaea into a new age. Eventually, they found a way to immortalize their prized prototype in a solution charged with heavy amounts of Geothermic energy. Her body fed off of it enough to sustain her life without air or food. They drew from her like a battery to support all their new technology, while she aged only very slowly. From planet to human to machine . . . the corrupted exhaust of which returned to the earth—thus was the cycle of Mother Gaea's service to her planet, and the economy of energy in the new world of Neo-Gaea.

But poor Lhinde was a broken vessel, no true immortal—a first-time experiment that should never have been expected to handle all that they wrung out of her. Her body slowly decayed from the high energy, and she began to age faster. That was when the Mother Project took a turn:

They removed her from the solution, impregnated her with human sperm, and then placed her into a new tank with purer energy and less toxic chemicals. They also infused her with even more Cydenges DNA using advanced methods. The baby grew in her womb, and eventually I was born. I was like no other human in history, hailed as a genetic marvel and a victory for humankind—human by birth, yet a Cydenges hybrid. I was still incapable of what they originally intended—a human queen bee—but more than able to provide power for them. Power, power and more power. The tool they didn't want became the tool they'd craved all along. My body did not decay, but instead the pure energy of Gaea renewed it even as it aged. I was a meta-human, a transcendent being.

Using this power, the Anier—who now referred to themselves as the Senate—developed their own way of reproducing humans. Or rather, they sought to create their own race. They discarded Lhinde, their failed prototype, and experimented with cloning, genetic modding and artificial intelligence, among other things, and at last settled on a certain brand of cyborg—which they labeled biomachina, or biomachines. These eventually became what we know today as the Hellebes. Seeing their success, the last generation of Anier leaders used this technology to develop new, younger bodies for themselves as a means of transferring their consciousness to an artificial vessel. This technique they did not seek to replicate on others, out of selfishness.

The process used to keep their precious Mother Gaea alive with pure planetary energy became the key to sustaining these new 'Elite' bodies eternally. Essentially, indefinite maintenance done on a frequent basis, like a living machine—for that is exactly what they are. The Gaean Senators, with their army of Hellebes soldiers, waged a quiet war on the entire world and purged humanity from Gaea, supplanting them with Hellebes. They made all the Hellebes male in order to pretend that females had truly died out, but also to emulate the Cydenges species, an army of sterile males to work the entire world and not question the system. It is said that they kept a remnant of humans as a failsafe, but only so many as could easily be contained and controlled.

So my life continued as their conduit, which they falsely called Mother Gaea. They started a cult among their new Hellebes populations that worshipped me as some kind of goddess, the ultimate slap in the face. I was kept abreast of most of the goings-on in the world—little did they know— obtaining information organically from Geothermic energy circulating through Haccolces and the broader world. A trace of all data filtered back to me. It was too much to handle for the first many years, but I learned to filter out the important things from the normal noise. Picture, instead of reading a book to glean information from it, being the book itself and watching the words form on your pages, having no say in the matter. Yet not in tens of words, nor pages, but thousands of pages per second. A book cannot speak back, only be written upon by an outside will.

The nine cities were erected around the nine bases of power the Anier had established over generations, built over Geothermic hotspots, and the shield walls were put in place to keep out the Cydenges—all powered by my unwilling contribution alongside everything else in the world. Raids came and went, and I cared less and less each time. Perhaps one of my moon brethren would one day break his way in here and put an end to my miserable life. I prayed that that day would come, but it never did.

Fast forward seven hundred years, and I heard the first piece of news in centuries . . . a human had come to our world from Mani, a real live Legaleian. This startling news stirred my mind, slowly rousing me from a long slumber. I even began to hope, hope that somehow this could be an indication that I may one day be freed of my prison. My world was six feet in diameter and ten feet tall. My world was wet and thick, as though I was waiting to be born and it never came. Bright, yet I could see nothing. Outside lay a world dominated by my enemies, run by arachnids in the dark known as the Anier, then the Elites, and most recently, Senators.

To my surprise, I found there were simultaneous skirmishes happening between the Elites and a group of renegade Hellebes that had somehow figured out how to free themselves of the programming that compelled them to obedience. Together, these two developments gave me hope. When at last I saw the face of the human who had come to rescue me . . . I couldn't possibly describe the emotion in words, though you can feel it through my memories. I watched in fascination as his magic flames lit up the biolab, destroying computers and exits, and then . . . the liquid was drained and the glass walls came down. I was paralyzed and helpless as a newborn, but Kallyn somehow bore me out. Perhaps he pulled me along with great effort, or his enhanced suit gave him the strength; my consciousness was fuzzy at best. Rebel Hellebes helped to carry me out of the facility, and I watched my world pass away behind me. Its sights and sounds gone, but its nightmarish memories lingering forever.

The Red Horizon, who were working in tandem with the Legaleian, took me to their base of operations and nursed me to health. My body took a full week to acclimate, at which point Gaea's energy gave me more than enough strength, and afterward I learned what these rebels had planned. I couldn't take my eyes off of Kallyn, however. Not only was he the first human I'd seen in almost a millennium, but he was not so bad to look at and could spin fire in the air. And . . . human. No mere replicant. Most of all, he was my rescuer, and I clung to him like a lifeline. I felt that if I was separated from him, I would be back in bondage, regardless of my physical state.

Before I knew it, my devotion became love. I never thought it could happen to me—a specimen, an experiment, a mutant abomination that should not exist, born in captivity and kept alive for near a millennium by miracle technology. This love fought with a growing sense of paranoia that I could not help. I still can't say what it was, and I may never find out, because I am slowly dying. But it lingers even now.

Your father and I escaped from the Red Horizon headquarters after he realized how anxious they made me. When we were finally alone on the run,

I told him how I really felt about him. That secretly, I'd always wished to marry a man like him, and to have a daughter of my own, no matter how selfish that was.

Before I knew it, I was pregnant with you. As my body slowly deteriorated, I've prayed dearly that I could at least see you. It's been very hard on my body, which lived for far too long in an artificial world. But now I have a new goal: To get you back to Mani. Kallyn is going to help me escape, and he had better come home with me as he promised. The ever-helpful Captain Zent is going to back us up as well, should the Elites send soldiers to stop us. I'm sending this data, encrypted with my key, back to the computers in the Haccolces labs. I don't know how they're going to replace me once they recover their systems, but . . . that's on them. I'm taking you with me, my dear daughter, and nothing will stop me.

Now, the time has come for you to do what I couldn't—to change this world. I believe that you will be the one to accomplish it, Lynchazel. Perhaps you can even bridge the gap between worlds and bring the Legaleians back to Gaea. Just remember that I'll always—

α Chapter 53 α

Mother Gaea

In ways, my time in the tank was eye-opening. Before, I had run calculations for them, small experiments, projections. I'd read the work of Anier scientists whom I'd never or barely seen. But to go in and be the experiment . . . that shook my very understanding of biology, and of self.

— From Lhinde's Vault

My vision cut, just like the previous time in the labs, and everything went black. "I didn't think she was ever going to shut up," said a husky feminine voice. I knew that voice; I'd heard it before. But this time, her voice was clear, up close and personal, as though she stood right beside me.

My sight flashed into whiteness, blinding me for a moment. A howl as of wind tore through, and the world around me seemed to spark and rumble. A dark shape flickered across my vision, and I got only the general impression of a female form. I clutched my ears and attempted to brace my legs, but as soon as I did so, it all stopped. Everything went black once more.

I looked around me, struggling to see anything. "Who are you?" I asked, though I already knew the answer.

"How much of a fool are you?" the voice shot back. "You know who I am, girl. I am your predecessor, the first Mother. I am the voice of Gaea, the widow in the darkness, the mourning virgin, cursed of the ancient ones. They—"

"They shall know your pain. I know."

I felt an unmistakable malevolence, like an angry wind or a thunderstorm given flesh. "You would mock me? And you don't even know who I am. Allow me to clarify."

Suddenly, a blinding light turned on in the darkness, revealing a naked girl with long black hair draping down her back. She clutched her shoulders, shivering, and whispered over and over, "Don't hurt me. Don't touch me. Don't hurt me." The sight of her and the sound of her voice pierced my heart. I looked away with a gulp, or whatever the equivalent of that is in a dream.

"You're Lhinde," I said quietly. "Not Gaea." I had known it all along, and my mother had confirmed it, but it was how personal and vulnerable this scene felt that drove it home.

"Wrong," she replied. "I am Gaea." Slowly, the girl rose to her feet and turned, now wearing a black gown, with straight-cut bangs attempting to hide her dark eyes. She looked almost like a gaunt version of Mydia Kalceron. "I was the Mother before Lynchazel, the first to discover Gaea's power. My attachment to the earth is not as simple as yours. I seek vengeance on my enemies, the Anier, for what they did to me, but also for what they did to Gaea. They robbed her of something precious and upset the balance of life for their own gain. They rose to power on the blood of my brethren and the blood of my planet. I am bitterness, I am anguish. I am the wrath of Gaea."

She pronounced those last six words with firm, slow precision. I took a step back, feeling chills. At first it was hard to take her seriously, but . . . her intensity was overwhelming. Even in the presence of eight superbeings back in the Senate Hall, I had not felt an aura like this. Such pure, cultured malice. No wonder I had mistaken her for a goddess of evil. I still couldn't be certain what she was. My mother had told me not to trust anything she said.

"What's the matter, girl?" Lhinde asked, condescension and flippancy overlapping in her voice on the word 'girl'. "Trying to decide whether to believe me or not? You think I'm trying to mislead you. What I say is not false. Gaea is angry for what Lldsaor and the other Anier have done, and her wrath—my wrath—will not be appeased until they are annihilated. You see it, too, the more you use my power, that it is tainted by the Anier's meddling. We can purge this taint and restore balance to Gaea."

"How?"

She smiled a cold, hollow smile. "With blood. Blood for blood."

"How much? When will it end? When will you be satisfied?"

"When this earth is swept clean of all artificial life," she answered.

"Then we can bring back the Cydenges, the original keepers of Geokinesis. Humanity is long gone. Let us sweep all remnant of that sorry race from Gaea."

"Wait, wait . . . so we kill all the people and then the space dragons come back and kill whoever's left . . ."

"Exactly. They and they alone are the rightful heirs of Gaea's power. They were the first exiles. You think them demons, predators of mankind, but man was the first aggressor. They are not of Luna, not the moon anyway, yet they have made her their home until they can reclaim Gaea."

"So . . . you, a human, want humans to be wiped out in favor of the Cydenges."

"I am not *human*." She growled the words gutturally as though rolling each letter like an exotic R sound, hair flaring around her. "I renounced that title long ago. I am the pain of Gaea."

This woman was growing tiresome. Malevolent, mad, certainly creepy, but . . . exhausting as well. Perhaps it was her too-evident god complex. "What if I just refuse to heed you?" I asked. "What will you to do? You're just a voice in my head, my grandmother's lingering memories." More like lingering emotions, but I didn't say that.

Lhinde laughed in response. "You still don't understand. I won't simply allow you to go against me. Sooner or later, I will bring you down from the inside and use you to accomplish the will of Gaea. I will make them know my pain, and inflict one thousand times the suffering on this world."

I would be the one laughing now, if I didn't know she was absolutely serious. I didn't have to know it; I could feel the intense anger . . . "Then I'll prevent you," I said stubbornly. "Once and for all. I will find a solution. I'll go to Luna if I have to. One way or another, I'll end this conflict for good."

Lhinde laughed again, far longer and scarier than before. "Oh, you humans. Always with your ambitions. Such pride was the cause of every war in history, every massacre, every evil thing you despise. You will never understand. The only thing that can purge uncleanness from the world is a pure, unquenchable fire that consumes all. You have tasted this power and felt its consuming breath, have unleashed it through your own body, the

Vessel of Gaea. No more tampering, squabbling, warring humans, hungry for power and thirsty for blood. Oppression, deceit, war . . . all this comes from humans."

I shook my head, eyes squeezed shut, trying to redirect the passion of her words. It didn't work. Every consonant bit into me like lashes from a barbed whip, every vowel a howl of madness, her anger rubbing off on me. I tried to redirect it back at her.

I wanted out of this dream—this waking nightmare—but I couldn't move. Dimly, I heard my mother's voice: *Endure. She can't go one like this forever.*

Indeed, within what passed for another minute, Lhinde finally stopped, crossed her arms and turned to the side, hair rippling like black smoke behind her. "I will leave you to consider for now, but I will be back." The rest of her body faded into smoke and was gone.

I was left wondering whether I had made a huge mistake in unlocking my mother's memories. Was it worth it?

α   Chapter 54   α

A Prize

What of these Beta Beasts? And the whispered Gamma Beast? I keep asking them, receiving only vague replies. Why can these creatures not provide enough energy yet? If not as a singular unit, then perhaps multiple linked in sequence. Yes, I understand that these are originally humans just like me, but one day—so they claim—our scientists can create them artificially just like the Hellebes.

— From Lhinde's Vault

They were shaking me. Someone was trying to wake me up. My first thought was that I'd been here before—in this oversized, underground laboratory. I didn't . . . kill anyone again, did I? Slowly, I opened my eyes, shaking my head, finally making sense of their words:

"Lyn, come on!" Zent's voice. There he was, bending over me and slapping my cheeks.

"Not much time left!" shouted Kinneson from somewhere on my left.

I lurched to my feet, dizzied by the sudden recall of my successive dreams. No time to think about them, though. Something urgent was going on. "What's . . . Did they find us?" I asked blurrily.

"Someone did," Zent confirmed. "Let's go."

Even as he said it, a Red Horizon soldier by the main door shouted, "It's him!"

Shots were fired, and I saw blood splash on the wall of the corridor where our soldier had been. I leaned over far enough to see if the man was correct, and ducked back quickly as I saw *him*. The very hound who had attacked me just an hour earlier: The Hunter. His left arm seemed to be back to normal, too. "It's him!" I hissed at Zent, and shouted, "Stay back from him! You don't stand a chance."

It was too late, however, as he sliced open more of our soldiers with his blade, its silver edge reflecting the eerie green light of the lab where it wasn't covered in blood. Red Horizon blood. The blood of my loyal companions and friends. "Get back!" I repeated, approaching the Hunter.

"Lyn, be careful!" Zent called. He started to run over to back me up, but I simply motioned him back. This was my fight. I wasn't about to accept Gaea's—Lhinde's—radical ideology, but that didn't mean I wouldn't remove an obstacle from my path if he insisted on being my nemesis, and more importantly . . . killing my friends.

He lunged for me at the speed of sound, and I reacted just as quickly, dodging to the side and unleashing a Geokinetic wave. Or at least, I tried to.

The ground did not respond.

The Hunter cackled, circling me. "Too bad, huh? They replaced these floors with copper."

No wonder it had felt weird stepping in here this time.

We exchanged more attacks. He struck again and again for my head, chest and legs with the Heart of Mani, while I dodged and sought an opportunity to retaliate. The copper floor did not hamper our Geokinetic movement, but only prevented the earth-moving powers that Geokinesis provided. I managed to avoid his blade, but only thanks to the breathing training I'd undergone with the Earth Sage. The Hunter was fast, faster than Zent or old man Musha.

He did not go after my allies this time, presumably only out of single-minded focus on me. That and the fact that the soldiers swarming in behind him were engaging them already. There was nothing our men could do against him from range anyway. Energy weapons would not work, and we had no snipers with bows. There was no one left to the Red Horizon with any bow skills, especially not like Seidrake's.

I tried the hook-kick technique to disarm my enemy, but he saw it coming this time, reacting with a fulminous sword swipe that nearly separated my foot at the ankle. Only an awkward jerk backward saved me from getting hit. He used this opportunity to land a kick of his own, his heel drilling into my chest and driving my whole body down to the floor. He didn't have my speed, but he had a significant weight advantage.

My head rang against the copper, jolting my neck with pain, and I rolled to the side to avoid a lethal thrust of his sword. He followed it up with a disrespectful kick, which hit home even as one of the Red Horizon soldiers tackled him. I grabbed hold of his boot as it drove into my stomach, forcing the air out of my lungs, and wrenched with my whole body while he toppled, heaving myself up by throwing him down in my place. As the black-armored soldier hit the copper floor, I grabbed his right wrist, twisting the blade from his hands and snatching it in my own right hand.

Laying the point at his neck, I prepared to drive the tip through and pierce his throat. His voice stopped me, however.

"Go ahead, finish me." Then he switched to Hellebes. "You're just a coward on the inside anyway."

He . . . switched. Switched languages. A brief flash of memory reminded me that the last time he spoke, on that hill . . . he had also spoken in the Manese tongue. Could it be?

"Zent!" I shouted, holding the blade's tip as steady as I could. "Quick, help me bind this man."

"But—"

"Do it!" I screamed.

Zent sprang into action, along with another soldier from my other side—Vester, the one who'd made capturing the Hunter possible—grabbing hold of the Hunter's arms and flipping him over onto his back. Using the sword's too-sharp silver edge, I bit into the floor and carved out a long strip of copper a half-inch thick. Prying it up and tearing it off at the end, I bound the Hunter's wrists in a coil and tied it off. Then I did the same for his feet while he thrashed in my companions' grip. When we got his mask off, I saw that his face . . . sort of resembled my friend. His features were larger with a more pronounced jaw and darker hair for some reason, cropped close to his head, but the similarity was uncanny.

Zent let out a curse as he saw his face.

"Uh, we should really be getting out of here," Kinneson said, looking at his radar. "Did you get the data key you needed, Heiress?"

I nodded and dialed in Sylleo's number. "Come on, come on . . ." A moment later, he answered, and I said, "Sylleo, can your men come pick us up at the lab? ASAP would be good. Got a prize for you here."

I heard him sigh on the other end. "All right, since this is still your favor. Hang tight."

Don't remind me about that . . .

We got out safely, somehow. Security was close, but a squad of Sylleo's men had already been posted near a hidden exit, and they funneled us out, bypassing most of the soldiers. Then they transported us by tram to the nearest gate while the remaining squads scrammed. Lldsaor would know at this point that Sylleo had helped us escape, but I was *really* hoping that he wouldn't catch on that they'd helped us get in in the first place.

The Hunter wasn't, you know, too happy about all this. We initially knocked him out, and subsequently gagged him with a copper wire and some cloth and voila, the angry curses became indistinguishable, muffled angry curses. Meanwhile, Zent worked to disable our captive's communication features, which he said was always a pain in the neck to do on the fly, no pun intended.

Soon, we were winging it back to Ccamos—the newly-established Red Horizon base—and Zent was giving me yet another lecture on how ridiculous my agreement to marry a Senator was. I had no choice, man. I would say it as many times as I had to. I didn't want to marry an immortal monster, no matter his artificial attractiveness. Or height. Or . . . ugh, it was a mess. I really didn't want to think about it.

The worst part about it all was that . . . we'd found Kaen. Sort of. I was 96.7% certain that they had transferred his consciousness to one of their new line of Hellebes bodies in a gamble to try and use the power of the sword against me. What that meant for his identity now . . . who could say? The joke was on Strongs, though, so long as we could successfully free him from the loyalty programming. As terrible as it sounded, I almost wished he had just stayed dead, because now I would feel guilty and embarrassed . . . no, not just feel; I would have to *tell* him to his face that I was marrying a monster. I was pretty sure his last words to me in the garden had been meant as a confession of sorts, despite the influence of that disgusting sword . . . hopefully his feelings for Mydia were stronger than for me. But who was I kidding—she wouldn't even recognize him. Would he recognize us?

Because . . . if my theory was right, this Hellebes warrior may be Kaen. But he may just be one of the monsters.

Pulling my legs up onto my seat, I hugged them to my chest. It was a silly, girlish posture, but it worked. Sort of. It's an old trick to gain a negligible modicum of emotional stability, one I'd seen a certain princess use on multiple occasions. I just wanted out of this whole situation. I wanted to reverse time. To find a new planet of my own and hole up there until the end of time. Zent just looked over at me from the pilot's seat, not saying a word. His face said it all. He might not understand human emotions well, but he was smart enough to see when further words weren't going to help.

Please, Kaen, just . . . be all right. If I could rescue my friend from the grip of that dictator general, at least that would be a step. One small step back to the way things should be.

α Chapter 55 α

Return from Insanity

What do these Hellebes feel, I wonder? What is it like to be a creation with a molded body, birthed by machines? For that matter, the process the Anier, or . . . Senate . . . speak of, to transfer one's mind—if such a feat is possible, what must that be like? To look upon one's own body and see a stranger? And then . . .

— From Lhinde's Vault

"Lyn."

That one small word was enough to make me jerk my head up sharply to stare at my friend. I held his massive hand in both of mine, and he squeezed them now. "Oh, Kaen, you're awake," I said in relief. I'd sat here at his side in the infirmary since the moment they'd let me in. The surgery was a success, or so the doctors said.

"Kaen?" he repeated. He sat up with a groan, making to unroll the bedsheets with his left hand, and then apparently thought better of it, leaving the sheets to lie at his waist. His body was completely different, that of a large Hellebes in his prime, abdomen layered with muscle. I was used to the sight of these Hellebes meat hunks, so I'd like to say it didn't do much to me. "Is that really my name?" he asked.

I nodded. "Come on, Kaen. I know you haven't lost everything. They were calling you the Hunter while you were under Strongs' control, but you're my friend from Mani. You found that silver sword, and then you came all the way to Gaea with me." I realized belatedly that I'd been speaking in Hellebes. So had he. His ability to speak it must have improved a lot, and perhaps had been programmed right into his Hellebes brain. I didn't know how that worked.

He shook his head. "It's all . . . fuzzy. Yes . . . it's coming back to me.

Give me a moment."

I nodded again, letting go of his hand. He stared down at it, turning it over, mouthing something like, *They gave me a new body* in awe. I could see his brain working, could see it in his eyes as they darted back and forth over the same spot, staring at something in the past. Finally, he looked back up at me. "I remember it all. I've got it. I'm . . ." He gulped. "I'm sorry for the way I treated you that day, in the gardens at Ccamos. I . . . I treated everyone horribly." He held his lower jaw as though to stop it from shaking.

It was him. Oh, bright, glimmering auroras, my friend was back.

"Kaen, it's all right," I said softly. "I forgive you. It was the sword's influence."

He shook his head. "No. It just . . . amplified my emotions. My negative ones. It's not an excuse. I lost myself when Mandrie died. Where is it, anyway?"

"It's right here," I said hesitantly, gesturing at the wall where it leaned, complete with the new black sheath Strongs' men had made for it.

"I think I'm over it now. Finally. I think Strongs helped me out more than he realized. My thanks for rescuing me. I need to thank Zent and the others, and . . ." He made a disgusted sound. "I can't believe I did the things I did." He squeezed his eyes shut, pinching his forehead. "Even with the mind control. I killed so many . . . I'm a murderer."

"That wasn't your fault. It wasn't your fault, okay? There was no fighting against your programming. You needed outside help. You couldn't change yourself."

It was at that moment, conveniently enough, that Zent walked into the room. "Oh. You're awake," he said. "Looks like it went smoothly."

When I realized Sylleo had come in behind him, I sat up in my chair, trying to act slightly less attached to Kaen. Why, though? What would I care if I made my husband-to-be jealous?

Kaen nodded, fingering the back of his neck. "I'm back. Better than before, really. Captain, I'm-I'm sorry for what I did to your men. I'll accept whatever—"

Zent waved a hand. "In the past. This is war, and in this war, we drop all charges in the old life when we free a Hellebes. That was the mind-controlled Kaen. This is your new life as a free man. I will ask for a detailed explanation, however, because that's crucial information. Right, Senator?"

Sylleo nodded.

"Of course, sir," Kaen said, dipping his head toward Sylleo respectfully. He seemed to be quickly piecing together his situation. "Do we—is there . . ." He toggled a finger at me and the door. "Something I can put on?"

"Oh." I cleared my throat, catching his drift. Picking up a package from the floor, I handed it to my friend and scurried out. When they called me back in, he was dressed in a well-fitting, relaxed Ccamos soldier uniform, emblazoned with the seal of Ccamos: The flying heron with a crown and arrow overhead. He was to be a soldier for Sylleo now; that was part of the deal.

Kaen looked over at me, clearing his throat. "So, um . . . well, I got captured on the way from Chronala to Ccamos in that cheap ambush, and I assumed I was done for. Under the influence of that sword, I was almost ready to break. I don't know what I was thinking, but I just charged straight into the enemy. They couldn't do anything to me with their energy weapons, but it didn't take them long to knock my sword right out of my fragile human hands. And . . ." he sighed. "Next thing I knew, I was in chains. My sword was nowhere, and I was going crazy. The whole trip back to Haven, it was all I could think about.

"Then Strongs himself came and talked to me. Before throwing me in a cell, that is. He told me that I was to serve him as his new personal weapon. I didn't understand what he meant, and of course I thought I must be missing something due to the language barrier . . . but when I saw the scientists coming in to scan my brain, I got really nervous. Then they told me I would have to die. Before I could . . . could serve my new master." He took a deep, calming breath. I could understand how nervous he was, and how traumatic this must be even to retell.

"After that," he continued, "I'm not sure how long it was—my memory gets pretty fuzzy in the in-between. But I remember having this feeling like I was outside my own body. And then I *saw* myself, and they were holding me down. And—" he swallowed again. "Well, I think you've probably all seen the footage. They sent it to you to scare you. For me, the most terrifying part was that I didn't feel anything. I still don't know if that was another me—if *I'm* another me, a copy—or if I simply switched bodies, but it was . . . horrifying. My new body was under harsh restrictions. I'm sure it's similar to most Hellebes, just—they don't have to watch their old bodies die."

"I did," Sylleo said softly. "And I remember it clearly." He said no more on the subject. The two locked eyes for a moment and seemed to share something in the silence. I shivered and hugged my short ribs. I'd be glad to be off this topic.

Kaen continued after a brief pause. "From there, I did exactly as commanded. It was odd being under the command program, but I simply did whatever my superiors told me to do, to the letter. First, it involved learning if and how I could still use the human Kaen's sword, which of course it turned out I could, and training in combat, flying aircraft, stuff like that. They'd already pre-coded my new body to speak fluent Hellebes and have a good grasp on most subjects, and even imprinted the body with matching muscle-memory, but I had to be . . . broken in, so to speak."

"Who were your superiors?" Sylleo asked. "Who was over you?"

"Well, sometimes it was Strongs himself, but usually one of his generals, called Sada."

Sylleo nodded. "I know him. Was he the one spearheading the project to capture and recruit you?"

"Mm . . . I'm not sure. There were a lot of scientists involved, and it was all in collaboration with Daedalus. I know that much."

"I'm sure your body was made there in Chronala," Zent added. "Lyn said you saw them being made in the labs, right?"

He nodded, as though at a painful memory.

"If only we knew how many more he has like you," Sylleo mused. "Did you interact with any others of the new type?"

"Actually, yes. He has at least two more, named Zwei and Kolm, but I don't know their origins, nor their intended purpose."

"Well, I doubt they were converted from humans," Zent said with a chuckle. "I think we know that much."

"He's not trying to make copies of that sword, is he?" Sylleo asked with a frown.

Kaen shook his head furiously. "No way. It can't possibly be copied, even if you could get your hands on the exact metal it's made from."

"Isn't it enchanted Manese silver?" I asked, stepping into the ring of speakers. It felt odd to be the short one by so much.

"Nope. Not . . . you know, not that they have a way to get that easily." Kaen walked over and almost picked the sword up, but he stopped himself first. "Is it okay if I pick it up, sir?" he asked Sylleo.

The Senator looked at Zent and shrugged. "He seems significantly changed. Go ahead, son."

Kaen took the blade by its pommel and spun it in the air, catching it in a backhanded grip. "I don't know its exact composition, but I don't think it's the same as the rest of the silver on Mani. It's . . . *older.* I gathered that much from Mani's words."

I frowned, staring at the gleaming blade. We had wiped the blood off, and there was no sign that it had ever been stained. Something about his analysis troubled me. If it came from Mani, and it was a token of great power and inhabited with the spirit of Mani, then why would it be different from the silver that made up the moon?

A sudden thought struck me. "Is it trying to speak to you?"

Kaen shook his head. "No. Like I said, I think Strongs did me a big favor by giving me a new body—at least, now that you guys saved me—because it severed my mental connection with the moon."

Zent nodded, looking over at Sylleo. "And what about the rest of the Senate? How long till they're onto us?"

Sylleo sucked in a breath. "Oh . . . not very long. I'll be hearing from Lldsaor soon, I'm sure. I'll just tell him you guys contacted me and I pulled you out because I wanted to keep the Mother Heiress safe, blabitty bla. And I will make *sure* to tell him about Strongs' multiple attempts on your life using a new model of Hellebes assassin. Along with the other Senators, but of course . . . carefully. It will be a busy few days."

"Any developments on the Mani invasion plan?" I asked.

Sylleo's expression soured. "They're playing their cards close to their chest. And when I say they, I mean the Emperor and his two cronies. But I know they've been making strides toward that over the past month, now that the Cydenges are out of the way again."

"For now," I added with a shrug of my hands.

"I know," replied the Senator. "I've tried to warn them to be on their guard. It's hard when everyone has their own agenda. Some are better at pushing their agenda than others. For now . . . we wait. I have some negotiations to settle, and it won't be long before I have to take you to the Senate Hall." He pointed at me as he said it, and then pointed at Kaen. "And possibly you. You're part of this now, whether you like it or not."

β PART FOUR β

Anticipation

Gaea

Hunter No More

Kaen mashed the buttons on his controller. He was trying to win this time, but fighting games were difficult, and he didn't know the characters' moves well enough. His life bar depleted at last, and victory text showed up on the screen in big gold letters. Victory for his opponent, not himself. "Aw, come on! Not again."

"It's okay, just try again," Plato encouraged him with a pat on the shoulder. "I'll beat you, but it'll at least be fun for me."

Kaen fixed him with a glare. "I'm sick of this stupid game." He had to will his hand not to throw the metal game controller as he set it down in frustration. Everything he did now was with the strength of a giant, so he had to be careful. They were playing together in the common room at the Ccamos military base on their free time. These video games . . . frustrating hardly described them. Plato and the others insisted that the old ones were the good ones, since updates in graphical technology were only ever followed with more and more laziness on the developers' part and less creativity. Therefore, this one only looked realistic if you didn't inspect the screen too closely, because Kaen could make out flat parts of the background scenery, flat features on the characters' faces and unnatural lighting, not to mention the animations.

With a sigh, he got up from his chair. "That's about all I can handle for now," he said, stretching. "I'm going to do some training."

"All right," Plato the Hellebes replied, joining an online arena.

Kaen's mind was already wandering as he stalked the halls in search of a good training room. This base wasn't too dissimilar to the rebel base he'd stayed in for a week as a human while trying to learn to walk and speak Hellebes. It was crazy to think that that had all been bypassed so easily by simply . . . transferring his mind to a new body. He shuddered at every recollection of it.

But no, what occupied his thoughts now was the queen he'd left behind in Nytaea, with the midnight hair and the beautiful smile. She had tried to say goodbye to him, even to just talk to him, but he had let that cursed sword infect his mind, dulling it and turning him paranoid. Worst of all, he hadn't even cried for his sister. He had obsessed over her safety each day, and yet as soon as she was gone, he'd turned to despair and anger without a drop of sadness.

Ducking inside a vacant training dojang, he removed his jacket and hung it up, preparing to let out some of his frustration on a heavy bag. If he couldn't hit Plato's stupid character, then he could at least hit this. The whole time, though, he thought of Mydia and his own failures. He had pushed her away, not realizing his own feelings for her. Now . . . what he wouldn't give to see her face. That dimpled smile. He'd been thinking on it more, replaying his last conversation with Lyn in his Vault. She was a friend, a sister. And a better one than he deserved. But he needed to respond to the one who truly loved him.

The only problem was that he was a Hellebes now. Kaen didn't even know if he could ever father a child, much less an heir to a throne. But it wouldn't stop him from returning home to apologize to Mydia and sort things out. At this very moment, she was surely agonizing over his well-being, hoping and praying that the sword had not taken over his mind completely—not knowing that it had very literally cost him his life.

Possibly my soul?

And yet, he was alive. Imposter or not, he had to move forward.

Kaen threw punch after punch at the sandbag, knocking it around like a hanging doll. He had left his sword back in his locker, as he simply didn't need it at the moment. It was freeing to be able to do so. While he worried over what the sword's silence meant, he was glad to not have to deal with the "Heart of Mani" anymore. *What a headache that was.* He did have to wonder . . . what would it do with Rhidea now? Would Mani press her even further about becoming his new Vessel? He had a feeling it had done so at least once in the past. Surely she would not accept it. He knew her that well.

Kaen was broken from his reverie as another Hellebes walked in behind him. He could tell it was a Hellebes, because Lyn's steps were lighter and more graceful, while Sylleo and his ilk had a different presence entirely, a palpable aura that could be sensed from afar.

It was Zent.

"Captain Zent," Kaen said in his best approximation of friendliness. "How did you find me?"

"I tracked you down by your smell. Nah. Didn't realize you were in here, son." The old Hellebes, stripped to the waist, set a bag down near the door and slipped off his shoes. "Up for some sparring, kid? Or maybe just a workout battle?"

"I'm good. Been in excellent condition lately." *Better than I ever hoped or wanted to be.* Kaen went back to slamming the sandbag with his heavy fists. Too heavy, created and conditioned for violence. The hands of an elite warrior Hellebes.

Zent walked over and caught the hundred-kilo bag with one hand as it swung toward him. "Oh really? Let's see about that." At the captain's insistence, they trained together for the next half hour, and Zent pried his personal feelings out of him the whole while with conversation. Had he really come to train, or did he just want to check in on his emotional progress as a biomachine? Considering how bad the man was at understanding human emotion, he was a fair conversationalist, seeming to draw out Kaen's inner conflict naturally and expose it in the light.

Inevitably, the topic of Lyn and Mydia came up. "It's not that I don't like Lyn," Kaen admitted. "We're very close. I think in my head I always assumed we'd end up together. But now I'm realizing how awkward and . . . odd that feels. And Mydia, she's—well, she's a queen, so naturally not on my "future spouse" radar. But I like her. A lot. They're so . . . different. Lyn is a tomboy, an old friend, almost a sister; she's like family. Mydia is a lady. Feminine. Sweet, but not cloyingly so like some noblewomen. And not stuffy."

Kaen realized as he paused to catch his breath that he'd been rambling for well over a minute and had hardly touched the dumbbells he'd been lifting. Zent had paused, too, watching and listening quietly.

"And you'll do everything you must to get back to see her," Zent finished. Kaen knew the man didn't understand the first thing about women, yet he tried to his best.

"Yes. I think so." Kaen lifted his dumbbells, then stopped with a frown. "Wait, which one?"

Zent only grinned.

Kaen scoffed. "A lot of help you are. I guess . . . I'm only sounding foolish, huh?"

"A bit. Perhaps getting the words out just helped you to see them more clearly for yourself."

Kaen stared blankly at the floor. "I suppose," he said softly. "You're right, Zent. I'd do anything to get back and see her. I don't—I don't care if she's a queen. And I'm . . . this. She already made it plain that she loves me, and I owe it to her to return and tell her how I feel."

"Good soldier. Sylleo needs men like you. If there's one thing I've learned as a soldier, it's that having a reason to fight, a powerful reason— that's everything." Zent briefly held up a set of eighty-kilo dumbbells as he said the words before continuing his reps.

Kaen followed along, not stopping. "And how much longer do you think it will go on like this? How long before a full civil war breaks out? Sylleo seems certain that something will happen soon."

Zent snorted. "Something, yes. But who can say what? I still don't know his long-term plan, but for now, I'm willing to trust him. Having worked with the other rebel leaders for fifteen years now—before they all died—I can safely say I agree with Lyn: They were far too distrusting of her, too controlling and secretive. I went along with it . . . no, I was just the same. I tried to help both the Red Horizon and Lyn to succeed, but . . . well, let's just say Sylleo may be one tyrant running a city his own way, but he's a better tyrant than most of us ever were as freedom fighting paragons."

Kaen nodded, setting down his dumbbells. As strange as it was to hear the man admit it, it seemed almost obvious to Kaen. True, he would not have expected such honesty and commitment to justice from one of the Elites, particularly after what he'd been through, but the Red Horizon was . . . far from perfect. "Zent," he asked after a moment, "what was Mother Gaea like? Lyn's mother? I know you knew both her parents."

Zent paused, a strange expression of amusement crossing his face, as though he'd been waiting for this subject to come up. Then he nodded. "She was . . . she was a gentle soul. It took her time to adjust after we freed her, but her mind became ever more unstable. She was fearless, but paranoid when it came to anything regarding the experimentation she'd been through over countless decades and centuries. And that paranoia only grew. Such a tragic story. But I can't blame her for being the way she was."

And Lyn said she *was hearing voices in her head,* Kaen thought to himself. It hurt to realize that her mother had likely been through the same thing Kaen had. But . . . that would indicate that Lyn and her mother had some influence from Planet Gaea, just as Kaen had been set upon by Mani. A chill ran up his spine. Why had he not made that connection before? Had Lyn's mother Lynchazel been the 'Vessel' of Gaea? And now . . . was it Lyn?

Somehow, it didn't seem to be affecting her mind yet . . . unless she was simply far stronger than he. But would it eventually?

<h1 style="text-align:center">β   Chapter 024 β</h1>

<h1 style="text-align:center">Incompetence</h1>

Abraham Strongs growled in frustration. "Why wasn't I informed of this limitation?" he asked his advisors angrily. Scientists and politicians, a useless lot, they had assured him that this precious new Hunter would be able to neutralize any and all energy thrown at him, whether airborne or on the ground. Not only that, but the new genetics Daedalus had used coupled with the advanced biointegrated armor should have guaranteed this Hunter's victory over even the Mother. Yet he'd been captured on his second assignment. Captured! Strongs had to remove some men from office, that much was certain.

"Sir," said one of the scientists, a smaller Hellebes named Akbar. "Sir, we weren't certain on the weapon's capacity. I tried to tell them that his ship was not protected by the sword the last time."

"Tried?" Strongs asked testily. "A little more than 'trying' would have been appropriate."

"Yes, sir."

Strongs looked around at his half-dozen lead scientists who had been involved with the Hunter Project, in conjunction with Daedalus' scientists. "You're all too afraid to show me any bad results, even if they're the real ones. Now our experiment is worse than dead; he has been *repossessed* by the enemy! Another thing I was misled on." *No, not misled. I merely left too much to incompetent hands.* These days he liked to delegate as much as possible—too much in some cases, it would appear.

The men looked at one another uncomfortably, the politicians as well this time. The loyalty programming was not a topic any Hellebes liked to discuss, as it crossed a sort of line in their brains' logic. They were fully capable of comprehending it, and indeed every high-ranking officials in the city of Haven was required to undergo seminars involving the 'obedience gene,' but it was a bit like being told you were a puppet in a puppeteer's hands: No one wanted to believe or acknowledge that. Worse, the strings themselves made it . . . delicate.

"Sir," ventured another one of the scientists, responsible for neurodigital research. "We still haven't figured out how the rebel group does it, though we have theories. These theories seemed to be rebuffed by our suppositions about the Hunter, but we had nothing more to go on."

"Pathetic," Strongs scoffed. These were the best scientists the biomanufactories were churning out these days? He might as well start hiring iguanas. Of course, he knew that these were *not* the best. He was trusting Daedalus on most of the science, because his own was a city with one purpose: War. "And what of Daedalus' scientists?" he asked.

"A lot of this data came directly from them, Senator. And Dr. Dekla, of course."

Dekla . . . speaking of incompetence. He nodded, before barking, "Then contact them! Come up with a way to neutralize the Hunter or hack his brain from afar."

Again, the disturbed looks, though some of these came simply from the volume at which their Senator spoke. It wasn't the first time, and it wouldn't be the last. Oh, no it wouldn't. Not as long as he had to put up with these noodle-spines.

Strongs turned away from his advisors with a huff. "I'm trusting you to sort this out. I'll be making some calls. We may ready for war sooner than I thought." With that, he stalked away. As he walked, he cursed himself mentally for being foolish enough to trust the assurances of lab coat-wearing Hellebes. They knew nothing of war. How could he be so stupid?

I need her dead. That girl has to die, and soon. Before she could become a true dragon.

There remained one more scientist to chastise, however, and that was his friend the rebel traitor. As soon as Dekla outlived his usefulness, he would be executed immediately, and that time may be very soon indeed. Most likely the reason he had failed to show up at this meeting.

Strongs sent the scientist a summons with exactly one expletive, and headed for the closest lobby to the military science branch of the Haven Elite military base. The fat Hellebes was there when Strongs arrived, huffing and puffing, seated in the softest chair he could find. "Dr. Dekla," Strongs greeted him.

"My lord," Dekla said, almost demurely. "I assume this is about the man with the silver sword—the Hunter?"

"That's correct, rebel. He's in the enemy's hands now. I'm sure you've heard."

"Indeed, my lord. Indeed. While I'm sorry to hear the way things turned out, I distinctly recall telling you it wouldn't work. He needed more time, and backup to boot, to ensure that this exact scenario did not happen."

Strongs flashed his eyes. "If I hear one more of my subjects say that . . . Look, *Doctor,* I'm not sure you understand just how precarious your situation is right now. What province did you desert from when you went to the rebels?"

"Haven, my lord."

"Ah, that's right. And that means that I don't have to consult the Senate before executing you tomorrow. It will alleviate my foul mood just a bit."

Now the fat man was sweating beads. "B-but . . . I gave you all the information I could, and—"

"And that's exactly why I don't need you anymore, insect. Security!" Strongs pinned Dekla down in his seat with his eyes alone. The doctor didn't move an inch until the uniformed guards arrived and closed in to detain him. "Wait! Wait! This is a mistake, you imbecile! You don't know what you're throwing away."

"Guards, take him to a fresh cell on death row."

Ignoring the man's pathetic cries for mercy, Strongs left the lobby and headed for his own office in the military HQ. Here, he called Daedalus. The Senator of Chronala was apparently busy at the moment, so he turned to looking over reports on Haven's martial growth and upcoming strategy plans.

Strongs knew that each day was a day closer to the time to launch his attack on the world. No longer would the Senate fear the Cydenges, but the threat they should have acknowledged long ago: Haven, the supreme military force of the planet.

As he looked over his generals' reports, Strongs surveyed his city through the tall windows of his command office. It was beautiful, not as an artist would describe it but a conqueror. Haven was a masterwork of military perfection. Each sector of the city housed nearly one thousand Hellebes troops of different specialties, and the city was compartmentalized and interconnected so as to allow maximum efficiency in housing, training and employing those troops, all while transporting resources and equipment back and forth.

One sector built weapons, another vehicles, others power suits that enhanced the fighting abilities of an elite squadron of soldiers, while others managed the food and energy supplies of the city. The true might of Haven did not reach the reports of the other seven cities, which was intentional. Daedalus, his main supporter, provided his large supply of troops. Unlike other cities, Strongs kept a tight and distinct command structure, all pointing back to him at the top. That fool of a First Minister, Phelps, was pretending to oversee much of the business, infrastructure and foreign affairs. He really ought to replace the man soon . . . not because he was particularly incompetent, just too free with his opinions. Like a dog attempting to serve his master better.

Finally, Daedalus got back to him. Soon, they had a video stream going.

"Senator Strongs? What is the situation in Haven? I heard your project piece was captured." The rhinoceros seemed half-worried, half-annoyed.

"Correct. The setup was all for nothing. By all reports—which are few— they have reconditioned him already." Strongs was no longer looking at the screen, but downward, blinking rapidly. Something he did when particularly upset.

"I . . . do wish I had been in on that, Strongs," Daedalus said, his high voice sounded more reserved than usual.

"Yes, yes. I was clearly too hasty. If my men weren't such lousy planners, this wouldn't have—never mind, it's fine. We'll just go with Plan B. I'll make an announcement to the Senate soon, so don't worry. The mole I was working with will be executed tomorrow, as he can offer no more help to me. What of Lldsaor's response to Sylleo? We all know he orchestrated that last attack. Does he still have the Mother?"

"I hadn't heard the rumors, just that she was sighted in Ccamos recently," Daedalus mused. "Presumably, she's back in his custody, or Lldsaor would be bragging about her by now. But I'd say if the Emperor can't charge Sylleo with something soon, she could remain in his grasp indefinitely. If I find out anything more before you do, I'll let you know."

"Indefinitely?" Strongs repeated, the word tasting unpleasurable on his tongue. "It might take him some time and careful planning. If something . . . unexpected . . . were to happen, however, then I might have something in mind."

Daedalus' frown took on a more worried look. "What might you be expecting to happen?"

Strongs grinned. "I'm not. That's the point. But if it did . . ."

β   Chapter 025   β

For the Sake of Humanity

Hans swung at the vertical log and missed. His axe struck its edge and skipped, throwing his arms to one side. With an angry grunt, he dug the axe head out of the ground and picked the log back up to put it on his splitting stump.

The boy had been at it all morning, and his hands were raw to show for it. He had huge stacks of wood piled up at Mrs. Craws' house—the lady he was staying with currently—and plenty to share with others who would need it. His family's house had not been rebuilt, though Mr. Todson, one of their resident builders, had already offered to do the necessary labor. Hans would have helped him raise it, he just . . . didn't have the willpower yet. So he was helping everyone else instead. It was easier.

Hans split his target, looked at his blistered hand, and decided enough was enough. He laid the axe up against the crude woodshed and set about gathering his last round of split wood. As he did so, he began whistling one of his mother's favorite tunes, but it died after the first few bars. Just like her. He . . . tried not to think of her. It just made him sad and lonely, and worst of all, he might start crying again. He was a man now at fourteen, and men did not cry. His father had always said that.

"Hans dear!" came Adina Craws' voice from out front. Hans looked to see her walking toward him beside the house. With a too-large nose and wispy brown hair that never wanted to grow long, Mrs. Craws was far from the prettiest lady Hans knew, but she and her husband were very kind people. Having lost their own son years back, they had offered him shelter now that both his parents were dead. He was already used to living without Father, and now he would just have to get used to one more hole in his life. Simple as that.

Seeing the large amount of wood he had already piled up, Mrs. Craws nodded appreciatively and said, "Honey, Mr. Todson is here again."

"Oh." Hans tried to think of something better to say, but he came up short. Instead, he nodded in reply and followed her out to where the tall man stood, wearing traditional hempen attire and a leather tool belt.

"Ahoy, Hans!" the man greeted in his scratchy voice. "I just got done with the Harpers' new house, and I'm going to start rebuilding Greta's now. You don't have to help if you don't want to."

"No, no, I'll—" Hans' voice caught, and he coughed awkwardly. Pounding his chest and swallowing, he said, "No, I'll help you with it, sir. I . . ." He trailed off.

Hal Todson stepped forward and took Hans by the shoulder with one gloved hand. "My boy, it's all right to grieve. Many in the village are grieving. But you're strong, just like your parents were. You'll get through it. Work will help you."

Strong . . . were they? If Mother was strong, then why did she leave me?

Hans clenched his hands so that Mr. Todson couldn't see his blisters. Work was the only way he knew to cope with loss. "Thanks," he mumbled.

"I'm going to get started now," Hal said. "Come on. We'll finish clearing the area and then take some measurements. Wes will help as well."

Wes was Hal's son, a few years older than Hans. Hans knew him fairly well, as there were only a dozen boys in the village. One less now, since Khoi had died in the bombings two weeks ago. "All right," Hans said a little more enthusiastically. At least, he meant it to be so. He ducked inside the house to gather a few things—especially his gloves—and ran back out to meet Mr. Todson, who had already headed for Greta's house.

Cleaning up the village would be a long process, and they would be at it a while, so he should put himself to work rather than dwell on his losses. For Master Long, and for Gaea. For his family. Someday, Gaea would be his to reclaim. *Miss Lyn . . . I hope you're safe out there. You'd better change this world.*

Long sat in the outlying field underneath the massive pear tree, meditating. Legs folded and eyes closed, he battled his own conflicted thoughts. Not exactly inner peace, but that was hard to find these days. The damp grass helped to keep him awake.

The ancient, fading man was still recovering from his exertion two weeks back, though he liked to think that his body was still young and spry. He was far from the condition he was once in, and that was fine with him. As he had tried to impress on young Lynchazel, there was more to life than chasing eternal health, youth, money, anything like that. One day down the line there would still be a coffin, or worse. No matter how much the Gaean Senate liked to delude themselves. Man was not meant to live forever.

Long sighed and cracked his eyes open. The sun had already risen well past the horizon, yet the hazy clouds attempted to obscure it from view, allowing the dew more time to hang around. The temperature was just right. The truth was that Long was anticipating another attack, whether he liked it or not. The villagers rebuilt as he sat there, restoring the village, yet it could be wiped clean once more in a matter of weeks . . . even days, though he doubted that. He didn't want to believe it, but the Senate was both fickle and cruel . . . and he wasn't sure how much they knew about this place.

One thing was certain, however: If it came down to it, he would struggle till his last breath to save these humans. To the bitter end. He was done with this body anyway, and had escaped death for far too long. Perhaps he could even be out there like Lyn, fighting for the freedom of Gaea and the sad people that were the Hellebes clones . . . but no, he'd made his choice long ago—and he had a duty here.

End of Part Four

α PART FIVE α

A

Civil War

Gaea

To Fell a Titan

It almost amuses me how far my own mind has fallen from all human ideals. Human life means fair nothing to me at this point, as the entirety of my world revolves around transcending and replacing that dated race. All while providing sustenance for the ever-ravenous machine of progress.
— From Lhinde's Vault

"So . . . let me get this straight," Kaen said, making precise hand motions to get his point across better. "You agreed to marry Sylleo, Senator of Ccamos, just so he would do *one* mission with you guys? Getting you into Haccolces so I could ambush you twice?"

I winced. "Look, I know it sounds bad if you put it like that, but . . . he's not that bad. I could do worse."

"Do worse?" he said incredulously. "You could do worse? Is that how you look at this?"

We were arguing outside the Ccamos military base, where Kaen was staying in the special forces division. He had called me there, saying we had something urgent to talk about. The stone exowall of the barracks was to my back, and the sun threatened to blind me whenever I looked up at Kaen— who now stood six inches taller than I. Instead, I glared down at the stone courtyard beneath his feet, smushing my lips together, chewing on the bottom one. I knew this would happen when he found out. I also knew it wouldn't be easy to explain. "Look, it's my life I'm ruining, okay? Or maybe there's a loophole, and I can just divorce him soon after."

"Divorce him. Did you read the fine print?"

"Uh . . . no?"

"Then just assume you can't. He's a dictator, Lyn. Get real."

I sighed. "Look . . . I'm sorry, Kaen. If you hadn't gone and died a month before, then maybe I wouldn't have . . . never mind. Sorry."

My friend didn't get angry, as he would have while under the influence of the Heart of Mani. Instead, he cocked his head, staring sidelong at me. "Are you saying what I think you're saying?"

"That I loved you more than a brother? I-I don't know. Maybe I did. But now that you're alive . . . Look, Mydia is waiting back on Mani. You really should go see her again."

He looked like he'd been slapped. Crossing his arms, he leaned back against a sign behind him. His stance was far less certain, more vulnerable and awkward than his heavy body looked capable of. "Lyn, I . . ." He cut off and tried again a second later. "I don't even know what to say to that. I'm not trying to tell you how to live your life, and it's none of my business, I just . . . this doesn't seem like you. I know Mydia loves me, I do. What am I saying? It's fine. That sword messed with my head for so many months that I still can't trust my feelings."

"Then go sort them out while you fight bad guys for Sylleo." I pumped my fist playfully. "I'll be waiting to hear what you'll say to Mydia, so let me know when you come up with something good."

He snorted and gave a weak smile.

I punched him in the chest, hard enough to cause him to take an involuntary step backward. "And make sure you tell me."

Kaen socked me back, his fist thudding into my chest just below the collarbone. I was ready for it, so I didn't have to step back to brace myself. "What was that?" I asked mockingly. "A girl punch?"

"You are a girl. You get girl punches." He shrugged and turned to walk away.

Annoyance flared up in me, but I kept myself from a hotheaded response. Kaen would get over it.

I left the barracks, messaging my future husband as I went. *Updates on the Senate?*

I've talked with most of them by now. No one is willing to support our side—not openly. Lldsaor in particular is taking his sweet time responding to me, probably trying to find the best possible threat to leverage against us. But of course, I have you, so I think I'll be all right.

Right. Yeah, he had me, the best leverage in the whole world . . . Man, I loved being a political pawn. *And what about Strongs?* I asked. *Think he's going to attack?*

More than likely. He'll figure out a way.

Then maybe we should just take the fight to him, before he strikes. While we wait for the Senate to make up their minds.

After a delay, he replied: *It's a possibility.*

Not a half hour later, Sylleo informed me that we would move forward with the preemptive strike. I couldn't help a bit more fist-pumping when I heard the news. And not only was I going to get out of Ccamos after three days of sitting around, but Sylleo was *letting* me go. I'd assumed he would be more protective of me after our 'bargain'. He knew how I felt about the arrangement, so he wasn't going to keep bringing it up. I certainly wasn't going to, though I wished I knew when he was hoping to have this ceremony . . .

Later that day, we met with a few of Sylleo's generals to plan how best to break into Haven and what to do about Strongs. We decided that trying to capture Strongs or sabotage his preparations—whatever their extent— was too dangerous. We would find incriminating evidence that we could show to the Senate to prove what Strongs was trying to do. If we could prove beyond a shadow of a doubt that he was actively attempting to kill the Mother that everyone else wanted alive, then that would be enough for him to be formally punished.

So we began planning for the attack. Sylleo would have come himself had he not had political obligations. Kaen and I would handle any other Hunters he had, provided there was not an entire army's worth of them, and together we were reasonably certain we could handle most any opposition thrown at us. "Just remember," Sylleo warned on that count, "that Strongs is exceedingly dangerous. Nowadays he's known for sitting back and letting others do the heavy lifting, but should he join the fight . . . well, he is an Elite, and as such, possesses powers that no one else does. Strongs was always the best warrior of us, save perhaps for Lldsaor."

"What are his powers?" I asked. I knew that Sylleo was able to move at blinding speeds that should be physically impossible.

"I'm not certain on all of them, but I know that he can read thoughts and intents when someone is nearby. Aside from that, his Geokinetic abilities are largely defensive."

"That shouldn't be too bad, then," Kaen said. "As long as we don't give him a way out, he won't be able to do anything against us. I'd take that over actual mind control any day."

Sylleo smirked. "You say that now. Just . . . protect Lyn. That's an order, soldier." He clapped Kaen on the shoulder. "Keep her safe." He pronounced those three words with the utmost precision and emphasis.

"I will, sir."

"Good man."

α Chapter 57 α

Haven

Nature is but a stepping stone we've long bypassed. The natural order serves us, and not the other way around . . . or so we would like to believe.
I have my doubts.
— From Lhinde's Vault

Two hours before next dawn, we left with General Inecc and General Frauss. Kaen was with Frauss's team, while I was with Zent and Inecc. As soon as the city came into view, it was clear why Strongs was called the military man of the Senate: It was not a city, but a giant fortress. Inside the bloodred shield, the city walls created an imposing barrier with defense towers placed close together. Haccolces and even Ccamos had the same, but these were heavily outfitted with weaponry, as though Strongs was expecting a war any day. And perhaps he was, the way he was going. *Is this why he so boldly opposes the Emperor?*

Well, we would see today what it took to get past his defenses.

We utilized the same shieldbuster/missile combo that the Red Horizon had used on the Haccolces shield wall when they first broke me out of prison. Auroras, that brought back memories. Once inside, I saw that the city really was laid out like one huge military base. Interesting that he chose to call it Haven when it looked like such a hellish place to me.

We were immediately targeted with all manner of automatic energy cannons. Alarms blared from multiple towers, but we ignored them. Inecc and Fraus took us into a dive and wove between the large, square buildings of Haven, heading for the command center at the middle. *Wait . . . is that a thing? Having your command center at the literal center?*

Sometimes I'm the last to pick up on things.

Someone radioed our ship. "Haven security. Stand down now, or you will be destroyed."

Inecc did not respond. Those were his orders. He would follow them whatever the cost.

"Will we make it there before they shoot us down, General?" I asked.

"Oh yeah. Don't worry."

Within another minute, both of our ships were docking at central command, our shields having sustained considerable damage but holding up thanks to Geokinetic pooling from our crews. We piled out of the ships, spotting no soldiers on the premises. Alarms blared about the place nonetheless, and we soon saw the first of the security force. Not wishing to take any excessive lives, I said, "Hang on." I felt for Gaea's quavering breath beneath my feet, probing for Geothermic signatures. Yes, this was a hotspot. Of course it was. I pulled on it and unleashed a Geokinetic shockwave that slammed into the soldiers, flinging them backward. It was the same trick I'd performed back in Haccolces shortly after obtaining my new power, before learning to control it.

We split up and broke into the main complex, tracing mental maps memorized at the mission briefing. It was labyrinthine like most Gaean superstructures, functional and heavily built. Despite the surprisingly light security force outside, it wasn't long before we met more serious opposition:

Two black-suited Hunters. The suits, according to Kaen, were biointegrated in ways that no previous models were, bearing patterns like veins that crisscrossed over their armor plates and limbs, with helmets carved like menacing monster faces. He wore his own now. Their visors glowed green. Well-armed, they fanned out around us, dodging fire from our soldiers. More Hellebes filed in behind them, and soon we had a full-out firefight. I was forced to back off and prepare an energy beam. I vaporized an entire wall and some ten Hellebes soldiers, including one of the obsidian warriors, but they kept coming. The black Hellebes were so much faster than our soldiers that the remaining one was able to kill one or two each in the time it took to dodge a single shot from Inecc's energy rifle.

My vision was creeping toward the dangerous white. I pushed back, breathing with concerted evenness, shoving it away. I circulated Gaea's blood through my own using Geothermic breathing, and the world came back into focus. In and out, breath for breath. *You've got this, Lyn.*

The scene was chaos. I had never pictured having to fight them in these enclosed spaces. I could have buried them all or melted them into obliteration if I could get in a clean shot without hitting my comrades. Instead, I used my Octobug to pelt the enemy with heat rounds, each one nearly capable of penetrating a personal shield. Seizing an opening, I jumped in and grabbed hold of the closer black-armored Hellebes, throwing him to the ground before putting two rounds through his back. I didn't want to kill any soldiers, poor pawns as they were, but with these there was just no other choice.

No more Hunters.

I unleashed another rippling wave into the enemy, peeling wall and floor off to crash into them, and we took the opposite hallway, proceeding on our course. I couldn't be certain, but I thought we had lost five men back there in that skirmish. Five allies dead, but two black-suited experiments down.

Two floors up, we were closing in on the administrative office. Strongs should be within the vicinity . . . in fact, I could feel his presence close by.

Too close. We should have been fine. Just as Inecc kicked in a door, a massive figure loomed before us in the hallway. He caught the broken door in one hand as it crashed inward, and then threw the entire door behind him with a dragging motion. A two-inch thick, brass-worked door, like a hunk of wood. "Looking for something?" asked Senator Strongs.

Hellsbreath!

Inecc took a step back, and Strongs seemed to cover two meters in a blink, kicking the general so hard that he flew backward, knocking over two of our soldiers and slamming against the far wall with a cluster bomb of crunches. Inecc groaned as he slid to the floor along with concrete dust, revealing a hole in the wall behind him.

Strongs unclenched and re-clenched his fist, as though thinking on how pleasurable it felt to hit someone for the first time in a while. "Well? What is your business—thought you could waltz in and infiltrate my city? Or have you just come to deliver an offering?"

"Senator Strongs," I said loudly, "You are coming with us. You'll face the justice of the Senate."

No, it had not been the plan . . . but it was now.

The Elite only laughed menacingly. "Almost funny. But I think I'll kill all of you instead. That will send a clearer message to Sylleo. You are the aggressors here, after all."

He rushed Zent, who dodged his blow, seeing it coming in time. One of our soldiers opened fire on the Senator, but the beams only reflected off of a strong shield. More fire, and every beam glanced off or reflected right back. *An advanced Geokinetic shield, for Gaea's sake* . . . Or was this Strongs' defensive ability Sylleo had warned of?

"Wait!" I shouted. "Stop—he can repel energy weapons."

Kaen stepped in with his sword to defend Zent, and Strongs turned on him with a derisive snort. "So you've come as well, Hunter. I should have known I'd lose you sooner or later. You had so much potential. But now that I've got her right in my grasp, I don't need you." He unleashed a flurry of attacks at Kaen, who backed off and tried to get in a swipe with his blade. But every time he tried . . .

It was as though Strongs could see his attacks coming. And he did.

Any others who got close enough, Strongs would take a bare moment to turn on him and deliver a crushing blow with precision, each with the power to break bones and snap necks. I didn't know if there was a limit to how many minds he could read at once, but it certainly made for an unfair advantage. No wonder he was so confident. Or was he simply reading all incoming attacks, no matter the source?

Either way, I determined to give him no opening, as Sylleo had said. I attacked from behind while Kaen kept him busy from the other side, and the Senator was forced to deal with us both at once. Kaen had the range and I had the speed to keep up with an Elite, but still neither one of us could land a hit on him . . .

Before I could see his movements, Strongs spun and grabbed me by the neck. I'd thought him distracted by Kaen, but he knew exactly where I was the whole time. I gasped in his grip, struggling to breathe. His hands were so large that his pinky and ring finger pinched each collarbone while his thumb and middle finger met at the back of my neck, cinching tight my throat. With his pointer finger, he pressed my chin up.

He didn't stop, but kept moving radially, whipping my body with him, and I was flying through the window. All I felt was painful lacerations and complete disorientation as I sailed through the air, landing on my back on the concrete five stories below. The world seemed to crack with my impact. My vision pulsed black and red. I struggled to breathe, as though lacking the strength to open my lungs again. Dazed, cervical vertebrae on fire, I dimly wondered if my skull had split. If it had, and my brain were showing through . . . how big would it look? As small as Phoebe used to say?

Lyn, shut up and focus! Come on! screamed a girlish voice in my head.

A second later, Strongs landed with one foot on each side of me. I couldn't move, so he grabbed me easily by the front of my suit, hoisting me into the air and preparing to strike. Before he could, Kaen had landed as well and was on him with his sword.

Somehow, I caught myself, wobbling on my legs as my chest heaved for breath. I was getting it. My vision was clearing. I didn't know how . . .

Up above, my friends were firing their weapons at the Senator to distract him, and I took the opportunity to gasp for breath and recover. I drew in Geothermic energy to my limits, listening to it pulse through my blood, feeling the fire in my veins. It was just soothing enough to take the edge off my pain. It would also heal me if I held it long enough, though this would be a big job even for Gaea. I was leaking blood onto the concrete in disturbing amounts, and the back of my suit was . . . *Oh, right. The window.* Wasn't ballistic glass supposed to be softer than normal . . . ?

Springier, White corrected. *Not the same thing.*

Sucking in a long, shuddering breath, I breathed with the ebb and flow of the earth. *There we go.* I was back in action. I made a move toward Strongs, and even as I did, I could see in his stance that he knew I was coming, so I backed off and waited.

Zent and Frauss peppered him with their guns as Kaen held him at bay, eliciting a curse from the Senator after many swings of his argent blade. In that instant, I went for it. I leapt with all my strength, taking hold of the giant's arm before he could dodge away. I used it like a fulcrum, his own kinetic energy as the power, to rotate his huge bulk and throw him to the ground. Kaen held his sword at Strongs' neck while I grabbed both arms in a full nelson, snaking under his armpits to clasp his neck from behind. It didn't matter how Strong he was—he couldn't get out of it this time, and reading our attacks wouldn't help him.

I ignored the blood pooling between my bunched shoulder muscles. Let it drip . . . I could last.

I hope.

Strongs responded with only a chuckle as the rest of our men came down to help us out. Knowing he was beaten, he put up little fight. "To think you amateurs had it in you. I haven't been bested in combat in centuries, much less by two semi-humans." His mannerisms suggested an adult whose children had beaten him in a kid's game and was playing along.

Zent bound the Senator's ankles, wrists, upper arms and neck in copper, just to be extra certain, and we called the ships. Sure enough, they came straight over on autopilot. Apparently, the security force had been too preoccupied to take control of our ships.

"Senate," Kaen muttered through heavy breaths, "Meet your new prisoner."

"There's only one thing left," Zent said. "Let's find that evidence. Shouldn't be too hard, given our hostage here."

α   Chapter 58   α

Prisoner of the Senate

Of the matter with the Legaleians, I know little other than that the conflict escalated while I was incarcerated by the Anier. Or . . . perhaps it's over? I know they sent prisoners to the grey moon—I durst not even inquire as to how—and supposedly they will soon move the fabled Font that gave them their powers over the earth. The Anier blamed them and their god for bringing the Cydenges upon us, but if they truly exile them all . . . would the attacks really lessen?
— From Lhinde's Vault

"Bah! I told you already," Strongs said tiredly, "There is no ulterior motive. I wanted you dead, girl. I still do."

The man was chained up in thick copper back at the Ccamos military prison, awaiting the next Senate convention. He almost looked resigned to his lot—the loser in a conflict he started—like he had given up. He certainly sounded the part right now, but I wasn't convinced. Kaen and Zent stood beside me in the prison hallway, arms crossed.

"You're a liability and a danger to our world," Strongs continued. "An enemy to progress. Fools the world over worship you, while the rest fight for control over you. It's been proven that we no longer need a Mother Gaea, and all your existence does is cause division and waste resources, so you have to die."

He said it all so matter-of-factly. It was nothing personal, I just needed to die for his vision of Gaea to come to pass.

"Are you admitting," Zent cut in, "that you crave more power? Maybe world domination?"

Strongs snorted. "I'm not going to give you ammunition to use against me before I'm even tried. What I said already is true and obvious, and the

Senate has heard it before. I insist, there is no ulterior motive."

"He's lying," I said. "And he's going to keep lying until we use those documents against him in court." I turned to leave. We were done here.

"You realize, girl, that Lldsaor and Sylleo both want to use you."

Strongs' words nearly stopped me in my tracks. I slowed, thinking about turning around and giving a response, but instead lengthened my stride. Taking such bait would be the childish thing to do. I'd been immature enough over the last few months. If I wanted anyone to respect me, I knew I would have to keep my emotions in check.

When I found Sylleo in the comms room back at the main military complex, he was in the middle of a conversation with one of the Senators. I couldn't tell at first until I caught some sharp words about me in a distinctive deep voice: Emperor Lldsaor.

"That has nothing to do with it," Sylleo answered into the mic. "I sent her to Haven for proof because I knew she could bring him in if need be. And she did, with the help of that human that Strongs turned into a Hellebes. If I let him go, I guarantee he will send all the military might that it takes to kill her. That is his goal."

Lldsaor was silent on the other end for a moment. "You are adamant about having him tried, then. Very well, we will meet tomorrow in Ccamos." He paused for a moment, waiting for Sylleo to reply. When he didn't, the Emperor said, "What's the matter? Is that not enough? We can meet at your own court."

"Yes. Yes, that will be fine. Thank you for taking this matter seriously." Sylleo hung up shortly, turning to me with an annoyed expression. "He's up to something. Otherwise he wouldn't try to hold the trial here. It should be in Haccolces."

I shrugged. It didn't matter to me. This way, we didn't have to travel, and they could take Strongs back to Haccolces themselves. Or . . . would they just put him under house arrest back in Haven? I would find out soon enough.

Sylleo's expression softened suddenly, and he approached me. "How are you holding up?"

I tensed, trying not to show it. "I'm fine. A little beat up, but I've had much worse."

Sylleo turned me around and pulled up my shirt, looking at the bandaged cuts that laced my back. I tried not to squirm. Next, he massaged my neck with one hand, feeling at the muscles and vertebrae. It was still sore enough to make me wince, and he pulled back his hand. "I'm sorry for sending you by yourself, Lyn," he said finally. "That was poor judgment on my part. I thought you and Kaen would be able to overpower him effectively."

I tried not to take that as an insult. I let him pull me close, resting my head against his short ribs. Just to go along with it and make him feel better, although it did feel . . . nicer than I wanted to admit.

"Two weeks from today," he said softly. "Is that all right?"

I stiffened on reflex, taking a nervous gulp before replacing my head against his side. I didn't have to ask what he referred to. *You're fine with this, Lyn. Just go along with it, at least pretend.* "Yes, that's fine. I was . . . hoping for a little longer. I wanted to at least make it back to Gaea and see my friends first."

He chuckled. "You make it sound like you'll never get another chance. This isn't your funeral we're talking about."

I turned my head away, but the movement only rubbed my forehead against his massive arm. "I don't know if I ever will get a chance, though. I feel trapped every moment I'm on Gaea. Maybe it's the fighting, the constant conflict. Or like a . . . feeling of fate calling me to something, something inevitable."

"It's probably just because you're the famous Mother Heiress who came back from Mani," he reasoned. "Everyone is holding you to some kind of standard, expecting something of you."

Especially you, I grumbled in my head. Fortunately, he couldn't read thoughts like Strongs. He finally let me go, and I tried not to step away too quickly. Wouldn't want to offend. "Thank you," I said as I left, unsure why. "I'll, uh, I'll make sure I get plenty of rest before tomorrow."

"That's my girl."

Gaea

Your girl . . . please . . . don't say it like that.

Tomorrow rolled around, and the custom aircraft began to arrive. The Emperor's airship was particularly impressive, painted in an elaborate red-and-gold design resembling a rack of swords. I couldn't believe the ruler of the most drab, ugly city on the planet had a ship so stylish.

Strongs' ship, of course, was the only one missing. But I was confident it would be hideous and utilitarian, probably shaped like a flying box. Well, okay, that wouldn't be utilitarian. But you get my point.

The early autumn leaf fall from the vibrant yellow-and-orange trees near the mansion spread a glorious backdrop for the arrival of the Senators—steadily landing one by one. I stood by outside to greet them, trying my best to look pleased to see each and every one. Relatively speaking, I was, since none of them—hopefully—were out to kill me like a certain favorite tyrannical biomachine.

Following refreshments for the guests at the residential manse, we gathered at the enormous assembly hall adjoining the main administrative complex. After that point, it was all business. Each of the Senators had brought lawyers versed in all things law-related, who reminded me of referees at a sports event. We produced the prisoner—unchained, since Sylleo said it would be shameful to treat him like that among fellow Senators.

I watched from the back of the hall along with Kaen. We would be acting as witnesses. There was a whole lot more complexity to the proceedings, but most of that had gone—and would continue to go—over my head.

Most of the trial, unsurprisingly, consisted of arguing, disputing and a bit of bickering back and forth between the seven Senators not standing on trial. The rest was all formality. Or was the bickering part of the formality? Lldsaor went livid once we brought out the documentation of Strongs' communications with Daedalus' scientists. The way Sylleo's lawyer spun it, he was only working with the scientists, and Daedalus had no actual part in it. That was intentional, meant to give Daedalus an escape card to side with us, should he be brave enough.

He wasn't, of course. Sweating and jittery, the rhinoceros of a man kept stealing glances at Strongs throughout the meeting as though expecting him to turn him in. At this point, however, that would look like desperation on Strongs' part, especially since he hadn't said much in his own defense so far. Throwing out accusations in retaliation would get him nowhere.

Disturbingly enough, when he was given a proper chance to speak, Strongs spent most of it trying to sway them to his point of view. I needed to die, they needed to forget about the Mother and move on into the future, entering the next stage of humanity, yada yada . . .

In the end, Strongs was sentenced to one month of prison to atone for his crimes against Gaea and the Senate, whilst a Haven official of the Emperor's own choosing would take his place for the time being. This couldn't have been any more of a relief for me. Not only did the majority of them take Sylleo's side, but we would have one month of freedom from Strongs' insane ambitions—after which he would have to be more careful.

That left two weeks for my honeymoon.

Lyn, you idiot. How could I think about that at a time like now? I spent most days trying to actively avoid thinking about the eventual fate I'd consigned myself to, but now there was a date in place. I was getting married. So little time, yet I had a feeling it would crawl.

Pronouncement made, Kaen and I shared relieved glances across the room while Strongs ground his teeth. Lldsaor addressed the Senate once more, but not to adjourn the meeting. "Men, we must make a decision on one more matter. I think this situation only proves that the Mother is not safe in Ccamos. I am not accusing anyone else of conspiring to kill her, but her safety is not something to take lightly."

I blinked. Did I just hear him right? My safety? *This* man?

"Now, hold on just one . . ." Sylleo began, but the Emperor cut him off with an outstretched hand, voice growing firmer, bordering on harsh:

"This is not a sudden thought, Senator Sylleo. You have kept her long enough, under the umbrella of the guest provision. We have allowed that, but the time has come to take other things into consideration. On top of that, she was nearly killed when you *personally* sent her to capture the one you knew was after her. This shows a severe lapse in judgment; it is up to us to decide on a better place to keep her. Gentlemen, who agrees?"

Brant and Vladimir's hands shot up, along with Daedalus, DeWitt . . . even Holman. The only hands left down were Sylleo's and Strongs'. The Haven Senator watched the vote with dark amusement.

"Excellent," said Lldsaor, clapping his hands. "Sylleo, we will be respectfully taking her off your hands, not as a punishment but as an act of better judgment. I propose Haccolces."

Oh, not that place again. Anywhere but there. It seemed every time I turned around I was heading back to that capital of steel and smog.

After much hemming and hawing, the Senate came to a consensus: I was going to Haccolces. They would ship Strongs back on the imperial aircraft and return for me in two days.

If there was one thing to be gained from this turn of events, it was that I might—*might*—just get out of this whole honeymoon thing.

α   Chapter 59   α

From the Inside

The titans, however, are what I'm most curious about. Mani I have heard whispers about . . . the Silver Titan . . . but he was exiled sometime before my birth. There are many stories explaining the "young" silver moon, and I do not know what to believe. But Luna . . .
— From Lhinde's Vault

We went along with it. Even Sylleo admitted there was nothing to be done; the Senate had unanimously decided, so to Haccolces I would go.

The next day, he called me in to his office to talk to me. Margill let me into the manse and gave me directions—but did not follow. I tiptoed into the room, one palm on the ornate crown molding of the door. Sylleo was pacing back and forth when I entered, dressed in a checkered red suit with khaki pants and a dark suit coat. Sweat beaded on his brow, and he looked uncharacteristically nervous, maybe more so than the day he'd proposed to me.

Shutting the door behind me, I asked, "Sylleo? What is this about?" I hadn't been too concerned, but seeing him like this certainly gave me pause.

The Senator cleared his throat. "Lyn. I'm glad you came. I was just . . . well, I wanted to apologize." His words came out as though relinquished grudgingly. It wasn't that he looked unhappy with me, more as though the apology triggered some deep Senatorial pride he'd been trying to bury.

Not deep enough, apparently.

"For? Is this about our wedding?" My tone was probably . . . a bit harsher than necessary.

"Sort of. That is out of the question now, Heiress. You needn't worry about any wedding. I . . . I wanted to marry you. I . . ." He coughed and held his hand to his forehead, wiping at the sweat. His skin tone was a shade more flushed than usual. He lowered his voice to a near whisper. "I had it pretty bad for your mother too, Lyn, even though I only got to meet her a few times after she entered adulthood. I was crushed when, after all those years, she vanished. It was a foolish and distant fantasy. But then you came along, and . . . reawakened that same desire. I'm sure everyone says it, but you look just like her. To many, you are the same woman. I couldn't help but fall in love with you. But I'm good at putting on airs, so I did my best to look the virtuous gentleman. The truth is that I'm no different from other Senators. I sought to use you in more ways than one, and despite my best efforts, I thought of you as a thing, a resource, a prize. Just like all the other Elites.

"I felt some pain after sending you to capture Strongs, but I told myself it would be easier once I was legally bound to you. Easier to use you as what you are—a weapon. The greatest this world has ever known. You are the closest we ever came to creating the Cydenges weapons we always wanted."

I swallowed, feeling a mix of emotions at his confession but unsure what to make of it. No, not just unsure—baffled beyond words. Angry, certainly, and hurt. Slightly flattered when he said I looked like my mother, but the compliment was squashed flat by the rest of his ramblings, as though purposely trying to derail every picture I'd had of him. Every one except the realization that had been building since the day he proposed: He was selfish and cold on the inside, like Lldsaor. Like Strongs. Vlad. Brant. Daedalus. Like Dekla.

He was not wrong there.

"Why are telling me all this now?" I demanded through a suddenly-hoarse throat.

He gave a shaky sigh. At length, he admitted, "Because Lldsaor has ruined my plans, perhaps for good. They've bested me. If there is a way to recover you after this, it will never be the same. The Senate is against me."

"So not because you actually feel sorry."

"Not . . . not really, no." He shrugged, crossing his arms. He looked *very* uncomfortable. "As I explained, I'm not who you think I am. I was there when the plan was made to change out Lhinde's broken body for a new one—

the one we named Lynchazel—and to carefully guide the growth of the new child, making her into the ultimate energy supply. I was one of the heads of that project."

"But so was Long!" I protested, unsure of why I was suddenly defending him. "He changed, so—"

He cut me off. "No, he's different. He got out of it; in fact, he never truly was into it. He opposed us all along the way."

I wanted to argue that he shouldn't be so hard on himself, that he wasn't making sense, that I knew him to be better than that, but . . . I found myself only growing in anger. Because he was right—he was a tyrant. He thought of the Hellebes as ants in his anthill, dogs in a kennel, serfs in his fields. And the way he looked at me, possessively as though of an object, or an animal that was prettier than the rest of her herd. *Well, let's not go that far. There's no 'prettiest' in a herd of one.* One human, anyway. No, he was like Vlad, simply not as vulgar with his comments.

"Fine, then," I said at last. My voice sounded only hoarser, and for some reason I was blinking rapidly. "I-I'd rather marry you than be locked up in that dungeon of Lldsaor's again, but you know as well as I that that's desperation, not love. I'll go. I'll be Lldsaor's pet. You can stay here in Ccamos and live your pitiful life, pretend you're a gentleman . . . I'll manage somehow."

I stalked from the room.

The day of leave-taking arrived, and I sat on the rooftop of Sylleo's manse, watching the sun rise over Ccamos' eastern skyline. I was still angry. I didn't consider myself the bitter type, but we women are good at holding grudges. I told myself I'd keep this one till the day I or Sylleo died—and I knew full well which one would come first.

Not if they put you in that tank, Lyn . . .

I sighed, checking the time on my wrist console. Roughly four hours until Lldsaor's men would get here, and I vacillated on whether I wanted the remaining time to slow or hasten. Neither phenomenon would help the gnawing unease gestating inside me.

Kaen was the one to find me, unsurprisingly. I heard the footsteps on the roof behind me, and within a few, I recognized his walk. Heavier bulk, but still the same rough gait. I turned, trying not to frown too much while also hoping he could see the hurt on my face. Perhaps I just wished I could blame it all on him.

"Nice sunrise, huh?" he said, taking a seat beside me on the metal shingles.

"Yeah," I mumbled, picking at a fresh-trimmed fingernail.

"They go by quick, though, huh?"

"What?" I looked up at him with wrinkled brows.

"The sunrises. Here on Gaea."

"Oh. Mm-hmm." A lot faster than one-to-two days, the span of early morning on Mani.

"C'mon, Lyn. We have a few more hours together. Can't spend it being all moody."

I glared at him. "You understand that's not how you cheer a girl up, right?"

He shrugged. "Wouldn't know. I'm a Hellebes."

I scoffed. "Yeah, right. You still walk like an ox."

"Huh?"

I smiled. Not a happy one, just a personal smirk. I knew he was trying, I just . . . no. I was wrong, and I knew it. I hesitated, allowing one side of my brain to growl in frustration at the other, and then said, "I'm-I'm sorry, Kaen. Nothing's going my way, so I just feel like being a jerk. It's . . . hard not to."

He nodded, scratching his elbow absently. "I suppose I can relate. I'd like to think I'm done with that, but I don't think any of us can ever shake our faults."

I sighed. "I guess. So . . . you're just going to be working for Sylleo now? Strongs isn't going to try to claim you as his property or whatever?"

He snorted. "Illegal property. I'm pretty sure most of the Senate doesn't like what he was doing behind the scenes with those Hunter Hellebes. Man,

I'm glad to be free of that. It was like having a vivid dream you can't control. You try, but nothing happens, and things go however you don't want them to. I'll never be able to shake those memories."

"And yet we've both killed plenty of Hellebes," I said dully. "Some humans as well."

"True. I didn't—I didn't say that was okay. Or normal. Or enjoyable. But . . . it's different when they're not your enemies—just targets to kill. Obstacles in the way of an overlord who sees them like bugs."

"Kind of like being a soldier in Lord Kalceron's army," I said with a small, ironic laugh.

"Kind of like that," he repeated softly.

Way to bring up bad memories, Lyn, I chided myself. But who was I kidding? The present was sadder than any memories from Mani. Mandrie lost, Kaen transfigured into a biomachine, and me about to be sent off on a platter to the tyrant emperor of my mother's world.

And then . . . the truly horrific memories, the ones I'd inherited. I tried to shove them away every time they rose to the surface, because I had too much to deal with now.

"So, is there a reason you came up here?" I asked, placing my chin over my folded arms, staring off into the rising sun.

"To give you a hug, obviously," he said, holding out his arms. "You don't want a hug? Okay, you don't want a hug. Actually, there is a reason. Sylleo told me to find you, because there's something we need to discuss before they come and get you."

"We as in more than just him and me?"

"I'll be there. Zent will be there. It's important, trust me."

I looked at him skeptically.

"Also, Sylleo told me to give you a hug. That you'd probably need it."

"Sylleo told you to give me a hug," I repeated flatly.

He nodded.

"Then I'm really glad you didn't."

When I entered the command room, I saw that Zent was indeed already here, along with Frauss and another general. Kaen followed me in and said, "I apologize for our tardiness, sir."

Sylleo merely gave him a nod. "Now," he said, addressing the gathering. "We are shipping the Mother Heiress off in three hours. Lyn . . . I'm truly sorry for the way things have played out. But know that we are not going to let you go into captivity without an attempt to turn the situation in our favor. In your favor. You will not be going without a plan. So listen close; this will not succeed without participation from all parties here, as well as complete secrecy outside this room."

I shared a look with Kaen, then Zent. Both men seemed to be encouraging me with subtle gestures to hear him out. I supposed I could listen for one more hour, or however long this took, if it meant that somehow he could help me win my freedom.

"Lynchazel, be careful."

Mother's words gave me pause. It had been a while since I'd dreamed of her, and I was overjoyed to see her phantom again, but when she greeted me so, my smile dropped and I knew she was here for a reason. As though a spell had broken, my brain began to work again. "I . . . thought you said you wouldn't be appearing anymore."

"Indeed. But Lhinde is already winning the battle in your mind—and she manipulated me into encouraging you to find the key."

"I know. But Mother, what is this really about?"

She looked down, silent for a moment. "I don't know. Just . . . be careful. I sense danger in your coming days."

I crossed my arms. "So you can read the future now? My future?" I wasn't sure why I was treating this like an argument all of a sudden.

"No. You know this is only a reflection of my mind lingering within yours, daughter. But I can see the thoughts that trouble you below the surface.

Layers of them. You're frightened of what may come, and for good reason. Lldsaor is a man corrupted long ago by power. Given over to it."

"I know," I whispered, and this time not out of frustration. My grudge was not with her, but with Sylleo—and the Emperor. "I'll . . . try to be careful, Mother."

She smiled. "I should go, love."

I nodded sullenly, feeling the dream slipping away. *I'll try to make you proud, Mother. I'll try.*

I know you will. The returning impression of her voice was soft as petals before joining the darkness of sleep.

Willing Experiment

She is an even greater mystery. The Lady of Gold, they called her, one of many names. The Lady of Proliferation, worshipped as a fertility goddess in a nation long ago. Before it was called Luna Halcyon. Before . . . well, there are many theories. I believe she was once a titan guardian of Gaea, just like Mani, but was embittered against humanity and fled to the moon. The greater moon.

— From Lhinde's Vault

Lldsaor came to get me personally. A bit of pomp followed a dash of formality, but nothing excessive: He brought just one ship, his personal cruiser that had come for the court meeting the other day. And with him were none other than Vladimir and Brant. It was almost like he didn't know my abilities well enough yet to trust that he could keep me in line.

Of course, he didn't mention anything like that. When we came out to meet them, the Emperor stepped down from the airship while his cronies stayed on board the vessel, staring down at my companions with measured distaste. "My good lady," Lldsaor said with a small bow. "It is our honor to escort you back to safety."

"Of course," I said, returning the bow. I made mine excessively long and gratuitous. Nothing wrong with making the Emperor feel just a little silly for his pretense of hospitality. It would soon be gone, after all.

I turned, waving at my friends. "See ya, guys." I blew Sylleo a little kiss, causing him to frown and Frauss to turn on him with the same expression. In some corner of my mind, I knew that was going a bit far. Following Lldsaor into the shuttle, I tried without success to shove down the rising sense of panic in my chest. I was giving up my freedom here in the one city that welcomed me. Willingly giving it up, and my companions were letting me.

Brant and Vlad picked on me surprisingly little on the way there—that is to say I was surprised they didn't have me dancing in my underclothes while the soldiers gawked. It wasn't *quite* that bad.

Lldsaor himself was unusually quiet, riding in his front-row passenger seat as his captain flew us, looking our way just often enough to remind me that I shouldn't get any ideas about a one-woman mutiny. I tried to take his fear of me with a bit of pride.

I had questions I'd have asked my captors on the long ride, but I stayed mostly silent for a few reasons. I didn't want to look desperate, and I also didn't want to look friendly. These were no friends of mine, no sir. Most of all, however . . . it just felt pointless.

When we finally reached Haccolces, I made out the skyline, the shield wall, the smoggy atmosphere . . . a sight I never wanted to see again. What a disgusting city. The shield wall opened right up for our official vessel, and we docked at Lldsaor's personal airport next to the Capitol Building. It would seem that this complex was as much the Emperor's home as his office.

When we landed, I was informed of a meeting in the lab complex. I paid attention as he led me through the dimly-lit halls, noting turns and doorways. I had been through here for my tests when they imprisoned me and Zent, but we were coming from the opposite direction and at least one floor up. Would they lock me up there or somewhere else?

We entered an innocuous room, and Lldsaor followed me in only by himself. No guards. But I noticed that both Brant and Vlad were waiting outside the door just . . . you know, in case.

I took a seat across from the Emperor at a plain metal table. His powerful aura seemed to beat against mine, tangible and threatening, but it didn't frighten me as it had when I'd first met him. The rest of the room was empty and hollow, and might as well have not existed. The only important things in this room were Lldsaor and the doorway out.

"It's good to see you again, Little Gaea" he lied. His booming voice seemed to split the still air like thunder.

"Nice to see you again, too," I lied back.

The Emperor cleared his throat purposefully. "Let's get down to business. We need you, and we especially need to perform some examinations on you to see where your body is at health-wise and what Geokinetic potential you have unlocked. The Red Horizon and Senator Sylleo were kind enough to do some of that for us. But Strongs and his little mole kept the data largely secret."

I thought about making another snide comment, but decided against it. I'd try and abide by Sylleo's guidelines for now and see how the conversation went. Not for the first time, however, I couldn't help wondering what further experiments they had to run.

Really, Lyn, White chided me. *They're just interested in your progress—just like Dekla. You're not the same idiot you were three months ago; you're a more powerful idiot.*

She had a point.

"This is important for a few reasons," the Emperor continued, oblivious to my internal ramblings. "Obviously, we need to know how dangerous you are, as well as how capable you are in the ways we originally intended: To power our world as your mother once did. But we also need to know how effective the unplanned circumstances surrounding your birth, childhood and training were."

How effective . . . very well put. I'd bet they were ticked already to see that I was able to take down Strongs. And yet . . . "And what if it turns out I'm not up to par?" I asked. "What if I'm not any more powerful than your creation that you're currently using? This Zeta Beast? Are you going to breed me like the first Mother and try for a purer bloodline? Will you . . . get rid of me altogether?" I had to force the words out of my mouth. I wasn't sure which possibility sickened me more.

Lldsaor blinked, and possibly even flinched, at my words. "So he did tell you some things. I can say with confidence that the current conduit is like a cow is to a lion, or a sheep to a mountain lion. We will never be able to replicate what we achieved with the Mother Project."

And why is that? It was one of those sticking points that made no sense to me still: With the advanced cloning methods available to them, and of course DNA storage and bioengineering . . . why couldn't they just print a dozen of me? Who needed the real Lyn when they could just duplicate me?

Foregoing that entire route of argument, I asked, "But you're not going to use me? You don't have to mince words. I know what we're talking about now."

The Emperor stared into me for a moment. "We will use you. But we might not put you back in that tank." He leaned in. "Depending on how you comply, we might find other uses for you."

That was . . . a good sign. Maybe. They needed my willing help, not just my body. Or was he toying with my mind to keep me on my best behavior?

"How was your stay with Sylleo?" he asked, seeming to take my silence for a favorable response. Why the sudden diversion of topic? "Was he everything you hoped he would be? The perfect gentleman none of us could ever be?"

Perfect gentleman . . . uncanny wording. I thought about it for a moment. There was what I thought, and what would be in my best interest to get the Emperor to think, and right now . . . those two aligned pretty well. "No. He's a prideful liar, full of duplicity—just like all of you."

"You seem particularly upset with him."

I set my jaw, trying to keep my face neutral. "I am. And I'd rather not talk about it." Hopefully my little 'performance that was not a performance' was sufficiently convincing to keep him from asking more questions for now. My relationship with Sylleo was complicated enough that I wasn't at all confident in my ability to conceal my last hope of a plan—not in the face of more questioning.

"And what does he think I'm planning right now?" he asked. "What does he think about it?"

Another good sign. Worthy of a small sigh of relief. Hopefully too small for the Emperor to notice. I shrugged, showing nothing with my face. "He didn't really tell me anything. He and I had a sort of falling-out, and I'm glad to be gone."

Lldsaor sat back in his chair. I couldn't tell if he believed me or not, but it was almost the truth. "Interesting. Most interesting. And what do you think of your return to Haccolces?"

"Seriously? As glad as I am to be away from Sylleo, I hate this place. And I don't want to 'work with you'. But I don't have a choice, do I?"

The Emperor seemed to consider this. "Not really, no. But I do think you'll eventually come around to our way of seeing things."

I was pretty sure he was lying with that statement. We both knew the truth there, but hopefully he thought me just desperate and annoyed enough to actually believe him. Never in a thousand years would I rather be here, talking with Lldsaor and his cronies, than back in Ccamos.

Just as I'd told Sylleo . . . as much as it galled me, I'd rather marry a genocidal Elite than be a prisoner again.

Rising from his seat, Lldsaor said, "We're done for now. We will put you in confinement for one day, Lynchazel. We have our reasons. Respect them, and we will also respect you. Tomorrow, we will begin more tests to gauge your body's growth, and I expect good behavior from you. Unless you resist our authority, I promise not to harm you or threaten you with weapons. Keep in mind, you'll be in copper most of the time; my guards will not make the same mistake as last time."

I almost smiled at that. They had been fools. "Yes, sir," was all I said.

Within another ten minutes, I was back in copper and sitting in a cell. Not the same one as before, but no better furnished. Or warmer. What was wrong with these people? One more day, and supposedly I'd get better accommodations . . . if I'd heard him right. But who was to say if the Emperor would keep his word? After all, he'd been talking to a science experiment, and despite anything he might say, I knew the troll saw me that way, not as a woman, nor even a lower person, but a mere thing with intelligence.

Naturally, I took this opportunity to sink into my memories, looking back over the past week or so. I skipped some things, like my frustrating conversations with Sylleo. I began flipping through my mother's memories, as I had during that first day of waiting for Lldsaor to pick me up. The message she had left me, the one that put me into a trance back in the underground lab, had been just that, a message left for her daughter to find, but there was a wealth of knowledge spanning the long centuries of Lynchazel's imprisonment. I was still trying to wrap my head around the idea that her mother before her, this Lhinde, was somehow still hanging around like a vengeful spirit. I didn't believe in things like that, and yet . . .

Lhinde's story was one of the saddest I'd ever heard, enough to make my treatment at the Senate's hands seem insignificant and unworthy of complaint. She had suffered emotional torment every day, witnessed the tortuous death of twenty-three friends, and then watched as her own body fell apart—only to at last be discarded like a rag. Would they do the same to me one day? When I was no longer useful? Doubtless, they'd have done it to my mother.

I could hear her voice now as I listened. The self-proclaimed Voice of Gaea: *Child of pain, you are searching for answers in the past, no?*

I made no answer. I didn't know how interaction with her worked, nor what the consequences could be.

You think that by ignoring me, you can change your story so that it does not reflect mine, and yet your recent memory only confirms mine. You see how corrupt the Anier are. That they must be brought down. They must die at your hands, for my sake. For Lynchazel's sake. For Gaea.

I shook my head. It sounded right, but I knew it wasn't. Slowly, I managed to shake myself from the memories . . . or whatever it was when Lhinde got involved. Lynchazel had called her memories dangerous, as her mind had been tainted by her predecessor's, and therefore so had mine. Lhinde's hatred for her tormentors was strong enough to persist through generations—centuries—undiminished. The very thought made me shudder.

One more day and they would begin. One more day of this cold cell . . . one more day of having my body to myself.

For now, I waited.

α Chapter 61 α

In the Lion's Jaws

*Does she bear as bitter a grudge against Mani as the stories say? If so,
then why is it against Gaea that her anger manifests? Probably because of
the Anier, as in my case . . . We are not so different, perhaps. In any case,
being the mother of the Cydenges, I'd bet anything that their aggression
toward Gaea began around the time she fled to her moon. But who can say?*
— *From Lhinde's Vault*

My door rattled, waking me instantly.

"Who's there?" I called, one foot already on the floor. I couldn't move
as fast with the copper bands on, but my muscles were still trained to respond
instantaneously when needed.

The lights were all off, which I thought odd. Only a faint glow
illuminated the tall figure of an Elite in the doorway, but I couldn't tell which
one. The cell door creaked open, and heavy footfalls sounded as the Senator
walked in. Something was very, very wrong. Every internal alarm rang in
my body, and panic seized me. As he approached, I acted on instinct, lunging
from my cot and swinging a foot to trip his leg while—

His hand caught me by the throat. His grip was so firm that my neck
jolted from my body's inertia. Auroras, that hurt. I wouldn't have hit him
anyway, as my reactions were not as fast without any Geokinetic access. Why
would I try to fight a Senator in this state? His other hand took hold of my
face almost gently, stroking it with two fingers, and I knew who it was before
he even spoke.

"There, there," came that fake, silky voice, hushed as though to keep his
words private and intimate. "Don't be frightened, dear. It's only me, Vlad. I
see pretty well in the dark. Oh, but don't make too much noise, now, or I'll
make this a bit more painful. Plus, no one will hear you anyway. I bought off

the guards and cut the power in this wing. No alarms, no lights, no prying cameras . . . just us. Will you be good?"

I glared in the general direction of his face. His iron grip held my chin up at a terrible angle that prevented me from possibly moving my head even to nod, but I tried to make an "mm-hmm" of affirmation.

"What's that? You'll be good? All right." He stroked my cheek one more time with his foul fingers before letting go, causing me to drop awkwardly and painfully to the floor. I struggled to my feet and fumbled for my bed, which I clambered onto once more. What did this creep want, anyway? Just to torture me, or . . . ?

"Now," he said, kneeling down. Or at least I was pretty sure he did, because the source of his voice dropped. "I came to have a chat with the princess, me and you. Like I said, no one will bother us. I'd ask you to entertain me a little bit, but I think we can save that for some other time. You see, I hear things. I have eyes and ears around the world, and some of them say you might have made a, hmm . . . a promise? To old Silly-O?"

I said nothing.

"Now, see, I was kind of heartbroken to hear that, but I didn't want to tell him as much, because he's got such sensitive feelings and . . . I knew you'd be coming here anyway. The Emperor doesn't know I'm here at the moment, of course, but he'd come around and let us have some quality time together before you go back in that tank. But there is one more idea I had." He paused, and though I couldn't see his face, I could imagine a look of pretend pondering. "I couldn't guarantee you the best living conditions, but it would get you out of your eventual fate in the labs."

"How can you be so certain I'll end up there?"

He laughed. "Oh, come now, darling. You don't think I know Old Sour well? We are best friends, or at least I like to think so. I go along with whatever he wants to do, and he counts me his faithful lapdog, so he tells me everything. He thinks this whole Mother Project has simply gotten, mmm . . . off the rails, and needs to go back on track."

Yet that's not what Lldsaor said. "And so . . ." I coughed, an aftereffect of having my throat crushed by Vladimir's hand. "Do I believe him or you?"

"Why, I suppose that's up to you. I'll leave you for now, but I'll be back sometime. Oh, and if you tell anyone about our little chat, I will make things less pleasant next time. And quite possibly kill you. Good night!"

I shook, grinding my teeth. He wasn't serious about that last part. That at least had to be false . . . right? The amount of loathing I felt for the biomechanical tormentor in that moment was more than can be described in words. Unclenching my right hand slowly, I found it to be . . . hot. Not sweaty. I couldn't see anything, but the sensation was far too familiar to be . . . no, it *had* to be coincidence. Just to prove my fear-induced hallucination false, I turned away from the cameras and snapped my fingers, pretending to call up a flame with my mind.

A flame sprang to life in my palm.

I gaped at it. Then a slow smile spread over my face. *Okay, maybe imprisonment won't be so bad after all.* Although . . . could I trust him about the cameras being deactivated? It sure looked like the power was out.

Better safe than sorry.

After some careful experimentation, I laid back down for the night. Needless to say, my sleep was fitful at best. I hadn't been scared of the dark since early childhood, but Vladimir had stirred a deeply buried terror that kept my heart beating rapidly and my breathing shallow, newly-reawakened magic notwithstanding. The Trident Senator possessed inhumanly keen night vision—perhaps one of the Elites' special Geokinetic abilities? Every time I almost got to sleep, I pictured Vladimir showing up in the darkness and strangling me in my sleep . . .

Finally, I awoke to morning light filtering in through the slitted windows. Had I . . . ? No, I hadn't dreamed that nightmare. I was still in the jaws of the lion. For now, I would ignore Vlad's words and focus on getting through one day of torture at a time. What type of tests and how many they had in store for me, we would soon see.

The Hellebes scientists were accompanied by guardsmen armed with stun rifles. They took me to a medical lab similar to the one where I had staged my escape the last time I'd been here. The medical gown fit me as well as ever, the time-honored attire for enduring all manner of torture. For some reason, the doctors seemed surprised at the data they found. Some of the readings they obtained from special copper bands that measured the strength of the energy draw I would have had—you could say, the potential pull that strained against my bonds. Of course I did not release my full strength, no matter what they said. What even was my "full strength"? What is the upper limit of infinity?

Lldsaor showed up two hours later, beckoning me. I followed him out of the facility and up one floor, where living quarters were situated in neat apartments. He informed me that these were home to some of the officials who worked at the Capitol. I was given an apartment all to myself. He gave me leave to order food if I wanted it; the servants would bring it. Best of all, I would have my own private bathroom, not that the bath itself was anything too fancy. In fact, he told me to make sure I was cleaned up and ready for a meeting tomorrow morning.

The Emperor left me there for the rest of the day, and I wondered at the necessity of putting me in a cell for just one night. He had to know it would make me upset. No, he must have been in on it. *But . . . better than indefinitely. Buck up, Lyn.* I took the opportunity to get a soothing bath and unwind—particularly the cervical region of my spine—and then I called a servant to get me some lunch. He came, of course, flanked by two guards. I could never overpower such a force in copper. One Hellebes, probably. Two or three armed with energy blasters? No.

Just bide your time, Lyn, White whispered to me. *This won't last forever.*

For now, I slept.

In the morning, they picked me up early for the meeting. I don't know why they bothered having me clean up if I didn't have time to do my hair or anything. At least they provided me with some decent—if comically oversized—clothing to wear. It seemed Lldsaor's tailors weren't as well-prepared as Sylleo's. *Wonder if they have any female staff here . . .*

They weren't going to let me have my gillsuit, I told myself. *Won't be seeing that for a while.*

They brought me to a conference room occupied by the Emperor, Brant and Vladimir. I glanced at each Senator before taking the seat they indicated. Vlad gave no outward sign that we'd exchanged any words recently.

"Little Gaea," said Lldsaor in his deep, commanding voice. "It is time to discuss some things with you."

"Indeed!" Brant said cheerily. "Important things, no less!" I couldn't tell if he was mocking the Emperor or simply adding his own spin.

Vlad shot him an annoyed glare. It seemed to say, *You weren't supposed to open your mouth till later.*

Lldsaor went on. "Mani. We want to take control of it. I believe you know this very well, Lynchazel, and you voiced some contrary opinions in the last Senate meeting before your escape. The first strike was a partial success, but I have to say, you were right: The Legaleians are truly formidable. So . . . we're going to require some cooperation from you, since we'd prefer not to keep throwing our resources away without a gauge of our odds."

I laughed. "Cooperation? You guys are all the same. You throw me in a cell and treat me like a cut of meat, and then expect me to give you what you want? To betray my own kin?"

"In a way, yes," said the Emperor. "All we need from you are a few details about Mani, and in exchange, we can strike a deal that will not involve you going into long-term imprisonment in the labs."

I shared a glance with Vlad. So he *had* been lying. Or Lldsaor was lying now.

"Keep in mind," Brand interjected brightly, "We're going to throw whatever is necessary at your home planet to bring it to heel, regardless of your level of cooperation."

I set my jaw. "What's the deal?"

Lldsaor raised a thick-knuckled finger. "Instead, we will use your body's genetic data to create military weapons capable of destroying the Cydenges en masse. That is our primary end goal. Mani is but a stepping stone along the way, a necessary piece that should allow us to eventually conquer Luna."

Right. Necessary. *Why do they need my consent . . . ?* "Then how do you benefit by putting me back in the tank? If I refuse to help you, that's all you can do, right?"

"Or we could kill you," Vladimir said in a honeyed voice.

I suppressed a shiver. Something was severely wrong in that man's head. The long centuries had not done his sanity any favors.

Yet, at the same time, a realization was dawning in my mind, and I could feel White brimming with excitement at it: These men needed my consent. Did that mean that somehow, in some way, I had control over my own genetic data? Was that even possible?

"He's right," the Emperor agreed. "Once we have the weapons we need, we could easily dispose of you, Lynchazel. You are not irreplaceable, after a certain point. Worse comes to worst and you refuse all compliance, we have at least two ways of creating a new generation of Mother, perhaps Mothers if we're lucky, out of you."

I scoffed, mostly to suppress a retch. "Right, because your goal had nothing to do with preserving humanity, but only creating the ultimate military force to conquer Luna and the whole universe. You were trying for a superhuman Cydenges-inspired race that could obliterate anything."

Close?

Lldsaor blinked, surprise and annoyance flashing on his face in quick succession. "So you've been . . . learning. Yes, that is correct."

Very close.

"And you can't do away with me until you're sure you have something better, because right now, I'm the closest thing you have to a Cydenges. I represent that ultimate power. You don't think you guys should have thought about trying to recruit me, rather than making an enemy by threatening me?"

Vladimir stood up. "Would you like to say that again?" All diabolical playfulness was suddenly gone, only raw irritation vibrating his tenor strings.

"Peace," Lldsaor said, waving a hand. "She has a point, Vlad. Lynchazel, we did indeed consider that option, and there is a simple reason for rejecting it: We can't trust you."

Trust. *Pheh.* Well, at least he was being honest. "To you, I'm an animal to cage, a bitch to tame. You realize you're trying to fight a war with venomous insects, right? If you create a line of rabid Cydenges creatures who can destroy everything, how will you control them?" Surely they weren't stupid enough to think they could get an army of creatures with my level of control or better. No, I had a feeling they couldn't fathom what such a product would look like.

"Mani is the missing piece," Brant cut in, holding up a finger. "Capturing it is vital. We have our reasons, lassie."

Real anger broke through the half-façade of my building irritation. "But you can't take Mani! You think you can, but the Magi there are stronger than you realize. You didn't see the actual footage; you just heard the reports. I was there."

"And I know you're stretching the truth to stall for time," Lldsaor said, waving a hand. "Why wouldn't you? The people of Mani are weak, mere bugs. It doesn't matter if they can control the elements if we come in force and squash them with the overwhelming power of technology. No, girl, we will conquer them. We will allow them to live after taking control. If you don't tell us what we want to know, then things can only go worse for you."

"You'll let them live? Like you did with the people of Gaea?" I asked sharply. "When you created your new Hellebes race and rose to power? When you built nine cities and razed the rest of your own world? You discarded them just like you discarded Lhinde."

Lldsaor actually seemed taken aback. "How do . . . ?"

"Oh yes," I went on, pressing my advantage. "Don't you know that the Cydenges DNA *you* grafted into my mother allows us inherited memories? I know what you are—the same scheming Anier."

Lldsaor's jaw was set, forming a snarl as he shifted from perplexity to rage. "So maybe you do. It seems you already know the whole story of the Mother Project. But it changes nothing. We will develop the weapons we need, whether you go along with us or not. And we will wipe the face of Mani, returning the Font to its rightful place here on Gaea."

Ah . . . That sounds more like him. "Oh, right, because you realized that was a huge mistake to blame the Legaleians for the Cydenges. And did you ever figure out what was truly the issue? What drew them to Gaea?"

"Not exactly—" Lldsaor began.

"Then *how* can you possibly hope to defeat them if you don't even understand them?" I fumed.

"That," he answered, emphasizing the words heavily, "is one of many things the Mother Project was set up to answer."

"Well, it's been a thousand years already. You'd better try harder."

The hulking Emperor breathed heavily in and out, and the other Senators seemed to await his reaction. Slowly, he got a hold of himself and even forced an ugly smile, spreading his hands in a satisfied gesture. "Very well, then. We will."

Vladimir flashed me a leer that said, *Have it your way.*

Disruption

O Mother, Lady of Gold, removed of the earth, I shall soon see you. When this flesh is done and dispensed, at last the part of me that is of you will return. This thought brings unexpected ecstasy. And together . . .
— From Lhinde's Vault

"Breathe, Lyn. Breathe. You can do this." I muttered the words through a hair tie held between my teeth as I put in one . . . two . . . I spat out the hair tie. Three. *There we go.* Checking myself in the serviceable mirror provided by my host, I turned to the side and brushed a stray lock of metallic grey hair—closer to white since my time on Gaea—over my ear. Good enough. I had to look close to godliness for all the sleazebags on the Senate, because this was the big day. Well, at least mostly spiffy, bordering on dashing . . . no, wrong word. The Hellebes language was strange sometimes.

Stunning. Was that the word? They definitely didn't deserve stunning, not that I'd be achieving it.

Besides, it might not be *the* big day, depending on how it went; just *a* big day.

Lldsaor himself came to get me at oh-seven-o'clock, and I was ready. He looked me up and down, noting my tidier look, as though noticing for the first time that I was a lady. He made no mention of it, however. Instead, the Emperor said, "It's time, Lynchazel. Don't let us down."

I followed close on his heels as he took me out to the nearest elevator ascending to the administrative floors. He and Brant had already impressed on me that it was in my best interest to go along with whatever they said and not cause trouble. They couldn't very well keep me from speaking during the meeting, just . . . I supposed they could punish me afterward? Vladimir had yet to make another personal visit, and I suspected the three of them had coordinated their separate threats to intimidate me from different angles and make me feel cornered.

That, or they were all simply immature backstabbers.

When we reached the Senate Hall, Brant and Vlad were already there, but Sylleo was not yet. To my understanding, my friend the Ccamos Senator was usually one of the last ones there. But in this case, I was glad, as it gave me a better chance to distance myself from him, or at least pretend to. People would talk, but I would let them.

I took the empty podium next to Brant after a permissive nod from the Emperor. While socially adept and certainly not as overtly sinister as Vladimir, Brant still rubbed me the wrong way every time I saw him. His charisma pulled you in until you were right where he wanted you, but an intensity lurked behind his light-hearted demeanor.

More weighty footfalls came from the doorway, and I glanced over to see Senator Sylleo striding in, posture as relaxed yet confident as ever. He was one of the tallest Senators, even taller than Lldsaor, and his suit was as flattering to his physique as ever, tailored to precision. What he lacked in sheer bulk he made up for with quiet presence and style.

And still I was annoyed to see him. I didn't even have to feign indifference to his arrival. Sure, my heartrate went up a notch and I felt just a tad closer to sweating, but it was hot in here anyway. Right?

"And here I thought I was fashionably late," Sylleo said with an impassive face. "Where is DeWitt hiding?" There remained two empty spots plus Long's, but Strongs was suspended from the Senate for the next couple of meetings. That left only DeWitt.

Vladimir made an elaborate pointing gesture as though smugly blaming someone, and we looked to see the door open once more, announcing the smaller Senator from Lenardda.

"See, even more fashionably," Brant said.

When DeWitt had taken his spot, Lldsaor commenced the meeting with a few rote lines. He then bulldozed his way to today's central topic:

"This rebel organization is out of the way, Strongs' misconduct has been appropriately punished, and we return to an important issue. The Mother Heiress has confirmed that the 'magi' who populate Mani's surface are not only dangerous but rapidly growing in power."

I opened my mouth to object, but the Emperor fixed me with a knowing stare. He'd planned this. But who was I kidding? Of course he had.

"But aren't there more pressing matters?" Sylleo asked.

"Yes, what about the Cydenges?" DeWitt put in.

"Or the Mother herself?" Daedalus asked, gesturing at me. "We still haven't figured much out about her. Perhaps it's time we moved her to Chronala so the real scientists can look at her."

Lldsaor waved his hand as though lazily brushing away a bug. "All valid points, but only distractions. The Cydenges will not be back for some time, statistically speaking, so we have time to prepare. And Lynchazel is being kept here in Haccolces, where my scientists are doing their best to decrypt her genetic code. It will take time, during which she'll be kept safe."

"And how large of a force are we sending this time?" Sylleo asked. "How much money are we wasting?"

"One hundred vessels are at the ready, my good Senator," Lldsaor replied in a tight voice. "And we will send one hundred vessels. They should be able to at least stake out a sizable area for us, from which we can work as an off-world base." He looked around the room. "It is more than possible. We can begin to crush these Manese ants and claim the moon for ourselves. Then we will investigate how to take back the miraculous Font that was once ours."

The Wellspring of Life . . . the same "Ancient Fount" that you guys sent away, I noted ironically.

A few murmurs of agreement sounded from around the room, mostly from Brant and Vladimir. Holman, Daedalus and Sylleo looked nonplussed, and DeWitt seemed unsure where he stood on the matter.

"I believe the Mother has something to say on this," Sylleo said, pointing at me.

I cleared my throat as all eyes turned to me. "The people of Mani will oppose you strongly. But I've told you before, they are weakening, not growing stronger. Emperor, you are making them out to be our enemies, but have you ever thought that they could be our allies? I was raised there. I could be an ambassador. I know their language and their customs."

Lldsaor narrowed his eyes at me, slowly shaking his head. I wasn't entirely clear on the meaning, but it was something along the lines of, *I hate you and I want to kill you right now.* I gave him only a small shrug in response, while Sylleo gave me a surreptitious nod of approval.

"The girl has a point," Holman said. "Why are you so intent on wiping out the Legaleians when their abilities could prove useful?"

"We have no need of their magic!" Lldsaor spat. He said the word with deep, loathsome revulsion that surprised me. "The people of Mani are weak, and we have far outstripped them."

Then why do we need to reclaim the Wellspring?

Brant started to say something, but I paid him no heed, looking up toward the ceiling and calling forth a flame. Lldsaor's words had struck a chord, and I was about to improvise to it. I caused the flame to begin dancing some thirty feet above our heads, twirling and circling, slowly descending. Brant cut off, and most of the Senators stopped to watch the display. I stretched upward my hands, swaying them as I pulled and stretched the flame, demonstrating to my onlookers that it was my doing.

I stepped out from behind Long's podium and slowly made my way to the center of the room, sweeping my feet gracefully as I went, transitioning into a full dance. It was a dance that Mydia had tried to teach me almost a year ago, and my newly-enhanced memory and agility allowed me to execute it flawlessly, bringing the flames to accompany me. They rested on my shoulders and trailed behind me, spinning with my skirts and hair and sweeping alongside my hands. Only due to precise spacing did they not singe my clothes. I accelerated my spinning dance, making it my own, and caused the fire to flare, pulsing and rippling in color and intensity.

One of the Senators said something from the circle of onlookers, but I ignored them all. It didn't sound upset, just a bit concerned. Others sounded awed in their comments. Finally, I ended with a billow of multicolored flames that licked toward the ceiling, lingering in the air before blinking out. I left some flames on my forearms, however, because it would help me in a minute, not to mention it looked imposing.

I slowly strode back to my podium, only slightly dizzy and jittery from nerves. I tried to ignore the eyes on me, though I noticed that Sylleo in particular looked dumbfounded. He couldn't have expected me to find my flames in this world, and never a display like that. Frankly, I wasn't sure where I had gotten the inspiration to do it all of a sudden.

Vladimir, believe it or not, was the first to clap, and then the others did as well. When the applause settled down, he said, "Well, I certainly don't think any of us expected *that*. It was quite pretty, wasn't it?"

Lldsaor was fuming now. "How were you able to do that?" he demanded. "That's impossible!"

I shrugged. "I'm considered weak back on Mani. But I managed to figure out how to use my magic on Gaea as well. Do you recall a certain Legaleian man who once came to Gaea? My father? If you continue to insult my people and threaten them, I can show you what this power is capable of."

The room went silent. The Senators looked at one another with various reactions. Would they see through my ruse, realizing how small a difference my flames could make against Elites? Or did they fear the unknown? Sylleo gave me a wide-eyed look that said, *Now you* may *have gone too far.*

"She has a point, Emperor," said Daedalus, shattering the silence like a window of ice. My performance seemed to have a profound effect on the mastodon Senator.

"I am with her as well," said Holman, seemingly speaking against his better judgment. "Proceeding with the invasion may be rash."

I watched Sylleo as he scanned the Senators' faces, judging the support each side had in the room. Each did the same. It was in that moment that I realized Sylleo's plan was quite possible; there might well be a war amongst the Senators.

The question was . . . would it be Plan A or Plan B?

Locking eyes with my former fiancé, I gave a nod and furtive glance downward.

"I would advise each of you to speak extra carefully now," Lldsaor said coldly. "I believe we all want to preserve peace within our imperium."

"Or do we?" Sylleo asked in reply. Looking back at me, he returned the nod.

Plan B it was.

Suddenly, a blast sounded close to the Capitol Building, followed by a chorus of others.

Sylleo's plan was in motion. This was all about to go to chaos, one way or another. I crossed my hands behind my podium, extinguishing the flames and wrenching off both copper bands at once. The heated metal peeled and tore with a beautiful groaning screech. Then I reached down and broke off each band from my ankles, and lastly the band around my neck.

As one, the Senators stared at me, their expressions ranging from shock to horror to anger. I immediately sent my Geothermic feelers out, reaching down as far as I could and throughout our room, sucking all the energy I could into my core.

Lldsaor, seeing what I was doing, shouted for Vladimir to bind me, but I threw out a shockwave pulse that knocked him right off his feet. Then I crouched, hand to the floor, and unleashed a blast of piercing devastation from my hand that rocked the entire building. I felt the floor shudder and undulate as the power rippled throughout every floor of the Capitol tower.

The Senators stumbled, looking around as though torn whether to go for me or escape. Lldsaor and his cronies rushed me in anger, but I made to release more energy straight into them, and each assailant hesitated. The building shook and began to topple, and soon one of the massive stained-glass windows shattered, revealing a black ship hovering outside.

"Come on, Lyn!" Sylleo shouted to me, making a break for it.

With a parting blast that shattered the floor between me and my pursuers, I turned and ran, jumping into the flying ship behind Sylleo as the pilot began to take off. It was Kaen. He tore away from the building, and I clutched my seat, wishing the door would take less than a whole second to close. I watched the Capitol Building crumble under its own weight behind us, hardly able to believe the sight. I had done that with one Geokinetic pulse. And I knew I could do it again if needed—on a larger scale.

Kaen showed off his new flying skills by taking us into a dive between two of the larger buildings of the capitol complex, weaving around one to boost down a straight avenue. Even now, the Capitol's automatic defense cannons kicked in, targeting us. *Fortunately, Kaen is a good pilot now,* I thought to myself, *or we'd all be—*

Something slammed into our vessel, piercing one side and nearly spearing my calf: A meter-and-a-half arrow, solid steel and tipped with machine-grade carbide. It had pierced our shield in one hit. Immediately, alarms rang in the ship, and Kaen muttered a classic Hellebes curse. They seemed to have grown on him.

"Keep flying," Sylleo said, glancing backward out the window. "That sniper is a good shot. He's about to shoot in two, one, now!"

Kaen swerved down and then up, and the arrow plowed through a concrete building to our left instead, borne from the opposite side.

I watched as a ship pursued us, another on its tail, both of tellingly intricate design. "I think we've got a couple Senators on our tail," I said.

Now it was Sylleo's turn to curse, uncharacteristically in his case. "Probably Vlad and Brant."

Kaen kept course for the southern gate, despite the fact that the guards were surely securing it even now, zigzagging in his flight as the enemy opened fire on us. Even once out of range of the sniper, we had multiple guns to dodge in addition to the Senators' ships gaining on our tail. Kaen's gunship was only so fast, no custom-made Elite craft. It was only a matter of time before more shots struck our hull and it reached critical condition, shieldless as we were and vulnerable to any lucky shot.

"Kaen, take us down for a landing!" Sylleo ordered.

"Yes, sir." Kaen slammed the engines into reverse and turned sharply down a nearby street. Even as he did, one more shot clipped our tail.

This time, the ship exploded.

α Chapter 63 α

A Test of Power

Together, we shall return to rule the earth in steel and fire. And when Mani returns at the end of the millennium, then we shall have our perfect vengeance.
— *From Lhinde's Vault*

It was a strange experience, as I'd never had the pleasure of being in a ship when it detonated, but in the moment all I could think was how best to land. I got my bearings in midair even as I was being carried forward by the centripetal force of our ship's turn, and managed to kick off the wall of the closest building, landing on all fours on the ground. Disoriented, ears ringing, I rose to my feet and glanced about, taking in my surroundings.

"Lyn!" Sylleo shouted from down the street, where he had landed on the road. "Think you can sweep them out of the air?"

"I'll try. Where's Zent?"

"On his way," Kaen said from behind me.

I nodded, scurrying over to the street corner closest to where our enemy would appear. Unless they sailed right over . . . "Hang tight, guys," I said, feeling beneath me for Geothermic activity. There wasn't as much here as in the center of the city, or rather, it was not as easily accessible. But it was enough. I drew on it, closing my eyes as I listened for the approaching engines. They would be here in a matter of seconds.

They came directly overhead. As soon as the ships crossed over the buildings into my line of sight, coasting while they pinpointed our location, I raised my hands and unleashed a wide blast of white energy, sweeping it from one ship to the other. Both vessels burst into flames in a chain reaction, erupting in twin explosions and plumes of smoke. The wreckage sailed past us, crashing into the far buildings, and . . .

Oh yes, they were still alive. The two titans walked out of the flaming ash, Vladimir with a maniacal grin and Brant with a look of molten anger on his face. "Sylleo, you *traitor*," Brant growled, stalking toward us. All trace of the posturing dandy had evaporated.

"Leave the Mother to me," Vladimir said. "I'm glad she didn't die to my bullets, so that I can kill her a bit more personally now. That's right, darling. Personal is my favorite way."

I held up my hands, giving Kaen a look that was supposed to say, *Not quite yet.* "What, you're giving up on Lldsaor's orders?" I called.

"Who's to say?" Vladimir responded. "I might not *actually* kill you, just leave you wishing for it. Well, sweetheart? What do you say? You and me."

Vlad attacked, darting in with a fencer's stomp and a knife-hand thrust. Back to the cement wall, I flicked away his hand and went for his footing with my own feet. Vladimir saw this coming and jumped, executing a double midair front kick and following it up with a series of flashy fist combos. I wasn't sure why he was using such forms until I realized he was just being his normal self: Showy and presumptuous.

Meanwhile, Sylleo traded blows with Brant while Kaen pressured him with his silver sword, possessing just enough speed to keep away from any counterattacks. Brant seemed unable to do much offensively because of it, and had taken at least one nick from the blade.

Vladimir finally landed a strike on me, clipping my shoulder. It was enough to throw off my balance, but nothing more. I recovered and retaliated, but he soon made contact again, this time grabbing my wrist. He whipped me around and thrust me back-first into the wall, right hand driving upward under my ribcage.

Under this force, the wall shattered. My body, the medium of its destruction, screamed in pain, remembering the half-healed glass wounds as my frame either cut out a shape in the concrete wall or was pulled through, tearing my skin. *Okay, he's stronger than I thought.* How did he put so much power into a single punch? A normal human would have been gouged by the concrete, but for me it was less—though some protective armor would have gone a long way in place of this pathetic dress. Why had I even put it on? I landed on top of the rubble, gasping for breath and alight with pain. My dress hung at the shoulder, streaked with blood from gashes along my back. But I was out of his grip. Gritting my teeth, I forged through the pain and handsprang over the wall's rubble, unleashing a quick Geokinetic ground attack to keep Vladimir at bay.

He leapt over my attack. "Very good, sweetheart," he said, stalking toward me. Then he reached out and let loose a Geokinetic pulse into the light switch, instantly killing the lights in a shower of sparks. Direct Geoelectric transfer? According to the jade steam that curled upward after the sparks, it was. What I had been able to catch of my surroundings indicated that this was an old military warehouse, now a warehouse bathed in dark. Vladimir approached me smugly, face lit faintly by the windows on the main street. "Now this is more like it."

I backed up, watching the Senator as best I could in the darkness. But the blur I was tracking was faint and fuzzy at best, shifting unpredictably as he dodged about to lose me. I would have to rely on my memory and situational awareness to stay alive. I tried to circle around to my left, into the next room where there was a bit more light, but he easily saw what I was doing and pressured me away from there. He feinted with Geokinetic stomps and then closed in. With each movement and attack, Vlad's body leaked faint wisps of green smoke, the byproduct of Geokinesis.

I fought to keep him away, but it was impossible with my back still pulsing like the sting of a dozen hornets. Soon, he had me from behind in a chokehold, bloodying his own expensive attire. I kicked and struggled to no avail, feeling my pulse wink out in my neck. He was cutting off my circulation; I had to act quickly.

So I did the unexpected—I burst into flames. As I did so, I turned with a shout and grabbed the tall man in a bear hug, hanging on tightly as I combusted. He dropped to the floor, shouting incoherently, and I fell on top of him, breathing flames into his face.

Vladimir finally threw me off, cursing, and charged out of the room. I let him go, watching my flames eat at the last of his clothes. *Burn, my little friends, burn . . .* They also provided a bit of light to see by. I had transferred as much of the fire as I could from my body to his. He would recover, at least after some regenerative procedures—Gaea's healing technology was incredibly advanced, and he was an Elite—but his dignity would not.

What about Brant? asked White.

I made my way back to the hole I'd made in the wall, dripping blood and wincing with every step, beating the temperamental flames from my sorry dress. I found Brant struggling in a hold from Sylleo, Kaen's sword point at his throat. Standing behind the thrashing Senator, Sylleo had him by the neck and one arm. "Stand down," he said firmly. "You're beaten."

The Maldunech Senator stopped struggling and hung his arm limply, and we bound him with copper. Sylleo stood up, turning to me. "Let's get out of here."

I looked up to see a ship—piloted presumably by Zent—hovering above the road. The three of us climbed in and sped off toward the south gate once more, which was only a quarter mile away.

"Time to leave this place behind," Zent said.

No sooner had he begun accelerating than Kaen shouted, "Look out!"

Twin missiles rocked our ship with explosions. Our shield was instantly down, and warning lights flashed. We bailed soon after, and not a moment too soon. As I sailed through the air, the ship exploded in a plume of smoke. I landed on a rooftop next to Kaen and Zent. Sylleo was facing the opposite direction, looking up at the ship that had shot us down. In the cockpit was a grimly smiling Lldsaor. He did not press the attack, but instead hovered in close and jumped out as well, leaving the ship to hang nearby. Unlike his angry attack bees, he didn't want me dead.

I could feel his presence even before he hit the rooftops, powerful as ever, an almost godlike aura that told a story of absolute power. His thick black hair whipped in the wind as he stared us down. One man versus three powerful fighters including an Elite and the Mother, yet he didn't look afraid. He had not brought Vlad and Brant to Ccamos that day for protection; I could see that in his bearing now.

"Sylleo, you have disobeyed for the last time," he said, voice crackling with thunder. "You are an enemy of the Senate—now a terrorist as well, caught in the act. Give me the Mother, and I'll make your sentence lighter. Resist . . . and I'll kill you right now with my own hands."

Sylleo stepped in front of me. "I cannot oblige. This woman, whom you consider but a resource that happens to breathe, has reawakened a sense of honor I thought I'd lost centuries ago. You fight for power and control while she fights for freedom." The Emperor had paused to listen to his speech, but Sylleo gave him no more chance before using his lightning speed to close in for an instant chokehold.

Lldsaor fought back like a lion beset by a pesky dog. Despite his strong start, Sylleo did not look confident. He clung to Lldsaor's tree-trunk neck, kicking for his legs, but the Emperor was like an immovable titan. "Go! Go, Lyn!" Sylleo shouted. "Everyone, *go!*"

I turned to move, sparing an uncertain glance at Kaen. "Come on!" he said, taking my hand and bolting toward the city gate. Zent followed, leaping across the first street along with us and down onto the following street. We approached the wall directly, where I summoned the Mother's power and sliced a half-circle wedge out of the wall with a blazing white beam. I gathered my strength and, with the help of the others, threw the earth forward beneath it, carrying the cut-out section through the wall, and we were free.

"Hang tight," Zent said tensely, watching his wrist console. "Reinforcements will arrive shortly . . ."

Soon, ships appeared on the southwestern horizon, and the city's defenses kicked in, attempting to shoot them down. One was hit, but three more made it, two of them circling for distraction while the other came straight for us, picking us up and then shooting into overdrive.

In the backseat of the speeding airship, I let out a shaky breath, gingerly feeling at my back as I looked over at Kaen. I tried to give him a reassuring grin, but I couldn't say what it looked like. My dress was an inappropriate mess of blackened cloth and soot-covered stripes, and I couldn't care less given the circumstances. Kaen's helmet was off now, revealing a resolute but troubled face.

"Lyn, you look, uh . . ."

I shook my head tightly. "I'm fine. Fine. I just—Sylleo . . ." I struggled to find the words to voice what I wanted to say. "Did he really just give himself up for us?"

Kaen nodded. "But he's Sylleo; he'll be fine." I could tell as he said it that he didn't mean the words. Lldsaor was done with Sylleo's rebellion, and our act at the Senate Hall was more than enough to justify killing another of the nine. Zent glanced over from the front passenger seat, not saying anything.

"So . . . he really did care about me," I said numbly. Not obsessively, nor even romantically . . . he actually cared enough to lay down his life so that I could escape. For my sake, not his. The realization of how I had treated the man bore down on me suddenly, how I had returned him spite and malice for his attempted honesty, hatred for his love, evil for good. He couldn't fight Lldsaor. But if I had stayed, if I had only disobeyed him and *stayed* to help him fight the Emperor . . . would we have had a chance?

Probably not. They said Lldsaor was more dangerous than he looked, and I could feel his Geokinetic presence from fifty meters away. I didn't know how I managed the feat at the wall, because I should have been out of operation in my condition. Adrenaline. Fear.

I knew in that moment that I would forever look back and wonder if we could have taken on the Emperor together.

But the way from here was not backward, but forward. To Ccamos we went. There, we would decide our course of action.

α Chapter 64 α

Strength

Do I regret my course? I ask myself all the time, and sometimes waver.
But the answer is ever unchanging: No.
— From Lhinde's Vault

We reached Ccamos within two hours, radioing in first and relaying the situation. Despite Sylleo not being with us, the Ccamos soldiers—including General Frauss—accepted us as trustworthy. A terse exchange ensued as we admitted that we were not sure whether their Senator was alive or not. As expected, he was not answering any calls.

We landed at the military base and met first with General Frauss and other high-ranking officers. They asked for more details on the Senator, and we gave them, although I was beginning to lose my strength, vision fading. Realizing my condition, the officers called medics to take me away for treatment. I resisted all the way, knowing I was foolish for it. I just felt so helpless after letting Sylleo stay behind in my place.

I walked out of the infirmary in bandages, having received a heavy dose of Geothermic energy in addition to a few medications. I would keep drawing planetary energy to slowly heal my body, just as Zent had taught me to do all those months before. Even unconscious, my body could siphon what it needed.

A fine mist was sifting down from somber clouds high above. The shield walls did not keep out rain, and in this case it fit the mood perfectly.

I found Kaen and the officers in the command room, sitting around the same desk where I'd once found Sylleo and his generals. Now, two of those generals and Sylleo himself were missing, with Kaen and Zent in their place. "Mother Heiress," said General Frauss with a dip of the head.

"Any updates on Sylleo?" I asked, knowing the answer.

"Haccolces radioed just minutes ago," replied another general. "They said that our Senator is dead and this is what we get for betrayal."

"Ccamos will become the next Mei Shan," Zent said softly.

"No," I insisted. "There's got to be a way out of this. Sylleo wouldn't let it end like that, so we can't either. We can find allies in the Senate, right?"

Frauss held up a hand. "Hold on. We'll get to that. For now . . . there's more pressing news. We just received a transmission from Senator Strongs. He says he's coming for you. To finish what Lldsaor should have. He offered two options: Be wiped out by his military or surrender you."

I felt a chill run down my spine. How could he even know about what happened in Haccolces yet? "Wait, he just—he escaped from prison? I thought they had him securely confined."

Kaen shrugged. "He probably set it all up in advance. I guess we shouldn't have left him alive."

"What about that stand-in guy?" I asked.

"First Minister Phelps?" Frauss asked. "No word back from him yet, but I assume Strongs has overridden his authority already. Or he was in on it."

"So what should we do?" I asked.

They all looked at one another, as though sharing a secret I didn't know. "Well," Frauss began, "We obviously must defend Ccamos. We are mobilizing troops as we speak and readying all defense cannons."

"But . . . I don't like that," I said. "I mean, defending the city, sure. That's only smart. But I won't let hundreds of troops die for my sake if there's something I can do about it. Plus, we're just weakening two militaries."

"Something like what?" Kaen demanded. "We've been over a lot of different options."

Zent held up a hand. "Easy, soldier. We'll figure something out. Lyn, we cannot give you up. That's simply not an option."

"What if I challenged him to a duel?"

Kaen raised his eyebrows. "You think you can beat him? After you and I barely managed to subdue him?"

"I'd need the right battleground. But . . ." I flexed my right hand, staring at the creases in my palm as they mushed together. I felt the itch of my thousand half-healed cuts from the other day, which had been weeping blood mere minutes ago. "Yes. I can beat him. I can kill him." *Once and for all.*

There was a heavy silence for a couple seconds, before Zent said, "Out of the question, Lyn. That would be foolish."

"I beat Vladimir by myself."

Zent shook his head. "Strongs is much more formidable. He's the best warrior among all of the Elites except for Lldsaor. And they're close."

"I know that. But I think I can take him."

"You *think*—" Kaen started.

"I *know* I can take him," I corrected. "Trust me, guys. Now . . . do you think he'll agree to it?"

Frauss took a long, slow breath. "There's one way to find out."

Strongs agreed.

He also made sure to mention that he was bringing most of his legions of trained Hellebes fighters with him. Strongs was well known for his tactical prowess in addition to his harsh training regimen, possessing the best overall military in the world. Some had begun to question whether he might be considering taking on the entire Senate in a play for world domination, and this very well might be the beginning of that. If so, it would make sense that he would want me out of the way for starters.

We met him outside the city wall with a delegation of about a dozen Hellebes, many with cameras to film the ensuing combat. As we watched Strongs' army approach, I began to realize why people feared him. The armada of ships overtook the entire horizon. Strongs' flagship flew front and center. The air force stopped behind it some three hundred yards out, and the flagship descended, flanked by a pair of vessels—likely piloted by his foremost generals.

"Lynchazel, Mother Gaea, this day the world is our witness," boomed Strongs' voice over an external speaker. "Let us decide through honorable combat whether Gaea wants you to live or not."

He got out of his ship along with a small retinue of Hellebes officials, who stood by watching just like my companions. We approached one another until we were about ten meters apart. My heart fluttered rapidly in my chest, trying to beat its way free. I took up a fighting stance, and the people behind me cheered.

Strongs stood ready with hands straight at his sides. "Today, you die."

"Let the combatants begin in five," a Hellebes aide called from behind Strongs, "Four, three, two, one." A gunshot rang out, signaling for us to begin.

Strongs did not immediately move in; that approach didn't favor his abilities. He circled me, and I circled him, watching my opponent's eyes and movements. I was certain he was just toying with me, however. If he wanted to crush me, he could do so quickly—or so he thought. He wasn't just sizing me up, but waiting for whatever mental signals tipped him off to my next move.

For my part, my strategy was simple: Don't plan. Any I did make, I purposely canceled. He couldn't read the future, just intentions. I pulled more potential energy from Gaea, flooding my veins with planetary fire. I did not unleash my elemental flames yet. That would be my secret technique, the one he hadn't witnessed. He probably sensed that intent, but hopefully he would get too caught up in the fight.

As I continued to wait, Strongs finally made the first move, closing half the distance between us and throwing out two swift Geokinetic attacks that split and shattered the ground beneath my feet, throwing up spikes of rock. I dodged these easily and responded with an attack of my own, causing the stone beneath his feet to melt. He danced backward, avoiding the softened stone and circling me once more. Then he rushed forward with an uppercut aimed directly for my chin. Only my quick reflexes saved me from being launched right off my feet. *Such speed . . .*

I avoided his aggressive follow-up combo, deflecting strikes by reflex and following up with a massive Geokinetic heave—with the most random timing I could manage, so that he couldn't read my movements before they happened. I tore up the earth in front of me, causing the stone to thrust upward to chest level. The move almost seemed to surprise Strongs—perhaps he'd gotten distracted as I'd hoped—throwing him to the side. As I let the stone fall, I unleashed a white blast of destruction, filling the air with wisps of green smoke. I looked and saw that he had gotten out of range, though my blast had struck and heavily weakened his personal shield. Or so I hoped.

I advanced on him, letting out an even heavier blast that shattered the ground and sent debris in all directions, following it up with a sweeping Geokinetic beam. This time, I struck his side as he dodged, burning through his shield and armor. Other than a small curse, however, he seemed unfazed.

Strongs retaliated with a multipart Geokinetic offensive, ripping up the ground and sending it to crash against me. I broke through it and stilled the next miniature earthquake, but his next one caught me, thrusting a whole plateau of dirt and stone upward in a three-meter radius beneath me. I found my balance midair, but a stone fist nearly smashed my legs off before I broke it. Arms and legs of stone jutted up out of the earth in quick succession, nearly hitting me and also creating an array of obstacles between me and the Senator.

As I dodged his attacks, I tried to keep aware of how much planetary energy I was using, because there wasn't nearly as much available here as in the city. My true strength lay in my ability to draw in more than most others, but that was limited by the amount that was actually available. So instead I stored it, pulling as much as possible from the land around us, drawing up the wisps of green smoke like steam through an exhaust vent.

I spent my stored energy in small bursts, once per dodge, before closing in to engage the Elite head-on. Strongs' martial style was brutal and relentless, much like Musha's had been—he was simply far stronger, more than I was even now. There was one way I could beat him, and I had to be close for it to work.

He anticipated my attack, observing my charge and moving to grab my wrist for a throw. When I twisted away, he turned it into an elbow strike, driving the front of his elbow under my right arm and spinning me off-course.

He then caught my foot, grabbed my arm—successfully this time—and threw me to the ground. Within the space of two seconds, I had gone from attacking to landing on a broken spire of rock with the massive Senator on top of me, attempting a submission. His weight and brute strength were enough to make the struggle a joke, and he soon had one arm under my right arm and choking off my air supply . . . and then my blood supply. I had just seconds . . .

I grabbed his arm and held on with all my strength—making sure that he couldn't get away—and stoked the fire within. The real fire, the raging flames of Mani. An inferno engulfed the both of us, and Strongs roared in pain, nearly deafening me. I transferred the heat from my own flesh to his. The Senator's grip slackened, and indeed he tried his best to get off of me, but I clung tightly, levering my own body on top as his own burned. My own skin was fine for now, though my gillsuit would be nothing but ash within half a minute.

With a roar of my own, I took hold of the flaming Senator and heaved his body in a somersault by the very arm that had choked me seconds ago. He landed flat on his back on spears of stone of my own making, which pierced his kidneys as he landed. I knew there would be no yielding, no second chances, so I aimed a concentrated blast of white-hot energy at his neck and sheared his head from his body with a searing beam.

It all happened faster than I could really think, too fast for me to make decisions. Decisions could have been my death, so I had acted before I could second-guess myself. After a few moments of staring at his giant head, which lay lifeless next to a blackened stump that was once his neck, I tried to make sense of what I was seeing. I had killed an Elite. Not only my greatest enemy in the world, but one of the most powerful beings to ever walk the face of Gaea. He was dead, and I had . . . killed him.

Then the cheers arose from behind me. I rose slowly, turning to see my companions' glad faces. I mustered a smile of relief before looking in front of me, whence the delegation that represented the largest army in the world stared me down. They were neither smiling nor laughing . . . but neither were they upset. Rather, they simply looked stunned.

Zent strode forward, taking me by the shoulder and clasping it tight. "Well done, lass." Then he addressed the enemy representatives. "Men of Haven! We have a proposition."

α Chapter 65 α

War for Gaea

Yes, Lynchazel, I can see you even now. It has taken time to come to a full understanding of my foresight, but now I know who it is that shall carry on my legacy. Lynchazel II, you shall be the final Vessel of our Mother, and the purest tool to enact great reforms upon Gaea. Your biological mother was greater, but she was wrung out by our oppressors. But you . . . Oh, I can hardly wait. The day of reckoning shall come.
— From Lhinde's Vault

"You're really okay with those soldiers just camping outside the city?" asked Kaen as we strode up to Sylleo's personal manse. Margill had requested I come, and I had asked Kaen to join me just because.

"Well, the officials agreed not only to sign a treaty but to undergo the operation to remove their programming. So yeah, I'm all right with it." I couldn't have asked for a better outcome, all things considered.

We ascended the large stone stairs of the manor house and approached the door. After two raps on the knocker, Margill was there to open it up for me. "My Lady," he said formally. "Come right in. You are welcome as well, Master Kaen."

He motioned for us to take a seat in the foyer, proceeding to serve us tea and take an opposite seat in a rigid posture. "Lady Lynchazel, I'm sure you've heard the news about my former master."

I nodded. "Yes, he's dead."

"And that makes you my next mistress. I doubt he told you that part."

"I . . ." The word caught in my throat, and I attempted to clear it out, shaking my head. *He did what?*

"Master Sylleo left me clear instructions on what I was to do in the event of his death," Margill explained, making motions with his hands. "First and foremost, all authority in the city and province of Ccamos was to be left to you at your earliest convenience, as well as this house and my service. The city is now yours to do with as you please."

After ten seconds of being too stunned for words, I let out a small, "Oh." It was all I could think to say at the moment. I looked to Kaen, who didn't seem quite as surprised by the news. "You . . . knew about this, didn't you?"

"A bit. Sylleo told me the day they shipped you back to Haccolces, right after they left. He said you'd make a far better leader than he ever did. He didn't know he would die, just that it was a possibility."

"I don't know about that. He . . ." I ran a hand through my silver hair, trying to blink away a tear. "He was a good leader. Far better than I gave him credit for. I don't think I can say that about any of the other Elites save Long. Margill, is there any way I can just . . . have some time to think about it? You're asking a lot. *He* asked a lot."

"But of course, madam. And . . ." He rose and proffered a small envelope for me to take.

I reached out and took it gingerly, staring at it suspiciously. Unrelated? Or just an explanation from the Senator, perhaps? I opened up the envelope to reveal a folded parchment. Unfurling it, I read its contents as quickly as I could:

Dear Lyn,

I'm sorry I was too much a coward to tell you all this in person. I tried, and I failed. I have come to terms with my role in the future of this world, and I can't say when it will be, but I feel I will not be around much longer. I want you to know that I love you and respect you as a woman, not as a historical figure and not as the Mother. Not even as Lynchazel's daughter. Being around you has inspired me to wake up and see the world for what it really is—an apocalyptic nightmare caused partly by my own hands.

I also know you'll probably see that as empty flattery, but I'm thanking you nonetheless. I know it is too much to ask, but I'm trusting you to bring about a solution. I believe only you have the unique upbringing and vision to see my dream to fruition, and that is why I'm leaving you all of Ccamos. Margill and the generals will help you and give you advice. Be wise, be alert, be diplomatic. Try to get some of the Senators on your side, because I know some of them will join our cause. It is time for the world to wake up and come out from under Lldsaor's heavy hand.

If I may make one last request, it is that you seek out a long-term solution to the conflict here on Gaea, to the war against the Cydenges, and to the coming war with your Legaleian brethren. I realize that is a tall order, but I know deep down that all three are connected on some level. If you can only find the common denominator between them all, then I think a solution may be within your grasp. Don't waste your strength on short-term skirmishes and political maneuvers . . . those won't help anyone in the long run. Be smart and safe, and be kind to Margill. He may be a free man, but he's more loyal than a dog.

I was nodding along with the letter, many different emotions racing through me, but . . . when I got to the end, I jolted upright, trying not to show my surprise. That last comment . . . it was pointed right at me. He was trying to say something. "Margill, are you . . . are you under the control gene? The loyalty programming?"

The butler looked at me with a strange expression. "No, madam. Many in Ccamos are not. Ever since Lord Sylleo discovered the way the rebels had bypassed it—which was months ago—he has been using the operation to ensure authentic loyalty from his subjects, working from the top down. True loyalty."

He "discovered" it? "And what did he do with those who didn't want to obey him?"

"I don't recall any, my lady. In today's world, given the choice, which one would you make?"

"Okay, I . . . can understand that. Did you know about this, too, Kaen?"

He shook his head. "News to me. But it kind of makes sense."

I stood up. "Margill, I accept. Thank you for your many years of service to Sylleo. Would you do me the honor of being my steward and advisor?"

He rose from his own seat, taking a formal bow. "It would be my honor, my lady."

"Thank you," I said, feeling short of breath. "All right, Kaen. We've got more talking to do."

"Right. We, uh, we do," he answered, looking uncomfortable. Yet he seemed to be straining to keep a straight face. Was something funny? "There's just one more thing. He didn't put it in the letter, did he, Margill?"

"Ah, no. I believe you suggested it afterward."

A weight of apprehension settled on me. "What am I missing? Come on, spill. Don't mess with me like this."

The two shared a look, and then Margill said, "You're a widow, Lady Lynchazel. I'm sorry to hear about your husband."

Over the next hour, I coasted through a strange dream in which I was the new leader of a city called Ccamos. In this dream, I spoke with generals and commanders in the Ccamos military, each of whom swore allegiance to me. We secured a tentative agreement with the squadron of Haven soldiers who had been posted outside the city for the meantime, until we knew what the Emperor was planning to do about us. As the new Senator, I was the biggest prize in the world. I also spoke directly with Phelps, the Hellebes who was in charge of Haven—and whom Strongs had bypassed to bring his pre-prepared force to Ccamos—and he agreed to continue in his line of duty despite the danger from the Senate, provided we lend our support.

The first of the remaining Senators that I reached out to was Daedalus, and we had a long conversation that ended in an agreement to meet and discuss a potential alliance. He was in a delicate position as the second in line of blame for Strongs' attempted matricide, and also Strongs' right-hand man who had supported him from the sidelines and developed new Hellebes for him.

While we could not trust him yet, Daedalus' support would be invaluable, as he controlled the world's population to a large degree.

Chronala was far more important than people gave it credit for. We sent out messages to all other world leaders, informing them that I was the new Senator of Ccamos and would be working with the new Haven Senator in the wake of unexpected and unplanned events. Holman and DeWitt were possible additions to our alliance, but it was likely that neither one of them would agree to join, being too scared of Lldsaor to do anything risky.

I also made a personal call to former Senator Long, explaining the situation and expressing our support. Strongs would no longer be able to raid his village, but I couldn't say what Lldsaor might try to do. I didn't see any reason why the Emperor would try to annihilate the humans, if indeed he knew about them. But he had ordered the bombing of the Red Horizon base and the attack on Nytaea, and he was every bit as much an animal as Strongs had been. Men like that seemed to lack any human emotion or empathy. Lord Kalceron had been the same way. There were many words to describe that: Egotism. Corruption. Selfishness.

If there was one sure fact about Emperor Lldsaor, it was that he needed to be stopped.

❧⁊

And now we reach the end of the second leg in my journey. I will make sure to upload my memories for future generations, but this record is just in case. I still await word from most of the Senators, and we are working on a way to get a message to Mani. For now . . . I think we're safe, but it's definitely tense. Oh, how I miss my old friends. Mydia . . . Rhidea . . . Phoebe, Oliver.

Will I ever get back there? As a Senator?

I cannot say if the Elites will relaunch their attack on Mani now that world war is imminent. But I know one thing regarding this coming war: I don't want to just fight. I don't want to simply win a war and lose many soldiers. I don't want to conquer: I want to free an enslaved people . . . and protect my own people back on Mani. We will seek to bring things to an end peacefully and diplomatically if at all possible.

But there are other loose ends as well, ones that only I may be able to tie up: The Cydenges are still at large, and we need to learn what they are really after and how they can be neutralized. And . . . I need to get Lhinde out of my head. I fear she will invade my dreams more and more until I go down a dark emotional spiral like Kaen. I fear the part I must play to right these events.

But one thing at a time. One war at a time.

β PART FIVE β

Epilogue

Heralds of the War

Queen Mydia Kalceron soaked in a relaxing bath. She was not, however, relaxed. This was an exercise she had recently taken up but had yet to perfect: Pretending to do a relaxing leisure activity while her mind raced, thinking and mulling and planning. Running a country, and running it well, was no simple task—particularly when war of unknown scale loomed on the horizon.

She thought mostly on her last conversation with Rhidea, during which the old mage had made a troubling announcement: She was now working hand-in-hand with the planet itself. Himself. Mani, a sentient force with a mysterious will of his own. It was such an outlandish thought, but then again, nothing was too outlandish to believe anymore, not to mention Mydia had seen the influence of this being firsthand through Kaen.

That was what worried her.

She tried not to dwell on her love's death, though it haunted her, the pain barging in every time she let her guard down. *Focus, curse you, focus!* she told her brain. Rhidea. She was the one who had to deal with Mani's influence now, and she should have been all along. If only . . .

A hiccupping sob escaped her lips, but she quickly cut it off. The shuddering briefly threw off Teli's slender fingers, which were attempting to massage her back as she leaned against the silver tub.

"Milady," the handmaiden said hesitantly, "You're tensing up something terrible again. Please do try to relax."

The girl's honest concern brought a flickering smile to the queen's lips. "I know. I'm sorry." She was instantly lost in thought again, sparing nary a second to try and relax her shoulder blades.

Rhidea. Mani. Something about the whole relationship—the . . .

symbiosis—felt wrong to Mydia. She could explain that doubt no more easily than banish it. Something bad would come of it, possibly disastrous. It seemed an unusual lapse in the Wandering Mage's judgment, unless she truly saw no other choice. Not to mention she had not consulted Mydia's advice before consenting, and the queen assumed that went for Fenwel as well. To a monarch and trusted friend, that stung like a slap in the face.

What did Mani want? Mydia was of the opinion that Mani was not a planetary entity at all, but rather a more specific one that had, in some way, possessed himself of a planet—or rather, a moon. There was a difference there. Perhaps he was even a huge charlatan, a powerful Perception mage dwelling in secret who convinced certain people that he spoke on behalf of the world. But . . . why? Ever that question . . .

Why?

She sighed quietly. Apparently in more angsty a fashion than she meant, for Teli silently began massaging just a bit more forcefully, causing her to clench her shoulder blades and then slowly release them as she concentrated on doing that thing . . . relaxing. Exhale. Slow inhale.

Ah, it did feel good. Like the old days.

"My Lady," came a young feminine voice from the doorway behind her, then a hesitant, "My apologies."

"None necessary, Julia," said Mydia, raising her head and turning half round to glance at the girl over her shoulder—moving only her neck for modesty's sake, as well as to not rob her back of Teli's kneading massage.

"It's your delegates—they've returned, My Lady," Julia said in a more excited tone.

"Alive? That's a relief. Which ones?"

"Ti'Vaeth and Dotham. Apparently with a favorable report."

That took some of the tension out of her shoulders. And her wrists, too. Why did one's wrists tense up, without even realizing it? "That is good to hear. I'll meet with them both in five minutes."

Julia said nothing, as if waiting for the queen to correct herself.

She did. "Perhaps . . . ten minutes."

The delegates were both waiting in her audience hall when she swept in, bedecked in her royal robes: Shimmering blue with long sleeves, a modest neckline and matching earrings. Her royal tiara pierced her conservative hair. Only with the help of the finest handmaidens in the realm was she able to get ready so fast, and they had indeed managed it in ten minutes.

"Tenna, Sylvia," she said as she approached her seat, having remembered the women's names on the way in. She brushed aside her skirts as she sat, adjusting them beneath her once and almost twice before thinking better of it. *Relax, Myds.*

"My Lady," said Sylvia with a proper curtsy to match her colleague's, early-greying hair rippling as she did so. "I bring good tidings from Dotham. And," she gestured at Tenna, "from Ti'Vaeth as well. It seems the empire is now willing to consider a wartime pact with us. In fact, the Archlord recently sent word back to Argent with that express command."

Mydia raised her eyebrows. *Command? Not a simple reply.* That was intriguing. That indicated that Rhidea's bargain with Domon had gone through. The very idea of making another deal with that treacherous viper made Mydia's skin crawl with displeasure, but peace with the tyrant Archlord was plenty favorable to further hostilities when it came to uniting against the Gaean invasion. It was shocking how few people in the world seemed to see the need to band together.

But what did it cost her? What had Rhidea offered the man? She would have to contact her at the first opportunity.

"That is excellent news," Mydia said genuinely. "Tenna, I'd like the details from the Ti'Vaeth regent, Kelleva."

The tall woman took a breath, then shrugged. "She extends a similar offer. I believe the orders were unilateral between provinces. The Archlord ordered that all Kystrea was to cease hostility with the five outlier nations and begin negotiations for temporary alliances."

Temporary. As though that was necessary to add.

"Regent Kelleva instructed me to inform you that you will soon receive word on the specifics of Ti'Vaeth's offer," the envoy added.

"Hopefully through direct communication," Mydia said under her breath. "We can't delay too much. Sylvia, anything else?"

The woman scratched her grey hair. "No, Milady. I fully expect identical responses from all twelve. I would advise that you prepare form responses for each, but perhaps also prepare further in case they want some manner of roundtable meeting—particularly if we can get the other outlier nations involved."

Mydia suppressed an eyeroll. She half wondered if Domon's plan was to feign making peace, yet delay long enough to purposely allow the Gaeans time to invade. It wouldn't make any sense, but . . . this was Domon, after all. The man who had sent her and her companions across the world just to demolish the gateway he'd sent them to find.

"Very well," she said after both women had finished. "We will await further reports. Thank you, ladies." As the delegates departed, Mydia turned to Secretary Keuda, who had been present for the entire report. "Could you fetch Captain Straif and the others?"

Keuda hesitated only a moment before giving a quick, "Yes, Queen," in her typical fast speech. She knew who "the others" were.

Mydia turned to Julia. "And, ah . . . now that no one is around, what kind of goodies do you suppose they have in the kitchens?"

Julia gave a hint of a playful smirk. "I shall scout the area and assess the goodies, Milady."

Mydia smiled, twirling her black hair behind her ears—the furthest she could properly twirl said locks—and looked down at her blue dress. It was of a fine material, sewn by a tailor whose name she could almost recall. She had multiple, but this woman was particularly skilled.

But no, she had more important things to think on than snacks and dresses. In truth, she wanted a minute alone. She should have somewhere between two to five minutes to herself here, seated on her deceptively uncomfortable carved wooden chair, pondering the defensive preparations Nytaea would be taking. She really was no tactician, possessing neither the head nor the knowledge for it, but she'd learned some, particularly where magic was involved.

But that was what she had tacticians for. For her part, she knew what needed to be done, just not precisely how. Having Domon's city-states no longer slavering at her borders was a huge relief, even if she did not entirely trust whatever offer of alliance his delegates brought to her. If only she had Kaen here—

No. *No, Mydia . . . why?* She cursed herself for letting her attention slip. She'd been doing so well. Her face melted into a pained grimace, eyes squeezing shut and lips trembling at the corners as she held a hand to her forehead. He was gone. He was gone. Why couldn't she just get over it? Why couldn't she simply brush it aside?

Tears streamed down her cheeks, and she fumbled about her, padding her dress as though for pockets, and lighted upon her handkerchief sitting on the small stand next to her chair. Oh, blessed handkerchief. She snatched it and dabbed madly at her face, trembling and sniffing. *Come on, Mydia, get hold of yourself! You're a child no longer, and no stranger to grief.* She'd been through this twice already. Why did it have to *hurt* so much?

She padded the tears from her skin, tasting salt on her lower lip, and gently pressed against her eyes to make certain the flow had stopped. Her makeup should be fine. Julia had put on only the minimum, as they'd had time for no more. Kaen had always liked her natural look, so why should she bother too much?

Oh, you fool! Was a queen allowed to kick herself? She did it anyway, thudding her right foot into the opposite calf. She let out a growling sigh and blinked rapidly, returning her handkerchief to her eyes and glancing about the room. She tried hard to not cry in public nowadays—not with a queenly image to uphold. She had ever been the reclusive, chubby princess who played by herself in her tower and attempted to chat with her surly handmaidens; now she represented an entire nation, one that had undergone not two but three regime changes in the last year.

Footfalls sounded from the front-facing double doors. Mydia hastily returned her now-crumpled hanky to the stand and cleared her throat, just enough to make sure her mouth could access her voice box.

It was Secretary Keuda, who curtsied formally with a proper greeting and gestured in Captain Straif and a shorter but heavily built man called Enchro, who had recently been appointed Marshal in Lanthar's stead. May his soul rest in peace; that man would be missed, although Enchro was doing an admirable job so far and seemed loyal.

Next came Ethas Gandel, tall and blond, regal as ever. He was recently married to Aldyr, Syneria Tolruin's sister. He was now her permanent co-regent, although she still debated letting him have the throne if she didn't . . . find a husband soon. The thought brought a brief, unwelcome grimace to her face.

"My Lady," said Enchro in a gravelly voice with a stiff bow. Everything he did was stiff, though not in a rude way nor, she thought, an uncomfortable way. Rather, old wounds from his days as a soldier and then an officer in her father, Lord Kalceron's, employ coupled with natural habits to make the man almost entertaining to watch. Not entertaining enough to smile in an unqueenly way, particularly given her current mood.

"My Lady," echoed Straif with a bow-curtsy hybrid. Mydia usually got a kick out of the way she and other female mage soldiers didn't know which one to do. Mydia wasn't sure herself. Standing beside Marshal Enchro in her red cape, the two seemed a perfect pair, short and thickly built.

Mydia motioned the two officers forward, swallowing down what she hoped were the last of her tears. Did they notice she had been crying? Almost certainly. "We just received favorable reports at last from our delegates in the empire," she informed them. "Which means we can begin formulating more focused defense strategies, as well as proposals for a joint defense system with Kystrea and the surrounding countries."

Straif shared a look with Enchro. "We're . . . talking about Domon's people, My Lady. With all due respect." She punctuated her words by clearing her throat.

Mydia nodded. "I know. Which is why I said begin to plan, not put anything into action."

"That . . ." Enchro seemed to be considering something hard. "Yes, that is wise, My Queen. We already have some sketches, yes?"

Ah, that's right. "Yes, we do in fact. Keuda?" Mydia prompted.

The woman gave an almost startled nod and zipped away. Mydia really wondered what she drank every morning. She was back in record time with multiple parchments, scrawled with plans.

Marshal Enchro took one and pored over it, glancing up at his queen. "Perhaps we can continue this in the strategy room soon?"

"Yes, yes," she agreed. "It was quite short notice."

Straif nodded absently, her eyes following Enchro's on the large page he held. The captain puffed away a stray lock of blonde hair that had escaped her leather hair band. "Perhaps we should focus on defensive measures here in Nytaea, then on the world at large in this eastern region. We don't know yet what this . . . alliance . . . will look like." She said the word *alliance* with distinct distrust.

Mydia nodded. "I agree. We can respond accordingly to their offer once we receive it."

"We're going to need a few more heads looking at this," Enchro muttered.

Black and Silver

Rhidea dreamed.

She swam in an infinite expanse, lit evenly from every side and none at all. The sun was an indistinct heavenly light, and nothing was recognizable amidst the omnipresent grey mist, yet she knew that she was somewhere. She glided along effortlessly, half guiding herself and half pulled by a mysterious force, ever deeper.

That force was Mani, and he was speaking to her:

Child of Silver, we are almost there.

She made no reply. Mani had nearly full access to her mind right now, and thus knew all her emotions and reactions, dimmer though they were in this dream world. Only she was not sure whether she was in the planetary entity's dream, or he in hers.

An apt question, favored soul. The currents of dreams ever change and shift, and to know oneself and be fully aware is a rare thing, indeed impossible, within one.

Rhidea could only think of Lyn, who had been having nocturnal visions for months before going to Gaea, and only recently had figured out that hers were memories.

Memories, yes . . . this is not so different. Ah, and here we are.

Mani brought Rhidea to what must have been the bottom of the misty ocean, and she alighted on an inky floor, indistinct and seemingly incorporeal. She walked lightly forward, and the mist swirled around her, changing and shifting the distant silhouette that was her destination. It materialized in seconds, however, and she made out pillars and columns. She reached out to touch them, but they phased out of reach as she did so.

She arrived at a tall structure, a silver temple. She knew this place, these stones and monuments. *The Down Under. Beneath the falls.*

Indeed. Do you know what this place truly is? He paused expectantly, but she merely waited for him to continue: *This is the old Temple of Mani, where the Silversmiths worshipped me. This was their home, these structures and monuments built by their own hands.*

She nodded in wonder, realizing that it made perfect sense. She had the slightest flicker of doubt at the word *worship*, but shoved that down quickly enough that Mani didn't see it. She could hide some things from him, even within his own dream.

Long ago, he continued, *the Silversmiths were my servants. The first humans on Mani.* As he spoke, the scenery began to change, time reversing as buildings rose from the smoky earth and formed together. The shattered pieces of pillars formed large monuments, arranged neatly leading up to the temple, and other structures were clearly houses. Time kept on reversing, and the massive, unexplained stone outcroppings and hills rose up and into the heavens.

What are they? she asked, eliciting what felt like a smile from her symbiotic partner.

Once, they were suspended as one across the divide between continents, my two halves. How do you think the humans traveled between? Soon after all the human pilgrims were situated, I tore down the land bridge. Best to let the peoples grow used to their millennial dwelling.

Rhidea did not respond, but only watched as her surroundings continued to change. The mist was clearing a bit as details became clearer, giving her a wider and better range to see what was going on . . . or ungoing. Eventually, even the monuments and buildings disappeared, vanishing into the earth, and then . . . silver poured down from the sky in streams, joining the core of Mani in the Down Under. *Fascinating . . .* She watched in stupefaction as the metal poured over the surface, surrounding the temple structure and lifting it from its place.

Rhidea rose with it. She shivered as the Silver poured around and even over top of her, though she did not really exist here in this backwards time lapse and could not feel it. *What is this? What happened to this world?*

We are nearing the dawn of Mani, he said cryptically.

The dawn of Mani . . .

Mani stripped the dream down, taking away the mist entirely and allowing her a panoramic view on a grand scale as the liquid silver poured down from the sky round about. She began to float away, faster and faster, phasing right through the pouring silver as it shaped and swelled Mani's core. Above . . . the continents were dissolving, dripping back to the surface of one round whole. She passed right through one of them, and was finally able to glimpse the scene in its entirety.

The Energy Field surrounding the planet was gone, as were the clouds and auroras. She watched as the barren surface of both continents streamed inward in a falling spiral, eventually eating them whole until the planet was one perfect sphere. Zooming in a bit allowed her to observe Mani's surface: Bubbly and imperfect. The silver was also fading, simple grey swirling through the metallic surface until it became ordinary rock.

The planet . . . transformed?

In a way, Mani confirmed. *What you see took place before the human settlers crossed from Gaea.*

And . . . the temple?

The temple was here at this point. Mani took her down to the surface of the moon, zipping across the barren plains at a blistering pace. She got the impression that time had finally stopped unraveling, but whether that was because they had arrived at the beginning or Mani had simply stopped it, she couldn't say. *Beginning . . .* What did that even mean?

There: A square temple, crafted of silver and standing out amidst a crater, the only landmark on the whole surface. Rhidea knew somehow that the Wellspring was not here this early on Mani.

There it is, he said. *And so you see that I have been here the whole time. Humans are the interlopers, but I took them in and welcomed them. My mother cast them out, but I gave them sanctuary. The Silversmiths served me faithfully until an unfortunate event tore them from my grasp, and then you know what that black soul . . .*

Domon.

Yes, Domon. What he did to your people. I understand why working with him is almost necessary now, but I do not like it. We are enemies, he and I. However, these silver beasts must be stopped, along with my mother's illegitimate offspring.

Rhidea set her jaw. *Indeed. And the Silver Beast. Stop them we shall, at any price.*

Again that sensation of a smile. It was not such a bad sensation.

Well said, daughter.

Domon awoke to a pain in the back of his skull. Not sharp, but more a dull, unwelcome ache. As he possessed a body that was over two hundred years old, aches and pains were nothing new, but this specific one was.

Rhidea. Could it have something to do with her? He had the High Mage roomed only three doors down from his in the castle intentionally. He was adept at deciphering elemental auras, and he wanted to know as soon as she might try something against him. He had awoken twice in the night, anticipating something—a tickling of his sense—yet nothing had happened. Three days had passed now since their tentative bargain.

What he sensed was not magic, certainly not of the dark varieties. He quested out with tendrils of Dark Magic, feeling at the earth beneath him, deep below the castle. Nothing was stirring.

Perhaps he was starting to lose it finally.

With a groan of age, he arose from his bed and began to dress himself. Calling one of his attendants, he demanded breakfast. Whether the castle servants loved him or cared for him was a question for its own day, but they were loyal.

With his mind, he continued to scan the world around him. He may be half asleep, but that did not limit his magical capabilities much. Yes, there was something coming from a few doors down. The signature was small, almost infinitesimal, but it was there. He would have to speak to her soon anyway. She was up; he knew that much.

But first, breakfast.

A few minutes later, he was crunching down on hard, crumbly toast smeared with some manner of tart fruit sauce, with small sausages on the side. The Halstar idea of a breakfast. Not half bad, just not exactly breakfast material. Too much work to chew.

As soon as he was done, he stretched and waited for his attendant. There he was. "You're late!" he snapped. "And for the last time, the toast is overdone."

"Apologies, Emperor," said the man with a groveling bow. What was his name? Cameron? "Anything else?"

"Yes. Contact the traveling mage, Rhidea, and have her meet me immediately in my lower study."

"Yes, Emperor." The man bowed low again.

"That is all, Cameron."

"It's . . ." the servant began, then hesitated, thought better of it, and turned to go.

As though I had time to learn all the servants' names here. With a small sigh, he strode forward as though following the man, but his feet fell in spontaneous pools of darkness, descending as he went. Within a few seconds, he was gone.

In his lower study—where he frequently performed his experiments on Mani's magic—he located the scrolls he had open from yesterday. There was one in particular . . . ah, there. *The Darkness Within,* read its title. Penned by himself. He didn't particularly want her looking at that one. He had perhaps ten minutes before she arrived, maybe less, and he wanted to perform a couple of experiments in preparation.

He had shown her this study yesterday, and they had worked together to test the reactions of Silver and Dark magic. The results had been suitably fascinating, and the two High Magi had kept from tearing one another's throats out—another bonus.

As expected, Silver magic had appeared at first glance to be unaffected by the corrupting effects of Dark, and repelled it to a small degree. The darkness he had forced upon her molded silver items was unable to penetrate, proving that the metal worked as a sort of insulant. He assumed this meant that she could theoretically shut off the Wellspring's power entirely from the world—or at least Dark Magic.

However, he sensed something deeper, a small panic within her, an excitement in her companion force, and a . . . stirring within her silver items, like a trembling vibration. Mani? The Archlord had not voiced his discovery, so as to hear her side of it first, but there was no mistaking it. She had not said much on it, only, "There could be something there, something faint."

Next, they had applied Dark Magic to a spell of her own that used her Silver Authority in addition to another, substituting Dark for that other element. These effects had been more readily visible. Best of all, at least in the way of preparing to defend Mani from foreign threats, was the revelation that the two powers could work just as smoothly in tandem, and as far as he could tell were roughly equal in strength.

But what other, what greater, powers had been born of Mani's influence within her? Perhaps she herself had yet to see. Today, they would test that.

And he would do his best not to prod her too much. Best not to anger a silver dragon.

β Chapter 028 β

The Mother's Fury

(Planet Gaea—Anier headquarters
Soldor 14, A.E. 1318, E120)
Mother Gaea rose to her feet and stretched. She teetered briefly and held out
a hand to her bed for balance, her other hand on her greatly pregnant belly.
"Oof," she grunted heavily. Her body was far too old and weak to be having
a baby, yet she had less than a week by all counts. A week till her baby girl
was born . . .

A week till Lhinde herself could finally die. She would get one glimpse
of her daughter, if all went well, before they took away the next Mother and
discarded the old one like a used rag.

And that was more than fine with Lhinde.

Sad as it was, she did not care that they would take Lynchazel from her.
She was too tired to care, too steeped in pain, too angry at the Anier and the
entire world. Lynchazel was a piece in the Anier's plans, an evolution in
bioexperiments, and a tool to Lhinde. A tool of vengeance. That was all. She
was ready to die and let another generation take her place.

She was done.

Lhinde approached the window of her chambers, a sad little window,
double-paned and thick-framed—in copper, of course, the same metal that
lined her entire room. Wouldn't want their pet Mother to accidentally stage
an escape while exhausted, dying and pregnant, now would they?

To be fair, she still could if not for the copper. She just wouldn't make it
very far, and would indeed soon die, along with the only other living
female . . . Hellebes. Lynchazel almost counted as one. But as for herself . . .
she still preferred to identify as one of *them*.

Lhinde tapped the glass of the window absently, looking out over the
twilit Steel City. An ugly, festering metropolis of industry and eternal

modernization, it grew like cancer. One day, that cancer would run its course and the growth would stop. It would merely be a sprawling, hideous city of smoke and oppression. She rubbed her abdomen distractedly. Lynchazel would soon come forth into the world and go directly into the laboratories here in Haccolces, growing in her artificial and accelerated childhood before they put her into their fully developed power grid. For now, their Gamma Beast made a flimsy but sufficient substitute. She felt that twinge again, that unshakable fear for her daughter.

No, she told herself. *Stop that, Lhinde. Whatever this child goes through, it won't be half as bad as what you endured.* Of course, she was no monster; she cared for her child, and indeed that was in large part her reason for hating the Anier. She just couldn't let it get in the way of her vision—her revenge. Because of what they did to her and would do to her daughter for potentially centuries to come . . . she must sacrifice her daughter to their schemes and ignore the pain that a mother was supposed to feel. She didn't feel it. She couldn't.

The girl, the next Mother Gaea, would bear her burden, but for the good of future people. Lhinde felt neither guilt nor pain at that. The horrible wrenching in her gut was just practice contractions. Yes, and the queasiness too. It would pass.

Lhinde looked upward through the window, above the sun's setting light that came from the far left, bathing the city in somber gold. Luna was up there, and would soon fall within her sight. She could feel it. Home of the Cydenges. Even now, she could remember her first encounter with one, the first time she had seen one ravage a city and wreak destruction, snapping humans in its metallic jaws and leaving untouched the pieces, unneeded for its sustenance. She remembered the time her keepers had accidentally let her dangerously close to one, and she'd watched its rippling scales as it closed on her, red eyes laser focused on hers. It had crept up close and then . . . brushed at her mind. Pushed at it. She'd panicked, lashing out with Geokinetic energy. Uselessly, as the silver beast only absorbed it.

The Anier called Sylleo had taken care of it, finding them just in time.

She remembered the time long after that when she had freed a captive Cydenges and attempted to escape on its back. It had let her, too, and indeed had . . . *communicated* its plan to her in advance. The creatures seemed to consider her someone special, or . . . probably more just curious. Strange. But perhaps almost . . . family.

But then there had been that one time, some two years back, when she was outside the shield domes, away from copper and buzzing technology. She had *heard* her. Not Gaea—her voice was different—but Luna. Her voice was deep, primeval and grinding, yet it echoed in her mind like the ring of metal on metal.

But she knew it was a she. "Mother?" she had answered after the briefest hesitation, wondering why she said it.

The voice responded in that same metallic growl, which she envisioned as the echo of sound reverberating off metal walls in a long hallway, coming from an infinite expanse filled with a thousand slow-grinding gears driven by one person, one . . . woman? Girl? No. Something else . . . deep in the darkness.

Lost in reverie, Lhinde could vividly reconstruct the image that had come to her mind then: A glimmering creature sheathed in pale metal with beautiful lines etched into its hard plates, its eyes golden flames. Not red, but burning gold. Larger than life and older than man, the majestic titaness stood on a black backdrop pitted with lonely stars, amidst a desolate landscape to which Lhinde felt a connection then . . . and even now as she glimpsed her once again.

"Mother," she whispered.

End of Book Two

To be continued in . . .

THE MOTHER TRILOGY: BOOK THREE

LUNA

JACOB GAMBER

AUTHOR'S NOTE

- 651 -

Two books down, one more to go . . . Thank you so much for reading! I hope you enjoyed it, as this novel has definitely been a long-coming passion project of mine. If you did, there's no better way to show support for the Mother Project than by leaving a review on Goodreads or wherever you may have found it online. Reviews are highly important for visibility and reader growth, but I'm also excited to see people's reaction to this book and the direction it took. How will Lyn tie together the broken threads of the past? Who or what is the Silver Beast? Find out in Book Three! For now it's time to step away from editing and reflect on this second installment.

As with last time, I'd encourage you not to read this if you haven't read the book yet, because I'll be discussing **spoilers** below.

Background

Gaea, in a way, was the first of the trilogy that I really had ideas for. Or rather, there are a lot of foundational ideas I had for the series that didn't show up until *Gaea*—the Cydenges, the Hellebes Mother, the energy weapons and other sci-fi tech. As I said in my last author's note, a main inspiration for this series was Superman, while aesthetically it's 'Final Fantasy meets Metroid'. Additionally, while the design of the Cydenges is entirely my own, the idea of a species coveted as a super weapon was taken directly from the Metroids.

I've been up-front about the sci-fi nature of the series, but I still tried to include enough hints in *Mani* that most readers won't be shocked to suddenly discover the genre-switch. I honestly don't think I'll ever write something quite as Sci-Fi as *The Mother Trilogy* again, unless I continue the series after *Luna*. (Which . . . might happen.) Fantasy was always my home territory, but this was just way too much fun to let go of, and I promised myself I'd finish it before moving on to older worlds.

Naturally, I don't think I can say I pioneered any new Sci-Fi ideas—if such a thing exists anymore—but rather pulled from numerous inspirations, taking what I liked. An exception to this would be the Hellebes design as explained in Chapter 37: Biodigital Convergence, which came later after much deliberation. It seemed the right choice for the story. I kept going back and forth on how far I wanted to take it, and ended up erring on the stranger side. Granted, I've always been fascinated by paradoxes of identity: What makes us human? The book of Ecclesiastes says this in the third chapter:

Who knows whether the spirit of man goes upward and the spirit of the beast goes down into the earth? So I saw that there is nothing better than that a man should rejoice in his work, for that is his lot. Who can bring him to see what will be after him?

On the topic of the two moons . . . where did that come from? I genuinely can't say, other than that it came as a slow realization, one of those "Hmm . . . the story needs this" sort of things. Some choices were made, I suppose, out of a deliberate desire to be different, such as the disparity between sexes on Mani and Gaea. I didn't have any grand designs for story impact, nor did I intend any deep exploration of sexism, historical patriarchy, etc.—I just said, "What's the *one* thing I've never seen anybody do with fantasy worldbuilding . . ."

Brief note on the politics of the novel: Very little is meant to reflect real-world politics one-to-one. I generally dislike that in fiction. In fact, the terms I use are often in fictitious context as well. For instance, "imperialism" in Gaea is more like a brand of globalism, and really just emphasizes a singular, worldwide power as originally intended by the Anier. "Militarist," for that matter, would be a slightly different brand of globalism. They look at Sylleo as a rebel, almost a traitor, for this reason.

Research

The astute reader has already noticed this is a Science Fiction story. However, I use the term Science Fantasy, or Sci-Fantasy, because very little is built on grounded science. In fact, despite *Gaea* being far more heavily Sci-Fi than *Mani,* I really have less to say on my research because . . . well, there's no great secret like in Book One. At least, none that can be explained using real-world science. And not as much astronomy stuff to figure out. Frankly, most of my research amounted to Googling things like "melting point of copper vs. steel" to see if Lyn could realistically break her bonds without Geokinesis, only to say, "Phooey with that, she just does it anyway."

It's worth mentioning here that Gaea is both like and unlike our own world. Its moons are similar in orbit and scale, yet—seeing as they orbit the planet opposite one another coequally—they pull on two ends of the world at once. Thus, the tide changes twice per day instead of once.

The fictional Geothermic energy that circulates through Gaea will likely be a sticking point with anyone actually versed in earth science . . . not only did I make up nonsensical properties and uses for it, but its name is very similar to geo*thermal* energy, which is an actual thing and completely different (it's a process that relies on water and heat). While I did do a fair bit of research into geoscience for this novel, I abandoned most of it, deciding it would be far more fun to go full-on fantasy, relying heavily on what my Linguistics Department thought sounded cool. There are also some inevitable inconsistencies involving Gaea's tectonic, radiation, and atmospheric effects from the . . . well, the exact causes are purposefully vague, but perhaps I could have been more consistent in description.

As for the inclusion of AI, quantum computing and the like within the story, I'm well aware that it might not age all that well. It's a risk one has to accept with science fiction. Then of course there are the technologies that are conscicuously *not* present, such as various forms of entertainment or more advanced communication that utilizes the unique capacities of biomachines . . . Or the internet—there are really only a couple allusions to it, but Gaea does in fact have a web similar to ours. This would realistically pervade the story, but I didn't want to overdo it.

Before I wrap up my ramblings, I should note that I intended to put the rules for the fictional game of Gogi here in the back matter, but alas . . . I never got around to playtesting it and I don't yet have a solid ruleset for it. In concept, it is two of my favorite strategy games—Go and Shogi—put together, literally mashing nearly every aspect of the two. The manga artist Yoshihiro Togashi made up a rather similar game called Gungi for his series *Hunter × Hunter,* which I only later discovered can be fully learned and even played online (unofficially, I believe). It is far, *far* more complex, however, incorporating aspects of chess and even some stacking mechanics.

I mention Gungi because I designed this game very similarly, yet entirely unintentionally. I intended Gogi to be more in the spirit of Go, in that the pieces and rules are quite simple but the strategy is complex, probably around the complexity of chess. When I develop a full ruleset, I'll post it on my website for dweebs like me to check out.

— Here end my tangential ramblings —
See you on Luna!

— Jacob G.

APPENDIX A
Characters
(And how on Gaea you're supposed to pronounce them)

<u>Underlined</u> names are from Gaea.
Names in **bold** are from Mani.

<u>Adina Craws</u>—A woman of Mei Shan.

Adullus Ta (uh-DOOL-us TAH)—A famous High Mage credited with creating the modern classifications of magic in the year 782.

Aldyr Tolruin (ALL-deer TOLL-roo-in)—Syneria's elder sister, engaged to Ethas of House Gandel.

Alfred—A mage from Snowbell, Fircas, employed by Lyn for a stunt.

Andra—Mydia's former handmaiden.

<u>Balfour</u>—A captain in the Red Horizon.

Bart, Big—Real name: Bartimaeus. Once a leader of the Nytaean Underground, more recently tied for second-in-command under Mydia.

<u>Bddo</u>—A corporal in the Red Horizon, serving under Captain Zent.

Ben—Called Uncle Ben by most, he is Oliver's uncle and a member of the Scathii Council.

Berta—A hearty young woman who started an orphanage with Phoebe.

Betty—The maid who showed Lyn the ways of the Palace maid.

<u>Brant</u>—Senator of Maldunech.

Carth—A veteran sky sailor who doesn't take quickly to mainlanders.

<u>Ccal</u>—A corporal in the Red Horizon, serving under Captain Zent.

Chara (CARE-uh)—Former handmaiden disliked by Mydia for years.

Charta (CHAR-tuh)—A bear-like, good-natured sky sailor.

<u>Chimeth</u>—Third General of Haccolces.

Christoff—A lieutenant in the Nemental military.

Cort Flanning—A noble student from the Nytaean Mage Academy introduced by Rhidea to the scholars of Randhorn. Thin and blond.

Curtis—A Hellebes soldier of the Red Horizon.

Daedalus (DED-uh-lus)—Senator of Chronala.

Dekla—Head biologist at the Red Horizon.

DeWitt—Senator of Lenardda.

Domon, Archlord (ARK-lord DOME-uhn)—Archlord (emperor) of Kystrea, long feared for his magical strength and his ruthlessness, despite being a fair ruler overall.

Dudley—Duke of Halstar, recently executed and dethroned.

Eivael Badon-Kalceron (AY-ih-vale BAY-duhn)—Mydia's late mother, and previous wife of Lord Kalceron. After her death eight years ago, he remarried to a sorceress named Lieda. [See **Kalceron**]

Enchro—Mashal of Nytaea, appointed by Mydia after Lanthar's death.

Ethas Gandel (EETH-us GAN-del)—Heir of his house, Ethas is 20 years old, tall and blond. He can't help being a bit better than most people, much like his fiancée, Aldyr Tolruin.

Feln—A sky sailor.

Fenwel—King of Nemental. He is aged and wise, possessing a keen wit and a good sense of humor. His hair and beard are white but not thin, his frame still strong, and he has some innate magic, though only a bit. Possesses the Perception-based gift of Truthseeing.

Fors—A general in the Ccamos military.

Fraid—A deranged fire mage and murderer, leader of a thieving band in Nytaea—the same who burned down Lentha's orphanage.

Frath—An elder of the village of Scathii.

Frauss (FROWSS)—A general in the Ccamos air force.

Gaela (GAY-luh)—A noblewoman serving directly under Queen Mydia, once a leader in the Underground. Tall, blonde hair streaked with white, her mild temperament often conceals dark anger. Skilled at keeping a straight face.

Gendric—Master of the Nytaean Mage Academy, wise mentor of Rhidea. Disapproved of Lord Kalceron's rule but tried to stay out of it. He once led a band of mage mercenaries who worked for whichever Kystrean State would pay the most money. The Archlord offered to build him a school in Nytaea if he'd teach aspiring magicians the art of war magic for Kystrea's armies. Gendric came to detest the idea of using the arts to kill. He made the school into a great academy where one could study Coaction and Authority and only pursue a soldier's career if one so chose.

<u>Getts</u>—Director and founding member of the Red Horizon.

Glenidar—King of Ti'Vaeth until Lord Domon rose up and killed him in a duel, naming himself Archlord of Ti'Vaeth and setting out to conquer the other Kystrean city-states.

Gorman Sedler—A servant in the employ of Lord Kalceron who secures Kaen and Lyn a position among the staff at the Palace.

Hamia (HAY-mee-uh)—A Palace maid who bunked with Lyn for a while. Stocky and chubby, she comes from a line of farmers.

Harcost—A carpenter in Nytaea. Formerly employed Lyn and Kaen.

Harold—A corporal in Archlord Domon's palace guard.

Hespian—Captain of the Nytaean Mage Guard, answering to Lord Kalceron himself. Despite his air of joviality, he can be quite cunning.

Hetta—A female water mage scholar from Randhorn.

<u>Hodge</u>—Quartermaster at the Red Horizon.

<u>Holman</u>—Senator of Luna Halcyon.

Humphret—A nobleman of some standing in Ti'Vaeth. His main hobbies include pestering the Archlord and eating.

<u>Inecc</u>—A general in the Ccamos air force.

Inno—A soldier who joined the Queensguard to protect Nytaea's new ruler.

Itoll (EE-toll)—An elder of Scathii.

<u>Janus</u>—A Hellebes soldier of the Red Horizon.

<u>Jed</u>—A Hellebes soldier of the Red Horizon. Loves Gogi.

Jinna—A scholar friend of Eivael Kalceron. She died tragically in a magical experiment, prompting the queen to abandon her alchemical experiments.

Julia—A handmaiden to Princess Mydia, about the same age as Lyn, though she's been in her position for years now. She came from a poor home to the Palace to pay off her father's debts, but Lord Kalceron had them killed off a year ago, stranding her in service to House Kalceron.

Kaen (KANE)—Lyn's longtime friend from Lentha's orphanage. Mandrie is his little sister. When Kaen infiltrates the Palace with Lyn to try to free Mandrie and Phoebe from the inside, he assumes the name of Roger. He has curly dark hair and intense expressions, and, despite his 17 years, carries himself like someone who has been through rough times and learned to harden himself against the world around him.

Kalceron, Edrius (EE-dree-us KAL-sir-on)—Governor of Nytaea, known for being crueler than the Archlord of Kystrea himself. His daughter is Princess Mydia. She and his firstborn son, Kallyn, were born to him of Lady Eivael Kalceron, his late wife. He remarried eight years back to a sorceress called Lieda. It is said that his first wife, Eivael, kept the worst of him in check, while his second, Lieda, only fostered that dark side.

Kallyn Kalceron—Son of Lord Kalceron and heir to the throne of Nytaea, Mydia's brother Kallyn disappeared fifteen years back and was presumed dead.

Kath—A fire mage soldier who joined the Queensguard to protect Nytaea's new ruler.

Kelleva—Regent of Ti'Vaeth for Domon during his campaign in Darsor.

Keuda (KYU-duh)—Royal secretary of Nytaea.

Kidd—A sergeant in the Red Horizon.

Kinneson—A captain in the Red Horizon.

Kyal (KYAHL)—Lord of the province of Imdek.

Kymhar (kih-MAHR)—Former member of the Dalim, the Archlord's lethal servants. Dresses in dark leathers with many layers to hide knives and kunai. Trained in stealth, assassination and martial arts.

Lanna—A female mage soldier assigned by the queen to guard Phoebe's orphanage.

Lentha—A kind woman who raised Lyn at the orphanage.

Lester—Oliver's father.

Lester, Little—Once a Nytaean Underground leader. Real name: Tomas.

Lhiard (lee-ARD)—Lord of the city-state of Uphel.

Lhinde (LIN-duh)—The first Mother Gaea, grandmother of Lyn, once a peasant girl from the Sovereignty of Starklett.

Lieda (LEE-duh)—The magician noblewoman to whom Lord Kalceron remarried eight years back, following the mysterious and sudden death of his former wife, Eivael. . . . Lieda is not well liked by Mydia, nor by the people of Nytaea. She is as much a thorn in the city's side as her husband. Hates Mydia and the sight of blood.

Lina—One of the senior Palace maids.

Lldsaor (ill[d]-SAW-ohr—just don't really pronounce a vowel sound on the first syllable)—Emperor of Gaea who rules from Haccolces.

Long (LUNG)—Former Senator of Mei Shan.

Lorta—A caustic, vulpine mage lieutenant who works closely with Captain Hespian in Lord Kalceron's Mage Guard.

Lyn (Lynchazel II)—A young woman with white hair and inexplicable strength. Said to have been brought by her destitute mother to Lentha's orphanage, where she was raised. Lyn barely remembers her real name, Lynchazel, for Lentha stopped using it early on when the other children at the orphanage picked on her for its 'noble' sound.

Lynchazel I (LINK-uh-zel)—???

Mandrie—Kaen's younger sister, who gets abducted by Captain Hespian of the Mage Guard.

Mant—A lieutenant in the Armed Guard of Nytaea.

Margill—Butler and steward to Senator Sylleo.

Marnie—Lester's mother.

Musha (MOO-shuh)—Board member, general and a founding member of the Red Horizon.

Mydia Kalceron (MID-ee-uh)—Sole daughter of Lord Kalceron, heir of Nytaea ever since her brother Kallyn died fifteen years back (or . . . went missing). Her mother, Lady Eivael, died eight years ago of a disease. Mydia's hair is jet black, her form a bit padded from her pampered life, her skin a pasty white. She is shy but very talkative when encouraged, and has a mischievous side. Mydia possesses illusionary magic as well as green magic. Inherited from her mother, the latter is a type of water magic which includes accelerated growth and renewal of plants/trees/flowers, as well as healing.

Oliver—A twelve-year-old boy, sandy haired and freckled, who lives in the village on the eastern Isle of Scathii. He is an orphan and a rebel who loves to fly, characterized by his daring and cleverness.

Orlando—A sergeant in the Red Horizon.

Phelps—An administrator working under Strongs.

Phoebe—A friend of Kaen and Lyn from back at the orphanage. She is sixteen years old and has brown hair that hangs down just past her shoulders, expressionless eyes and a beaklike, hooked nose. Phoebe dreams of having a family someday in a better Nytaea, but is also an incurable pessimist. No one knows the exact details of how she came to the orphanage, but she holds bitterness against someone close to her in her past.

Phreska—Lyn's biology instructor at the Red Horizon.

Podda—A common girl's name that Lyn uses as an alias in the Palace.

Rhidea, Cae (KYE rye-DAY-uh)—A traveling magician, tall with deep red hair, once High Magister to King Fenwel of Randhorn. Now, she wanders about from place to place, seeking a solution to the dwindling magic of the world. She carries herself with confidence and addresses everyone equally, often as 'child.' Her features are beautiful but hard, her hazel eyes focused. Rhidea is also the most powerful mage to be seen in many decades. As a High Mage, she is versed in many branches of magic, but one of her specialties is gravitational control.

Ridda—Rhidea's alias in Redufiel.

Rissius—A founding member of the Red Horizon who made it possible for the rebel organization to exist.

Rodessa—A contact of Rhidea's at the Imperial Archives in the Ti'Vaeth citadel.

Roger—Kaen's alias in the Palace.

Ruel (ROOL)—A soldier who joined the Queensguard to protect Nytaea's new ruler.

Sam, Skinny—Deceased leader of the Underground in Nytaea.

Seidrake (SEE-drake)—The Red Horizon's top sniper. Devastating with a Hellebes bow.

Shanagel (shuh-NAY-guhl)—A very strange sky sailor.

Skye, Admiral—Fleet commander and Board member of the Red Horizon.

Solomiya (so-lo-MEE-uh)—A mysterious sorceress of great power recruited by Domon soon after dominating Darsor.

Sor the Lark—A deceased scholar, author of the book *Secrets of Mani*.

Stenek (steh-NEK)—A major in the Red Horizon who leads a team into Maldunech along with Zent and Musha.

Stessa Valiant—A water mage scholar from Randhorn.

Strongs—General of the Anier forces, now Senator of Haven.

Sylleo—Senator of Ccamos.

Sylvia—A delegate sent by Mydia to Dotham.

Syneria Tolruin (sih-NEER-ee-uh TOLL-roo-in)—A friend of Cort Flanning from the Mage Academy. Sixteen years of age, blonde, blue eyed. Coming from wealthy House Tolruin, she carries a chip on her shoulder.

Task—A Hellebes soldier of the Red Horizon.

Teli (TEL-ee)—Handmaiden to Queen Mydia of Nytaea, formerly a young maid who suffered a rough upbringing.

Tenna—A delegate sent by Mydia to Ti'Vaeth.

Teuchan (TOO-kahn)—A nobleman who led the Anier in the late thirteenth century.

Thames—A scholar friend of Eivael Kalceron.

Todson—A carpenter of Mei Shan. His son, Hal, is friends with Hans.

Tom, Tall—Once a Nytaean Underground leader. Real name: Dossam.

Tommy—A young boy from Lentha's orphanage.

Trevias Lhordes (TREV-ee-us LORE-deez)—A famed general of Ti'Vaeth who fought for High King Glenidar along with a coalition of city-states to repel the invading Torlegans. Credited with bringing an end to the war and driving them over the Styrite Mountains for good in 794.

Tyiv (TEEV)—Lord of the southern Kystrean city-state of Dotham, and a member of the Umbra Council.

Vass—Board member and founding member of the Red Horizon.

Viktor Amma—A water mage scholar from Randhorn.

Vladimir—Senator of Trident.

Vyss—Stewardess to Domon in Redufiel.

White—Lyn's cognitive assistant who oversees her Vault.

Zama—Governor of Nytaea appointed by a vacationing Archlord.

Zent—Former captain in the Haccolces air force who worked with the Red Horizon secretly. Affectionately called Cap at HQ, but he's a colonel. Lyn's main friend and benefactor on Gaea.

APPENDIX B
Glossary of Terms and Locations
(And how on Gaea you're supposed to pronounce them)

Andeir (AN-dare)—A town in the province of Fircas.

Anier (uh-NEER)—An enigmatic organization existing before the year E1. Founders of the Mother Project.

Anteleth—A noble beast like a far larger gazelle, whose branching horns are breakable at every joint and could once be found scattered about the rocky outcroppings of the Plains of Nandaer where the Anteleth roamed. Now, they are thought to have been exterminated by monsters, and more recently humans, who hunted them to extinction, and their horns are prized items that serve to remember them by.

Aptitude—Magical talent.

Ardencaul River—One of the Four Rivers, fed by the Wellspring's water and flowing eastward from Ti'Vaeth. It passes through Fircas, Nytaea, Storklance, and finally the country of Nemental, before rushing over the eastern coast of Argent.

Argent (AHR-jent)—The major continent of Mani where the Legaleians dwell.

Auroras—A phenomenon that lights up the sky beneath the clouds during nights of the Sunlit Cycle (very dimly and not consistently) and during daytime of the Sunless Cycle usually without cloud coverage—thus creating light for the people of Mani to see by.

Authority—One of two schools of magic present on Mani, alongside Coaction. The two appear similar, except that Authority is far more powerful, but are quite different in practice. [See **Coaction**, also see Appendix C]

Balrun—Situated along the banks of the Ardencaul in Nytaea, the

Balrun sector is home to most of the Nytaean shipping industry, docks, warehouses, etc.

Biomanufactories—Facilities for raising Hellebes. [See Appendix C]

Branch—Magical term for one of the eight major classifications of magic present on Mani: Water, Fire, Lightning, Wind, Earth, Perception, Reality and Silver. Both Authority and the less powerful Coaction are categorized under these eight branches, though there are many subclasses, such as green magic (plant magic) and healing, Mydia's specialties born of her Water Aptitude. [See Appendix C]

Castanor—An outlier nation of Darsor lying to the north.

Ccamos—One of the Nine Cities of Man, ruled by Sylleo and situated in western South Terrol.

Chronala—One of the Nine Cities of Man, ruled by Daedalus and overseeing the world's population from northeastern Nestra.

City-State—One of thirteen small regions of Kystrea, each ruled by a king and dominated by one large, usually central, city. In the center of the empire is Ti'Vaeth, Archlord Domon's own city-state and the first of the thirteen to come under his control one hundred years ago. Before the Archlord took over, they were independent city-states ruled by a king, but now he likes to use the terms "governor" and "province."

Coaction—The lesser school of magic present on Mani, with Authority being its greater cousin. The two appear similar, except that Authority is far more potent, but are quite different in practice. [See **Authority**]

Constellation—A phenomenon of the Sunlit night skies, created by the Energy Field as Sol reaches certain angles, creating a shimmering image upon the thick cloud coverage not altogether unlike the auroras. They also appear in the Night Season, coming in different times of the day than in the Sunlit Cycle. [See **Auroras**]

Craglands—A vast wasteland stretching from the Rooting Valleys westward.

Cryvad (crih-VAHD)—Westernmost city-state of the Kystrean Empire and birthplace of Mydia's mother, Eivael Badon. It is a land of plenty, as the

Rudaens River forms a wide delta that spreads throughout it before spilling into the Sea of Emptiness.

Cydenges (sigh-DEN-jeez)—**???**

Cynnith Ocean (SIH-nith)—Spans between the eastern and western hemispheres of Gaea.

Dark Magic—A theoretical transversion of the power that flows from the Wellspring of Magic. Anti-life, anti-magic. It is extremely potent and destructive, but don't worry—Archlord Domon must have a good reason for creating it.

Darsor (dar-SORE)—The native name for a certain continent on Mani.

Dalim (duh-LEEM)—An elite order of assassins who work for Archlord Domon, trained in many ancient martial arts. Can refer to singular or plural assassins of the order, or to the order at large—though they are not many, and hold tightly to their bloodline.

Day Season—See Sunlit Cycle.

Dojang—A martial training room, ranging from small one-on-one rooms to larger ones for group instruction.

Dotham (DOE-thum)—A southern province of Kystrea, bordering the Styrite Mountains on the south.

Down Under—A land deep below, or rather between, the continents of Mani.

Energy Field—The outer portion of Mani's sky (atmosphere) that pulses with energy and is believed to contain much of the elemental power born of the Wellspring that is tapped by magi. The Energy Field is responsible for the auroras—the shifting heavenly lights that come and go along with thick cloud coverage, keeping the regular days distinguished throughout each Sol Cycle—as well as constellations and other such phenomena. [See **Sol Cycle**, **Auroras**]

Element—One of the five Elemental Branches of magic: Water, Fire, Lightning, Wind and Earth. Can also refer to any one of eight major forces at work in the world of Mani, though the magical term is 'branch.' [See **Branch**]

Elite—A name for Emperor Lldsaor and Senators of the Gaean League.

Eltar—A Darsorian outlier nation to the southwest of the Duchy of Halstar.

Escatar—The smallest continent on Gaea, found in the Kholon Ocean, home to the city of Luna Halcyon.

Faliday (FAL-uh-day)—A Nementali town located just south of Randhorn.

Felmani (fel-MAW-nee)—An outlier nation of Darsor lying in the northwest region.

Fircas—A Kystrean province bordering Nytaea on the east and Ti'Vaeth on the west.

Four Rivers—The great rivers of the world that spring from the Wellspring of Life in Ti'Vaeth and flow in the four cardinal directions to the edges of Argent.

Gaea (GUY-uh, JEE-uh)—Homeworld of the Hellebes, ancient home of the Legaleians and all mankind. Gaea is a large planet with much water and diverse biomes, a thick atmosphere and heavy gravity.

Gaean Senate—The nine leaders of all Gaea, each ruling one city.

Gantz River—One of the Four Rivers, running southward out of Ti'Vaeth through Imdek, under the Styrite Mountains, and through the country of Torlega before spilling over the southern coast of Argent.

Gate (of Mani/Gaea)—Two linked archways, one on each world, crafted by ancient Legaleian Reality magi. The exact workings are no longer known.

Gatewatch Isle—A forbidden island which lies in the northeastern hemisphere of Gaea. On it stands the Gate of Gaea.

Geokinesis—The Hellebes ability to manipulate stone underfoot and to move their own bodies using Geothermic energy as fuel.

Geothermic Energy—Also called planetary energy. The pure lifeblood of Gaea, which is utilized as the foundation of most technology in the modern world as well as personally by Hellebes.

Ghartu (GAR-too)—Northwesternmost of the Kystrean provinces, bordering Uphel on its eastern side. Home to one of the harshest climates of

Argent, dry and arid.

Gogi (GO-gee)—A strategy game originating in the eastern continent of Tai'Xi, played on a 10x10 steel grid with dark and light pieces that can be surrounded, captured and used for oneself.

Governor—Official title of the king of a city-state (province) of Kystrea. Sounds less nationalist.

Great Exile—The Legaleians' "pilgrimage" to Mani one thousand years ago.

Haccolces (huh-COLE-seez)—One of the Nine Cities of Man, seat of the Emperor and capital of the Gaean League. Monikered "The Steel City", this industrial supercenter lies at the center of North Terrol.

Hall of Eternity—The imperial palace of the Archlord, nestled deep within the Ti'Vaeth citadel. Three walls enclose it, rising higher toward the very center, where a tall stack rises from the Wellspring into the sky, whence issues the Sky Funnel. [See **Wellspring of Magic**, **Sky Funnel**]

Halstar—A duchy spanning the broad central region of Darsor.

Haven—One of the Nine Cities of Man, ruled by Strongs and situated in southeastern North Terrol.

Heart of Mani—An unknown force occupying the sword that Kaen found in the waterfall ruins.

Hearth—The one and only town occupying the Down Under.

Heiress—Or Mother Heiress. Refers to Lyn, the returned daughter of Mother Gaea thought to be lost forever. Many hopes ride on her.

Hellebes (HEL-uh-beez)—The Hellebes are a race of people indigenous to Gaea.

Hellebes Mother—Often simply called the Mother or Mother Gaea, this name refers to a line of revered figures vital to the operation of the Gaean League—one woman at a time, the sole female in existence—for she alone has the capacity to create the egg cells from which all Hellebes are made. [See **Biomanufactories**] This process is a closely guarded secret, and she herself is never seen—for these reasons and others, she is worshipped as a goddess worldwide.

Helstrom—A desert region on the eastern coast of North Terrol.

High Legaleian—An old language spoken by the first people of Mani, largely similar to the currently spoken dialect but different enough to baffle the uneducated.

High Mage—A title given only to magi who have proven themselves both academically and in the arts of Authority. A High Mage possesses strong talent, carefully honed over decades, and is required to have mastered Authority in at least three branches of magic.

High Magister—Entirely separate, this is a royal court position bestowed on Cae Rhidea by King Fenwel some forty years back.

Imdek (EEM-dek)—A province of southern Kystrea.

Imperial Highway—A long road spanning the continent of Argent from west to east and breaking only with each major city encountered along the way. Highly traveled because it is safe, and vice versa.

Iron Dojang—The Red Horizon's best training room, outfitted with steel floors and ample equipment for harsh but effective combat training.

Kholon Ocean—The vast seas spanning from western Nestra to the continent of Tai'Xi, with Escatar in the middle.

Kysedon (kih-SEE-duhn)—An island in the middle of Lake Lucia upon which the city of Ti'Vaeth stands. [see **Lake Lucia**]

Kystrea (KISS-tree-uh)—An empire spanning most of the map of Legalei (Argent) and comprised of thirteen city-states, ruled over by twelve lords called governors and an Archlord.

Land of Storms—A circular, barren rockscape which lies at the heart of Darsor, concealing the Tower of Mani at its center. Overhead is a great conflagration of thunderstorms, ever roiling and spewing deadly lightning everywhere, and no one ventures near for fear of being struck dead.

Legalei (leh-GAHL-ay)—An old term for the world of Mani. [See **Mani**]

Legaleia (LEE-guh-LAY-uh)—Ancestral Gaean home of all current day Manese folk. Now has a different name.

Legaleian (LEE-guh-LAY-un)—The language spoken by people all across Argent.

Legaleians—The humans who inhabit the magical world of Legalei, which is also called Mani. [See **Mani**]

Lenardda—One of the Nine Cities of Man, ruled by DeWitt and occupying South Terrol's southern tip.

Loftus—A northern Kystrean province.

Lor'Hav (lore-HAWV)—The first village encountered in Darsor, just east of the ancient forest that borders Darsor's western cliffs.

Lucia Lake—The largest standing body of water on the continent of Argent, this lake—affectionately called the Sea of Ti'Vaeth by idiot outsiders—surrounds the isle of Kysedon, and thus the city of Ti'Vaeth. Tall cliffs form a wall around the lake, which is fed from underground by the Wellspring. The Four Rivers run in each cardinal direction from Lake Lucia.

Luna—Mani's golden twin, the second moon of Gaea. In truth, it was the first. Home to the Cydenges, yet to be explored by Hellebes.

Luna Halcyon—Only of the Nine Cities of Man to occupy the small continent of Escatar, ruled by Holman.

Lygellis (lie-GELL-iss)—An outlier nation to the southwest of Kystrea, partially bordering Torlega on the southeast. Lygellis is the largest of the outlier lands but sparsely populated. There isn't much there apart from the northern delta shared with Cryvad.

Monsters—Naturally, this word can be used to mean many different things, but to most Legaleians it refers to a range of specific, actual monster species that once roamed the face of Mani: Fire-breathing snakes, enormous lions and bull-bears, to name a few. Some say dragons.

Magic—A force that drives the world of Mani and gives it breath. All magic comes from the Wellspring of Magic in Ti'Vaeth, which lies at the very center of the continent of Argent.

Maldunech (MAL-du-nek)—One of the Nine Cities of Man, ruled by Brant and situated in southeastern Nestra.

Manese (maw-NEEZ)—Legaleian; of Mani. [See **Legaleian**]

Mani (MAW-nee)—A silver world pulsing with magic, with which the Legaleians (the inhabitants of Mani) were blessed—or some say cursed.

Mani's white sun, Sol, makes her rounds only once per month, so one Sol Cycle is four weeks long (28 days exactly). There is a reactive, pulsing Energy Field that surrounds the planet, creating powerful displays called auroras to light the two-week nights and also strange constellations that recur periodically. [See **Auroras**, **Energy Field**, **Sol Cycle**]

Mani Halcyon—A Gaean city of old. Not many remember the name.

Mannet—A large town immediately south and within sight of Redufiel, capital of Halstar.

Mei Shan—Formerly one of the Gaean League's nine cities, now destroyed and lying presumably in nuclear waste in far-off Tai'Xi.

Memory Vault—See **Vault.**

Moon—???

Mother Project—The purposes of this project are unknown throughout Gaea today, but it centered around the creation of the first Mother Gaea.

Nandaer (NAHN-dare)—A large plain in southern Sorfaen, near the southern edge of Argent, where the proud Anteleth once roamed.

Nemental (NEM-en-tall)—The kingdom bordering Kystrea's eastern flank, sandwiched between Storklance and the eastern cliffs of Argent. Her king is Fenwel of Randhorn.

Nestra—A midsize continent of Gaea's western hemisphere, bordered by the Cynnith Ocean on the east and the Kholon Ocean on the west. Home to Trident, Ccamos and Maldunech.

Night Season—See Sunless Cycle.

Noduin (NO-dwin)—The largest of the Sky Islands, not far off the shore of Argent.

Nomu—Another Sky Island, lying just farther out than Noduin and not quite as large.

Nytaea (nigh-TAY-uh)—A city-state in Kystrea ruled by Lord Kalceron, the governor. Lyn grew up in this city, where she was raised from a baby by the kind woman Lentha.

Perception—The branch of Coaction/Authority that governs manifest (perceived) reality.

Polestone—A reddish stone whose natural properties cause it to point toward the center of Argent—more accurately, toward the Wellspring of Life. Not always as useful as it sounds, but using one in conjunction with the current angle of the sun can make pinpointing directions easier.

Province—See **City-State.** These terms are interchangeable.

Randhorn—Capital of Nemental, where King Fenwel rules and Rhidea has a seat as High Magister.

Reality—The branch of Coaction/Authority that rules physical reality.

Rudaens River (roo-DENZ)—One of the Four Rivers of the world, running westward from Ti'Vaeth through Thyria and eventually ending in a wide delta in the province of Cryvad.

Redufiel (ruh-DOO-fee-el)—Capital city of the Duchy of Halstar.

Rooting Valleys—Winding valleys that spread out from Haccolces and Mount Beides.

Secrets of Mani—A book of magical history once possessed by Princess Mydia's mother, given to Mydia by Cae Rhidea upon her return to Nytaea.

Scathii (SKAH-thee, with a hard 'TH')—Well known but rarely seen, the Isle of Scathii is hidden at the farthest reaches of the Sky Islands. Scathii is home to the world's highest density of wind magi, a secret they like to keep to themselves, and is also one of the few providers of wool to the outside world.

Silver—The most common metal in Mani, said to comprise a large portion of the continent of Argent deep below its surface. In places such as Nytaea, the ancient order of Silversmiths used their Silver Authority to wrest the raw metal from Mani's belly and create wonders such as the Nytaean Palace. In addition to being both a metal and a magical element, the word Silver (always capitalized) is also used to refer to a living force that is believed to represent the breath, or the will, of Mani himself.

Silver Beast—A mythical creature or force of great malevolence.

Sky Funnel—A twisting waterspout that pours upward from the Wellspring at the very center of Ti'Vaeth. It issues from a long stack, walled in by the Hall of Eternity, but no one seems to know the exact source of the

Wellspring's water.

Snowbell—A town in which Lyn and company stop on their way through the province of Fircas, experimenting with a new money-making stunt.

Sol—The white sun of Mani, which makes her rotation once every twenty-eight days. She shines for around two weeks during what is called the Sunlit Cycle, before dipping over the horizon and bringing on the Sunless Cycle.

Sol Cycle—A pattern of 28 days during which Sol passes around the world of Mani, providing two weeks of day and two weeks of night. [See **Sunless Cycle**, **Sunlit Cycle**]

Sorfaen (SORE-fane)—Southeasternmost province of Kystrea, bordering Torlega on the west, Nemental on the east, and Fircas, Storklance and Nytaea on the north.

Soul River—A river said to run in a circle around the continent of Darsor. To an outsider, it would sound mythical.

Starklett—A kingdom that no longer exists on Gaea, and whose last prince was assassinated one thousand years ago.

Storklance—The easternmost province of Kystrea, which borders Nytaea on the west and Nemental on the east.

Stormhawk—An aerial assault vessel developed by the Haccolces Air Force. The latest model is decades old and has yet to be surpassed in speed and offensive weaponry.

Styrite Wars—A long war waged from 778–794 between a coalition of three Kystrean city-states (Ti'Vaeth, Dotham and Fircas) and the ruthless warriors of Torlega, who were attempting to expand over the mountains by conquering Dotham and other regions.

Sun Dancer—A constellation of the Sunlit night sky. [See **Constellation**]

Sunless Cycle—A period of two weeks on Mani where the sun drops below the western horizon and vanishes, causing the auroras and clouds to change their patterns. At dawn, the Sunlit Cycle, or Day Season, begins.

Sunlit Cycle—A period of two weeks on Mani where the sun travels from the eastern horizon to the west. At dusk, the Sunless Cycle, or Night Season, begins.

Synergist—One who practices Coaction, which is also called synergy. [See **Coaction**]

Synergy—See Coaction.

Tai'Xi (TIE-SHEE)—Far eastern continent, once home to the great city of Mei Shan.

Terrol—A large continent divided between South Terrol and North Terrol.

Thyria (THEER-ee-uh)—A western city-state of Kystrea lying between Ti'Vaeth and Cryvad.

Ti'Vaeth (tih-VETH)—The Capital of Kystrea, wherein dwells Archlord Domon. Encompassing the lush, vibrant surrounding lands both inside and outside the shimmering water wall called the Veil, Ti'Vaeth is the largest city-state of Kystrea.

Torlega (tor-LEE-guh)—A land to the south of Kystrea, hemmed in against the southern coast of Argent but defended by the jagged Styrite mountains. The Torlegans are well known for their earth magi, who use stonesung armor to protect themselves, insulating from most kinds of magic.

Tower of Mani—The mythical tower that lies in the center of the Land of Storms.

Trident—One of the Nine Cities of Man, ruled by Vladimir and located on Nestra's western shore.

Umbra Council—The Archlord's trusted friends whom he allows in on his plans and with whom he discusses them.

Underground—A rebel faction in Nytaea, funded partly by Mydia. They plotted to overthrow Lord Kalceron and give his rule to the people.

Uphel (OOH-fel)—A northern Kystrean province.

Vault—A permanent memory bank possessed by all Hellebes, which cannot be forgotten or misplaced. Lyn inherited hers, but her mixed blood gave her trouble accessing it for a while.

Veil—A wall of water that covers Ti'Vaeth in a sheet, spraying upwards from the Wellspring at the center of the city and streaming outward, making the sky like the roof of a greenhouse. The water flows outward from there, forming the Four Rivers, and also feeds the giant lake that surrounds the capital city of Ti'Vaeth.

Vessland—A mountainous land surrounding the city of Maldunech.

Wellspring of Life/Magic—The source of all magic—and water, therefore life itself—on Mani. The Well has begun to dry up lately, and with it the magic of Mani, in part due to the Archlord's meddling with it.

Yan'Vala (YAHN-vuh-LAH)—A nation lying to the northeast of Kystrea, hidden in a mountainous region of crags and gorges that reach down to infinity, as though the continent were tearing itself apart. The locals assure any travelers that the cracks have stayed exactly the same for at least two centuries, mind you.

Yartel River (yar-TEL)—One of the Four Rivers, running northward from Ti'Vaeth and ending at the continental coast of the Uphel province.

APPENDIX C
Notes on the Worlds

Coaction and Authority

Magic has existed on Mani for many centuries. How long exactly is often debated, but presumably for at least the one thousand years that humans have dwelt on the silver world. Magic is the essence of life and nature and the bond that holds the planet together—literally and figuratively.

Manese magic is split into two main classifications: Coaction and Authority. Coaction is the lesser art, a means of prompting the magical nature of Mani to produce for the wielder some effect, while the greater art, Authority, allows one to forcibly bend nature to heel and command the elements. The process is only technically different; it is mostly a difference in the strength of the results—and a prerequisite thereof. Any Authority at all generally takes years of practice to achieve.

High Magi such as the famed Cae Rhidea or the deceased Prince Kallyn (and his father, Lord Edrius Kalceron, for that matter) are skilled in even the highest arts of Authority, able to bend the elements to do their bidding. To be called a High Mage, one must demonstrate mastery in no less than three branches of Authority. Lesser magi like the average mage soldier can only perform relatively small feats of Coaction, prompting nature into responding to their own actions in order to produce a certain effect. This is far less potent than actual Authority, but easier for those with little potential or training.

Those born with the gift—or Aptitude—of magic are called Adepts. This Aptitude is not distributed to all, though some Adepts miss their talent by not realizing they ever had it (the ability will eventually disappear if never utilized by adulthood), but those who have it also experience a longer life. It is for them to decide whether that is a blessing or a curse. Stronger Aptitude means longer lifespan. Some ancient High Magi lived for multiple centuries.

The Eight Branches of Magic

Elements of Mani:
- Water—The element of water and the essence of life.
- Fire—The element of heat, combustion and flames.
- Lightning (Thunder)—The element of electricity and lightning.
- Wind—The element of air pressure and wind control.
- Earth—The element of terra firma—stone, ground, earthquakes.

The Dimensional Branches:
- Perception—the force governing perceived reality.
- Reality—the force governing physical reality.

Ancient:
- Silver—Manipulation of silver and its associated properties.

Silver is its own special case, as it predates elemental magic (while dimensional magic appears to have followed the elements to Mani). Since silver is embedded deeply into the makeup of the very planet, Silver magic is the most powerful by far, allowing the wielder near-complete control of the metal. As for its various abilities and the extent thereof . . . they are unclear, as the Silversmiths—the ancient order of magi who exclusively had this gift—died off long ago.

Dates and Times

On Mani, the Sol Cycle is twenty-eight "days" long. Since these days are divided by the great auroras and the clouds, they are separate from the Sol Cycle. Each day in the Cycle, Sol progresses farther in her rounds, creating two seasons: Sunlit and Sunless; Day Season and Night Season.

The Sol Cycle:
- 1–2: Dawn (Full sunrise on 2nd day)
- 3–8: Waxing Day
- 9–10: Zenith (Full Day)
- 11–14: Waning Day
- 15–16: Sunset (Dusk on Day 16)
- 17–28: Night Season

Naturally, all these figures vary depending on where on Mani you live. The farther north or south of the equator one lives, the shorter each Sunlit Cycle will be. The farther east, one will experience each stage of the Sol Cycle before those in Ti'Vaeth, Kystrea; the farther west, later:

Ti'Vaeth: ±0	Mid-Sea (East):-7
Mid-Sea (West): +7	Tower of Mani: -14

There are thirteen months in the year, each with their own two seasons—Day and Night—which are warmer and colder. There are no traditional seasons on Mani, so constellation cycles tell the passing of a full year.

Dating Systems:
- Years of the Exile (E1–E1000): Begins at the time when the first prisoners were sent to the grey moon (some contest this, claiming it started when the Titan of Growth was sent there). Counts upward to the end of the silver world. Used on Mani as well, but they leave off the E. It is the year E997 when our story begins.
- A.E. (1–23XX+): Used before the Anier rose to power, and refuses to die despite their attempts. Counts from a significant historical event.

Months of the Manese Year:	*The Gaean Equivalent:*
• Mani'Tor	• Manidor
• Ae'Tor (AY-tore)	• Aidor
• Fynle (FIN-lee)	• Finhal
• Dri'Shal (DREE-shahl)	• Dirhal
• Firvaen (FIR-ven)	• Firven
• Norvaen (NOR-ven)	• Norven
• San'Hal (SAHN-hall)	• Svenhal
• Quoi	• Koii
• Ver'Ta	• Verda
• Herch'Ta (HER-(k)-tah)	• Hersta
• Vendale (VEN-duh-lee)	• Venidal
• Henavaen (HEN-uh-ven)	• Henaven
• Sol'Tor	• Soldor

Gaea's Planetary Energy:

Geothermics:

Gaea's natural planetary energy (called **Geothermic energy**) is tapped by deep wells all over the planet, most notably in nine locations where it rises closest.

Geokinesis:

Various Hellebes-developed methods to convert Geothermic energy into work. Many machines do this, such as propulsion engines, Geoelectric generators and energy rifles, but Hellebes themselves are the most efficient at transmuting the power. They use it on a daily basis, drawing it in through their skin to enhance their own physical capabilities and even, with training, to return into the earth with a portion of their will, reshaping it. Many combat styles and techniques center around these uses.

Geokinetic Transfer:

Each Hellebes can only hold in himself so much energy at a time, and can only draw so quickly. This statistic refers to how much Geothermic energy a Hellebes is able to metabolize at once. It is said that female Hellebes have a vastly greater capacity for Geokinetic transfer than their male counterparts.

Hellebes Biomanufacturing:

Long ago, a population crisis led to the near-extinction of the people of Gaea, who were left with only a handful of female citizens. Thus, one was selected to be the sacrifice for proliferation. Preserving her in a solution rich with Geothermic energy, scientists found a way to use her egg cells and her DNA to generate indefinite generations of Hellebes in their **biomanufactories**. This did not, however, solve the problem of birth ratios, and thus only through great labors are they able to create a new female when the old expires.

They called her Mother Gaea, among other titles, and she became not only a way forward for humanity, but a symbol of hope, a goddess worshipped by the new wave of mankind.

Hellebes Traits:

The Hellebes race, as they came to be called, are not ordinary humans but taller, stronger, lacking many of the weaknesses of old humanity—for the scientists of the Gaean League, over many centuries, tweaked their genetics freely, even insinuating into each one a "loyalty gene" that discourages disobedience and keeps the order of the League. Hellebes are the ultimate machine when it comes to manual work, as they are many times stronger than a human and can use Geokinesis to further bolster their bodies. All are born male in the biomanufactories, but are said to lack reproductive capacity. One of the key Hellebes traits is their inability to forget information due to their **Memory Vault**.

Hellebes Development:

Hellebes production, the miracle that sustains Gaea. Not only bypasses sexual reproduction entirely but allows for a high level of customization against novel diseases and environmental anomalies. Each Hellebes is formed using a cocktail of genes catalogued over a long span of human history, pooling from various geographical and ethnic sources.

- **Stage 1:** Embryo–Fetus
- **Stage 2:** Fetus–Baby
- **Stage 3:** 0–10 months
- **Stage 4:** 10–24 months — Walking, learns basic words.
- **Stage 5:** 2–4 years — Physical training/basic tutelage begin.
- **Stage 6:** 4–6 years — Speaking/writing fluently, Vault training.
- **Stage 7:** 6–Puberty — Advanced phys. training, Geokinetics.
- **Stage 8:** Puberty–Full adult — Specialized training by assignment.

In all, the process takes about nine years and six months.

The Gaean Senate:

After the Great Exile, at the height of the population crisis, the Gaean League arose to save the world, uniting each major surviving sector of Gaea under nine cities—with one Senator for each. While little is known about each Senator, they are men of great renown and stature, powerful beings that have surpassed the limitations of the Hellebes and are thus fit to rule them.

- Lldsaor, Emperor of Gaea, Senator of Haccolces
- Brant, Senator of Maldunech
- Strongs, Senator of Haven
- Sylleo, Senator of Ccamos
- Vladimir, Senator of Trident
- Holmon, Senator of Luna Halcyon
- Daedalus, Senator of Chronala
- DeWitt, Senator of Lenardda

The ninth Senator is little spoken of, as he and his city were destroyed one hundred years ago.

Gaea

ABOUT THE AUTHOR

Jacob Gamber grew up in Araluen, Alagaësia and Fablehaven, and spent the remainder of his childhood in rural Pennsylvania, telling stories to sheep. When the time came to embark on his own journey to a fantasy world, he botched it thoroughly several times and eventually got a full-time factory job. Presently, he lives in eastern Ohio with his wife and children. He enjoys music, role-playing games and puzzles, and is reportedly allergic to bad love triangles.

Visit www.jacobgamber.com for more info on his works, progress, and upcoming stories. You can also check out his personal blog, www.ideaengine.blog, where he posts monthly newsletters, behind-the-scenes content, and a weekly fantasy web serial called *Tales from the Earthen Sky*. You can also find him on Royal Road, where he posts *Earthen Sky* and other original works.

Sign up for Jacob's newsletter at **www.ideaengine.blog/subscribe-today** —or by scanning this QR code:

Gaea

Gaea

Gaea